READER'S DIGEST
SELECT EDITIONS

READER'S DIGEST
SELECT EDITIONS

The condensations in this volume
are published with the consent of the authors
and the publishers © 2006 Reader's Digest.

www.readersdigest.co.uk

The Reader's Digest Association Limited
11 Westferry Circus Canary Wharf London E14 4HE

For information as to ownership of
copyright in the material of this book,
and acknowledgments, see last page.

Printed in Germany
ISBN 0 276 44104 4

SELECTED AND CONDENSED
BY READER'S DIGEST

THE READER'S DIGEST ASSOCIATION LIMITED, LONDON

CONTENTS

Hidden on a remote island is a top-secret facility housing former US intelligence operatives who present a security risk to their government. One of them, Hal Ambler, escapes— only to discover that little of his former life is as he remembers it, and every detail of his past, has been erased. On the run, he draws on his old skills to learn the truth about who he once was and, in so doing, uncovers a high-level conspiracy to bring about a major shift in the balance of world power.

THE AMBLER WARNING
ROBERT LUDLUM

Jeremy Marsh, a science journalist, has made a career out of rationally explaining the supernatural, so when he receives a letter telling him about the ghostly lights that appear on foggy nights in a cemetery in North Carolina, he sets off to investigate what he assumes is a hoax. On arriving in Boone Creek, however, he is charmed by the locals and, in particular, by librarian Lexie Darnell. Through her he soon discovers that logic is no help when it comes to unravelling matters of the human heart.

Nicholas SPARKS
True Believer

TRUE BELIEVER
NICHOLAS SPARKS

By the author of The Notebook

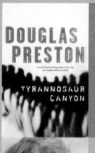

TYRANNOSAUR CANYON

DOUGLAS PRESTON

321

There are many theories about what caused the extinction of the dinosaurs, and this colourful, Indiana-Jones-style adventure homes in on one of the most intriguing. When a fossil hunter makes the discovery of a lifetime in a remote canyon in New Mexico, he soon has a host of interested parties on his tail, including a greedy collector, a passionate scientist, a sinister official, and local vet Tom Broadbent, who just wants to do right by a dead man's daughter.

John Mortimer's knowledge of the legal system and sharp eye for character are put to good use in this lively new novel. When well-meaning volunteer Lucy Purefoy sets out to help ex-con Terry along the road to reform, she finds it isn't that easy. She hatches a bold plan to prove her dedication to the cause, which results in the tables being turned in a most unexpected way. With a cast of characters as colourful as those in the author's famous Rumpole stories, *Quite Honestly* sparkles with wit and wisdom.

QUITE HONESTLY

JOHN MORTIMER

469

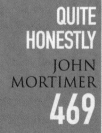

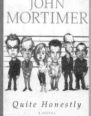

THE AMBLER WARNING

ROBERT LUDLUM

Imagine waking up to find that the face staring back at you from the mirror is not your own. Imagine finding that all evidence of your past life has disappeared and even old acquaintances don't remember you any more.

That's the situation in which former intelligence agent Hal Ambler finds himself when he escapes from a top-security hospital on Parrish Island off the coast of Virginia . . .

Chapter 1

The four-storey building had the invisibility of the commonplace. It looked like countless others erected in the fifties and sixties and a casual passer-by would not have given it a second look.

Yet there was no such thing as a casual passer-by on this barrier island, six miles off the coast of Virginia. The island was, officially, part of America's National Wildlife Refuge System, and anyone who enquired learned that, owing to the extreme delicacy of its ecosystem, no visitors were permitted. Part of the island's leeward side was, indeed, a habitat for ospreys and mergansers. But in the centre was a fifteen-acre campus of manicured green slopes and the bland-looking facility.

The boats that stopped at Parrish Island three times a day had NWRS markings, and from a distance it would not be apparent that the personnel ferried to the island looked nothing like park rangers. If a fishing vessel tried to land on the island, it would be intercepted by khaki-clad men with genial smiles and hard, cold eyes. No one ever got close enough to see the four guard towers or the electrified fencing.

Few people in the government knew of the Parrish Island Psychiatric Facility, yet simple logic had decreed its establishment: a secure environment was needed to treat someone who was out of his mind when that mind was filled with state secrets. At Parrish Island, security could be carefully managed. Staff members were thoroughly vetted and the clinical staff was rotated every three months, minimising the chance of inappropriate attachments developing. Security protocols stipulated that patients be identified by number, never by name. Any patient deemed an especially high risk, either because of the nature of his psychiatric disorder or because of the sensitivity of what he knew, would be housed in a separate, locked ward.

On the western wing of the fourth floor in Ward 4W was one such patient, No. 5312: six feet tall, perhaps forty years of age with cropped brown hair and eyes of unclouded blue. The intensity of his stare could be unnerving.

The patient's troubled dreams grew in vividness as sleep ebbed from him. Images buckled like a film strip before an overheated projector bulb. A political rally on a steamy day in Taiwan. A political candidate, struck down by a blast and sprawled on the rostrum in a cowl of his own blood. He lifted his head and gazed out at the crowd one final time, and his gaze settled on a *chang bizi*—a Westerner. The one person who was not screaming, crying, fleeing. The one person who did not seem surprised, for he was, after all, in the presence of his own handiwork. The candidate died staring at the man who had come from across the world to kill him.

The image buckled, shimmied, burned into a blinding white, as Hal Ambler opened his eyes to see the soft fluorescent lights recessed into the ceiling of his windowless room. A pretend day, at least, was beginning. Ambler's room was nine feet by twelve, the floors tiled with white vinyl, the walls covered with white PVC foam. Before long, the door would slide open with a hydraulic sigh. These details were the stuff of life in a high-security facility, if you could call it a life. He experienced intervals of grim lucidity when he felt that he had been abducted—not just his body but also his soul.

In the course of a two-decade career as a clandestine operative, Ambler had occasionally been taken captive and endured periods of solitary confinement. It wasn't conducive to deep thoughts. Rather, the mind filled with scraps of advertising jingles, half-remembered pop songs and an acute consciousness of small bodily discomforts. Those who had trained him had prepared him for such eventualities. The challenge, they had insisted, was to keep the mind from attacking itself.

Yet he wasn't in the hands of his enemies now; he was being held by his own government. And he did not know why.

As a member of the Consular Operations branch of US intelligence, Ambler had heard about Parrish Island. He understood why such a facility had to exist. It was dangerous to allow just any psychiatrist access to a patient in possession of highly classified information. Yet this did not explain why Hal Ambler found himself here. How long had it been? Six months, a year, more? Somehow he had failed to keep track of time. There was so much he did not know.

Ambler completed his callisthenics regimen, finishing with a hundred one-armed pushups and, at a small sink in a corner, brushed his teeth. The toothbrush handle was made of a soft, rubbery polymer that could not be sharpened into a weapon. He pressed a touch-latch, and an electric razor slid from a compartment above the sink; he was permitted 120 seconds of use before returning the sensor-tagged device to its compartment, or an alarm would chime. After he finished, Ambler splashed water on his face and ran his wet fingers through his hair. There was no mirror, no reflective surface anywhere. All to some therapeutic end, no doubt. He donned his 'day suit', the white cotton smock and loose trousers that were the inmates' uniform.

He turned slowly when he heard the door slide open, and smelt the disinfectant that lingered in the hallway. His visitor was, as usual, a heavyset man with a brush cut, dressed in a dove-grey uniform, a cloth tab fastened over his ID badge: another precaution taken on this ward. He carried a black nylon mesh belt in one hand. 'Raise your arms,' he grunted, as he placed the belt round Ambler's waist.

Ambler was not permitted to leave his room without the device, which was known as a REACT belt—the acronym standing for 'remote electronically activated control technology'. Inside the thick fabric were several flat lithium batteries; once the belt was in place, two metal prongs were positioned just above his left kidney. The belt could be activated from as far away as 300 feet and set to deliver an eight-second charge of 50,000 volts, which would knock even a Sumo wrestler to the floor.

Having fitted the device, the orderly escorted Patient 5312 down the white-tiled hallway for his medications. Ambler's movements, slow, lumbering, were belied by the swift efficiency with which his gaze took in his surroundings. That was one of the many things the orderly failed to notice.

There were few things that Ambler failed to notice. The building was decades old, but it had been refurbished with up-to-date security technology: doors were opened by chip cards containing transponder wafers, and major gateways used retinal scans. About thirty yards down the hall from his cell was the Evaluation Room, which had a one-way observation window. There he would sit for regular 'psychiatric evaluations', the purpose of which remained elusive. The staff had, he sensed, come to regard him as a lifer, someone who would be interned at the facility long after they had left it.

Several weeks ago, however, everything had changed for him. The plain fact was that he had *reached* someone, and that would make all the difference. More precisely, *she* would. She already had begun to. She was a young psychiatric nurse named Laurel Holland. And she was on his side.

A FEW MINUTES LATER, the orderly and his leaden-footed patient arrived at a large semicircular area called the Surveillance Atrium. At one end was some exercise equipment, at the other was the dispensary: a long counter, a sliding window of wire-mesh glass and, visible through it, a shelf of plastic bottles. Ward 4W had been designed for a dozen patients; it currently served a population of one. As a result, the Surveillance Atrium had become an informal rest-and-recreation centre for orderlies, and half a dozen were gathered there this morning.

As Ambler turned an unfocused gaze towards a pair of them seated on a low, cushioned bench, he allowed a rivulet of drool to roll down his chin.

'Candy time,' one of the orderlies said; the others sniggered.

Ambler made his way slowly to the dispensary, where the auburn-haired nurse was waiting with his morning's pills. An imperceptible flicker—a fleeting glance, a fractional head nod—passed between them.

He'd learned her name by accident; she'd spilt water on herself, and the fabric that was supposed to conceal her ID badge had become wet and translucent: LAUREL HOLLAND. He'd said her name aloud in a low voice; she seemed flustered, yet not displeased. With that, something sparked between them. He studied her face, her posture, her voice. She was in her thirties, he figured, with hazel eyes flecked with green, and a lithe frame. Smarter and prettier than she realised.

Over the past six weeks, conversations between them had been murmured and brief, but a great deal of information had been conveyed. And Patient 5312 was now more than a number to her.

She recognised something about him—recognised his *sanity*. Knowing this had bolstered his faith in himself, and his determination to escape. 'I don't want to die in this place,' he'd murmured to her one morning. She made no reply, but her stricken look told him all he needed to know.

'Your meds,' she'd said brightly the next morning, placing three pills on his palm that looked different from the usual neuroleptics. *Tylenol*, she mouthed. As clinical protocol required, he swallowed the tablets under her supervision, then opened his mouth to show that he had not secreted them anywhere. Within an hour he had proof that she had helped him. He was lighter on his feet, lighter in spirit. Within a few days, he felt brighter-eyed—more himself. He had to make an effort to appear medicated, to feign the heavy-gaited, Compazine shuffle that the orderlies were accustomed to.

Now, with her body shielding her movements from the camera, Laurel Holland slipped her keycard into the waistband of his white-cotton uniform. 'I'm hearing there could be a Code Twelve this morning,' she said quietly.

The code referred to a major medical emergency, requiring a patient's evacuation to a hospital on the mainland. Ambler remembered a previous Code Twelve, and recalled the security procedures that had been followed. As formidable as they were, they represented an irregularity in routine: an irregularity that he might be able to exploit.

Two hours later—hours of glazed silence and immobility on Ambler's part—an electronic chime sounded, followed by an electronic voice: *Code Twelve, Ward Two East*. At once, the orderlies were on their feet and most of them left for the second-floor ward.

Ambler felt a hand on his shoulder. The same heavyset orderly who had been at his door earlier in the morning. 'Patients return to their room during emergency protocols,' the man said.

'What's going on?' Ambler asked, thick-tongued and dull.

'Nothing you need worry about. You'll be safe and sound in your room.'

Minutes later, he and the grey-uniformed orderly were in front of Ambler's door. The man presented his chip card to the grey plastic reader device at waist level near the door, and the hatch-style door slid open.

'In you go,' he said.

'Need help to . . .' Ambler gestured at the porcelain commode.

'Oh, hell,' the orderly said, and followed Ambler into the room.

You only get one go. No mistakes.

As the orderly came over to him, Ambler stooped, bending his legs at the knees, as if he were starting to crumple. Suddenly he shot upwards, ramming the man's jaw with his head. Bewilderment showed in the orderly's face as he absorbed the force of the impact, and fell heavily to the floor.

Ambler went through the man's pockets. He collected the chip card and the ID badge, then changed swiftly into the man's dove-grey shirt and trousers. It was impossible to get rid of the stun belt in the time he had—but he cinched in the uniform's grey fabric belt, hoping that the REACT device would remain concealed.

Holding the orderly's chip card up to the card reader inside his room, he opened the door and glanced out. There was nobody in the hallway. Ambler stepped out and held the card to the outside reader. After a couple of clicks, the door slid shut.

Now he raced to the door at the end of the hallway. Locked, of course. He presented the keycard he had just used, heard a few clicks, then nothing.

This wasn't a passageway authorised for orderlies.

He tried Laurel Holland's keycard. This time the door opened.

Finding himself in a dimly lit service corridor, Ambler turned right, towards a linen cart at the far end. The janitors hadn't visited the area yet. There were cigarette butts and cellophane wrappers on the floor—and an empty Red Bull can that someone had stomped on and flattened. Responding to intuition, Ambler stuck it in his back pocket.

How much time did he have? More concretely, how long before the orderly's disappearance would be noted? Within a few minutes, the Code Twelve would be concluded, and someone would be sent to retrieve Ambler from his room. He had to get out of the building as fast as possible.

Looking around, he found the laundry chute and climbed inside, holding on to the entrance ledge with both hands and exploring with his legs. There was no side-mounted scuttle ladder, as he'd hoped. Instead, the chute was lined with smooth steel. To stop himself from falling, he had to brace his hands and his sneaker-clad feet against opposite sides of the chute.

Repositioning each limb in sequence, he lowered himself down the chute. By the time he had reached the bottom, his muscles were spasming in agony. He pushed through bags of soiled laundry and finally reached a concrete floor. He was in a hot, low-ceilinged basement space, loud with the rumble of laundry machines. He craned his head. At the end of a row of white industrial washers, two men were loading a machine.

Ambler knew he had to find his way onto the loading dock, where the laundry was collected. He stood up and stepped across the aisle of laundry machines, forcing discipline on his quivering muscles. If he *were* seen, his steps had to be confident. Once he was out of sight of the laundry workers, he stood beside a row of wheeled laundry carts and assessed his location.

'Hey,' called a voice. 'What the fuck are you doing here?'

Ambler forced an easy-going smile as he turned towards the small, bald man who was obviously a mid-level ward attendant, someone whose life consisted of taking shit from his bosses and giving it to those he bossed. 'Take it easy, dude,' he said. 'I swear I wasn't smoking.'

'This is a joke to you?' The supervisor walked over and glanced at the badge on Ambler's shirt. 'I can have you busted, you—' He broke off, realising that the face on the ID badge was not that of the man in the uniform, and started to unhook a device from his belt. It was a radio transmitter that activated the stun belt.

No! Ambler couldn't let it happen. Reaching for the flattened can in his back pocket, he slid the metal under the belt, hardly conscious of it scraping his flesh. The belt's two prongs now rested on the conductive metal.

'Welcome to a world of pain,' the supervisor said, as he pressed the stun-belt activator.

Ambler heard a buzzing from the rear of the belt. But his body was no longer the path of least resistance between the prongs; the flattened can was. A wisp of smoke, then the buzzing ceased. The belt had been shorted out.

Ambler charged at the supervisor and tackled him to the floor. The man's head slammed against the concrete and, concussed, he let out a low moan.

Glancing at the initials underneath the man's name, Ambler saw that he had inventory-management responsibilities: overseeing things entering and leaving the building through its service entrances. Ambler replaced the badge he'd been wearing with that of the supervisor. The man would be his ticket out.

The steel gate at the west service exit bore a white and red sign: NON-AUTHORISED PERSONNEL STRICTLY PROHIBITED. By the push bar there was a wall-mounted retinal scan device.

Ambler put his arms beneath those of the unconscious supervisor, hoisting him before the scanner and holding his eyes open with his fingers. He pushed the button with his left elbow and two bursts of red light came from the scanner glass. A motor whirred inside the steel door and it swung open. Ambler let the man drop to the floor and walked through the gate.

He was soon at a loading dock at the west side of the building, breathing unfiltered air for the first time in a long while. The day was cold, wet, foggy. But he was *outside*. And he was in greater danger than ever. He knew about the electrified perimeter fence from Laurel Holland. The only way out was to be officially escorted out—or to be one of the official escorts.

He heard the distant sound of a motorboat—it had to be the one they used for medical evacuations—approaching the island. Then, from closer by, came another motorised sound as an electric vehicle, like an oversized golf cart, drove up to the building. In short order, a stretcher was wheeled up to the back of it. The cart would take the patient to the boat.

Ambler took a deep breath, strode up to the vehicle and banged on the driver's side. The driver regarded him warily.

'They told me to stick with the guy all the way to the medical centre,' Ambler said, climbing aboard. 'Newbies get all the shit jobs.' The tone was of mild complaint, the message one of apology. He folded his arms on his chest, concealing his badge and its ill-matched photo ID.

'You with Barlowe's team?' the driver grunted.

'You got it.'

AT THE WHARF, the men in the express cruiser—the boat's pilot, a paramedic and an armed guard—grumbled when they were told that the body was to be accompanied by an attendant from the facility. Weren't they trusted to do the job right? Besides, the paramedic pointed out, the patient was already dead. This was going to be a morgue run. But Ambler's blasé manner reassured them, and nobody wanted to loiter in this weather. They each grabbed a corner of the aluminium-framed stretcher, shivering in their navy windcheaters as they transported the body below decks.

Making sure that the photo on his ID badge got flecked with shore mud as he climbed onto the jetty, Ambler joined the paramedic and the guard on a bench behind the helm. He watched the pilot as he adjusted the stern and bow thrusters, then shifted the throttle to full. The forty-foot boat was soon riding high in the water, pressing past thirty-five knots.

'They didn't say anything about the body being accompanied,' the young paramedic said irritably. 'You realise the guy's dead, right? I checked myself. So it ain't like he's gonna escape, you know?'

Ambler adopted an officious air. 'Until they got a notarised certificate, your say-so counts for nothing. Nobody at Parrish has that authority. So the rules are the rules.'

'Quit busting his balls, Olson,' the guard said to the paramedic.

Ambler gave the guard a friendly glance. He was in his mid-twenties, with a military haircut, and a hip-holstered HK P7 pistol. He was the only armed man on the boat, but Ambler could tell he was no slouch.

As the three resumed an uncompanionable silence, Ambler allowed himself to feel a touch of relief.

The boat had gone only a few miles from Parrish Island when the pilot, wearing headphones, gesticulated to get the attention of the others, and pressed a lever that broadcast the radio through a loudspeaker.

'Cruiser 12-647-M, this is a Five-Oh-Five from Parrish Island.' The radio dispatcher's voice sounded agitated. 'We have an escaped-inmate situation. Repeat: an escaped-inmate situation. The inmate may have stowed himself on your vessel. Please confirm or disconfirm immediately. Over.'

Ambler felt his stomach contract as the guard gave him a hard look. He jumped to his feet.

'Now you know why I'm here,' he grunted. 'They've put security reps in every vehicle leaving the island. We've been hearing static about some kind of escape attempt for the past twenty-four hours.'

'Could've told us,' the guard said sullenly.

'Not the kind of gossip the facility's looking to spread,' Ambler said. 'Gonna check that body right now.'

He scrambled down the steps to the below-deck berth. Just inside, recessed into the hull, was a tool closet, he noticed. It was almost empty.

He would have to work fast, before the others decided to follow him . . . The body bound to the stretcher looked bloated, the grey pallor of death unmistakable.

Moments later, he raced to the cabin. 'You!' Ambler thrust his forefinger at the paramedic. 'You said the patient was dead. I just felt the guy's neck, and guess what? He had a pulse same as you and me.'

'You don't know what you're talking about,' the paramedic said indignantly. 'That's a corpse down there.'

'A corpse with a pulse rate of seventy? I don't think so.'

The guard's head swivelled, and Ambler could tell what he was thinking: *This guy sounds like he knows what he's talking about.*

'Are you part of it?' Ambler demanded, fixing the paramedic with an accusatory glare. 'You *in* on it?'

'What the hell are you saying?' The paramedic's cheeks reddened. He turned to the guard. 'Becker, you can't be taking this guy seriously. I know how to take a pulse, and that's a goddamn *stiff* we got there.'

'Show us,' Ambler said grimly.

The paramedic led the way down to the berth. Ambler followed, and the guard brought up the rear with his pistol out of its holster. The medic swung open the door, then said in a stunned voice, 'What the . . .?'

The two others peered inside. The stretcher lay askew, its Velcro straps undone. The body was gone.

'I don't understand,' the paramedic said, his voice unsteady.

'Well, I think the rest of us do,' Ambler said icily. He glanced at the tool-closet door, hoping nobody would notice how the latch was bulging with the strain of keeping the door shut.

'You're telling me a corpse walked out of here?' the guard demanded, turning towards the paramedic and gripping his pistol firmly.

'Probably just slipped over the side and went for a nice swim,' Ambler sneered. 'We'd never have heard, and in this fog, we'd never have seen. Three miles to shore . . . not too strenuous. Typical corpse behaviour, right?'

'This is *crazy*,' the paramedic protested. 'I had nothing to do with it! You gotta believe me.'

'Guess we know now why he was so pissed off to find me tagging along,' Ambler said to the guard, just loudly enough to be heard over the engines. 'Listen, you better call this in. I'll keep a watch on the suspect.'

The guard looked confused. Ambler could read the conflicting impulses on his face. He leaned over and spoke confidingly into his ear. 'I know you had nothing to do with it,' he said. 'My report's gonna make that clear. So you got nothing to worry about.'

'Understood,' the guard said, reassured.

'Give me your pistol and I'll keep an eye on this joker,' Ambler said, his voice level. 'But you need to radio this in *right now*.'

'Will do.' The guard hesitated only for a moment before handing over the fully loaded Heckler & Koch P7.

IN THE CIA headquarters building in Langley, Virginia, hidden away in the sort of windowless interior space that usually housed copying machines or stationery supplies, was Clayton Caston's office. He liked it because no one disturbed him there, but most Agency veterans tended to assume that Caston was the victim of internal exile. They looked at him and saw a man who had surely not accomplished much in his three decades of service, a time-server in his fifties, ticking off the days until he could retire with a pension.

Anyone who saw him at his desk this morning, his eyes fixed on his clock, pens and pencils arrayed neatly on his blotter, would only have had such preconceptions confirmed. The clock said 8.54: six minutes before the working day began. Caston pulled out a copy of the *Financial Times* and turned to the crossword puzzle, filling in the boxes, seldom pausing for longer than a second or two. At 8.59 he was done.

He heard the door rattle as his new assistant, breathless from having jogged down the hall, entered. Adrian Choi opened his mouth as if to deliver an excuse, then thought better of it and slid into his seat before his smaller, lower work station. There was a hint of slumber about his almond-shaped eyes, and his thick black hair was damp from the shower. He was cutting it fine, Caston thought.

At 9 a.m. on the dot, Caston put the *Financial Times* in the wastepaper basket and activated his secure email. Several of this morning's messages were Agency-wide notifications of little interest. But one was from an Internal Revenue Service clerk in St Louis who, though mystified by Caston's request, was happy to oblige with the details of the special-purpose divisions formed by a light-industrial firm over the past seven years.

Caston realised how drab his activities seemed to most of his colleagues. Those who used to work in the field, or still hoped to, treated him with genial condescension. 'You gotta go if you wanna know' was their watch-word. Caston never went anywhere, but a sheaf of spreadsheets could often tell him everything he needed to know without him having to leave his desk.

Then again, very few of his colleagues actually knew what Caston did. Wasn't he one of the guys who audited people's travel-and-entertainment accounts? Or were requisitions of paper and toner cartridges his area? Either way, it was a job just slightly above the menial in prestige. There were a few, however, who treated Caston with deference, even awe. They tended to be members of the top tier of the counterintelligence directorate. They knew how Aldrich Ames was really apprehended in 1994. And they knew about how a slight discrepancy between reported income and expenditures became a thread that led to the exposure of Gordon Blaine. They knew about dozens of other victories that would never come to public attention. Caston made inroads where whole bureaus failed. He had an accountant's preoccupation with columns of digits that didn't add up; a trip booked but not taken; a receipt for travel that was at odds with a reported itinerary; a credit-card charge for an unreported cellphone. There were a thousand small slips to which the devious were prone. Yet those who wouldn't brave the tedium of collation would never detect them.

Adrian came over to Caston's desk clutching various memos, animatedly explaining what he had sorted through and thrown out.

Caston glanced up. 'Be sure to send out the quarterly 166 forms for processing,' he said. 'As for this morning's incoming, anything . . . irregular?'

'A voicemail came in from Caleb Norris. I have a feeling it's urgent.'

Caston leaned back in his chair. 'You *feel* that?'

'Yes, sir.'

Caston studied the young man, like an entomologist scrutinising a new specimen. 'And you're sharing your feelings. Interesting. Now, am I a member of your family, a parent or sibling? Are we pals? Am I a girlfriend of yours? No? In that case, please don't tell me what you *feel*. I only care about what you *think*. What you have reason to *believe*. What you *know*, by observation or inference. Keep these nebulous *feelings* to yourself.' He paused. 'You were saying. About nonstandard incoming messages.'

'Well, there's this yellow inter-office thing from the—'

'You should know the CIA colour codes by now. There's no "yellow".'

'Sorry,' Adrian said. '*Canary*.'

'Which signifies what?'

'It's for . . .' He paused, his mind temporarily a blank. 'It's for a stateside incident with security implications. Ergo, non-CIA. Something to do with the other governmental agencies.'

Caston nodded briskly and accepted the bright-yellow envelope. He broke the security seal, put on his reading glasses and quickly scanned the report. Potential security breach relating to an inmate escape. A patient resident at a high-security clandestine treatment centre.

It was strange, Caston reflected, that Patient 5312 wasn't named. He reread the report to see where the incident had taken place.

The Parrish Island Psychiatric Facility. It rang a bell. A warning bell.

Chapter 2

Ambler pushed through the thorny scrub scratching at his sodden clothing towards a stand of salt-stunted trees. He shivered as the cold wind gusted, and tried to ignore the gritty sand in his shoes. Given that the local air-force base was probably twenty miles to his north, and the naval base about the same distance to his south, he expected, any moment now, to hear the low *whomp-whomp-whomp* of a military helicopter.

He quickened his pace until he heard the thrumming of traffic on

Highway 64. On the hard shoulder, he brushed himself down, put up a thumb and smiled. He was wet and bedraggled, and wearing a strange uniform. The smile would have to be pretty damned reassuring.

A minute later, a truck pulled over. Ambler had his ride.

A truck, a car, a bus: a few transfers later, he was in the suburbs of Washington. In a strip mall, he found a sporting goods store, where he hurriedly bought a few garments from the sale bins, paying with cash that was in the pockets of his uniform, then changing behind a hedge near the store. His new garb consisted of khakis, flannel shirt and windcheater.

Rip Van Winkle was coming home.

As he caught a bus heading for the city centre, Ambler found himself in a contemplative mood. Faces and voices from the past swirled through his consciousness.

The last psychiatrist who had 'evaluated' him had been a lean man in his early fifties with black-framed glasses and brown hair greying at the temples. But when Ambler looked at him, he saw other things, too. He saw a man who resented his job, who dreamed of a different sort of life, perhaps a book-lined office on Manhattan's Upper West Side, a leather couch and wing chair, a clientele of writers, artists and musicians. The hardest part was simply getting through his rounds at a place he despised.

The psychiatrist was made uneasy by Ambler. His expertise was supposed to give him special insight into his patients, and with that, usually, went a sense of authority. But he did not experience that around Ambler.

'Let me remind you, these sessions are strictly evaluative,' he had told Ambler. 'My job is to monitor progress, keep an eye on the medications. So, any new side effects I should be aware of?'

'It would be easier to talk about side effects,' Ambler had said, 'if I knew what the *main* effect was supposed to be.'

'The meds are meant to control your psychiatric symptoms, as you know. Paranoia, dissociative disorder, ego-dystonic syndromes . . .'

'Words,' Ambler said. 'Without meaning. Sounds without sense.'

The psychiatrist typed a few notes on his laptop. His pale grey eyes were chilly behind his glasses. 'Several psychiatric teams have wrestled with your dissociative identity disorders. We've been through this.' He pressed a button on a small remote control and an audiotape played, the sound emerging bright and clear through recessed speakers. Ambler's voice was audible, spewing conspiracy theories with an unhinged sense of urgency: 'You're behind it. All of you. And all of them. Opus Dei . . . the Rockefellers . . .' On and on the recording went.

To Ambler it was almost physically painful. 'Stop it,' he said quietly. 'Please stop it.'

The psychiatrist paused the tape. 'Do you still believe those . . . theories?'

'They're paranoid fantasies,' Ambler said, groggily but distinctly. 'And the answer is no. I don't even have a memory of having held them. That's not me, OK? I mean, that's not who I am.'

'You're somebody else, then. Two different people? Or more?' The psychiatrist removed his glasses. 'The question I'm putting to you is the question you need to put to yourself: Who are you?'

'The problem with the question,' Ambler said after a pause, 'is that you think it's multiple choice. You want me to choose from your list of options.'

'Is that the problem?' The psychiatrist looked up from his laptop. 'I'd say the real problem is that you're checking off more than one answer.'

IT TOOK AMBLER a few moments to rouse himself when the bus came to the Cleveland Park stop, but he made it out in time. On the street, he looked around him.

He was back.

This was not the weather he would have chosen for a homecoming. The skies were grey; drizzle kept the pavements slick. Still he remained hyper-alert. It was an ordinary street on a dismal day, yet there were dangers. If he could just reach his apartment, he could retrieve the ordinary detritus of his existence—its very ordinariness was now what made it precious.

Would they dare to come after him *here*—where there were people who actually knew him? Surely it was the safest place for him to be? His enemies, whoever they were—a rogue element in the government, he suspected, who had tried to bury him alive among lost souls frenzied with delusion—could not afford to confront him in the open, where the local police would inevitably get involved.

Ambler saw the newsstand he used to pass every morning when he was in town. He smiled at the grizzled, gap-toothed man behind the counter. 'Reggie,' he called out. 'Reggie, my main man.'

'Hey.' It was a reflex, not a greeting.

Ambler strode over to him. 'Been a long time, right?'

The man looked at him again, not a flicker of recognition in his face.

Ambler glanced down at a stack of *Washington Post*s, the top copy dappled with rain, and noticed the date. The third week of January—no wonder it was so cold. He blinked. Nearly *two years* had been taken from him.

But now was not the time to dwell on loss.

'Come on, Reggie. How you been? Working hard, or hardly working?'

On Reggie's face, puzzlement was hardening into suspicion. 'I ain't got no change for you, bro. And I don't give out free coffee, neither.'

'Reggie, come on—you *know* me.'

'Move along, big guy,' Reggie said. 'I don't want any trouble.'

Ambler turned away and walked the half block to the 1920s red-brick apartment block where he had been a tenant for the past decade: Baskerton Towers. A sort-of home for a man who really had none.

A career in the highest tier of operational security was a career spent under an alias. No division of Consular Operations was more secret than the Political Stabilisation Unit, and its operatives only knew each other by a field name. It was not a job that lent itself to deep civilian ties either. Indeed, the paltriness of his domestic existence had given special importance to his casual street acquaintances. And although he spent little time in Baskerton Towers, the apartment was a badge of normality for him.

The tower block was set back from the street, an oval drive permitting cars to come up to the lobby. Ambler looked around the nearby streets and pavements, saw no sign of anybody taking an interest in him, and walked up to the building. Someone would know him—one of the doormen, if not the building superintendent—and would let him into his apartment.

He looked at the long list of tenants: black plastic letters on a white board, names in alphabetical order.

No Ambler. ALSTON was followed by AYER.

They'd taken his apartment, then—a disappointment, but not a surprise.

'Can I help you, sir?' It was one of the doormen, emerging from the vestibule: Greg Denovich.

'Greg,' Ambler said, jovially. Greg was for Gregor, he'd always assumed; the man was from the former Yugoslavia. 'Been a real long time, huh?'

'Do I know you?' Denovich asked. But it wasn't a question. It was a statement in the negative.

'I guess not,' Ambler said softly. Then his perplexity gave way to panic as he heard the sound of tyres braking hard on the rain-slicked street behind him. He turned round quickly and saw three men in Parrish Island guard uniforms emerging from a white van. One carried a carbine; the others had pistols. All three were running towards him.

The van was obviously part of an emergency 'retrieval service', a device used by clandestine branches of the government for sensitive domestic 'pick-ups'. And on this wet and cold January morning, Harrison Ambler was the target. In showing up here, he had let wishful thinking swamp his better judgment. He could afford no more mistakes. Think—he had to *think*. Or rather, he had to *feel*.

After two decades as a field operative, Ambler had mastered escape and evasion. It was second nature to him. But he never relied on the grids of logic and 'decision trees' foisted on you by the trainers. The challenge was to feel your way out of situations, improvising as necessary. To do otherwise was to fall into a routine that could be anticipated by adversaries.

Ambler scanned the street. He could now see armed men, some uniformed, striding purposefully towards him from either end of the block. Now what? He could bolt into the building and search out a rear exit. But the move would have been anticipated.

Staring at the face of the man with the carbine who was hastening across the boulevard, Ambler instinctively did the most dangerous thing of all. He ran directly towards the man.

'What *took* you so long?' Ambler bellowed. 'He's *getting away*!' He gestured vigorously with his thumb towards the lobby of Baskerton Towers.

'We got here as soon as we could,' the man with the carbine replied.

The other two, Ambler could see now as they hurried past him, carried tactical .45s, which would have twelve rounds in the magazine. It was a lot of firepower to capture one man.

Ambler walked across the street to the idling retrieval van. As he was approaching, he flipped open the wallet that had belonged to the Parrish Island supervisor, and held it up for a brief moment, as if displaying a badge. He was too far away for the driver to make anything out; the authority of the gesture would have to convince. As the driver lowered his window, Ambler took his measure. The man's eyes were watchful.

'You guys get the change in orders?' Ambler demanded. 'It's kill, not capture. And what took you so long? If you'd been in place a minute earlier, we'd be all done.'

The driver said nothing for a moment. Then his gaze hardened. 'That thing you showed me? I couldn't see it.'

Suddenly, Ambler felt the man's big, beefy hand grab his right wrist. 'Show me again.'

With his left hand, Ambler reached into his jacket for the pistol he'd taken from the guard on the boat, but the driver smashed the heel of his free hand into the P7, sending the weapon flying into the air. Ambler immediately wrenched his wrist round, yanked it up towards his shoulder, then sharply down, using his forearm like a crowbar, and smashed the driver's arm against the edge of the partly lowered window.

The driver yelped, but his grip was like steel. With his other hand, he was beginning to feel for an under-the-dashboard compartment, no doubt where a weapon of some sort was stored.

Ambler let his right arm go limp, let the driver pull him part of the way into the cab. Then, with his other hand, he spear-punched the man's larynx.

The driver released him and leaned forward, struggling for breath, both hands tearing at his collar. Ambler opened the door and pulled the driver from his seat. The man took a few steps before collapsing to the ground.

As Ambler climbed aboard, he could hear the cries of alarm among the men of the second unit. But it was too late for them to take action. He gunned the engine and sped down the street.

The van was serving admirably as a getaway car; within minutes, though, it would become a glaring beacon to his pursuers. A few miles further down Connecticut Avenue, Ambler eased the van into a side street and left it idling, with the keys in the ignition. If he was lucky, someone would steal it.

He took a cab to Dupont Circle, a thriving, populous neighbourhood at the intersection of three of the city's major avenues. It was a place with a brisk pedestrian traffic, even on this dismal morning. Getting out at New Hampshire Avenue and 20th Street, Ambler swiftly lost himself among the day-trippers and headed for the cybercafé three blocks east of the Circle.

He found a computer station with a good view of the street from the storefront window. With a few keystrokes, he brought up the Watchlist, a collective database coordinated by the Justice Department for use by federal law-enforcement agencies. Dimly remembering passcodes that luckily still functioned, he typed his full name, Harrison Ambler, into the internal search engine. He wanted to see if there was any flag on his name.

After a few moments, a message was displayed.

No records match **Harrison Ambler**.

It was an odd glitch; any federal employee, even one who was no longer on the payroll, should have had at least a perfunctory listing, even though Ambler's Cons Op identity would be omitted from such databases.

With a shrug of annoyance, he keyed his way to the State Department website, then to a password-protected internal employee database which should contain details of his civilian cover job at the State Department. For years, Hal Ambler could always explain, if anyone asked, that he was a mid-level staffer, working at the Bureau for Educational and Cultural Affairs. It was a subject he could hold forth upon at eye-glazing length, if required to. Never mind that it had nothing to do with his real career.

He used to wonder what would happen if he gave a candid answer when someone at a cocktail party asked him what he did. *Me? I work for an ultra-clandestine division of an already clandestine intelligence service called Consular Operations. A special-access programme, with maybe twenty-five people in the government cleared for it. It's called the Political Stabilisation Unit. What does it do? Well, a lot of things. Often enough, it involves killing people. People who, you hope, are worse than the people you save from them. Can I get you another drink?*

Typing in his name, he clicked RETURN, and waited a few long seconds.

Employee **Harrison Ambler** not found. Verify spelling and try again.

Feeling himself breaking out in a cold sweat, he keyed his way into the Social Security database, and ran a search for his name.

Harrison Ambler not found.

It made no sense! He summoned more databases, conducting search after search. All yielded a maddening refrain, variations on a theme.

Your search did not match any documents.
No records were located for **Harrison Ambler**.

It was as if he had never existed.

Like a distant echo, the voices of various Parrish Island psychiatrists returned to him, with their spurious diagnoses. It was all nonsense, of course. He knew precisely who he was. His memory of his life before his institutionalisation might not be vivid, clear and continuous, but it felt real. There must have been some technical error: he was certain of it.

Although he was beginning to wonder whether certainty was a luxury he could no longer afford.

A white car—no, a van—moving too fast, faster than the stream of traffic, suddenly came into view. And then another. And a third, pulling up directly in front of the café. How had he been located so fast?

If a digital trigger had been installed in the State Department database, his probing would have activated a warning signal—and the system would have uncovered the registered address of the computer he was using.

Ambler sprang to his feet, pushed through an EMPLOYEES ONLY door, and raced up the stairs. If he were fortunate, he would find his way to the roof, then to the roof of an adjoining building. As his muscles pumped, a thought entered his mind. *If Hal Ambler doesn't exist, who are they after?*

LOCATED AT THE BASE of the Sourland Mountains, Lake Aswell was surrounded by stands of willow, birch and hickory. In spring and summer, the ground was dense with foliage, flowers, berries. Even now, in January, when most of the trees were leafless, there was a sombre elegance to it all.

A quarter of a mile south of the access road to the lake, Ambler pulled the twelve-year-old Honda Civic that he'd found in a train station parking area off the road. It had been as anonymous a model as he could hope for, with a StorAKey box inside the wheel well. The box was a foolish contraption, used by drivers who valued the security of a spare key more than the security of their vehicles. Now he left the Honda hidden in a copse of cedar trees. The fibre-filled tan jacket he had picked up en route kept him warm, and as he walked along, his footfalls softly crunching on the carpet of leaves and pine needles, he felt the tension beginning to drain from him.

He was bone weary from the long hours of vigilance during the drive away from the capital, but his mind was still churning. The clandestine facilities of the United States government had been mobilised against him. Which meant that someone had set him up. Or that someone, or some group, with access to the powers of state, had sought to make him vanish.

There were colleagues at the Political Stabilisation Unit who could help him, but they were not men and women who reported for work at desk jobs; they changed their location regularly . . .

Harrison Ambler not found—it was madness. They had locked him out of every electronic forum he knew about. They had tried to lose him, to bury him. *They!* The exasperating bare plural—*They!*

Nearing the lake, Ambler heard the fluttering of an owl in an enormous cypress tree. He could just make out the chimney of old man McGruder's cabin, perilously close to the water on the far bank. A few yards further on, and in a dense stand of spruce trees, was the glade where, seven years ago, he had decided to build his own cabin. Curtained by magnificent old evergreens on three sides, it provided not only seclusion but tranquillity.

It was a single-roomed timber shelter almost as primeval as the nature that surrounded it. The ceiling and floor joists, the eaves, beams, even the stick-and-mud chimney—he had done them all himself, one warm, buggy June, using little more than a pile of wood and a gas-powered chain saw. He had only ever been there alone, and had never spoken of it to anyone. In violation of the rules, he had not told his employers about the acquisition of the lakeside land, arranged through a hard-to-trace offshore company. There had been times when he'd arrived back at Dulles International Airport, unable to face the world, and would drive nonstop to the cabin, covering the 180 miles in just three hours. He'd take his boat out and go fishing for small-mouth bass, and try to save some part of his soul from the deceit and subterfuge that was his vocation.

Taking a deep breath, he stepped through a gap in the firs and looked around at—a small, empty glade where his cabin should have been.

A wave of dizziness overtook him. His memory of where he had sited the structure was indelible—and yet all he could see were patches of moss, a sprawl of juniper and a deer-cropped yew tree. He circled the area, eyes alert to any sign of human habitation, past or present. Nothing. In a daze of incomprehension, he sank to his knees on the cold, mossy ground. Even to frame the question filled him with fear, yet he had to: Could he trust his own memories?

He let out a low guttural roar of fury and frustration. He had lost his sanctuary. He rose to his feet and began to pace, listening to the chirps and whistles of winter birds. Then he heard a faint, whistling noise of a different kind, and felt a sharp sensation of pain from a blow at the base of his neck.

He reached for the area, felt an object projecting from his body, and yanked it out. It was a long, penlike dart, and it had hit the top part of his sternum, an area of thick bone. He just might have been very lucky.

Diving into the low-draping branches of a hemlock tree, he examined the projectile. It was made of steel and moulded plastic; the now-empty syringe barrel bore small black lettering identifying its contents as carfentanyl—a synthetic opioid 10,000 times more powerful than morphine. He could feel an angry welt where the dart had struck him, yet, so far, he still felt alert.

He had been dosed with similar narcotics before, many times, on Parrish

Island. It was possible that he had built up a measure of tolerance. And, of course, the dosage contained in the syringe must have been designed to be sublethal; otherwise a bullet would have been less troublesome.

He became aware that his thinking was growing unfocused, woozy. The carpet of pine needles beneath him now seemed like a good place to lie down and take a nap . . . *just for a few minutes*.

No! He could not succumb. He had to feel the fear. Epinephrine, better known as adrenaline, was an effective counter-agent to carfentanyl.

Feel the fear, he repeated to himself, crawling from beneath the apron of the hemlock and craning his neck to see all around him. And suddenly he did feel it, as he heard a faint whistling sound again, the sound of a fast-moving projectile, missing him by inches. Adrenaline coursed through his bloodstream: his mouth went dry, his heart hammered wildly and his stomach knotted. Someone was still after him.

Both darts had come from further up the bank. In his mind, Ambler walked to his southwest, trying to visualise every detail of the terrain. There was the large stand of hemlocks; a procession of boulders; a gulch where, during the summer, lady's-slippers flourished in the wet shade. And, lashed maybe twelve feet off the ground to an old, ailing elm, a portable tree stand for deer hunting. It had been placed there years ago and never dismantled. The seat was on a platform about three feet square; the heavy straps that held it up were secured round the tree and kept in place by a couple of eye-bolts threaded through the trunk. Of course. Any professional would have taken advantage of it. How long had his pursuer been studying him before he squeezed the trigger?

The uncertainties were beginning to tire Ambler. *I could rest here. Just for a few minutes*. No! He wrenched himself back to the present crisis. So long as he was free, he had a chance.

Rising to a crouched position, Ambler slowly moved forward. *Slow and steady*, he told himself.

He completed an elliptical course that led him past the elm, then back towards it. As he drew closer, he found a line of sight through bramble, trunks and branches, and looked where he expected to find the stand. But though the tree was as he had imagined, there was no stand on it.

The wind gusted and he heard a sound, faint but distinct, of wood scraping against wood. He turned towards it and finally made it out. Another deer stand—bigger, higher and newer, lashed to the vast trunk of an old plane tree. As quietly as he could, Ambler moved towards it. Sitting in it was a big man, dressed in camouflage fatigues, and, luckily, facing the opposite direction. Dangling round his shoulders from a strap was a long rifle. It had to have been the dart gun. But the man also had a small sidearm—from its outline, probably a Beretta M92, US military issue usually reserved for members of the Special Operations units. Ambler strained to see in the late-afternoon gloom. The rifleman was holding to his eyes a pair of autofocus binoculars with a green, rubberised waterproof casing.

Was the man alone? He *seemed* to be: he had no walkie-talkie, no visible communicator, no earphone. But assumptions could not be made.

Ambler's view of the gunman was partly blocked by a thick branch, which projected horizontally from the trunk of the old plane tree for maybe fifteen feet, and which was strong enough for his purposes. If he could swing himself up on it, he could propel himself over the brambles that encircled the base of the tree, and be within reach of the tree stand.

He waited for the next gust in the right direction—away from the gunman, towards him—and sprang up, his hands grasping the branch silently, as he swung himself up and onto it. A low groaning noise came from the wood itself, as the bough flexed under his weight, but the gunman on the stand—Ambler could see him now—gave no sign that he noticed.

Ambler inched his way down the bough. He'd hoped to release the stand's heavy nylon strap, sending the platform crashing to the ground. But the strap's buckle was on the other side of the trunk and he could not get much closer without giving himself away. He clenched his jaw, willing himself to focus. *Nothing ever goes according to plan. Revise, and improvise.*

He raised himself to another branch, filled his lungs with air, and pushed off, throwing himself at the gunman in a flying tackle.

Alerted by the noise, the man rose and turned. Ambler hit him too low—at knee rather than waist level—and instead of being knocked out of the stand the man fell forward and grabbed hold of Ambler. It was the most Ambler could do to get his hands on the Beretta.

With a powerful blow, the man knocked the pistol from his hand and into the brambles below. As the two men fought on the small stand, Ambler could tell he would have the worst of it. The man was six foot five, heavily muscled, and yet astonishingly agile. Ambler protected his head, but his body was left exposed. He stepped back, slammed himself against the tree trunk and dropped his hands. He couldn't have said why. As he gulped air, his entire body quaking, a flicker of his opponent's eye told Ambler what he needed to know: the big man was going for the *coup de grâce*—a single punch to the jaw.

Ambler did the one thing he was capable of doing: he dropped to the ground, with exquisite timing. And the punch connected with the trunk.

As the man howled in pain, Ambler sprang up, butting his head into his opponent's solar plexus, then grasped the man's ankles and heaved. The gunman spilled out of the stand and Ambler plunged down after him.

With fast, deft movements, Ambler detached the long-barrelled rifle from its sling, and used the sling to tie the gunman's hands behind his back. The centre two knuckles of his right hand were red, bloodied and beginning to swell, obviously broken. The man moaned in agony.

Ambler looked around for the Beretta. It glinted from beneath the brambles, and Ambler decided to put off retrieving it.

'Kneel, GI Joe,' Ambler said. 'You know the position. Cross your ankles.'

The man did so reluctantly. 'I think something's broken, man,' he said in a low, strangled voice, clutching his ribs.

'You'll live,' Ambler said shortly. 'Or not. That's for us to decide, isn't it?'

'I don't think you understand the situation,' the man said.

'Which is exactly where you come in,' Ambler replied, working to control his breathing. He began to pat the man's trouser pockets and extracted a military-style pocketknife. 'Now we're going to play a little game of truth or dare.' He swung out the blade and held it close to the man's face. 'First question. Are you working alone?'

'No way. A bunch of us here.'

He was lying. Even dulled by the carfentanyl, Ambler knew it, the way he always knew it. When colleagues asked how, he would give them different answers in different cases. A tremble in the voice. Or a tone of voice that was too assertively smooth in another. Something around the mouth. Something around the eyes. There was always something.

Consular Operations had once assigned people to study his peculiar faculty; nobody had managed to duplicate it. Intuition was what he called it.

'So you're alone,' he told the kneeling operative. 'As I'd have expected.'

The man protested, but without conviction. Ambler realised that they must have figured it was a long shot that he'd show up here. There were fifty other places he might have gone to, and he guessed there were watchers positioned at those places, too.

'Next question. What's my name?'

'I wasn't informed,' the man said, almost resentfully. 'Assignment arrived a few hours ago. No photo. They said you were forty, six foot tall, brown hair, blue eyes. Basically, if anybody showed up in this godforsaken place today, it was going to be you. That's how they explained it, OK?'

'Well done,' Ambler said. 'You told me the truth. I can always tell.'

'Whatever you say,' the man said. He was not a believer.

'Who are you working for?'

'They'll explain. It's not for me to say.' Confidence was starting to return to the man's voice.

'You don't seem to understand. They're not in charge of you right now. I am.' He pressed the edge of the knife to the gunman's right cheek.

'Please,' the man moaned.

'A word of advice. If you're going to take a gun to a knife fight, make sure you win.' Ambler focused on the long-barrelled rifle. A Paxarms MK24B-A .509-calibre syringe-projection rifle. 'A pretty fancy piece of equipment,' Ambler said. 'Not part of GI Joe's usual kitbag. What's the deal?' He pressed down again with the blade.

'*Please*,' the man said, and it was as if all the air had come out of him.

'Instructions were to knock me out—and then what?'

The man sounded almost sheepish. 'Seems the people I work for have taken a real interest in you. They said you might show up, and if so, I was to make an approach. They said to use my discretion if I thought you might be dangerous.' He shrugged. 'So I took the tranquilliser gun just in case. They were going to radio further info to me once I reported in that you were in custody. Assuming you showed.'

'*They?* The government, you mean.'

'Huh?' A puzzled look. 'I don't work for a government pay grade, that's for damn sure. We're talking about a strictly private outfit, OK? These people hire me to do jobs, but they do it at a remove. The sense I got was, they learned you were on the market, and they want to sign you up before someone else does.'

'Nice to be in demand.' Ambler struggled to process what he was hearing. 'Method of contact?'

'I got an encrypted email with the instruction. Partial payment wired into an account. The deal was on. No meetings. Total breakaway security.'

The man was telling the truth—and his words told Ambler even more.

Breakaway security. Jargon from US intelligence. 'You're an American operative,' he said.

'Retired. Used to be in military intelligence. Special Forces for seven years. Now I'm freelance.'

Ambler unzipped a pouch attached to the man's camouflage vest. There was a battered-looking Nokia cellphone inside and Ambler pocketed it. He also found a military version of a BlackBerry text-messaging device.

'So here's the barter,' Ambler said. 'You tell me the email protocols and your passcodes.'

There was a pause. Then, a new look of resolve. 'Dream on.'

'Do you know what a man's face looks like when it's flayed?' Ambler said evenly. 'I do. Now then. Shall we begin?'

The kneeling man's eyes constricted in fear. 'You said a barter,' he said. 'What do I get?'

'Oh, that. You get to . . . how shall I put it? Save face.'

The man swallowed hard. 'Passcode is 1345GD,' he said hoarsely.

'A friendly reminder. If you lie, I'll know,' Ambler said. 'Get a single detail wrong, and we'll return to our anatomy lesson. Understand?'

'I'm not lying.'

A wintry smile. 'I know.'

'Email encryption is automatic. Subject line must say: "Seeking Ulysses". Capitalising doesn't matter. Signoff is "Cyclop".' The man continued to detail the communication protocols. After Ambler had made him repeat everything three times, he said, 'You got to let me go, man.'

Ambler took off his tan jacket and put on the man's combat vest and Kevlar-lined camouflage jacket, which seemed likely to come in handy. He took the man's belt wallet and strapped it on himself; most off-the-books operatives carried substantial sums of cash, and that, too, might come in handy. As for the rifle, its bulk would make it more of an impediment than an advantage, at least in the short term. He field-stripped it and tossed the six remaining tranquilliser darts into the brambles. Only then did he untie the man's hands and toss him the tan jacket. 'So you don't freeze,' he said.

As he moved, Ambler felt a slight sting at the side of his neck and absently slapped at it with a hand. It was only a moment before he realised that there would be no mosquitoes around at this time of the year, and by then he had noticed that his fingertips were wet with his own blood. Not an insect. Not a dart.

A bullet.

He whirled round. The man he had just untied had crumpled to the ground, blood spilling from his mouth, the fixed stare of death on his face. A sniper's bullet—the same bullet that grazed Ambler's neck—must have hit him in the head.

Had the bullet been meant for Ambler?

He had to run. Ambler plunged through the woods at top speed. His gift of the tan coat might have flagged the man for execution. A distant sniper would have homed in on the colour. But why send someone to 'make an approach' if the plan was to kill him?

Ambler had to leave the Sourlands. The Honda had no doubt already been located. What other vehicles were in the area? He remembered seeing a tarp-covered Gator, an off-road utility vehicle, a quarter of a mile up the hill. When he reached it, he wasn't surprised to find that the keys were in it. This was still a part of the world where nobody locked his front door. The Gator started easily, and Ambler drove through the woods as fast as the vehicle could manage, gripping the steering wheel when the vehicle bounced over rocks, ducking his head to avoid low branches.

The windscreen of the Gator suddenly exploded. A second bullet had arrived.

He steered crazily, hoping that the bouncing of the vehicle would make it harder to keep him in the cross hairs of the sniper's scope. The line of fire told him that the shot had been fired from across the lake—somewhere in the area of McGruder's old house. Or the grain silo a little further up the hill. Yes, that's where he'd set up if he were running an op.

Gunning the engine, he drove up the steepest slopes of the Sourland Mountains with ease; ten minutes later, he reached a road. The Gator was too slow to keep up with traffic, and the shattered windscreen would attract attention, so he parked behind a dense stand of cedars and turned off the engine. There was no sound but its ticking and the rushing of cars nearby.

He took out the slain man's text-messaging device. *They want to sign you up.* Was it a ruse? Whatever outfit had recruited the American ex-operative clearly intended to keep itself at one remove, yet Ambler had to learn what they knew. Now it was up to him to make an 'approach'. After a few moments' thought, he typed a terse message.

An encounter with the subject, he explained, had not gone as planned, but he now found himself in possession of some 'interesting documents'.

A meeting would be necessary. *Awaiting instructions*, he typed. Then he sent the message off to whoever was on the receiving end.

He made his way to the side of the road. In the camouflage jacket, he would look like an out-of-season hunter. A couple of minutes later, a middle-aged woman driving a GMC picked him up. She talked nonstop—Ambler making polite noises but barely hearing a word—before dropping him off at the Motel Six near Route 173.

Seventy-five dollars for a room. He worried that he wouldn't have enough, then he remembered the belt wallet. Checking in under a false name, he struggled against an exhaustion that would have threatened to engulf him even without whatever carfentanyl remained in his system.

In the nondescript room he went through the contents of the belt wallet. There were two sets of identification cards; most useful would be the driver's licence from Georgia. It looked unremarkable, but Ambler could tell that it was designed to make alteration easy. He would have no difficulty getting a passport-size photograph of himself at a shopping mall, and adapting the already spurious licence. The operative's height and eye colour were different from his, but not enough to arouse suspicion. Tomorrow . . . but there were so many things he would have to deal with tomorrow. Things he was too exhausted to contemplate right now.

He forced himself into the shower, made the water as hot as he could tolerate, and remained there, sudsing off the sweat, blood and grime until nothing remained of the small motel-issue bar of soap. Then he staggered out and dried himself.

As he towel-dried his hair vigorously he stepped over to the mirror above the sink. It was fogged with steam, and he heated it with the hair dryer until an oval was cleared. He could not remember the last time he had looked at his own face, and he braced himself for a haggard countenance.

When he finally saw himself in the mirror, vertigo overcame him.

It was the face of a stranger.

The man in the mirror was unrecognisable to him. The high, angular cheekbones, the aquiline nose . . . it was a handsome face—more handsome than his own. *His* nose had been broader, the cheeks more convex, the chin cleft. And what he read in it was the same emotion that filled his own breast: terror. Dread.

The psychiatric jargon to which he had been subjected during his months of captivity—'dissociative identity disorder', 'personality fragmentation' and so on—suddenly filled his mind. He could hear a chorus of murmured doctors' voices insisting that he had suffered a psychotic break and was drifting through fictive identities.

Could they have been right? Was he mad after all?

Chapter 3

Sleep finally overtook Ambler, but unconsciousness provided no sanctuary. His dreams took him to Changhua, Taiwan, a city surrounded by mountains on three sides and facing the Taiwan Strait.

On the outskirts, near a paper factory, a makeshift platform had been assembled. The man many believed would be the next president of Taiwan, Wai-Chan Leung, was about to appear before a crowd of thousands of supporters who had flocked from nearby townships. Never in living memory had a political candidate inspired such excitement.

Leung was, in many ways, an unlikely figure. For one thing, he was much younger than most candidates: just thirty-seven years of age. He came from a wealthy merchant family, and yet he was a genuine populist. He had founded the country's fastest-growing new political party, a party committed to reform. Having led successful anti-corruption campaigns at the local level, Leung now asked to be given the authority to cleanse national politics of corruption and cronyism. And where other candidates exploited a long-standing fear and resentment of the 'Chinese empire' represented by the mainland, Leung spoke of a 'new policy towards the new China'—a policy centred on conciliation, trade and shared sovereignty.

To many old China hands, the young man sounded too good to be true. According to a dossier painstakingly compiled by Consular Operations' Political Stabilisation Unit, he was.

Ambler had been deployed at Changhua as part of an 'action team' dispatched by the Political Stabilisation Unit—one of the 'Stab boys', in the sardonic shorthand. Which meant he was there not as Hal Ambler but as Tarquin, his field name. Tarquin, he sometimes felt, was a person in his own right. When he was in the field, Ambler *became* Tarquin. It was a form of mental compartmentalisation that enabled him to do what had to be done.

As he moved through the crowd, keeping his eyes on the platform, the Western-faced Tarquin was presumed to be a member of the foreign media.

At any moment, the man would appear. Taiwan's great hope. The youthful idealist. The visionary.

The monster. The PSU dossier had revealed the fanaticism that lay beneath the candidate's pose of moderation and reasonableness. It exposed his ideological ties with the Khmer Rouge, his personal involvement with the drug trade—and with a string of political murders throughout Taiwan. He could not be allowed to succeed, to take his place at the helm of Taiwan's National Congress. It was to ensure the survival of democracy itself that Leung had to be removed from the democratic arena.

The Stab unit specialised in that kind of job. Undersecretary Ellen Whitfield, the unit's director, was single-mindedly devoted to the idea that unpalatable action was sometimes necessary to fend off even more unpalatable consequences. Where other unit directors were content to analyse and assess, Whitfield would act—early. She did not believe in endless diplomatic temporising when peace could be kept by means of a swift, surgical intervention. Seldom, though, had the stakes been so great.

Tarquin's earpiece crackled softly. 'Alpha One in position,' a voice said. Translation: the team's explosive-ordnance technician was now a safe distance from where he had secreted his device, ready to activate the radio-controlled detonator on Tarquin's signal.

From the murmurs of the crowd, Tarquin knew that the candidate had appeared. He looked up as Leung stepped smartly onto the dais.

Applause grew; the candidate beamed. Tarquin waited, holding the props of a journalist's notepad and pen.

Awaiting your signal: a metallic voice prompted from his earpiece. *Awaiting your signal.*

The sound seemed to change to another, a faint noise that Ambler now realised had woken him and brought him back to the here and now. His motel bedsheets were knotted and clammy with sweat. The noise—a rattling from the bedside table—was the vibration from the slain man's text-messaging device. He reached for it and, after pressing a few buttons, confirmed that a reply to his email had arrived. The brief message conveyed precise instructions. A rendezvous had been arranged for 2.30 that afternoon, at Philadelphia International Airport, Gate C19.

They were clever. They were using the airport's security staff and metal detectors to ensure that he would arrive unarmed. Though the arena was public, the hour selected was when relatively few people would be waiting for flights, and the gate was in a quiet part of the terminal, so they would have some measure of seclusion. They knew what they were doing. It was not an entirely comforting thought.

CLAYTON CASTON sat at the breakfast table, dressed in one of his dozen identical grey suits, bought from a clothier's catalogue. They had been marked 50 per cent off, which seemed very reasonable to him, and the wool-and-polyester blend minimised wrinkling, which was very practical. 'Year-round executive three-button suit', the catalogue said: an 'all-season blend'. Caston took the clothiers at their word; he wore the suits all year round. So, too, the rep ties, red with green stripes, or blue with red stripes. He realised some of his colleagues considered his unvarying attire eccentric. But what was the point of variety for its own sake? You found something that did what it was supposed to do, and you stuck with it.

It was the same with his breakfast. Cornflakes were what he had in the morning; cornflakes were what he was having now.

'That is such *bull*!' his sixteen-year-old daughter, Andrea, exploded. She was talking to her brother Max, older by one year. 'Chip is *gross*. Anyway, he's into Jennifer, not me—thank God!'

'You are *so* transparent,' Max said implacably.

'Use a grapefruit knife if you're cutting grapefruit,' their mother said, mildly reproving. 'That's why we've got them.' She was dressed in a towelling bathrobe, her feet in towelling slippers, her hair held back in a headband. To Clay Caston, she was a vision of loveliness.

Max accepted the curved knife without a word; he was still needling his sister. 'Chip hates Jennifer and Jennifer hates Chip; you made sure of it when you told Chip what Jennifer said about him to T.J. By the way, I hope you let Mom know about what happened in your French class yesterday.'

'Don't you dare!' Andrea jumped up in a rage. 'Why don't we talk about the little *scratch* on the side of the Volvo? Think Mom's noticed yet?'

'What kind of a scratch?' Linda Caston asked, putting down her coffee.

Max gave his sister a smouldering look. 'You know something?' he said. 'I think it's time your friend Chip and I had a talk.'

'You wouldn't dare, you little toad.'

Caston looked up from his *Washington Post*. The others at the table were going at each other as if he didn't exist. Caston was used to it. Andrea and Max were self-absorbed adolescents; an undisciplined, rambunctious couple of brats, who squabbled over the slightest scrap. That they were his own children was something of a mystery to him. But Clayton Caston loved them like life itself.

'Is there any orange juice left?' Caston's first words at the breakfast table.

Max handed him the carton. 'There's a swallow or two left, Dad,' he said.

'One swallow does not make a spring,' Caston replied.

Max shot him an uneasy look. 'Whatever.'

THERE WAS A LOT LESS shouting in Caleb Norris's office at the CIA two hours later, but the hushed voices only emphasised the heightened tension. Norris was Associate Deputy Director of Intelligence, and when he had summoned Caston for a 9.30 a.m. meeting he hadn't needed to tell him what it was about. Since the Parrish Island bulletin had arrived the previous morning, further signals—conflicting and vague—had come in, suggesting that there had been additional disturbances related to the incident.

Norris was barrel-chested, with a broad face and small, wide-spaced eyes. Although he was the Agency's most senior intelligence analyst and a member of the Director's inner circle, anyone who saw his photograph would place him in a different profession—that of a bouncer, say. Norris was too impatient for a traditional career, and at the Agency his impatience became a virtue. He pushed through the log jams and bottlenecks that left others in his wake. Caston admired that about him.

Norris was in a characteristic state of agitation—pacing his office, his stout arms folded on his chest—when Caston had appeared in the doorway. Norris was annoyed by the Parrish Island incident; it reminded him how much of the intelligence establishment was outside the purview of its titular director. Every division of the military had its own internal intelligence unit, as did the Department of Defense, the White House's National Security Council and the National Security Agency in Fort Meade. Even the State Department supported a bureau of intelligence and research, in addition to its clandestine-service division, Consular Operations. And every organisation was further partitioned internally. The fissures and fault lines were numerous, and each held the potential for catastrophic failure.

Hence this bulletin bothered him. It was one thing not to know what was happening in Uzbekistan; it was another to be in the dark when it came to your own back yard. The Parrish Island facility was a 'joint resource' used by all of America's clandestine services. A man kept isolated in a locked ward was presumably very dangerous, either because of what he was capable of disclosing or what he was capable of *doing*. But when Norris had enquired as to the escaped man's identity, nobody had had an answer.

'Here's the thing,' the ADDI blurted out to Caston when he entered, as if they were already in the midst of conversation. 'Every patient in that facility goes with a requisition signature and a twelve-digit billing code. If Langley checks in a loony-tunes analyst, Langley foots his bill. If it's someone at Fort Meade, Fort Meade gets billed. The records are supposed to give the name of the officer who authorised the custodial detention. Only, not this time. The accounts guys say they can't find the billing code in their database. Ergo, we haven't even figured out who authorised his detention. Either they're telling us the truth, in which case they're screwed. Or they're stonewalling, in which case they're screwing us. What I want from you, Clay, is a lantern in the darkness. My usual request, right?'

Caston bowed his head. 'If they're stonewalling, Cal, it's on a very high level. I can tell you that already.'

The ADDI turned an expectant gaze towards him. 'More,' he said.

'It's pretty clear that the fugitive is a former high-value agent.'

'Who went off his rocker.'

'That's what we're told. Best I can figure, Consular Operations has given us "file front" info on Patient 5312. And we got a psych profile zapped over from Parrish Island. Basically, he's a severe dissociative. He thinks he's someone he isn't.'

'Then who is he?'

'That's the question of the hour, isn't it?'

Another gust of indignation filled Norris's sails. 'Goddammit,' he cried. 'How can you just lose somebody's identity, like a sock in the dryer?'

Caston shrugged. 'Like I say, psychiatric files we've got, all indexed under the patient number, 5312. But that information doesn't lead to any Cons Op personnel files—no matter what root you probe in the system.'

'Meaning they've been erased?'

'Meaning, more likely, they've been disconnected. The data probably exists somewhere, but it isn't linked to a digital ID anybody has access to.'

'Sounds like you've been roaming through the computer system there.'

Caston looked disapprovingly at Norris's messy desk. 'The major systems at State aren't integrated, but they use the same back-office program we do for accounts management. If you know your way round that, you get the equivalent of a plank you might use to board one ship from another.'

'So what did you learn once you galloped across that plank?'

'Not a lot so far. We're still combing the records. There's a partial ops record, under his field alias, Tarquin, so we do know that Tarquin was a member of the Political Stabilisation Unit. But the rest of his record has been delinked from the Tarquin folder.'

'So, what's your gut tell you? What do your instincts say?'

It took Caston a moment to realise that Norris was goading him.

Early in their working relationship, Caston had made his scorn for the notion of 'gut instinct' abundantly clear. It was something of a hobbyhorse with him. As far as he was concerned, to go on hunches was to go off half-cocked. It prevented one from analysing the data logically; it impeded the workings of reason and the rigorous techniques of probability analysis.

Caston watched as Norris's face split into a grin; the ADDI enjoyed needling him into delivering his firmly held convictions on the subject.

'I'm just kidding,' Norris said. 'But, tell me, what are we supposed to make of this Tarquin?'

'Several data points suggest that he's a bad egg. You know my views about agents who colour outside the lines. If you're on the payroll, you should comply with parameters established by federal decree. The way I see it, either a practice is authorised or it isn't. There's no middle path. I want to know why we have people like this "Tarquin" in the employ of the federal government. When will our intelligence services learn that it never works?'

'Nothing in creation ever works to plan. Including Creation itself. And God had seven days to get it right. I can only give you three.'

'What's the rush?'

'The intelligence directorate has been getting signals about some sort of irregular off-the-books activity going on. We think it involves highly placed members of the government, and that it's been fast-tracked. So we're all on alert. We can't know it's connected to this "Tarquin" but it's dangerous to presume otherwise. So we need a report from you in three days. Find out who Tarquin is. Help us bring him in.'

Caston nodded stonily. He did not need encouragement. He detested anomalies, and the man who had escaped from Parrish Island was an anomaly of the worst kind.

AT MOTEL SIX, New Jersey, Hal Ambler used the Nokia to place a number of phone calls. He could not use the emergency numbers he had memorised as a Stab operative, in case they triggered a tracing mechanism. Instead, it would be safer to knock on the front door.

Accordingly, the first call he made was to the State Department Communications Office. Pretending to be a reporter from Reuters, he asked to be connected to the office of Undersecretary Ellen Whitfield. Could she confirm a statement that had been attributed to her? Her assistant, to whom he was connected, was apologetic. The Undersecretary was travelling as part of an overseas delegation. Was it possible to be more specific? the Reuters correspondent asked. The assistant was sorry but she could not.

Ellen Whitfield's official designation as an 'Undersecretary' in the State Department concealed her real role as the Director of the Political Stabilisation Unit: his boss. What did Ellen Whitfield know about what had happened to him? If she did not know, she would want to know, wouldn't she?

He struggled to recall the days before he found himself a captive at the Parrish Island facility. He could remember the commencement of the Stab operation at Changhua—preparing for the 'removal' of Wai-Chan Leung—but then? His mind was like a torn page. There was no sharp line separating recollection from oblivion; rather, it feathered irregularly to an end.

Perhaps he needed to go further back, to a time when his memories of his life were vivid. If only he could find someone who could corroborate those memories. Someone who could provide the reassurance he desperately needed: that he was who he thought he was.

On impulse, Ambler called directory assistance for Dylan Sutcliffe, in Providence, Rhode Island.

Dylan Sutcliffe was someone he had met when they were freshmen at Carlyle College in Connecticut. Dylan had the gift of the gab and a great store of tales about growing up in Pepper Pike, Ohio. Ambler remembered the Charlie Brown-style shirts Sutcliffe favoured, with their colourful horizontal stripes. He recalled attending Sutcliffe's wedding just a year after graduation; knew that he had a good job at a Providence community bank.

'This is Dylan Sutcliffe,' a voice now said.

'Dylan!' Ambler said. 'It's Hal Ambler. Remember me?'

There was a long pause. 'I'm sorry,' the man said, sounding confused. 'I'm not sure I caught your name.'

'Hal Ambler. We were at Carlyle together two decades ago. You were in my suite, freshman year. *I was at your wedding.* Coming back now?'

'Listen, I don't buy things from strangers over the phone,' the man said curtly. 'I suggest you try this on somebody else.'

Could this be the wrong Dylan Sutcliffe? Nothing about him *sounded* like the Sutcliffe who Ambler remembered. 'Maybe I got the wrong guy. You didn't go to Carlyle, then?'

'I did. It's just that nobody in my class was named Hal Ambler.' There was a click as the man hung up on him.

Prompted by a mixture of anger and fear, Ambler called Carlyle College and got transferred to the registrar's office. To the young man who answered, he explained that he was a human resources officer for a major corporation, the prospective employer of one Harrison Ambler, and they were verifying certain items on the applicant's résumé. All he needed was confirmation that Harrison Ambler had graduated from Carlyle College.

'Certainly, sir,' the young man said. He asked for the spelling and entered the name; Ambler could hear quiet, swift clicking on a keyboard. 'Could you give me the spelling one more time?' the voice asked.

With a growing sense of apprehension, Ambler did so.

'I guess it's a good thing you called,' said the voice on the phone. 'Nobody by that name has ever matriculated here, let alone graduated.'

'Is it possible that your database doesn't go back far enough?'

'Nope. We're a small college. Believe me, sir, if this guy was enrolled here at any time during the twentieth century, I'd know.'

'Thank you,' Ambler said, his voice hollow. 'Thank you for your time.' His hand was trembling as he pressed the OFF button on the cellphone.

It was madness! He shut his eyes, and allowed the memories of four decades to swirl in his mind: the time, exploring his own back yard as a child, when he had stumbled on a nest of wasps; the hot July in summer camp, learning to do the butterfly stroke in Lake Candaiga; the August he spent, aged fifteen, working in a fairground restaurant ten miles south of Camden, Delaware, where he had grown up. There were less comfortable memories, too: a sophomore-year crush at Carlyle turned sour: the breathlessness of their early encounters, then the tears, the stormy recriminations.

All these things he remembered with clarity and precision. Or was it simply a delusion? A throbbing was building in his head as he left his room.

In one corner of the motel's lobby, an Internet-enabled computer was available for guests. Ambler sat down in front of it and, using a passcode held by the State Department's analytic bureau, logged onto the newspaper database LexisNexis. The local newspaper in Camden once ran a small item about him when, as a sixth grader, he won the county spelling bee.

He ran the Nexis search. Nothing matched the description. As far as LexisNexis was concerned, Harrison Ambler did not exist.

AMBLER DROVE to the airport and bought a ticket to Wilmington. The woman at the ticket counter stifled a yawn as she stamped his boarding card. The photo ID he submitted—the Georgia licence, altered to display a photograph of Ambler—would not withstand close scrutiny, but it received none.

Gate C19 was at the end of a long walkway and adjoined two others. He glanced around; fewer than a dozen travellers were visible. It was half past two. The next flight at any of these gates would not be for another ninety minutes. It was a dead period.

You'll know who I am, the message had said. Ambler walked around the seating areas, taking in the stragglers and early birds: the plump woman feeding candy to her plump daughter; the man in the ill-fitting suit, thumbing through a PowerPoint presentation; the young woman with piercings. No contenders. Finally, his eyes alighted on a turbaned Sikh gentleman, moving his lips as he read *USA Today*.

As Ambler walked over to him, he saw no evidence of any hair under the turban—not a single stray strand. A gleam of adhesive on the man's cheek suggested that the beard was recently applied. Was the man really moving his lips as he read, or was he communicating on a fibre-optic microphone?

Ambler stepped behind the seated figure and, with a lightning-swift movement, grabbed the turban and lifted it up. Beneath it, he saw the man's pale, smooth-shaven pate—and, taped to it, a small Glock.

Ambler seized the gun and let the turban drop back into place. The seated man remained stock-still, only his raised eyebrows registering surprise. The manoeuvre had taken no more than two seconds, and had been concealed from anyone's view by Ambler's own body.

The pistol was oddly light, and Ambler recognised the model at once. The body was made of plastic and ceramic, the slide containing less metal than a typical belt buckle. The odds that it would set off a metal detector were low; the odds that the security guards would interfere with a Sikh's religious headdress were even lower.

'Bravo,' the fake Sikh said in a low voice. 'A fine defensive move. Not that it changes anything.' He spoke English with the perfect enunciation of someone who had learned it abroad at an early age.

'I'm the one with the weapon. That doesn't change anything?'

'Sometimes you make best use of a weapon by giving it up,' the man said, his eyes twinkling. 'Tell me, do you see the guy in the airline uniform, standing at the gate counter?'

Ambler glanced over. 'I see him.'

'He's with us. He stands ready to shoot you, if that proves necessary.' The man looked up at Ambler, who was still standing. 'Do you believe me?'

'I believe he'll try,' Ambler responded. 'You'd better hope he doesn't miss.'

The fake Sikh nodded. 'But then, unlike you, I'm wearing Kevlar, just in case.' Again he looked up at Ambler. 'Do you believe me?'

'No,' Ambler said, after a beat. 'I don't.'

The man's smile widened. 'You are Tarquin, aren't you? You see, your reputation precedes you. They say you're devilishly good at reading people. I needed to be sure.'

Ambler took the seat next to him; the meeting would be less conspicuous that way. 'Why don't you explain yourself?' he asked.

The other man extended a hand. 'The name's Arkady. You see, I'd been told that a legendary field agent, alias Tarquin, might now be "available" for recruitment. And, no, I don't know your real name. I am aware that you seek information. I do not have that information. What I have is access to those who possess the information.' Arkady cracked his knuckles. 'Or rather, to those with access to those who possess it. In the organisation to which I belong, information flows only where it must.'

As he spoke, Ambler watched him intently. The man was not lying.

'I have to say the speed of the invitation is puzzling,' Ambler said.

'We don't like to waste time. The squawk went out yesterday morning.' In the trade jargon, an alert radioed to all intelligence services went out on 'the squawk'. It was a leaky form of communication, used when urgency overrode secrecy. 'Clearly, your admirers have been waiting for this,' Arkady went on. 'And, no doubt, they think they have competition for your services. They don't want to let the moment pass.'

'You're speculating.'

'I know what I have to know. I can surmise a certain amount beyond that. And, of course, there is a great deal I must be content not to know. The system works for us all. It keeps them safe. It keeps me safe.'

'But it doesn't keep me safe. One of your guys tried to kill me.'

'I very much doubt that.'

'The large-calibre bullet that grazed my neck would beg to differ.'

Arkady looked bemused. 'That doesn't make any sense.'

'Yeah, well, the other guy looked pretty surprised, too, the moment before the bullet travelled on through his head.' Ambler's voice was a low rasp. 'What kind of a crazy game are you guys running?'

'Not us,' Arkady murmured. 'This sounds like a case of interference. It just means we weren't the only people to hear the squawk and respond. There has to have been a second party involved. We'll do the analysis, make sure there's been no breach. But it very much sounds like a parasitic visitation, so to speak. It won't happen again. Not once you're with us. My employers would very much like to keep you safe—so long as they can be assured that you will do the same for them. Trust must run in both directions.'

'That they can trust me,' Ambler said steadily, 'is something they'll have to take on trust.'

'That's the one thing they never do.' Arkady sounded apologetic. 'Such a bore, I know. But they have a little test for you. It's all terribly "win-win", as my employers like to say. The job we have for you is small, but . . . ticklish. It has defeated others, yet it must be done. You see, my employers are careful people, but maybe not all their friends are quite so careful. And maybe an undercover agent made some inroads and, having collected some evidence, is about to testify in a legal proceeding. All very messy.'

'You're talking about an undercover federal agent?'

'It's awkward, isn't it?' Arkady said. 'ATF, in fact.'

If the investigator was with the Bureau of Alcohol, Tobacco and Firearms, the investigation quite likely involved gun smuggling. The obvious assumption was that gunrunners who supplied the organisation which Arkady worked for had been ensnared.

'Like all of us, this agent is mortal,' the fake Sikh went on, 'and one day he will die. We simply wish to place a rush order on that eventuality.'

'Why me?'

Arkady made a face. 'This is so embarrassing. The truth is, we don't know what he looks like. The person he had direct dealings with isn't in a position to help us out—the reason is irrelevant. We've got a venue, we've got a time, but we don't want to take out the wrong person. You'll be able to tell at a glance who the mark is. Because, being the mark, he *knows* he's marked. That's the sort of thing you'll be able to pick up on.'

'I see,' Ambler said, and he was beginning to. Some sort of rogue outfit wanted his services. By killing a federal agent, he would prove that he had severed all loyalties to his former employers. They must have had reason to believe that he was sufficiently disaffected to entertain the assignment.

Perhaps they knew more than he did—perhaps they knew why he had been committed to Parrish Island.

'Then do we have a deal?'

Ambler thought for a moment. 'If I say no?'

'You'll never know, will you?' Arkady smiled. 'Maybe you *should* say no. And resign yourself to ignorance. There are worse things.'

Not to know was the one thing Ambler could not survive. He glanced at the blue-jacketed man behind the gate counter. 'I think we can do business.'

It was madness, and it was the one thing that might save him from madness. At the moment, this man was the closest thing he had to an escape route.

'At ten a.m. tomorrow, the undercover agent has a meeting scheduled with the US Attorney for the southern district of New York,' said Arkady. 'We believe that an armoured limousine will bring him to the corner of One St Andrew's Plaza in Lower Manhattan. In a rare moment of vulnerability, the agent will have to traverse a pedestrian area on foot. You must be there. At the appropriate time, one of our people will pass you a weapon. The rest is in your hands. All we insist on is that you follow the instructions exactly.'

'It's highly exposed,' Ambler protested. 'A lousy plan.'

'You don't know the facts of the case,' Arkady said, a glint of steel in his voice. 'My employers have studied them. The target is a cautious man. He isn't skulking under bridges for your convenience. This is actually an extraordinary opportunity. We may not get another for a long time, and then it will be too late. Remember, you're free to walk away. But if you complete the assignment, you will be introduced to someone up my line of command—someone who has worked beside you.'

Someone, then, who might know what happened to Harrison Ambler.

'I'll do it,' Ambler said.

Arkady leaned forward and patted Ambler's wrist. 'We don't ask so very much. Only that you should succeed where others have failed. It wouldn't be the first time.'

CLAYTON CASTON was looking thoughtful when he returned to his windowless office. Not *lost* in thought, Adrian Choi decided; *found* in thought was more like it. He looked as if he had his hooks in something, probably something to do with a spreadsheet. So many things around Caston seemed to involve spreadsheets.

'Anything I can do?' he asked his boss, eternally hopeful.

'Yes,' Caston said, 'there is. When we requested the Consular Operations files pertaining to the alias "Tarquin", we were given only partials. I need anything they can scrounge. Tell them to verify clearance with the office of the Director of Central Intelligence. Also, I need more from Parrish Island. I want personnel records for everyone who has worked at Ward 4W in the past twenty months.'

'I got the sense that they were dragging their feet at Consular Operations,' Adrian said. 'They didn't seem too happy with the request.'

'Of course not. They'd have to acknowledge that the Central Intelligence Agency is, in fact, this country's central intelligence agency. It offends their sense of pride. But the fact remains that I need them to cooperate. Which means I need you to get them to cooperate. In fact, I'm counting on it.'

Adrian nodded soberly, hairs pleasantly raised on the back of his neck. *I'm counting on it.* That sounded almost like *I'm counting on you.*

An hour later, a large, compressed digital file arrived from the system at Parrish Island. After decompressing and decrypting, the main component turned out to be some sort of audio file.

'You know how this thing works?' Caston grunted.

Adrian did. He made a few software adjustments, then set the audio file to play on Caston's computer. Apparently it had been recorded at a psychiatric session with Patient No. 5312, and represented his state of mind.

Patient No. 5312, they knew, was a highly trained government operative. An agent in possession of two decades' worth of operational secrets.

He was also—the recording made plain—stark raving mad.

AS CHIEF of the Second Bureau of the Ministry of State Security—the bureau devoted to foreign operations—Chao Tang visited Zhongnanhai on a regular basis. It was a capital within a capital. A heavily guarded complex in Beijing, where China's top leaders had lived and ruled in secrecy and seclusion since the Yuan Dynasty of the fourteenth century. The question, in Chao's view, was whether the old traditions would give way before a man who was intent on overturning them: China's youthful President Liu Ang.

The meeting tonight had been foisted upon Liu Ang by his own supporters. For what was at stake was nothing less than Liu Ang's own survival, and the future of the world's most populous nation.

Fear galvanised five of the six men gathered round the black lacquered table on the second floor of Liu's residence.

The intelligence reports from the First Bureau, which specialised in domestic intelligence, were shadowy and indistinct, but when they were combined with those from Chao's own bureau, the shadows deepened into something black indeed.

Liu Ang's adviser on security matters, seated to his right, exchanged glances with Chao, and then addressed the President. 'Forgive me for speaking forthrightly, but what good are all your plans for reform if you are not alive to carry them out?'

'You have made the case before,' Liu replied. 'And my answer remains that I refuse to be paralysed by fear. And I refuse to take action against people based solely on suspicion, not evidence. To do so would make me indistinguishable from my enemies.'

'When your enemies destroy you, you will be easily distinguished from them,' Chao interjected. '*They* will be the victors, and *you* the vanquished.'

'Some of those who oppose me are men and women of principle,' Liu Ang said. 'They cherish stability and regard me as a threat to it. When they see they have been in error, their opposition will subside.'

'There are powerful men, even within the inner councils of state, for whom the enemy is change,' Chao countered. Everyone knew about hardliners who were opposed to any movement towards transparency and fairness, having prospered from their absence. Especially dangerous were those hard-liners who had grudgingly acquiesced to Liu's appointment in the belief that he could be controlled, then discovered that he was nobody's puppet. So far, none had dared to move publicly against him, but a small cadre had decided that Liu was only growing more powerful over time— that they had to act soon, before it was too late.

'You who proclaim your loyalty to me—why would you turn me into the very thing I despise?' Liu Ang protested. 'They say that power corrupts, and now I know how. The reformer starts to listen to the counsel of fear. Well, I *refuse* to do so.'

It was all Chao could do not to pound the table. 'Are you *invulnerable*?'

he demanded. 'If someone fires a bullet at your reformist brain, does the bullet bounce off? The counsel of *fear*? How about the counsel of *sanity*?'

Chao's devotion to the young President was as personal as it was professional. Even before Liu Ang's elevation, Chao had respected the man's agility and integrity. But he did not have any illusions about the apparatus that Liu hoped to dismantle. It fostered insularity and self-deception, and to Chao there was no greater sin. Hence his heated words at this evening's meeting. He simply wanted Liu Ang to survive.

'You know that Comrade Chao and I have disagreed about many things,' said fifty-year-old Wan Tsai, his large eyes further magnified by his wire-rimmed glasses. 'Yet about this we are in agreement. The precautionary principle must be upheld.'

'Let us drop the euphemisms, Wan Tsai,' Liu Ang reproached. The old man was one of his oldest friends. 'You want me to launch a purge.'

'Just weed out the disloyal!' cried Wan Tsai. 'It is a matter of self-defence!'

The President gave him a sharp look. 'As the sage Mencius asks: What good is self-defence if it comes at the expense of the self?'

It was a mixed blessing that, at forty-three, Liu Ang was far younger than any who had previously occupied the position, and so beloved by the multitudes beyond Zhongnanhai's gates. Their adoration, like the Western media's enthusiastic coverage, only heightened the hard-liners' suspicion.

'Do not mistake me,' Liu Ang said gravely. 'I'm not discounting the worries you raise. But if I resort to purges to protect my position, my administration will not be *worthy* of protection.' He paused. 'Those who oppose me for reasons of principle, I shall endeavour to persuade. Those whose motives are less wholesome, well, they are opportunists. And if my policies succeed, they will do what opportunists always do: they will see which way the wind is blowing, and realign themselves accordingly. Just you see.'

'Is this the voice of humility or hubris?' asked a man at the other end of the table. The man, Li Pei, had white hair and a face as wrinkled as a walnut shell. A generation older than the others, he was in some ways the most incongruous of Liu's allies. He came from humble origins in the provinces, and was known by the sobriquet *jiaohua de nongmin*, or 'wily peasant'. He had kept a place in the Zhongnanhai compound through Mao and Mao's successors. Many assumed he was simply a cynic who adjusted to whoever was in charge. That was only part of the story. Like many of the most corrosive cynics, he was a wounded idealist.

At the head of the table, President Liu Ang took a sip of tea. 'Maybe I am guilty of both hubris and humility. But not ignorance. I know the risks.'

Another voice spoke quietly. 'We should not only look within. Among your enemies are foreigners who do not wish China well.'

'And these are not theoretical concerns,' Chao Tang said, exasperated. 'The intelligence reports I refer to are *deeply* worrying. Have you forgotten what happened to Wai-Chan Leung, in Taiwan? Many viewed the young man as a kindred spirit of yours. You may be facing some of the same enemies: the kind who fear peace more than war. The dangers are real. Indeed, as I say, it would appear that some sort of conspiracy is already in motion.'

'"Some sort"?' Liu echoed. 'The merest conjecture!'

'Plainly, members of your own government are involved,' Chao said. It took an effort to keep his voice level. 'Nor can we disregard evidence suggesting that certain elements in the US government may also be involved.'

'Your intelligence is not *actionable*,' Liu protested. 'I do not see what I can do that is consistent with the example I wish to set.'

'Please consider—' Wan Tsai started.

'Feel free to continue your discussion,' the youthful President said, rising to his feet. 'But I have a wife upstairs who is beginning to think she has been widowed by the People's Republic of China. In this particular, partial information *shall* suffice for action.' The laughter that followed was perfunctory, hardly leavening the atmosphere of anxiety. Perhaps the young President did not *want* to know the threats against him; he seemed to fear those threats less than he feared the consequences of paranoia. The others could not afford to be as sanguine. What Liu Ang did not know could kill him.

Chapter 4

Ambler was seated on a bench in St Andrew's Plaza, Lower Manhattan, on a concrete plaza between three looming federal buildings. He shifted to get comfortable. His muscles ached and the jackhammer of a street-repair crew, somewhere nearby, was prompting a headache. He checked his watch; he had already read the *New York Post* from cover to cover. A vendor across the plaza was selling sugared nuts from his cart; Ambler was thinking about buying a bag, simply to give himself something to do, when he noticed a middle-aged man in a Yankees jacket emerging from the back of a black car parked in the street below.

The mark had arrived.

He was paunchy, and sweating despite the cold. He looked around agitatedly as he climbed the steps to the plaza. This was someone who knew himself to be acutely vulnerable and was filled with a sense of foreboding.

Ambler stood up slowly. Now what?

A woman in heels and a green vinyl raincoat was walking rapidly towards him. She had a mane of blonde hair, full lips, grey-green eyes. Incongruously, she was carrying a brown lunch bag. As she approached, her attention seemed distracted and she stumbled into him.

'I'm sorry,' she murmured in a raspy voice.

Ambler found that his hands were now clutching the paper bag, which, his fingers quickly confirmed, did not hold lunch.

The man in the Yankees jacket had reached the plaza and was starting to walk towards the most northerly federal building.

Ambler pulled the weapon from the bag, opened his tan raincoat—on every block of the city, one could see a dozen just like it—and slipped the gun into the inside pocket. It was a Ruger .44; more powerful than the job required, and certainly too loud.

He turned and saw that the blonde was seated at another bench near the building. She had given herself a ringside view.

Ambler's heart was pounding. It was madness to have agreed to do this.

The mark stopped abruptly, looked around, and started to walk again. He was no more than thirty feet away from Ambler.

Intuition flared in Ambler's mind like the sun passing from behind a cloud. Now he understood what he had previously only vaguely, subconsciously surmised. *They never would have asked him.*

No doubt Arkady believed what he had been told, but the story made no sense: a risk-averse organisation would never give someone of uncertain loyalties an assignment of this nature. He could so easily have tipped off the authorities and ensured the mark's safety. *Ergo . . .*

Ergo the whole arrangement was a test. The gun was empty.

The mark was now twenty feet away, walking steadily to the building. Ambler strode rapidly towards him, withdrew the Ruger from his coat, and, aiming at the back of the man's baseball jacket, squeezed the trigger.

There was the quiet click of an empty gun, a sound largely swallowed by traffic noise. Feigning dismay, Ambler squeezed again and again, until all six chambers had been hammered.

He was sure that the blonde woman had seen the cylinder rotate, the firing pin twitch without effect.

Detecting sudden movement in his peripheral vision, Ambler turned his head. A security guard across the plaza had seen him! The guard pulled out his own gun, and Ambler heard the hard, popping sound of a .38 pistol, and the higher-pitched *twang* as a bullet zinged by his ear. Then he noticed another sudden movement: the vendor had pushed his wheeled cart into the guard, knocking him over. Ambler heard the metallic skittering of the pistol that had been knocked from his hand.

No mere bystander would ever move *towards* gunfire. The man posing as a vendor was surely part of a team.

He heard the roar of the motorcycle before he saw it, seconds later: a powerful black Ducati Monster emerged from nowhere, the face of its rider hidden behind his helmet's visor. Friend or foe?

'Jump on!' the rider bellowed, slowing down without coming to a stop.

Ambler followed instinct and threw himself onto the large rear section of the motorcycle's seat. The Ducati roared off again.

'Hold on tight!' the rider bellowed again. Moments later, the bike was bounding down the steps on the opposite side of the plaza.

Pedestrians on the pavement had already scattered. The man knew what he was doing, however, and soon the bike had zipped into traffic. Two blocks north, he turned onto Duane Street and pulled over, beside a limousine.

It was a Bentley; the driver was attired in olive-drab livery. The back door opened for Ambler and he got inside, settling back on the light tan leather seats. Another man was seated there, and now he moved forward and opened a window in the glass partition and spoke to the driver in front in a soft foreign tongue.

The limousine set off gently into the city traffic. Ambler's fellow passenger then turned and greeted him with a cheerful 'Hello'.

Ambler felt a jolt of recognition—Osiris. Arkady had promised Ambler he would meet 'someone who has worked beside you'. A man he had known only as Osiris, and who had known him only as Tarquin.

Osiris was a large man in his sixties, bald save for a fringe of red hair around his ears and the nape of his neck. He had been soft around the middle when they'd worked together in the Political Stabilisation Unit, but was surprisingly fast on his feet. Especially considering his other incapacity.

'It's been a while,' Ambler said.

Osiris smiled, his blue, filmy eyes almost but not quite meeting Ambler's. 'Long time no see,' he agreed.

Osiris was skilled at making people forget that he was blind. Consular Operations had had no more brilliant linguist. Not only could he speak and understand all the major languages, he was expert at dialects and regional accents too. He knew whether a German came from Dresden, Leipzig or Thüringen; he could differentiate thirty strains of 'street' Arabic.

'Our driver doesn't have any English, I'm afraid,' Osiris told Ambler. 'But he speaks Albanian like a prince.' He pressed a button and a drinks compartment slid out from the partition; without groping, he removed a bottle of water and poured some into two glasses. He waited for Ambler to take one before taking the other.

'Apologies for all the monkey business,' Osiris went on. 'I'm sure you've figured out the score. My employers needed to confirm that you weren't a sawbuck on a string. It wasn't as if they could exactly check references.'

Ambler nodded. It was as he had thought. 'What happens to the mark? The guy in the Yankees jacket?'

'Who knows? Apparently, the Feds launched an investigation into price-fixing in the construction industry, and that guy got flipped, turned state's evidence. If you sensed he was running scared, you were right. Lots of scary people would like to see him go down. Just not us.' Osiris laughed. 'What Arkady told you is what we told him. I lied to him, he lied to you, but it got purified in the pass-along, because he believed what he was saying.'

'So, do you know my name?' Ambler said.

'How many jobs did we work on together? Three, four? You'd think I would have picked up a thing or two. Tarquin. Real name Henry Nyberg—'

'Nyberg's another cover name,' Ambler interrupted. 'Used a few times and discarded. What's my real name?'

'Look, I'm not the information desk. I don't have *all* the answers.' Osiris's opaque eyes looked curiously alert beneath his almost porcine eye-brows. 'Some of them are above my pay grade. And you may not want to know what you think you want to know, my friend.'

'Try me.'

Osiris's sightless eyes fixed on him. 'I know a better place to talk.'

PRESIDENT LIU ANG had retired to his private quarters, but in another wing of the compound, the meeting continued.

The Second Bureau chief, Chao Tang, removed a dossier from his black portfolio and spread several photographs across the table. 'I have already shown this to Liu Ang, and I have asked him to cancel his foreign appearances for the sake of security. He refuses. But the rest of you should see.' He tapped one of the photographs: a crowd before a wooden platform. 'Taken a few minutes before the assassination in Changhua, Taiwan, a little more than two years ago. Please notice the Caucasian in the crowd.'

He tapped another photograph, a digitally enhanced close-up of the same man. 'The assassin. In other photographs, you'll see him at the location of other killings. Our spies have learned a thing or two about him.'

'What is his name?' the elderly, white-haired Li Pei demanded.

'We have only a field alias,' the spymaster, Chao, admitted. 'Tarquin.'

'Tarquin,' Li Pei repeated. 'An American?'

'We believe so, though we are not certain who controls him. Yet we have reason to think he may be a pawn in the plot against Liu Ang.'

'Then he must be eliminated,' said Li Pei.

'Precautions have already been taken,' Chao Tang said. 'We've had a signals intelligence team working on it. Yesterday, when we gained credible information about his possible whereabouts, we were able to take action. Trust me, the finest this country has to offer is on the case.'

It sounded like empty rhetoric, Chao knew, yet he believed it to be true. Agent Joe Li had never disappointed. And though he did his work with professional dispatch and dispassion, his loyalty to his country was beyond question. China's most formidable operative reported only to Chao.

'So this Tarquin—he is dead?' asked the economist Wan Tsai, drumming his fingers on the black lacquered table.

'Not yet,' Chao said.

A CLEVER RENDEZVOUS, Ambler judged, as he and Osiris disrobed and changed into swimming trunks provided free by the swimming pool of the Plaza Hotel in New York. It would be hard to conceal a listening device under these conditions—and nearly impossible to make an audible recording over the ambient noise of splashing water.

'So who are you working for these days?' Ambler prompted, treading water in the deep end beside Osiris. An elderly woman towards the shallow end was lazily swimming widths. Otherwise the pool was vacant. A few dowager types in one-piece swimming suits were sipping coffee as they reclined on poolside chaise longues.

'They're people like us,' Osiris replied, 'just organised differently. Former covert-ops people, lots of old Stab hands, in fact, who might not have been using their skills to full advantage. Now they're still serving American interests, but they're paid for and deployed by a private concern. We're all organised as a network. Agents work independently, but are coordinated and deployed by their "upline". And these people are intent on bringing in unique talent. Puts *you* in a good bargaining position, you know. You're something of a mythic figure among the Stab boys. The bosses figure if only half the stories they tell about you are true . . . and I've seen you work, so I know the score. It's an amazing skill. A *gift*. So what's the deal? Some witch doctor give you an amulet one day?'

Ambler allowed himself to float peacefully on the water for a moment. 'I'm not the best person to ask,' he said, soberly. 'But I think it has to do with this: most people see what they want to see. They simplify things. I don't. I can't. It isn't something I can turn on or off.'

'I don't know whether that's a blessing or a curse,' Osiris said. 'The condition of knowing too much.'

'Right now my problem is knowing too little. You know what I'm after. Enlightenment.'

'But enlightenment comes in steps,' Osiris said. 'What I've really got to offer is judgment, rather than information. Tell me the relevant facts, and I may be able to help you make sense of them.'

THE CHINESE MAN in the well-tailored merino suit attracted little attention as he came into the lobby of the Plaza Hotel. He was slight of build, handsome, with delicate features. He nodded at one of the receptionists at the desk, and she returned his nod, assuming that the man had confused her with whatever girl had checked him in. In an 800-room hotel it was a safe bet that someone who looked like he belonged did indeed belong.

Within a few minutes, Joe Li had ascertained that his quarry was not in any of the public spaces of the hotel—the art galleries, shops or dining rooms. He had ruled out the possibility that the quarry had taken a room; an establishment like this would demand ID, take impressions of credit cards, and so on. That left two other possibilities. One was the fitness centre.

None of the hotel's staff saw him turn down a corridor between two elevator banks and step through a service entrance. They did not see him open his briefcase and assemble the equipment it had carried. They did not see him step into a janitor's grey overalls and board a service elevator with a wheeled bucket and mop.

'DON'T YOU SEE,' Osiris was saying. 'There's an alternative hypothesis.' He trod water with small, graceful movements. 'You've been baffled by the fact that your memory of who you are doesn't square with the world you inhabit, and you assume it's the world that has been manipulated. What if it's your *mind* that has been manipulated?'

Ambler listened with a rising sense of dread as Osiris began to explain.

'It's easier to alter the contents of your head than it is to change the whole world. The best and the brightest have been fascinated by the possibilities of mind control since the 1950s. They've spent millions on research, inside and outside the government. Scientists developed modified versions of the old electroconvulsive therapy machines. Built on breakthroughs in "depatterning", these new machines mess with someone's mind so hard that they start to lose all sense of space and time and, basically, their sense of self. In the old days they'd combine that with a technique called "psychic driving", where a patient would be put in a stupor and bombarded with messages on a tape loop—sixteen hours a day for weeks on end. All very crude. Our agents could be, had been, captured by the enemy, the contents of their minds plumbed by means of stress, trauma and psychopharmacology. But what if you could alter the contents of human memory?'

'That's impossible.'

'The Pentagon didn't think so. In their Strategic Neuropsychology Division, they developed a technique known as *mnemonic overlay*. We're way beyond the old tape loops now. It involved "rich feed"—video, audio, olfactory stimuli—and discrete memory vignettes. Subjects would be put under the influence of a variety of infused psychotomimetic chemicals, then exposed to the *feed*: a stream of vivid episodes, in a constantly changing order, from pre-school to high-school graduation.

'A name, that of the overlaid identity, would be repeated again and again. The result was an alternate self that an agent would automatically retreat to under conditions of extreme stress or altered consciousness.'

'How do you know so much about it?'

Osiris shrugged. 'My background is in psy-ops. The idea was that you'd produce an interrogation-proof agent. But you know how the clandestine services work. Once you've developed a technique, it's anyone's guess how they'll put it to use.'

'And you're suggesting . . .?'

'Yeah,' said the sightless operative. 'I'm just suggesting, just putting it to you. What makes most sense of what you know?'

Ambler was beginning to feel prickly heat, despite the cool water. *Identity fragmentation . . . abreactive ego dystopia . . .* the psychiatric jargon returned to him in sharp, lacerating shards.

NOT IN THE FITNESS CENTRE, then. Joe Li had checked the area carefully, including the locker room. Now he pushed his bucket through the changing rooms adjoining the swimming pool. Still no sign of his quarry. The last place to look was the pool itself.

Walking with a shambling gait, Joe Li made his way into the swimming pool area. Nobody gave him a second look; nobody gave the long, modified handle of the squeeze mop a second look, either. As he wheeled his bucket along the tiled floor, he casually glanced around him. The man he was after had narrowly evaded him in the Sourlands. It would not happen twice.

If his quarry were here, his work would soon be finished.

AMBLER CLOSED HIS EYES and dived to the floor of the pool, then let himself ascend quickly, feeling the chill of the water around him, the ache in his muscles, trying to anchor himself in the real. He took in all the particulars of his surroundings. The old lady swimming her short, side-to-side widths; she had to be eighty. The plump coffee drinkers seated on poolside chaise longues were no doubt discussing diets and exercise routines. On the other side of the tiled deck, a stooped custodian with a bucket and mop. Chinese guy, indeterminate age . . . except there was something off.

Ambler blinked. The stoop was not quite convincing—and, as he studied the scene before him, neither was the mop.

'Osiris,' Ambler said suddenly. 'There's a janitor. Chinese. One of yours?'

'Not remotely possible,' Osiris said. 'This was a spur-of-the-moment decision, coming here. Nobody was notified.'

'There's something odd about him. Something . . . I just don't know.'

Ambler dived under water again, intending to resurface a few yards away, so that he could take another look at the janitor without being obvious about it.

Moments later, the water nearby had grown clouded, dark.

On instinct, Ambler stopped himself from resurfacing. He looked up and saw blood gouting from Osiris's body and spreading through the water like billowing clouds.

KEVIN MCCONNELLY, the Plaza's pool attendant, was trying to be patient with the red-faced, middle-aged man in the changing area. 'If you think someone stole your wallet,' he told him, 'we have to take that seriously. All I'm saying is that we've never had a problem with theft here.'

'Always a first, though,' the red-faced man grumbled.

'Did you check your jacket pocket?' McConnelly asked, gesturing towards the lump in the lower left pocket of the man's navy blazer.

The man glowered, but patted the pocket. Then he pulled out the wallet and actually opened it up, as if to verify that it was really his.

McConnelly refrained from smiling. 'All right, then,' he said.

'I never keep my wallet here,' the man said petulantly. 'Strange.' He gave McConnelly a suspicious look. 'Sorry to waste your time.' But the tone somehow said that McConnelly was to blame.

McConnelly just shrugged. 'No worries. Happens a lot.' *Especially with arrogant bastards like you who won't admit when you screw up.* The Plaza was full of cosseted rich people who liked to think the world was designed just for them.

He was about to fetch a clipboard and file an 'incident' report when he heard screams coming from the pool area.

ANOTHER BULLET pierced the water, trailing a shaft of bubbles like a string of pearls and missing Ambler by a few feet. The index of refraction had put the gunman off his target. But he would not make the same mistake again.

Staying well below the surface, Ambler pulled himself along with powerful strokes to the side nearest the gunman: closer was safer. The gunman would have to reposition himself to have an angle on Ambler now. He glanced towards the deep end: Osiris was already dead, he could see, hovering near the surface with his limbs spread out.

Where was safety? Ambler had been under water for perhaps fifteen seconds. He could hold his breath for fifty or sixty seconds. But in the crystalline blue water, there was no place to hide. Except—the cloud of blood a few yards away . . . Osiris's own lifeless body offered the only protection he had. Ambler shot to the surface, close to the side of the pool nearest the assailant, and took a few deep breaths. The others in the pool area were screaming and fleeing.

Ambler dived deep again and, when he moved towards the surface, hid himself in the cloud of blood beneath the lifeless operative. Then he dragged the body towards the diving boards. Another shot zipped into the water, just missing his shoulder. A rifle that could be easily disassembled and reassembled, with a barrel that passed as a mop, was a compromised weapon. Most likely, it was of a stripped-down single-bolt design that had to be reloaded before each shot. Hence the five-second lag between bullets.

Through the bloodied water, Ambler glimpsed the high diving board overhead. The concrete stanchion supporting it would offer some protection.

Another *crack* as the Chinese man squeezed off a bullet; Ambler thrashed violently to evade its path, then plunged deep into the water again.

Timing was all. Could he make it to the concrete stanchion before he fired again? And if he did, what would he do next?

KEVIN MCCONNELLY was out of shape, but the fifteen years he had spent in the military police had given him sharp survival instincts. He ducked his head into the swimming-pool area, then stepped back. What he had seen was a professional, firing from an odd-looking rifle; clearly not someone to be confronted. He charged into the locker area and looked around desperately. Something had to be done, and he would have to do it. But what?

He did not consider himself much of a brain, but the next thing he did, he decided later, was very, very smart. He found the circuit breaker for the hall, and turned off all the lights. An inky darkness shrouded everything, and a curious silence, too, as fans and motors stopped running. He realised that it might help the gunman to escape, but nobody went shooting in the dark, did they? Now, there had to be a flashlight around somewhere.

He heard the sound of someone streaking towards him. He stuck out a leg and tripped the man. The runner crashed into a stand of lockers.

As McConnelly turned the lights on again, he saw a six-foot-tall man in swimming trunks, short brown hair, a smoothly muscled body—late thirties, early forties. He was massaging a bruised shoulder.

The man glared. 'What the hell did you do that for?'

Not the shooter. The shot-at, more likely.

McConnelly took a quick look around; no sign of the gunman. He had fled the scene, they both knew. McConnelly, anyway, was relieved.

'Here's the deal.' McConnelly liked to say those words. It was the voice of authority. 'I'm going to get the police to come and secure the area. Then you're going to explain to me and to them exactly what went down.'

'Is that what you think?' The man went to his locker, where he scrubbed at his head with a towel and started to change into his street clothes.

'That's what I know,' McConnelly said levelly, following him.

Then a curious thing happened; the man caught a glimpse of himself in the wall-mounted mirror and blanched, like he'd seen a ghost. He took a deep breath. 'Here's the deal. You never saw me.' He turned and walked away.

CASTON WAS STARING UNHAPPILY at a list of State Department civilian covers. The trouble, of course, was that it almost certainly did not contain the name he was after. That name had been deleted. How was he supposed to find something that did not exist?

His eyes drifted over to that morning's *Financial Times*, which reposed in the wastepaper basket by his desk. It went to show how damned distracted he was that, for the first time he could remember, he made a mistake in filling out the crossword puzzle. *Nothing important; thrice before the transport begins* was the clue. He'd written down *trivia* and he had to erase it; *trifle* was plainly the right answer. He pulled the paper out of the basket and glared at the puzzle. Tiny eraser crumbs still adhered to the page. In Caston's head the cogs were starting to turn. To erase was to take something away. But when we did so, didn't we always end up *adding* something, too?

'Adrian,' he called out, dropping the paper again.

'Master,' Adrian said, bowing his head with light-hearted irony. If it were less affectionate, it would be just shy of insubordination.

'Prepare a Requisition 1133A to send to Joint Intel Resources, would you?'

Adrian pursed his lips. 'That's, like, offline archival retrieval, right?'

'Very good, Adrian.' The young man had been doing his homework.

'The clerks hate like hell to do those. A major pain in the ass.'

Caston was glacial. 'Is that what the manual says?'

His assistant coloured. 'I know somebody who works there.'

'And who would that be?'

'Just some girl,' Adrian mumbled, regretting that he had said anything.

'Girl, meaning a female of your approximate generation?'

'I guess so,' Adrian said, his eyes downcast.

'Well, Adrian, would you call me a charming man?'

Adrian gave him a doe-frozen-in-the-headlights look. 'Um, no?' he finally said, realising he could not say yes and maintain a straight face.

'Correct, Adrian. I am happy to know that you haven't lost touch with reality. The advantage of being a newcomer. Someone here once described me, accurately, as having a "charm deficit", and that was someone who actually *liked* me. Now, I really am in a great hurry for my Requisition 1133A, so I want you to call your young friend in Archives and'—he cleared his throat—'charm the pants off her. Can you manage that?'

'I—I think I can, yeah.' Adrian swallowed. His country was calling on him! With greater conviction, he added, 'Definitely.'

Caston then reached for the telephone; he needed to have a word with the ADDI. He had not moved from his seat in hours. But he was closing in.

Chapter 5

The one-storey ranch-style house in Gaithersburg, Maryland, was distinguished from its neighbours only by the holly bushes that grew round its foundations. It seemed an unlikely place of safety, but Ambler had to find out. He rang the doorbell, and waited. Would she even be home?

The front door was opened a few inches, a chain stretched across the opening. A pair of eyes met his, and widened.

'Please, just go away,' Laurel Holland said in a quiet, frightened voice.

The nurse who had helped free Ambler from Parrish Island shut the door on him.

She had stepped away from it, but, he could tell, was still standing near it, as if frozen by uncertainty, indecision.

The door was cheap, brown-painted fibreboard with glued-on detailing. The chain was a joke. One shove and it would have broken off the latch. Yet that was not an option. Ambler had only one chance; he had to play it right.

He rang the bell again. 'Laurel,' he said. 'Laurel, I *will* go if you want me to, and you'll never see me again. I promise you that. You saved my life. You saw something nobody else saw. You had the courage to listen to me, to risk your career—to do what no one else did. And I'll never forget it.' He paused briefly. 'But I need you, Laurel. I need your help again.'

He waited several long moments. Then he turned from the door, his heart sinking, and walked down the porch steps, scanning the street. He had made the trip down from New York using a cab and two rented cars, and, throughout his journey, he had monitored the traffic for any sign of a tail. He had scouted out the entire area where she lived before making his approach. And there was nothing awry. At midafternoon, the street was deserted apart from a few cars belonging to people like Laurel Holland who worked an early shift and were home.

He heard the door opening behind him before he reached the drive, and turned round.

'Come inside quickly,' she said. 'Before I come to my senses.'

Wordlessly, Ambler entered the house and followed her into the kitchen. It had not been changed since the house was built. The counters were melamine, the appliances harvest gold, the floor harlequin-patterned vinyl.

Laurel looked scared and angry with him, but angrier with herself. She also looked beautiful. In Parrish Island, she had been the brusque, pretty nurse; at home, with her hair down, dressed in a sweater and jeans, he could see that she was more than just pretty. She was lovely, elegant even, her strong features softened by her wavy auburn hair. Ambler realised he was staring, and averted his eyes.

With a pang, he saw the small revolver—a Smith & Wesson .22—mounted on a bracket near the spice rack. Someone must have put it there for her. A husband, a boyfriend. It was the kind of gun a man would have obtained for a girl. A certain kind of man, anyway.

'Why are you here?' Laurel demanded. 'Do you realise what can happen to me?'

Ambler flinched and bowed his head. 'I brought you trouble, didn't I? Because of what you did. I want to say thank you, and I want to say I'm sorry. I'll go,' he whispered.

'No,' she said. 'I don't want . . . I don't know what I want.' There was anguish in her voice—embarrassment, too, that he was witness to it. Absently, she ran a hand through her hair. 'The keycard wasn't actually mine. The night-shift nurse always leaves hers in the dispensary drawer.'

'So they figured I'd palmed it from her somehow.'

'You got it. The video made it pretty obvious what happened, or so they thought. Everyone got a reprimand, and that was the end of it, aside from the two guys on the hospital boat. So. You left. And now you're back. They told us you were dangerous. Psychotic.'

'But you didn't believe them,' Ambler said. 'Otherwise you wouldn't have let the dangerous psycho in your house. Especially since you live alone.'

'Don't be so sure,' she said.

'You didn't used to,' Ambler said. 'Tell me about your ex.'

'You seem to know so much, why don't you?'

'He is, or was, ex-military. A veteran, in fact.'

She nodded, looking slightly startled.

'Maybe a little paranoid,' Ambler said, tilting his head towards the gun bracket. 'So let's think this through. You're a psychiatric nurse, in a secure facility. Why would that be? Maybe because your man came back from a tour of duty—Somalia, Desert Storm?—a little messed up in the head.'

'Post-traumatic stress disorder,' she said quietly.

'And so you tried to heal him, make him whole.'

'Tried,' she said. There was a tremor in her voice.

'And failed,' Ambler said. 'But not for lack of effort. So they encouraged you to specialise. You threw yourself into the subject, and you're smart, so you did well. Psychiatric nurse, military background. Parrish Island.'

'You're good,' she snapped, resentful of being reduced to a case study. 'But why the *hell* are you here?'

'Because . . .' Thoughts swirled in Ambler's head. 'Maybe because I'm worried that I *am* mad. And because you're the one person I know who looks at me as if I'm not.'

Laurel shook her head. 'You want me to say you're not psychotic? I don't think you're psychotic. But what I think doesn't mean a thing.'

'To me it does.'

She gave him a long, level look.

'Want some coffee?'

'If you're making it,' said Ambler.

They sat together, drinking coffee, and suddenly Ambler knew exactly why he had come. There was a warmth and humanity to her that he craved. Where others sought him as an operative for hire, Laurel was the one person he had found who believed in him as he wanted to believe in himself.

'It was Desert Storm,' she said.

'Your ex?'

'Ex-husband. Ex-Marine. It's an identity in itself, being ex-Marine. It never really leaves you. Any more than what happened to him in Desert Storm ever left him. So what does it mean? Am I attracted to trouble?'

'He wasn't post-traumatic when you met, was he?'

'No, not then. But he did two back-to-back tours, and came back different. Started to drink, a lot. Started to hit me. I kept trying to reach him, like there was a broken little boy inside him, and I could somehow make him better if only I could *love* him enough. I did love him. And he loved me, too. He wanted to protect me. He got paranoid, started to imagine enemies everywhere. And he was afraid for me, not just for him. Only thing that never occurred to him was that, for me, *he* was what there was to be afraid of. That gun on the wall—he put it there, insisted I learn how to use it. Sometimes I thought about using it to protect myself . . .'

'Against him.'

She closed her eyes, nodded, embarrassed. She was silent for a while. 'I should be terrified of you. I don't know why I'm not.'

'You're like me. You go by your instincts.'

She gestured around her. 'And see where it's got me.'

'You're a good person.' Ambler spoke simply. Without thinking about it, he reached over and placed a hand on hers.

'That what your instincts say?'

'Yeah.'

The woman with the green-flecked hazel eyes just shook her head. 'So tell me, is there a shell-shocked vet in your background?'

'My lifestyle wasn't conducive to relationships. Hard to keep a lover if you're disappearing for seven months to Sri Lanka, or Chechnya, or Bosnia. Hard to have civilian friends when you know you're dooming them to an intensive period of surveillance. It's a good life for a loner. It was a sacrifice. A big one. But it was supposed to make you less vulnerable.'

'And did it?'

'I've come to think it had the opposite effect.'

'I don't know,' Laurel said, the recessed overhead lights burnishing her wavy hair. 'With my luck, I'd have been better off if I'd always been alone.'

Ambler shrugged. 'I know what it's like to have people change on you.

I had a dad who drank. He was really good at holding it, and then he wasn't.'

'An angry drunk?'

'At the end of the day, most of them are.' Ambler looked away. 'It's tricky, because they can turn on a dime. Giddy, laughing, then suddenly it's *smack*, with an open hand or a closed fist. He was always sorry afterwards. Really sorry. You know what it's like—the guy says he's going to change, and you believe him because you want to.'

She nodded. 'You have to believe him. So much for instincts.'

'I'd call it self-deception. *Ignoring* your instincts. See, if you're that little boy, you get real good at watching your old man's face. You learn to recognise when he seems to be in a bad mood but it's only because he's down on himself. You ask him then if you can have your allowance, if he can buy you a new action figure. Other times he seems happy, and you look at him cross-eyed, and suddenly it's a cloudburst, and he's going to belt you for sure. I learned to tell the difference, learned the subtleties. By the time I turned six, I knew his moods like I knew the alphabet. Knew when to get the hell out of his sight. Knew when he was lying to me or to my mom.'

'A heavy thing for a kid.'

'He left by my seventh birthday.'

Laurel was quiet for a while, as they sipped coffee. 'You ever had another job? Other than being a spook, I mean.'

'A couple of summer jobs. Serving up barbecue at a fairground outside of town. And I used to be pretty good at drawing. I did a year in Paris, trying to make money as a street artist.'

'Your road to riches, huh?'

'I had to take the first exit. People got upset because the way I saw them wasn't necessarily the way they wanted to be seen. Somehow on my sketch-pad they ended up looking scared, or eaten by self-doubt, or despairing. A lot of the time, it freaked them out or pissed them off. Back then, I didn't fully understand what was happening.'

Her lynx eyes drew him in. 'Do you understand what's happening now?'

He stared at her. 'Ever get the sense you don't really know who you are?'

'All the time,' she replied. 'What did they do to you?' She put a hand on his, and the warmth from the contact seemed to travel up his arm.

Slowly, he told her about his disappearance from the databases and electronic archives, and then, in broad strokes, the essentials of what Osiris had told him. She listened contemplatively, and finally said, 'I think they tried to mess with your mind when you were on the inside. In fact, I'm sure of it. With drugs and electroshock and Lord only knows what else. But I don't believe you can ever really change who a person is.'

Quietly, he said, 'When I was . . . inside . . . I heard a recording. Of myself. But it was as if it was someone else.'

'How do you know it was you?'

'I just . . . know,' he said.

Laurel's focus was razor-sharp. 'That can be explained,' she said. 'I did a unit on pharmacology in nursing school. Let me get my textbook.'

When she returned a few minutes later, she was carrying a thick book. 'The sort of psychosis you're talking about could be drug induced.' She turned to a chapter on anticholinergic drugs. 'Look, here, in the discussion of overdose symptoms. It says anticholinergics can result in psychosis.'

'But I don't remember getting doped up.'

'They could have combined the anticholinergic with another drug.' She flipped through the pages. 'Look.' She tapped a passage with a finger. 'Drugs like Versed interfere with memory formation. There's a whole warning about amnesia following the injection. With the right drug cocktail, you could have been plunged into an episode of madness, but you'd have no memory of it.'

The hairs on the back of Ambler's neck were prickling with excitement.

'You'd be a raving lunatic for a few hours,' she went on, 'and they'd record you while you're in that state. And make believe that you're crazy. Persuade you that you're crazy. For whatever reasons of their own.'

Reasons of their own. The larger questions: *Who? Why?* yawned like an abyss. Grappling with *What?* was exhausting enough.

'How do you explain about the databases?' Ambler pressed. 'It's as if I never existed.'

'It wouldn't be that hard to erase someone's records.' There was certainty in Laurel's voice, a certainty that dismissed Osiris's hypothesis out of hand. 'They want to put off any casual enquiries.'

'What about what I saw in the Sourlands? There was no sign of my cabin, no sign that it ever really existed.'

'And you think that's beyond the landscaping skills of a powerful government agency?'

'Laurel, listen to me,' he said, his voice almost breaking. 'I look in the mirror and I don't *recognise* myself.'

She reached over and touched his cheek. 'Then they changed you. Plastic surgery. You can keep people anaesthetised for weeks at a time. They do it in burn wards, sometimes. They could have changed your face, then kept you under until you'd healed. Even if you had conscious intervals, therapy, again, could stop memories forming. How would you ever know?'

'That's crazy,' Ambler said.

She stood very close to him and placed her hands on his face. She examined the skin along his jaw, his ears, then felt for scars behind his hairline. He could feel the warmth of her own face near his, and as she ran her fingertips over his features something stirred within him.

'See anything?' he asked.

Laurel shook her head. 'Haven't found any scars—but that doesn't mean anything. There are all sorts of minimally invasive techniques they do now, through the mucosa of the nose, the reverse of the eyelids . . .'

'But you don't have any evidence for your theories.'

'It's the only way to make sense of what you've experienced.'

'That's assuming, of course, that my experience—my memory—makes sense.' He fell silent. 'I feel like such a goddamn *victim*.'

'Maybe that's how they want you to feel. I don't think they put you in Parrish Island because you're weak. They put you there because you were too strong. You'd started to see through something you weren't meant to see through.'

'You're beginning to sound as crazy as me.' He smiled.

'Can I ask you a personal question?' she said, almost shyly.

'Bring it on,' he said.

'What's your name?'

For the first time that day he laughed. He extended a hand, mock-formally. 'Pleased to meet you, Laurel Holland,' he said. 'My name is Harrison Ambler. But you can call me Hal.'

'I like that better than Patient No. 5312,' she said. She placed both her hands in his short brown hair, and then, once more, brushed them lightly over his face. She turned his head in one direction and another, as if playing with a mannequin. Then she leaned forward and caressed his cheek.

It took him a few moments to respond at all. When he did, he clasped her in his arms and it was as if she was all he had in the world.

When they broke off, there were tears in both their eyes.

'I *believe* you,' she said, her voice resolute. 'I believe you're *you*.'

'You may be the only one,' he said quietly.

'What about your friends?'

'I told you—for the past twenty years, pretty much of the time my only friends were my colleagues, and there's no way to track them down.'

'What about friends from childhood, college?'

He told her about his call to Dylan Sutcliffe.

She was stopped by that, but only for a few seconds. 'Maybe he always hated you. Maybe he thought you were trying to borrow money. Who knows? Don't give in to them.'

'*Them.*' That empty, unpalatable word again.

'Whoever's responsible for the whole charade. Maybe they're trying to drive you round the bend. Well, we're not playing their game. Deal?'

Ambler shakily rose to his feet. 'Deal,' he said, his voice thick with emotions he could no longer control.

She took him into her arms and pressed her forehead to his. 'We have to choose what to believe, sometimes. And I choose you. Instincts, right?'

'But, Laurel—'

'Shut up, OK? I believe you, Harrison Ambler. I believe you.'

As HE DROVE his rented Pontiac away from Laurel's house some time later, it was dark. Ambler felt a relief that was real yet also precarious. He desperately wanted to prolong his visit, but Laurel Holland had done enough for him: he could not let her make any further sacrifice.

At the next intersection, he waited patiently at a red light and glanced at his rearview mirror—

Oh Christ—the van! The hatchet-faced driver. A retrieval team. Or worse. How had they found him? As the light turned green and he drove across the intersection, he wanted to veer round immediately in a U-turn, but cars were clogging the opposing lane of traffic.

There was no alternative, Ambler thought desperately. Seeing a small gap in the oncoming traffic, he made a 180-degree turn. He heard the blaring horn of the car he had cut in front of, heard its tyres skid as it slowed to avoid collision. Every second seemed to pass with agonising slowness as Ambler gunned the Pontiac down the highway as fast as he could. Finally, when he trusted himself to look, there was no longer any sign of the van in his rearview mirror.

Moments later, however, Ambler found himself behind a slow-moving station wagon. Crazed with frustration, he leaned on his horn, but the wagon maintained its speed. Ambler veered into the opposing lane, overtaking the wagon with immense acceleration. By the time he swerved into Orchard Lane, his shirt was soaked with sweat. He tore through the quiet street, then brought the sedan juddering to a halt in front of Laurel Holland's house, where—

Oh Christ!—the same van had already pulled up, diagonal to the driveway, and the rear double doors were ajar and facing her porch. He heard screams—Laurel's—and heard her front door crash open. Two large men, muscles stretching at their knitted black shirts, had bound her to a canvas stretcher and were hoisting her into the back of the van.

Just two of them, but—*dear God, no!*—one of them was pulling out a hypodermic, the needle glinting in the streetlights. He knew what would follow. Laurel knew too much now. She would never be released.

He could not let it happen.

The hatchet-faced driver, suddenly realised it was Ambler in the sedan and started to run towards him. Ambler floored the accelerator while in neutral, and then, as the engine revved and roared, engaged the clutch and shifted into gear. The car leapt up and shot towards the van, just forty feet away. The man was now at Ambler's left, preparing to grab him from the vehicle. At the last moment, Ambler opened his side door, heard it smash into the man, walloping him unconscious. Then he ground the brakes and turned the steering wheel all the way to the left. The back of the Pontiac slewed round in the opposite direction, slamming into the van.

Ambler scrambled out of the car and charged to the rear of the van where Laurel, trussed up in canvas straps, was kicking and thrashing with all her might, struggling with her captor.

'Step away from her or you die!' Ambler bellowed. 'One head shot, one gun shot.' That would cinch it. In these shadows, a weapon would be assumed. 'Now!'

The man did as instructed. Holding his hands up, he walked slowly round the van, and as he neared the front, he did what Ambler expected: he suddenly dived inside, and, keeping his head ducked down, gunned the motor, lurching across the lawn and back onto the street.

He had fled the scene, but there would soon be others.

Ambler undid the canvas straps that bound Laurel.

'Are they gone?' she asked in a voice tremulous with fear.

'We need to get out of here,' was all he said.

'I knew you'd come for me,' she said, clutching him with quivering arms.

'We've got to get out of here,' Ambler repeated urgently. 'Is there someplace you can stay? With someone you know they won't have on file?'

Laurel's face was drawn. 'There's a woman who's like an aunt to me. She was my mom's best friend when I was growing up. She lives in a place outside Clarksburg in West Virginia.'

'That'll do,' Ambler said. 'I'll take you there.'

THE RIDE TO CLARKSBURG took a few hours. They were driving her car, an old Mercury, and Ambler remained alert to any sign of pursuit or surveillance. Laurel spent some of the time weeping, some of the time in stony silence, processing what had happened and responding ultimately, with rage and resolve. Ambler, meanwhile, was berating himself.

When they parted she almost flinched, as if a plaster were being ripped from a wound. He felt something of the same.

'I brought this on you,' Ambler murmured. 'I'm to blame.'

'No,' she said fiercely. 'Don't say that. *They're* the ones, dammit.'

'Will you be all right?'

She nodded slowly. 'You get the bastards,' she told him through gritted teeth, before she turned and walked towards 'Aunt Jill's' Victorian house. A porch light cast a warm, yellow glow.

THAT NIGHT, in a motel near Morgantown, old memories from his days as Tarquin seeped through the chambers of Ambler's mind.

You'd started to see through something you weren't meant to see through. Laurel's words echoed in his head, as he saw himself in Changhua again, positioned in the dense crowd of supporters, waiting for the Taiwanese candidate to reach the optimal position before he was supposed to signal to the munitions tech to detonate the explosive device.

'My friends,' Wai-Chan Leung began. He had a wireless microphone clipped to his lapel and walked freely on the stage. 'My greatest hope is that you may call *me* your friend. For too many years, our leaders have not truly been our friends. They have been the friends of foreign capital, of wealthy rulers, of the International Monetary Fund. But I do not feel that they have always been *your* friends.'

He paused, as a round of applause interrupted his words, and moved towards the podium. 'In an era of globalisation, some countries are more vulnerable than others. They call Taiwan the little tiger. What worries me is that tigers are an endangered species.'

Tarquin watched him intently. Nothing about the human being twenty yards in front of him matched the Stab dossier given to his team. The dossier had described someone cunning, prone to wrath, cynical. Someone whose public display of compassion was disingenuous. Tarquin detected none of these traits, not a trace of artifice, not a flicker of deceit. The man who was speaking believed what he was saying.

You'd started to see through something you weren't meant to see through.

'Self-sufficiency is a fine ideal,' Wai-Chan Leung was saying. 'But is it realistic? We need both—ideals *and* realism. Some people will say that you must choose between them. Do you know who they remind me of? The man, of ancient times, who set up shop in a village selling both a spear he said would penetrate anything, and a shield he claimed nothing could penetrate.'

A rumble of applause and laughter.

'The people of Taiwan—*all* the Chinese people—have a wonderful future ahead of them, if they choose it. So let us choose wisely. The mainland is changing. Shall we alone stand still?'

Leung was now just a foot or two from the wooden podium, a foot or two from death. Tarquin felt his heart speeding. Every nerve in his body told him that the operation was *wrong*. Wai-Chan Leung was not their enemy.

The candidate held his arms before him, and moved his fists together, knuckle against knuckle. 'Simply to *oppose* leads to immobility. Paralysis. Should this really be our relation to our cousins across the Taiwan Strait?' Now he interlaced the fingers of both hands. 'In cooperation, we can find our strength. In integration, we can regain our integrity.'

Tarquin's earpiece crackled: 'I don't have your sight line, but seems to me that the target's in position, no? Awaiting your signal.'

Tarquin did not speak. It was time to activate the device, to end the young man's role in the world, but Tarquin's every instinct fought against it.

The noise in the earpiece: 'Tarquin, you dozing? I'm going to click—'

'No,' Tarquin whispered into his concealed mike. '*Don't do it.*'

But the ordnance tech was impatient and would not be deterred. When the tech replied, Tarquin could hear the jaundiced cynicism of a man who had been in the field a few years too long: '*One for the money, two for the show, three to get ready, now go, cat, go . . .*'

The explosion, when it came, was far softer than Tarquin had been expecting. The inner sides of the podium had been reinforced with steel in order to minimise collateral injuries; the cladding helped muffle the sound and focus the force of the explosion towards the figure standing behind it.

As if in slow motion, Wai-Chan Leung, the great hope of so many Taiwanese, stiffened, then toppled forward on the dais, his body outlined with the spray of his own viscera.

For a few moments, in the midst of the smoke, the man's body was still. Then he lifted his head and looked at the crowd. And his eyes came to rest on Tarquin's. They were devoid of anger, and held only bewilderment and sadness. It was the face of a man who knew he was dying and wondered why.

As Tarquin, too, now wondered why.

The crowd was roaring, wailing, screaming, and, amidst it all, he somehow made out the sound of a bird trilling loudly . . .

Across the earth, across the years, Ambler stirred in his bed, suddenly conscious of the stale motel air. He opened his eyes: the trilling continued.

The Nokia he had taken from the stalker in the Sourlands.

He pressed the ON button and brought it to his ear. 'Yes?'

'Tarquin,' a hearty voice brayed.

'Who is this?' said Ambler, suddenly wary. A cold fear washed over him.

'I'm Osiris's controller,' said the voice.

'That's not much of a recommendation,' Ambler replied.

'You're telling me. We're terribly concerned about the security breach.'

'Someone opens your mail, that's a breach. Somebody shoots your operatives dead, that's something a little more serious.'

'Damn right. And we've got some ideas about what happened. Point being, we need you, and we need you now.'

'I don't know who the hell you are,' Ambler said. 'For all I know you killed Osiris.'

'Listen. Osiris was an extraordinary asset. I mourn his loss—we all do.'

'And you expect me to take your word for it?'

'Yes, I do,' the man said. 'I know your abilities.'

Ambler paused. Like Arkady, like Osiris, the man had confidence in his ability to detect deception. He had no choice but to play along. The further he could burrow into the organisation, the greater his chance of reaching the truth about what had happened to him—and who he truly was.

Yet a thought nagged at him. During his career, he'd sometimes been involved in what was known as a sequence operation: one piece of information leading to another, more critical than the one before, in a chain designed to draw in and ensnare an adversary. Every sequence operation, he knew, depended on the utmost air of credibility; the more skilled the adversary, the higher the level of credibility required. The wiliest adversaries of all, however, would set about *reversing* the sequence operation, sending information back up the chain that was specially crafted to tantalise US intelligence. A newfound zeal for the unexpected windfall would obscure the Agency's original objectives; the hunter would become the quarry.

What Ambler could not determine was whether he was being ensnared within a sequence operation, and, if so, whether he would be able to exploit it for his own ends. There was no more dangerous game. Yet what was his alternative?

'All right,' Ambler said. 'I'm listening.'

'We're going to meet tomorrow morning in Montreal,' the man said. 'Use whatever ID you've got—the one Osiris gave you should work fine. But it's your choice.' The man went on to give more detailed instructions.

Shortly before Ambler left the motel a couple of hours later, the phone rang again in his motel room: Laurel. She sounded calmer and yet there was still concern in her voice. He explained quickly that he had an appointment to keep; that he had received a call from Osiris's controller.

'I don't want you going,' she said, and he could hear her fear.

'I'm afraid, too. But I'm more afraid *not* to go.' He paused. 'I'm like a fisherman with something tugging on the line. I don't know what it is, but I don't dare let go.'

After a long pause, she said, 'Even if it sinks your boat?'

'Even if.'

ON THE FLOWER-DECKED TERRACE of a luxurious villa in Hong Kong's New Territories, two diners sat at a table, its white linen cloth covered with a dozen delicacies. The calm waters of Discovery Bay shimmered beneath the rosy sun of the early evening. As the aromas mingled in the faint breeze, the silver-haired American inhaled, and reflected that, in previous centuries, such a banquet would be available to few outside China's royal courts.

Ashton Palmer sampled a dish made from hatchlings of the Mountain Bulbul; the bones of the tiny songbird were as undeveloped as those of a sardine, providing a pleasing texture. 'Extraordinary, don't you agree?' he said to his dining companion, a Chinese man with broad features and hard, gimlet eyes.

The man, a long-time general of the People's Liberation Army, smiled, grooves forming in his leathery skin. 'Extraordinary,' he agreed. 'But from you, one has grown to expect nothing less.'

'You are too kind,' Palmer said, responding to General Lam in the Hakka dialect spoken in the general's native village. 'Still, I know that you, like me, appreciate attention to details. This dish was last served in the final decades of the Qing Dynasty. I fear that your friends in Zhongnanhai would find it *decadent*.'

'They prefer Burger King,' General Lam grunted. 'Pepsi-Cola served in silver goblets. Not that I have been spending much time at Zhongnanhai.'

'If President Liu Ang had his way, all the warriors would be exiled to the provinces. He regards the PLA as an enemy, and so has turned it into one. But then, as Chinese history shows, in exile lies opportunity.'

'That has been the case for you,' the general said.

Palmer smiled, and did not deny it. When he was still a young PhD graduate on the State Department's policy-planning staff, the smart money had him pegged as the next Henry Kissinger. But, as it emerged, he had a fatal flaw: a zeal for the truth. With startling abruptness, the *wunderkind* came to be the *enfant terrible*. The mediocre men and women of the department expelled the one who threatened their comfortable assumptions. In some ways, Palmer reflected, his exile and retreat to academia had indeed been the best thing that ever happened to him. His disciples gradually took sensitive policy positions in the Defense Department, the State Department and Washington-based think tanks and, as the years had passed, their guru had been patiently biding his time. Now he was counting the days.

'I am pleased that we still share the same perspective on these matters,' he said.

The general touched one cheek and then another as he intoned a Hakka proverb: 'Right eye, left eye.' It meant that two people were as close in their views as a man's two eyes.

'Right eye, left eye,' Palmer echoed. 'Of course, to *see* is one thing. To *act* is another. You have not developed second thoughts, I trust?'

The general responded with another Hakka proverb. 'The wind does not move the mountain.'

'I am pleased to hear you say so. For there *will* be winds, of gale force.

Sometimes great disruption is necessary to ensure a greater stability.'

'Exactly so.' The general raised the Bulbul hatchling to his lips and his eyes narrowed as he savoured its crispy perfection.

'*Six days remain*,' said the silver-haired Palmer, with emphasis. 'Your people must know when to act, and do so unfailingly.'

'Certainly. After all, the course of history is at stake.' The general raised his finger again. 'Right eye, left eye,' he repeated quietly.

Chapter 6

T he voice on the cellphone had told Ambler to be at Montreal's Promenades de la Cathédrale at 11 a.m. He took a cab there, hoping the camera round his neck made him look like just another tourist. Famously, the cash-strapped Anglican diocese had bailed itself out by selling the land underneath Christ Church Cathedral and it was now a vast shopping mall.

Ambler had just taken the escalators down to the Promenades and was trying to orientate himself in the cavernous mall when he felt a pair of hands on his shoulders, spinning him round.

A burly, ginger-haired man smiled at him. 'Face to face at last,' he said.

Ambler did a double take. He knew this man—not personally, but by reputation and from many a dossier. His name was Paul Fenton.

Fenton had made his name as the founder of a Texas-based electronics firm with major defence contracts. His business concerns had expanded, and by the late eighties he had earned notoriety for funding right-wing insurgencies around the world. To some, he was a patriot; to others, a dangerous zealot who played fast and loose with the laws governing the foreign export of munitions. That he was a savvy entrepreneur was undoubted.

'You *are* Tarquin, aren't you?' Fenton took Ambler's silence for assent, and extended a hand. Yet the question had not been rhetorical—there was a measure of uncertainty. Fenton had not known what he looked like.

Ambler took Fenton's hand, and spoke in a low, harsh voice. 'It's idiotic to meet me in public this way. You're too goddamn recognisable.'

Fenton just winked. 'People don't see what they don't expect to see.

Besides, sometimes the best place to hide is in a crowd, don't you find?' He gestured around him. 'Welcome to the world's largest underground pedestrian network.' His voice was a honeyed baritone. He looked athletic, rugged, and also rich. His skin was weathered, but . . . moisturised.

'The Underground City,' Ambler said. 'Perfect for the underground man.'

Fenton had not been exaggerating: the so-called Underground City consisted of twenty miles of passageways, over 1,600 boutiques, 200 eateries, dozens of cinemas. Despite the freezing temperatures above ground, it was warm and brightly lit. Ambler realised why Fenton had chosen the venue—the risks of violence were small in such a public place.

'Tell me something,' Ambler went on. 'Are you actually here by yourself? A man of your . . . stature?'

'Why don't you tell me?'

Ambler swept a glance around him, across dozens of faces. A square-faced man in a duffle coat, mid-forties, short hair; another, twenty feet to his left, in a camel's-hair overcoat over a dark flannel suit. They were too inconspicuous. 'I see just two. And one of them's not used to this sort of posting.'

Fenton nodded. 'Gillespie's basically a secretary.' He nodded at the man in the camel's-hair coat, who nodded back, colouring slightly.

'But you were going to tell me about Osiris. And this doesn't seem the ideal setting for a tête-à-tête.'

'I know just the place,' Fenton purred, and led Ambler to an exclusive-looking clothing boutique a little further down the promenade.

At the entrance there was the usual antitheft portal, the two plastic-clad towers, though placed a little further from the door than was usual. A low beep sounded when Ambler approached.

'Sorry about that,' Fenton said. 'Probably doesn't like your camera.'

Which meant it wasn't an ordinary antitheft portal at all. Ambler removed his camera and stepped through.

'Actually, if you could just stand there for a moment longer,' Fenton said. Ambler did so. The door sucked closed behind him.

'Welcome to my humble little shop,' the industrialist said. 'If you were a fashionista you'd be damned impressed. There isn't a single price tag in this place that doesn't have a comma.'

'Get a lot of customers?'

'Nary a one,' Fenton said, his cheeks broadening in a smile. 'We're almost never open. And when we are, I've got the world's scariest shop girl—Brigitte's her name. She doesn't exactly tell folks that they're not worthy to be shopping here, but they get the message.'

'I guess it's more discreet than a big sign saying KEEP OUT! And the door tower isn't really for inventory control, I presume. It's bug repellent.'

'Wide spectrum. Real powerful. Not that it would matter if anyone did sneak in a listening device. Go check out the window glass.'

Ambler walked to the storefront window; peering closely, he made out a fine-mesh metal screen within the glass. 'This whole place is a screen room,' he marvelled. A screen room was a space enclosed by ferromagnetic gauze that blocked radio-frequency signals. Ambler turned. 'You're a careful man,' he said. 'So how do you explain what happened to Osiris?'

Fenton's ruddy face paled a little. 'Listen, what happened to Osiris was a goddamn *tragedy*. I've got a crack team looking into it and we'll have answers soon. The man was a prodigy, one of the most remarkable operatives I've had the privilege of knowing. And he was a big-time admirer of yours—you should know that. Soon as it went on the squawk that Tarquin was out and about, Osiris was the one who said I needed to bring you in.'

'You seem to know a lot about me,' Ambler said.

'Everything and nothing, it seems. Tarquin's the only name anybody has for you. You're exactly six feet tall. Weight a hundred and ninety pounds. Age forty. Brown hair, blue eyes.' He smiled. 'But that's just data.'

Ambler sat down on a brushed-steel stool. 'You're too modest,' he prodded. 'I think you know a lot more than you're saying.'

'I've heard tales from the field. I got a lot of contacts.' Fenton paused. 'Obviously you had some powerful enemies—and some powerful friends. I'd like to be one of them.' He grinned again. 'You impress the hell out of me. In my book, you're a goddamn magician. *Poof*—the elephant vanishes from the stage. *Poof*—the magician's gone, cape, wand and everything. How did you manage that?'

'How do you mean?' Ambler kept his voice low-key.

'Professional secret, huh? You realise we ran your prints?'

Ambler flashed back to the water tumbler that Osiris had given him in the back of the Bentley. 'And?'

'And *nothing*. You got yourself deleted from every database in existence. We ran all the digital identifiers—and nothing comes up.' Fenton grinned. 'We've got access to *all* the State Department personnel files—the deep-down hidden stuff. I've got insider privileges. So it should be easy for me to get the 411 on Tarquin, right? But I got nada. Because you're a magician. Which, of course, makes you all the more valuable as an operative.'

Ambler hesitated; he would not disabuse Fenton. But Fenton himself was no small game either. *I got a lot of contacts*: an understatement if anything.

'Do you have any idea what you're worth to me?' Fenton went on. 'According to your former colleagues, you're the closest thing they've ever met to a mind-reader. I don't know what you did to get yourself in trouble. Don't much care, either. You see, Tarquin, I like to surround myself with the best. And you, my friend, are off the charts.'

'Sounds like you've been putting together the Dirty Dozen.'

'We're bigger than that. You've heard of the Strategic Services Group?'

Ambler nodded. It was one of those management-consulting firms that seemed to offer spurious solutions to spurious problems.

'Glad to hear it, because I'm thinking it's your future.'

'I'm not exactly the MBA type.'

'I'm not going to beat around the bush with you. SSG is kind of like this place—it provides one kind of service publicly, but that isn't why it exists. See, they call me the show runner.'

'Then what's the show?'

'Ostensibly, it's an international management-consulting firm—a bunch of people in suits who travel the world, racking up frequent-flier miles. But you know how the ads talk about the "SSG difference"? The real difference is that our core team is actually composed of former covert operatives. And not the bottom-of-the-barrel types, either. I've been creaming off the best. I've hired the Stab boys en masse. And now they're doing what they used to do. *Better*. Difference is, now they're free to do their *real* job. Working for truth, justice and the American way. Not filling out paperwork in triplicate and falling on their sword every time they stub the toe of a goddamn foreign national, the way the Washington bureaucrats would have it. When things need to get rough, they get rough. No apologies required. I'm a true-blue patriot. But it drives me crazy the way we've let ourselves get shackled by federal regulations and UN accords and what have you. Our people are the best in the business—then the bureaucrats put leg irons on them! My thing is, I'm taking those leg irons *off*.'

'Which should make you an enemy of the very government you're trying to protect.' Ambler's words were pointed, his voice level.

Fenton raised his eyebrows. 'Plenty of bureaucrats in Fort Meade and

Langley, not to mention Foggy Bottom, disapprove, no doubt about it. But there are good men and women in Washington, too. The people who really count.' Fenton glanced at his watch. 'Listen, there's a well-established model for this sort of relationship. You know how crucial private military firms—PMFs—have been over the past couple of decades? Well, the PMFs do overt. We do *covert*.'

'Spies for hire.'

'We're making the US of A as strong as she ought to be, Tarquin. We can do what the US government can't.' Fenton's eyes sparkled.

'You must have close ties with some pretty high-ranking officers.'

'Absolutely. Officers who actively enlist our services. For them it's a matter of outsourcing covert ops.'

'All the flavour, none of the calories,' Ambler said, forcing down a gorge of revulsion. Zealots like Paul Fenton were all the more dangerous because they viewed themselves in a heroic light. Placing themselves above the laws of men, above justice itself, they threatened the very security they prized.

'We're after bigger game now.' There was excitement in Fenton's voice. 'Now we've been given a truly major commission.'

'Is that so?' Ambler had to play Fenton carefully: he could not appear overly interested, but he could not be too cool, either.

'Which is why we need you.' Fenton stopped. 'So where do I stand with you? Can we do business? Can we help fix this rattletrap world together? What do you make of my enterprise? Be honest!'

'Before we met,' Ambler said, fingering one of the dresses on a rack, 'I had no idea what could be done with pleated voile.'

Fenton's laughter was high-pitched. He stared at Ambler. 'Tarquin, I'd like you to come with me now. I got something to show you.'

'Glad to hear it,' Ambler said, looking around the brushed-steel and grey-carpeted boutique. 'Because there's nothing here in my size.'

The two men left the boutique and re-entered the cavernous world of the Underground City. They made their way down a triple-tiered bank of escalators, and pushed through the crowds along several blocks' worth of passageways. Finally, they reached the exit for the Palais des Congrès and rode up a couple of escalators to ground level. The Palais itself was a leviathan of chilly glass, steel and concrete.

Fenton brought Ambler to the pavement in front of it. There were extensive security cordons round the building.

'What's going on?' Ambler asked.

'A meeting of the G8,' Fenton said. 'Trade ministers from the United States, Canada, France, Britain, Italy, Germany, Russia and Japan, plus special guests.'

'I don't recall having been invited.'

'You're with me,' Fenton said, eyes twinkling. 'Come along.'

HIGH UP in an adjacent office tower Joe Li adjusted his power binoculars. He had received a warning that his quarry might try to penetrate the international meeting. Next to him was a Chinese sniper rifle that had been carefully zeroed that very morning. At the moment, the man known as Tarquin was visible, exposed. But who was he with? Li focused his binoculars on the ruddy-faced, powerfully built man who was Tarquin's companion and immediately felt a twinge of concern.

He dropped the binoculars and picked up a digital camera, fine-tuning its focus until the image of the man was sharp. The picture must go for analysis. Further intelligence would be required before he could take action.

Liu Ang's enemies had, he suspected, found themselves a formidable new asset.

AMBLER FOLLOWED Fenton into the conference centre. The hall of the Palais was a high atrium of mitred glass above hexagonal granite tile, and the lobby was bathed in the silver glow of the winter sky. An old-fashioned sign—white letters affixed to a black plastic pegboard—indicated which spaces had been allocated for the various meetings.

'Any moment now,' Fenton murmured, 'you're going to see proof of what our operation can do.'

Ambler heard the rumble of conversation from an adjoining hall—the sound of a meeting breaking up. People were standing up, chairs were being moved, some attendees rushed forward to introduce themselves to others. Some went for coffee, or headed outside for a smoke.

'What time do you make it, Tarquin?'

'Eleven fifty-nine.' A beat. 'Twelve noon.'

Abruptly, loud shrieks echoed through the atrium. The conversational rumble ceased at once, replaced by screams: *Oh my God! Oh my God!* The keening swelled in volume. Fenton stood by a carpeted staircase, an arm hooked round Ambler's shoulders, while black-jacketed security guards hustled in; paramedics a few minutes later. Somebody at the meeting had been killed.

Controlling his shock, Ambler asked Fenton, 'What just happened?'

Fenton spoke briefly into a cellphone, then turned to Ambler. 'The dead guy's name was Kurt Sollinger,' he said in a low voice. 'A Brussels-based trade negotiator. According to our intel, he was a real menace. Fell in with some Baader-Meinhof remnants when he was in grad school, started living a double life. He was exploiting his EU position to set up international companies, laundering money and diverting significant sums to terrorist cells. They called him "the Paymaster". And what he paid for was bombings and, especially, assassinations.'

'But why would you—?'

'Today's a special day.' Fenton's eyes were hard. 'An anniversary, of sorts. Do you recall the murder of the US Deputy Treasury Secretary?'

Ambler nodded. One of the brightest lights in the American government, he'd been gunned down before a crowd several years ago in a São Paulo hotel. Despite an extensive international investigation, the assassin had never been apprehended.

'It happened five years ago today. At *exactly* twelve noon. His killers prided themselves on their timing. Kurt Sollinger was the Paymaster. We learned this not long ago. Trust me, the message won't be lost on those bastards. They'll know they've been rumbled, and their own paranoia will do them more damage than we'd be able to.' Fenton lit up a cigarette.

Ambler swallowed hard, amazed that Fenton was simply hanging around an assassination that he had orchestrated.

'We've got a much bigger fish for you.' Fenton handed Ambler a sheet of filmy paper. The scent told Ambler that it was highly combustible security paper. 'Or shark, I should really say.'

Ambler read carefully. The target was Benoit Deschesnes. The Director-General of the International Atomic Energy Agency. A very big deal indeed. Other details were provided, including a description of his daily routine.

'This the guy you want me to take out?' Ambler's stomach churned, but he fought to keep his voice even.

Fenton nodded gravely. 'He's been taking advantage of his position as head of the IAEA to transfer nuclear expertise to countries like Iran, Syria, Libya, Algeria, even Sudan. He's dirty. He's dangerous. And he's got to go.'

Fenton drew on the cigarette. 'You've absorbed what's on the data sheet?'

Ambler nodded.

His companion took the sheet back and touched it with the tip of his cigarette. For a brief moment, it blossomed into pink-white flame, then it vanished. 'Trust me, Tarquin, this is going to be the start of something very special. You take care of Benoit and you'll go to the head of the class.'

Ambler closed his eyes for a moment. His predicament was exquisite. He could alert the government about Deschesnes, but government officials had 'outsourced' the task to Fenton in the first place. Besides, his words would carry no credibility. His former bosses believed he was insane, and there was no evidence that Harrison Ambler had ever lived. Then, too, if Ambler passed on the assignment, Fenton would find somebody else for it.

A few minutes later, the two walked outside in front of the conference centre. Snow lay heavily on the ground, frosting rows of boxy shrubs to either side of the path, and the skies had grown darker.

'So have we got a deal?' Fenton asked, dropping his cigarette butt.

It was *madness*—there was no sense, no logic, in joining an enterprise whose basic legitimacy he rejected. Yet to refuse would be to lose himself again—and that was one thing Ambler could not do.

'You'll pay me in *knowledge*, show runner,' Ambler heard himself say.

Fenton nodded. 'It's the usual story, isn't it? Somebody messed with you. You want me to find out who, why. Like that, right?'

'Like that,' Ambler said softly.

CLAY CASTON was looking disapprovingly at a coffee stain on the oatmeal carpeting in the ADDI's office. It had been there on his last visit. Caleb Norris had no doubt ceased to see it. Many things were like that. One failed to see them because one was accustomed to them.

'I think I'm following you so far,' Norris was saying. 'You find the patient's intake date, and then you do a . . .'

'A variance analysis.'

'Right. A variance analysis. Looking at subtle patterns in expenditures. Good thinking.' An expectant pause. 'So what did you find?'

'Nothing.'

'Nothing,' Norris repeated, downcast. 'Oh, well.'

'Which I found pretty fascinating. It's like the dog that didn't bark, Cal. A special low-level operation means a lot of paperwork for authorisation, all sorts of special requisitions. Nobody drives up to Parrish Island and checks himself in. You're bundled in by men in white coats. That means the redeployment of vehicles, the possibility of overtime, and so on. If a junior-grade staffer does anything that involves Agency resources, he fills out requisition forms. Spoors in the forest—a trail. The higher up you go, the less of a trail there is, because you don't need to requisition; you've already got the resources at your command. The absence of any irregularities at all surrounding this inmate suggests the presence of a high-level mover.'

'How high, do you think?'

'At least an E17 level,' Caston said. 'Someone your rank, or higher.'

'That should narrow things down. What about the career coverage? Learn anything more about the escape artist?'

'A thing or two,' Caston said.

'Because we've got to figure out a way to lure him in.'

'That won't be so easy,' Caston said. 'We're dealing with an unusual customer. I'll tell you one detail I found suggestive: seems that, in the field, nobody would play cards with the guy.'

'He cheated?' Caleb Norris unknotted his tie.

Caston shook his head. 'You know the German word *Menschenkenner?*'

Norris squinted. 'A person-knower? Someone who knows a lot of people?'

'Not exactly. A *Menschenkenner* is someone with a knack for figuring people out, for taking their measure. You wouldn't want to get near this guy when you've got something to hide.'

'A walking lie detector. I'd like to get me some of that.'

'The people I spoke to doubt Tarquin himself knows how he does it. But their research indicates that people like him are particularly attuned to "micro-expressions"—facial expressions that last only a millisecond. The subject's looking mournful—then, just for an instant, they look triumphant. There's nothing mystical about what Tarquin does. He's just responding to clues that are so fleeting that, with most of us, they don't register.'

Norris frowned. 'Makes this Tarquin a formidable weapon. For twenty years, he was working for us. Now we've got to assume he's working against us.' He shook his head. 'This isn't a man you want to have on the other side.'

'No,' Caston said. He did not voice his suspicion that there was a connection between Tarquin's uncanny gifts and his hospitalisation—indeed, the erasure of his civilian existence. He hadn't worked out the logic yet. But the day was young.

THE GLOOM of the Montreal afternoon brightened momentarily when Laurel called Ambler on his cellphone.

'Are you all right?' he asked, urgently.

'I'm fine, Hal,' she said. '*Everything*'s fine.' She muffled the phone with her hand, having an exchange with someone nearby, then said, 'Aunt Jill wants to know whether you like peach preserves.'

Ambler tensed. 'What did you tell her about—?'

'You? Not a thing.' She lowered her voice. 'She assumes I'm talking to a boyfriend. A "beau", as she would say. Imagine.'

'And you're sure you haven't noticed anything off? Anything at all.'

'Nothing,' she said. '*Nothing*,' she repeated, too quickly.

'Tell me about this "nothing",' Ambler said.

'Just—oh, it really *is* nothing. Some guy from the oil company called a little while ago. They were updating their customer records, asked me all sorts of silly questions, then when they got into stuff about oil usage and the type of equipment we use, I went and checked and saw Aunt Jill uses natural gas, not oil. When I came back to the phone—they'd hung up. Must have been some sort of mix-up.'

'What was the name of the company?'

'The name?' She paused. 'You know, they actually didn't say.'

Ambler recognised the hallmarks: the innocent-seeming, professional phone call, probably with a voiceprint analyser on the other end. *It was a probe.* 'Laurel,' he said, forcing himself to speak calmly. 'When was this?'

'Maybe—twenty minutes ago?'

'Listen to me very carefully. You need to leave *now*. *Right now*.' He gave her precise instructions. She was to drive her car to a car-repair shop, tell them that the steering alignment needed to be fine-tuned, and drive off with whatever 'replacement' car they'd lend her. It was an easy way of getting a vehicle that could not readily be traced to her.

Then she was to drive somewhere—anywhere she had no connections to.

'I'll do this,' she said, taking a deep breath. 'But I need to see you.'

'That won't be possible,' he said, as gently as he could. 'I'm leaving the country tomorrow.'

'I'll see you tonight, then.'

'Laurel, I don't think that's a good idea . . .'

'I can't *do* this otherwise,' she said. 'I just . . .' she faltered. 'I just can't. I need to see you tonight.'

LATE THAT NIGHT, at a motel near Kennedy Airport, outside New York, Ambler stood in his room on the twentieth floor, studying the traffic far below. The rain was coming down in sheets, flooding culverts and forming layers of slick on all the roads.

At 11 p.m., squinting through binoculars, he saw a sedan drive up, a Chevrolet Cavalier, pummelled by the downpour. He knew it was Laurel because she waited for a minute in front of the hotel, as he had instructed, then drove to the next exit, then returned. He peered at the patterns of traffic surrounding her. If she were being tailed, he should be able to tell.

When she got back to the hotel, he called her cellphone to reassure her that she had no visible tail. She emerged from the car, holding a plastic bag. Some minutes later she knocked on his door.

As soon as the door was closed, she dropped her sodden blue nylon parka to the floor and put her bag down beside it. Wordlessly, she stepped up to him, and they held each other close. Then she pressed her lips to his.

He pulled away after a few moments. 'Laurel—all that's happened—you need to step back. You need to be careful. I'm not sure that we . . .'

She looked at him wordlessly, her eyes imploring, and he knew he could not push her away without wounding her. The truth was that he did not want to. Desire washed over him, and they sank down onto the bed, creating the warmth they both craved.

When their bodies finally parted, their hands sought out each other, and they interlaced fingers, as if neither could bear to be wholly separated.

After several minutes of just being quiet together, Laurel turned to him. 'I made a stop on the way,' she whispered. She rolled from the bed, got to her feet, and retrieved the plastic bag. She removed something from it and handed it to him. A large, heavy volume.

'What is it?' Ambler asked.

She was trying not to smile. 'Take a look.'

He switched on the bedside lamp. It was a clothbound yearbook with the Carlyle College logo embossed on a tan cover, and still in its original shrink-wrap, now looking slightly brittle. His eyes widened.

'Pristine,' she said. 'Untouched, unaltered, untampered with.' She handed it to him. 'This is your past. This is what they could never get to. You told me where you went to college, you told me what class you were in, and so I got to thinking. The way they'd tried to erase your past—I figured they'd done enough to put off a casual investigator. They could have altered the computer records at the provost's. But they couldn't do more than that, right? So I went to the alumni office, and I bought a copy of your yearbook. The real, physical object. Paid sixty dollars for it.'

'Laurel,' he whispered. He felt a surge of gratitude. 'You did this for me.'

There was pain in her eyes, and something like love, too. 'I did it for us.'

He took the book into his hands, slit open the age-stiffened shrink-wrap and leaned back against the headboard of the bed. He paged through, struck by how skinny most of the kids looked. As he must have.

'Brings back memories, huh?' Laurel snuggled beside him.

Ambler's heart began to pound as he flipped through the book. He turned to the A's, thinking back to his open-faced, twenty-one-year-old visage, and ran a finger along the rows of black-and-white images, an array of bushy hair and braces. ALLEN, ALGREN, AMATO, ANDERSON, ANDERSON, AZARIA.

His smile faded. There was no question where the HARRISON AMBLER photograph should have appeared. But there was nothing. Not a blank space. Not a 'photograph unavailable' notice. Just the face of another student.

Ambler felt light-headed and a little sick.

'What's wrong?' Laurel asked. She looked where his finger rested. 'I got the wrong year, didn't I?' she said. 'I'm so stupid.'

'No,' Ambler muttered. 'The year isn't wrong—I'm wrong.' He exhaled heavily and shut his eyes. Osiris's words returned to him. *It's easier to alter the contents of your head than it is to change the whole world.*

Harrison Ambler was a lie, a life assembled from a thousand fragments, and funnelled into the mind of someone else. An artificial life designed to supplant an authentic one.

Ambler cradled his head in his arms, seized by a sense that something had been taken from him that he would never recover: his very identity.

When he looked up, he saw Laurel staring at him, her own face tear-stained. 'Don't give in to them,' she said, putting her arms round him.

'Laurel . . .' he started, but he felt himself collapsing in on himself.

She took hold of his shoulders as if to bring him back from whatever distant place he had drifted to. 'It's a matter of *instincts*, right? Sometimes we *know* what's true even if we can't prove it. Well, I look at you and I feel *safe*. I know you're a good man, because I know the other kind all too well.'

'But if it wasn't for me—'

'*Stop it!* Saying that is like saying *they're* not to blame. But they are, and they're going to pay. Listen to your instincts, and you'll get to what's true.'

'What's true,' he echoed. The words sounded hollow in his mouth.

'*You're* true,' she said. 'Let's start with that.' She pulled him close. 'I believe. You need to believe, too.'

The warmth of her body strengthened him. For a long while, neither spoke. 'I have to go to Paris, Laurel,' he said finally. And he explained to her why and how he was to do Fenton's dirty work. 'At the end of it, maybe I'll find out that I'm not who I think I am. That I'm someone who's a stranger to us both.'

'You're frightening me,' Laurel said quietly.

'Maybe you *should* be frightened,' Ambler said. He held both her hands in his, gently. 'Maybe we both should be.'

SLEEP THAT NIGHT was a long time coming, and when it came Ambler was once again hurtled back to the innermost recesses of his mind. Memories flooded him, and a face came into focus—first just the eyes. They belonged to Wai-Chan Leung and, as he held the gaze of the dying man, he was possessed with a great rage. He and his colleagues had plainly been manipulated. The dossier had been a tapestry of lies.

You'd started to see through something you weren't meant to see through.

By the day's end, the Taiwan government announced that it had taken into custody members of a left-wing radical cell who were behind the assassination. Tarquin was familiar with the so-called cell: a dozen or so graduate students who got up to little more than distributing photocopies of Maoist pamphlets from the 1950s.

For the next four days, Tarquin had set out to expose the truth. The pieces of the puzzle were not difficult to locate. He raced around the island's various power centres, meeting 'assets' in the Taiwanese military who scarcely disguised their glee at Leung's murder, and visiting the confederates of the corrupt politicos and businessmen who held the true reins of power. Sometimes he inveigled information—sometimes he extracted it through a measure of brutality he had not realised he possessed.

It was as Tarquin had begun to suspect: the 'intelligence' in the dossier had been manufactured by Leung's political rivals and they'd woven in enough accurate detail about other malefactors to give it plausibility. But that left a larger mystery. How did this crude disinformation find its way into the Consular Operations intelligence network? How had the Political Stabilisation Unit been tricked into acting on this farrago of deception?

WHEN AMBLER AWOKE, his eyes were inflamed, and his head pulsed. Laurel was already up, and dressed in khaki trousers and a blue shirt. He looked at the bedside clock, reassuring himself that he remained on schedule.

'You've got plenty of time—we won't miss our flight,' she said, as he staggered to the bathroom.

'*Our* flight?'

'I'm going with you.'

'I can't let you,' he said. 'I can't expose you to—'

'I accept that there are dangers,' Laurel interjected. 'That's why I need you. That's why you'll need me. I can help. I can be an extra pair of eyes. I'm an amateur, I get that. But that makes me the one thing they won't be looking for. Besides, you're not frightened of them. You're frightened of yourself. And that's where maybe I can make things easier, not harder.'

'How would I live with myself if anything happened to you over there?'

'What if something happened to me here and you weren't around?'

Ambler cupped her face with his hands. It was madness. But it might well save him from another form of madness. And what she said was true: on another continent, he would not be able to protect her.

'If anything should happen to you . . .' he began.

Her gaze was steady. 'I'll pick up a toothbrush at the airport.'

Chapter 7

As the train pulled into the Gare du Nord two days later, Ambler felt a wave of nostalgia. The smell of Paris took him back with full force to the nine months he had spent in the city. He deposited his case at the left-luggage office and walked through the crowd at the station. Laurel was seated in a waiting area, as they had arranged, and her eyes lit up when she saw him.

As a precaution, they had travelled separately. He had flown to Brussels, using identity papers Fenton had provided in the name of Robert Mulvaney, and arrived in Paris by train. She was using a passport adapted from one he'd hurriedly purchased on the black market in the Bronx.

His heart swelled. She was as beautiful as he had ever seen her.

They walked together out into the Place Napoléon III, and Laurel stared in wonder at the station's magnificent façade. 'It's amazing,' she breathed.

An hour later, he left Laurel at his favourite café, the Deux Magots, with a cappuccino, a *Blue Guide* and a view of the oldest church in Paris. He explained that he had some business to do and would return before long.

Ambler walked west into the 7th arrondissement. He made a few detours, checking in windows to see if he could identify anyone following him. There was no sign of surveillance. Finally, he made his way to an elegant nineteenth-century building on the rue St Dominique and rang the bell.

The Strategic Services Group logo was incised on a rectangular brass plaque on the door. Mounted on the door frame was a dark glass square—part of a third-generation audiovisual security system.

A man's voice sounded from the speaker: '*Est-ce que vous avez un rendezvous?*'

'My name is Robert Mulvaney,' Ambler said. It was almost more comforting to have a name he knew was fake than one he only hoped was real.

After a few moments, during which a computer no doubt compared his image to a digital image supplied by Fenton, Ambler was buzzed into the foyer. To a balding factotum, he itemised the equipment and documents he would need—including a passport in the name of Mary Mulvaney, the page with the photograph left blank.

Half an hour later, he was presented with a briefcase. Ambler did not inspect its contents; he had no doubts about the efficiency of Fenton's outfit. While his 'order' was being fulfilled, he had studied the updated dossier on Benoit Deschesnes. He mulled over its contents as he walked back to the Deux Magots.

Three high-resolution pictures showed a grizzled, sharp-featured man in his mid-fifties. There were also a few pages that summarised the man's life.

Deschesnes, whose address was an apartment on rue Rambuteau, had studied nuclear physics and gone on to work at the European nuclear research centre in Geneva. In his early thirties, he moved back to France and joined the faculty at Paris VII, where he became increasingly interested in nuclear policy. Then, when a slot opened for a nuclear arms inspector at the UN's International Atomic Energy Agency, he applied and was accepted. His rise was swift, and, when he was proposed as Director-General of the IAEA, he worked hard to make sure that the members of the French mission were solidly behind him.

There had been some concerns in the Ministry of Defence about Deschesnes's youthful involvement with the Actions des Français pour le Désarmement Nucléaire, a pressure group that argued for the total abolition of nuclear weapons, but it was, evidently, a storm that Deschesnes had weathered. He was generally deemed a success. In his three years as Director-General, he had shown a gift for sidestepping controversy while carefully husbanding the IAEA's prestige. According to an article in *Time*, reproduced in the dossier, he was a 'cerebral Frenchman with a heart as big as his brains', who was 'bringing new brio to bear on the most important threat to global security: loose nukes'.

The public had no idea about the real story. About a year ago, the CIA had observed the IAEA Director-General meeting secretly with a renegade Libyan nuclear scientist, and had captured enough of the conversation to deduce that his high-profile role was a cover for a profitable sideline in helping non-nuclear states acquire nuclear weapons technologies. The analysis had all the hallmarks of a CIA report. Evidence never 'proved' a conclusion; it 'made plausible' or 'provided additional support for' the hypothesis advanced. Clearly, none of that worried Fenton. He would, it appeared, do for his country what its official defenders were too cautious to do.

Just over an hour later, Ambler was back at the Deux Magots. Inside the café, the air was fragrant with coffee and cigarettes. Laurel was visibly relieved when she caught sight of him. Ambler seated himself at her table, stood the briefcase by his chair and took hold of her hand.

He explained, giving the minimum of detail, about the document work. Laminating her photograph into the passport would take a minute. 'Now that Mr and Mrs Mulvaney have their papers in order, we can behave like a married couple.'

'In France? Doesn't that mean you have to take a lover?'

Ambler smiled. 'Sometimes, even in France, your wife *is* your lover.'

As the two walked towards a taxi rank, Ambler sensed that they were being followed. Abruptly, he rounded a corner and turned up an adjoining street, Laurel keeping pace with him. The presence of a tail was not itself a cause for alarm. No doubt Fenton's people wanted to make sure that Ambler didn't disappear again. In the next minutes, he and Laurel turned down several streets at random—to find the same broad-shouldered man traipsing behind them.

But the man was making it too easy. He was failing to keep an appropriate distance between himself and them, and he was dressed like an

American, in what looked like a dark Brooks Brothers suit, and a candy-striped tie. The man *wanted* to be seen. That meant that he was a decoy. Identifying the real tail took several minutes longer. It was a stylish brunette in a dark, mid-length coat. There was no point in losing either of them. Ambler wanted Fenton's people to *know* where he was going; he had even called the Hotel Debord from the SSG branch office to confirm his reservation. So he and Laurel grabbed a taxi, collected their cases from the left-luggage office at the Gare du Nord and checked into the Hotel Debord.

The hotel was a little dank—a slight mildewy smell emanated from the carpet in their third-floor room—but Laurel voiced no misgivings. Ambler had to stop her before she set about unpacking. He motioned to her that she should remain very quiet.

He opened the hard-sided case provided by the SSG. The pieces of the collapsable TL 7 rifle were lodged in compartments slotted into stiff black foam. A Glock 26 pistol was secured in place as well. The documents he had asked for were in a side compartment.

Ambler removed the packing foam and felt every square inch of the case's lining. He detected nothing out of the ordinary. He tapped the handle with his fingernails and examined the stitching along the top. Finally, he squeezed the black foam with his fingers until he detected a small lump. Using a pocketknife, he prised the two layers of foam apart and uncovered an object, shiny and oval, like a vitamin pill wrapped in foil. It was a miniature GPS transponder, designed to signal its location by pulsing radio signals on a special frequency.

As Laurel Holland stared at him in perplexed silence, Ambler studied the room. There was a small green sofa beneath the window. He lifted the seat cushion and secreted the transponder among the scattering coins and dust beneath it. He was probably the first person to lift the cushion in a year, and he doubted it would be lifted for another year.

Now he took the briefcase along with his garment bag, and gestured to Laurel to take her own luggage. Wordlessly, they walked out of the room.

FORTY MINUTES later, they were settling into a new room at the Hotel Beaubourg, on the rue Simon Lefrance, a stone's throw from the Pompidou Centre, and just round the corner from Deschesnes's apartment. Ambler paid for the room with the remaining cash he had taken from the operative in the Sourlands.

Laurel broke the silence. 'I was going to ask you what *that* was all about. But I guess I kind of know.'

'A needless precaution, let's hope.'

As Laurel took a quick bath, Ambler heated the small iron that the hotel had provided and carefully laminated her photograph onto the passport.

She came out of the bathroom, covering herself shyly with her towel. 'I have a feeling that there's a lot you're not telling me,' she said. 'And I should probably be grateful for it.'

He kissed her lightly on the neck. 'We'll have dinner and get an early night. Tomorrow we can have breakfast in one of the cafés round the corner. The man I'm looking for lives a few blocks away.'

She looked into his eyes. 'In your career, you've had to . . . do things that must have been hard to do.'

'I had a Cons Op instructor who used to say that there are really two worlds,' he began slowly, softly. 'The world of the operative, and the normal, everyday world. And sometimes these worlds intersect. Suppose a man is prepared to sell technology that can be used to kill hundreds of thousands of people. The safety of the normal world, the everyday world, depends on making sure the bad guys don't succeed. If we operated by policeman's rules, we'd lose the war. And there *is* a war. Beneath the surface of every major city in the world there are battles going on every minute of every day. If things work the way they're supposed to, people like me spend their lives keeping that battle from erupting into view.' Ambler stopped. So many questions remained unanswered. Was Benoit Deschesnes really a part of this war? Could he kill him in cold blood? *Should* he?

'And if they *don't* work the way they're supposed to?' Laura asked.

'Then the great game becomes just that, another game, only a game played with human lives.'

'YOU MAKE ME feel safe,' Laurel said to him that night, as they lay together beneath the sheets. 'But then you already know that's how I feel, don't you? Because of the way you see. It must make some people uncomfortable. That sense of being seen through.' She paused. 'I guess I ought to feel that way, too. But I don't. Maybe I *want* you to see me for what I am.' She interlaced her fingers with his. 'It reminds me of what kids say: "I know that you know that I know that you know . . ."' A slow smile appeared on her face. 'Tell me something about myself.'

'You're one of the most sensitive people I've ever met,' Ambler said.

'You should get out more.' She grinned.

'When you were a girl, you were different from the others, maybe a little bit on the outside of things. Not an outsider, exactly, but you maybe had an ability to see things that others didn't.'

Laurel was not smiling any longer. She lay back and gazed at the ceiling. 'My dad was a Vietnam vet. A good man, I think, but damaged, like my husband got to be.'

'He hit your mom?'

'Never,' she said sharply. '*Never*. He knew he'd have lost her for ever if he raised a hand to her.' Laurel closed her eyes. 'My dad worked in an electrical equipment plant in Virginia, my mom was a doctor's receptionist. The place where I grew up wasn't much, but it had a good school district and that's something Mom cared a lot about. Maybe too much. She kept telling Dad to ask for a raise, a promotion. Then one day, at some school event, she ended up talking to some people at the plant, and, well, I guess she was led to understand that the plant was only keeping Dad on the payroll out of kindness. His Vietnam service, and all. So a promotion wasn't really on the cards. Mom changed after that. Like she'd given up on him.'

'She's dead, isn't she?' Ambler said gently. 'They both are.'

Tears rolled from her cheeks. 'There was an icy patch on an intersection and a municipal trash lorry fishtailed there. Dad wasn't paying attention; he'd had a couple of beers and they were both happy. He was driving a company truck, filled with electrical equipment, when he ploughed into the other vehicle. The truck stopped; the equipment flew forward. Crushed them both.' She squeezed her eyes shut, striving to regain control. 'Maybe it changed me. Maybe it didn't. But it became part of me, you know?'

It was not the kind of wound that could ever heal fully, Ambler knew. He knew, too, why it was important to her that he should know. She wanted him to know her—not just who she was but how she became who she was. Her *identity* was composed of a hundred thousand incidents and memories, and yet it was a single, unquestioned thing. An entity that was *hers*.

Ambler felt a churning sense of envy.

AT SEVEN THIRTY the next morning, the receptionist at the Hotel Beaubourg was greeted by the American couple with a cheerful *bonjour*, as they set off for the Café Saint Jean on the rue Rambuteau. Once they had settled at a wrought-iron table from which Ambler made sure he could see the entrance to Deschesnes's apartment building, they ordered croissants, poached eggs, orange juice and coffee. Ambler stepped out for a moment to grab a copy of the *International Herald Tribune* from a news vendor.

He glanced at the headlines when he returned. Various business and political leaders were soon to address the annual World Economic Forum at Davos, Switzerland. A strike had hit Fiat, crippling production at its Turin plants. A bomb had gone off at a religious festival in Kashmir; Hindu extremists blamed. Talks failed in Cyprus. *The more things change*, Ambler reflected mordantly.

They did not have to wait long. Deschesnes appeared at about eight o'clock, briefcase in hand, and scanned the street for a few moments before getting into the black limousine that had arrived to pick him up.

'Sorry, honey,' Ambler said loudly. 'I guess I left my guidebook at the hotel. You go ahead and eat your breakfast and I'll go get it.'

Laurel looked puzzled for a moment—but just a moment. Then she beamed at him. 'Why, thank you, dear, that is so sweet.'

She was almost enjoying this, Ambler thought. He handed her a shopping list—items of clothing that would come in handy—and he was off.

A couple of minutes later, Ambler went into the Rambuteau metro station, and took the metro to Ecole Militaire—Deschesnes had to be headed for his office, which was located nearby at 7 Place de Fontenoy.

Ambler turned himself into a birdwatcher at the Square Cambronne, gazing about with compact field glasses, occasionally feeding pigeons with the crumbs of a pastry acquired from a street vendor.

At one o'clock, Deschesnes strode purposefully out of the modernist building that housed the regional office of the IAEA and entered the Ecole Militaire metro station—a peculiar move for the Director-General of a powerful international agency; one that carried a suggestion of subterfuge.

Ambler trailed the UN administrator as he made his way south, emerged at Boucicaut station, strode to the end of the block, took a left, and, in the middle of a quiet residential street lined with classic *parisien* houses of weather-stained limestone, took out his keyring and let himself in.

It was 1.20 and it looked as though Deschesnes was conducting an affair. From across the street, Ambler took out his field glasses and peered at the windows of the drab building. A flicker of light at a curtained window on the third floor told him that it was the apartment Deschesnes had entered.

Then he saw Deschesnes's figure shadowed against the unlined curtains. He was alone. His mistress had not yet arrived. Ambler felt the small Glock 26, fitted invisibly in his waistband holster.

He had noticed a florist on the corner. A few minutes later, he buzzed the third-floor apartment, a bouquet of elegantly wrapped flowers in hand.

'*Oui?*' a voice said warily through the loudspeaker a moment later.

'*Livraison des fleurs.*'

'*Pour qui?*' Deschesnes demanded.

Ambler kept his voice bored, impassive. '*Pour M. Benoit Deschesnes. Si vous n'en voulez pas . . .*'

'*Non, non.*' The buzzer sounded. '*Troisième étage. A droite.*'

Ambler was in.

The building was in poor repair, the steps worn, the banister broken in a couple of places. When Deschesnes came to his door, he saw a man in a respectable winter coat holding out a bunch of flowers with his left hand. Ambler hardly looked like a deliveryman, but his smile reassured the Frenchman, and he opened the door wider to take the bouquet.

Ambler dropped the bouquet and extended his right foot into the door. His right hand was holding the Glock, aimed at the Frenchman's abdomen.

Deschesnes cried out, and tried to slam the heavy door, but Ambler lunged forward, shoulder first. The Frenchman had been hurled back several feet and Ambler swiftly closed the door, securing the chain and dead bolt with his free hand. Now he stepped towards Deschesnes, forcing him back into the living room.

'Be quiet or I *will* use this,' he said in English.

The man before Ambler was large framed but soft, with an expanding girth from too many expensive meals, too little exercise. Fenton's brief had described a man who was truly a force for evil in the world. If Fenton was correct, the UN dignitary *deserved* death, and by arranging that death, Ambler could infiltrate the very heart of Fenton's enterprise. He would obtain the knowledge he sought, learn who he really was.

The winter sunlight was beaming through the large window opposite the door, casting a silvery glow onto a sparsely furnished living room. There was a bookshelf with a few books, a coffee table covered with newspapers.

'Bedroom?' Ambler asked.

Deschesnes jerked his head to the left towards a doorway and Ambler marched him across to it.

'You're alone?' Ambler asked as he scanned the bedroom.

Deschesnes nodded. He was telling the truth.

Keeping the physicist within his sights, Ambler pulled down the blinds and sat on the arm of a sofa by the window. 'Sit,' he said, pointing the gun at the bed. 'I'm told your English is pretty good, but if you don't understand anything I say, just tell me.'

'Why are you here?'

'Didn't you know this day would come?' Ambler said quietly.

'I see,' Deschesnes said, sitting down on the bed as if winded. 'Then you are Gilbert. It's funny—I always assumed you were French. Joelle never told me you were not. Not that we ever talked about you. But I do know that she loves you. What we have is not *sérieuse*. I don't expect you to excuse or forgive, but I—'

'Monsieur Deschesnes,' Ambler broke in, 'I have no connection to Joelle. This has nothing to do with your personal life. It has everything to do with your professional life. Your *covert* professional life. I refer to your connections with those whose hearts are set on nuclear weaponry.'

A look of bewilderment appeared on Deschesnes's face and Ambler detected no trace of deception. 'My role in nuclear proliferation is a matter of public record. I have spent a career working against it. What in God's name is this about?'

'Tell me about your meeting with Dr Abdullah Alamoudi in Geneva, last spring.'

'What are you talking about?'

'Are you pretending you don't know who Dr Alamoudi is?'

'Certainly I know who he is,' the Frenchman replied. 'You refer to a Libyan physicist who is on our watchlist. We believe him to be involved in a secret weapons programme involving various Arab League nations.'

'Then why would the Director-General of the International Atomic Energy Agency be meeting with such a person?'

'Why indeed?' Deschesnes spluttered. 'Alamoudi would no more be caught in the same room as me than a mouse would curl up with a cat.'

'Then how do you explain your trip to Harare last year?'

'I cannot,' the UN eminence said simply. 'I have never *been* to Harare. Who sent you? Where are you getting this information? Who has supplied you with such *lies*?' He paused. 'Was it Actions des Français?' he asked. 'Do they not realise how counterproductive this is—acting as if *I* am the enemy? Tell them they would do more good if they put honest pressure on our elected officials.'

'I'm not with Actions des Français,' Ambler replied steadily.

Deschesnes's gaze fell on Ambler's gun. 'No, of course not,' he said. 'They would never entrust anything important to an American. Then you are—CIA? I suppose their intelligence is bad enough to explain such a blunder. Perhaps you should give your employers a message from me. They should fill their intelligence dossiers with the truth, for a change. The *truth* is that hundreds of nuclear bombs are stored in conditions of risible security. It's a moral obscenity. The great nations of the West have been criminally negligent, and America is the prime culprit. The world should be terrified, and yet you people couldn't care less!' Deschesnes was breathing hard, his fear and confusion forgotten as he voiced the fury that had driven his career.

Ambler was shaken; he could no longer doubt the man's sincerity. Someone had set Deschesnes up.

Now, through the window, he saw a small, black-haired woman approaching the building's entrance. Joelle, no doubt.

'Is there anyone home in the apartment upstairs?' Ambler demanded.

'There's never anyone home before six,' Deschesnes said. 'But, Joelle . . .'

'I'm afraid we haven't finished our conversation,' Ambler said. 'I would prefer not to involve Joelle. If you agree.'

Deschesnes nodded, ashen.

Pistol still in hand, Ambler followed the Frenchman out of the apartment and up to the floor above. The door was locked but the latch was flimsy. Ambler slammed his hip into the door and it gave way.

The two walked inside. The living room looked scarcely inhabited—there was an oval jute rug, a few battered items of furniture—but it would suffice. At Ambler's insistence, the two spoke in hushed voices.

'Let's assume that I have been supplied with false information,' Ambler said. 'That your enemies mean to set you up. The question for us is *why*?'

'The question for me is why you don't get the hell out of my life?' Deschesnes replied. 'And why do you insist on waving that gun in my face?'

'I'll put the gun away,' Ambler said. As he did so, he added, 'But it won't make you any safer. There are many more where I come from.'

Deschesnes blenched. 'And you are from—where?'

'It's not important. Powerful officials have been assured that you pose a major risk to international security. Again, why would that be?'

Deschesnes shook his head. 'I can't think of any reason why. As the Director-General of the IAEA, I am something of a symbol of the international resolve on this issue. My views are common sense and shared by millions of people and thousands of physicists.' He paused. 'The main work I am doing now is on the Chinese role in nuclear proliferation.'

'What have you found?' Ambler, looking out of the window, watched as the petite black-haired woman walked hesitantly from the building.

'Nothing. Despite what the American and French governments say, there is no evidence at all that China is currently involved in proliferation.'

Ambler felt his frustration rising. Deschesnes was an innocent man, an irrelevance. Just another ageing Frenchman of dubious private morality but undoubted public probity. Yet there had to be a reason for someone to have ordered his death.

Ambler shut his eyes for a moment, then saw what he had to do.

'*Vous êtes fou! Absolument fou,*' was Deschesnes's first response when Ambler explained the situation.

'Perhaps,' Ambler replied placidly. 'But consider. The people who sent me are serious. If I don't kill you, they'll send someone else. But if we can persuade them you're dead, and you can disappear for a while, I have a chance of finding out who's set you up. It's the only way you'll be safe.'

Deschesnes stared at him. 'And exactly how could such a thing be done?'

'I'll contact you in a few hours when I've worked out the details,' Ambler replied.

'And what if you don't call?'

Then I'll be dead, Ambler thought. 'I'll call,' he said. 'You have my word.'

CLAYTON CASTON BLINKED. Dust motes were visible in the morning light that filtered through the window of Caleb Norris's office at the CIA's Langley headquarters. 'Our man's last assignment in the field turned out to be in Taiwan,' he reported. 'The question is, who was the officer in charge? Because the final report should have had the authorising signature of the OIC. I figure the OIC is going to know who Tarquin was before he was Tarquin. Maybe he was the person who recruited Tarquin in the first place.'

'So who signed at the X?'

'No signature. Authorisation was coded. Officer-in-charge alias was Transience.'

'So who's Transience?'

'Couldn't get that.'

'Our jobs would be a lot easier if the CIA was entrusted with the identity of Cons Op agents,' Norris said grumpily. 'Their precious "partition principle" too often means you end up pinning the donkey tail to your own arse.'

The auditor turned to face him squarely. 'I want *you* to call the person who runs the Political Stabilisation Unit, Ellen Whitfield, and ask her directly. You're an ADDI; she has to pay attention.'

'Transience,' Caleb Norris repeated. 'I'm starting to get a bad feeling about this . . .' Caston's scowl made him hesitate. 'I just mean that there are a lot of unknowns. And my worry is that we don't even know how much we don't know.'

BY LATE AFTERNOON, Ambler had begun to collect the items he would need. There was a great deal to do and little time to do it in. And Ambler could no longer turn to Fenton's people for supplies; ingenuity and opportunism would have to replace the well-supplied stockroom.

He appropriated Deschesnes's pied-à-terre near Boucicaut station as a workshop. Using a can opener on three bouillon containers, he produced three circular pieces of steel and backed these with rubber cement and a thin layer of foam—packaging material that accompanied a cheap radio. He fashioned the blood packs out of extra-thin latex condoms and a bottle of FX blood that he bought at a costume shop in the 9th arrondissement.

Finally, he removed the primer charge from a couple of the 0.284-inch rifle cartridges supplied by Fenton's armourer, using pliers from the nearest hardware store. The work was slow, laborious. The primer contained less than a grain of priming compound; he would need the primers from four cartridges to produce one workable squib.

It was another hour and a half before he completed the ensemble.

When he met up with Laurel in the gallery on the top floor of the Pompidou Centre, he had been away for hours, assembling the props for the drama—a theatre of death meant to substitute for death itself.

Laurel's first response to his explanation was incredulity, but then her self-possession came to the fore. Yet he knew there was a problem with the plan, and she saw it too when they talked it through.

'If people see a man shot,' she said, 'they'll summon an ambulance.'

Ambler nodded. 'It would take a paramedic two seconds to discover what was going on. The whole ruse would be blown. So, we've got to use an ambulance of our own. Set the whole thing up. Hire a driver somehow.'

'"Somehow"?' Laurel echoed. 'Is that one of those spycraft terms?'

'You're not helping, Laurel,' he complained.

'That's the problem,' she said. 'Or maybe the solution. You need to let me help. *I'll* drive it.'

He did not bother to argue. She was right. It was the only way.

'OK,' he said. 'So now all we need to do is to commandeer an ambulance.'

THE CLINIQUE DU LOUVRE, situated in an elegant building between the Louvre and the Samaritaine, the city's premiere department store, was the perfect place to go looking for an ambulance. It had a large fleet of emergency vehicles far in excess of its actual needs.

At Ambler's signal, Laurel walked over to the guard who sat in a glass booth at the entrance to the parking garage. She was a tourist seeking directions. The guard gave her a look that was wary but not hostile—a pretty woman was scarcely an unwelcome sight. Soon she was unfolding a Michelin map of the city and holding it up to him.

While the guard's view was blocked by the map, Ambler vaulted over the low safety barrier, strode up the ramp to the first-floor parking level, and walked over to a small fleet of boxy Renault ambulances. These were back-up vehicles, seldom used, and he chose the most elderly model. Ten minutes later the work of getting into the vehicle, dismantling its key cylinder and replacing it with one for which Laurel would have the key, was done.

TWO HOURS LATER, at the Hotel Beaubourg, Ambler stripped the TL 7 rifle, making sure that all the parts were lubricated and clean. Then he reassembled it, except for the muzzle. With the hinged stock in collapsed position, the object was inconspicuous in a sports bag. He changed into a track suit.

In the lobby, he waved at the concierge. '*Le jogging*,' he said, smiling.

The man at the hotel desk laughed. It was obvious what he was thinking. *Americans—obsessed with fitness*. 'See you later, Monsieur Mulvaney.'

Laurel joined him in the plaza outside the Pompidou Centre. As they reviewed their plan, Ambler's eyes swept the arena.

At a quarter to five, Benoit Deschesnes appeared, as he did most evenings, for a walk in the formally arrayed Luxembourg Gardens. Ambler watched, relieved that the dignitary's movements were unselfconscious and fluid.

He had already spotted one of Fenton's agents following him—dressed in a Brooks Brothers suit, he was pretending to read the plaques at the base of various statues. A few hundred feet away, a small group of Frenchmen were engrossed in a game of boules.

Deschesnes was walking as instructed, his coat open to display his white shirt. He sat for a moment on a bench, apparently admiring a fountain, then shivered. The day was cloudless and cold, and the evening sun cast shadows across the empty flowerbeds.

Ambler hoped that Deschesnes would make his reaction to the 'gunshots' convincing. When the tiny explosive charges beneath his white shirt were detonated, and the hidden bloodpacks burst, it was bound to be startling and somewhat painful, despite the piece of metal shielding his chest.

'Remember,' Ambler had cautioned, 'when the squibs go off, don't try anything overly dramatic. Just slump gently to the ground.'

It took Ambler several more minutes to locate another watcher: the man with binoculars in the window of an apartment building overlooking the gardens. He and the Brooks Brothers' guy were Ambler's audience, though he could not swear there were no others.

When Ambler was sure no civilians were watching, he disappeared silently into the evergreen bushes sixty yards from the fountain and set up the rifle. He had Deschesnes plainly in view. Activating the small walkie-talkie in his bag, he held the microphone close to his mouth and spoke quietly. 'Deschesnes. If you can hear me, scratch your ear.'

A moment later, the physicist did so.

'I'm going to count down from five. When I reach one, squeeze the device in your pocket. Don't worry. This'll all be over soon.' He looked around. A group of people was now approaching from thirty yards away. They would make good witnesses. He raised the rifle and let the barrel emerge a couple of inches from the bushes. He wanted Fenton's agents to see it. 'Five, four, three, two, one . . .' He fired three times. A distinct spitting sound punctuated each squeeze of the trigger. The human eye would not be able to detect that no actual projectile came from the muzzle.

A spurt of red fluid burst through the front of Deschesnes's shirt, then two more. Deschesnes made a loud grunt—Ambler could see, through the scope, the startled look in his eyes—and slumped to the ground.

The men playing boules saw what had happened and ran first towards the body, then, as one of them realised the danger, away. Ambler swiftly dismantled the rifle and put it back in his bag. Then he waited. For a long minute, nothing happened. Then he heard the sound of an ambulance. He took a white coat from the sports bag and put it on.

Laurel brought the ambulance to a halt nearby, as they had arranged, and ran towards the body. Ambler moved swiftly to the vehicle, his white coat flapping, dropped the sports bag by its rear bumper and grabbed a stretcher. It took him about thirty seconds. When he got to the body, Laurel, white-coated like him, was standing mute and pale, staring down at Deschesnes.

'He's dead,' she said in a quavering voice.

'Right,' Ambler said, and heaved the body onto the stretcher.

'No, I mean he's really dead.' Laurel gave him a stricken look.

Ambler stopped. He felt a wave of vertigo. *It was impossible.*

Yet the body had the limpness, the heaviness, of death.

'We need to get him inside,' Ambler murmured, his eyes only now seeing the tiny trickle of blood at Deschesnes's hairline and the small-calibre bullet hole a few inches above. It was the kind of shot that bled little and caused instant death. Someone, somewhere in the park or the surrounding buildings, had shot the UN's chief arms inspector.

The two moved the body quickly into the ambulance, closed the rear door and began to remove Deschesnes's shirt and the makeshift squib vest. Next, they wiped the fluids off the official's chest. Then, with lightning speed, Ambler pulled Laurel out of the ambulance and signalled to her that they needed to get away as fast as possible.

As they slipped into the gathering crowd, he could see the man in the Brooks Brothers' suit talking on his cellphone, and hoped he was reporting only that Ambler had accomplished his mission. But then he noticed something that sent a chill through him. Ten yards behind Fenton's agent, in a group of bystanders, was a face he recognised. A handsome, Chinese face.

The gunman at the Plaza Hotel.

PRESIDENT LIU ANG looked at the familiar faces gathered round the black lacquered table. Chao Tang, of the Ministry of State Security, Second Bureau, was looking especially serious this morning.

'We have new intelligence,' Comrade Chao said.

'True, or just new?' Liu Ang asked, lightly.

'Both, I fear.' From a leather portfolio, Chao withdrew a number of photographs, showing them to Liu Ang before passing them to the others. 'Here is the man they call Tarquin,' he said. 'In Canada, at the G8 meeting some days ago. Notice the time stamp. Just a few minutes previously, a member of the European delegation was assassinated. Kurt Sollinger. A friend of ours, economically speaking—he was working hard on an agreement that would have facilitated trade between this country and the European Union. And here is another photograph of Tarquin, taken in the Luxembourg Gardens, in Paris, minutes before the IAEA Director-General, Benoit Deschesnes, was shot dead. Dr Deschesnes was preparing an arms-inspection report that would have cleared this regime of the false notion that we have been contributing to nuclear proliferation.'

The soft-spoken man who sat to Liu Ang's left, his special adviser on security matters, shook his head glumly. 'Here is an assassin who has the future security of China itself in his sights.'

'The vital question,' Liu Ang said, 'is *why*?'

'That is optimistic. The vital question may be *when* will he turn his attention to you?' Comrade Chao laid two photographs of Tarquin side by side. 'Here is a magnification of Tarquin, taken at the Changhua incident. Here he is again in Canada.'

'Why, they are different men,' the President exclaimed.

'No,' Comrade Chao said. 'Our analysts have scrutinised the images for those aspects of physiognomy that cannot be altered—distance between the eyes, distance from eye to mouth, and so forth—and they have concluded that this is the same man. He has had plastic surgery, obviously in an attempt to elude his enemies. Some reports say he has gone rogue. Others insist that he remains in the employ of his government.'

'There are many ways of working for one's government,' said Li Pei, the man nicknamed 'the wily peasant', grimly.

President Liu Ang glanced at his watch. 'I appreciate the update, gentlemen,' he said. 'But I cannot be late for my meeting with the PLA Industrial Committee. They will take it poorly.' He stood up and, with a quick bow, excused himself.

The meeting, however, did not adjourn.

'Let's return to the President's question,' the economist Wan Tsai said. 'It is not to be brushed aside. Quite simply: Why?'

'*Why* is indeed an important question,' said Li Pei, as he turned to Comrade Chao. 'In particular, why is the assassin still alive? When we last met, you said you had taken measures.'

'Perhaps he is even wilier than you,' Comrade Chao said softly.

WHEN THEY HAD spoken in Montreal, Fenton had given Ambler the address of a safe house in a quiet, residential neighbourhood in the 14th arrondissement. It was where Ambler was to report in, following the Deschesnes assignment.

Ambler pressed the doorbell of 45 rue Poulenc, then waited for nearly a minute, during which his visage was doubtless being scrutinised by a hidden camera. A low thrumming indicated that the door was unlocked. He turned the knob and walked into the carpeted foyer. There was no one visible in the hallway, but he heard a voice through an intercom near the foot of a narrow staircase on the right. Fenton's voice: 'I'm downstairs. End of the hall.'

Ambler made his way through a door and down another narrow staircase. On the landing, he saw a closed pair of double doors and knocked.

Paul Fenton opened the door and motioned Ambler into a study lined with books, many faded by the years.

'Have a seat,' Fenton said. He gestured towards an office chair.

Ambler was oddly calm. 'They say two heads are better than one,' he said, swivelling on the chair to look straight at Fenton. 'I suppose you figure that two pairs of *hands* are better than one.'

'How's that?'

'I'm just saying I don't work with back-ups, not if I don't know about them.'

'What back-ups?'

Ambler studied his features for any flicker of dissemblance. There was none whatever. 'The Chinese gentleman . . .'

'What Chinese gentleman?' Fenton interjected blandly.

Ambler paused. 'You have no idea what I'm talking about?'

'Afraid not,' Fenton said. 'Was there someone else at your rendezvous, Tarquin? If you've any reason to suspect a security lapse, I need to know.'

'Believe me, if I had, you'd be the first to hear,' Ambler replied smoothly. 'No, nothing like that. I appreciate your need to have observers in position.'

'But that's standard protocol,' Fenton protested.

'Not a problem. In Stab operations, I usually knew the full complement, but that was then. Forgive an old jungle cat for being on edge. Really, it's nothing to be concerned about.'

'Good,' Fenton said. 'You've lived up to your reputation. Deschesnes's death has been reported. I'm very pleased. You did the job swiftly and cleanly. I think you've got a future in my inner circle.' He stopped, raised a hand. 'But I haven't forgotten our conversation. There was stuff you wanted to find out. I'd told you that you had powerful enemies and powerful friends, and it seems I was right. I spoke to my principal partner at State and the good news is, he has agreed to a meeting with you, promises to fill you in completely. We'll schedule it soon as we can. Maybe even here.'

'Who's the partner?'

'I promised not to say. Not yet. One thing you'll learn about me, Tarquin, is that I'm a man of my word.'

'And I'm holding you to it,' Ambler snapped. 'Dammit, Fenton—I told you I was to be paid with *knowledge*. You think you can fob me off with a cheque's-in-the-mail excuse like that?'

Fenton's ruddy face coloured further. 'It's not like that, Tarquin,' he said steadily. 'My partner very much wants to meet you. All the more now. That's going to happen within a matter of days. And it's not like you'll be cooling your heels in the meantime. I know that an operative like you must be eager to get back to work. At this point, there's no assignment I wouldn't entrust you with. Got a *real* exciting project for you coming up. But don't pack your skis just yet. One more assignment for you here.'

'One more?'

'A man who really needs killing,' Fenton said. 'Apologies for being so plain-spoken. But this one's going to be tricky.'

'Tricky,' the operative echoed.

'A Cons Op "beyond salvage" order has already gone out on this guy and they've put their in-house best on it. But when the rubber hits the road, they still come to me. You bring in Fenton, you're guaranteed results. So now I'm putting *my* best on it—and that means you.'

'Tell me more about the target.'

'We're talking about somebody with top-notch skills and training. A high-flying covert-ops ace gone bad. A sociopath with reams of government intel in his head, because of his experience in the field and in the office. Firsthand knowledge of all kinds of official secrets. And he's *out of his mind*. Every day this guy draws breath is a day his country is at risk.'

'Thanks for narrowing it down. But I'll need to start with a name.'

'Of course,' Fenton said. 'The target's name is Harrison Ambler.'

Ambler's face paled.

Fenton raised an eyebrow. 'You know him?'

'Let's just say we have a history.'

CLAYTON CASTON RETURNED to the patient file that had arrived this morning, and briefly scrutinised the small photograph. A handsome but unremarkable face, though with something almost cruel about the sharp features.

'Adrian?' he called across to the other desk.

'Yes, *Shifu*,' Adrian replied, pressing his flattened hands against each other, in a prayerful gesture of mock homage. *Shifu*, Caston had learned meant 'instructor', and was an honourific used in martial-arts movies.

'Any progress with the personnel list for Ward 4W?'

'No,' Adrian said. 'They're saying that the lists are being updated.'

'We'll take whatever they have.'

'That's what *I* said. No go.' Adrian bit his lower lip contemplatively. 'I gotta say, it's been tough. I swear, they're literally battening the hatches.'

Caston arched an eyebrow. '*Literally* literally, or figuratively literally?'

'Don't worry, I haven't given up.'

Caston shook his head and leaned back in his chair. His unease was growing. The data he had received felt artificial somehow. As if it had been specially prepared for eyes like his. More information had been furnished concerning Tarquin's assignments as a member of the Political Stabilisation Unit of Consular Operations—but there was nothing about his civilian identity or how he had been committed to Parrish Island. His every attempt to get personnel records from Tarquin's ward had been stymied. Caston doubted that his counterparts at the State Department would dare to circumscribe his investigation. Which meant that the blocking agents were at another level: either lower, beneath the radar, or higher, above scrutiny.

Caston's phone chirped with the double tones of an internal call. Caleb Norris was on the other line. Caston was to come to see him immediately.

When Caston arrived at the office of the ADDI, Norris's broad face wore a look of distraction. 'Word from the top. We've got to bring this investigation to an end.' Norris's eyes did not meet Caston's as he spoke. 'There it is.'

'What are you talking about?' Caston controlled his surprise.

'Thing is, there have been some high-level communications between State and the DCI,' Norris said. 'And the message we're getting is, our enquiries are interfering with a live special-access operation.'

'And what are the details of that operation?'

Norris shrugged. 'Special access, right? We haven't been entrusted with that information,' he said, sounding flustered. 'They say Tarquin's in Paris. They'll pick him up there.'

'Pick him up or pick him off?'

'Who the hell knows? It's like a gate has slammed down.'

'The proper response to an outrage,' Caston said, 'is to be outraged.'

'Goddammit, Clay. We've got no choice in this. The DCI himself is saying hands off or heads off. You hearing me? The DCI himself.'

'It's *wrong*,' Caston snapped. 'And I really don't like to be interrupted. Once I begin an investigation . . .'

Norris shot him an exasperated look. 'What *you* think, or *I* think—that's really the least of it. There are procedural principles at stake. But the fact is, the DCI has made his decision and it's our job to fall into line.'

Caston was silent for a long moment. 'Don't you find this *irregular*?'

'Well, sure.' Norris began to pace unhappily.

'It's *damned* irregular,' Caston said. 'Doesn't sit well with me.'

'Clay, you gotta choose your battles,' Norris said in a defeated tone.

'Don't you find,' the auditor replied, 'that it's always your battles that choose you?' He turned on his heel and walked out of the ADDI's office.

Caston continued to brood as he returned to his desk. Perhaps one irregularity deserved another. His eyes darted from the files on his desk to those on Adrian's less tidy work space, and the wheels in his head kept turning.

They say Tarquin's in Paris. They'll pick him up there.

He took out a yellow pad of paper and began to make a list. Pepto-Bismol. Ibuprofen. Maalox. Imodium. It wouldn't do to travel without such medicinal precautions. He shivered, as he contemplated the prospect of getting into an aeroplane. It wasn't about heights, the fear of crashing or the sense of enclosure. It was the prospect of breathing in the endlessly recycled breath of his fellow passengers . . . some of whom could well have tuberculosis or some other airborne infection. The whole affair was so *insanitary*. Intestinal parasites could lurk in every crevice. He shuddered. It was a very heavy burden he was taking on. He would not do so if he had not been sure that the stakes were very high. After filling most of the front sheet with his neat script, he looked up. 'Adrian, I'm going to be travelling. To Paris. On vacation.' He tried to keep the dread out of his voice.

'Paris—that's *super*,' said Adrian, with inappropriate enthusiasm. 'You'll have an incredible time.'

'I very much doubt that.'

'Then why are you going?'

'I told you, Adrian, vacation. Nothing to do with our investigation, which, I have just been officially instructed, is to be discontinued.'

Comprehension dawned on Adrian's face. 'You must find that *irregular*.'

'Highly.'

'Verging on the *anomalous*.'

'Quite.'

'Got any instructions for me?' Adrian brandished a ballpoint pen. There was a glint of excitement in his eyes.

THE CLERICAL SERVICES offered by the US Consulate at 2 rue St Florentin, within a few hundred yards of the Place de la Concorde, were a perfect cover for the Paris Cons Ops station. On the ground floor, hapless tourists with lost passports lined up and filled out forms, and visa applications were processed at a snail's pace. None of the visitors or regular employees ever thought to wonder what took place on the upper floors; to wonder why they insisted on a separate cleaning service and used different exits and entrances. Yet it was on the upper floors that Cons Ops, Paris Sector, had decided that a former agent known as Tarquin was beyond salvage.

Ambler planned to enter the lion's den—but only if he could be certain that the lion had left it. The lion in question was one Keith Lewalski, a man of sixty who ran the Consular Operations's Paris Sector with an iron fist. Ambler had no intention of putting his formidable reputation to the test.

He took a chair at a nearby café and glanced at his watch. It was all in Laurel's hands. If everything had gone according to schedule, she would already have presented herself to the Cultural Affairs Section of the American Embassy at 2 avenue Gabriel as the assistant of a museum curator involved in the International Partnerships Among Museums programme, who had dispatched her to retrieve an agenda for an upcoming meeting. She would have been sent up to the fourth floor and, while there, she would have asked to use a private embassy telephone to call her boss.

Then her instructions were to dial the Consulate and, using a script that Ambler had prepared for her, convey an urgent message: a State Department dignitary from Washington had arrived at the Embassy seeking an immediate debriefing with Mr Lewalski. The Consulate switchboard would have authenticated the call as originating from the US Embassy; the words employed would convey the urgency.

He glanced at his watch again, trying not to think of all that could have gone wrong.

Five minutes later, he watched an ageing bureaucrat emerge from 2 rue St Florentin with a harried air and get into a limousine. He felt a pulse of relief. She had done it. Could *he*?

As soon as the limousine turned the corner, Ambler strode into the building with a resolute air. Ignoring the lines at the other counters, he walked up to the 'Official Enquiries' desk. A heavyset woman sat at the counter, ticking boxes on a preprinted list of office supplies.

'Arnie Cantor around?' Ambler said.

'Just a sec,' the woman said, and wandered through a back door.

An efficient-looking young man trotted up to the counter moments later. 'You wanted Arnie Cantor?' he said. 'Who can I say was asking for him?'

Ambler rolled his eyes. 'Either he's here or he's not here,' he said.

'He's not here at the moment,' the young man said carefully. He had the open-faced look that junior clandestine types made a point of cultivating. 'Maybe *I* can help you. If you'll tell me who you are—'

'If you don't know who I am, then assume you're not *supposed* to know.'

The young man smiled crookedly. 'What do you want me to do?'

'You got a couple of choices. You can get Arnie on the phone, or you can rustle up one of your desk cowboys upstairs. I'm the bearer of news, and the sooner you get me out of the sight lines of the civvies out here, the better. In fact, let's go now because I really don't have any more time. If you guys were on the ball, I wouldn't have had to come here in the first place.'

'But I'll need to see some identification?' The request turned into a query; the young agent felt wrongfooted, uncertain.

'Man, I got no shortage of identification—for four different identities. I told you I got dragged in here from the field. You think I got my real papers on me?' Ambler broke off. 'Hey, don't let me give you a hard time. I was once standing exactly where you are now. Ambler slipped behind the counter and pressed the button to the elevator that stood a few yards away.

'You can't go up there by yourself,' the young man said.

'I'm not,' Ambler replied breezily. 'You're coming with me.'

The young man looked bemused but followed Ambler into the elevator. The authority in the stranger's voice was far more effective than any form of identification could have been. Ambler pressed the button for the third floor. When the elevator door opened, he stepped into what looked like an entirely different building. One that was very familiar to him.

Ambler viewed the room, identifying the most senior officer there moments before the man rose to his feet. Keith Lewalski's second-in-command. He was seated at a corner desk in a room that had no private offices.

'You,' Ambler called brusquely. 'Come over here. We need to talk.'

The man rose to his feet and walked over with a look of perplexity.

'How long have you been stationed here?' Ambler demanded.

A brief pause before he spoke. 'Who are you, exactly?'

'How *long*, goddammit?'

'Six months,' he replied cautiously.

Ambler spoke to him in a low voice. 'You get the Tarquin alert?'

A fractional nod.

'Then you know who I am—who *we* are. And you know better than to ask any more questions.'

'You're with the retrieval team?' The man spoke in a hushed voice.

'There is no retrieval team, and you never met me,' Ambler said, his voice like gravel, even as he assented to the query with a fractional nod of his own. 'You understand? Any problems with that, you take it up with the Undersecretary. Though if you're interested in career longevity, I'd think twice about it. If our investigation reveals that you've been slacking on the job, I'm going to be ripshit. And so's everyone in my chain of command. Let me remind you: time *is* of the essence.'

The man extended a hand. 'I'm Sampson. What do you need?'

'It's mop-up at this point,' Ambler said. 'Target's been eliminated, as of oh nine hundred hours. Faster than we feared. Messier than we'd hoped.'

'I understand.'

'I doubt that, Sampson.' Ambler's voice was imperious. 'We're concerned about your little boat over here. Worried you may have sprung a leak.'

'*What?* You can't be serious.'

'It's only one possibility—but we have to check it out. Tarquin knew too much. Like I said, it got messy. I'm going to need a secure communications hookup to Washington. I'm talking end-to-end security.'

'We should really discuss this with—'

'*Now*, goddammit.'

'Then you want the keep—the secure datasphere chamber, upstairs. Swept every morning. I guarantee its security personally.'

THE 'KEEP' was situated behind two blast-resistant doors, made of thick steel with a rubberised flange that ensured a tight, soundproof seal. Its walls were made of alternating layers of fibreglass and concrete.

Ambler stepped into the chamber, a space of approximately 400 square feet, and pressed the button that clamped the doors closed. For a moment, there was silence; the room was hot and dimly lit. Then the ventilation system kicked into gear and the halogen lights blinked on. There were two work stations, side by side. By means of a continuous high-speed fibre-optic connection, highly encrypted data was exchanged on an hourly basis with the digital storage complex in Washington.

Ambler turned on one of the flat-panel monitors and it flickered to life; the connection was already live. Lewalski's trip to avenue Gabriel would only take twenty minutes, or less. Ambler would have to use his time wisely.

Wai-Chan Leung, he typed. A few seconds later, a biography appeared, prepared by the State Department's Bureau of Intelligence and Research. There was no hint of the allegations that had been in the dossier prepared by the Political Stabilisation Unit. The analysts were mainly interested in how Leung's prospects as a national political figure in Taiwan had been affected by his 'determinedly nonbelligerent rhetoric' on the subject of relations with China. The words of the biography were dry, carefully phrased, but they reflected the idealistic young candidate Ambler had seen—someone who had spoken up for his ideals, regardless of political expedience, and who had been respected for it.

Kurt Sollinger's file was far more cursory. A trade negotiator, he had spent fifteen years involved in European economic affairs. Ambler focused on the section that concerned his chairmanship of a committee tasked with East–West trade issues. The group had been making notable strides in hammering out a special trade accord between Europe and China; an accord that had been derailed by Sollinger's death.

Next he keyed in the name of Benoit Deschesnes. He found what he was looking for towards the end of the file. The State Department's own analysts had concluded that Deschesnes's report into the charges that the Chinese government had been engaging in nuclear proliferation would exonerate the Chinese government. The latest update, posted only several hours earlier, stated that the release of the special commission's findings would be postponed due to the violent death of the principal investigator.

China. The orb of the web centred over China. The word told Ambler everything, and nothing. What seemed crystal-clear was that the assassination of Wai-Chan Leung was part of a pattern of attempts to eliminate influential people who seemed well-disposed towards China's new leadership. But *why*?

Ambler glanced at his watch. He had already stayed too long.

THE DAIMLER that took Undersecretary Ellen Whitfield to the Chateau de Gournay, just forty minutes to the northwest of Paris, waited in a gravelled parking area while she strode into the magnificent building. Less ostentatious than Versailles, it was no less impressive and was often used by international conferences of governmental and nongovernmental organisations, and by high-level conclaves of industrialists and their information-age successors. At the moment, it was being rented by a lavishly funded conservative think tank based in Washington. Professor Ashton Palmer, who chaired the think tank's Pacific Rim programme, always preferred settings that expressed the very finest that civilisation had to offer.

A liveried manservant greeted Undersecretary Whitfield in the foyer. 'Monsieur Palmer will see you in the blue room, madame,' he told her.

The blue room was octagonal and overlooked a beautifully contoured landscape. The vaulted ceiling was sixteen feet high; the carpets the finest broadlooms of the period; the chandeliers of museum quality. The Undersecretary glanced at herself in an elegant Venetian mirror. The pewter light of a French winter shafted through the leaded window, accentuating her high cheekbones and carefully coiffed chestnut hair, her cerise suit and single strand of pearls. As she returned her gaze to the view, she heard a voice say, 'They understood craftsmanship, didn't they?'

Ashton Palmer. Ellen Whitfield turned and smiled at the elegant man walking towards her. 'As you always say, "It is not the skill, it is the degree of skill."'

'That was the striking thing about the Sun King's court: the level of civility, the appreciation of accomplishments in literary, artistic, scientific and architectural realms. At the same time they were oblivious to the seismic instabilities of the social order—the basis for the revolution that would consume their children a century later. Theirs was a spurious sort of peace, which contained the seeds of its own destruction. People are quick to forget what Heraclitus taught us: "War is common, strife is customary, and all things happen because of strife and necessity."'

'It's good to see you, Ashton,' Whitfield said warmly. 'These are—dare I invoke the old Chinese curse?—interesting times.'

Ashton Palmer's silver hair was thinner than it had been when Whitfield was his student but no less tidy above his high and impressive forehead and intelligent slate-grey eyes. There was something ageless about him. Whitfield had encountered many figures deemed historic, but she believed that he was the one truly great man she had ever met.

'What have you to tell me?' he asked. Whitfield knew he had just flown straight from Hong Kong, but he looked remarkably rested.

'So far, everything has been happening exactly as you envisioned.' There was a gleam in the Undersecretary's eye. 'Quite a place you've got here.'

'The Center for Policy Studies is ostensibly holding a conference. "Currency Regulation: an East/West Perspective." What did you tell your people?'

'Meeting with scholars on currency liberalisation.' The Undersecretary sat down at a gilt-wood table in the centre of the room, and Palmer joined her. 'I remember the first time I heard you lecture,' she said, looking off through the leaded window. 'I was an undergraduate, you were teaching a course on "global dominion", and you wrote three words on the board: *Machtpolitik*, *Geopolitik* and *Realpolitik*. Someone at the back called out, "Are we going to have to speak German?" And you said no, but that there *was* a language we'd need to learn: the language of politics. You announced that only a few of us would gain fluency in it, while the rest would fall into the clichés of the historically insignificant. Strong stuff for young minds.'

'You had the mental sinews, even then,' Palmer said.

'I remember you showed us on a map that the Mongol empire almost exactly covered the same area as the Communist empire: from North Korea and China all the way to Eastern Europe. The "footprint of history", you called it. And you showed us that there was a pattern, that the Eastern empires were always dangerous to the West in proportion to how liberal they were internally. For several centuries, China had never posed a threat to the West even though it could have been its greatest rival. Chairman Mao was only a paper tiger. In China, the more totalitarian the regime, the more cautious, defensive and inward-looking its military posture.'

'A good many people have been unable to read the writing on the wall,' Palmer said. 'Especially when it's in Chinese. Your State Department colleagues still refuse to see that as China has become more Western in its governance it has also become more of a menace—militarily as well as economically. The President of China has a pleasant face, and that has blinded our government to his determination to awake the slumbering dragon.'

A liveried manservant entered the room and cleared his throat. 'Professor Palmer,' he said. 'You've received a transmission.'

Palmer turned to Ellen Whitfield with an apologetic look. 'Excuse me.'

He got to his feet and disappeared down a long hallway. When he returned, a few minutes later, he looked both anxious and energised. 'Everything is falling into place,' he told Whitfield. 'Which raises the pressure.'

'I understand.'

'What about Tarquin? And his newfound "companion"—any concerns on that front?'

'No cause for concern. We're keeping an eye on things.'

'Seventy-two hours remain. All must play their roles to perfection.'

'So far,' Undersecretary Ellen Whitfield assured him, 'everybody has. Especially Tarquin.'

AMBLER'S EYES were fixed ahead as he left 2 rue St Florentin; he wanted to look like a man with no time to waste. Once he was out on the street and away from the Consulate, he adjusted his gait to that of an aimless stroller, lost in his own world. Then he heard the sound of someone hurrying in his direction, someone with legs significantly shorter than his, and, to judge from the faint panting sounds, in poor physical condition.

Ambler lengthened his stride and turned left at the end of the block into the rue Cambon and then into the rue du Mont Thabor. Ahead was an alleyway. He paused, and pretended to check his wristwatch. Reflected in its dial, he saw his pursuer. With a sudden movement, he whirled round and grabbed the stranger, wresting him into the alley.

The man was perhaps five foot six, pasty-faced, with thinning black hair and faint hollows beneath his eyes. He was out of breath and his forehead gleamed with sweat. He looked entirely out of his element. His clothing—cheap raincoat, nondescript wool-and-polyster grey suit and poly-blend white shirt—was clearly American. Ambler watched his hands to see whether he would make a move towards a concealed weapon or device.

'You're Tarquin, right?' the pallid stranger asked, breathing hard.

Ambler slammed him against the cinder-block wall—'Ow,' the man protested—and ran his hands over his clothes, alert to any kind of weapon. Nothing.

Ambler studied him, looking for a flicker of guile. 'Who wants to know?'

'Take your hands off me,' the man spat.

'I said, who wants to know?'

The man drew himself up, a look of affronted dignity on his face. 'The name's Clayton Caston.' He did not offer to shake hands.

Chapter 8

'Don't tell me,' Ambler said with unconcealed scorn. 'You're a friend. You're here to help me.'

'You've got to be kidding,' Caston replied testily. 'I'm no friend of yours. And I'm here to help myself.'

'Who are you with?' Ambler demanded. The man's ineptness at basic field manoeuvres was genuine, but he could be part of a team, drawing Ambler out while others moved in for the kill.

'You mean my place of employment?'

'I mean right now, right here. Who else is out there?'

'About eleven million Frenchmen,' Caston replied.

'You're telling me you're operating alone?'

'Well, for the moment.'

Ambler found himself starting to relax; there was no hint of dissembling in the man's face. He *was* operating alone. In saying so, Ambler sensed, he was admitting an awkward truth.

'But I'm with the CIA,' the man cautioned, sounding nettled. 'So if you hurt me, it would be bad for you. The Company hates paying medical bills. They wouldn't take it sitting down. So just let me go.'

'You're joking.'

'A common assumption, frequently erroneous,' he said. 'Listen, there's a McDonald's near the Paris Opéra. Maybe we could talk there.'

Ambler stared at him. '*McDonald's?*' He shook his head. 'This some new Agency rendezvous point?'

'I wouldn't know. It's just that I'm not sure I can stomach the local grub.'

Ambler's eyes scanned the street. 'Fine, we'll talk at a McDonald's. But not that one.'

He plunged his hand in the suited man's breast pocket and pulled out a cellphone. An inspection revealed that it had a prepaid French SIM card. Probably he had rented the device at Charles de Gaulle Airport. Ambler pressed a few keys and the phone displayed its number, which he memorised.

'I'll give you a call in fifteen minutes with an address.'

The man glanced at his watch. 'Fine,' he said, with a slight harrumph.

Twelve minutes later, Ambler got out at the Pigalle metro station opposite McDonald's. The milling crowds would make it easy for Ambler to maintain a discreet scrutiny of the venue. He phoned the man who called himself Caston and gave him the address. Then he waited, and within a few minutes had satisfied himself that there was no surveillance team.

The pasty-faced man arrived in a taxi, getting out at the corner just before the McDonald's. He craned his head around, a useless gesture that was more likely to identify himself to anyone following him than it was to identify the followers. Then, as the cab disappeared, he entered the restaurant.

Ambler waited another five minutes, then crossed the busy street and walked into the McDonald's, which was dark inside and illuminated with reddish lights. Caston was seated at a corner booth, nursing a coffee.

Ambler bought a couple of Quarter Pounders, and sat down at a table that was in the rear third of the restaurant but afforded a clear view of the door. Then he caught Caston's eye and gestured for him to join him. Caston had evidently selected his booth because it was the least visible. It was the sort of defensive mistake that no field agent would have made. Only amateurs blinded themselves to stay out of sight.

Caston sat down opposite Ambler. He looked unhappy.

'Who knows you're here with me?' Ambler asked.

'Just you,' the man replied. There was a grumble in his voice but, again, not a trace of dissembling. Caston's eyes settled on the hamburgers on the tray in front of Ambler. 'You going to eat both of those?'

Ambler shook his head.

The CIA man picked up a hamburger and started to wolf it down. 'Sorry,' he said after a while. 'Haven't eaten for a while.'

'Hard to get a good meal in France, huh?'

'Tell me about it,' the man said, earnestly, oblivious to Ambler's sarcasm.

'No, you tell me. Who are you really? You don't look like a CIA agent. You don't look like any kind of field agent or law-enforcement officer.' He regarded the stoop-shouldered, soft-bellied figure before him. The man was obviously out of shape. And out of place. 'You look like an accountant.'

'That's right,' the man said. He took out a silver pencil and pointed it at Ambler. 'So don't mess with me.' He smiled. 'Actually, I was a CIA before I joined the CIA. Certified Internal Auditor, you know. I've been with the Agency for thirty years.'

'Back office?'

'That's what you front-office types would say.'

'How did you end up at the Company?'

'Do we really have time for this?'

'Tell me,' Ambler said, an insistent note in his tone.

'The quick story is that I started out working on corporate fraud at the Securities Exchange Commission. Then I did a stint at Ernst and Young, except somehow that seemed too much like *doing* corporate fraud. Meantime, some bright spark in Washington figured that the Company really *was* a company, on some basic level. Decided they needed to bring in someone with my peculiar skill set.' He drained his coffee. 'And they did mean peculiar.'

Ambler studied the man as he spoke and, again, detected no deceit. 'So I was found by a rank amateur in the field,' Ambler said. 'A complete desk jockey. I don't know whether to be amused or mortified.'

'I may be a complete desk jockey, Tarquin. That doesn't make me a complete idiot.'

'Quite the contrary, I'm sure,' the operative said. 'Tell me how you found me, and tell me *why*.'

A smile flickered at the corner of the man's mouth, a moment of suppressed vanity. 'It was simple, really—once I heard you were Paris bound.'

'As you pointed out, it's an area with a population of eleven million.'

'Well, I started to think about the probabilities. Paris isn't a good place to hide out: it's still a major sector for the intelligence communities of several nations. So you weren't here to go to ground. Maybe you had a job to do— but then why wouldn't you decamp at your earliest opportunity? That left decent odds that you were here in pursuit of information. Now, what would be the last place in the world that a former Cons Ops employee, one now classified as "rogue", would make an appearance? Obviously, the Paris offices of Consular Operations.'

'So you made your way there and kept vigil on the bench across the street.'

'Because the information you needed had to involve Consular Operations in some way, and it was the world you were most at home with.'

'So it was just a feeling you had, huh?'

Caston's eyes flashed. 'A "feeling"?' He was majestic in his scorn. 'A "feeling"? Clay Caston does not proceed by *feelings*. He does not dabble in hunches or intuitions or instincts or—'

'You want to keep your voice down?'

'Sorry.' Caston flushed. 'I'm afraid you touched a nerve.'

'Anyway, by your wonderful succession of logical inferences—'

'It's more a matter of a probabilistic matrix than strict syllogistic logic.'

'By whatever screwy juju you rely upon, you decided to stake out one particular doorway. And got lucky. But the harder question is *why* were you looking for me?'

Caston hesitated. 'A few days ago, all I was interested in was finding you so that you could be put out of business—an irregularity eliminated. But I've come to think that there's a *larger* irregularity to contend with. I was being *stonewalled*, is what it comes down to. There are some bad actors who want to find you. I want to find them. That might give us a shared interest—by pooling our information, we may both be able to make progress.'

'Let me see if I've got this straight,' Ambler said, keeping his voice quiet. 'You wanted to track me down to take me out. Now you want to track down others who want to track me down.'

'Exactly.'

'Then what?'

'Then it will be your turn. After I turn them in, I'll want to turn you in.'

'You're telling me that *eventually* you hope to "turn me in"? Put me out of business? Why would you *tell* me a thing like that?'

'Because it's the truth. See, you represent everything I detest. You're a cowboy, and you're deployed by other cowboys, people who have no consideration for rules and regulations, people who will take the short cut every time. But that's not all I know about you. I also know that you pretty much always know when someone is lying to you. So why bother?'

'What you heard is right. It doesn't spook you?'

'Makes life easier, I figure. Prevarication was never my strong suit.'

'Let me ask you one more time: have you told anyone where I am?'

'No,' Caston replied.

'Then tell me why I shouldn't kill you.'

'Because in the short run, we have certain shared interests. In the long run, we're all dead. I figure you'll take your chances on a temporary alliance.'

'The enemy of your enemy is your friend?'

'That's *hateful* philosophy.' Caston started to fold up the paper wrappings into an origami crane. 'Let's be clear. You're not my friend. And I'm sure as hell not yours.'

HALF AN HOUR LATER, the two men, operative and auditor, arrived separately at the Hotel Sturbridge, part of an American-based chain, where Caston was staying. Caston's room was large, by Parisian standards, albeit boxy and institutional in feel. He invited Ambler to sit on an armchair, upholstered in mustard velveteen, while he set about arraying papers on a small desk.

Caston asked Ambler a few pointed questions about experiences since leaving Parrish Island; Ambler's responses were matter-of-fact.

'A bizarre . . . condition,' Caston said after a while. 'I mean this whole erasure thing. If I weren't in the bottom decile for empathy, I'd have to think that the experience would be unsettling. Like some strange identity crisis.'

'An *identity crisis*?' Ambler scoffed. 'Please. That's when a Fortune 500 marketing executive decides to quit his job and start a business selling vegan muffins to organic food stores. We're way beyond that—can we agree on this?'

Caston gave a shrug. 'Listen, I've spent the past few days assembling all the data I could, with the help of my assistant, and I've retrieved a good deal of your performance record at the Political Stabilisation Unit.' He handed a sheaf of pages to Ambler. 'You see anything that looks faked, let me know.'

Ambler thumbed through it. It was a curious sensation, to see, in an abbreviated form, the product of blood, sweat and tears. It filled him with a sense of bleakness. What if this life—a life that had forced him to sacrifice all close human ties—was without any real and enduring consequences, or at least any good ones?

Caston went on. 'You've got an extraordinary faculty for "affective inference". A walking polygraph. Gives you a lot of value in the field. The Stab team snaps you up early on in your Cons Op career. You're in the rough-and-tumble, engaged in the kind of assignments that the PSU likes to get up to.' He was not trying to hide his distaste. 'Then we've got the job at Changhua. Successfully completed, according to the files. Next thing, you drop off the map. Why? What happened?'

Ambler told him briskly.

Caston didn't speak immediately, but then his gaze sharpened. 'Tell me exactly what happened the evening you were taken away. Everything that was said. Everything and everyone that you remember seeing.'

'I'm sorry, but I don't . . .' Ambler's voice trailed off. 'It just isn't there. Laurel says it's something to do with drug-induced retrograde amnesia.'

'It has to be in your head somewhere,' Caston said. 'Doesn't it? Maybe you're not trying hard enough.'

'Dammit, Caston. I lost *two years* of my life. Two years of mind games, desolation, hopelessness. You have no idea what I've been through . . . I cast my mind back and there's nothing, OK? No picture.' A wave of exhaustion swept over him. He was too tired to talk. Too tired to think. He walked over to the bed and lay down, staring miserably at the ceiling.

Caston snorted. 'Screw the picture. Start with the small facts. How did you get back from Taiwan. What means of conveyance?'

'God*dammit*, I told you *I don't know*,' Ambler exploded.

Caston was undeterred. 'Did you swim? Take a steamer?'

The operative's head was pounding; he struggled to moderate his breathing. 'Did you hear a word I said?' he asked, more quietly.

'What means of conveyance?' Caston repeated impatiently.

'Obviously, I must have flown.'

'So you *do* have some idea, you self-pitying bastard. Where would you have flown from, exactly?'

Ambler shrugged. 'I guess Chiang Kai-shek Airport, outside Taipei.'

'What flight?'

'I don't . . .' He blinked. 'Cathay Pacific,' he heard himself say.

'A commercial flight, then.' Caston evinced no surprise. 'A commercial flight. Twelve hours. You have a drink on board?'

'Must have.'

'What would you have had?'

'A Wild Turkey, I guess.'

Caston picked up the telephone and dialled room service. Five minutes later, a bottle of Wild Turkey arrived at the door.

He poured a couple of fingers into a tumbler, handed it to Ambler. 'Relax, have a drink,' he said stiffly. The offer was an order: the auditor had turned into the bartender from hell.

'I don't drink,' Ambler protested.

'Since when?'

'Since . . . since Parrish Island.'

'You used to drink, though, and you're going to drink now. Bottoms up!'

'What's this about?'

'A science experiment. Just do it.'

Ambler drank, the bourbon burning slightly as it went down. He felt no euphoria, only a sense of dizziness, a growing queasiness. Caston poured him another drink and Ambler downed it.

'What time did the plane get in?' the auditor demanded.

'Morning arrival.' An eel of unease squirmed in Ambler's bowels. Knowledge was coming to him, as if from another dimension.

'Did you do a debrief with the operation's OIC?'

Ambler felt frozen. He must have done one.

'Next question,' Caston asked, relentlessly. 'Who's Transience?'

Ambler felt as if the room was spinning around him, and, when he shut his eyes, it spun faster still. Blackness overcame him. And then, out of the blackness, a glimmer of memory.

ONCE MORE he was in the past that shadowed his present. In a frenetic blur of images, he saw the flight attendant on the Cathay Pacific plane who kept him well supplied with bourbon; the taxi driver at Dulles, a Trinidadian with strong views about the quickest route; his apartment at Baskerton Towers, which felt, that day, so small, so sterile. Little more than a place to bathe and dress, and prepare himself, so it seemed, for battle.

What battle? Fog swept over his memories again, a hovering opacity. Ambler . . . no, he was *Tarquin* . . . had felt a flicker of distant emotion. If he could retrieve the emotion, he could retrieve the memories that came with it. The emotion was partly guilt, mostly rage.

The fog thinned. Buildings and people came into view: headquarters in Washington, DC. He went straight to the top, to the Undersecretary in charge of the Political Stabilisation Unit—to Transience, who had to be told. Tarquin lacked the moral narcissism to suppose that his hands were ever clean; but he was outraged to discover that they had just been made bloody by an unfathomable lapse of professionalism.

Undersecretary Ellen Whitfield, the Director of the Political Stabilisation Unit, was someone he knew well, arguably too well. She was a handsome woman; once, to him, she had been beautiful. Many years ago, near the beginning of his career, when she was still involved in field ops, they had had an affair, consummated mainly in Quonset huts in the Northern Mariana Islands. It had lasted less than a month.

Ellen had applied for an administrative posting at the State Department soon afterwards; he accepted his next assignment in the field. At Cons Op, she became known for her surpassingly well-organised mind, and showed herself to be adept at office politics—flattering her superiors and wrong-footing those who stood in her path, without ever betraying her intent. Just six years after receiving her first DC posting, she became a division direc-tor, and rapidly revivified the Political Stabilisation Unit.

Within Consular Operations, Stab was regarded as highly 'proactive'—critics said 'reckless'—and now it became far more so. To its critics, the Stab operatives treated the edicts of international law with all the respect a Boston driver gives to traffic signs. That someone who seemed as prim and controlled as Ellen Whitfield had presided over this transformation took some of her colleagues by surprise. Not Ambler. He knew she had a streak of wildness, something that would once have been called devilry. In another place, during a humid August, he had found it arousing.

Yet Whitfield—who had earned the civilian rank of Undersecretary—was now proving curiously elusive. By the fourth time Ambler was told that Undersecretary Whitfield was 'in a meeting', he knew he was being shut out. He had already written up and transmitted his report on the Leung debacle. What he wanted now was accountability. He wanted her to say that she would conduct a full and proper inquiry. He wanted an acknowledgment that Stab had gone awry, and would take steps to set its house in order.

Ambler learned through informal channels that Whitfield had not even filed an official memorandum about his complaint, as protocol stipulated. It was an *outrage*. Was Whitfield so embarrassed by her failure that she refused to make a clean breast of it to the Director of Consular Operations? Did she think she could arrange a cover-up? He needed to confront her.

He felt a surge of the fury he had known in Changhua. A fury at betrayal. It was a Friday afternoon, the end of a Washington working week. *I'm sorry, Undersecretary Whitfield is in a meeting. You can leave another mes-sage, if you like.* When he phoned an hour later, the assistant's reply was equally impassive. *I'm sorry, Undersecretary Whitfield has left for the day.*

Livid, he got into a car and drove to Whitfield's home, on the outskirts of Fox Hollow, a village west of Washington. He knew where she lived and there would be no evading him there.

Half an hour later, he nosed his car past a white fence into the curving drive of a stately house, with an elegantly corniced façade of weathered red brick, and large bay windows. Broad stone steps led to the carved oak door.

Ambler pulled up and got out of his car. He rang the doorbell. Moments later, a Filipina woman in a maid's uniform came to the door.

'I'm Hal Ambler, and I'm here for Ellen Whitfield,' he said.

'Madame not seeing anybody,' the uniformed woman said. Then, more stiffly, she added, 'Madame not here.'

Ambler knew she was lying, Whitfield's voice could be heard from an adjoining room. He pushed past the protesting maid, strode down the tiled hall, and barged into a wood-panelled library.

There was Ellen, sitting in front of an array of documents, with an older man who looked familiar. He was silver-haired, scholarly-looking, with a prominent forehead.

'Madame, I *tol'* him you no—' As the silence was broken by the noisily protesting maid, Whitfield and the silver-haired man looked up suddenly, startled and dismayed.

'God*dammit*, Ambler!' Whitfield yelled. 'What the *hell* are you doing here?' The older gentleman had turned away as if he had developed a sudden interest in the books on the shelves.

'You know damn well what I'm doing here, *Undersecretary* Whitfield,' he returned. 'I want answers. I'm fed up with your delaying tactics. What are you trying to hide?'

Whitfield's face was mottled with fury. 'Get out of my house! How *dare* you violate my privacy like this!' An outstretched arm pointed to the door. Ambler noticed it was trembling.

'You got my memorandum,' he replied icily. 'It contains the truth. You think you can bury that truth? You think you can bury me? Well, forget it. Believe me, I've taken precautions.'

'Listen to yourself. Don't you hear how *crazy* you sound? In my job, I've got to deal with more things than you can *possibly* imagine. If you want a conference, we can meet first thing Monday. But if you're not out of this house immediately, I *will* have you banished from the services of this country—permanently and irrevocably. Now get the *hell* out of my sight.'

Ambler stood, breathing hard, his own anger somewhat pre-empted by her stormy ire. 'Monday,' he said heavily, and turned to go.

A few miles outside Fox Hollow, an ambulance with pulsing red lights and siren suddenly appeared behind him, and he steered to the side of the road. Swiftly, the vehicle pulled over in front of him, and another car, a Buick, blocked him in behind. Several men poured out of the ambulance; others emerged from the Buick. They pulled him from his car, and one man jabbed a hypodermic into his arm. As he was strapped onto a stretcher, he heard tense exchanges, then his consciousness began to waver and dim.

IT WAS TWILIGHT when Ambler opened his eyes again. He focused on the pallid auditor, and began to speak, providing as clear an account of his movements and observations as he could. Time had fogged the details, yet the outlines of the episode were now vivid to him.

'I was afraid you'd blacked out there for a while,' Caston said after Ambler had spoken for five minutes without pausing. 'Glad to have you back among the living. Now will you get the hell off my bed?'

'Sorry.' Ambler got up, and sat down on the mustard-coloured chair. He must have nodded off. According to his watch, four hours had passed.

'So Transience was Ellen Whitfield herself?'

'It was the alias she used at the time she was in the field. When the files went digital, all that stuff was lost. No official records were to be retained—she wanted a total scrub. She said it was a security precaution.'

'Explains why the name didn't pull anything,' Caston said. He regarded the operative silently for a moment. 'You want another drink?'

Ambler shrugged. 'They got some mineral water in the minibar?'

'Oh sure, they got some Evian. With the current exchange rate, it comes out to $9.25 for 500 millilitres. That's, what, 16.9 ounces. So it's like fifty-five cents an ounce. Fifty-five cents for an ounce of *water*?'

Ambler sighed. 'Please tell me you don't have a family. You must drive them crazy.'

'Not at all,' the auditor said, smiling. 'Because, you see, they don't listen to a word I say. Which suits me just fine.' There was a contented look on the auditor's face for a moment, and Ambler realised with surprise the dry-as-dust auditor was a doting father. Then Caston returned to the matter at hand, abruptly businesslike. 'The man who was with Undersecretary Whitfield, seated in her library—describe him to me in as much detail as you can.'

Ambler brought the image to mind. A man in his sixties. Silver hair, carefully groomed, a studious-looking face.

Caston listened, then stood up, agitated. 'It can't be,' he breathed. 'You're describing . . . but it's impossible.'

'Out with it.'

Caston fiddled with his laptop computer, which he had plugged into the phone jack. After typing a few commands into a search engine, he stepped aside and gestured for Ambler to take a look. The screen was filled with an image of the very man Ambler had seen at Whitfield's house.

'That's him,' Ambler confirmed. 'Who is he?'

'His name is Ashton Palmer. Whitfield studied with him as a graduate student. Later she repudiated him and everything he stood for. Had no contact with him whatever. She wouldn't have had a career otherwise.'

'I don't understand.'

'There was a time, twenty, twenty-five years ago, when Ashton Palmer was the brightest star of the foreign policy establishment. Wrote some widely reprinted articles in *Foreign Affairs*. Gave seminars in the West Wing, in the Oval Office. People hung on his every word. He was given an honorary appointment in the State Department, but he was bigger than that. He was destined to be the next Kissinger.'

'So what happened?'

'A number of people would say he self-destructed. Or maybe he just miscalculated. He came to be recognised as a dangerous fanatic. He gave a particularly incendiary speech at the Macmillan Institute for Foreign Policy, in DC, and afterwards, a number of countries, thinking that he represented the government, actually threatened to recall their ambassadors. The Secretary of State spent all night working the phones. Overnight, Palmer became *persona non grata* because the views he expressed would have put America on a collision course with history. He took up a teaching position in the Ivy Leagues, was appointed to the board of a somewhat fringe think tank in Washington. This image is taken from their Harvard website. But anyone at State who was closely associated with him became an object of suspicion.'

'So none of his people got anywhere?'

'Actually, there are lots of Palmerites throughout government. But if you want to have a career, you can't admit to being one. And you certainly can't maintain any connection with the old rogue.'

'Makes sense.'

'Yet you saw the two of them together—and that doesn't. A major player of the State Department in the company of Professor Ashton Palmer? Do you realise how utterly ruinous that could have been to her?'

Now Ambler understood the fear that he had sensed in Ellen Whitfield. He told Caston. 'So this is what it was all about.'

'I wouldn't hazard that it was *all* about that.' Caston was precise, as ever. 'But as head of the Political Stabilisation Unit, maintaining ties with Palmer was career suicide.'

Ambler leaned back and reflected. Whitfield, a glib and fluent liar, could probably have explained away Palmer's presence to anybody else. But Ambler was the one person she could never hope to deceive. That's why he was railroaded. That was the intelligence she couldn't afford to have leaked. The tape of his paranoid ravings was an insurance policy, establishing that nothing he said could be taken at face value.

She must have panicked that night, and activated a 918PSE, the rarely used protocol for a psychiatric emergency involving a clandestine officer. Because he had spoken of having taken precautions—implying that damaging information would be released in the event of his death—she must have concluded that the only solution was to make him disappear.

His heart hammering, Ambler excused himself and used his cellphone to call Laurel. He gave her the names of Whitfield and Palmer; at the Bibliothèque Nationale de France, they agreed, she would be able to search the archives for relevant material. He felt calmer by the time he'd rung off.

Caston turned to him. Something was on his mind. 'Can I ask you a personal question?'

Ambler nodded.

'What's your name?'

NOTHING BUT THE BEST for Paul Fenton, Undersecretary Whitfield reflected as he invited her into his suite at the elegant Hotel George V located midway between the Arc de Triomphe and the Seine. Aside from the walls, which were upholstered in a yellow-gold fabric, the early Empire theme was rendered in green hues and dark woods. From the window, one could see a breathtaking skyline, with Les Invalides, the Montparnasse Tower and, of course, the Eiffel Tower clearly visible.

Fenton led her into the salon, where they sat on green-striped chairs at a small glass table.

The Undersecretary leaned forward confidingly. 'I don't know whether I've ever fully told you how grateful I am—how grateful we all are—for everything you've done for us over the years.'

Fenton shrugged modestly. 'Would you like some coffee?'

Whitfield turned her head towards an ebony sideboard. 'I noticed you had a tray of coffee ready—so thoughtful. But let *me* get it.' She stood up and returned with the tray. There was a silver pot of freshly brewed coffee, a ceramic milk jug and a bowl of sugar. 'I'll be mother,' she said, pouring coffee into two delicate Limoges cups.

She reclined in her chair and watched Fenton as he shovelled spoonful after spoonful of sugar into his cup, the way he always did. Then he took a sip and smiled. 'You know I've always been honoured to provide whatever help I could. It's a pleasure to work with someone who sees the world the way I do. We both understand that one has to combat tomorrow's threat today, right?'

'Early detection, early treatment,' she agreed. 'And nobody does it better than your people. You're not just a private contractor, in our view. You're really a full partner in the mission of preserving the American ascendancy.'

'We're similar in a lot of ways,' Fenton said. 'We both like to win.'

Whitfield watched Fenton finish his coffee and return the empty cup to its saucer. 'It's easier to win,' she said, 'when your opponents don't even know you're playing the game.'

Fenton nodded vaguely; he closed his eyes and opened them again, as if having a hard time keeping them focused. 'But I know you didn't want to meet me here just to congratulate me,' he said, slurring his words slightly.

'You were going to give me a progress report on Tarquin,' she said. 'He doesn't know you're at this hotel, I assume. You've taken precautions?'

Fenton nodded, sleepily. 'I met him at a safe house. But he did real good.' He yawned. 'Excuse me,' he said. 'I guess jet lag is catching up with me.'

Whitfield refilled his cup. 'You must be *exhausted*, with everything that's gone on over the past several days.'

Fenton yawned. 'This is so strange,' he murmured. 'I just can't keep my eyes open.'

'Don't fight it,' Whitfield said. 'Just let it come.' Her agents had had no difficulty in lacing the sugar with a fast-acting central nervous system depressant that, even in levels great enough to produce unconsciousness, would elude forensic detection.

Fenton made a sound like a sleeper's muted groan.

'I really am sorry.' She glanced at her watch. 'It was a difficult decision for Ashton and me to make. It's not that we doubt your loyalty. It's just that you know who I am. You'd be able to connect the dots—and we weren't sure you'd like the picture.'

The upcoming event was too important to allow anything to go wrong. Everyone had to play their part to perfection. As she stared at the motion-less body before her, she reflected that Paul Fenton already had.

Chapter 9

'I don't have a good feeling about this,' Ambler said. The two men were walking along, Caston with his hands in his overcoat pockets for warmth.

'You *what*?' Caston gave him a withering look.

'You heard me.'

'Did your horoscope say your stars were in a bad alignment? I mean, look, if you know something I should know, let's talk about it. But we're grown-ups. We should be responsive to facts. Not *feelings*.'

'Reality check: you don't have the home field advantage here. We're not in spreadsheet land. Those are real buildings around you, and if somebody takes a shot at one of us, it'll be with a real bullet. Anyway, how would a pencil-neck like you even know about an Agency safe house? On the prin-ciple of need-to-know, it should be off your radar screen.'

'Nothing that costs the Agency money is off my radar screen.'

Ambler frowned. 'How do you know the place isn't going to be occupied?'

'Because the lease comes up at the end of this month and we're letting it expire. And because we've got a budget item for the cleanup crew that's slated to arrive next week. Ergo, it's empty, but still equipped. I reviewed requisition items for Paris before I left.'

The building on rue Bouchardon looked oddly desolate; the stone façade dappled with lichen and soot, the windows grimy, the black metal door grille battered and chipped.

'How do we get in?' Ambler asked Caston.

'Not my department.' Caston looked affronted. 'What, you expect me to do everything? You're the operative. Operate.'

The site was exposed, so Ambler knew he'd have to try something that worked fast. He knelt down and untied one of his shoes. When he stood up again, he was holding a thin key, flat like a normal key, except for five small elevations between the grooves. It was called a bump key. Ambler had picked it up when he'd noticed it lying around in the Cons Ops offices, and had secreted it into his shoe for safe-keeping. 'Stay here,' he told Caston.

He loped over to a dustbin at the end of the street, and returned a few minutes later with a thick paperback novel someone had thrown out.

A bump key was designed to hit the bottom pin in the lock chamber hard, so that the top pin bounced clear of it long enough for the key to turn. But getting it to work required skill and luck.

Ambler positioned the bump key in front of the hole and banged it with the spine of the paperback, shooting it through the lock as hard as he could and then twisting it the instant it was in.

He could not believe it. It worked—first time! The key turned, retracted the latch, and he pushed the door open. He felt a surge of pride at his hand-iwork, and, smiling, turned to Caston.

'At last,' the auditor groused. 'I can't believe it took you so long.'

With great effort, Ambler remained silent.

They stepped inside the lobby of the apartment building. It seemed entirely vacant, which meant Ambler would be able to work on the apartment's front door without fear of being observed.

But the CIA team that had equipped the apartment had also taken care to given it a proper mortise lock. Ambler scrutinised it for a few minutes before giving up. He lacked the tools for the job.

Caston was openly scornful. 'Can't you do anything right? You're supposed to be the hotshot operative. Twenty years at the PSU. And now—'

'Caston? Put a sock in it.'

Ambler walked to the building's cramped courtyard. The ground-floor apartment had a couple of windows that faced onto it. With the spine of the paperback, Ambler smashed a rectangular pane of glass and removed all the remaining shards. He stood stock-still for a moment, listening.

'You just cost the United States of America four hundred dollars,' Caston said softly. 'At least. Labour costs for a glazier in Paris are astronomical.'

Ambler placed both hands on the stone ledge and pulled himself up, then through the glassless window. A sturdy-looking bookcase stood on the other side, and he somersaulted over it gently and landed on his feet.

Walking carefully in the gloom, he made his way to the door, turned on some lights, and then retracted the dead bolt. At last he opened the front door, where Caston, arms folded across his chest, was standing impatiently.

'It's freezing outdoors,' he said. 'And you had to break a window.'

'Just get in.' Ambler closed the door behind Caston and locked it again.

The two men wandered through the apartment until they found a small room with a large television in it. Beneath it was what looked like a regular cable box. Ambler knew better. The roof of the building would have satellite equipment, connected to the ground floor by a non-interceptible fibre-optic cable; the box contained complex decryption equipment.

Caston pulled at a drawer in the monitor stand and found a keyboard. Then he turned on the monitor and busied himself with typing for a few minutes. The screen blinked to life, but it displayed interference.

'Let's see if I can remember how this is done,' Caston said, mainly to himself, as he punched more keys. Abruptly the screen filled with digits, displaying sizes and download times for a series of large files.

'I'm taking these from Open Source sector,' Caston explained to Ambler. 'Non-classified, public-domain materials, for the most part. I just want you to see Ashton Palmer in his element. You're the face expert, OK? I want you to see that face full-sized, in colour, and at maximum resolution.' He fussed with the keyboard for another minute and suddenly the screen was filled with the image of Palmer.

'This is from the mid-nineties,' Caston went on. 'A speech he gave at a conference sponsored by the Center for Policy Studies.'

On the screen, in a navy suit and dark red tie, Ashton Palmer looked confident, magisterial, almost serene. Dark curtains were visible behind him. He looked up from the lectern, his slate-grey eyes glittering. 'The traditional form of Chinese housing in cities was the *siheyuan*—literally, "four-sided enclosed courtyard", and it was composed of inward-facing dwellings on all sides. The very architecture of the *siheyuan* has proved an apt symbol of the national character. The Middle Kingdom was a profoundly inward-looking realm. A pervasive xenophobia was perhaps the most constant element of Chinese culture. Chinese history contains no Peter the Great, no Napoleon, no Queen Victoria. Since the collapse of the Tatar yoke, there has been nothing we can call a Chinese empire: there has only been China. Vast, yes. Powerful, without question. But ultimately a four-sided enclosure, an enormous *siheyuan*. What is beyond debate is that this ingrained xenophobia has served the rest of the world well.'

Ambler moved nearer to the screen, riveted by the image of the eloquent scholar and the intelligence he seemed to radiate.

'Some believed that China would change once the Communists seized control,' Palmer went on. 'But Chairman Mao maintained the tightest control over his countrymen of any leader in history. And for all the bellicosity of his rhetoric, he was deeply conservative, his obsessions inward-looking. It is only in recent years that we have begun to see a seismic shift within China—a genuine turning outwards, fuelled by its incredibly swift entry into the system of global capitalism, a development that one American administration after another had sought to promote.'

Palmer's gaze grew eerily intent. 'China is on fire, and it is the West that has provided the fuel, in the form of hundreds of billions of dollars of foreign capital. We're seeing a GDP growth rate upwards of ten per cent a quarter, as well as gigantic increases in consumption: within a few years China will be consuming ten per cent of the world's petroleum, a third of its steel. So, our conglomerates depend increasingly upon the Chinese dynamo for their own growth. Does any of this sound familiar, ladies and gentlemen?' Palmer's eyes scanned the audience before him. 'Consider a country where labour was cheap, capital and resources abundant—a country that was able to transform its economy into the most efficient and swiftest growing in the world. I refer'—he raised his voice—'to the United States of America, as it was in the early twentieth century. We all know what ensued. A period of military, industrial, economic and cultural supremacy—a period of power and prosperity that we call, in shorthand, the American century.' He glanced down at the lectern before resuming. 'But nobody ever promised that the American century would be permanent. Indeed, there is every reason to believe that it will not be—every reason to believe that the twenty-first century will, in retrospect, be identified as the Chinese century.'

Murmurs from the audience were audible.

'This development, ironically, will be the fruit of our own labour. A sceptic might hold that it would be a better thing for America, and the world, if China's integration into the community of nations were slowed, and brakes put on the engines of her growth. Of course, it is not my place, as an impartial scholar, to root for one outcome or another. But if, as I believe, we have reached a fork in the road, perhaps I can help direct our attention to what lies at the end of each path. Conflict with China is inevitable. What is not inevitable is whether we lose. That will depend on choices we make today.'

Ambler shuddered. Ashton Palmer had an urbanity, a spurious civility, that made him, potentially, even more dangerous than obvious fanatics.

Clay Caston knelt down and typed a series of commands on the keyboard again, until another video clip began to play. This feed was fuzzier, apparently copied from a C-SPAN broadcast.

'Here, you'll hear him singing a different tune,' Caston said. 'The Center for Strategic Studies conference a couple of years ago was a closed event—it was Palmer speaking mainly to acolytes.'

The clip began with a question from a young, bearded man in the audience. 'Do you feel, Professor Palmer, that America's policy towards China is sufficiently attuned to our national interests? Because many people in the State Department today would look at the rise of President Liu Ang and call it a great success, a tribute to their policy of "constructive engagement".'

Palmer smiled, showing white, even teeth, as the camera returned to him. 'And that's fair enough,' he said. 'Liu Ang is a marvellously appealing politician. I have only the greatest hopes that he represents the future.'

Despite Palmer's smooth avowal and easy manner, Ambler felt a chill. He reversed the clip until it reached the moment where Ashton Palmer said the name of the Chinese President. Then he advanced the video frame by frame. *There*. In a micropause between the two parts of the Chinese name, Palmer's face settled into a radically different expression. The eyes were drawn, the corners of his mouth pulled down, the nostrils flared: it was an expression of outrage and disgust. By another frame or two, it had been replaced by a look of smiling approval.

Caston shook his head. 'I'd never have picked up on that.'

'There are a lot of things in heaven and on earth that don't show up on your spreadsheets,' Ambler said.

'Don't underestimate me,' Caston said. 'I get there in the end.'

'You would.' Ambler stood up, and started to pace. 'OK, you want to talk logic? What's happening in China these days—what does it all mean for a guy like Ashton Palmer? Why does he hate Liu Ang so much?'

'I'm a numbers man, Ambler. I don't do geopolitics. But I read the papers. And the main thing about Liu Ang seems to be that he's enormously popular among his people, and an incredible force for liberalisation. He's opened markets, established fair trading systems. But follow the logic of Palmer's argument—all that stuff about what could happen if an inward-looking kingdom starts to become integrated in the community of nations—if you're Palmer, Liu Ang is your worst nightmare.'

'If you're Palmer,' Ambler added, 'you'd want to do something about it.'

'I read somewhere that Liu Ang's making some big state visit to America next month,' Caston mused. He fell silent for a moment. 'I'm going to have to make some calls.'

Ambler's gaze returned to the frozen image of the scholar as he tried to extract everything he could from his visage. *Who are you? What do you want?*

Then the image vanished. The monitor exploded—blossoming into a cloud of glass fragments.

Ambler whirled round and saw a black-clad gunman, crouched in the hallway outside the room. The military assault rifle he was holding was a model Ambler recognised. The Heckler & Koch G36. Standard issue for the Consular Operations armoury.

Ambler threw himself down a split second before a triple burst drove more bullets in his direction. Caston, he saw, had hurled himself towards the far side of the room, away from the commando's sight line. For now.

The commando was not alone; Ambler could see it in his eyes. He had the confidence of a member of a team. How many? Four to six would be standard for a special-ops squad with a civilian target. If this were rapid response, it could be as few as two or three. They would have arrived using different routes of entrance—some through the door, some through the window. With a heat scope, it would have been a cinch to determine their exact position in the safe house.

As a second black-clad gunman ran past the first—a standard flanking manoeuvre—Ambler suddenly kicked the study's door closed.

Caston was cowering, his usually pallid face now sheet white. 'Believe me,' he breathed, 'I had nothing to do with this.'

'I know that,' Ambler said. 'One of the downloads must have triggered an alarm. Like you said, this place was supposed to be unoccupied.'

'So what now?'

'It isn't good. We're dealing with pros.'

A blast of bullets tore away at the upper half of the door, filling the air with splinters and the smell of carbonised wood. Ambler leapt up and switched off the lights before throwing himself on the floor again.

The question was, Why was he still alive?

Because the infrared scopes would have told the gunmen there were two people in the study. Identify, then kill: that would be the order of business.

They had not shot Ambler because they had not been able to verify that it *was* him. Their instructions did not cover the presence of a second party.

'We don't have anything to hold them off,' Caston said. 'We've got to surrender.'

Another triple burst punched a large hole in the door. Ambler knew that he had just seconds to put them off their game plan. His only weapon was the small Glock 26—utterly useless against an assault rifle.

Revise and improvise.

'Actually, you do have something you can use,' Ambler said in a low voice. 'What you've got is a hostage. You need to shout that you've got a hostage and you're going to shoot him if they take another step. *Now.*'

'You're mad. I can't do that.'

'You can, and you *will*.' Ambler mouthed the word *Now*.

Caston took a deep breath. 'I have a hostage,' he bellowed to the gunmen, in a surprisingly steady voice. 'You take another step and I'll shoot him.'

Silence, followed by a barely audible exchange among the gunmen.

Ambler removed the small Glock 26 from his back holster and pressed it into the auditor's hand. 'You hold it to the back of my head, OK?'

'Easy for you to say,' Caston whispered. 'I'm the one they'll shoot dead.'

'You're just going to have to trust me on this. You've done well so far.'

Ambler could tell that Caston was pleased by the reassurance.

'You're going to use my body as a shield,' Ambler said. 'Don't let them see you, if you can avoid it. Keep me between you and them at all times. I'll help with that, but you need to understand the manoeuvre.'

'Except *you're* the one they're after, right? It doesn't make any sense.'

'Just go with me on this,' Ambler repeated. It would take too long to explain. In the midst of a tension-fuelled operation, nobody would think to second-guess identities. They were men pumped with adrenaline, trying to complete their orders without a career-destroying mistake like letting the hostage die. Noting the position of hostage and hostage-taker would swamp other considerations, details like hair colour and height.

Ambler whispered further instructions in Caston's ear.

Finally, Caston took another deep breath. 'Let me speak to your commanding officer,' he roared.

No response came.

Arranging his countenance into a look of sheer terror, Ambler hurtled himself towards the ravaged door, as if he had been shoved, and pressed his face against the large, jagged hole. 'Don't let him kill me,' he whimpered, with the hysteria of a civilian caught in a nightmare beyond his imagining. 'Please don't let him kill me.'

The two commandos: square-jawed, dark-haired, were trying to look *past* him, into the darkened room, oblivious to the fact that their quarry was, literally, staring them in the face.

'I want to speak to the commanding officer,' Caston repeated, in a loud, confident voice. '*Now*.'

The two men exchanged glances, and Ambler felt his pulse quicken. There was no commanding officer present. Not yet.

'Don't let him kill me,' Ambler repeated, in a snivelling mantra of terror.

'You're going to be OK,' the larger commando said in a low voice.

'Let the hostage go,' the other commando shouted. 'And we'll talk.'

'Do you think I'm a moron?' Caston immediately shouted. Ambler was astonished: the auditor was extemporising.

'If you hurt him, it's all over for you,' the second commando yelled back.

Suddenly, Ambler dropped to the floor, out of the commandos' view. 'Ow!' he bellowed, as if he had just been struck.

Now he and Caston conferred quietly, hurriedly. Then Ambler showed his face at the jagged hole once more. 'Please let me out of here,' he wailed. 'I don't know who you people are. I don't want to know. Just don't let him kill me.' He contorted his features and let his eyes become moist. 'He says he'll blow me to shreds. I got a wife, kids.' He was speaking in short, breathless sentences. 'I'm in the movie business. I came here to scout locations. The Ambassador's a good friend . . . *Oh, please*—'

'Here's the plan,' Caston boomed. 'One of you can come to within five feet of the threshold. A foot nearer, and he dies. I'm going to let the civilian walk towards you so you can see that he's fine. But I'll have a red-bead on him all the time, understand? You make a wrong move, and my .338 Lapua Magnum gets to show you what it can do.'

Ambler flung open the door and took a few unsteady steps into the hallway, his face a study in terror. The commandos would assume that their target was situated in a darkened corner of the room, out of their sight line, holding a sophisticated, long-range rifle. Their plan, now, would be to stall as long as possible, to allow the other members of the team to assemble.

Ambler took a step towards the larger commando and said beseechingly, 'He's going to kill me, I know it. I can see it in his eyes.' As he spoke, the words rushing out with mounting hysteria, Ambler began to wave his hands around in agitation. 'You need to help me. Please help me. Call the US Ambassador, Sam Hurlbut. He'll vouch for me. But please don't leave me with that . . . that *maniac*.' As he spoke, he leaned forward, towards the commando, as if to try to speak to him in confidence.

'You need to calm down,' the commando barked, scarcely concealing his distaste for the panicking civilian, who was coming too close and talking too much as he continued to flail his hands wildly.

At that point Ambler pitched himself forward and, with cobra-strike swiftness, wrested the G36 from the commando and slammed the silencer-cuffed barrel against his head. As the large man slumped to the ground, Ambler trained the assault rifle on the man's startled partner.

He saw a man trying to revise all his assumptions, utterly bewildered.

'Drop yours now,' Ambler ordered.

The man did so, backing up slowly.

Ambler knew what the man was preparing to do. 'Freeze,' he shouted.

But the man kept backing away, hands raised. When an operation had gone wrong, you evacuated. That was the rule. So Ambler just watched as the man turned and ran out of the apartment, no doubt to rejoin his squad.

He and Caston, too, would now need to evacuate immediately, and regroup in their own way.

IN BEIJING, early the next morning, Chao Tang was in the communication room at the Ministry of State Security, poring over a communiqué that had arrived overnight, his eyes only. What he had learned was profoundly disturbing. If Comrade Li's description of the incident in the Luxembourg Gardens was correct, the situation they confronted was even more dire than he had imagined. New operating assumptions had to be arrived at swiftly.

Chao could not wait any longer for Liu Ang to come to his senses. He had to take direct action on his own. As he transmitted his encoded instructions, he tried to reassure himself that he was merely taking the desperate measures that the situation required. If he had miscalculated, however, he had just made the biggest mistake of his life.

Who else knew about Joe Li's dispatch? The young man who had delivered it, Shen Wang, was bright-eyed and bushy-tailed as he was every morning. At first Chao had been wary of him. He was effectively 'on loan' for twelve months from the People's Liberation Army, which had taken to 'seconding' junior officers to the civilian branches of government.

Shen Wang was known to be a protégé of General Lam, a stiff-necked figure whom Chao regarded with distaste. Yet despite a suspicion that the intern would report back to his PLA master, the young man had steadily grown on Chao. He was industrious and seemed to be a true idealist.

Now Shen Wang appeared at the doorway, clearing his throat discreetly. 'If you will excuse my presumption, sir,' he said, 'you seem concerned.'

Chao looked up. Had Shen Wang looked at the communiqué? He seemed so innocent it seemed impossible he was guilty of any such thing.

'Matters have long been complicated,' Chao replied. 'This morning, they grow more so.'

Shen Wang bowed his head. 'I cannot know the complexities of the state matters that burden you,' he said. 'But I know that your shoulders are broader than any burden.' He was alluding to an old proverb.

'Let us hope so.'

'Comrade Chao recalls his lunch appointment?'

Chao smiled distractedly. 'You'll have to remind me.'

Shen Wang glanced down at Chao's daily schedule. 'A luncheon celebration of the People's Heroes. At the Peninsula Palace.'

'I suppose I'd better get going, then,' Chao said, thinking of the city's impossible traffic. Even a short trip involved an inordinate amount of time.

Later, as Chao climbed into the back of his armoured limousine, he reflected on Shen Wang's perceptiveness. Chao prided himself on recognising potential, and he believed that this young man had a considerable future.

After ten minutes of sludge-like traffic, the sedan finally roared over an overpass at a reasonable speed. But in the lane opposite, an enormous yellow bulldozer was visible up ahead. Roadworks of some sort, Chao thought. It was unfortunate that they could not have been postponed until a more reasonable hour of the day. At least they were in the opposite lane.

'Traffic's not so bad going our way, eh?' Comrade Chao's driver said.

The chief of the Second Bureau of the Ministry of State Security never replied. Instead, a scream exploded from his throat as the bulldozer, with its shovel blade low to the ground, suddenly veered into their lane. The windscreen was smashed and metal screamed against metal, as the car was lifted off the ground by the blade and pushed against the guardrail until it catapulted over it and plunged onto the concrete below, where it burst into flames.

High in the unseen cab, the bulldozer's driver spoke into a cellphone.

'The cleanup is completed,' he said, in a rough northern dialect.

'Thank you,' Shen Wang told him. Given the soaring number of traffic accidents in Beijing these days, the death on the overpass would be dismaying but not altogether surprising. 'The general will be very pleased.'

'WHAT'S THIS?' Laurel asked, eyes widening in alarm as she ran her fingers along a purplish bruise on Ambler's shoulder.

They were in the hotel room and Ambler had removed his shirt.

'Caston's safe house wasn't all that safe, it turned out,' he admitted.

'Can you really trust that man?' Laurel asked, with a sharp look.

'I have to. If I can't trust him, I can't trust myself.' He stopped. 'It's hard to explain.'

She nodded. 'I understand. I don't know why I'm worrying about it. The world stopped making sense a long time ago.' She ran her fingertips over his chest, his shoulders, his arms, as if confirming that he was real, a person of flesh and blood. When she met his gaze again, her eyes were moist. 'I've never met anyone like you before. You're a good person.' She tapped the centre of his chest. 'With a good heart. They tried to erase you, but you know what? You're realer than any man I've ever met.'

'Laurel,' he said, stopping when he heard the catch in his own voice.

'When I'm with you, it's like . . . it's like discovering I'd been all by myself my whole life without fully realising it, because I never knew what it was like to be *together* with someone—*really* together. I can't go back to the way it was before.' Her voice thickened with emotion. '*That's* what you've done to me.'

His mouth was dry. 'Nothing frightens me more than losing you. Nothing makes sense without you, Laurel. Not for me. Without you I'm—'

'Harrison Ambler,' she said, smiling as she spoke the name aloud.

THE MUSÉE ARMANDIER, with its collection of second-rate rococo art from the early eighteenth century, scarcely qualified as being worth a visit, Ambler remembered. It was among the least-visited public spaces in Paris, and thus a good place for a private encounter. Its plentiful windows would also enable Ambler to detect any tails, and, better still, the Armandier foundation hired only a single guard for the whole museum.

Ambler mounted the stairs to the fourth floor and turned down a hallway to the large room at the end, where he and Caston had agreed to meet.

His footsteps were muffled by the peach-coloured carpet, and he could hear Caston's voice as he approached.

He felt a prickle of apprehension. Was Caston with someone?

Silently, he came closer, until he could make out the words.

'Good,' Caston was saying. And: 'Is that right?' And: 'So they're doing OK?' A man talking on a cellphone. There was a long moment of silence. 'Good night, hugglebunny,' Caston said. 'Love you, too.' He closed the flip-phone and pocketed it as Ambler entered the room.

'Glad you made it,' Caston said.

'"Hugglebunny"?' Ambler asked.

Flushing, the auditor turned and looked out of the window. 'I had my office check the Border Control database,' the auditor said after a pause. 'Dr Ashton Palmer arrived in Roissy yesterday. He's here.'

'Your office—can you trust their discretion?'

'I say "my office", but it's really just my assistant. And yes, I trust him.'

'What else did you learn?'

'I didn't say I learned anything else.'

'You did,' Ambler corrected him. 'Just not in words.'

Caston scowled. 'The thing is, it's messy, and I'm not sure what to make of it yet. It's what they call "chatter"—small interceptions, some fragmentary, each inconclusive on its own. Something's going on—or maybe I should say that something's about to happen. Something involving—'

'China,' Ambler broke in.

'Well, that's the easier part of the conundrum. The harder part is *you*. You've become entangled in something that involves Chinese politics. And the question is: Why you? What information did the Strategic Services Group have about you? Which data points were pertinent?'

'Paul Fenton decided I was a magician because I'd "erased" myself.'

'When, in point of fact, you'd been "erased", if you want to put it that way. But this suggests that they had a particular need for an agent who couldn't be identified. And not just any agent. An agent with fantastically honed skills at inferring emotion. A walking polygraph.'

'Fenton has my Stab records, or some of them. He doesn't know my real name, but he knows my assignments, what I've done, where I've been.'

'So there are your inherent characteristics, and there are the historical facts: who you are and what you've done. Either or both could be relevant.'

'Wouldn't want to leap to conclusions, huh?'

Caston smiled wanly. 'I'm simply trying to get you to look for patterns. Because the fact is that there's a pattern here. Changhua. Montreal. And now Paris—the Deschesnes incident.'

'Changhua . . . I tried to stop it. Too late, but I tried.'

'You failed. But you were there. Meaning there's very likely photographic evidence of your presence. The question is why they wanted you. And what they really wanted you for. Changhua. Montreal. Paris. It's not just a string of events, Ambler. It's a *sequence*.'

'Fine,' Ambler said testily. The overheated museum was causing him to perspire. 'It's a sequence. What's that mean?'

'Meaning we need to see how each event is connected to the one before, because then we'll know what the next event is going to be.' Caston gave him a wintry look. 'Then again, we can just wait for the next event to happen. That might make all things clear. From every indication we've got, we're about to see what it's all leading up to. If I were superstitious, I'd say you were bad luck.'

ADRIAN CHOI FIDGETED with his ear stud as he sat at his boss's desk. It felt good, sitting there, and there couldn't be any harm in it. Besides, it wasn't as if anybody ever passed by. He made another phone call, and smiled his sunniest smile as he spoke to an assistant at the Joint Intel Resources Center, someone at his level. Caston had asked her boss about those Parrish Island personnel files, but to no avail. He'd grumbled and protested and blustered. So now he would try another approach.

The young woman who answered sounded immediately wary. 'PIPF. Ward 4W—yes, I know,' she said. 'I'll have to process the request forms.'

'No, see, you guys already gave us a copy of the files,' Adrian lied. 'I'm just asking for another copy.'

'Oh,' the woman said, a little less frostily. 'Sorry. Bureaucracy, right?'

'Tell me about it,' Adrian said. 'I'd like to say it was a matter of national security. But it's really a matter of saving my own skin.'

'How do you mean?'

'Well, Caitlin—it's Caitlin, right?'

'That's right,' she said. Was he imagining it, or was she warming up?

'You sound like the kind of person who never messes up, so I don't expect much sympathy from you.'

'Me?' She giggled. 'Are you *kidding*?'

'Hey, it's important for me to have somebody to look up to,' Adrian said. 'Thing is, I forwarded the file directly to the DDI's office without keeping a copy for my boss. Which means my boss is going to pitch a fit.' He paused. 'Listen, that's my problem, not yours. I didn't mean to lay this on you. Never mind. Really.'

The young woman on the other end of the line sighed. 'It's just that they've been really uptight about the whole thing, God knows why. Everything's in some Omega-level sequestered database. But, listen, I'll see what I can do, OK?'

'You're a lifesaver, Caitlin,' said Adrian. 'I mean that.'

BURTON LASKER looked at his watch yet again, as he prowled the Air France lounge. It wasn't like Fenton to be late. Yet the flight had already started to board, and Fenton had still not appeared. Where was he? Why wasn't he answering his cellphone?

Lasker had been Fenton's staunchest lieutenant for a decade, and considered those years with Fenton the most valuable and gratifying of his life. Every visionary required someone who devoted himself to the tightly focused task of *execution*, of *follow-through*, and Lasker excelled at that. Fenton, who truly *was* a visionary, respected him for it.

Where was the man? As the Air France attendants, with an apologetic shrug, closed the ramp doors, Lasker felt an icicle of fear within his gut. Something was wrong. He phoned the front desk of the hotel where he and Fenton had both been staying. 'No, Monsieur Fenton has not checked out.'

Something was very wrong.

LAUREL HOLLAND joined the two men on the still-deserted fourth floor of the Musée Armandier a few minutes later than they had planned—her errands had taken her longer than she had expected.

'You must be Clayton Caston,' she said to the auditor, extending a hand.

'I'm Clay,' he replied, 'in your hands, anyway. Nice to meet you, Laurel.'

'Your first time in France, Hal tells me. Mine too.'

Ambler glanced down at the newspaper Laurel had brought with her: *Le Monde diplomatique*. On the front page, alongside a picture of snow-capped mountains, was a headline referring to the World Economic Forum.

'What's that about?' he asked, pointing to the article.

'Oh, some meeting of global titans in Davos, Switzerland.'

'I was there once,' Caston said. 'The World Economic Forum wanted my expertise for some panel on money-laundering. They like a smattering of people who actually know what they're talking about.'

Ambler peered through the window at the street, confirming that nobody suspicious had entered the vicinity. 'This is the thing. I'm tired of playing blindman's bluff. We know there's a pattern here—a sequence, like you say, Caston. But I need to know the next step, ahead of time.'

'My assistant is working on getting more information from Joint Intel Resources,' Caston said. 'I think we should wait to see what he finds out.'

Ambler gave the back-office man a flinty look. 'You're along for the ride, Caston. Nothing more. Like I say, this isn't your world.'

BURTON LASKER entered the George V lift with the young manager on duty. When they reached the seventh floor, the manager knocked on the door of Fenton's room, then unlocked it with a special keycard. The two men strode through the suite, seeing no sign of habitation. Then the hotelier stepped into the bathroom; his face was ashen as he stepped out. Lasker rushed in to see what the other man had seen. He gasped. It felt as though there were a balloon inside his chest, making it hard to breathe.

'You were a friend of his?' the hotelier asked.

'A friend and business associate,' Lasker confirmed.

'I am sorry.' The man paused awkwardly. 'Help will arrive shortly. I will make the calls.'

Lasker stood rooted to the spot. Fenton's body was slumped in the tub of bathwater, the emptied bottle of vodka propped by the basin—stage dressing that might confuse the gendarmerie, but did not fool Lasker.

He had a strong suspicion who was behind the murder, and when he went through Paul Fenton's PDA, his suspicions were confirmed. Fenton had come to Paris to meet 'Tarquin', a man Lasker knew all too well.

Tarquin had served in the Political Stabilisation Unit; Lasker—field name Cronus—had had the misfortune of serving with him on a couple of assignments. Tarquin was known for his peculiar gift of reading people, a gift that some strategists at Consular Operations were overly impressed with. They couldn't grasp what seasoned operatives like Cronus knew: that operational success always came down to firepower and muscle.

Now Tarquin had killed the greatest man Lasker had ever known, and he would pay with his life.

He would send a message to Tarquin on Fenton's wireless PDA. First, though, calls would be made to the dozen or so 'associates' that SSG had on the ground in Paris. A rendezvous with the condemned man would be established for sunset.

Chapter 10

Caleb Norris pressed the OFF button of his cellphone. It was foolish that the CIA permitted the use of cellphones in headquarters, he reflected. It nullified a great many of the elaborate security precautions that were taken. But, at the moment, that suited him well.

He fed various papers into the shredder beside his desk, retrieved his coat, and, finally, unlocked a steel-lined case secreted in his credenza. The long-barrelled handgun fitted neatly into his briefcase.

'Have a *great* trip, Mr Norris,' his secretary said.

'Thank you, Brenda,' the ADDI replied heartily. 'I intend to.'

'Don't get sunburnt,' she cautioned. 'I looked up the weather forecast for the Virgin Islands, and it's supposed to be nothing but clear skies.'

'Just what we like to hear.'

'Your car is waiting at the 2A bay with your luggage,' Brenda added. 'Dulles should take half an hour this time of day. It'll be smooth sailing.'

She was right, but Norris had left himself plenty of time at the airport. Even with the right paperwork, checking a weapon through airport security could take some time. In the event, the line at Business Class moved fast.

'Good afternoon,' the airline clerk behind the counter said. 'And where are you headed for today?'

Norris slid his ticket across the counter. 'Zürich.'

'Skiing, I bet.' The clerk glanced at his passport and ticket invoice before stamping his boarding card.

Norris took a glance at his watch. 'What else?'

ON THE STREET outside the Musée Armandier, Ambler felt the BlackBerry vibrating in his inside pocket. It had to be a message from Fenton or one of his people. He scanned the screen quickly. A deputy of Fenton's had called to arrange a meeting this evening—an outdoor rendezvous. As he returned the device to his pocket, he felt a faint sense of unease.

'Where?' asked Laurel, when he told her about it.

'Père-Lachaise,' the operative replied. 'Not the most imaginative venue.'

'Worries me,' Laurel said. 'I don't like the sound of it.'

'Because it's a cemetery? It might as well be an amusement park—it's a prettily heavily trafficked area. Trust me, I know what I'm doing.'

'I wish I shared your confidence,' Caston said. 'Fenton's a wild card. His arrangement with the federal government is a can of worms. Had my office look into it, and it seems its deeply buried. Nothing I can penetrate while I'm here, but I'd love a chance to review the accounts. Irregular, I'd bet.'

Laurel reached a hand over to Ambler's. 'I'm just saying be careful,' she said. 'You still don't know what these people are really up to.'

'I'll be careful. But we're getting close.'

'Close to finding out what they did to you?'

'Yes,' Ambler said. 'And close to finding out what they may have planned for the rest of the world.'

'Take care, Hal,' she said. 'I *really* don't have a good feeling about this.'

'WE MUST GET THE MESSAGE to President Liu,' Wan Tsai said, the horror in his gaze further magnified by his thick-lensed, wire-rimmed glasses.

'But what if Comrade Chao's death really *was* an accident?' Li Pei asked.

The two were in Wan Tsai's office, in the Hall of Diligent Government.

'Do you believe that?' Wan Tsai demanded.

A faint chest rattle was audible as the older man exhaled. 'No,' he said. 'I don't.' Li Pei was in his late seventies, but suddenly looked older still.

'We have all gone through the proper channels,' Wan Tsai said, not for the first time. 'We have all raised the alarm. Yet I find that President Liu is already in the air, halfway there. We must get him to come back.'

'He will *not* come back,' Li Pei wheezed. 'We both know he is as stubborn as a mule.' A mournful look passed over his age-etched countenance. 'And who knows whether he might confront even greater dangers at home.'

Wan Tsai swallowed hard. 'Who is in charge of Liu Ang's security retinue?'

'You *know* who,' the wily peasant said.

The economist closed his eyes briefly. 'The PLA, you mean.'

'A unit under PLA control. It comes to the same thing.'

Wan Tsai looked at the façades of Zhongnanhai that were visible from his window. The doors, the walls, the gates, the bars—every implement of security struck him as a tool of imprisonment. 'I will speak to the general in charge,' he said abruptly. 'I will appeal to him personally. Many of these generals are men of honour, whatever their political views may be.'

A few minutes later, he was on the phone to the man currently in charge of President Liu Ang's security. He made no secret of his anxieties, but admitted that they were not yet founded upon clear evidence. He implored the man to convey to Liu Ang an urgent message.

'Have no worries on that score,' said the PLA official. 'Nothing could be of greater importance to me than Liu Ang's security.'

'I cannot stress enough that all of us who work with Liu Ang are *extremely* concerned,' the economist said.

'We are in complete agreement,' General Lam, said reassuringly. 'Trust that our beloved leader's safety will be my personal priority.'

At least Wan Tsai thought that was what the general said. The man's heavy Hakka accent made the word 'priority' sound almost like another, seldom-used Mandarin word, which meant 'plaything'.

LE CIMETIÈRE DU PÈRE-LACHAISE was the resting place of many legendary figures—Marcel Proust, Oscar Wilde, Sarah Bernhardt, Edith Piaf, Chopin, and others. Deathstyles of the rich and famous, Ambler mused as he entered. The meeting was to take place at 5.10 p.m. and already the light was fading rapidly. He shivered, only partly because of the cold.

The cemetery was well over 100 acres and criss-crossed with cobbled walkways. On the map, it was sectioned off into ninety-seven 'divisions', but the main routes had names, and the instructions had been specific about which to take. Carrying a black rucksack, Ambler had dutifully followed the avenue Circulaire, on the periphery, to the avenue de la Chapelle, then turned left onto the avenue Feuillant. The roads and walkways, lined with mausoleums and tombstones, made it seem like a village of the dead.

He walked the paths surrounding the specified rendezvous. Most of the trees were leafless, of little use for concealment. Still, Fenton could have positioned security guards behind the larger edifices, or interspersed, in plain clothes, among the tourists and visitors.

He approached a nearby bench and, with an inconspicuous motion, left the black backpack underneath it, then strolled away. He ducked into a kiosk marked 'WC', removed his jacket and put on a grey sweatshirt and horn-rimmed glasses with clear lenses. He exited swiftly, stepping round the kiosk and behind a ten-foot stone memorial.

A minute later, a young man in jeans and a leather jacket sat down on the bench and yawned. When he stood up and walked away, Ambler could see that the backpack was gone.

The young man was one of the watchers and had done what Ambler had predicted. They had observed Ambler leaving the backpack in place and, intent on learning why, had dispatched someone to retrieve it. The item was, in fact, filled with birdseed—that being the tradecraft term for anything of no actual value that might be used to attract the attention of enemy agents. They would understand the ruse as soon as the pack was opened.

Meanwhile, Ambler had identified one of the sentries—one of the watchers. He would follow the young man and see whether he led him to others.

Walking down another cobbled path, his other clothes in the nylon zip-bag he carried on a shoulder strap, he hoped he was inconspicuous. He kept pace twelve yards behind the leather-jacketed watcher, and followed him through a square full of people. The young man sauntered along, glancing left and right; few would have registered the nearly imperceptible looks of acknowledgment, from a woman to his left and a weedy-looking man on his right. But Ambler did. They were watchers, too, then.

Ambler proceeded to the next memorial square. There were more of them. He *felt* it as much as anything, and his skin began to crawl. There were far too many watchers in place; it was too elaborate. People were situated in non-defensive positions, deployed as for rapid, aggressive actions.

Ambler's mind reeled, but he forced himself to focus. Ahead of him, the man in the leather jacket was passing the nylon backpack to two stone-faced men in dark overcoats. They received the package and hurried off.

Was the rendezvous a set-up? Had Fenton been lying to him all along? Ambler could not rule it out. Perhaps Fenton was a spectacularly good actor. Ambler's powers of perception may have been unusual and uncanny, but he had no illusions that they were infallible. Perhaps, though, Fenton himself had been misinformed. That seemed the more likely.

Whatever the circumstances, Ambler knew that a swift retreat was the only safe move. He quickened his stride and took an immediate right, towards Père-Lachaise metro station.

Too late he saw the two bulky men in dark overcoats closing in on him from opposite directions and now stepping into him, their broad shoulders catching his, spinning him round in a fluid, well-choreographed movement. The operatives were tall and broad and their bulk helped conceal the disciplined ferocity with which they propelled Ambler off the cobbles and round the back of a mausoleum. Moments later, hidden from view, they stood to either side of him, hands gripping his upper arms. The man on Ambler's right had a hypodermic in his other hand.

'Not one word,' the man said in a hushed voice, 'or I sink this in your arm.' He was an American, stocky-framed and broad-faced.

Now a third man sprang into view, and it was a few seconds before Ambler recognised him. His hair was greying, his forehead deeply creased. When Ambler had known him, his face had been smooth, his head of hair full. But the equine cast to his features was unchanged. There was no mistaking the man he had known as Cronus.

Now Cronus—Burton Lasker—smiled. 'It has been a while, hasn't it?' he said in a conversational tone. 'Too long, Tarquin.'

'Maybe not long enough,' Ambler replied neutrally. His eyes flickered among all three men. Already it was obvious that Cronus was the figure of authority here; the others were looking to him for a signal to act.

Lasker's eyes gleamed with pure hatred. 'Did you really think you could get away with it?'

'With what?'

'Killing a great man doesn't make you any less insignificant. You're still a worm. And you'll be stepped on like a worm.'

Ambler peered into the black depths of Cronus's eyes. Rage glinted there, but something else too: sorrow. Grief.

'Cronus, what happened?' Ambler said softly, intently.

'You murdered Paul Fenton,' Lasker said. 'The question is why.'

Fenton—*dead*? Ambler's mind began to churn rapidly. This whole rendezvous, he saw now, had never been anything other than a deathtrap, revenge plotted by a faithful lieutenant half-crazed with grief. 'Listen to me, you're making a big mistake—'

'No, you listen to me,' Cronus said, cutting him off. 'You will tell me what I want to know. I'll find out the hard way or the easy way. And I'm kind of hoping it'll be the hard way.' His face twisted into a dark scowl.

RESTING ON THE PITCHED stone roof of a Napoleonic general's tomb, concealed by the parapet, Joe Li stretched like a cat and gazed through his powerful binoculars. The tomb was one of the highest elevations in the immediate vicinity, and the view was extensive. His rifle, modified to make it mobile, was a QBZ-95 sniper rifle.

He studied the knot of men around Tarquin. The operative had demonstrated a remarkable ability to escape difficult situations. With professional dispassion, Joe Li had to grant him that. But he was only flesh and blood and, in all likelihood, there would soon be a great deal of both on display.

Joe Li's last communication with Beijing had been unsatisfactory. His controller was growing impatient; in the past, Li had achieved results with considerable dispatch. But he was not used to the sorts of complications that his latest assignment had presented him with. He had an incisive mind. He collected and correlated information. And he knew Tarquin was a formidable target and that there was no room for mistakes.

He peered through the scope again, the focus electronically perfected to maximal sharpness at the precise point where the cross hairs met.

'JUST CURIOUS. How many "associates" do you have here?' Ambler asked.

'A baker's dozen,' Cronus replied.

'Not bad for something so last-minute,' Ambler said, impressed.

'The Strategic Services Group has resources everywhere,' Cronus said. 'Fenton's legacy. We'd all give our lives for him. That's what people like you could never grasp.'

'People like me?' Carefully, casually, Ambler took a step back. He composed his face into an expression of resignation and glanced at the man to his left, who was looking at Cronus, getting his signals from his leader. Ambler started speaking heatedly, testily—the sort of verbal protest that was normally inconsistent with physical aggression. 'You're making a lot of assumptions, Cronus. You're wrong about Fenton, but you're too blind or too stupid'—Ambler swivelled fluidly round—'to admit your mistake'— *now*, with explosive force, he slammed his rigid fingers into the throat of the giant to his right.

He could feel the impact of his knuckles against cartilage. Even as the syringe dropped to the ground, he lashed out at the other muscleman, but the man dodged the blow, and reached into his jacket for a gun. Both Ambler and Cronus dived out of the way, racing in opposite directions.

Which meant that Ambler was in the field of fire.

As he dropped to the ground, he heard four muted reports—from where?—and marble and earth exploded all around him. He forced himself to survey the terrain opposite, and saw, in a dense mound of rhododendrons, fleetingly, a glimpse of khaki-clad shoulder.

He yanked the gun, a silenced Beretta 92 Centurion, from the downed man's shoulder holster, took careful aim, and fired a tight, rapid cluster of three shots. The weapon made a quiet spitting sound.

A bloodied arm flailed out of the foliage. Moments later, a wounded man lurched to the safety of a stone edifice nearby.

Ambler had to *move*—every moment at rest was a moment in someone's cross hairs. He tucked the gun into the top of his jeans and sprang off in the direction Cronus had run in, felt the stinging spray of marble against his ear. Another bullet had been aimed at him, this one, he sensed, from a sniper in an elevated location.

A baker's dozen, Cronus had said, and he had not been bluffing. All would be seasoned killers. Ambler needed to shift the odds. But how?

He raced over to another cobbled walkway, the avenue Aguado. He was now nearing the northwestern section of the cemetery, approaching a large chapel in a Moorish style. He darted into a pillared walkway of limestone and slate. To his left was a Japanese man with a digital camera and a malevolent gaze. Ambler did not give him a second thought; the tourist was annoyed because Ambler had just ruined his shot. In the next alcove, a woman was reading a book. She glanced up at Ambler briefly.

It was a ruse that would have been more persuasive ten minutes ago, when the light was still adequate for reading. The woman had a broad, masculine face, and her thick legs were planted in the manner of a trained operative. He saw her slip a hand into her nylon parka, as if for warmth.

Ambler turned into her alcove, and as he passed her, he suddenly veered, crashing his body into hers so that the two of them tumbled heavily to the stone flooring. He twisted her body as they fell, and thrust the muzzle of the silenced Beretta against her throat.

'Not one word,' he said. He grabbed her book and opened it. A miniature radio transmitter was lodged in a space carved out of the pages.

'Tell them you have seen me,' Tarquin whispered. 'Tell them I have ducked down into that underground vault over there.'

Uncertainty flickered in her eyes.

He pressed the muzzle of the Beretta harder against her throat. 'You try anything, I'll know.'

Pressing a button on the transmitter, she said, 'Constellation Eighty-seven. Constellation Eighty-seven.' The chapel was in the middle of Division 87.

Tarquin grabbed the small flesh-coloured wireless earbud from her right ear and placed it in his own.

'What's your report?' the metallic voice crackled through the earbud.

Tarquin nodded to the woman.

'He's hiding in the underground vault,' she said.

He whispered into her ear, 'And he's armed.'

'And he's armed,' she added.

Without warning, Ambler whipped his arm back against her neck and forced her head forward into the crushing vice. She would be unconscious for several minutes. He propped her body on the marble bench, letting her head loll back against the wall, as if she were napping. Next he removed her shoelaces and made a loop that encircled her ankles. As soon as she attempted to stand, the loop would tauten.

He moved to another alcove that was now darkly shadowed but permitted a view of the steps down to the vault. He did not have long to wait.

The first on the scene was the leather-jacketed youth who had retrieved his backpack. He raced down the steps into the vault, a hand inside his jacket. A bald, middle-aged man with a pitted face was next. He stationed himself near the top of the steps. A third man arrived two minutes later, the second of the two men who had grabbed him. His face was reddened and glazed with sweat.

There was a low tone from the earbud, then the metallic voice again: 'Constellation Eighty-seven, confirm subject remains in position.' The sweat-slicked man, Ambler saw, was moving his lips as the voice was transmitted. Obviously he was wearing a hidden mike. A look of perplexity crossed the man's face. 'Constellation Eighty-seven, come in,' he said.

Ambler levelled the Beretta on the stone ledge of the nearest bay, peering through the deepening gloom with a sinking feeling. The distance was too great for an accurate hit using a handgun. The odds were greater that he would give his own position away.

He waited for one more member of the team to appear in Division 87, then made his retreat, sliding through a low arched aperture and through a bramble-ridden area of the quadrant to his north. In the distance he could see a guardhouse and the tall, dark green gates that let onto the city.

He hurried past countless tombs and statues as shadows lengthened and the setting sun's rosy glow began to ebb. His muscles were coiled, his senses on full alert. His ploy had reduced the pressure of the hostile forces, yet others would remain in position. He put on another burst of speed, and then stumbled briefly on the uneven ground. He felt, rather than heard, the double tap: another spray of stone, sharp, stinging fragments. Had he not stumbled, one of those bullets would have struck him in the upper body. He rolled behind a six-foot-tall obelisk.

Another spray of stone—this time the bullets came from the opposite side. He whipped his head round; the angle of the shot was too low to have come from any distance.

'Stand up like a man, why don't you?'

Cronus's voice.

The burly operative stepped out from behind a large memorial stone.

Ambler desperately scanned the area in front of him. He saw, some yards away, the back of a green-uniformed groundsman, PÈRE-LACHAISE ÉQUIPE D'ENTRETIEN stencilled in white across his shoulders and on the cap. Through the green gates—so close and yet a million miles away, it seemed—he could hear the faint bustle of a Paris street.

Cronus's gun was trained on him. Ambler could try to grab for his Beretta, yet the long, silenced muzzle would add a fatal split second to the time needed to deploy it.

All around him, the business of everyday life proceeded. The groundsman kept steadily working his way closer with his rubbish spike; some tourists started to flow through the gates. Suddenly a shaft of light from the setting sun dazzled off the windscreen of a passing car, and, for an instant, the groundsman's face was illuminated. Ambler felt another jolt of terror. He remembered the Plaza swimming pool, the Luxembourg Gardens.

The face he had glimpsed was that of the Chinese assassin.

'The thing you'll never understand, Cronus,' said Ambler, desperately trying to buy time, 'is that—'

'I've heard enough out of you,' the burly man said, his finger curling round the trigger of the silenced pistol. Abruptly the expression of hostility left his face, replaced by an oddly vacant look.

At that same instant, a plume of red droplets seemed to erupt from Cronus's left ear. The Chinese man had dropped to one knee, the rubbish spike in his hands replaced with a long, silenced rifle. Then he whirled round, towards Ambler, and squeezed off a shot—and for a moment Ambler wondered if this was the last thing he would ever see . . . but the man was peering through the scope, and a professional did not use a scope for a target only fifteen feet away. Tarquin heard the *plink* of an ejected cartridge.

The assassin was not firing at him, but at a sniper somewhere out of sight. *It made no sense.*

The man before him aimed his rifle again, peering through the scope. A double tap: two *plinks*—two more cartridges ejected. Ambler heard the distant moan of an injured man. The green-uniformed marksman rose from his crouching position and folded the stock of his rifle.

Ambler was dumbfounded, dazed with disbelief.

The assassin was letting him live.

'I don't understand,' Ambler said to him numbly.

The marksman turned to him, his brown eyes solemn. 'I know that now. It is why you are still alive.'

Ambler looked at him anew and saw a man who was doing what he believed duty demanded, a man who took pride in his formidable skills but no pleasure in their deadly consequences.

A moment later, the Chinese man's throat exploded into a cloud of blood. The unseen sniper, however badly wounded, had had at least one more shot in him, and he had trained it on the man who posed the greatest threat.

Ambler had to seize the opportunity. He charged towards the double green gates and through them into the street, not stopping until he found the rental car he had left nearby.

As he veered through the Paris traffic, taking pains to be sure that he was not being followed, he tried to process what he had learned. Someone had killed Fenton. Was it a member of Fenton's organisation—a mole? Was it someone in the United States government?

And the Chinese assassin: an adversary who had become an ally—indeed, someone who had given up his life to protect Ambler.

Why?

'I DON'T UNDERSTAND,' Laurel repeated. All three of them were gathered in Caston's oatmeal-bland hotel room.

'I don't, either,' Ambler said. 'None of this feels right.'

'It doesn't add up,' Caston put in.

'Wait a minute,' Laurel said. 'You said the killings were all linked to China. You said it looked like a sequence, like it was leading up to something imminent. You figured that Liu Ang was the probable target.'

'He's supposed to be visiting the White House next month,' Caston said. 'Big history-making thing. But the timing seems wrong. There's too much of a delay after the last event.'

'There's no delay,' Laurel said. She opened her large handbag and pulled out her furled copy of *Le Monde diplomatique*. 'The World Economic Forum takes place in Davos this week,' she said. 'Tomorrow is President Liu Ang's big address.'

Ambler began to pace, as he thought out loud. 'Liu Ang leaves the security of the Beijing cocoon for the first time since taking office. He comes to the West, and, in the middle of his big speech, he's gunned down . . .'

Caston looked contemplative. 'By whom?'

Fenton's voice: *Got a* real *exciting project for you coming up. But don't pack your skis just yet.*

Ambler did not speak for a long moment. 'Could Fenton have thought I would do it?'

'Is that possible?'

'Alternatively, the assassin may well be someone I know. Stab prided itself on hiring the best of the best and Fenton prided himself on hiring the best of Stab. If you were entrusting someone with the assassination of the Chinese President, wouldn't you get the best trained person you could?'

'And if it were a Stab operative,' Laurel said slowly, 'the odds are that you'd have had some dealings with the person.'

'The consequences . . .' Caston said glumly. 'My God. The consequences. President Liu Ang is an incredibly beloved figure in China. If he's killed, the people will be outraged. And the hysteria will turn into wrath. If *anything* should connect the assassination to members of the US government it could plunge the nations into war.'

'To risk that you'd have to be a fanatic,' Laurel said.

'Like Ashton Palmer.' Ambler felt the blood drain from his face.

Caston leapt from his chair and started to pace. 'They'll have thought this through from every angle. An operation like this, there'll be a deep-cover agent in place, and a back-up, too.' His gaze sharpened. 'And some strategy of misdirection. There's always got to be a fall guy. It would simplify matters if that was also the gunman, of course. But we've got to assume they've done a thorough assessment of all the parameters.'

'An operation always involves human beings,' Ambler said, a hint of defiance in his voice. 'And you can't quantify the human factor, Caston. Not with any precision. That's what people like you never understand.'

'And what people like *you* never understand is that—'

'Guys,' Laurel interjected impatiently, tapping on the newspaper. '*Guys*. It says here that he's speaking at Davos at five tomorrow afternoon.' She looked bewildered, desperate. 'Can't we just alert everyone?'

'Trust me, they're already operating on top alert,' Ambler said. 'The trouble is, there've been so many death threats against this guy that there's a serious boy-who-cried-wolf problem at this point. They know about the threats. And Liu Ang refuses to be immobilised by them.'

'Can you explain that this time the threat's really, really serious?'

Caston shot Laurel a glance. 'I'll do that,' he said. 'I'm sure it'll make all the difference.' He turned to Ambler. 'You really think there's a chance you'd recognise the assassin?'

'Yes,' Ambler said simply. 'I think they'd meant to recruit me for the job. But you're right, of course: Fenton doesn't work without an understudy "backstop". He's bound to be from the same talent pool. From Stab.'

'Even if he wasn't,' Laurel said hesitantly, 'you'd still be able to pick up on him. You've done it before—you have that gift of seeing.'

'I've done it before,' Ambler acknowledged. 'It's just that the stakes were never this high. Still, what choice is there?'

Laurel flushed. 'You don't owe anyone anything, Hal,' she said, suddenly agitated. 'Don't be a hero. Let's just disappear, all right?'

'Is that what you really want?'

'Yes,' she said, and then she murmured, 'No.' Tears welled up in her eyes. 'I don't know,' she said in a muffled voice. 'All I know is—if that's where you're going, that's where I'm going. There's no other place I feel safe.'

Ambler pulled her close and squeezed her tightly. 'OK,' he whispered.

Caston looked at Ambler stonily. 'Just so you're clear about this. You've got less than twenty-four hours to elude whatever lethal operatives Strategic Services and/or your own beloved Consular Operations have on the lookout, make your way into Switzerland, infiltrate a heavily guarded conclave of the global elite, and identify the assassin before he strikes. You have any idea of how you might accomplish this?'

'Sure,' Ambler said, his voice hollow.

'Well, let me tell you something.' Caston arched an eyebrow. 'It's not going to be as easy as it sounds.'

Chapter 11

When a roadside sign indicated that the Swiss border lay thirty kilometres ahead, Ambler veered off onto a small rural road. He knew he could not afford to drive the rented Opal coupé through the border checkpoint.

Laurel and Caston were travelling by high-speed rail to Zürich, which would take just over six hours, the bus to Davos adding another couple of hours. Ambler had no choice but to drive, to seek anonymity among the hundreds of thousands of cars on the autoroute. So far so good. But the border checkpoint would be the most hazardous part of the trip.

At the town of Colmar, in Haute Savoie, he found a cab driver, who, once Ambler had flashed a peacock's fan of hard currency at him, agreed to drive him to the hamlet of St Martin on the Swiss side of the border.

They were seven miles away when Ambler began to pick up signs that he might have been detected. There was a tarp-covered Jeep, maintaining a constant distance behind them—and there was a helicopter, in a place and at a time when no helicopter would normally be present.

Unease congealed into anxiety. The sun was a ribbon of red, glimmering over the horizon, but the mountain air was chill. Ambler told the cab driver that he'd had a change of heart, that he felt like going on an early-morning hike; yes, right here, what spot could be lovelier?

After the transfer of more hard currency, which softened the driver's look of suspicion to one of wry amusement, Ambler tightened the laces of his heavy leather climbing boots, zipped up his microfleece-lined winter jacket and got out of the car. A border crossing on foot was not an unexpected eventuality. Within minutes he had disappeared among the snow-laden firs, pines and larches lining the road.

After jogging for half a mile, he glimpsed two lampposts either side of the road, alongside a dark wood customs house with green shutters and a steeply raked roof, surrounded by French and Swiss flags. There was a low, bright orange barrier to control the flow of vehicles, with doorless booths on either side. A little past the customs house, the driver of a malfunctioning food-service lorry had pulled over, and Ambler could make out the belly and legs of a short, paunchy mechanic bent over its engine.

Opposite the customs house was a parking area, set lower than the road. Ambler strained to see: a cloud had passed over the once-glimmering sunrise; he saw a match flare, a border-patrol guard lighting a cigarette. He glanced at his watch. It was a little past eight o'clock; sunrise came late in January, and the mountainous terrain postponed the sunrise even further.

He could now see the canvas-topped Jeep. It must have ferried over the French border guards for the morning shift. Ambler positioned himself behind a copse of young spruce trees and raised his compact field glasses to his eyes. The border-patrol guard was taking a deep drag on his cigarette. Through the windows of the customs house, Ambler could see a number of the other guards drinking coffee and trading gossip. Seated among them was a man in a bright red flannel shirt with a pear-shaped body that told of a sedentary existence: the truck driver, Ambler guessed.

Whatever the rulebook might say, it was hard to persuade men to stand outside in the freezing cold keeping watch when traffic was sporadic. Even without hearing the banter, Ambler could tell from the men's faces that a spirit of joviality reigned. One man, though, remained apart from the others. Ambler turned his field glasses towards him. The man wore the uniform of a senior officer in the French customs authority: it would be his job to make occasional inspections of such checkpoints.

As Ambler fine-tuned the focus of his field glasses, the man's face came into sharper view, and Ambler saw how wrong he was. The man was not an officer with the customs authority. Ambler recognised him. The man's name—but it did not matter what his name was; he used innumerable aliases. He had grown up in Marseilles and served as a henchman for one of the drug mobs there before drifting into employment as a mercenary. He was an efficient killer, most useful for the non-attributable kill: *specialist*. The last time Ambler had seen him he had been blond; now he was dark-haired. The hollowed cheeks beneath high, ridge-like cheekbones and slash-like mouth remained the same.

Any sense of advantage Ambler had enjoyed evaporated at once. The specialist would not have been dispatched alone. If he was inside, it meant that others had been deployed in the surrounding woods.

Now, two border guards, one French, one Swiss, emerged: a white Renault van was pulling up to the checkpoint, idling before the low orange barrier. One of the guards bent down to speak to the driver. A face was matched with a passport photograph. The two guards glanced at each other. A decision was made. The barrier rose, and the van was waved on.

The two men split up and went to sit on plastic chairs, one in each of the outside booths. They adjusted their ear mufflers and padded jackets. Now the killer from Marseilles emerged from the customs house and walked over to the lower parking lot, where he disappeared behind a low brick structure—of the kind where maintenance equipment was stored. Was he conferring with someone? There was no time to analyse the options. The growing daylight would only help his enemies. Ambler had to act.

CALEB NORRIS NEVER had troubled dreams; if anything, when under pressure he seemed to sleep more deeply and peacefully. When he woke, an hour before landing, and disembarked at Zürich he looked no more rumpled and tired than he did on any other day.

Ironically, his weapon made luggage retrieval faster than it would have been otherwise. He reported to a special Swiss Air office that handled just such matters, affixed his signature to two sheets, and was given both his firearm and his overnight bag. A few other government types had also assembled in the office. One of them, a man dressed in a dark grey suit, smiled at him. Norris remembered him from various security briefings he'd attended at the White House. Stanley Grafton was his name, and he was a member of the National Security Council.

'Caleb.' Grafton extended a hand. 'I didn't see your name on the agenda.'

'And I didn't see yours,' Norris replied smoothly.

'Last-minute substitution,' Grafton said.

'Same here,' Norris said. 'What can you do? We've all come to mouth sonorous nothings.'

'It's what we do best, right?' Laughter crinkled Grafton's eyes. 'Hey, you want to hitch a ride with me?'

'Sure. You got a limo?'

Grafton smirked. 'A 'copter, baby. I'm NSC, we gotta travel in style.'

'Glad to see our tax dollars at work,' Norris jested. 'Lead the way, Stan.'

He hefted his bag as he followed the NSC man. It felt better balanced with the long-barrelled 9mm pistol back inside it.

AMBLER HEARD a man's low voice only a few yards away from the copse of spruce trees where he was hiding. 'This is beta lambda epsilon. Have you located the subject?' He spoke with a Texan accent. 'Because I didn't get out of bed to freeze my goddamn johnson off.'

The response was inaudible, no doubt piped through earbuds. He was speaking on some sort of walkie-talkie. The Texan yawned and started to pace on the shoulder of the road, to keep his feet from getting cold.

There were sounds of shouting from the checkpoint. Ambler looked over at the car idling before the orange security barrier. An irate passenger— bald, pink-faced, expensively dressed—had been ordered to step out of a chauffeured car while the vehicle was inspected. *Bureaucratic madness*, the rich man charged. It was a trip he made daily.

The guards were apologetic but firm. There had been reports. They were required to take special precautions today. The pink-faced businessman sighed, his protests subsiding into general peevishness. Moments later, the orange barrier rose and the luxury car went on its way.

Yet the man's noisy protests had provided Ambler with cover.

He crept along a path towards the road, until he spied a burly man wearing a black leather coat and an expensive gold wristwatch—the Texan. Stepping from behind a bank of snow, Ambler sprang towards him, encircled his neck with his right arm and hooked his hands together on the man's left shoulder. Then he squeezed the man's neck between his bicep and forearm, clamping down the carotid arteries. The man coughed and went limp.

Swiftly, Ambler patted the man down, looking for his walkie-talkie. He found it in the pocket of the leather coat. It was a small model, with a limited range but a powerful signal. Ambler placed the tiny earbuds into his own ears, took a deep breath and pressed SPEAK. Then, in a plausible Texan drawl, he said, 'This is beta lambda epsilon, reporting in—'

A thickly accented voice—the harsh French of the Savoyard province— cut him off. 'We told you to cease communications. You jeopardise operational security!' The voice was not that of the Marseilles assassin. It had to be a third man.

'Shut up and *listen*,' Ambler drawled angrily. 'I *seen* the bastard. On the other side of the road. Saw him dart across the parking lot like a goddamn red fox. He's *taunting* us.'

There was silence on the other end. Then, cautiously, urgently, the voice returned: 'Precisely where is he at this moment?'

Ambler drew a blank. He had not thought this through. 'He crawled inside the Jeep,' he blurted. 'Yanked up the canvas and crawled inside.'

'And he's still there?'

'I'd have seen him if he wasn't.'

'OK.' There was a pause. 'Good work.'

If Ambler's cheeks hadn't been numb with cold, he would have smiled.

After a few moments, the killer from Marseilles strode from his booth towards the lower parking lot, where the canvas-topped Jeep was stationed. A powerful-looking, silenced firearm was in his hand.

Ambler looked around for something he could throw. But ice had cemented everything to the ground: pebbles, gravel, rocks. He retrieved the Texan's magnum pistol, and removed a heavy lead bullet from the chamber. Then he whipped it high into the air. The bullet fell on the other side of the road, landing on the Jeep's canvas top. The sound it made was disappointingly faint, yet the specialist's reaction was extreme. Without warning, he dropped to his knees and fired repeatedly into the truck, perforating the canvas with a fusillade of silenced, high-energy bullets.

Ambler watched through his field glasses. Of the other man—the Savoyard—there was no sign. The mechanic, sheltered from the wind by the raised hood of the *camion*, continued his wrenchings. In their outdoor booths, the Swiss guard and his French counterpart sat on their plastic chairs, sipping coffee.

Ambler swallowed hard. For a few seconds, he would be able to cross the road without being glimpsed. Impetuously, he decided to do so.

He rushed behind the low brick storage building, then approached the parking lot. The specialist had ascertained that nobody was in the Jeep after all. He backed away from it, then turned round, towards Ambler.

'Don't make a move,' Ambler said.

'Whatever you say,' the specialist lied in passable English. 'You're in charge now.'

'What the hell is going on here?' A booming voice came from behind them. One of the Swiss border guards had wandered over.

The specialist turned round, almost out of curiosity.

'What the hell is this?' the Swiss guard demanded in French.

A small circle of red suddenly bloomed on the guard's forehead and he crumpled to the ground.

An instant later—an instant too late—Ambler squeezed the trigger . . .

Nothing happened. He remembered too late the bullet he had thrown, remembered that the firing chamber had been empty. By then the specialist had swivelled back to Ambler, his long-barrelled pistol held perfectly level, perfectly still, and aimed at his target's face.

Ambler's nerves shrieked at him in reproach. He shut his eyes briefly. When he opened them again, he forced himself to see, to speak. His mien— his voice, his gaze—would be his weapon. These were the crucial seconds.

'How much are they paying you?' Ambler demanded.

'Enough,' the specialist replied impassively.

'Wrong,' Ambler said. 'They're playing you for a fool, *un con.*' He tossed the heavy .44 pistol to the ground. Ironically, he felt much safer now. The fact that he was unarmed would lessen the pressure for an immediate kill. *Sometimes you make best use of a weapon by giving it up.*

'Don't talk,' the specialist said, and took a step towards him.

'Because after you kill me, they're going to kill you. This operation has been designed so that all the participants kill each other off. It's a sort of auto-erase feature.' Ambler let out a short laugh. 'That's why you're per-fect—for their purposes. Cunning enough to kill. Too stupid to live.'

'You would say anything,' the specialist said, testing him. 'Men in your position always do.'

'Men facing death? That describes both of us, my friend—and I can *prove* it.' The look Ambler gave the assassin was disdainful.

A micro-flicker of confusion and interest. 'How?'

'First, let me show you a copy of the Sigma A23-44D transmission. I've got a copy in my inside jacket pocket.'

'Don't make a move.' The specialist's knife-thin mouth turned into a sneer. 'You must think I'm an amateur. You'll do nothing at all.'

Ambler shrugged and held up his hands. 'Take it out of my pocket your-self,' he said evenly. 'It's in the right inside pocket—yank down the zipper. I'll keep my hands in view. Or are you afraid to find out the truth?'

'You *move* and I blow your brains out,' the specialist barked as he approached, holding up the gun in his right hand, reaching for the zip with his left. The metal tab lay concealed under the collar of Ambler's jacket. It took two tries before the slider moved down the row of teeth. Now the man stepped closer, groping around inside the jacket. Ambler composed him-self. To make his move too early or too late would be fatal.

The specialist discovered that the inner pocket was itself zipped up, hor-izontally. As the man fumbled with his left hand, Ambler bent his knees slightly, like an exhausted man collapsing further. Frustrated, the specialist removed his left hand and started to switch his gun from his right hand to his left. As he bent his knees a little further, Ambler was no longer thinking, just giving himself over to instinct altogether, and—*now*—he surged forward and upwards, the coiled strength in his legs immense, his lowered head ramming into the other man's jaw. He felt, and heard, the man's teeth slamming together, and then the neck snapping back, the reflex causing the man's hand to spring open. Ambler heard the sound of a gun clattering to the ground as the man from Marseilles collapsed onto the road.

Picking up the silenced gun, Ambler snaked his way through the woods behind the customs house, then crept back to the road. Technically, he supposed, he had just crossed the border between France and Switzerland. The food-service truck was still parked on the paved shoulder, but the mechanic was no longer bent over the engine. He was some distance away from it, one finger pressed to his ear, walking calmly towards Ambler. He looked up, as if he had just noticed Ambler, and gave him a wry nod.

A wave of dread swept over Ambler. Without consciously deciding to, he yanked the silenced pistol from his jacket and levelled it . . . even as he found himself staring into the bore end of a large-calibre gun that had materialised in the other man's beefy hand.

'*Salut*,' the man in the overalls said. He spoke with the slightly Teutonic vowels of Savoyard French.

'*Salut*,' Ambler replied, as—he kicked out his legs from under himself, and, in free fall, squeezed the trigger three times, the spitting sound of each round accompanied by an incongruously forceful recoil. Simultaneously, the Savoyard's long-barrelled magnum blasted away where Ambler's head had been an instant before he had dropped to the ground.

Ambler landed rockily, but with more grace than the gunman in overalls who now lay still.

Swiftly, Ambler detached the Savoyard's key ring from his belt, and found the key to his van, which was parked thirty yards east of the checkpoint. Minutes later, Ambler headed down the road into Switzerland, towards the hamlet of St Martin. The checkpoint soon vanished from his rearview mirror.

THE RESORT TOWN of Davos was essentially a mile or so of buildings clustered along a single road, snow-laden conifers surrounding it like frosted sentries. Geographers knew it as the highest-altitude resort town in Europe;

for a few days every year, it represented the pinnacle of financial and political power as well. Indeed, the town had become synonymous with the annual meeting of the World Economic Forum—a gathering of the world's global elite that took place there in the last week of January. Although the forum was dedicated to the free movement of capital and labour and ideas, it took place in a heavily guarded encampment. Swiss military police surrounded the sprawling steel-fenced Congress Centre.

Ambler left the van in a parking lot behind an old church and trudged up a narrow road to the town's main street, the Promenade, which was lined with one shop after another—up-market outlets of international brands like Bally, Rolex and Prada—and the occasional hotel and restaurant.

Checking his watch, Ambler made his way towards the Steigenberger Hotel Belvedere on Promenade 89, a giant pink structure diagonally opposite the main entrance to the Congresszentrum. His pulse quickened as he approached. Lining the hotel's circular drive, alongside the usual luxury cars, were military transport vehicles and a large-tyred SUV with a blue police light on top and a Day-Glo red band along the side, bearing the white letters MILITÄR POLIZEI.

Caston, he knew from a voicemail he'd listened to en route, had successfully used his influence as a senior CIA officer to have himself officially added to the roster of conference guests.

A brisk walk through the Belvedere's vestibule and the carpeted area beyond, revealed several lounges that flowed one into another, as well as a roped-off dining room. Ambler took a seat on a leather chair not far from the front desk and glanced at himself in a mirror across the wall, satisfied that, dressed as he now was in an expensive-looking charcoal-grey suit purchased recently, he looked the part. He would be taken for one of the many businessmen who, though not so illustrious as the 'participants', had paid significant amounts to attend.

Ambler ordered a coffee, black, from one of the attendants, and lingered over the business publications on the small table nearby. When he picked up *The Economist*, he felt a small twinge: on the cover was a photograph of Liu Ang looking cheerful, above the sprightly legend BRINGING THE PEOPLE'S REPUBLIC BACK TO THE PEOPLE. He flipped through the cover story, his eyes flicking up at frequent intervals, watching the guests come and go.

Before long, he found a promising candidate: a man in his early forties, with greying blond hair; someone in banking, to judge by his immaculate cotton shirt, his finely patterned yellow tie. He had just entered the hotel and looked slightly annoyed with himself, as if he had left behind an item he needed. His cheeks were pink from the cold, and his black overcoat bore a few flakes of snow.

Ambler left a few francs by his coffee cup and caught up with the man as he strode into a waiting lift, stepping into the car just moments before the door closed. The businessman had pressed the fourth-floor button. Ambler pressed it again, as if he had not realised it was already lit. He glanced at the man's conference badge: MARTIN HIBBARD.

Moments later, he followed the businessman out of the lift and down the corridor, noting the number of the room where the man stopped but walking past him and disappearing at the end of the hall. Just out of sight, Ambler stopped, listened as the door shut behind Hibbard, and then, a minute later, opened again. Ambler peered round the curve in the wall and saw the man emerge, clutching a leather portfolio, then return to the elevator bank. Given the time of day, and his late-for-a-meeting air, it was a safe assumption that he had a lunch appointment, and had a need of whatever documents were in the portfolio. In all likelihood, he would then head to the Congress Centre for one of the 2.30 sessions, and would not be back to his hotel room for hours.

Ambler returned to the lobby and scanned the receptionists at the elegant mahogany-and-marble front desk. One of them, a woman in her late twenties, with too much lipstick and eye shadow, would be his best chance.

When the woman had finished with the guest she had been dealing with, Ambler stepped forward with a sheepish grin. 'I'm such a moron,' he said.

'I'm sorry?' Her English was only lightly accented.

'I'm sorrier. Left my keycard in my room.'

'Not to worry, sir,' the woman said pleasantly. 'It happens all the time.'

'Not to me, it doesn't. The name's Marty—Martin Hibbard.'

'And the room number.'

'What is it now?' Ambler pretended to search his memory. 'Oh, yes—room 417.'

The woman keyed a few codes into her computer. Moments later, a new keycard emerged from a machine behind her and she handed it to him. 'Hope you're enjoying your stay,' she said.

'You know, I am, actually,' Ambler said. 'Thanks to you.'

She smiled gratefully at the rare compliment.

Room 417 turned out to be spacious, with light, airy colours and delicate furniture. There was not a room for rent in the whole Davos-Klosters area during the last week of January, but the one Ambler had taken momentary possession of would serve, at least for a while. He made the phone call, turned off the lights, drew the curtains shut and waited.

The knock at the door came ten minutes later. Ambler pressed himself against the wall adjacent to the door, unlatched it and opened it a crack.

'Hal?' she whispered, as she slipped in and closed the door behind her. He did not have to see; he could smell her shampoo, the honeyed scent of her skin.

He spoke quietly, too, in order not to startle her. 'Over here,' he said, and she stepped towards his voice, reached a hand out to his face, caressed his cheek. He could feel her lips brushing his.

The contact was electric. 'Laurel,' he breathed, 'I—'

She pressed her mouth to his, silencing him, and seeming to draw courage from his kiss. 'I know,' she said, after a pause. 'You don't have to say the words.'

He put his arms round her and drew her close, kissing her hair, her eyes, her neck, inhaling deeply. He had to savour every moment he had with her. He felt her clutching him, no longer desperately but with a serenity that somehow suffused them both.

After a moment they both relaxed and stepped back. He flipped the switch near the door. Laurel was exactly as he had pictured her: the large green-flecked hazel eyes, filled with love and concern; the porcelain skin.

'Thank God you're safe, my love,' she said quietly. 'Thank God.'

'You're so beautiful.' He spoke the thought aloud without intending to. 'I don't want to lose you.'

'Let's just leave,' she said, a wild sense of hope transforming her features. 'Let's ski down that mountain and never look back.'

He shook his head, for there were words he could not speak. His life had been cheap before, but now it contained something of infinite value. Yet it was *because* of Laurel that he was here; it was because of her that he would do what had to be done. A world that contained Laurel was a world that intensely *mattered* to him. These were the things that Ambler could not say.

'Soon,' he said. 'In just a few hours.'

Laurel blinked slowly. 'I have a bad feeling about this. I can't shake it.' Her eyes glistened moistly.

Ambler moved to the window and peered out at the low-slung complex of buildings across the street: the Congress Centre. Military policemen stood in clusters. Tall steel fences, partly buried in snow, funnelled visitors to a precisely indicated point of egress. Ambler had seen maximum-security prisons that were more inviting.

The fear that ran through him now was fear for Laurel—for her safety. 'Did you talk to Caston about it?'

She smiled ruefully through her tears. 'Talk to Caston about feelings? He just talked about odds and probabilities.' She was no longer smiling. 'He says you're going to do what you're going to do, no matter how long the odds of success are.'

Ambler shook his head. 'He's not wrong.'

'Maybe Caston will figure out a way,' Laurel said. 'He got *me* in. Not that I learned a damned thing.'

'He got you in?' Ambler was astonished.

She nodded. 'He figured out that, technically, I've got an intel-service classification. High-level clearance, right? Fact is, the groundsmen at Parrish Island have that clearance, too. It's the rules at a facility like that. It's all about these letters and numbers that go after your name, and Caston's a whiz at working the system.'

'Where *is* he, by the way?'

'Should be here any minute,' Laurel said. 'I came early.' She did not have to explain why. 'But maybe he's found one of those "anomalies" of his.'

Someone rapped on the door three times; Laurel recognised the tattoo and let Clayton Caston in. He looked exhausted, even more pallid than usual. His raincoat bore epaulettes of snow, which were dissolving into rivulets down the front. He had a black tote bag in one hand, silk-screened with the logo of the World Economic Forum.

'You find out anything?' Ambler asked him.

'Not a whole lot,' Caston said soberly. 'I was inside the conference centre this morning went in and out of the technical seminars. Laurel got around, too, but it sounds like she didn't strike gold, either.'

'I kept feeling that everybody could tell I didn't belong,' Laurel admitted. 'And the thought that one of them—just one of them—might be this maniac . . .'

'We're not dealing with a maniac,' Ambler said carefully. 'We're dealing with a professional. Far worse.' He paused. 'But there's good news, too—

the simple fact that both of you were able to gain entrance,' Ambler said. 'That was your doing, Caston, and I'm still not sure how you pulled it off.'

'I had my assistant call the office of the executive chairman, got my name added to the DC retinue,' Caston explained. 'An official-sounding call from Langley, security assurances. They didn't argue.'

'They don't mind having spooks at the table here?'

'*Mind?* They love it. Davos is all about power. Power of every kind. They'd be *delighted* to have the DCI himself—he was here a couple of years ago—but they're quite pleased to have a senior CIA official, too.'

'And you got Laurel on the books the same way?'

'My assistant swung it, actually. We described her as a psychiatric specialist with the Joint Intelligence Services—which happens to be her technical designation. She's also got a high level of clearance, which happens to be mandatory for Parrish Island personnel. The last-minute request was slightly irregular, but not remarkably so. The WEF people called my office through the Langley switchboard—standard callback procedure—and had a second discussion with my assistant. He provides a pass code for verification, transmits a digital photo for the security card, and we're in like Flynn.'

Ambler tilted his head. 'So can you do the same for me?'

'Um, let me think. Are you on the employee rolls at the CIA?' Caston's eyes blazed. 'Harrison Ambler does not *exist*. Or have you forgotten? All this time I figured you were holding back on some grand scheme you had. The hell of it is, you're even more reckless than I'd imagined. You race pell-mell into a potential disaster area without a *plan*! You don't *think*.'

Ambler's limbs felt like lead. 'Just break it down for me—tell me how the badge system is organised physically.'

'You can't bullshit your way in, if that's what you're thinking,' Caston grumbled. 'The system is very simple, and damn near impossible to spoof.' He unbuttoned his suit jacket and showed them the white plastic identification badge he was wearing on a white nylon string round his neck. It bore a photograph of Caston to the left of his name, a silvery hologram below, a blue colour stripe above. He turned it round, exposing the magnetic strip on the back. 'When you enter, you swipe the card through a reader. The card encodes a digital signature that calls up a guest record from the computer—which is a stand-alone, not connected to the Internet, so you can't hack into it. There's a guard stationed at a monitor, and every time a card is read, the name and photograph from the computer record gets displayed on the screen. If you're not in the computer, you're out of luck. And then there's a metal detector you've got to pass through, like at the airport. Jackets, keys and such go through a conveyor belt.'

'Enough to keep out an assassin?' Laurel asked.

'We're talking about someone who has been planning this for months, or longer.' Caston glanced at Ambler. 'You've got about two hours.'

'What if you say you've lost your card?' Laurel asked.

'Then they apologise and escort you to the exit,' Caston replied. 'These people haven't had a security breach in some three decades.'

Laurel looked at Ambler expectantly. 'There's got to be something, right? The human factor—like you always say.'

Scenarios flitted through Ambler's mind, and his eyes fell on the black WEF tote bag that Caston had been carrying, filled with material that delegates were given at check-in. He picked it up and spilled its contents onto the bed. There was a white binder with the schedule of events, page after page with titles such as 'Whither Water Management?' and 'Towards a New Bretton Woods'. There was the schedule of addresses by the UN Secretary General, the President of Pakistan, and others; Liu Ang's address was clearly the keynote event. Ambler closed the binder and picked up a small thick book, listing all the 'participants' in the WEF meeting—nearly 1,500 pages of photographs of each followed by a career biography.

'Make a hell of a police line-up,' Laurel put in.

Suddenly Caston sat bolt upright. 'A police line-up,' he echoed.

Ambler looked at him. 'What?'

'They're responsible for numbers of false convictions,' Caston said. 'Line-ups, I mean. Eyewitnesses are highly fallible. You're led to believe that one of the people in the line-up may be the fellow that you saw. So you look—and you choose the one who looks most like the person you remember. But the *closest* person isn't necessary the *same* person.'

As Caston stood near him, Ambler began to flip through the book. 'I want you to look at the pictures, too,' he told Laurel. 'If it's close enough, you'll know it at once. Don't think about it. *Experience* it.'

The faces flew by, about two per second. 'Wait,' Laurel said.

Caston stuck a small Post-it on the page, and said, 'Keep going.'

Ambler did, whisking through the pages until he paused at one. Caston placed another adhesive flag on the page and Ambler resumed flicking through. By the time he had finished, four pages had been flagged. He handed the book to Caston. 'You're the fresh eye. Take a look.'

Caston flipped to each of the four. 'The third one,' he said, passing it to Laurel, who did the same.

'Probably the third,' she said, a little more hesitantly.

Ambler opened the book to the third Post-it, and tore off the page, scrutinising the man's biography. 'Not the *strongest* resemblance, I wouldn't have thought,' he said, half to himself. 'But then I have a hard time remembering what I look like these days.' He glanced again at the photograph, the severe eyes. Jozef Vrabel was his name, and he was the president of V&S Slovakia, a Bratislava-based company that specialised in 'wireless solutions, services and products, and network security'.

'I don't mean to puncture the mood,' Laurel said. 'But how are we going to get the guy's card in the first place?'

'Don't ask me,' Caston said, shrugging. 'Ask Mr Human Factor there.'

'Can we find him?' Ambler looked at Caston.

The numbers man nodded. 'There's a computer terminal at the conference centre and a lot of the hotels, too. It's all designed so you can find people. Networking is key to the Davos experience. I can type in this name, and it'll say what programmes he's signed up to attend. Because you have to sign up, you see. Then . . .'

'Then you find him, and tell him that there's an emergency, and bring him outside the centre.'

Caston coughed. 'Me?'

'How are you at lying?'

Caston reflected for a moment. 'Mediocre.'

'Mediocre will be good enough,' Ambler said. He reached over and gave Caston an encouraging squeeze on the shoulder. 'Sometimes, if it's worth doing, it's worth doing badly.'

'If I can help . . .' Laurel began.

'I'm going to need you on the logistics front,' Ambler told her. 'I'll want binoculars or some high-powered device for vision enhancement. According to the agenda, the premier is scheduled to speak at the Congress Hall.'

'It's the biggest hall in the place,' Caston said. 'Seats over a thousand.'

'That's a lot of faces, I won't be able to get near them all.'

'You're going to stick out if you walk about with a pair of binocs around your neck,' Laurel cautioned. 'But that place is camera central, with all the broadcast cameramen everywhere. I had a chat with one of the camera guys, looked through the viewfinder of his camera, and you know the lenses on those things are amazing. I was thinking, you could use one of them—they're bulky but portable, and they have a powerful optical zoom. Plus, they wouldn't attract a second look.'

'Once you're inside, nobody's going to be paying you much attention,' Caston said. 'The badge doesn't display your affiliation, just your name.'

'But getting hold of a camera . . .' Ambler asked.

'Is not a problem,' Laurel said. 'The guy I spoke to showed me a store-room full of them.'

'Listen, Laurel, you're not trained for operational—'

'You're in a life raft, and you want to check whether someone has a boating licence?' Caston scoffed. 'I thought I was the rule stickler here.'

'Fact is, it's gonna be easier for me than for "Jozef Vrabel" to get into that store room,' Laurel said. 'And I've already had friendly chats with the boys who go in and out of it.' In a mock-vampish tone, she added, 'I may not have "skills", but I do have . . . assets.'

AMBLER'S FIRST GLIMPSE of Jozef Vrabel was disheartening: the man he had chosen for a doppelgänger was barely five foot five, with a small head, narrow shoulders, and a round, protruding belly over wide hips. If Caston was right, though, all that had to match was the face; and the face was—well, close enough for a quick glance.

'I don't understand,' the Slovak businessman, garbed in a suit of taupe gaberdine, was repeating as Caston led him from the Congress Centre.

'It's crazy, I know,' Caston was saying. 'But the Agency has already negotiated a deal with Slovakia Telecom, and it's our last chance to reconsider. Otherwise, contractually, it takes effect by the end of the day.'

'But why were we never contacted about this? This is ridiculously last-minute.' The Slovak's English was accented but fluent.

'You're asking how it could possibly be that the United States government could mishandle the bidding process?'

The Slovak snorted. 'When you put it that way . . .'

Ambler, who had stationed himself across the street, strode swiftly towards him. 'Mr Vrabel? I'm Andy Halverson, with the US General Services Administration. Clay here says we're about to make a pretty costly mistake. I need to know if he's right.'

Caston cleared his throat. 'The current offering costs out at twenty per cent over our existing telephony arrangement. Even with embedded security features, it seems to me that we're not getting the best possible value.'

'That's a preposterous deal!' the Slovak said. 'You should have been talking to *us*.'

'We've got an office filled with people whose job that is,' Ambler said steadily. 'Guess they never bothered to learn their way around Bratislava.'

'You're about to sign a two-hundred-million-dollar contract, Andy,' Caston said to Ambler, 'and your guys are relying on two-year-old market analyses?'

The Slovak's face relaxed into a genial smile. 'Gentleman—the hour is late, but it is not *too* late, I trust. I think we can do business together.'

The two Americans took him to a small second-floor conference room at the Belvedere, one they had ascertained would be unoccupied for an hour. Ambler knew that the room would be theirs, if only briefly, so long as they simply looked as if they belonged.

Laurel, dressed in a grey skirt and white blouse, met the two inside the small conference room, and approached Jozef Vrabel with a black, wand-like device.

Ambler made apologetic noises. 'Just a formality. Technically, when we're having an offsite discussion of what's officially classified information, we're got to do a scan for listening devices.'

Laurel waved the device—a thing fashioned out of two television remote controllers—along the man's extremities, then his torso. When she approached the badge, she paused, and said, 'If you'll let me remove that name tag, sir . . . I'm afraid the chip inside creates interference.'

Vrabel did so with a complacent nod, and she stepped behind him, pretending to scan his back. 'All right,' she said. She replaced the nylon rope round his neck, tucking the card inside his lapel; since nobody ever looked at their own badge while it was on, he would have no occasion to notice that his conference badge had been replaced by a Triple A membership card.

'Please, sit,' Ambler said, gesturing. He turned to Caston. 'You've got the terms of offering?'

'You mean here? We can download the encrypted files, but we'd have to use one of our machines.' Caston spoke his lines a little stiffly, but it passed as embarrassment. 'The station boys have the clear-connect.'

'At the Schatzalp?' Ambler retorted. 'You can't expect Mr Vrabel to ride the funicular up the mountain to the Schatzalp. That's just too far. He's a busy man. We're all busy. Forget about it. Just forget about it.' He turned to the Slovak. 'Sorry to waste your time.'

Vrabel broke in in a tone of lordly magnanimity. 'Gentlemen, please,' he said. 'Your country deserves the highest consideration, and should not be shaken down by a bunch of scheming *zeks*. My own shareholders have interests aligned with yours. Put me in the funicular. In truth, I was rather hoping for a chance to visit the Schatzalp. I'm told it's not to be missed.'

'Are you sure you want to take the time?'

'Absolutely,' said the Slovak, with a $200-million smile. '*Absolutely.*'

AT THE MAIN ENTRANCE to the Congress Centre, the fast-moving queue sluiced between two steel fences and a no less formidable human cordon of military policemen, their breath forming puffs of smoke in the cold air. Immediately past the entrance was a series of coat-check stations. Then came the security area, staffed by half a dozen guards. Ambler took his time removing his coat. He wanted to time his entrance, to be certain there were plenty of people ahead of and behind him. He wore a blazer without a tie; the ID badge hung from his neck near the shirt's third button.

Finally, he saw a crowd of men and women pushing through the entrance and he nimbly stepped into line at the security desk.

'Cold outside!' he said to the man at the computer monitor, with what he told himself was a passable mid-European accent. 'But I guess you're used to it!' He pressed his card to the card reader and patted his cheeks, as if they were frozen. The man glanced at the screen and at him. A light at the turn-stile pulsed green, and Ambler pushed his way through a gate bar.

He was in.

EVERY CORNER of the Congress Centre was brightly lit, the walls and floors all warm, glowing shades of cream, tan and ochre. The wooden ceiling was curved, giving the sense that one was inside an enormous ark. Ambler paused at a seating area where coffee was served on small glass-topped tables. Lettering nearby declared the area to be a WORLD CAFÉ.

He walked down a broad stairway to a sort of mezzanine. At the end of a long corridor snaking off behind the stairs was a blue sign that read TV STUDIO; evidently it was reserved for broadcast journalists to conduct inter-views. A sign in an alcove advertised 'bilateral rooms', presumably reserved for private discussions. The main flow of traffic on the mezzanine was to the left, towards an area with wicker chairs and a juice bar, where a couple of high-mounted television monitors displayed what looked to be video excerpts from the high-profile 'briefings'. At an adjoining computer bay, dozens of fingers clicked at dozens of keyboards.

Ambler descended another flight of stairs to a much larger space below, checked his watch, then pushed through the throng. A mid-afternoon crowd of people, between sessions, grabbing canapés from silver trays, or crystal glasses of conference-approved beverages.

Ambler slowed and began to take in his surroundings, picking up snatches of conversation and glancing at dozens of faces as he zigzagged through the crowd. Suddenly, a man stepped in front of him and looked at him with an expression of bewilderment. He spoke rapidly in a language Ambler did not understand. Something Slavic again, but different.

'I'm sorry?' Ambler placed a finger on his ear, miming incomprehension.

The man now spoke in laborious English. 'I said, I don't know who you are but you are not who your badge says.' He pointed to it. 'I know Jozef Vrabel. You're not him.'

AT THE OTHER END of the hall, Clayton Caston was quaking behind his icy smile. 'Undersecretary Whitfield?' he asked.

Ellen Whitfield turned. 'I'm sorry?'

'My name is Clayton Caston. I'm with the CIA, Office of Internal Review. I'm here with an urgent message from the DCI.'

'Will you excuse me?' Whitfield said apologetically to the dignitary with whom she had been speaking. To Caston, she said, 'How's Owen doing?'

'I think we've all been better,' Caston replied tightly. 'Would you come with me. It's *very* important.'

'Certainly.'

He took her swiftly down a rear hallway to a room by a sign that read BILATERAL ROOM 2. When they entered, Whitfield saw that Ashton Palmer was already seated on one of the room's white leather chairs.

She turned to Caston. 'What's this about?' she asked evenly.

Caston closed the door and gestured for her to have a seat. 'I'll explain.'

He took a deep breath before joining them. 'Undersecretary Whitfield, Professor Palmer, from time to time, a specialist in forensic and investigative auditing turns up things he wished he hadn't. In the intelligence communities in the United States, as you know, one division may be utterly oblivious of an operation authorised by another. So long as legitimate procedures have been followed, the nature of these operations is not my concern. But imagine if an analysis of data points leads you to uncover an inter-agency operation that is potentially explosive in its consequences—especially if the operation should come to be exposed.'

'Then I'd think the person who exposed that operation should consider himself responsible for those explosive consequences,' Whitfield replied smoothly. Her lips were pressed tightly together. 'That's logical, isn't it?'

'Is this something you've discussed with the DCI?' asked Palmer.

'I wanted to talk to you first,' Caston said.

'That's very wise,' said the silver-haired scholar, his eyes watchful but unintimidated.

'But my point is,' Caston went on, 'that if I have been able to connect the dots—align the data points—then so will others.'

'Data points?' Palmer blinked.

'They run the gamut, from—I'm speaking hypothetically here, you understand—plane tickets purchased and trips made to payments routed to foreign officials. They include accounting irregularities to do with the use of PSU resources—and many other items I'd prefer not to get into.'

Palmer and Whitfield looked at each other.

'Mr Caston,' the professor began, 'we both appreciate your concern. But I fear you've become involved in matters that are rather above your head.'

'Top-level command tier decisions,' Whitfield put in.

'You continue to miss my point. Quite simply, you've been *sloppy*. You've left a trail. What I have been able to find out, others—such as any investigating domestic or international commission—will be able to find out. And I wonder whether you factored that into your equations when you devised this harebrained operation.'

Whitfield bristled. 'I don't know what you're talking about, and I very much doubt you do, either. This indirectness is getting tiresome.'

'I'm talking about the termination of President Liu Ang. Is that direct enough for you?'

Palmer blanched. 'You're not making any sense—'

'Come off it,' Caston snapped. 'What I found out is what *any* competent investigation is going to uncover. You complete the operation, and our government is going to get blamed. You rogue warriors are all the same. You're so caught up in your subterfuges that you never think ahead. I've respected the inter-organisational boundaries, kept quiet to give you the benefit of the doubt. I see I was mistaken. I shall file my report with the DCI immediately.'

'Mr Caston, I'm impressed by the seriousness with which you take your work,' Whitfield said, suddenly cordial. 'Let me apologise if I've offended you. Of course we trust your discretion and your judgment. But we need you to trust ours as well. Please don't underestimate the level of calculation and planning that has gone into this. Or the benefits to be secured by it.'

'Which are?'

'We're talking about history, Mr Caston,' said Palmer. 'About history, and the making of it. The only thing more hazardous than trying to change the course of history is *not* to do so.'

'Enough with the abstractions,' Caston growled. 'We're talking about a head of state who's revered the world over.'

'Men must be judged by their consequences, not their intentions,' Palmer said. 'And consequences must be assessed by techniques of historical analysis and projection.'

'You're saying you prefer a Chinese despot to a Chinese democrat?' Caston asked, swallowing hard.

'From the viewpoint of the world, there's hardly any question about it. Despotism has kept the lid on Pandora's box.'

'Please note,' Whitfield added brightly, '*we're* not doing anything. Oh no. Do you see us in that hall? We're not even present at the scene of the prospective . . . incident. We're *here*. With you, Mr Caston.'

'In conference with a senior officer of the CIA.' A small, steely smile was playing on Palmer's lips.

'That's something plenty of people can vouch for.' The Undersecretary flashed a brief, perfect smile. 'So if we *were* up to something, the natural inference would be that *you* were up to the same thing.'

'Not that we expect anyone to be making such inferences at all,' Palmer said. 'They'll be making other inferences.'

'That's what I'm trying to tell you,' Caston started. 'The US government is going to be suspected immediately.'

'We're counting on it,' Whitfield said. 'I'm sorry, such geopolitical calculations aren't the usual province of an auditor. But all the eventualities have been explored by our finest minds—or perhaps I should say our finest mind.' She gave Palmer an admiring glance.

'Wait a minute. If the US is suspected—'

'Suspected, yes, but *only* suspected,' Palmer explained. 'We're aiming for constructive ambiguity. Blame, but not absolute knowledge, suspicion without hard evidence. Guesses piled upon guesses—but mortared by suspicion into a very strong wall.'

'Like the Great Wall of China?'

'Nicely put, Mr Caston. Another Great Wall of China. And, as history shows, there's just one way to wall China in.'

'Get the Chinese to build the wall themselves,' Caston said slowly.

'Why, Mr Caston,' the scholar said, 'it seems you're of our party without knowing it. We both understand the ascendancy of logic, don't we? We both appreciate that ordinary intuitions, including moral intuitions, must capitulate before the clean force of *reason*.'

'You still don't convince me,' Caston said. 'Maybe the world is messier and less controllable than you know. You think you're the masters of history. From where I sit, you're a couple of kids playing with matches. And it's a flammable world out there. The simple truth is, you're putting the nations on course for open warfare.'

'The United States has always performed best when it was on a wartime footing,' Palmer said. 'In fact, a period of endless small-scale skirmishes was what secured our global pre-eminence.'

'Americans do dislike the notion of dominating the globe,' Whitfield said. 'The one thing they like less is the prospect of someone else doing it.'

'Why be overtaken by events when you could help *shape* those events?' Palmer's voice was a soothing, professorial baritone. 'You see, Mr Caston, the course of history is too important a thing ever to be left to chance.'

AMBLER STUDIED the Slovak's face: confusion was steadily, irreversibly hardening into suspicion. He glanced at his badge: JAN SKODOVA. Who was he? A government official? A business colleague—or rival?

Ambler smiled broadly. 'You're right about that. We were on a panel together. Switched badges as a joke.' A beat. 'Guess you had to be there.' He thrust a hand out. 'Bill Becker, from EDS, in Texas. Now how do you know my new friend Joe?'

'I am also a businessman from Slovakia. Utilities. Where is Jozef, then?' *Goddammit—there was no time.*

'Hey, you got a card?' Ambler pretended to fumble for one of his own.

Warily, the Eastern European withdrew a card from the inside breast pocket of his suit jacket. Ambler glanced at it quickly before pocketing it.

'Wait—you're the cable guy from Kosice? Joe was telling me about you.'

A flicker of uncertainty appeared on Skodova's face; Ambler pressed the advantage. 'If you ain't busy, maybe you could come with me. Joe and I were just talking in that little private lounge out back. Had to nip out here to wet my whistle, but I ain't one for crowds. Seems to me we just might be able to do business. You know about Electronic Data Systems?'

'Jozef is where?' The question was polite but pointed.

'I'll take you to him,' Ambler said, 'but first I promised I'd snag him a bottle of slivovitz.' Skodova followed him to the bar, where he borrowed a bottle of the plum brandy from a gently protesting bartender, then led the Slovak businessman down a corridor that led to the small meeting rooms. He stepped into the first one where the door was ajar, indicating it was unoccupied.

Skodova followed Ambler in, looked around and said, 'Please explain.'

'He was here a moment ago,' Ambler said, shutting the door.

A minute later, he left the room alone. Skodova would be unconscious for at least an hour. Ambler had propped him in a chair, slumped forward on the table, his shirtfront drenched with brandy, the bottle nearby. Anyone who entered would draw the obvious conclusion. It wasn't perfect, but it would have to do.

Now Ambler swept through the crowd quickly, looking for anything unusual; any facial expressions beyond the usual range of human emotions. He glanced at his watch. It was 4.45—fifteen minutes before the premier's big speech. At a doorway to the rear of the hall, cameramen—dressed far more casually than the conference participants—began entering with their outsized equipment. He caught a glimpse of a woman in a simple button-down shirt and jeans, her auburn hair tousled, and his heart began to race. It was Laurel. She had done exactly what she said she would do, had arrived on schedule and secured the equipment. *You'll need me*, she had said. That was some understatement. He needed her in so many ways.

Moments later, the two of them had ducked into the still-deserted balcony above the seating area.

'The camera crews are going to be arriving in just a couple of minutes—lose the jacket and you'll blend right in.' They were the first words she spoke to him, but her eyes were alive with love.

He quickly stuffed his blazer into one of the equipment boxes that were lying around. Laurel reached over and mussed his hair appropriately.

'Looking good,' she said. 'Any leads yet?'

'Not yet,' Ambler said, feeling an upwelling of despair that he quickly tried to purge, both from his voice and from his heart. 'Where's Caston?'

'Probably talking to his assistant—he's been on the phone to him a lot.'

Ambler nodded, but said nothing; even the act of speaking was now an effort. In the next small sliver of time, he would succeed or he would fail. It was as simple as that.

'We've got two cameras here, one with a 48X optical zoom.' She handed him the bulky camera, which was secured to a folding tripod. Both were a sort of drab green. 'Think he'll be seated in front?'

'Could be,' Ambler said, hoarsely. He cleared his throat. 'Could be seated further back, too. Too many possibilities.'

'Well, you're here. Just do what you do.' She was maintaining a bluff, almost jovial tone. Yet Ambler could tell that, like him, she was terrified.

In the artificial 'courtyard' adjacent to them, the great and the good—and the not very good at all—began to fill the Congress Hall. They were excited, of course, though many of them were too grand to let on. Liu Ang was arguably the most important statesman on the planet. He was not just the hope of his people; he was the hope of the world. With the squeeze of a trigger, that hope would be extinguished. These thoughts raised dust storms within Ambler's head; he had to banish them—had to banish thinking itself—if he were to see clearly.

The stakes had never been higher. They could scarcely *be* higher.

AT EACH SEAT was a plastic-wrapped radio-frequency headset, which would receive and transmit a simultaneous translation in one of ten languages, depending on the channel selected.

While the crowd continued to drift into the hall, Ambler decided to make a first pass across the floor without the camera's zoom lens, relying on what his naked eyes could take in, but with the advantage of greater mobility. As he walked towards the front of the hall, he saw two blue panels on either side of the stage bearing the familiar World Economic Forum logo. A large screen hung two-thirds of the way down the central section of the stage; the video feed from the official WEF camera would be projected upon it.

Ambler checked his watch, then looked around him; the seats were nearly all filled now, and the Chinese leader would be making his appearance in a matter of minutes. He paced along the front row, as if looking for a vacant seat, his eyes darting from face to face, and he detected . . . only looks of self-importance, banal sentiments. A pudgy man with a stenographer's notebook exuded the sort of anxiety appropriate to a journalist with an impending deadline; a perfectly coiffed blonde looked distracted, as if rehearsing for an upcoming interview; a man with a forehead speckled with liver spots was scrutinising the booklet of headset instructions. Ambler walked slowly up the right-hand aisle, his eyes sweeping the rows. There were so many people—*too* many people. Why did he think he could . . .? He cleared his mind again, tried to achieve a state of pure receptivity.

A kaleidoscope of human emotion lay before him, but in none of the faces surrounding him did he see the expression he was looking for. He knew the type. He couldn't analyse it; he just recognised it when he saw it, or *felt* it, like the wave of cold you feel when opening a freezer on a warm day. It was the glacial deliberateness of the professional killer, the man who was too alert to his surroundings, whose anticipation was geared not simply to what he would witness but what he would do.

But now, when it mattered most, nothing. *Nothing.*

Panic swelled in his chest and he pushed it down. He race-walked to the back of the hall, then mounted the narrow stairs to the balcony. In the centre, he saw three stationary cameras from international media companies, and half a dozen others. The balcony was an ideal site for a gunman; it would take relatively little skill to hit the target from such an elevated perch. He met Laurel's eyes and then glanced at the others, his eyes seeking out each visage. *Nothing.*

Wordlessly, he came over to Laurel and took the camera with the 48X zoom lens that she had prepared for him. She had positioned herself at an older twin-lens camera. Struggling for calm, he angled the camera downwards. Its automatic focus provided immediate clarity of field and the level of detail was astonishing. He studied face after face in the viewfinder, waiting for the prickling of his senses that would tell him to pause, to look again. How had he ever imagined he'd have a chance? He felt as if a band were tightening around his chest, as if he were breathing against resistance.

Laurel stood close behind him. 'It'll come, my dear,' she murmured.

He felt the warmth of her breath against his neck, and it kept the panic from engulfing him. In a world of pretence, she was the one true thing.

Presently, he heard the sound of the side doors shutting, locked now to outsiders. The guards would not open the doors again until after the speech was concluded. A rustle went through the crowd as, briskly, the Director of the World Economic Forum, a tall, bald man in a dark blue suit, strode onto the stage to make a few introductory remarks.

Ambler could not, must not, give up. The killer was *here*, ready to derail human history with a squeeze of the trigger. It was up to Ambler—or Tarquin—to find him.

ADRIAN CHOI shuffled through the dossiers that Caitlin, the administrative assistant at the Joint Facilities Center, had given him. They contained the personnel records from the psychiatric facility that Caston had been so intent on getting his hands on. A bunch of résumés, for crying out loud. It should not have been so hard to get hold of them.

But it had been. That was why he'd figured he had better go through them with a magnifying glass.

And there was one—what would Caston call it?—*anomaly*.

Adrian dialled Caston's cellphone; it would be their fourth conversation within the hour.

Caston answered immediately. Adrian briefly gave him the update. Caston had him repeat certain details, urgently.

'And when you crosscheck,' Adrian said, 'the Social Security numbers don't match.' He listened to Caston's breathless reply.

'That's what I thought,' Adrian put in. 'Anomalous, huh?'

THE DIRECTOR of the World Economic Forum concluded his remarks, received a warm hand of applause, and took a seat to the right of the stage. Then the applause grew as Liu Ang himself walked on stage, and took his place before the lectern.

He was physically smaller than Ambler had expected, yet his mien conveyed an almost larger-than-life serenity; a sense of great patience and wisdom. He thanked the Director of the World Economic Forum in a lilting, melodic English, then began to speak in Chinese. He was addressing the world—but his own countrymen were a large part of that world, and when his speech was broadcast to them, he wanted them to know he had spoken his native tongue with pride and eloquence. Ambler could understand nothing of what the man said, but a great deal from the way he said it.

Liu Ang was wry and funny—the headset-equipped audience guffawed at just the moment Ambler would have guessed—and then he was sombre and impassioned. It was the voice of a genuine statesman, the voice of somebody who envisaged a future of peace and prosperity and wanted to invite the rest of the world to join that future. A man who was helping to bring tolerance and enlightenment not only to the Middle Kingdom but to the world at large.

A man who was slated for death at any moment.

Somewhere in the hall, the assassin was biding his time, and Ambler's peculiar gift had failed him utterly. Again, he scanned the rows beneath him, gazing so intently into the viewfinder that his vision began to blur, his neck to stiffen. Now, abruptly, almost involuntarily, he looked up and craned his head to look at those on the balcony around him, and his gaze came to rest on Laurel's face.

She had been peering through her camera at the man at the lectern, clearly as mesmerised as he had been, and it was a moment before she realised Ambler was watching her. Something rippled through her face and then she turned to him with an expression of love.

Ambler blinked hard. *What had he just seen?* He replayed it in his mind. Laurel, his beloved Laurel, studying the scene through the camera calmly—stonily, could it be?—and then the look in her face, a moment before it was wreathed in a loving smile. Again, he replayed that fraction of a second in his mind, and he saw another expression on her face, as fleeting as a firefly's glow, and as unmistakable.

An expression of pure contempt.

Ambler stole another look, and saw Laurel's right finger on what looked like a brace beneath the camera lens—in fact, he now realised, a trigger. A lightning bolt of comprehension struck him with devastating force.

How could he have been so blind?

All along, there had been a missing piece to the puzzle. Caston's voice: *There's always got to be a fall guy.* The realisation hit him like a body blow. He was not meant to prevent the assassination. He was meant to take the blame for it.

The cameras—Laurel's idea. Her 'inspiration'. The old models were steel-clad contraptions, and dozens of them went through the X-ray detectors every day. But the rays could not penetrate metal. And anyway, Laurel's camera didn't conceal a weapon; it *was* a weapon.

The twin-lens set-up was a ruse: protruding from the top hole was the bore end of a rifle. The long camera body and two-foot zoom served as a barrel, the functioning lens could double as the sight. And the trigger, of course, was exactly . . . where her finger was now.

Indeed, she was fingering the trigger with the assurance of experience. It had to have been she who had killed Benoit Deschesnes in the Luxembourg Gardens: the Chinese marksman must have seen her do it.

How slow Ambler had been to see what was before his eyes! Yet now, he saw with dizzying immediacy what would ensue. The shots would come from almost precisely where Ambler was standing. Security would tackle him; his adversaries would have found that easy to arrange. Circumstantial evidence would suggest that he was an American, but it would be impossible to prove. Because his identity had been erased.

Suspicion without proof would be the most explosive thing of all. The loss of the beloved Liu Ang to a suspected US agent would produce an instant conflagration. Riots—on a scale without precedent—would overrun the People's Republic; the PLA would be forced to step in. But the sleeping giant would not return to its slumbers: not before wreaking havoc on a sleeping world.

The thoughts filled his mind like a deepening shadow, yet all the while he and Laurel maintained eye contact. *I know that you know that I know that you know* . . . Ambler felt anguish, rage and regret, twined together like strands of steel.

All of it—starting with his 'escape', and everything that followed, was according to plan. Their plan. He had been nothing more than a puppet.

ON A SMALL, closed-circuit monitor in the bilateral room, an image of the Chinese leader was being broadcast, captioned with an English translation. Neither Palmer nor Whitfield paid more than casual attention.

Caston flipped his cellphone shut. 'Sorry. I need to pop out for a sec.' He stood up, shakily, and started for the door. It was locked—from the inside.

Now Ellen Whitfield flipped open her own cellphone. 'I'm sorry,' she said. 'Given the *delicacy* of our conversation, I thought it would be best if we weren't disturbed. You'd been worrying about our precautions. As I've been explaining, they're far more extensive than you seem to have realised.'

'I see.' Caston felt winded.

'Mr Caston, you *worry* too much. What we've arranged is a tidy little bank shot, strategically speaking. Liu Ang is assassinated. The US government, inevitably, is suspected. And yet deniability is maintained.'

'Because, after all, the assassin doesn't exist,' Palmer added.

'You're talking about . . . Tarquin.' Caston watched them carefully as he said the name. 'You're talking about . . . Harrison Ambler.'

'Harrison *who*?' Whitfield asked lightly.

The auditor stared straight ahead. 'You *programmed* him.'

'Someone had to.' There was no trace of self-doubt in Whitfield's eyes. 'Let's give the man his due, though. He's done a magnificent job. We'd set a difficult course for him. Few could have navigated it. Though we *did* think it prudent to give him a heads-up about the Cons Ops sanction. I'd asked our principal to commission Tarquin to take out Harrison Ambler. I'm almost sorry I wasn't around for that conversation.'

'How did you set Ambler up, then?' Caston asked. 'Don't tell me—Laurel Holland.'

Whitfield's countenance remained sunny. 'She's a true prodigy, Lorna Sanderson is. I suppose you could say it was a matter of matching one extraordinary talent with another. As you probably know, there normally isn't a person in ten thousand who could fool Harrison Ambler.'

Caston's eyes narrowed. 'But Lorna Sanderson is one in a million.'

'You got it. A hugely talented actress. Won the top drama prizes in college. She was the star protégée of a disciple of the legendary acting coach, Stanislavsky, who devised the concept of the Method. Method actors train themselves to experience the very emotions they're projecting. That way they're not really acting. Quite a skill.'

'So what happened?' And what was happening outside the door? As sturdy as it was, Caston was seated close enough to it that he could detect the vibrations from some sort of . . . scuffle.

'Lorna was a junkie. Speed, then heroin. Then she started to deal. When she was arrested, her life was effectively over. Sell two ounces of heroin in New York and it's a Class A felony, a sentence of fifteen to life. That's where we stepped in. Because a talent like that doesn't come along every day. We had a federal prosecutor broker a deal with the local DA's office. After that, we owned her. She was our special project, and she proved an apt pupil.'

'And so everything has unfolded according to plan,' Caston said heavily.

Abruptly, the door burst open. A barrel-chested man loomed in the door frame; others crowded immediately behind him.

Caston turned. 'Don't you ever knock?'

'Evening, Clay.' His hands on his hips, the ADDI stared at Whitfield and

Palmer without surprise. 'Wondering how I figured out what you were on-to?' he asked the auditor.

'What I'm actually wondering, Cal,' said Caston, 'is what side you're on.'

Norris nodded gravely. 'I guess you're about to find out.'

FOR A SPLIT SECOND they shared an instant of understanding, a connection no longer of love but of loathing, and—

Ambler *threw* himself at her even before he realised what he had done, threw himself at her at the very moment she squeezed the trigger.

The weapon's loud report exploded overhead a microsecond later. A popping noise, the shattering of glass, a perceptible diminishment of illumination told him that the bullet had gone awry, had struck one of the ceiling lamps. Even as that thought sunk in, Ambler felt a searing pain at his midriff, felt the pain before he registered the flashing motion of her hand, the shiny steel of the blade entering him a second time.

Blood poured from him, but with his remaining strength, he lunged at her and made her fall. His hands wrested her arms up and to her sides, pinning them to the floor. The screams around him sounded as if they were coming from far away. He was conscious of nothing other than her, the woman he had loved—struggling beneath him. Her face, inches from his, showed nothing but vicious determination. The loss of blood began to cloud his mind, even as he relied on his own body weight to prevent her escape.

A distant voice: *Recall the man, of ancient times, who set up shop in a village selling both a spear he said would penetrate anything and a shield he claimed nothing could penetrate.*

A man who saw through everybody. A woman whom nobody could see through. The spear. The shield.

Fragments of time past flashed dimly through Ambler's head. In Parrish Island, it was she who had planted the notion of his escaping in the first place, even the exact date—he realised that now. It was Laurel who, at every juncture, had kept him both off balance and on track. Tarquin, the *Menschenkenner*, had met his match. The realisation opened a wound more painful than those she had inflicted with her blade.

He closed his eyes briefly, then opened them and peered into her eyes, searching out the woman he had thought he knew. Before he lost consciousness, he saw only blackness and defeat, and then, in that blackness—faintly, flickeringly reflected—he saw himself.

Epilogue

Harrison Ambler closed his eyes and felt the gentle glow of the March sun. Lying on a chaise longue on the boat's deck, he could hear soothing sounds. The water lapping against the hull. The sound of a spinning reel, as a fishing line was cast. Other sounds, too.

He finally knew what it felt like to be a family man. On the opposite side of the boat, the son and daughter bickered playfully as they baited a fishing hook. The mother was reading the newspaper, intervening with a wry, loving look when the youngsters got too rambunctious.

He yawned, felt a twinge of pain. Bandages still ridged his midriff, but after two operations he was healing; he could feel his strength starting to return. The sun glittered off the lake in the Shenandoah Valley, and though it was not yet spring, the weather was balmy. He decided that he would probably never return to the Sourlands, but he still loved boats and fishing, and he was glad to be with others with whom he could share his expertise. Somehow it was better this way. More real.

'Hey, daddy-o,' the boy said. At seventeen, he was already broad-shouldered. 'Got you a ginger ale from the cooler.' He handed Ambler the can.

Ambler opened his eyes and smiled at him. 'Thanks,' he said.

'You sure you don't want a beer,' asked the woman, Linda. She was not young, but she was elegant and funny. 'There's a Guinness somewhere.'

'Naw,' Ambler said. 'Got to start slow.'

Yes, it felt good being a family man. He could get used to this.

Not that it was his family exactly.

As a gentle ripple moved the boat ever so slightly, Clayton Caston clambered up from below deck, green at the gills. He levelled a reproachful gaze at Ambler and dry-swallowed another seasickness pill.

'How I ever allowed myself to be talked into coming aboard this vomit-inducing vessel . . .' he began.

Only a high-grade hypochondriac like him could have convinced himself that he was suffering from seasickness on the nearly motionless lake.

'I envy you, Clay,' Ambler said simply.

'Do you realise that the actuarial odds of drowning on a domestic body of fresh water are actually greater than the odds of drowning while at sea?'

'Aw, come on. Fishing is one of the great American leisure-time activities. Just give it a chance. You might even turn out to be good at it.'

'I know what I'm good at,' Caston groused.

'You're full of surprises—bet you even surprise yourself sometimes. Who knew you were such an ace with the AV equipment?'

'I told you,' Caston said. 'My assistant walked me through all that. All I know about coaxial cables otherwise is their purchase price per metre.'

But from the satisfied look on Caston's face, Ambler could tell he was remembering what happened after Whitfield and Palmer discovered that the bilateral room had been turned into a closed-circuit TV studio, and their entire conversation fed to the Congress Centre's media centre. Hundreds of Davos participants had witnessed their fanaticism on the monitors mounted throughout the conference centre.

It took Palmer and his protégée little time to realise the implications—not merely for their own futures, but for their plan. Like many a dark venture, the one thing it could not survive was exposure to light.

As Caston had recounted to Ambler during one of a number of hospital visits, Caleb Norris was the one who had directed the Swiss military policemen to the bilateral room and had had the conspirators taken into custody. He had been alerted by an emergency message that a Chinese spymaster named Chao Tang had arranged to have delivered to him personally. It was an unusual step, but top-level spy officials often made a study of their opposite numbers. In such an extreme situation, Chao decided to enlist the personal assistance of an American. The fact that the Chinese spymaster was reported dead soon thereafter served as powerful authentication.

As a sedated Ambler had drifted in and out of consciousness during his time in hospital, Caston had to tell him what had happened several times before he understood that it wasn't just a dream, an effect of the narcotics. Later, when he was mentally alert, there were other visitors, including Dylan Sutcliffe—the *real* Dylan Sutcliffe, although, given the fifty pounds he'd put on since Carlyle College, it took Ambler a moment to recognise him. Caston himself had spent a fair amount of time figuring out the methods by which calls had been rerouted, and tricks played on Ambler.

'Well,' Ambler said after a while, 'your broadcast career might have been brief, but it was mighty effective. Sunshine is the best disinfectant, right?'

Caston blinked. 'Did the kids put on sunblock?' he asked his wife.

'It's *March*, Clay,' Linda replied, amused. 'Nobody's sunbathing here.'

A delighted squeal and a shout from the other end of the fishing boat: 'I caught it. *I* caught—it's *mine*.' Andrea's voice: proud and emphatic.

'*Yours?*' Max's not-quite-convincing baritone. 'Who cast the line? Who baited the hook? I just asked you to hold on to the goddamn rod while I—'

'*Language*,' Linda interjected warningly.

'Language? What, *English*?' Max grunted.

Their mother went over to the squabbling pair. 'Anyway, that fish is too small,' she went on. 'You kids better throw it back.'

'You heard what Mom said,' Andrea said gleefully. 'Throw your teensy-weensy fish back in the water.'

'Oh, so it's *my* fish now?' Max's voice broke in a squawk of indignation.

Ambler turned to Clay Caston. 'They always like this?'

'Afraid so,' Caston said happily.

Caston glanced at his wife and kids across the deck, and Ambler could see the pride and devotion that pulsed through him. But the auditor was not distracted for long. A few minutes later, when another gentle ripple swayed the boat, he plopped himself down on the canvas chair next to Ambler, and pleaded, 'Listen, can we just turn the boat round and go back?'

'Why would we want to do that? It's a beautiful day, the water's lovely, we've rented this incredible boat—how could we be doing better?'

'Yeah, but this was supposed to be a fishing trip, right? See, I think you'll find that all the fish are lurking around the dock. In fact, I'm sure.'

'Come on, Clay,' Ambler said. 'That doesn't stand to reason.' He arched an eyebrow. 'The most probable distribution of fish this time of the year—'

'Trust me,' Caston implored, cutting him off. 'The dock's the place to be. I've got a *good feeling* about this.'

ROBERT LUDLUM

Born: May 25, 1927
Deceased: March 12, 2001
Website: ludlumbooks.com

Drama, in all its forms, always appealed to Robert Ludlum who started his career as an actor, having acquired a taste for treading the boards during his time at school in New York. As a teenager he left home to take part in a touring play and, by the time he was sixteen, he had landed his first Broadway role in a comedy production. When the Second World War broke out, he applied, unsuccessfully, to join the Royal Canadian Air Force. Later, in 1945, he signed up for two years' service with the US Marine Corps, writing a 200-page manuscript about his experiences during his tour of duty in the South Pacific.

Back home in America, Ludlum took a degree course in Fine Arts at Weslyan University where he met his actress wife, Mary, with whom he would later have two sons and a daughter. After graduation, the couple both embarked on highly successful theatrical careers. Over the next two decades, Ludlum appeared in some 200 television roles, as well as on Broadway, and also masterminded some 300 stage productions for New York and regional theatres. His deep voice made him perfect for voice-overs and he once claimed that the line 'Plunge works fast', uttered during a commercial for a toilet cleaner, earned him the funds to put one of his sons through college. As a producer, he also ran what was thought to be America's first shopping-mall theatre, The Playhouse, in Paramus, New Jersey. For the theatre's 1960 production of *The Owl and the Pussycat* he famously hired a then unknown actor named Alan Alda.

In the late sixties, Ludlum turned his creative energies to writing books. From the start, he had a magic touch. His first novel, *The Scarlatti Inheritance* (1971) was an immediate hit and he followed it up with a new blockbuster almost every year thereafter. *The Osterman Weekend* (1973), was the first of his books to be filmed, under the direction of Sam Peckinpah. Interestingly, Ludlum attributed his meteoric success as a writer to his experience of the theatre. 'I understood about dialogue and the architecture of scenes . . . If I had tried to write ten years before I wouldn't have got anywhere,' he once said.

The heroes in Ludlum's books are often individuals battling against shadowy global corporations or military or government organisations—the kind of institutions that concerned him in real life. In an interview in 1997, when asked what political issues were uppermost on his mind, he said, 'Mega-mergers, national and trans-national . . . If this continues to its logical progression there will be fewer and fewer choices in this world . . . greater economic power will be in the hands of too few.'

Ludlum was a consummate storyteller who took the genre of the spy thriller and turned it into pure escapism by creating larger-than-life plots. One of the hallmarks of his work was painstaking research. Typically, he would spend three months on preparation before even setting pen to paper, and each book took some fifteen months to write. He could justifiably boast when he was done, that his readers would always learn something, whether it be about a new weapon or gadget, or the latest breakthrough in surveillance techniques.

During his thirty-year writing career, Robert Ludlum wrote over two dozen books and gained a vast and enduring international fan base. Following his death in 2001, it came to light that he had left behind several manuscripts, of which *The Ambler Warning*, published posthumously in 2005, was one.

BOURNE TO STARDOM

In 2002, the Bourne Trilogy, for which Ludlum is probably best known, got a new lease of life when the books were transferred to screen starring the Hollywood actor Matt Damon (below) in the role of Jason Bourne. *The Bourne Identity* was followed in 2002 by *The Bourne Supremacy*, and Damon will again star in the final part, *The Bourne Ultimatum*, in 2007.

TRUE
BELIEVER
NICHOLAS SPARKS

Late at night, when fog shrouds
the trees in Boone Creek cemetery,
North Carolina, it is said that ghostly lights
appear to dance among the headstones.

For science reporter Jeremy Marsh
the phenomenon seems at first like
just one more irresistible
news opportunity.
But, unbelievably, it completely
transforms his life . . .

ONE

Jeremy Marsh sat with the rest of the live studio audience, feeling unusually conspicuous. He was one of only half a dozen men in attendance on that mid-December afternoon. He'd dressed in black, of course, and with his dark wavy hair, light blue eyes and fashionable stubble, he looked every bit the New Yorker that he was. While studying the guest onstage, he managed to surreptitiously watch the attractive blonde three rows up. His profession often demanded effective multitasking. He was an investigative journalist in pursuit of a story, and the blonde was just another member of the audience; still, the professional observer in him couldn't help noticing how attractive she looked in her halter top and jeans. Journalistically speaking, that is.

Clearing his mind, he focused on the guest. This guy was beyond ridiculous. In the glare of television lights, Jeremy thought the spirit guide looked constipated as he claimed to hear voices from beyond the grave. He acted as if he were everyone's best friend, and it seemed that the vast majority of the audience—including the attractive blonde and the woman the spirit guide was addressing—considered him a gift from heaven itself. Which made sense, Jeremy thought, since that was always where the lost loved ones ended up. Never once had he heard of a spirit guide channelling from the other, hotter place. But he had to admit that it was a pretty good show. Timothy Clausen was far better than most of the quacks he had written about over the years.

'I know it's hard,' Clausen said into the microphone, 'but Frank is telling you that it's time to let him go now.'

The woman he was addressing looked as if she was about to faint. Her hands were clasped so tightly that her fingers were white.

Clausen paused and brought his hand to his forehead, drawing once more on 'the world beyond', as he put it. Everyone knew what was coming next; this was the third audience member Clausen had chosen today. Not surprisingly, Clausen was the only featured guest on the popular talk show.

'Do you remember the letter he sent you?' Clausen asked. 'Before he died?'

The woman gasped. 'Yes, but how could you know about—?'

Clausen didn't let her finish. 'Do you remember what it said?' he asked. 'It was about forgiveness, wasn't it?'

On the couch, the hostess of the show, the most popular afternoon talk show in America, swivelled her gaze from Clausen to the woman and back again.

As the woman in the audience nodded, Jeremy noticed mascara beginning to stream down her cheeks. She finally let loose a raspy cry. Tears burst forth like an automated sprinkler.

'Frank left something else for you, didn't he? Something from your past. A key of some sort, is that right?'

The sobs continued as the woman nodded. OK, here's the clincher, Jeremy thought. Another true believer on the way.

'It's from the hotel where you stayed on your honeymoon. He put it there so that when you found it, you would remember the happy times you spent together. He doesn't want you to remember him with pain, because he loves you.'

'Ooohhhhhhh . . .' the woman cried. The cry was interrupted by sudden, enthusiastic applause. The microphone was pulled away. The woman from the audience collapsed in her seat. On cue, the hostess faced the camera. 'Remember, what you're seeing is real. None of these people have ever met with Timothy Clausen.' She smiled. 'We'll be back with one more reading after this.'

More applause as the show broke for commercials, and Jeremy leaned back in his seat.

As an investigative journalist known for his interest in science, he enjoyed what he did and took pride in his work. For his regular column in *Scientific American*, he'd interviewed Nobel laureates, explained the theories of Einstein, and had been credited with sparking the groundswell of public opinion that led the FDA to remove a dangerous antidepressant from the market.

Unfortunately, as impressive as it sounded, his column didn't pay much. Freelance work helped pay his bills and, like all freelancers, he was always hustling to come up with interesting stories. His niche had broadened to include 'anything unusual', and in the past fifteen years, he'd investigated psychics, spirit guides and faith healers. He'd exposed frauds, hoaxes and forgeries. He'd visited haunted houses, searched for mystical creatures and hunted for the origins of urban legends. Sceptical by nature, he also had the ability to explain difficult scientific concepts in a way the average reader could understand. Scientific debunking, he felt, was both noble and important, even if the public didn't always appreciate it.

Jeremy knew the people chosen by Clausen weren't officially part of the act. But the audience was loaded with life-after-death believers. To them, Clausen was legitimate. How else could he know such personal things about strangers, unless he talked to spirits? But, like any good magician who had his repertoire off pat, the illusion was still an illusion, and right before the show, Jeremy had figured out how he was pulling it off and had the photographic evidence to prove it.

Bringing down Clausen would be a big coup and it served the guy right. Clausen was on the cusp of enormous celebrity and, in America, celebrity was all that mattered. Though he knew the odds were improbable, Jeremy fantasised about what would happen if Clausen actually picked *him* next. As the commercial break ended, he felt the slightest twinge of hope that somehow Clausen would zero in on him.

And, as if God himself wasn't exactly thrilled with what Clausen was doing either, that was exactly what happened.

THREE WEEKS LATER, winter in Manhattan was bearing down hard. Plumes of steam rose steadily from the sewer grates before settling over icy sidewalks. Not that anyone seemed to mind. New York's hardy citizens displayed their usual indifference to all things weather-related, and Friday nights were not to be wasted under any circumstance, especially when there was reason to celebrate. Nate Johnson and Alvin Bernstein had already been celebrating for an hour, as had a couple of dozen friends—some from *Scientific American*—who'd assembled in Jeremy's honour. Most were well into the buzz phase of the evening and enjoying themselves immensely, mostly because Nate was picking up the tab.

Nate was Jeremy's agent. Alvin, a freelance cameraman, was Jeremy's best friend, and they were celebrating Jeremy's appearance on ABC's *Primetime Live*. Commercials for *Primetime Live* had been airing that week—most of them featuring Jeremy and the promise of a major exposé—and interview requests were pouring into Nate's office. Earlier that afternoon, *People* magazine had called, and an interview was scheduled for the following Monday.

There hadn't been enough time to organise a private room for the get-together, but no one seemed to mind. With its long granite bar and dramatic lighting, the facility was packed with women straight from work, dressed in designer skirts and sipping flavoured martinis while pretending to ignore the men. Jeremy himself had his eye on a tall redhead standing at the other end of the bar.

'C'mon, Jeremy, pay attention,' Nate said, nudging him with his elbow. 'You're on TV! Don't you want to see how you did?'

Jeremy turned from the redhead. Glancing up at the screen, he saw himself sitting opposite Diane Sawyer, who was describing him as 'America's most esteemed scientific journalist'.

'Did she just call you esteemed?' Alvin asked. 'You write about Bigfoot and the legend of Atlantis!'

'Shh,' Nate said, his eyes glued to the television. 'I'm trying to hear this. It could be important for Jeremy's career.'

Flickering on the screen behind Diane Sawyer and Jeremy were the final moments of Jeremy's performance on the daytime television show, in which he had pretended to be a man grieving the boyhood death of his brother, a boy Clausen claimed to be channelling for Jeremy's benefit.

'Your mother never changed his room—the room you shared with him. And you still had to sleep there,' Clausen announced.

'Yes,' Jeremy gasped.

'But you were frightened, and in your anger, you took something of his, something very personal, and buried it in the back yard.'

'Yes,' Jeremy managed again, as if too emotional to say more.

'His retainer!'

'Ooooohhhhhhhhh,' Jeremy cried.

'He loves you, but you have to realise that he's at peace now. He has no anger towards you . . .'

On *Primetime Live*, the tape faded to black, and the camera focused on Diane Sawyer and Jeremy sitting across from each other.

'So nothing Timothy Clausen said was true?' Diane asked.

'Not a thing,' Jeremy said. 'I have five brothers, but they're all alive and well.'

'So how did Clausen do this?'

'Well, Diane,' Jeremy began. 'Clausen is good at reading people and he's expert at making vague, emotionally charged associations and responding to audience members' cues.'

'Yes, but he was so specific. How does he do that?'

Jeremy shrugged. 'He heard me talking about my brother before the show. I simply made up an imaginary life and broadcast it loud and clear. Con men like Clausen use paid "listeners" who circulate in the waiting area before the show. Before I was seated, I made sure to strike up conversations with lots of audience members, watching to see if anyone exhibited unusual interest. Sure enough, one man seemed particularly concerned.'

Behind them, the videotape was replaced by an enlarged photograph that Jeremy had taken with a camera hidden in his watch.

Jeremy pointed. 'This man was mingling with the studio audience. Zoom in further, please.'

On-screen, the photograph was enlarged. 'Do you see the USA pin on his lapel? That's actually a transmitter that broadcasts to a recording device backstage. I happen to have one just like it.'

Jeremy reached into his jacket pocket and pulled out the same USA pin, attached to a long, threadlike wire and transmitter.

Diane inspected it with apparent fascination. 'And you're certain that this was indeed a microphone and not just a pin?'

'A week after the show, I obtained some more photographs.'

A new picture flashed on the screen. It was the same man who'd been wearing the USA pin.

'This photo was taken in Florida, outside Clausen's office. As you can see, the man is heading inside. His name is Rex Moore and he's actually an employee of Clausen's.'

'Ooohhhhh!' Alvin shouted, and the rest of the broadcast, which was winding down, anyway, was drowned out as others joined in with hoots and hollers. Jeremy was deluged with congratulations after the show had ended.

'You were fantastic,' Nate said. At forty-three, Nate was short and balding. He was energy incarnate and, like most agents, positively buzzed with fervent optimism.

'Thanks,' Jeremy said, downing the remainder of his beer.

'This is going to be big for your career,' Nate went on. 'It's your ticket to a regular television gig. I've always said that with your looks, you were made for TV.'

'I'd have to say Nate's right,' Alvin added with a wink. 'I mean, how else could you be more popular than me with the ladies, despite having zero personality?'

Jeremy laughed. Alvin Bernstein, whose name conjured up a clean-cut, bespectacled accountant, didn't look like an Alvin Bernstein. As a teenager, he'd seen Eddie Murphy in *Delirious* and had decided to make the full-leather style his own. Fortunately, leather seemed to go well with his tattoos, which complemented his multiple-pierced ears.

'So are you still planning a trip south to investigate that ghost story?' Nate pressed. 'After your interview with *People*, I mean.'

Jeremy signalled the bartender for another beer. 'Yeah, I guess so. I was thinking I could use it for my column. I should be there less than a week. "Mysterious lights in the cemetery." No big deal.'

'Hey, you need a cameraman by any chance?' Alvin piped up.

Jeremy looked over at him. 'Why? Do you want to go?'

'Hell, yeah. Head south for the winter, maybe meet me a nice Southern belle while you pick up the tab. I'll be clear towards the end of the week. And if you're serious about television, you'll need some decent footage of these mysterious lights.'

'That's assuming there are even any lights to film.'

'You do the advance work and let me know. I'll keep my calendar open.'

'Even if there are lights, it's a small story,' Jeremy warned. 'No one in television will be interested in it.'

'Not last month, maybe,' Alvin said. 'But after seeing you tonight, they'll be interested.'

'He's right,' Nate said. 'If you can get some actual footage of the lights, it might be just the thing that *GMA* or *Primetime* needs to make their decision.'

Jeremy was silent for a moment before finally shrugging. 'Fine,' he said. He glanced at Alvin. 'I'm leaving Tuesday. See if you can get there by next Friday. I'll call you before then.'

Alvin reached for his beer. 'Well, golly,' he said, mimicking Private Gomer Pyle in the CBS sitcom, 'I'm off to the land of grits and chitlins.'

Jeremy laughed. 'You ever been down South?'

'Nope. You?'

'I've visited New Orleans and Atlanta,' Jeremy admitted. 'But for this story, we're heading to the real South. It's a little town in North Carolina, a place called Boone Creek. I'm staying at the Greenleaf Cottages, which the chamber of commerce describes as scenic and rustic yet modern. Whatever that means.'

Alvin laughed. 'Sounds like an adventure.'

'Don't worry about it,' said Jeremy, noting the leather, tattoos and piercings. 'You'll fit right in down there, I'm sure.'

ON TUESDAY, the day after his interview with *People* magazine, Jeremy arrived in North Carolina. It was just past noon; when he'd left New York, it had been sleeting and grey. Here, with blue skies stretched out above him, winter seemed a long way off.

According to the map, Boone Creek was in Pamlico County, a hundred miles southeast of Raleigh, and—if the drive was any indication—about a zillion miles from what he considered civilisation. On either side of him, the landscape was flat and sparse. Farms were separated by thin strands of loblolly pines.

But it wasn't all bad, he had to admit. The actual driving part, anyway— the revving of the engine, the feeling of acceleration. His ex-wife, Maria, would have loved a drive like this. In the early years of their marriage, they would rent a car and drive to the mountains or to the beach, sometimes spending hours on the road. She'd been a publicist at *Elle* magazine when they'd met at a publishing party. When he asked if she'd like to join him at a nearby coffee shop, he had no idea she would end up being the only woman he ever loved.

A year later, they were married. He was twenty-six, not yet a columnist for *Scientific American* but steadily building his reputation, and they could barely afford the small apartment they rented in Brooklyn. To his mind, it was young-and-struggling marital bliss. To her mind, he suspected, their marriage was strong in theory but constructed on a shaky foundation. While her job kept her in the city, Jeremy travelled, pursuing the big story. He was often gone for weeks at a time. Just after their second anniversary, as he readied himself for yet another trip, Maria sat down beside him on the bed.

'This isn't working,' she said simply, letting the words hang for a moment. 'You're never home and it isn't fair to me. It isn't fair to us.'

'You want me to quit?' he asked, feeling a small bubble of panic.

'Maybe you can find something local. Like at the *Times*.'

'It's not going to be like this for ever,' he pleaded.

'That's what you said six months ago,' she said. 'It's never going to change.'

Looking back, Jeremy knew he should have taken it as the warning that it was, but at the time, he had a story to write. The final split came a year later, a month after a visit to a doctor, one who presented them with a future that neither of them had ever envisioned. Far more than his travelling, the visit foretold the end of their relationship, and even Jeremy knew it.

'I can't stay,' she'd told him afterwards. 'I want to, and part of me will always love you, but I can't.'

The divorce had become final seven years ago and, to be honest, it was the only truly sad thing ever to have happened to him. He'd never been seriously injured; he'd emerged from childhood without the psychological trauma that seemed to afflict so many of his age. His brothers and their wives, his parents, and even his grandparents were healthy. They were close, too: a couple of weekends a month, the ever-growing clan would gather at his parents', who lived in the house in Queens where Jeremy had grown up. He had seventeen nieces and nephews, and though he sometimes felt out of place at family functions, since he was a bachelor again in a family of happily married people, his brothers were respectful enough not to probe the reasons behind the divorce.

And he'd got over it. For the most part, anyway. Besides, Maria had been right. In fifteen years, his workload hadn't changed a bit. He still had to produce a dozen columns for *Scientific American*, at least one or two major investigations and another fifteen or so articles a year—interviews with scientists, exposés about drugs and anything, absolutely anything, about the supernatural.

He had to admit the process wasn't anything like he'd imagined a career in journalism would be. At Columbia—he was the only one of his brothers to attend college—he'd double-majored in physics and chemistry, with the intention of becoming a professor. His career choice didn't change until his father was swindled by a bogus financial planner right before Jeremy graduated. With the family home in jeopardy—his father was a bus driver and worked for the Port Authority until retirement—Jeremy bypassed his graduation ceremony to track down the con man and write the first exposé of his life. In the end, the house was saved and *New York* magazine picked up the piece. The rest, as they say, was history.

Still, fifteen years of chasing stories and what had he received in exchange? He was thirty-seven years old, single and living in a dingy one-bedroom apartment on the Upper West Side, and heading to Boone Creek, North Carolina, to explain a case of mysterious lights in a cemetery.

He shook his head. The big dream. It was still out there, and he still had the passion to reach it. Only now, he'd begun to wonder if television would be his means.

THE STORY of the mysterious lights originated from a letter Jeremy had received a month earlier. His first thought was that it would make a good Halloween story. On the other hand, if the town was trying to cash in—like Roswell, New Mexico, with UFOs—the story might be appropriate for one of the major newspapers. Or, if he kept it short, he could use it in his *Scientific American* column.

The lights in Boone Creek were, apparently, predictable enough to enable the town to sponsor a Historic Homes and Haunted Cemetery Tour, during which, the brochure promised, people would see not only homes dating back to the mid-1700s but also, weather permitting, 'the anguished ancestors of our town on their nightly march between the netherworlds'.

The brochure, complete with pictures of the tidy town, had been sent to him along with the letter. As he drove, Jeremy recalled the letter.

Dear Mr Marsh,

My name is Doris McClellan, and I read your story in 'Scientific American' about the poltergeist haunting Brenton Manor in Newport, Rhode Island. I thought about writing to you back then, but for whatever reason, I didn't.

I don't know if you've ever heard about the cemetery in Boone Creek, North Carolina, but legend has it that the cemetery is haunted by spirits of former slaves. In the winter, blue lights seem to dance on the headstones whenever the fog rolls in. Some say they're like strobe lights. To me, they look like sparkly disco balls. Last year, some folks from Duke University came to investigate. They saw the lights, but couldn't explain them, and the local paper did a big story on the whole mystery. Maybe if you came down, you could make sense of what the lights really are.

If you need more information, give me a call at Herbs, a restaurant here in town.

After reading the letter, he had flipped through the brochure. There was information concerning a parade and barn dance on Friday night and an announcement stating that, for the first time, a visit to the cemetery would be included in the tour on Saturday evening. On the back of the brochure were testimonials from people who'd seen the lights and an excerpt from an article in the local newspaper.

After failing to find the article—there were no archives at the local newspaper's website—Jeremy contacted Duke University and found the original research project. It had been written by three graduate students, and though he had their names and phone numbers, he doubted there was any reason to call them. The report barely scratched the surface of the information he needed. And, besides, if he'd learned anything in the past fifteen years, it was to trust no one's work but his own.

He watched oak trees slide past the windows, wishing he'd researched the ghost story further. What if there were no lights? What if the letter writer was a quack? He shook his head. Worrying was pointless; it was too late now. He was already here and Nate was busy working the New York phones.

In the boot of the car, Jeremy had all the necessary items for ghost hunting: cameras, camcorders and tripods, audio recorder and microphones, microwave radiation detector, electromagnetic detector, compass, night-vision goggles, laptop computer and other odds and ends.

The traffic picked up near Greenville and he looped round the downtown area. He crossed the wide, brackish waters of the Pamlico River and turned onto a rural highway, squeezed on both sides by barren winter fields, denser thickets of trees, and the occasional farmhouse. About thirty minutes later, he was approaching Boone Creek.

After the first and only stoplight, the speed limit dropped to twenty-five miles an hour and, slowing the car, Jeremy took in the scene with dismay. In addition to the half-dozen mobile homes perched haphazardly off the main road and a couple of side streets, the stretch of blacktop was dominated by two run-down service stations and Leroy's Tyres. Jeremy reached the other end of town in a minute, at which point the speed limit picked up again.

Either the chamber of commerce had used photographs of some other town on its website or he'd missed something. He glanced in the rearview mirror, wondering where on earth Boone Creek was. The quiet, tree-lined streets. The first flowering azaleas.

As he was trying to figure it out, he saw a white church steeple peeking out above the tree line and decided to make his way down one of the side streets he'd passed. He soon found himself driving through a town that may once have been gracious and picturesque, but now seemed to be dying of old age. Wraparound porches decorated with hanging flowerpots and American flags couldn't hide the peeling paint. Yards were shaded by massive magnolia trees, but the neatly trimmed rhododendron bushes only partially hid cracked foundations. Still, it seemed friendly enough.

Meandering from one road to the next, he found the waterfront, recalling that the town had been developed at the confluence of Boone Creek and the Pamlico River. Dispersed among the vacant spaces and boarded-up windows were two antique shops, an old-fashioned diner, a tavern called Lookilu, and a barbershop. Most of the businesses looked as if they were fighting a losing battle against extinction. The only evidence of modern life was the T-shirts emblazoned with such slogans as I SURVIVED THE GHOSTS IN BOONE CREEK! that hung in the window of the department store.

Herbs, where Doris McClellan worked, was easy enough to find. It was located in a restored turn-of-the-century peach-coloured Victorian building. Cars were parked out front and tables were visible inside. Every table was occupied. Jeremy decided to swing by and talk to Doris after the crowd had thinned out.

He headed back towards the highway and, impulsively, pulled into a service station. After taking off his sunglasses, Jeremy lowered the window.

The grey-haired proprietor wore dingy coveralls and a cap. He rose slowly and began strolling towards the car. 'Can I hep ya?' His name tag read TULLY.

Jeremy asked for directions to the cemetery but, instead of answering, the proprietor looked Jeremy over carefully.

'Who passed?' he finally asked.

Jeremy blinked. 'Excuse me?'

'You look like you're heading to a burial.'

Jeremy glanced at his clothing: black jacket over a black turtleneck, black jeans. The man did have a point.

'I guess I just like black. Anyway, about the directions . . .'

The owner pushed up his cap and spoke slowly. 'I don't like going to burials none. Make me think I ought to be heading to church more often to square things up before it's too late.' He took a rag from his pocket and wiped his oily hands. 'I take it you're not from here. You got a funny accent.'

'New York,' Jeremy clarified.

'Heard of it, but ain't never been there,' he said.

'About the cemetery,' Jeremy prodded. 'Can you tell me how to get there?'

'I s'pose. Which one ya lookin' for?'

'It's called Cedar Creek.'

The proprietor looked at him curiously. 'You got kin buried there?'

'No. Actually, I'm a journalist.'

'You need some gas?' the man asked, moving towards the rear of the car. 'Premium or regular?'

Jeremy shifted in his seat. 'Regular, I guess.'

After getting the gas going, the man took off his cap and ran his hand through his hair as he made his way back to the window.

'You have any car trouble, don't hesitate to swing by. Name's Tully, by the way. And you are?'

'Jeremy Marsh,' he said. 'But anyway, about the directions to Cedar Creek . . .'

Tully glanced up the road. 'Well, you ain't going to see anything now. The ghosts don't come out till night-time, if that's what you're here for.'

'Excuse me?'

'The ghosts. If you ain't got kin buried in the cemetery, then you must be here for the ghosts, right? But if you want tickets, you'll have to go to the chamber of commerce.'

It took a moment to follow the train of thought. 'Oh,' Jeremy said. 'The Historic Homes and Haunted Cemetery Tour, right?'

Tully stared at Jeremy as if he were the densest person ever to walk the face of the earth. 'Whaddya think I was talkin' about?'

'I'm not sure,' Jeremy said. 'But the directions . . .'

Tully shook his head. 'OK, OK,' he said, as if suddenly put out. He pointed towards town. 'Head back downtown, then follow the main road north until you reach the turn about four miles from where the road used to dead-end. Turn west and keep going until you get to the fork, and follow the road that leads past Wilson Tanner's place. Turn north again where the junked car used to be, go straight, and the cemetery'll be right there.'

Jeremy nodded. 'OK,' he said. 'Thanks for your help.'

'Glad to be of service. That'll be seven dollars and forty-nine cents.'

'You take credit cards?'

'No. Never liked them things. Don't like the government knowing everything I'm doing. Ain't no one else's business.'

'Well,' Jeremy said, reaching for his wallet, 'it is a problem. I've heard the government has spies everywhere.'

Tully nodded knowingly. 'Which reminds me . . .'

TULLY KEPT UP a steady stream of talk for the next fifteen minutes. Finally, another car pulled in on the other side of the pump, interrupting their talk.

Jeremy used the opportunity to sneak away. He stopped at the department store to buy a map and a packet of postcards featuring the landmarks of Boone Creek, and before long he was making his way along a winding road that led out of town. With a bit of backtracking, he finally reached a narrow gravel lane almost hidden by the overgrowth of trees on either side.

Making the turn, he bumped his way through various potholes until the forest began to thin. He passed a sign that noted he was nearing Riker's Hill—site of a Civil War skirmish—and a few moments later, he pulled to a stop in front of the main gate at Cedar Creek Cemetery. Riker's Hill towered in the background.

Surrounded by brick columns and rusting wrought-iron fencing, the cemetery was set into a slight valley, making it look as if it were slowly sinking. The grounds were shaded with oaks that dripped with Spanish moss, but the massive magnolia tree in the centre dominated everything. The dirt pathway beyond the main gate was carpeted with decaying leaves. Tall weeds sprouted near the headstones, almost all of which appeared to be broken.

It wasn't much to look at. But for a haunted cemetery, it was perfect. Especially one that might end up on television. Jeremy smiled.

He stepped out of the car and stretched his legs before retrieving a camera from the boot. Above him, cumulus clouds drifted across the sky and a lone hawk circled in the distance. He pushed through the rusting main gate and wandered down the dirt pathway. Up ahead, a crypt looked as if it had been invaded. The roof and sides had toppled in, and just beyond that, another monument lay crumbled on the pathway. More damaged crypts and

broken monuments followed. Jeremy saw no evidence of purposeful van-
dalism, only natural, if serious, decay.

In the shade of the magnolia, he paused, wondering how the place would
look on a foggy night. Probably spooky, which could prompt a person's
imagination to run wild. But if there were unexplained lights, where were
they coming from? He guessed that the 'ghosts' were simply reflected light
turned into prisms by water droplets in the fog, but there weren't any streetlamps out here. They could come from car headlights, yet he saw only the
single road nearby, and people would have noticed the connection long ago.

He'd have to get a good topographical map of the area. Perhaps the local
library would have one. In any case, he'd stop by the library to research the
history of the cemetery and the town itself. He needed to know when the
lights were first spotted. Of course, he'd have to spend a couple of nights
out here in spookyville as well, if the fog was willing to cooperate.

For a while, he walked round the cemetery taking photographs. As he
was flicking through the digital images to make sure they were sufficient,
he saw movement from the corner of his eye.

Glancing up, he saw a woman walking towards him. Dressed in jeans,
boots and light blue sweater, she had brown hair that lightly swept her shoulders. Her skin had a hint of olive, but it was the colour of her eyes that caught
him: from a distance, they appeared almost violet. Whoever she was, she'd
parked her car directly behind his.

For a moment, he wondered whether she was approaching to ask him to
leave. Maybe the cemetery was off limits. Then again, perhaps her visit
here was simply a coincidence.

Come to think of it, a rather *attractive* coincidence. Jeremy straightened
as he slipped the camera back into its case. He smiled broadly as she
neared. 'Well, hello there,' he said.

She slowed her gait slightly. Her expression seemed almost amused, and
he half expected her to stop. Instead, he thought he caught the sound of her
laughter as she walked right by.

With eyebrows raised in appreciation, Jeremy watched her go. She didn't
look back. Before he could stop himself, he took a step after her. 'Hey!' he
called out.

She turned and continued walking backwards, her head tilted inquisi-
tively. 'You know, you really shouldn't stare like that,' she called out.
'Women like a man who knows how to be subtle.'

She turned again and kept on going. In the distance, he heard her laugh again.

Jeremy stood open-mouthed, at a loss how to respond.

OK, so she wasn't interested. No big deal. Still, most people would have at least said hello. Maybe it was a Southern thing. Or maybe she simply didn't want to be interrupted. And besides, he reminded himself, it's a cemetery. She was probably here to visit the departed. People did that all the time, didn't they? The only difference was that most cemeteries looked as if someone came by to mow the lawn now and then.

Jeremy tried not to stare as she disappeared behind an oak tree. It was only after she'd vanished that he was able to remind himself that pretty girls didn't matter right now. He had a job to do and his future was on the line here. Money, fame, television, yadda yadda yadda. OK, what next? He'd seen the cemetery . . . he might as well check out the surrounding area. Get a feel for the place.

He walked back to his car and hopped in. Turning round, he started back the way he had come, looking for a road that would lead him to the top of Riker's Hill, but he gave up in frustration. As he neared the cemetery again, the sharp-eyed journalist in him happened to notice that the woman's car was gone, which left him with a slight pang of disappointment.

It was after two, and he figured the lunch rush at Herbs was probably ending. Might as well talk to Doris. Maybe she could shed some 'light' on the subject. He smiled to himself, wondering if the woman he'd seen at the cemetery would have laughed at that one.

TWO

Only a few tables were still occupied when Jeremy reached Herbs. As he pushed through the door, he saw two main rooms on either side of the building, separated by a set of stairs. The peach walls were offset by white trim, giving the place a homely, country feel.

A waitress ambled out from the kitchen. In her late twenties or so, she was tall and reed-thin, with a sunny, open face. 'Just take a seat anywhere, hon,' she chirped. 'Be with you in a minute.'

After making himself comfortable near a window, he watched the waitress approach. Her name tag said RACHEL. 'Can I get you something to drink?' she asked.

'Do you have cappuccino?' he ventured.

'No, sorry. We have coffee, though.'

'Coffee will be fine.' Jeremy smiled.

'You got it. Menu's on the table if you want something to eat.'

'Actually, I was wondering if Doris McClellan was around.'

'Oh, she's in the back,' Rachel said, brightening. 'Want me to get her?'

'If you wouldn't mind.'

She smiled. 'No problem at all, darlin'.'

He watched her head towards the kitchen and push through the swing doors. A moment later, an older woman emerged. She was the opposite of Rachel: short and stout, with thinning white hair, she was wearing an apron over a flower-print blouse. Pausing at the table, she put her hands on her hips before breaking into a smile.

'Well,' she said, drawing out the word into two syllables, 'you must be Jeremy Marsh.'

'You know me?' Jeremy asked.

'I just saw you on *Primetime Live* last Friday. I take it you got my letter and you're here to write a story about the ghosts?'

He raised his hands. 'So it seems.'

'Well, I'll be.' Her accent made it sound like she was pronouncing the letters *L-I-B*. She pulled out a chair. 'I suppose you're here to talk to me.'

'I don't want you to get in trouble with your boss if you're supposed to be working.'

She glanced over her shoulder and shouted, 'Hey, Rachel, do you think the boss would mind if I took a seat? The man here wants to talk to me.'

Rachel poked her head out from behind the swing doors. 'Nah, I don't think the boss would mind at all. She loves to talk. Especially when she's with such a handsome fella.'

Doris turned round. 'See,' she said. 'No problem.'

Jeremy smiled. 'I take it you're the boss.'

'Guilty as charged,' Doris answered. Her eyes flickered with satisfaction as she leaned forward. 'You hungry? You should try one of our sandwiches. It's all fresh—we even make the bread daily.' She hesitated, looking him over. 'I'll bet you'd love the chicken pesto sandwich. It's got sprouts, tomatoes, cucumbers, and I came up with the pesto recipe myself.'

Rachel approached with two cups of coffee.

'And just to let you know . . . if I'm going to tell a story, I like to do it over a good meal. And I tend to take my time.'

'The chicken pesto sandwich sounds fine,' Jeremy said.

Doris smiled. 'Bring us a couple of the Albemarles, Rachel.'

'Sure,' Rachel answered. 'Who's your friend? Haven't seen him around here before.'

'This is Jeremy Marsh,' Doris answered. 'He's a famous journalist here to write a story about our fair town.'

'Really?' Rachel said with a wink. 'For a second, I thought you'd just come from a funeral.'

Jeremy blinked as Rachel moved away.

Doris laughed. 'Tully stopped in,' she explained. 'He figured I might have had something to do with you coming down. He rehashed the conversation and we thought his comment was a hoot.'

'Ah,' Jeremy said.

Doris leaned forward. 'I'll bet he talked your ear off. He'd talk to a shoe box if no one else was around, and I swear I don't know how his wife put up with it for so long. But she went deaf, and so now he talks to customers.'

Jeremy reached for his coffee. 'His wife went deaf?'

'I think the Good Lord realised she'd sacrificed enough.'

Jeremy laughed before taking a sip. 'So why would Tully think you were the one who contacted me?'

'Every time something unusual happens, I'm always to blame. Comes with the territory, I guess, being the town psychic and all.'

Jeremy simply looked at her, and Doris smiled.

'I take it you don't believe in psychics,' she remarked.

'No, not really,' Jeremy admitted.

'For the most part, I don't, either. Most of them are kooks. But some people do have the gift.'

'Then . . . you can read my mind?'

'No, nothing like that,' Doris said, shaking her head. 'My gift is different. I'm a diviner. And I can also tell what sex a baby's going to be before it's born.'

'I see.'

Doris looked him over. 'You don't believe me.'

'Well, let's just say you *are* a diviner. That means you can find water and tell me where I should dig a well. And if I asked you to do a test, with scientific controls, under strict supervision—'

'You can test me any time, in any way you'd like. But that's not why you came. You want to hear about the ghosts, right?'

'Sure,' Jeremy said, relieved to get straight into it. 'Do you mind if I record this?'

'Not at all.'

Jeremy reached into his jacket pocket and retrieved a small recorder. He set it between them and pressed the appropriate buttons. Doris took a sip of coffee before beginning.

'OK, the story goes back to the 1890s or thereabouts. Back then, this town was still segregated, and most of the Negroes lived out in a place called Watts Landing. There's nothing left of the village these days, but back near the turn of the century, I guess about three hundred people lived there. So Union Pacific came through to set the railroad lines. And the line they proposed ran right through the Negro cemetery. Now, the leader of that town was a woman named Hettie Doubilet. She was from the Caribbean, and when she found out that they were supposed to dig up all the bodies and transfer them to another place, she got upset and tried to get the county to do something to have the route changed. But the folks that ran the county wouldn't even consider it.'

Rachel arrived with the sandwiches. She set the plates on the table. Jeremy reached for his sandwich and took a bite. He raised his eyebrows. 'My compliments to the chef.'

Doris looked at him almost coquettishly. 'You *are* a charmer, Mr Marsh,' she said, and went on with her story.

'Back then, a lot of folks were racist. Some of them still are, but they're in the minority now. Hettie Doubilet was enraged by the folks at the county, and legend has it that she put a curse on us white folk. She said that if graves of her ancestors would be defiled, then ours would be defiled, too. The ancestors of her people would tread the earth in search of their original resting place and would trample through Cedar Creek on their journey, and in the end, the cemetery would be swallowed whole.'

Doris took a bite of her sandwich. 'And, to make a long story short, the Negroes moved the bodies to another cemetery, the railroad went in, and after that, just as Hettie said, Cedar Creek Cemetery started going bad. Little things at first. A few headstones broken. The county folks, thinking Hettie's people were responsible, posted guards. But it kept happening. And over the years, it kept getting worse. You went there, right?'

Jeremy nodded.

'So you can see what's happening. Looks like the place is sinking, right, just like Hettie said it would? Anyway, a few years later, the lights started to appear. And ever since then, folks have believed it was the slave spirits marching through.'

'So they don't use the cemetery any more?'

'No, the place was abandoned in the 1970s. The county owns it now, but they don't take care of it.'

'Has anyone checked into why it seems to be sinking?'

'I'm not certain, but I'm almost positive that someone has. I've heard stories that some folks from Raleigh came to find out what was happening.'

'You mean the students from Duke?'

'Oh, no, not them. They were here last year. I'm talking way back.'

'But you don't know what they learned.'

'No.' She paused, and her eyes took on a mischievous gleam. 'But I think I have a pretty good idea.'

Jeremy raised his eyebrows. 'And that is?'

'Water,' she said simply. 'I'm a diviner, remember. And I'll tell you that that land is sinking because of the water underneath it.'

'I see,' Jeremy said.

Doris laughed. 'You're so cute, Mr Marsh. Your face gets all serious-looking when someone tells you something you don't want to believe. You're so easy to read.'

'So what am I thinking?'

Doris hesitated. 'Well, I don't want to scare you.'

'Go ahead. Scare me.'

'All right,' she said. She took a long look at him. 'Think of something I couldn't possibly know. And remember, my gift isn't reading minds. I just get . . . hints now and then, and only if they're really strong feelings.'

'All right,' Jeremy said, playing along.

Doris reached for his hands. 'Let me hold these, OK?'

Jeremy nodded. 'Sure.'

'Now think of something personal I couldn't possibly know.'

'OK.'

She squeezed his hands. 'Seriously. Right now you're just playing with me.'

'Fine,' he said. 'I'll think of something.' Jeremy closed his eyes. He thought of the reason Maria had finally left him. For a long moment, Doris said nothing. Instead, she simply looked at him, as if trying to get him to say something.

He'd been through this before. Countless times. He knew enough to say nothing, and when she remained silent, he knew he had her. She suddenly jerked, and immediately afterwards, released his hands.

Jeremy opened his eyes and looked at her. 'And?'

Doris was looking at him strangely. 'Nothing,' she said.

'Ah,' Jeremy added, 'I guess it's not in the cards today, huh?'

'Like I said, I'm a diviner.' She smiled, almost as if in apology. 'I'm sorry. I shouldn't have done what I did. It was inappropriate.'

'No big deal,' he said, meaning it.

'No,' she insisted. She squeezed his hands again. 'I'm sorry.'

Jeremy was struck by the compassion in her expression. And he had the unnerving feeling that she had guessed more about his personal history than she could possibly know.

Doris reached for her sandwich. 'Well, anyway, maybe it's better if we just visited for a while. Is there anything I can tell you?'

'Tell me about the town of Boone Creek,' he said. 'I figure that since I'm going to be here for a few days, I might as well know a little about the place.'

For the next half-hour, Doris talked almost nonstop. She seemed to know everything that was going on in town. Not because of her supposed abilities—and she admitted as much—but because information passed through small towns like prune juice through an infant. In a lull, Jeremy glanced at his watch.

'I suppose you need to be going,' Doris said.

He reached for the recorder and shut it off. 'Probably. I wanted to swing by the library before it closes.'

'Well, lunch was on me. It's not often that we have a famous visitor come by.'

'Thanks,' he said.

She stood up and began leading him from the restaurant. 'I assume you're staying at Greenleaf Cottages?' When Jeremy nodded, she went on.

'Do you know where they are? They're kind of out in the back country.'

'I have a map,' Jeremy said. 'I'm sure I can find it. But how about directions to the library?'

'Sure,' Doris said, 'that's just around the corner.' She motioned up the road. 'Do you see the brick building there?'

Jeremy nodded.

'Take a left and go through the next stop sign. At the first street after that, turn right. The library's on the corner just up the way. It's a big white building. Used to belong to Horace Middleton, before the county bought it.'

Jeremy held out his hand. 'Thank you. Lunch was delicious.'

'Anytime you want to talk, just come by. I'm always available. But I will ask that you don't write anything that makes us look like a bunch of bumpkins. A lot of people—me included—love this place.'

'All I write is the truth.'

'I know,' she said. 'That's why I contacted you. You have a trustworthy face, and I'm sure you'll put the legend to bed once and for all in the way it should be done.'

Jeremy raised his eyebrows. 'You don't think there are ghosts out at Cedar Creek?'

'Oh, heavens no.'

Jeremy looked at her curiously. 'Then why did you ask me to come down?'

'Because people don't know what's going on, and they'll keep believing until they find an explanation. You see, ever since that article in the paper about the people from Duke, the mayor has been promoting the idea like crazy, and strangers have been coming from all over hoping to see the lights. It's causing a lot of problems—the place is already crumbling and the damage is getting worse. Nearly everyone around here except me thinks that promoting the ghosts is a good idea. Ever since the textile mill and the mine closed, the town's been drying up, and they think of this idea as some sort of salvation.'

Jeremy glanced towards his car, then back to Doris. 'You do realise you're changing your story from what you wrote in the letter.'

'No,' she said, 'I'm not. All I said was that there were mysterious lights in the cemetery that were credited to an old legend, that most people think ghosts are involved, and that the kids from Duke couldn't figure out what the lights really were. All that's true.'

'So why do you want me to discredit the story?'

'Because it's not right,' she said. 'People traipsing through, tourists camping out—it's just not very respectful for the departed. And combining it with something worthy like the Historic Homes Tour is just plain old wrong.'

Jeremy shifted from one foot to the other. 'If you believe that you can divine water and the sex of babies, it just seems—'

'Like I'd be the first to believe in ghosts?'

Jeremy nodded.

'I do. I just don't believe they're in the cemetery. I've been out there, and I don't feel the presence of spirits.'

'So you can do that, too?'

She shrugged without answering. 'One day, you're going to learn something that can't be explained with science. And when that happens, your life's going to change.'

He smiled. 'Is that a promise?'

'Yes,' she said, 'it is.' She paused, looking him in the eye. 'And I have to say that I really enjoyed our lunch. It isn't often that I have the company of such a charming young man.'

'I had a wonderful time, too.'

He turned to leave. The clouds had drifted in while they'd been eating and Jeremy tugged at his collar as he made his way to the car.

'Mr Marsh?' Doris called out.

Jeremy turned back. 'Yes?'

'Say hi to Lex for me.'

'Lex?'

'Yeah,' she said. 'At the reference desk in the library. That's who you should ask for.'

THE LIBRARY turned out to be a massive Gothic structure, completely different from any other building in town. It occupied most of the block and its two storeys were adorned with tall, narrow windows, a sharply angled roof and an arched wooden front door. A friendly, carved sign with italicised gold script welcomed all to *Boone Creek Library*.

In the cheerfully lit, pale yellow foyer sat an L-shaped desk. Jeremy saw a large glassed-in room devoted to children, and to the right was what appeared to be the main area. He nodded and waved to the elderly woman behind the desk, who smiled and waved back before returning to the book she was reading. Jeremy pushed through heavy glass doors to the main area, where he felt a surge of disappointment. Beneath bright fluorescent lights were only six shelves of books, in a room that wasn't much larger than his apartment. He saw only three people browsing the shelves, including one elderly man with a hearing aid who was stacking books on the shelves.

He made his way to the reference desk, but there wasn't anyone behind it. He paused at the desk, waiting for Lex. Turning round to lean against it, he figured Lex must be the white-haired man putting the books away. Jeremy nodded and waved, making sure the man knew he needed help, but instead of moving towards him, the man waved and nodded in return before going back to stacking books. No doubt he was trying to stay ahead of the rush. Southern efficiency was legendary, Jeremy observed.

IN THE SMALL, cluttered office on the upper floor of the library, she stared through the window. She'd known he would be coming. Doris had called the moment he left Herbs and told her about the man in black from New York City who was here to write about the ghosts in the cemetery.

She shook her head. She'd read Mr Marsh's stories before and knew how he operated. It wouldn't be enough to prove that ghosts weren't involved. He'd interview people in his own way, get them to open up, and then he'd twist the truth in whatever way he wanted. Once he was finished, people around the country would assume that everyone who lived here was gullible, foolish and superstitious.

Oh, no. She didn't like the fact that he was here at all.

She absently twirled strands of her dark hair between her fingers. The thing was, she didn't like people traipsing through the cemetery, either. Doris was right: it was disrespectful. Those lights had been around for decades, so why was it suddenly so important to increase tourism around here? People didn't live in Boone Creek because they wanted to get rich. Well, most of them, anyway. There were always a few people out to make a buck, beginning with the mayor. But most people lived here for the same reason she did: because of the awe she felt when the setting sun turned the Pamlico River to a golden yellow ribbon, because she knew and trusted her neighbours, because people could let their kids run around at night without worrying that something bad would happen to them.

She loved everything about the town: the smell of pine and salt on early spring mornings, the sultry summer evenings that made her skin glisten, the fiery glow of autumn leaves. But most of all, she loved the people and couldn't imagine living anywhere else. Of course, a number of her friends hadn't felt the same way, and after heading off to college, they'd never returned. She, too, had moved away for a while, but she'd always known she would come back. And she also knew she would be the librarian, just as her mother had been, in the hope of making the library something that would make the town proud.

No, it wasn't the most glamorous job, nor did it pay much. The library was a work in progress, but first impressions were deceptive. The ground floor housed contemporary fiction only, while the top floor held classic fiction and nonfiction. She doubted whether Mr Marsh even realised the library was dispersed through both storeys, since the stairs were accessed in the rear of the building, through the children's room.

Her office was upstairs. A small room next to hers contained the rare titles, books she'd accumulated through estate and garage sales, donations, and visits to dealers throughout the state, a project her mother had started. She also had a growing collection of historic manuscripts and maps. This was her passion. She was always on the lookout for something special, and her library was regarded as one of the best small libraries in the state.

And that's how she viewed it now. *Her* library, like this was *her* town. And right now a stranger was waiting for her, a stranger who wanted to write a story that just might not be good for *her* people.

Oh, she'd seen him drive up, all right. Seen him get out of the car and head round to the front. She'd recognised the confident city swagger almost immediately. He was just another in a long line of people visiting from someplace more exotic, people who believed that life could be more exciting, more fulfilling, if only you moved away. A few years ago, she'd fallen for someone who believed such things, and she refused to be taken in by such ideas again.

OK, she decided, she should probably go and talk to Mr Marsh from New York. Southern hospitality—as well as her job—required her to help him find what he needed. More important, though, she might be able to keep an eye on him.

Yes, she could handle Mr Marsh. And, besides, she had to admit that he was rather good-looking, even if he couldn't be trusted.

JEREMY MARSH looked almost bored. He was pacing one of the aisles. Every now and then he frowned, as if wondering why he couldn't find anything by Dickens or Chaucer. If he asked about it, she wondered how he would react if she responded with 'Who?' He'd probably stare at her all tongue-tied like he had when she saw him earlier in the cemetery. Men, she thought. Always predictable.

'I suppose you're looking for me,' she announced, forcing a tight smile.

Jeremy glanced up at the sound of her voice and, for a moment, he seemed frozen in place. Then all at once he smiled as recognition set in. His dimple was cute, but the smile was a little too practised. 'You're Lex?' he asked.

'It's short for "Lexie". Lexie Darnell. It's what Doris calls me.'

'You're the librarian?'

'When I'm not hanging out in cemeteries and ignoring staring men, I try to be.'

'Well, I'll be,' he said, trying to drawl the words like Doris had.

She smiled and moved past him to straighten a few books. 'Your accent doesn't cut it, Mr Marsh,' she said. 'You sound like you're trying out letters for a crossword puzzle.'

He laughed easily. 'You think so?' he asked.

Definitely a ladies' man, she thought.

'I know so.' She continued straightening the books. 'Now, what can I help you with? I suppose you're looking for information on the cemetery?'

'My reputation precedes me.'

'Doris called to tell me you were on the way.'

'Ah,' he said. 'She's an interesting woman.'

'She's my grandmother.'

Jeremy's eyebrows shot up. L-I-B, he thought, keeping it to himself this time.

She tucked her hair behind her ear and faced him, keeping her tone steady. 'What type of information were you looking for?'

He shrugged. 'Anything that might help me with the history of the cemetery. When the lights started. Any stories that mention the legends. Old maps. Information on Riker's Hill and the topography. Things like that.' He paused, studying those violet eyes again. 'I have to say, it's kind of amazing, isn't it?' he asked.

She stared at him. 'Excuse me?'

'Seeing you at the cemetery and now here. Your grandmother's letter, which brought me down here. It's quite a coincidence, don't you think?'

'I can't say I've given it much thought.'

Jeremy was not to be deterred. 'Well, since I'm not from around here, maybe you could tell me what people do for relaxation in these parts. I mean, is there a place to get some coffee? Or a bite to eat?' He paused. 'Like maybe a little later, after you're off?'

She blinked. 'Are you asking me out?' she asked.

'Only if you're available.'

'I think,' she said, regaining her composure, 'I'll have to pass. But thank you for the offer.'

'OK, fair enough,' he said, his tone easy. 'But you can't blame a guy for trying.' He smiled, the dimple flashing. 'Now, would it be possible to get started with the research? I was hoping I might read the article that appeared in the local paper.'

She nodded. 'It'll probably be on the microfiche.' She started to walk towards the foyer. 'You'll find what you need upstairs.'

Jeremy had to step quickly to catch up with her. 'Do you mind if I ask you a question?'

She opened the main door and hesitated. 'Not at all,' she said.

'Why were you in the cemetery today? I got the impression that few people head out there these days.'

She said nothing and, in the silence, Jeremy grew uncomfortable.

'Aren't you going to say anything?' he asked.

She smiled and winked before moving through the open doorway. 'I said you could ask. I didn't say I would answer.'

All Jeremy could do was stare. She was something, wasn't she? Confident and beautiful and charming all at once.

They made their way through the foyer, past the children's reading room, and Lexie led him up the stairs. Pausing at the top, Jeremy looked around.

L-I-B, he thought again. With oak-panelled walls and mahogany flooring, the cavernous, open room stood in stark contrast to the area downstairs. Along the far wall was a stone fireplace with a painting hung above it, and the windows, narrow though they were, offered just enough sunlight to give the place an almost homely feel.

'Now I understand,' Jeremy observed. 'Downstairs was just the appetiser. This is where the real action is.'

She nodded. 'Most of our daily visitors come in for recent titles by authors they know, so I set up the area downstairs for their convenience. The room downstairs is small because it used to be our offices before we had it converted.'

'Where are the offices now?'

'Over there,' she said, pointing behind the far shelf. 'Next to the rare-book room.'

'Wow,' he said. 'I'm impressed.'

She smiled. 'Come on—I'll show you around.'

For the next few minutes, they chatted as they meandered among the shelves. Lexie paused in front of a few lamps to turn them on. A yellowish glow spread through the room. As she leaned over, he caught a trace of her perfume.

Jeremy motioned to the portrait above the fireplace. 'Who's this?'

Lexie paused, following his gaze. 'My mother,' she said.

Jeremy looked at her questioningly.

'After the original library burned to the ground in 1964, my mother found a new building and began a new collection. She was only twenty-two, but she lobbied officials for funds, she held bake sales, went door-to-door, pleading. It took years, but she finally did it.'

As she spoke, Jeremy found himself glancing from Lexie to the portrait and back again. There was, he thought, a resemblance. Especially the eyes.

When Lexie finished her story, she tucked a loose strand of hair behind her ear. She seemed to do that a lot. Probably a nervous habit. Which meant that he was making her nervous. He considered that a good sign.

Jeremy cleared his throat. 'She sounds like a fascinating woman,' he said. 'I'd love to meet her.'

Lexie's smile flickered slightly and she shook her head. 'I'm sorry,' she said. 'I suppose I've rambled on long enough.' She nodded towards the rare-book room. 'I may as well show you where you'll be cooped up for the next few days.'

'You think it'll take that long? There aren't that many books to peruse, are there?'

'It's not just books. You'll find some of the information you're looking for in the diaries. I've collected as many as I can from people who lived in the area. I even have one by someone who viewed himself as an amateur historian. You can't check them out of the library, though, and it'll take some time to get through them.'

'I can't wait,' he said. 'I *live* for tedious research.'

She smiled. 'I bet you're quite good at it, Mr Marsh.'

'Jeremy,' he said. 'Call me Jeremy.'

She raised an eyebrow. 'I'm not sure that's such a good idea.'

'Oh, it's a great idea,' he said. 'Trust me.'

She snorted. Always on the make, this one. 'It's tempting,' she said. 'But I don't know you well enough to trust you, Mr Marsh.'

Jeremy watched with amusement as she turned away, thinking that he'd met her type before. Women who used wit to keep men at a distance usually had a sharp edge to them, but somehow with her it came across as . . . well, charming. And it wasn't just the accent. Or even her startling eyes and the way she looked in jeans. That was part of it, but there was more. It was . . . what?

He was here to write an article, but with a sudden sinking sensation, he realised that he'd rather spend the next few hours with Lexie. She was mysterious, and he liked mysteries. As he followed her towards the rare-book room, he couldn't help but think that his trip down South had just become a lot more interesting.

THE RARE-BOOK ROOM was small, divided by a low wooden wall that ran from one side to the other. Behind the wall were tall shelves of books. Opposite the door was a window with an antique roll-top desk beneath it. A small table with a microfiche machine stood just off to Jeremy's right, and Lexie motioned towards it. Going to the roll-top desk, she opened the bottom drawer, then returned with a small cardboard box.

Setting the box on the table, she riffled through the transparent plates and pulled one out. Leaning over him, she turned the machine on and slid the transparency in, and again he caught a trace of her perfume. A moment later, the article was in front of him.

'You can start with this,' she said. 'I'm going to look around to see if I can find some more material for you.'

Jeremy turned his attention to the article but learned very little that was new. The story covered the original legend, describing it in much the same way that Doris had, albeit with some minor variations. But all legends were like that: stories got passed around and altered slightly to make them more compelling.

Jeremy glanced over his shoulder. No sign of Lexie.

Looking back at the screen, he figured he might as well add to what Doris had told him about Boone Creek. He moved the glass-plate housing of the microfiche, watching as other articles popped into view. He read about a young man who landscaped the front of the Veterans of Foreign Wars building to earn the right to be an Eagle Scout, a new dry-cleaner opening on Main Street, and a recap of a town meeting.

The town was just what he expected. Sleepy and quiet, the kind of place that continued to exist more as a result of habit than any unique quality and that would fade from existence in coming decades as the population aged.

'Reading about our exciting town?' she asked.

He jumped, surprised he hadn't heard her come up behind him. 'I am.'

'Here,' she said, setting a stack of books beside him. 'These should get you started. And I found a book of ghost stories that you might find interesting. There's a chapter in there that discusses Cedar Creek. I'll be back in a while to see if there's anything else you need.'

'You're not going to stay?'

'No. I've got work to do. And keep in mind that even though the library is open until seven, the rare-book room closes at five.'

'Even for friends?'

'No. I let them stay as long as they want.'

'So I'll see you at seven?'

'No, Mr Marsh. I'll see you at five.' She took a couple of steps towards the door.

'Lexie?'

She turned. 'Yes?'

'You've been a great help so far. Thank you.'

She gave a lovely, unguarded smile. 'You're welcome.'

Jeremy spent the next couple of hours perusing information on the town. He thumbed through the books one by one, lingering over the photographs and reading sections he thought appropriate.

Most of the information covered the early history of the town, and he jotted what he thought were relevant notes on the pad beside him. He learned that the cemetery had been used for more than a hundred years without any sightings of mysterious lights. That lights first appeared about a hundred years ago and occurred regularly, but only when it was foggy. That many people had seen them, which meant that the lights were unlikely to be simply a figment of the imagination. And that the cemetery was sinking.

He learned that Boone Creek had been founded in 1729 and that for a long time it was nothing more than a tiny trading village on the banks of the Pamlico River. Towards the end of the nineteenth century the railroad boom hit North Carolina and forests were levelled while numerous quarries were dug. After that, the town tended to boom and bust along with the economy of the rest of the state. In the most recent census, the population of the county had actually dropped, which didn't surprise him in the slightest.

He also read the account of the cemetery in the book of ghost stories. The writer had added a postscript stating that the Cedar Creek Cemetery had begun to sink. The book had been written in 1954, and, by the way the cemetery looked now, Jeremy figured it had sunk even more since then.

Still, as he absorbed the information, he couldn't help glancing over his shoulder from time to time on the off chance that Lexie had returned.

ACROSS TOWN, on the fairway of the fourteenth hole and with his cellphone sandwiched against his ear, the mayor snapped to attention as he listened to the caller through the hissing static. 'He was at Herbs? Today? Did you say *Primetime Live*?'

The mayor pretended not to notice that his golf buddy, who was in turn pretending to see where his most recent shot had landed, had just kicked the ball from behind a tree into a better position.

'Found it!' his buddy yelled.

The mayor's buddy did things like that all the time, which frankly didn't bother the mayor, since he'd just done the same thing.

'Well, this is interesting,' the mayor said, his mind whirring with possibilities, 'and I'm glad you called. You take care, now. Bye.'

He flipped the phone closed just as his buddy was approaching.

'I hope I get a good lie with that one.'

'I wouldn't worry too much,' the mayor said, pondering the sudden development in town. 'I'm sure it'll end up being right where you want it.'

'Who was that on the phone?'

'Fate,' he announced. 'And if we play this right, maybe our salvation.'

TWO HOURS LATER, Lexie poked her head into the rare-book room. 'How'd it go?'

Glancing over his shoulder, Jeremy smiled. Pushing back from the desk, he ran his hand through his hair. 'Good,' he said. 'I learned quite a bit.'

'I'm glad. But as I said, I usually lock up about five o'clock.'

Jeremy stood up. 'No problem. I'm getting tired, anyway.'

'You'll be in tomorrow morning, right?'

'I was planning on it. Why?'

'Well, normally, I put everything back on the shelves daily.'

'Would it be possible to just keep the stack the way it is, for now? I'm sure I'll go through most of the books again.'

She thought for a moment. 'OK. But if you don't show up first thing, I'll think I misjudged you.'

He nodded. 'I won't stand you up. I'm not that kind of guy.'

She rolled her eyes, thinking, Oh, brother. 'I'm sure you say that to all the girls, Mr Marsh.'

'No,' he said, leaning against the desk. 'Actually, I'm very shy.'

She shrugged. 'Shows me what I know. Being that you're a journalist from the big city, I had you figured as a ladies' man.'

'First impressions can be deceiving.'

'Oh, I realised that right away.'

'You did?'

'Sure,' she said. 'When I first bumped into you at the cemetery, I thought you were there for a funeral.'

THREE

Fifteen minutes later, after heading down an asphalt road that gave way to yet another gravel road—they were fond of gravel round here—Jeremy found himself parking his car in the middle of a swamp, in front of a hand-painted sign advertising GREENLEAF COTTAGES. Which reminded him never to trust the promises of the local chamber of commerce.

Modern, it definitely wasn't. It wouldn't have been modern thirty years ago. In all, there were six small bungalows set along the river. With peeling paint, plank walls and tin roofs, they were reached by following small dirt pathways that led from a central bungalow that he assumed to be the main office. Debating whether he should even check in, he heard the sound of an engine coming up the road and watched as a maroon Cadillac came rolling towards him, spewing up stones as it slid to a stop beside his own car.

An overweight, balding man burst from the door, dressed in green polyester trousers and a blue turtleneck sweater.

'Mr Marsh?'

Jeremy was taken aback. 'Yes?'

The man scurried round the car. 'I'm glad I caught you! I can't tell you how excited we all are about your visit here! I'm Mayor Tom Gherkin. Like the pickle, but you can call me Tom.' He laughed. 'I just wanted to welcome you to our fine town. I came straight from the golf course once I learned you were here.'

Jeremy looked him over. At least it explained the clothes. 'You're the mayor?'

'Have been since '94. It's kind of a family tradition. My daddy, Owen Gherkin, was the mayor for twenty-four years. Knew everything there was to know about this place. Of course, being the mayor is only a part-time job here. I'm more of a businessman. I own the department store and radio station downtown. Oldies. You like oldies?'

'Sure,' Jeremy said.

He laughed. 'I figured as much from the moment I laid eyes on you. I said to myself, "That's a man who appreciates good music." Well, like I said, I can't tell you how thrilled we all are that you're here to write a story about our fine town. It's got people real excited around here. First the folks from Duke, then the local paper. And now a big-city journalist.'

Jeremy shook his head. 'How did you know I was here?'

Mayor Gherkin laid a friendly hand on his shoulder, and almost before Jeremy realised it, they were moving towards the office. 'Word gets around, Mr Marsh. Part of the charm of this place. That, and the natural beauty. We've got some of the best fishing and duck hunting in the state, you know. Folks come from all over, and most of 'em stay right here at Greenleaf. Your own quiet bungalow, out here in the middle of nature. I'll bet it makes you see those hotels in New York in a whole new light.'

'That it does,' Jeremy admitted.

Mayor Gherkin looked around. 'So, Jeremy . . . you don't mind if I call you Jeremy?'

'No.'

'That's mighty kind of you. So, Jeremy, I was wondering if you think one of those television shows might follow up on your story here.'

'I have no idea,' he said.

'Well, if they do, we'd roll out the red carpet. Why, we'd put 'em up right here at Greenleaf, free of charge. And, of course, they'd have a whale of a story to tell.'

'You do realise that I'm primarily a columnist? Normally, I have nothing to do with television . . .'

'No, of course not.' Mayor Gherkin winked, obviously in disbelief. 'You just do what you do, and we'll see what happens.'

A moment later, Mayor Gherkin pushed through the door of the office. The wood walls reminded Jeremy of what he might find in a log cabin. Just beyond the desk was a large-mouth bass mounted on the wall; in every corner and along the walls were stuffed critters: beavers, rabbits, squirrels, opossums. All had been mounted to make them appear as if they'd been cornered and were trying to defend themselves. The place was the Museum of Natural History transformed into a horror movie and squeezed into a closet.

Behind the desk, a huge, heavily bearded man sat with his feet propped up. Dressed in overalls and a plaid shirt, the man rose from behind the desk and grabbed a clipboard. He pointed to Jeremy and the clipboard. He looked as if he wanted nothing more than to pull Jeremy's arms from his body so he could use them to beat him before mounting him on the wall.

Gherkin laughed. 'Don't let him worry you none, Jeremy,' the mayor offered quickly. 'Jed here doesn't talk much to strangers. Just fill out the registration form, and you'll be on your way to your own room in paradise.'

Jeremy was staring wide-eyed at Jed.

'Not only does he own Greenleaf and serve on the town council, but he's the local taxidermist,' Gherkin went on. 'And, just so you know, the town will be happy to pay for your accommodations here.'

'That's not necessary . . .'

'Not a word,' he said, waiving the rebuff off. 'The decision's already been made by the higher-ups.' He winked. 'That's me, by the way. It's the least we can do for such a distinguished guest.'

ACROSS TOWN, in a blue-shuttered white bungalow, Doris was sautéing bacon, onions and garlic as a pot of pasta boiled on a nearby burner. Lexie was dicing tomatoes and carrots over the sink. After finishing at the library, she'd swung by Doris's, as she normally did a few times a week. Though she had her own house nearby, she often had dinner at her grandmother's.

Neither had said much. For Doris, the reason was her long day at work. For Lexie, the reason was Jeremy Marsh. Doris had always taken an acute interest in her personal life and Lexie had learned that it was best to avoid the topic whenever possible. She knew her grandmother meant no harm. Doris simply didn't understand why someone in her thirties hadn't settled down yet. Doris was from the old school; she married at twenty and stayed with a man she adored until he passed away three years ago. Lexie's grandparents had raised her, after all, and Lexie knew what Doris thought: it was time for her to meet a nice guy and settle down.

Lexie sometimes wished for that as well. But she wanted to meet the right guy first, someone who inspired her. That was where she and Doris differed. Doris seemed to think that a decent, moral man with a good job was all a woman should reasonably expect. Lexie didn't want to settle for someone simply because he was kind and decent and had a good job. Maybe she had unrealistic expectations, but Lexie wanted to feel passion. She wanted a man who was both sensitive and kind, but at the same time could sweep her off her feet. Someone romantic, the kind of guy who would buy her flowers for no reason at all.

It wasn't too much to ask, was it?

Doris, of course, had a ready answer. 'Trust me, honey, that passes after the first couple of years.' Yet Lexie's grandfather was one of those naturally romantic men. Until the very end, he would open the car door for Doris and hold her hand when they walked through town. He clearly adored her and would often comment on how lucky he was to have met a woman like her. After he passed on, part of Doris had begun to die as well. First the heart attack, now worsening arthritis; it was as if they'd always been meant to be together. Had Doris simply been lucky in meeting a man like him? Or had she seen something in her husband beforehand, something that confirmed he was the right one for her?

More important, why on earth was Lexie even thinking about marriage?

Probably because she was here at Doris's house, the house she'd grown up in after her parents had died. Of course, she'd always imagined that she would have a family of her own by now, but it hadn't worked out. Two relationships had come close: there was the long relationship with Avery, which had begun in college, and after that, another involving a young man from Chicago who was visiting his cousin in Boone Creek one summer.

He was the classic Renaissance man: he spoke four languages, spent a year studying at the London School of Economics, and had paid his way through school with a baseball scholarship. Mr Renaissance was charming and exotic, and she'd fallen for him quickly, but she woke up one morning to learn that he was on his way back to Chicago. He never even bothered to say goodbye.

And after that? Not much, really, unless you counted Rodney Hopper, a deputy sheriff in town. They'd gone on a dozen or so dates, one every other month or so, whenever there was a local benefit that she was encouraged to attend. Like her, Rodney had been born and raised here. He'd been pining away for her since they were kids. But Rodney . . . well, he was a little too interested in fishing and hunting and lifting weights and not quite interested enough in books or anything going on in the rest of the world. He was a nice guy, though, and she figured he'd make a fine husband. But not for her.

So where did that leave her?

Here at Doris's, three times a week, waiting for the inevitable questions about her love life.

'So what did you think of him?' Doris asked.

Lexie smiled. 'Who?' she asked, playing innocent.

'Jeremy Marsh. I heard he spent hours at the library.'

Lexie shrugged. 'He seemed nice enough.'

Doris waited for Lexie to add more, but when she didn't, Doris sighed. 'Well, I liked him. He seemed like a perfect gentleman.'

'Oh, he was,' Lexie agreed.

'Was he charmed by your sparkling personality?'

'Why would that matter? He's only in town for a few days.'

'Did I ever tell you about the way I met your grandfather?'

'Many times,' Lexie said. They'd met on a train that was heading to Baltimore; he was on his way to interview for a job, one that he would never take, choosing to be with her instead.

'Then you know that you're most likely to meet someone when you least expect it.'

Lexie brought the salad bowl to the table. 'You don't have to worry about me. I'm happy. I love my job and I have good friends.'

'And don't forget you're blessed with me, too.'

'Of course,' Lexie affirmed. 'How could I forget that?'

Doris chuckled and went back to sautéing. 'I thought he was quite handsome,' she opined. 'And just to let you know, there's more to him than you think. He's not what you imagine him to be.'

It was the way she said it that gave Lexie pause. Doris sometimes sensed things, she knew. Even though Doris seldom explained further, Lexie was aware that she always sensed the truth.

COMPLETELY UNAWARE that phone lines were buzzing all over as people discussed his presence in town, Jeremy was lying in bed under the covers, watching the local news while waiting for the weather report. He was surrounded by Jed's handiwork. In his room, there were twelve critters, representatives of the entire zoological species of North Carolina.

Other than that, the room wasn't too bad, as long as he didn't expect a high-speed connection to the Internet or to warm the room without use of the fireplace. He should have asked where he could find some firewood. This place was freezing.

Just then the meteorologist appeared on the news. Jeremy had been wondering whether he should head out to the cemetery but wanted to find out if fog was likely. If not, he'd catch up on his rest. It had been a long day; he'd started out in the modern world and then had gone back in time fifty years. It certainly wasn't something that happened to him every day.

And, of course, there was Lexie. Lexie whatever-her-last-name-was. Lexie the mysterious. Lexie who flirted and withdrew and flirted again.

She *had* been flirting, hadn't she?

The meteorologist said the skies were expected to be clear throughout the evening. He mentioned nothing about the possibility of fog tomorrow, either.

Figures, he thought.

THE FOLLOWING MORNING, after showering in a lukewarm trickle of water, Jeremy slipped on a pair of jeans, a sweater and a brown leather jacket and made his way to Herbs, which seemed to be the most popular breakfast place in town. At the counter, he noticed Mayor Gherkin talking to a couple of men dressed in suits. Rachel was busy working the tables. Jed was seated on the far side of the room, looking like the back side of a mountain. Tully was sitting at a table with three other men and was doing most of the talking. As Jeremy wound his way through the tables, the mayor raised his coffee cup in salute.

'Well, good morning, Mr Marsh,' Mayor Gherkin called out.

Jeremy waved and nodded back, trying to avoid getting corralled into a conversation. He'd never been a morning person, and on top of that he hadn't slept well. He took a seat in the corner booth and Rachel moved to the table, carrying a pot of coffee.

'No funeral today?' she teased.

'No. I decided to go with a more casual look,' he explained.

'Coffee, darlin'?'

'Please.'

After flipping his cup, she filled it to the brim. 'Would you like the special this mornin'? A Carolina omelette.'

'Sure,' he said, having no idea what was in a Carolina omelette, but with his stomach growling, anything sounded good.

'Be back in a few minutes, darlin'.'

Jeremy began nursing his coffee while perusing yesterday's newspaper. All four pages of it. He glanced through the window, wondering why he'd even bothered with the local paper. There was a vending machine out front offering *USA Today* and he was reaching into his pocket to look for change when a uniformed deputy took a seat across the table from him.

The man looked angry. His biceps swelled the seams of his shirt and he wore mirrored sunglasses. In his mouth was a toothpick, which he moved from one side to the other. He said nothing, giving Jeremy plenty of time to study his own reflection.

'Can I help you?' Jeremy asked.

The toothpick moved from side to side again.

'Jeremy Marsh?' the officer intoned.

Above the officer's breast pocket, Jeremy noticed a shiny bar with the name engraved on it. 'And you must be Sheriff Hopper?'

'*Deputy* Hopper,' he corrected.

'Sorry,' Jeremy said. 'Have I done something wrong, Officer?'

'I don't know,' Hopper said. 'Have you?'

'Not that I know of.'

Deputy Hopper moved the toothpick again. 'You planning to stick around for a while?'

'Just for a week or so. I'm here to write an article—'

'I know why you're here,' Hopper interrupted. 'I like to visit with strangers who are planning to hang around for a while.'

He put the emphasis on the word 'strangers', making Jeremy feel it was some sort of crime.

'I hear you intend to spend a lot of time at the library?'

'Well . . . I guess I might—'

'Mmm,' the deputy rumbled, cutting him off again.

Jeremy reached for his coffee cup and took a sip, buying time. 'I'm sorry, Deputy Hopper, but I'm not exactly sure what's going on here.'

'Now, you're not hassling our guest, are you, Rodney?' the mayor called out from across the room.

Deputy Hopper didn't turn his gaze from Jeremy. 'Just visiting, Mayor.'

'Let the man enjoy his breakfast,' Gherkin chided. 'Come on over, Jeremy. I've got a couple of people I'd like you to meet.'

Deputy Hopper scowled as Jeremy rose from the table and made his way to the mayor, who introduced him to the county lawyer and a heavyset physician. The mayor was going on about how exciting Jeremy's visit was for the town. 'Might even end up on *Primetime Live*,' he said.

'Really?' the lawyer said.

Jeremy shifted his weight from one foot to the other. 'Well, as I was trying to explain to the mayor yesterday—'

'And speaking of the town,' the mayor added, 'I'd like to invite you to a little dinner this evening with a few friends. Some of the people have seen those ghosts and you'll have the chance to pick their brains.'

When Jeremy hesitated, it was all the mayor needed to conclude. 'Say about seven o'clock?' he said.

'Yeah . . . sure. I guess that's fine,' Jeremy agreed.

'I'll let you know where the dinner's going to be. You'll be at the library, right?'

'Probably.'

Before the conversation went any further, Rachel came by, just a little too close. Holding a plate, she nudged Jeremy. 'Come on, darlin'. I've got your breakfast.'

Jeremy followed her back to the table. Thankfully, Deputy Hopper was gone and Jeremy slid into his seat.

Rachel set the plate in front of him. 'I told 'em to make it extra special, since you're visiting from New York City. I've always wanted to go there. It seems so . . . glamorous and exciting.'

'You should go. It's like nowhere else in the world.'

She smiled. 'Why, Mr Marsh . . . is that an invitation?'

Jeremy's jaw dropped. Huh?

'Well, I just might want to take you up on that,' she twittered. 'And I'd be glad to show you 'round the cemetery, any night you'd like to go. I'm usually finished here by three o'clock.'

'I'll keep that in mind,' Jeremy mumbled.

Over the next twenty minutes, as he ate, Rachel came by a dozen times, refilling his coffee cup, smiling at him unrelentingly. Jeremy wasn't sure eating at Herbs was worth it, even if the food was great. Small-town USA was way too much to deal with before coffee. Tomorrow would be coffee elsewhere. And not from Tully's service station, either. He didn't want to get stuck in a conversation when he had other things to do.

Good Lord, he thought, I'm already thinking like a local.

LEXIE FOUND HERSELF glancing out of the window when Jeremy Marsh pulled into the library parking lot.

Jeremy Marsh. Who'd continued to creep into her thoughts. And just look at him now. Trying to dress more casually to blend in. And somehow he'd almost pulled it off.

But enough of that. She had work to do. The budget was due at the end of the month, she had a stack of publishers' catalogues to go through, and she had to get everything set for the Historic Homes Tour—of which the library was a part, since at one point it was a historic home. But no matter how hard she'd tried to squelch it, her mind kept wandering back to Jeremy Marsh. She didn't want to think about him, but Doris had said enough to pique her curiosity.

He's not what you imagine him to be.

What was that supposed to mean? Last night, when she'd pressed, Doris had clammed up. Instead, they'd circled the topic: what happened at work, how the Historic Homes Tour was shaping up for the weekend. As her grandmother rambled on, Lexie kept thinking about her pronouncement.

He's not what you imagine him to be.

And what might that be? A big-city type? Someone in search of a quick fling? Someone who would make fun of the town the moment he left? And why on earth did she care? He was here for a few days, and then he'd be gone and everything would return to normal.

Oh, she'd already heard the gossip this morning. A couple of women talked about how he was going to make the town famous, how things might get better around here businesswise. They offered opinions as to whether he'd find the source of the mysterious lights.

Some people here, after all, actually believed they were caused by ghosts. But others clearly didn't. Mayor Gherkin, for instance. If Jeremy Marsh couldn't find the cause, it would be good for the town's economy, and that's what the mayor was betting on. After all, Mayor Gherkin knew something that only a few others knew.

People had been studying the mystery for years. Not just the students from Duke. At least two other outside groups or individuals had investigated the claim in the past without success. Mayor Gherkin had actually invited the students from Duke to pay the cemetery a visit, in the hope that they wouldn't figure it out, either. And, sure enough, tourist traffic had been picking up ever since.

She supposed she could have mentioned that to Mr Marsh yesterday. But since he hadn't asked, she hadn't offered. She was too busy trying to ward off his advances and make it clear she wasn't interested in him. Oh, he'd tried to be charming—well, OK, he *was* sort of charming in his own way— but that didn't change the fact that she had no intention of letting her emotions get the better of her.

And then Doris had made that ridiculous comment, which essentially meant that she thought Lexie *should* get to know him better. But what really burned her was that she knew Doris wouldn't have said anything unless she was certain. Sometimes she hated Doris's premonitions.

As she pondered, she heard her office door open with a squeak.

'Good morning,' Jeremy said. 'I thought I saw a light on.'

Swivelling in her chair, she noticed that he'd draped his jacket over his shoulder. 'Hey there.' She nodded politely. 'I was just trying to catch up on some work.'

'I like your filing system,' he said, gesturing at the piles of paperwork on the desk. 'I've got one just like it at home.'

A smile escaped her lips as he took a step towards her desk and looked out of the window.

'Nice view, too. Why, you can see all the way to the next house. And the parking lot, as well.'

'Well, you seem to be in a spunky mood this morning.'

'How can I not be? I slept in a freezing room filled with dead animals. Or rather, barely slept at all. And then this morning. Half the town was at breakfast.'

'I take it you went to Herbs,' she remarked.

'I did,' he said. 'I noticed you weren't there.'

'I like a little quiet time to start the day.'

'You should have warned me.'

She smiled. 'You should have asked.'

He laughed, and Lexie motioned towards the door. Walking to the rare-book room, he asked, 'Would you happen to know a Deputy Hopper?'

She looked over in surprise. 'Rodney?'

'He seemed a little perturbed by my presence here in town.'

'Oh, he's harmless. He probably heard that you'd be spending time at the library. He's kind of protective when it comes to things like that. He's been sweet on me for years.'

'Put in a good word for me, will you?'

'I suppose I could do that. Just don't do anything to make me take it back.'

They continued in silence to the rare-book room. She led the way inside, flicking on the light. 'I've been thinking about your project, and there's something you should probably know,' she said. She told him about the two previous investigations into the cemetery. 'If you give me a few minutes,' she added, 'I can dig them up for you.'

'I'd really appreciate that,' he said. 'But why didn't you mention them yesterday?'

She smiled without answering.

'Let me guess,' he said. 'Because I didn't ask?'

'I'm only a librarian, not a mind-reader.'

'Like your grandmother? Oh, wait, she's a diviner, right?'

'She is. And she can tell the sex of babies before they're born.'

'So I've heard,' Jeremy said.

Her eyes flashed. 'It's true, Jeremy. Whether or not you want to believe it, she can do those things.'

He grinned at her. 'Did you just call me Jeremy?'

'Yes. You did ask me to, remember?'

'I remember,' he said, '*Lexie*.'

'Don't push it,' she said, but she held his gaze just a little longer than usual, and he liked that. He liked that a lot.

FOUR

Jeremy spent the rest of the morning hunched over a stack of books and the two articles Lexie had found. The first was written in 1958 by a folklore professor at the University of North Carolina. The second, published in a 1969 issue of *Coastal Carolina*, reported the fact that the cemetery was sinking. The author also mentioned the legend and the proximity of Riker's Hill, and while he hadn't seen the lights, he speculated on a number of possibilities, all of which Jeremy was already aware of.

The first was rotting vegetation that sometimes bursts into flames, giving off vapours known as swamp gas. They could also be 'earthquake lights', which are electrical atmospheric charges generated by the shifting and grinding of rocks deep below the earth's crust. The car headlights theory was advanced, as was the idea of refracted starlight and fox fire, which is a phosphorescent glow emitted by certain fungi on rotting wood. The author even mentioned the possibility of the Novaya Zemlya effect, in which light beams are bent by adjacent layers of air at different temperatures, thus seeming to glow. And, in offering a final possibility, the author concluded that it might be St Elmo's fire, which is created during thunderstorms by electrical discharges from pointed objects.

In other words, the author said it could be anything.

However inconclusive, the articles did help Jeremy to clarify his own thoughts. In his opinion, the lights had everything to do with geography. The hill behind the cemetery was the highest point in any direction, and the sinking cemetery made the fog more dense in that particular area. All of which meant refracted or reflected light.

Going through the stack of books, he made notes regarding the changes in the town over the years. In the early twentieth century, there was a mini housing boom that lasted from 1907 to 1914, during which the north side of the town grew. The small port was widened in 1910, and again in 1916, and once more in 1922; combined with the quarries and phosphorus mines, excavation was extensive. The railroad was started in 1898, and a trestle bridge over the river was completed in 1904. From 1908 to 1915, three major factories were constructed: a textile mill, a phosphorus mine and a paper mill. Of the three, only the paper mill was still in operation.

He leaned back and glanced at the clock. Already it was nearly noon. A moment later, Lexie pushed through the door.

'Hey there,' she greeted him. 'How's it going? I was running out to grab lunch. Want me to bring you something back?'

He hesitated for only an instant.

'Would it be all right if I came with you? I'd love to stretch my legs. Maybe you could show me around. If that's OK, I mean.'

She almost said no, but she heard Doris's words. Despite her better judgment, she said, 'Sure. But I've only got an hour or so before I have to get back, so I don't know how much help I can be.'

He followed her out of the door. 'Anything at all is fine,' he said. 'It's important to know what goes on in a place like this.'

'In our little hick town, you mean?'

'I didn't say it was a hick town. Those are your words.'

'Yeah. But they're your thoughts, not mine. I love this place.'

'I'm sure,' he agreed. 'Why else would you live here?'

'Because it's not New York City, for one thing. I used to live in Manhattan. On West 69th.'

He almost stumbled in midstep. 'That's just a few blocks from where I live.'

She smiled. 'Small world, isn't it? Lived there with my boyfriend for almost a year while I interned in the NYU library.'

Jeremy was trying to fathom the thought of this small-town librarian living in his neighbourhood. Noticing his expression, she had to laugh. 'You're all alike, you know that?' she said.

'Who?'

'People who live in the city. You think that there's no place in the world as special as New York.'

'You're right,' Jeremy admitted. 'I mean, come on ... Greenleaf Cottages can't exactly compare to the Plaza, can it?'

She bristled at his smug attitude. 'People don't live in hotels,' she snapped. 'They live in communities. Where people know and care about each other.'

He raised his hands. 'Hey,' he said, 'I love communities. I lived in one growing up. I knew every family in my neighbourhood. New York City has that, too. Visit Park Slope in Brooklyn or Astoria in Queens, and you'll see kids hanging out in the parks, playing basketball and soccer, doing much the same as kids are doing here.'

'Like you've ever thought about things like that.'

'I have,' he said. 'If I had kids, I wouldn't live where I do. I have nephews and nieces who live in the city, and every one of them lives in a neighbourhood with lots of other kids and people watching out for them. In many ways, it's a lot like this place.'

She said nothing.

'Look,' he offered, 'I'm not trying to pick a fight. And besides, I'm not sure how we got on the subject of kids. All I was trying to say was that I was surprised that you lived in New York.' He paused. 'Truce?'

She stared at him before finally releasing her breath. Maybe he was right. And, she admitted, she'd been the one who escalated the whole thing. 'Truce,' she agreed. 'On one condition.'

'What's that?'

'You have to do the driving. I didn't bring a car.'

He looked relieved. 'Let me find my keys.'

Neither was particularly hungry, so Lexie directed Jeremy to a small grocery store, and they emerged with crackers, fresh fruit, and various cheeses.

In the car, Jeremy said, 'Riker's Hill. Is there a road that leads to the top?'

She nodded. 'But it's not much of a road.'

'No big deal. I'm getting used to bad roads around here.'

'OK,' she said, 'but don't say I didn't warn you.'

Neither said much as they headed out of town, past Cedar Creek Cemetery and over a bridge. The road was soon lined with ever-thickening groves of trees on both sides. The blue sky had given way to an expanse of grey, reminding Jeremy of winter afternoons much further north. Riker's Hill loomed off to the left.

Lexie told him to turn at the next intersection, which seemed to loop round towards the rear of Riker's Hill. Leaning forward in her seat, she peered through the windscreen.

'The turn is just up ahead,' she said, pointing.

She was right: it wasn't much of a road. Gravelled and rutted, kind of like the entrance to Greenleaf, but worse. As they neared the crest, the vegetation looked more weathered. Jeremy pulled over to the side and they stepped out of the car.

The air seemed colder up here, and the sky seemed closer. Down below, they could see the town, rooftops clustered together. Just beyond the town, the brackish river looked like flowing iron. He spotted both the highway bridge and the picturesque railroad trestle that rose behind it.

'The view is amazing,' he said finally.

Lexie pointed towards the edge of town. 'See that house over there? Kind of off to the side, near the pond? That's where I live now. And over there? That's Doris's place. It's where I grew up.'

He smiled. The breeze tossed her hair as she went on.

'As teenagers, my friends and I would sometimes come up here. During the summer, the heat makes the house lights twinkle, almost like stars. And the lightning bugs—well, there are so many in June that it almost looks like there's another town in the sky.'

She paused, realising that she felt strangely nervous. Though why she should be nervous was beyond her.

'I remember this one time when a big thunderstorm was expected. My friends and I got one of the boys to drive us up here in his truck. When the lightning started, it was beautiful at first. It would light up the sky, sometimes with a jagged flash, other times almost like a strobe light. Then the lightning started striking the trees around us. Gigantic bolts came down from the sky so close that the ground would tremble.'

As she spoke, Jeremy studied her. It was the most she'd said about herself since they'd met, and he tried to imagine what her life had been like back in high school. Even now, when she was lost in the memories, he wasn't quite able to put his finger on who she'd been.

'I'll bet you were terrified,' he said. 'Lightning bolts can reach fifty thousand degrees, you know.' He glanced at her. 'That's ten times hotter than the surface of the sun.'

She smiled, amused. 'I didn't know that. But you're right—I don't think I've ever been so terrified in my entire life.'

'So what happened?'

'The storm passed, as they always do. But I remember Rachel was holding my hand so hard she left fingernail marks in my skin.'

'Rachel? The waitress at Herbs?'

'Yeah, that's the one.' She looked over at him. 'Why? Did she put the move on you at breakfast this morning?'

He shifted from one foot to the other. 'Well, I wouldn't call it that. She just seemed a little . . . forward is all.'

Lexie laughed. 'It doesn't surprise me. She's . . . well, she's Rachel. She and I were best friends growing up. But after I went off to college and New York . . . well, it wasn't the same after I got back . . .'

She trailed off. Jeremy looked at her closely.

'You see the world differently these days?' he suggested.

She sighed. 'Yeah, I suppose that's it.'

'I think it happens to everyone as they grow up,' Jeremy responded. 'You find yourself moving on. It's perfectly normal.'

'I know. But in a town this size, there are only so many people in their thirties and even fewer who are still single.'

He nodded before breaking into a smile. 'Thirties?'

'Yep,' she said with a shrug. 'Getting old, I guess.'

'Or staying young,' he countered. 'Whenever I get worried about ageing, I just start wearing my trousers lower, flash the waistband of my boxers, wear my ball cap backwards, and walk around listening to rap.'

She giggled at the image. Despite the chill in the air, she felt warm with the recognition that she was enjoying his company. She wasn't sure she liked him yet—in fact, she was pretty sure she didn't—and for a moment, she struggled to reconcile the two feelings. Which meant, of course, that the whole subject should best be avoided. She brought a finger to her chin. 'Yes, I can see that. You do seem to regard personal style as important.'

'Without a doubt. Why, just yesterday people were particularly impressed with my wardrobe, including you.'

She laughed, and in the ensuing silence, she glanced at him. 'I'll bet you travel a lot for your job, don't you?' she asked.

'Maybe four or five trips a year, each lasting a couple of weeks.'

'Have you ever been in a town like this?'

'No,' he said, 'not really. Every place I go has its own charms, but I can say with all honesty that I've never been to a place like this. How about you? Other than New York, I mean.'

'I've been to the University of North Carolina, in Chapel Hill, and spent a lot of time in Raleigh. But I've never been overseas or anything like that.'

Even as she spoke, she knew how small her life would seem to him. Jeremy, as if reading her mind, flashed a hint of a smile.

'You'd like Europe. The cathedrals, the gorgeous countryside, the bistros. The relaxed lifestyle . . . you'd fit right in.'

Lexie dipped her eyes. It was a nice thought, but . . .

Why on earth was he telling her all this, anyway? To show her that he was more cosmopolitan than she was? Well, I hate to break it to you, she thought, but I already know that.

And yet, even as she digested those thoughts, another voice piped in, telling her that he was trying to flatter her. He seemed to be saying that he knew she was different, more worldly, than he'd expected her to be. That she could fit in anywhere.

Oh, he was difficult to resist, this Mr Jeremy Marsh. Well travelled but still grounded; worldly but still cognisant of the things that mattered. She had no doubt that he had an innate ability to make others—especially women—feel as if he was in kinship with them. Which, of course, led directly back to her first impression of him.

'Maybe I'm a romantic,' he said, glancing over at her.

'You know what I liked about New York?' she asked, changing the subject.

He watched her expectantly.

'There was always something happening, people hurrying down the sidewalks and cabs buzzing by, no matter what time it was. There was always someplace to go. It was exciting.'

'Why didn't you stay?'

'It wasn't the place for me. I went there to be with someone.'

'Ah,' Jeremy said. 'So you'd followed him up there?'

She nodded. 'We met in college. He'd grown up in Greensboro, was intelligent and really handsome, too. He looked my way, and the next thing I knew, I was following him up to the city. Everything was great for a year or so. We were even engaged.'

She seemed lost in thought before she let out a deep breath. 'I took an internship at the NYU library, Avery went to work on Wall Street, and then one day I found him in bed with one of his coworkers. It kind of made me realise that he wasn't the right guy, so I packed up and came back here. I never saw him again.'

The breeze picked up, sounding almost like a whistle as it rushed up the slopes. 'Are you hungry?' she asked.

'I'm starved,' he said.

They made their way back to the car and divided up the lunch.

'So you came back and worked at the library, and . . .'

'That's it,' she said. 'That's what I've been doing for the last seven years.'

'Well . . . you sound like you're happy,' he said.

'I am,' she was quick to agree. 'Aren't you?'

'Most of the time. Every now and then I go nuts, but I think that's normal.'

'And that's when you start wearing your trousers low?'

'Exactly,' he said with a smile. 'Would you mind if I asked a personal question? When we first got here, you pointed out your grandmother's house. And you said you'd grown up there.'

She nodded. 'I did.'

'Why?'

She looked out of the window; habit made her search out the highway that led out of town. When she spotted it, she spoke slowly.

'My parents were coming back from Buxton, on the Outer Banks. That was where they got married. My grandparents owned a beach cottage there. My mom swore that it was the most beautiful place in the world. It was their little escape. There's a beautiful lighthouse that you can see from the porch, and every now and then, I head out there, too, just like they used to, just to get away from it all.'

Her lips formed the tiniest of half-smiles before she went on. 'But, anyway, on their way back that night, the best guess is that my dad fell asleep at the wheel and the car went off the bridge. By the time the police dredged it out, they were both dead.'

Jeremy was quiet for a long moment. 'That's terrible,' he said finally. 'How old were you?'

'Two. I was staying with Doris that night, and the next day, she and my granddad told me I'd be living with them from now on. And so I did. I didn't feel like I was missing anything when I was growing up. To me, my grandparents seemed like everyone else's parents.'

When she finished, she looked over at him, noticing the way his shoulders filled out his sweater, and eyeing that dimple again.

'Now it's my turn to ask questions,' she said. 'What made you want to become a journalist?'

He told her about his college years, his plans to become a professor, and the turn of events that had brought him to this point.

'And you said that you have five brothers?'

He nodded. 'Five older brothers. I'm the baby of the family.'

'For some reason, I just can't see you with brothers.'

'It's a shame you didn't inherit the psychic abilities of the rest of your family.'

She smiled. 'Two hundred and forty-seven,' she said.

He looked over at her. 'Excuse me?'

'That's how many women have visited Doris to find out the sex of their babies. Growing up, I'd see them sitting in the kitchen. Doris would talk to them for a while to make sure they were sure they wanted to know, and then she'd take their hand; a few seconds after that, she'd make her pronouncement.' Lexie let out a soft breath. 'She was right every time. Two hundred and forty-seven women came by, and she was right two hundred and forty-seven times. Doris wrote everything down. She still has the book in her kitchen.'

Jeremy stared at her. Impossible, he thought.

'I know what you're thinking,' she said, 'but you can check it out with the hospital, too. Or the women. She stopped when ultrasound finally arrived in town. There was no reason for people to come to her any more.'

'And the divining?'

'Same thing,' she said. 'There isn't much demand around here. The eastern section of the state sits over a vast reservoir. You can sink a well anywhere and find water. But when she was growing up in Georgia, farmers would come to the house begging for her help, especially during the droughts. And even though she wasn't more than eight or nine, she'd find the water every time.'

AFTER FINISHING LUNCH, they bounced back down Riker's Hill.

'Do we have time to see a couple of other places?' Jeremy asked. 'I'd love to swing by the marina, the paper mill, and maybe the railroad trestle.'

'We have time,' she said. 'They're all in the same area.'

Ten minutes later, following her directions, he parked again. They were at the far edge of downtown, a few blocks from Herbs, near the boardwalk that stretched along the riverfront. The Pamlico River was nearly a mile wide and flowed angrily, the currents rippling to form tiny whitecaps as they rushed downstream. On the far side of the river, near the railroad trestle, the paper mill spewed clouds from duelling smokestacks. Jeremy stepped out of the car and struggled to catch up with Lexie as she set off for the boardwalk. She finally slowed, then stopped to lean against the railing.

She motioned towards the other end of town. 'The marina is over there, near the highway. Can you see where all those sailboats are docked?'

Jeremy nodded. 'Can big boats dock there?'

'I think so. Yachts from New Bern sometimes stop over.'

He followed her gaze, then turned round, coordinating locations. With Riker's Hill in the distance, the trestle and the factory seemed perfectly aligned. Coincidence? He stared in the direction of the paper mill, trying to figure out whether the tops of the smokestacks were lit at night. He'd have to check on that.

'Do they ship logs by barge or do they use the railroad, too?'

'I've never noticed, to tell you the truth.'

Jeremy nodded as he stared at the trestle.

Lexie smiled and went on. 'I know what you're thinking—maybe the light from the train shines as it goes over the trestle and that's what's causing the lights, right?'

'It did cross my mind.'

'That's not it,' she said, shaking her head. 'At night, the trains pull into the yard at the paper mill so they can be loaded the next day. So the light on the locomotive is shining in the opposite direction, *away* from Riker's Hill.'

He considered that as he joined her at the railing. The wind whipped her hair, making it look wild. She tucked her hands into her jacket pockets.

'I can see why you liked growing up here,' he commented. 'It must have been . . . idyllic. You seem to have thrived.'

She turned so that she could lean back against the railing, and stared towards the downtown area. The little shops festooned with American flags, a barbershop pole, a small park nestled at the edge of the boardwalk. For an instant, she seemed sad. 'Yeah, but I went off to college. A lot of people around here never do. They stay because it's impossible for them to leave.'

She smiled at him, then glanced away. Jeremy changed the subject. 'So this weekend,' he started. 'What's it like?'

'Won't you be here?' she asked.

'Probably. For part of it, anyway. But I was just curious how you felt about it.'

'It's . . . needed at this time of year. You go through Thanksgiving and Christmas in a rush, and then it's cold and grey and rainy . . . so, years ago, the town council decided to do the Historic Homes Tour. And ever since then, they've just added more festivities to it in the hope of making for a special weekend. This year it's the cemetery, last year the parade, the year before that, a Friday night barn dance.' She glanced at him. 'As forgettable as it sounds, it's actually sort of fun.'

Jeremy raised his eyebrows, remembering the barn dance from the brochure. 'They have a dance?' he asked, feigning ignorance.

She nodded. 'On Friday night. In Meyer's tobacco barn downtown. It's quite the shindig, with a live band. It's the only night of the year that the Lookilu Tavern is pretty much empty.'

'Well, if I happen to go, maybe you'll dance with me.'

She smiled before eyeing him with an almost seductive look. 'I'll tell you what. If you solve the mystery, I'll dance with you.'

'Fair enough,' he said. 'I can't wait. And when it comes to the foxtrot . . .' He shook his head. 'Well, all I can say is that I hope you can keep up.'

She laughed. 'I'll do my best.'

Crossing her arms, Lexie watched the sun trying and failing to break through the gloom. 'Tonight,' she said.

He frowned. 'Tonight?'

'You'll see the lights tonight. If you go to the cemetery.'

'How do you know?'

'Look across the river behind me,' she said. 'The tops of the smokestacks on the paper mill are already hidden by clouds. The fog is coming in.'

He looked over his shoulder, studying the outlines of the paper mill. 'You're right,' he said.

'Of course I am.'

She pushed herself from the railing. 'C'mon. I have to get back to the library to read to the children.'

As they made their way back to the car, Jeremy noticed that the top of Riker's Hill had become hidden as well. 'How can you be so sure the lights will be out tonight?'

It took a moment for her to answer. 'I just am,' she said.

'Well, I guess it's settled, then. I should probably head out there.' As soon as he spoke the words, he remembered the dinner he was supposed to attend, and he suddenly winced.

'What?' she asked, puzzled.

'Oh, the mayor is setting up a dinner with a few people he thought I should meet,' he said. 'I only found out this morning.'

'I wouldn't worry about the lights, even if you do go to dinner with the mayor. They don't usually come out until late.'

'Are you sure?'

'That's when *I* saw them. It was a little before midnight.'

He stopped in his tracks. 'You've seen them? You didn't mention that.'

She smiled. 'You didn't ask.'

ACROSS TOWN at Herbs, Deputy Rodney Hopper was stewing over his cup of coffee, wondering where on earth Lexie and that . . . city boy had gone off to. Oh, he knew exactly what City Boy saw in Lexie. It was impossible not to notice, Rodney thought. She was the prettiest woman in the county, probably the state.

Rodney scowled. Just where were they, anyway? Not at Herbs. He supposed he could ask around, but word would probably spread, and he wasn't sure that was such a good idea. All his buddies teased him about Lexie as it was. They'd tell him she was just spending time with him to be nice, but he knew better. They were just jealous.

He'd hoped that Doris would have some insight, but it just so happened that she wasn't around, either. Off at the accountant's, they said. Besides, she'd probably deny knowing anything about it. He'd heard that she actually liked City Boy.

''Scuse me, darlin'?' Rachel said. 'You OK?'

Rodney looked up and saw her standing at the table with the coffeepot. 'Just one of those days,' he said.

She smiled, looking pretty, though Rodney didn't seem to notice. He'd long since come to view her as something of a sister.

'Well, it'll get better,' she reassured him.

He nodded. 'You're probably right.'

Her lips went together. Sometimes she worried about Rodney.

'Are you sure you can't squeeze in a quick bite to eat?'

'No. I'm not all that hungry.' He extended his cup. 'A refill might be nice, though.'

'You got it,' she said, pouring.

'Hey, did you notice whether Lexie came through here?'

She shook her head. 'I haven't seen her all day.' She hovered over the table. 'I saw you sitting with Jeremy Marsh this morning.'

'Oh, yeah. I just thought I should introduce myself.'

'He's a handsome fella, isn't he?'

'I don't notice whether other men are handsome,' he growled.

'Well, he is. I could look at him all day. Everyone's talking about him. He invited me to New York,' she boasted.

At this, Rodney perked up. 'He did?'

'Well, sort of, anyway. He said I should visit.'

'Really?' he asked. 'That's great, Rachel.'

He took a gulp of coffee. Did City Boy really invite Rachel to New York? Or did Rachel invite herself? He could see how he might find her attractive, but . . . Rachel tended to exaggerate, and Lexie and City Boy were nowhere to be found. Something here didn't add up.

He began sliding from the booth. 'Well, listen, if you see Lexie, tell her I stopped by, OK?'

'Sure thing. You want coffee to go?'

'No, thanks. My stomach's feeling a little green already.'

'You poor thing. Want me to get some Pepto-Bismol for you?'

'To be honest, Rach,' he said, 'I don't think it's going to help.'

OUTSIDE THE ACCOUNTANT'S OFFICE, Mayor Gherkin hustled to catch up with Doris. 'Just the woman I wanted to see,' he called out.

Doris turned to watch the mayor approach in his red jacket and check trousers. 'What can I do for you, Tom?'

'Well, as you may or may not have heard, we're arranging a special evening for our guest, Jeremy Marsh,' he said. 'He's writing a big story and you know how important this could be for the town.'

'I've heard,' she said. 'And it's good for your businesses.'

'I'm thinking of the whole community here,' he said. 'And I was hoping you'd help us out with something to eat.'

'You want me to be the caterer?'

'Not for charity, mind you. The town would be happy to reimburse you for expenses. We're planning to hold it at the old Lawson Plantation. I figure we could sort of use it as a kickoff to the Historic Homes Tour.'

'When are you planning to have this get-together?' she asked.

'Well, tonight, of course . . . but like I was saying—'

'*Tonight?*'

'It's for a good cause, Doris. I know it's inconsiderate of me to drop this on you like this, but you and I both know you're the only one who could handle it.'

'Does Jeremy Marsh even know about this?'

'Of course he does. I spoke to him about it this morning. And I was hoping that Lexie might come as well. You know how important she is to folks in this town.'

'I doubt if she would. She hates doing these types of things any more than absolutely necessary. And aren't you forgetting that I'm against the whole idea of using the cemetery as a tourist attraction?'

'Not at all,' he said. 'But you do want your voice heard, don't you? If you don't show up, there's going to be no one there to represent your side of things.'

Doris stared at Mayor Gherkin. The man certainly knew what buttons to press. And, besides, he had a point. If she didn't go, she could imagine what Jeremy would end up writing if all he had to go on was the mayor and the town council.

'All right,' she capitulated, 'I'll take care of it. But it'll be a buffet, and I'm going to sit at the tables like the rest of you.'

Mayor Gherkin smiled. 'I wouldn't have it any other way.'

DEPUTY RODNEY HOPPER was sitting in his car across the street from the library, wondering whether or not to go inside. He could see City Boy's car parked in the lot, which meant that they'd returned from wherever they'd gone, and he could see lights from Lexie's office glowing through the window.

He could imagine Lexie sitting at her desk, twirling those strands of hair. He wanted to talk to her, but he didn't have a good reason. He never dropped by the library just to chat because, honestly, she had never suggested it.

He saw a figure pass by the window, and he wondered if City Boy was in the office with her. That would take the cake, wouldn't it? In less than a day, City Boy had moved right in, hadn't he? Well, maybe he'd just have to have another little talk with him about the situation. Spell things out for him, so that City Boy would understand exactly where things stood.

Then again, maybe Lexie was just being friendly. Everybody was going out of their way to make the guy feel welcome, right? And the mayor was leading the charge. This morning, when he had City Boy right where he wanted him, the mayor (the mayor!) helped the guy slink away.

He hated not knowing what was going on, and just as he was getting ready to head inside, he was interrupted by a tapping on the glass. It took an instant for the face to come into focus. The mayor. Mr *Interrupt at the Wrong Moment*. Twice now.

Rodney rolled down his window.

'Just the man I was looking for,' Mayor Gherkin said. 'We're going to need a representative from law enforcement this evening.'

'What for?'

'The little get-together, of course. For Jeremy Marsh. Tonight at the Lawson Plantation.'

Rodney blinked. 'You're kidding, right?'

'No, not at all. In fact, I'm making him up a key to the city. I sure would appreciate your presence.'

'I don't know, Tom. I'd have to call someone in to cover for me. I really don't think I'm going to be able to make it.'

'That is a shame. But I understand. Duty is duty. I'm sure Lexie would love to have seen you, though.'

'Lexie?'

'Of course. She runs the library, so that makes her one of the dignitaries who'll attend. I was just coming by to tell her about it.'

'Wait!' Rodney said. 'You said it's tonight?'

The mayor nodded.

'I just might be able to work something out.'

The mayor smiled. 'Glad to hear it,' he said.

AFTER MAKING a quick stop in her office, Lexie found herself surrounded by twenty children, some nestled in their mothers' laps. Lexie was sitting on the floor, reading her third book.

As she read, she felt her mind wandering back to the lunch she'd shared with Jeremy. Though it couldn't be described as a date, it almost had that feeling, which made it a little disconcerting. Thinking back on it, she realised that she'd revealed far more about herself than she'd intended. It wasn't as if he'd pried. Instead, it had just happened. But why on earth was she still dwelling on it?

No matter how much she tried to stop it, Jeremy's image kept popping up: the slightly crooked smile, his expression of amusement at things she said. Doris had been right. He wasn't what she thought he'd be. He was smart, and even if he held his mind closed to the possibility of mystery, he made up for it by being good-humoured about their differing beliefs and way of life.

If truth be told, she wanted to spend more time with him. But even that realisation didn't change the little voice in her head warning her not to get hurt. She had to tread carefully, for Jeremy Marsh would hurt her if she allowed it to happen.

JEREMY WAS HUNCHED over a series of street maps of Boone Creek, dating back to the 1850s. The cemetery, as he already knew, sat between the river and Riker's Hill; more important, he realised that a line drawn between Riker's Hill and the paper mill would pass directly through the cemetery. The total distance was a little more than three miles, and he knew that it was possible for light to be refracted that far. With the right layering of the fog, and enough brightness, everything could be explained.

He realised that he should have noticed the relationship between the paper mill and Riker's Hill when he was up there. Instead, he'd been caught up with Lexie. He was still trying to figure out the sudden change in her behaviour. Yesterday she wanted nothing to do with him, and today . . . well, today was a new day. And he couldn't stop thinking about her. He couldn't remember the last time that had happened. Maria, probably, but that was a long time ago. Today the conversation had been so comfortable that despite the fact that he should finish studying the maps, all he wanted to do was get to know her even better.

Strange, he thought, and before he realised what was happening, he stood up from his desk and began making his way to the stairs. He suddenly wanted to see her.

He walked down the steps and spotted Lexie sitting on the floor, surrounded by children. She read in an animated way, and he smiled at her expressions: the wide eyes, the 'O' she made with her mouth, the way she leaned forward to emphasise something in the story. The mothers sat with smiles on their faces. A couple of the kids were absolutely still.

'She's really something, isn't she?'

Jeremy turned. 'Mayor Gherkin. What are you doing here?'

'Why, I came to see you and Miss Lexie. About the dinner tonight. We've got everything just about set up. I think you'll be quite impressed.'

'I'm sure I will,' Jeremy said.

The mayor told Jeremy the location and offered directions. 'Do you think you'll be able to find it?' he asked. 'Those back roads can get kind of dark. You might consider coming with someone who knows where it is.'

When Jeremy looked at him curiously, Gherkin glanced knowingly towards Lexie.

'You think I should ask Lexie?' Jeremy asked.

The mayor's eyes twinkled. 'That's up to you. If you think she'd agree. A lot of men consider her the prize of the county.'

'She'd say yes,' Jeremy said, feeling more hopeful than certain.

The mayor looked doubtful. 'I think you may be overestimating your own abilities. But if you're so sure, then I suppose my business is through here. You see, I came to invite her myself, but since you're going to take care of it, I'll just see you tonight.'

The mayor turned to leave, and a few minutes later, Jeremy watched Lexie close the book and finish up. He felt a jolt of nervous adrenaline. When was the last time that had happened?

Lexie followed the kids out of the children's room. When she saw Jeremy, she headed over.

'I take it you're ready to look through the diaries,' she surmised.

'If you have time to get them,' he said. 'I still have a way to go with the maps. But there's something else, too.'

'Oh?' She tilted her head slightly.

As he spoke, he noticed butterflies in his stomach. 'The mayor came by to tell me about the dinner tonight. It's at the Lawson Plantation, and he's not sure if I can find the place, so he suggested I bring someone who knows where it is. And since you're the only one I know in town, I was wondering if you'd accompany me.'

For a moment, Lexie said nothing. 'Figures,' she finally said.

'Excuse me?'

'Oh, it's not you. It's the mayor. He knows I avoid events like this unless it has to do with the library. He figured I'd say no if he asked, so he finagled a way to get you to ask me instead. He might come across like he's no smarter than a sack of grass, but he has a funny knack of getting people to do exactly what he wants and making them think it was their idea all along.'

Jeremy pushed his hands into his pockets. 'Well, you don't have to come. I'm sure I can find the place on my own.'

She put her hands on her hips and looked at him. 'Are you backing off?'

'Well, I just thought that since the mayor . . .'

'Do you want me to come with you or not?' she asked.

'I do, but if you're not—'

'Then ask me again. For yourself this time, and don't use the excuse about needing directions. Say something like, "I'd really like to bring you to the dinner tonight."'

Jeremy fidgeted like a nervous schoolboy. 'I'd really like to bring you to the dinner tonight. May I pick you up later?'

She smiled and placed her hand on his arm.

'Why, Mr Marsh,' she drawled, 'I'd be delighted.'

FIVE

That evening, as the fog thickened, Rodney Hopper decided the Lawson Plantation looked like it was about to host a Barry Manilow concert. He'd been directing traffic into parking spots and watching in disbelief at the procession excitedly making its way towards the door. He'd seen all eight members of the town council, the mayor and the staff from the chamber of commerce, the volunteers from the Historical Society, the crew from Herbs, and the bartender from the Lookilu. Lawson Plantation wasn't this crowded during the Christmas season, when the place was decorated to the nines.

Tonight wasn't the same. This wasn't a celebration where friends and acquaintances got together to enjoy each other's company. This was a party meant to honour someone who had nothing to do with the town. Even worse, though Rodney was here on official business, he knew he shouldn't have bothered ironing his shirt and polishing his shoes, since he doubted that Lexie would even notice.

He knew all about it. After Doris had gone back to Herbs to get the cooking under way, the mayor had rolled in and mentioned the awful news about Jeremy and Lexie. Rachel had called him straight away. Rachel, he thought, was sweet in that way and always had been. She knew how he felt about Lexie and didn't tease him like a lot of other folks did.

And now the town was placing its bets on the existence of ghosts in the cemetery and that the city boy would bring the world to their doorstep because of them. Rodney strongly doubted it. And besides, he didn't honestly care if the world came or not, as long as Lexie stayed part of *his* world.

ACROSS TOWN and at about the same time, Lexie stepped onto her porch just as Jeremy was coming up the walkway with a bouquet of wild flowers. Nice touch, she thought, and she suddenly hoped he couldn't tell how frazzled she'd been until just a few minutes ago.

Tonight had been rough. First, of course, there was the question of whether this was even an actual date. Then there was the image question and how she wanted to be perceived. It became so confusing that she'd decided to go with a professional look: brown trouser-suit with an ivory blouse.

But here he comes waltzing up in his Johnny Cash look, as if he hadn't given the evening a second thought.

'You found the place,' Lexie observed.

'It wasn't too hard,' Jeremy said. 'You showed me where you lived when we were on Riker's Hill, remember?' He offered the flowers. 'Here. These are for you.'

She smiled as she took them. 'Thank you,' she said. 'Give me a second to put them in a vase and then I'll be ready.'

He opened his palms. 'I'll wait here.'

A couple of minutes later, in the car, Lexie directed Jeremy along the back roads until they came to a long winding drive. As he approached a towering hedge, which he assumed lined a circular drive, he leaned over the steering wheel, wondering which way to turn.

'You might want to park here,' Lexie suggested. 'I doubt if you'll find a space any closer, and you'll be able to get out of here when you need to.'

A moment later, they were walking round the curve of the drive near the hedge. All at once, the old Georgian mansion stood in blazing glory before them. Scores of cars were parked haphazardly, while numerous others were trying to squeeze into improbably tiny spaces.

Jeremy halted, staring at the scene. 'I thought this was supposed to be a little get-together with friends.'

Lexie nodded. 'This is the mayor's version of a little get-together. He knows practically everyone in the county.'

'Why didn't you tell me it would be like this?'

'Like I keep telling you, you keep forgetting to ask.' She smiled, looking towards the house. 'It is kind of impressive, isn't it? Not that I think you necessarily deserve it.'

He grunted in amusement. 'You know, I've really come to appreciate your Southern charm.'

'Thank you. And don't worry about tonight. Everyone's friendly, and when in doubt, just remember that you're the guest of honour.'

DORIS HAD TO BE the most organised caterer in the world, Rachel thought, since this whole thing had been pulled off without a hitch. Rachel was wiggling through the crowds in her best imitation Chanel party dress when she spotted Rodney walking up to the porch.

With his neatly pressed uniform, she thought he looked quite official, like a marine in one of those posters in the VFW building. Most of the other deputies carried a few too many chicken wings and Budweisers around the midsection, but, in his spare time, Rodney pumped iron in his garage. He kept the door open, and sometimes on her way home from work, she'd stop and visit with him for a while, like the old friends that they were.

Rachel took a lipstick from her bag and dabbed at her lips, conscious of the soft spot she had for him. Oh, they'd gone their separate ways for a while, but in the last couple of years things had been changing. Two summers ago, they'd ended up sitting near each other at the Lookilu, and she'd seen his expression as he watched a newscast about a young boy who had died in a tragic fire in Raleigh. Seeing his eyes well up over the loss of a stranger had affected her in a way she hadn't expected. She'd noticed it a second time last Easter, when the sheriff's department sponsored the egg hunt at the Masonic Lodge and he'd pulled her aside to tell her the trickier places in which he'd hidden the goodies. He'd looked more excited than the children, and she remembered thinking that he'd be the kind of father who would make any wife proud.

Looking back, she supposed that was the moment she realised that her feelings for Rodney had changed. It wasn't that she fell in love with him right away, but she'd stopped believing the possibility to be nil. Not that it was likely, though. Rodney was over the moon for Lexie. There were times when it didn't bother her, but lately the times it didn't bother her were fewer and further between.

Pushing through the crowd, she wished she hadn't brought up the subject of Jeremy Marsh at lunch. She should have known what was bugging Rodney. By now, it seemed, the entire town was talking about Lexie and Jeremy. She would still like to go to New York, but as she'd mentally replayed her conversation with Jeremy, she'd gradually come to the realisation that he might have simply been making conversation and not extending an invitation. Sometimes she read too much into situations like that.

But Jeremy Marsh was just so . . . perfect.

Cultured, intelligent, charming, famous and, best of all, not from here. There was no way Rodney could compete with that. But Rodney, on the other hand, *was* here and didn't plan to leave, which was a different sort of an advantage. And, she had to admit, he was responsible and good-looking, too, in his own way.

'Hey, Rodney,' she said, smiling.

Rodney glanced over. 'Oh, hey, Rach. How are you?'

'Good, thanks. Some party, huh?'

'It's great,' he said, not hiding the sarcasm in his voice. 'How's it going inside?'

'Pretty good. I saved a plate of food for you.'

Rodney hesitated for a moment before smiling. Rachel always looked out for him. 'Thanks, Rach.' For the first time, he noticed what she was wearing, his eyes alighting on the little gold hoops in her ears. He added, 'You look nice tonight.'

'Thank you.'

'You want to keep me company for a while?'

She smiled. 'I'd like that.'

JEREMY AND LEXIE wove through the mass of parked cars, their breaths coming out in little puffs as they neared the mansion. On the steps up ahead, Jeremy saw Rodney Hopper standing near the door. Rodney saw Jeremy at the same time, and his smile immediately changed into a scowl. Even from a distance, he looked large, jealous and, most important, armed, none of which made Jeremy feel particularly comfortable.

Lexie followed his gaze. 'Oh, don't worry about Rodney,' she said. 'You're with me.'

'That's what I'm worried about,' he said. 'I kind of get the feeling he isn't all that happy that we showed up together.'

She knew Jeremy was right, although she was thankful that Rachel was beside the deputy. Rachel had a way of keeping Rodney calm and Lexie had long thought that she'd be perfect for him.

Rachel brightened when she saw them coming up the steps. 'Hey, you two!' she said. 'I love your outfit, Lex.'

'Thanks,' Lexie said. 'You look like a million bucks, too.'

Jeremy said nothing as he tried to avoid the evil eye that Rodney was sending his way. Rachel and Lexie glanced at each other.

'And look at you, Mr Famous Journalist,' Rachel sang out. 'Lexie, would you mind if I escorted him inside? The mayor is waiting for him.'

'Not at all,' Lexie said, needing a minute alone with Rodney. She nodded to Jeremy. 'Go ahead, I'll catch up.'

Rachel clamped on to Jeremy's arm, and before he realised it, he was being led away. As they passed, Lexie mouthed a silent thankyou.

Lexie turned to Rodney. 'It's not what you think,' she began.

'Don't explain,' he said. 'I've seen it before, remember?'

She knew he was referring to Mr Renaissance, and her first instinct was to tell him he was wrong, she wasn't going to let her feelings run wild this time. But that was what she had said to Rodney when he'd warned her that Mr Renaissance had no intention of staying.

'I wish I knew what to say,' she said, hating the guilty note in her voice.

'You don't have to say anything.'

She knew she didn't. It wasn't as if they were a couple or had ever been a couple. But a little voice reminded her that she had played a role in keeping the spark alive these last couple of years, even if it had more to do with security and comfort than anything romantic.

'Well, just so you know, I'm actually looking forward to things getting back to normal around here,' she volunteered.

'Me, too,' he said.

'Rachel sure looks nice, doesn't she?' she said.

Rodney's chin dropped to his chest before he looked at Lexie again. For the first time, she saw the tiniest of smiles.

'Yeah,' he said, 'she does.'

Their eyes met for an instant, then Lexie turned away. 'Well, I should probably head inside,' she said. She began moving towards the door.

'Hey, Lexie?'

She turned. 'Yes?'

He swallowed. 'You look nice, too, by the way.'

The sad way he said it nearly broke her heart and her eyes dipped for an instant. 'Thank you,' she said.

RACHEL AND JEREMY moved round the edges of the crowd. He appreciated Rachel keeping him out of harm's way. He could hear people talking about him but wasn't quite ready to mingle yet, even if the whole thing did leave him feeling just a bit flattered. As he was pondering the situation, Rachel squeezed his arm to get his attention.

'Get ready, darlin'. It's showtime.'

'Excuse me?'

She looked past him, towards the rising commotion behind them.

'Well, Mayor Tom, how are you?' Rachel asked.

Mayor Gherkin seemed to be the only person in the room who was perspiring, his bald head shiny in the light. 'Rachel! You are looking lovely.'

'Thank you,' she said, smiling.

'I hate to ask you this, but would you mind?' he said, motioning to Jeremy. 'People are excited to get this fine event started.'

'Not at all,' she answered, and, in the next instant, the mayor began leading Jeremy through the crowd.

As they walked, people stared with wide eyes or oohed and aahed, whispering that it must be *him*.

'I can't tell you how glad we are that you finally made it,' Mayor Gherkin said, speaking from the corner of his mouth and continuing to smile to the crowd. 'I was beginning to worry.'

'Maybe we should wait for Lexie,' Jeremy answered, trying to keep his cheeks from turning red. This whole thing, especially being escorted like a prom queen, was just a little on the weird side.

'I've already spoken to her, and she'll meet us there.'

'And where's that?'

'Why, you're going to meet the rest of the town council, of course. You've already met Jed and Tully, but there are a few others. And the county commissioners, too. Don't worry—they've got all their ghost stories ready. You brought your tape recorder, right?'

'It's in my pocket.'

'Good. Glad to hear it.' For the first time, he turned from the crowd to look at Jeremy. 'I take it you are heading out to the cemetery tonight . . .'

'I was, and speaking of that, I wanted to make sure—'

The mayor kept on going as if he hadn't heard him, while nodding and waving to the crowd. 'Well, as the mayor, I feel it's my obligation to tell you not to worry none about meeting those ghosts. Oh, they're a sight, of course. But so far, no one's ever been hurt.'

'Ah,' Jeremy said. 'I'll try to keep that in mind.'

LEXIE WAS WAITING for him and Jeremy breathed a sigh of relief when she moved to his side as he was introduced to the town's power elite. Most were friendly enough, but he couldn't help watching Lexie from the corner of his eye. She seemed distracted, and he wondered what had happened between her and Rodney.

Jeremy didn't have a chance to find out, as the rest of the evening was akin to an old-fashioned political convention. After his meeting with the council—each and every one of them promised 'it could be the biggest story ever' and reminded him that 'tourism is important to the town'—Jeremy was brought to the stage, which had been festooned with a banner proclaiming WELCOME JEREMY MARSH!

The mayor made a long-winded speech praising Jeremy and mentioning the *Primetime Live* appearance. At the end, Jeremy was presented with a key to the city. He found himself smiling and actually enjoying himself. As he stood onstage, Lexie winked at him.

From there, the mayor led him off to the corner, where Jeremy spent the rest of the evening listening to one story after another about encounters with ghosts. Unfortunately, most of the stories began to run together. Everyone claimed to have seen the lights, but each one of them had a different description. Some swore they looked like people, others like strobe lights.

At the same time, Lexie was talking to various people, and every now and then, their eyes would meet. As if they were sharing a private joke, she would smile with raised eyebrows, her expression seeming to ask him, *See what you've got yourself into?*

Lexie, Jeremy reflected, wasn't like any of the women he'd dated. She didn't hide what she was thinking, she didn't try to impress him, nor was she swayed by anything he'd accomplished in the past. Instead, she seemed to evaluate him as he was today, right now, without holding either the past or the future against him.

It was, he realised, one of the reasons he'd married Maria. Her lack of pretence, the steely way she confronted him when he did something wrong, the patience with which she would listen to him as he struggled with a problem. And though he and Lexie hadn't shared any of the daily nitty-gritty of life, he couldn't shake the thought that she'd be good at dealing with it, if that was what she wanted.

Jeremy realised she had a genuine affection for the people here, and she seemed to be truly interested in whatever it was they were saying. Her

behaviour suggested that she had no reason to rush or cut someone's conversation short, and she had no inhibitions about laughing aloud when
something amused her. Every now and then, she'd lean in to hug someone,
and pulling back, she'd murmur something along the lines of 'I'm so glad
to see you again.' That she didn't seem to think of herself as different, or
even notice the fact that others obviously did, reminded Jeremy of an aunt
who had always been the most popular person at holiday dinners, simply
because she focused her attention so completely on others.

A few minutes later, Jeremy saw Lexie moving towards him with just a
trace of seduction in the gentle sway of her hips. And as he watched her,
there was a moment, just a moment, when the scene seemed as if it weren't
happening now but taking place in the future, just another little get-together
in a long procession of get-togethers in a tiny Southern town in the middle
of nowhere.

AS THE EVENING drew to a close, Jeremy stood with Mayor Gherkin on the
porch while Lexie and Doris stood off to the side. 'I sure do hope this
evening met with your approval,' the mayor said, 'and that you were able to
see what a wonderful opportunity you have when it comes to this story.'

'I did, thank you. But you didn't have to go to all this trouble,' Jeremy
protested.

'Nonsense,' Gherkin replied. 'Why, it's the least we can do. You'll get a
little bit more of the town's flavour this weekend, too. The small-town
atmosphere, the feeling of travelling back in time as you walk through the
homes. It's like nothing you can imagine.'

'I have no doubt about that,' Jeremy said. 'And thanks for this, by the
way,' he added, raising the key to the city.

'Oh, you're very welcome. You deserve it.'

Jeremy smiled as Gherkin pumped his hand. After Gherkin vanished
inside, Doris and Lexie approached, smirks on their faces.

'L-I-B,' Doris teased. 'You and your city slicker ways. You should have
heard the way these folks were talking about you. I just feel lucky that I can
say I knew you way back when.'

Jeremy smiled, looking sheepish. 'It was a little crazy, wasn't it?' He
looked around, noting that the fog had become even thicker. 'Well, I suppose I should be going. I'd hate to miss my big chance at getting a whiff of
the supernatural.'

'Don't worry. You won't miss the lights,' Doris said. 'They don't come out until later. You've still got a couple of hours.'

Jeremy turned to Lexie. 'You ready to go?'

Lexie nodded. She kissed Doris on the cheek and, a moment later, Jeremy and Lexie were walking to the car. She glanced towards him. 'Doris was right. People *loved* you.'

She sounded almost shocked by the admission, and Jeremy pushed his hands into his pockets. 'Well, you shouldn't have been surprised. I am very lovable, you know.'

She rolled her eyes, looking more playful than annoyed.

'Hey, it's none of my business, but how did it go with Rodney?'

'You're right.' She shrugged. 'It is none of your business.'

He looked for a smile but saw none. 'Well, the only reason I asked was because I was wondering whether you think I should sneak out of town under the cover of darkness so he doesn't have the chance to crush my head with his bare hands.'

That brought a smile. 'You'll be fine. And besides, you'd break the mayor's heart if you left.'

Reaching the car, he opened the door for her. As she climbed in, she brushed against him slightly. After rounding the car, he slid behind the wheel but hesitated before starting the engine.

'What?' she asked.

'I was just thinking . . . I know it's getting late, but would you like to come with me to the cemetery?'

'In case you get scared?'

'Something like that.'

She peeked at her watch, thinking, Oh, boy . . .

She shouldn't go. She'd already opened the door by coming with him tonight. There wasn't a single reason to say yes. But before she could stop herself, the words were already coming.

'I'd have to swing by the house first to change into something more comfortable.'

'That's fine,' he said. 'I'm all for you changing into something more comfortable.'

'I'll bet you are,' she said knowingly.

'Now, don't start getting fresh,' he said, feigning offence.

'Just drive, will you? Or I'll change my mind.'

'OK, OK,' he said, turning the key.

The car rolled along the foggy streets, the yellow streetlamps only making the night seem murkier. As Jeremy pulled into her drive, she opened her door. 'Wait here,' she said, tucking a strand of hair behind her ear. 'I'll only be a few minutes.'

He smiled, liking the fact that she was nervous, and watched her move up the path, certain he'd never met anyone quite like her.

Fifteen minutes later, they pulled in front of Cedar Creek Cemetery. He angled the car so the headlights shone into the cemetery. The fog was dense and impenetrable in places while thin in others, and the slight breeze made tendrils curve and twist, almost as if alive. The crumbling tombs added to the eerie effect.

Leaving the car idling, Jeremy popped the boot. As she peered in, Lexie's eyes widened. 'It looks like you've got the makings of a bomb in there.'

'Guys love their toys, you know.'

'I thought you'd just have a video camera or something.'

'I do. I have four of them.'

'What's this thing?' she asked, pointing to an electronic box.

'A microwave radiation detector. And this over here,' he said, 'sort of goes with it. It detects electromagnetic activity.'

'Ah,' she said. 'Why do you have all this stuff?'

'I like to use everything that paranormal investigators use,' he said. 'I don't want to be accused of missing anything. Besides, it seems more impressive when someone reads that you've used an electromagnetic detector. They think you know what you're doing.'

She laughed, then pulled out one of the camcorders and slung it over her shoulder. 'Which way?'

'That depends. Where do you think we should set up? Since you've seen the lights, maybe you have some ideas.'

She nodded in the direction of the magnolia tree, where she'd been heading when he'd first seen her in the cemetery.

'Over there,' she said. It was the spot directly in front of Riker's Hill. 'That's where they were when I saw them.'

Over the next hour, as Lexie filmed him with one of the camcorders, Jeremy set everything up. He arranged the other three video recorders in a large triangular pattern, mounting them on tripods, until the entire area was overlapped. He tested the remotes, then began setting up the audio equipment. Four microphones were attached to trees, and a fifth was placed near the centre, which was where he'd set the electromagnetic and radiation detectors.

As he was making sure everything worked properly, he called out, 'Well, I'm almost done here. All I still have to do is spread some flour and unwind the thread.'

'Flour? Like baking flour?'

'It's to make sure no one tampers with the equipment. The flour is so I can check for footprints and the thread will let me know if anyone else approaches.'

He opened the bag of flour and began pouring, circling the cameras and the microphones with a thin white layer. Then he tied the thread to a branch and formed a large square round the whole area. After he had finished, he made his way back to Lexie. 'I'm going to go and hit the lights on the car. And hopefully none of this will have been in vain.'

When he shut off the engine, the cemetery turned darker than a cave. After feeling his way to the gate, he stumbled back to her side and took a seat. For the next half-hour or so, they rehashed the events of the party. It was too dark for Jeremy to read Lexie's face, but he liked how close she felt in the enveloping darkness.

Changing the topic of conversation, he said, 'Tell me about the time you saw the lights. I heard everyone else's story tonight.'

Though her features were nothing but shadows, Jeremy had the impression that she was being drawn back in time.

'I was eight years old,' she said, her voice soft. 'I'd started having nightmares about my parents. Doris kept their wedding picture on the wall, and that was the way they always looked in the dream: Mom in her wedding dress and Dad in his tuxedo. Only this time, they were trapped in their car after it had fallen in the river. I could see the panic and fear on both their faces as water filled the car.'

Her voice was strangely devoid of emotion, and she sighed.

'I'd wake up screaming. I don't know how many times it happened. Finally, Doris woke me up one night and told me to put on a warm jacket, and the next thing I knew she'd brought me here. She told me she was going to show me something wonderful. We wound our way among the tombstones and sat for a while until the lights came. They looked almost alive—everything got really bright . . . until the lights just faded away. And then we went home.'

He could almost hear her shrug. 'When I got home, I couldn't sleep, because I'd just seen the ghosts of my parents. It was like they'd come to visit me. After that, I stopped having the nightmares.'

Jeremy was silent.

She leaned closer. 'Do you believe me?'

'Yes,' he said, 'actually, I do. Your grandmother was a smart lady. Doing what she did, I mean.'

'She *is* a smart lady.'

'I stand corrected,' he said, and just then Lexie shifted beside him, as if straining to see into the distance. 'I think you may want to turn your equipment on,' she said.

He suddenly realised that he could see not only Lexie but also the cameras in the distance. He squinted, trying to make sure his eyes weren't playing tricks on him, then aimed the remote at each of the three cameras, turning them on. Something actually seemed to be happening.

He glanced around, looking for passing cars or illuminated houses. When he looked towards the cameras again, he decided that he definitely wasn't seeing things. Holding his breath, he watched as the fog in front of them grew more silver by the moment, before changing to a pale yellow, then an opaque white and finally an almost blinding brightness. For a moment, most of the cemetery was visible—like a football field illuminated before the big game—and portions of the foggy light began to churn in a small circle before suddenly spreading outwards. Jeremy imagined that he saw the shapes of people or things, but then the light began to recede, as if being pulled on a string, back towards the centre, and even before he realised the lights had vanished, the cemetery had turned black once more.

He blinked, as if to reassure himself that it had really happened, then checked his watch again. The whole event had taken twenty-two seconds from start to finish. Though he knew he should get up to check the equipment, all he could do was stare at the spot where the ghosts of Cedar Creek had made their appearance.

'IT IS AMAZING, isn't it?' Lexie said, her voice soft. 'I'd almost forgotten how pretty it could be.'

Jeremy didn't respond. Finally, she poked him in the arm to get his attention. 'What do we do next?' she asked.

He shook his head, coming back to her.

'Is there a highway around here? Or another major road?'

'Just the one you came in on that runs through town.'

'I get the impression you already know what's causing them.'

'Why?' she said, playing coy.

'It's just a feeling I get. I'm good at reading people. A guy named Clausen taught me his secrets.'

She laughed. 'Well, then, you already know what I think.' She leaned forward, looking darkly seductive. 'It was my parents,' she whispered. 'They wanted to meet you.'

Perhaps it was the orphaned tone she used—simultaneously sad and resilient—but as a tiny lump formed in his throat, it was all he could do not to take her in his arms right then and there.

They loaded up the equipment. Neither of them said much on the way home. When they reached her door, Jeremy realised he didn't want the evening to end, not yet.

Hesitating before the door, Lexie brought a hand to her mouth, stifling a yawn before breaking into an embarrassed laugh.

'Sorry about that,' she said. 'I'm not normally up this late.'

'It's OK,' he said, meeting her gaze. 'I had a great time tonight.'

'So did I,' she said, meaning it.

He took a small step forward, and when she realised he was thinking of trying to kiss her, she pretended to fiddle with something on her jacket.

'I suppose I should call it a night, then,' she said.

'Are you sure?' he asked. 'We could watch the tapes inside. Maybe you could help me figure out what the lights really are.'

She looked away. 'Please don't ruin this for me,' she whispered.

'Did I do something wrong?'

'No. I had a great day, a wonderful day.'

'Then what is it?'

'We know what'll happen if I let you through that door. But you're leaving. And when you do, I'll be the one who's hurt. So why start something you have no intention of finishing?'

With someone else, with anyone else, he would have said something flippant. But as he looked at her on the porch, he couldn't form the words. Nor, strangely, did he want to.

'You're right,' he admitted. He forced a smile. 'Let's call it a night. I should go and find out where those lights are coming from, anyway.'

'Thank you,' she said.

'Good night, Lexie.'

She nodded, and after an awkward pause, she turned towards the door. Jeremy stepped off the porch. Then she heard his voice behind her.

'Hey, Lexie?' he called out.

In the fog, he was nothing but a blur. 'Yes?'

'You may not believe it, but the last thing I want to do is hurt you or do anything that would make you regret that we've met.'

Though she smiled briefly at his comment, she turned away without a word. For the first time in his life, Jeremy was not only disappointed in himself but wished he were someone else entirely.

SIX

Jeremy's cellphone rang as the harsh grey light of morning punched through the torn curtains. It was 8 a.m., way too early to talk to anyone, especially after pulling an all-nighter. He winced before groping for the phone.

'This better be important,' he grumbled.

'Jeremy? Is that you? Where have you been? Why haven't you called? I've been trying to reach you!'

Nate, Jeremy thought, closing his eyes again.

'You said you were going to keep in touch!'

'Sorry, Nate,' Jeremy said. 'I've just been tied up.'

'I tried calling you all day yesterday, but I kept getting your voicemail. You can't imagine what's going on. I've got producers hounding me left and right. Things are really moving. One of them suggested that you do a piece on these high-protein diets.'

'Nate, I saw the lights,' Jeremy said.

'The lights in the cemetery?' he asked. 'When? Why didn't you call me? This gives me something to run with. Oh, *please* tell me you got it on film.'

'I did, but I haven't seen the tapes yet.'

'So the lights are for real?'

'Yeah. But I think I found out where they're coming from. All I have to do is figure out how and why it happens when it does.'

Nate, for a rare moment, had nothing to say. Like the trained professional he was, however, he recovered quickly.

'OK, how's this?' he said. 'We open with the legend. Misty cemetery, a close-up on the graves . . .'

The man was the master of Hollywood clichés. Jeremy glanced at the clock. 'I'm tired, Nate. How about this? You think about it and let me know later, OK?'

'Yeah, I can do that. I'll be calling you in a couple of hours, so make sure you keep your phone on. Things could be moving quickly.'

'Goodbye, Nate. I'll talk to you later.'

Jeremy groaned as he got up and made his way to the bathroom. He turned the water in the shower as far as it would go and stayed under the single jet for twenty minutes. Only then did he begin to feel alive again. Sleeping less than two hours would do that to a person.

After throwing on his jeans, he grabbed the tapes, went outside and got into his car. The fog hung over the road and the sky had the same ugly tones as it had the day before, making him suspect the lights would appear again tonight, which not only boded well for the tourists this weekend but also meant that he should call Alvin. Even if the tapes were OK, Alvin was magic with a camera.

His first step, though, was to see what he'd caught on film. He'd seen a VCR in the rare-book room at the library, and as he drove towards town, he wondered how Lexie would behave towards him when he got there. Would she go back to being distant and professional? Would the good feelings from their day together linger? He had no idea what was going to happen, even though he'd devoted much of the night to trying to figure it out.

Sure, he'd found the source of the light. The moon, he'd learned, couldn't have been responsible for the lights. It was, in fact, a new moon, when the moon was hidden by the earth's shadow, and he had a sneaking suspicion that the mysterious lights only occurred in this particular phase. It would make sense: without moonlight, even the faintest traces of other light would become that much more obvious, especially when reflected in the water droplets of the fog.

But as he'd stood in the chilly air with the answer within reach, all he could think about was Lexie. It seemed impossible that he'd met her only two days earlier. Einstein had postulated that time was relative, and he supposed that could explain it. How did the old saying about relativity go? A minute with a beautiful woman would pass in an instant, while a minute with your hand placed on a hot burner would feel like an eternity? Yeah, he thought, that was it.

Part of him knew it was time for him to grow up, maybe even settle down and live the sort of life his brothers did. But in the past few years, since Maria had left him, it just seemed easier to not get to know women too well, to keep them perpetual strangers, when they could still project hope and potential on him.

And that was the thing. There wasn't hope or potential. Most women wanted a way of life he couldn't give them. Not because he didn't want to, but simply because it was impossible. Science could solve a lot of problems, but it couldn't change his particular reality. And the reality was that Maria had left him because he hadn't been the kind of husband she'd wanted. He admitted this painful truth to no one, of course. Not to his brothers, not to his parents, not to Lexie. And usually, even in quiet moments, not even to himself.

THE LIBRARY WAS OPEN, but Lexie wasn't there. He felt a pang of disappointment when he pushed open the office door only to find the room empty. She'd been in earlier, though: the rare-book room had been left unlocked, and when he turned on the light, he saw a note on the desk along with the topography maps he'd mentioned. *I'm taking care of some personal things. Feel free to use the VCR. Lexie*

No mention of yesterday or last night, no mention of wanting to see him again. She might have been in a rush, or she might have kept it short because she planned to be back soon.

Jeremy had work to do, so he forced himself to focus on chasing the tail end of the story. The audio recorders had picked up no unusual sounds, and neither the microwave nor the electromagnetic detector had registered the slightest energy variances. The videotapes had picked up everything he'd seen the night before, but they were far from television quality.

However, observing the way in which the lights had changed during the twenty-two seconds they were visible assured him again that he'd indeed found the answer. He popped the tapes out, perused the topography maps, and calculated the distance from Riker's Hill to the river. He compared his photographs of the cemetery with those he found in books about the town's history and came up with an estimate regarding the rate that the cemetery was sinking. He tapped a few words into a search engine on the Internet to look for the timetables he needed, then, finally, he spoke to a Mr Larsen at the paper mill, who was eager to help.

And with that, all the pieces came together. The truth had been in front of everyone all along. Like most mysteries, the solution had been simple, and it made him wonder why no one had realised it before. Unless, of course, someone had, which opened the door to another angle on the story.

But, despite the morning's success, Jeremy felt little sense of accomplishment. Instead, all he thought about was the fact that Lexie wasn't around to either congratulate or tease him about it. He rose from his seat to check her office again. It looked the same as it had the day before—stacks of documents, books scattered haphazardly, the answering machine flashing messages. But without Lexie, the room may as well have been completely empty.

'MY MAIN MAN!' Alvin shouted into the receiver. 'Life treating you good down South?'

Despite the static on Jeremy's cellphone, Alvin sounded remarkably chipper.

'I'm fine. I was calling to see if you'd still like to come down and help me.'

'I'm already gathering my gear,' he answered. 'Nate called an hour ago and told me all about it. I'll meet you at Greenleaf later tonight. This is the first day that flights are even close to being on schedule.'

'What are you talking about?'

'Haven't you seen the news? It's been an absolute blizzard since you left. Manhattan is practically buried.'

As Alvin explained, Jeremy tapped his computer keys, calling up the weather on the Internet. On the national map, the Northeast was a blanket of white. L-I-B, he thought.

'I guess I've been busy,' he said.

'Hiding's more like it,' Alvin said. 'I hope she's worth it.'

'What?'

'Don't pull my chain. Nate can't reach you and you haven't been watching the news. We both know what that means. Is she pretty?'

Jeremy hesitated. 'Yeah. But we're just friends.'

'I'm sure,' he said, laughing.

Jeremy felt a headache coming on and his tone took on an edge. 'I'm not in the mood for this, OK? I told you we're just friends.'

'I can't believe this. You're falling in love. I know you, so don't try to deny it.'

'Yeah, whatever. When will you be here?'

'I'm guessing around seven tonight. I'll see you then.'

Jeremy ended the call, shoving his phone back into his pocket. No wonder he'd been keeping it turned off.

Alvin didn't have a clue as to what he was talking about. The facts spoke for themselves. Love wasn't possible in a couple of days. True love needed time to grow into something strong and enduring. Love was about commitment and dedication. Lust was a possibility, but he couldn't *love* Lexie. Case closed. He smiled with satisfaction for a moment before his brow began to wrinkle.

The thing was, it didn't feel like lust, because even more than wanting to hold her or kiss her, he simply ached to see her again. To spend time with her. To talk to her. He wanted to watch her roll her eyes when he said something ridiculous, see her nervously tuck strands of hair behind her ear. He wanted to ask her about her dreams and hopes for the future, to know her secrets.

But if it couldn't be love and it didn't feel like lust, what was it? Did he *like* her? Of course, he did, but that word didn't come close to explaining why, for the first time, he felt the urge to tell someone the truth about his divorce. His brothers didn't know the truth, nor did his parents. But he wanted Lexie to know; and right now she was nowhere to be found.

Two minutes later, Jeremy's phone rang, and he recognised the number on the screen of his cellphone. Though not in the mood, he knew he had to answer, or the man would probably burst an artery. 'Hey there,' Jeremy said. 'What's happening?'

'Jeremy!' Nate shouted. Through the static, Jeremy could barely hear him. 'Great news! You can't believe how busy I've been. We've got a conference call with ABC at two o'clock!'

'Great,' he said.

'Jeremy! Are you still there? You're breaking up! You've got to use a public phone and call me here. At two o'clock! Your career depends on this! Your entire future depends on this! I can't hear a thing. Hit a button if you caught everything I'm saying.'

Jeremy pressed the 6.

'Great! Fantastic! Two o'clock! And be yourself!'

Jeremy hung up the phone, wondering how long it would take for Nate to realise that he wasn't on the line any more.

JEREMY WAITED. Then waited some more.

He paced the library, he wandered past Lexie's office, he peeked out of the window for signs of her car, feeling a growing sense of uneasiness. It was just a hunch, but nothing about her absence this morning seemed right. Now that he was finished with his research—other than possibly finding anecdotes in the diaries, which he hadn't finished going through—he wasn't sure what to do next.

He went downstairs and paused at the reception desk. 'Do you know where Ms Darnell is?' he asked the elderly volunteer. 'I got a note that said she was out.'

'She was here when I came in.' The volunteer checked the calendar on her desk. 'She doesn't have any appointments.'

'Would you know if she has a cellphone?'

'She doesn't—that I know for sure. Have you checked Herbs? She might be helping Doris get things ready for the weekend.'

'Thanks. If she comes in, will you tell her I was looking for her?'

Feeling more agitated than ever, Jeremy left the library. Before heading to Herbs, he swung by Lexie's house, noting the drawn curtains. Her car was gone. Although there was nothing out of the ordinary, it struck him as wrong somehow, and the uneasiness deepened as he retraced the roads back to town.

The morning rush at Herbs had died down, and it took only a moment to see that Lexie wasn't here, either. Rachel was wiping a table and waved when she saw him.

'Morning, darlin',' she said, approaching. 'It's a little late, but I'm sure we can whip up some breakfast, if you're hungry.'

'No, thanks,' he said, slipping his keys into his pocket. 'I'm not that hungry. But is Doris around?'

She smiled and nodded over her shoulder. 'She's in the back. I'll tell her you're here. That was quite a party last night. People were talking about you all morning. Do you want some coffee while you're waiting?'

'No, thanks,' he answered.

Rachel disappeared into the back, and a minute later, Doris emerged, wiping her hands on her apron. 'You caught me mixing dough. Last night set me back for the weekend and it's going to take a bit to catch up before the crowds tomorrow. Usually, a couple of hundred come in for the tour.'

He smiled. 'Life here never ceases to amaze me.'

'Don't knock it till you try it. I have a feeling you'd love it here.'

She sounded almost as if she were testing him and he wasn't quite sure how to respond.

'But, anyway,' Doris said, letting him off the hook, 'I'm glad you came by. Lexie mentioned that she told you about my notebook. She warned me that you probably wouldn't believe a word of it, but you're welcome to look through it.'

'I'd like that,' he said. 'Speaking of Lexie, have you seen her around? She wasn't at the library.'

She nodded. 'She came by the house this morning. She told me you two saw the lights last night.'

'We did. They were amazing, but like you said, they weren't ghosts.'

She looked at him, satisfied. 'And I take it that you've already figured everything out or you wouldn't be here otherwise.'

'I think so.'

'Good for you,' she said. 'I'm sorry I can't chat more now, but I'm kind of busy, so let me get my notebook for you. Who knows, maybe you'll want to do a story about my amazing powers next.'

'You never know,' he said. 'I just might.'

Jeremy watched her vanish into the kitchen. He noticed that Doris hadn't responded to his question about Lexie's whereabouts. Nor had she even ventured a guess, which seemed to suggest that she viewed the subject as off limits. He looked up to see her approaching again. 'Feel free to make copies if you want,' she said. 'But bring this back before you leave. It's pretty special to me.'

'I'll do that,' he promised. 'Can I return the notebook to Lexie if I see her today?'

'That's fine,' she said. 'But I'll be here, too, just in case.'

As he caught her obvious meaning, he felt his stomach sink. 'Did she say anything about me? Did she seem OK?'

'Lexie,' she began slowly, 'is hard to read sometimes. But I'm sure she'll be OK, if that's what you're asking.'

'Was she angry with me?'

'No, that I can tell you. She definitely wasn't angry.'

Waiting for more, Jeremy said nothing. In the silence, Doris took a long breath. 'I like you, Jeremy, but you're putting me on the spot. I know what you want and what you're asking. All I can say is that if Lexie wanted you to know where she is, she would have told you.'

With that, his mind began to absorb the fact that she was gone. 'I don't understand why she'd do something like this,' he said.

She gave a sad smile. 'Yes,' she said, 'I think you do.'

SHE WAS GONE.

Like an echo, the words kept repeating themselves. Behind the wheel on the way to Greenleaf, Jeremy tried to analyse the facts. He reminded himself there was no reason to panic. It wasn't as if something terrible had happened to her. It just boiled down to the fact that she didn't want to see him again. Perhaps he should have seen it coming. He'd expected too much.

So where did that leave him? He could sit back and accept her decision, or he could track her down. If there was one thing he was good at, it was finding people. He'd learned how to follow a trail of breadcrumbs to anyone's doorstep. He doubted, however, that that would be necessary. After all, she'd already given him the answer he needed, and he was sure he knew exactly where she'd gone.

The thing was, that didn't help him with the idea of what he should do. He had a conference call in a few hours, one with important ramifications for his career. Alvin would be arriving this evening, and though Alvin could handle the filming on his own tonight, they had to work together tomorrow.

On the other hand, he didn't want everything to end like this. He wanted to see Lexie; he needed to see her. A voice in his head warned him not to let his emotions govern his actions, and rationally, he couldn't see how anything good could come of him traipsing off in search of her.

In the end, the decision was simple. Now, he thought to himself, all he had to do was pack.

OK, SHE ADMITTED, she was a coward.

It wasn't the easiest thing for her to own up to the fact that she'd run away, but hey, she wasn't exactly thinking clearly these past couple of days. The truth was, if she had stayed around, things would have become even more complicated. She woke up this morning knowing that she had to end things before they went too far, and when she pulled in to the sandy driveway at the front, she knew she'd done the right thing by coming here.

The place wasn't much to look at. The old cottage was weathered and blended into the sea grass that surrounded it. The shingles had streaks of grey, the pipes groaned when she turned on the shower, and she had to light the stove burners with a match. But the memories here never ceased to calm her and, after storing the groceries she'd picked up, she'd opened the windows to air out the place. Then, grabbing a blanket, she settled into a rocker on the porch. When the sun broke through the clouds and beams of light stretched towards the ocean, she found herself holding her breath.

Last night ,she knew, she'd almost made a mistake, and she was pleased by how resolute she'd been when Jeremy wanted to come in. Part of her *had* wanted to let him inside, no matter what it might have led to. As she'd tossed and turned in her bed last night, she'd realised she might not have the strength to do the right thing again.

She should have seen it coming. As the evening had worn on, she'd found herself comparing Jeremy with both Avery and Mr Renaissance, and Jeremy more than held his own. He had Avery's wit and Mr Renaissance's intelligence and charm, but Jeremy seemed more comfortable with himself than either of them. No doubt the excitement and unpredictability of the day had reminded her of how happy she'd been when she still believed that Avery and Mr Renaissance were the men of her dreams.

But she'd been wrong then, just as she was wrong now. She knew Jeremy would solve the mystery today—since the answer was in one of the diaries, and all he had to do was find it—and she had no doubt that he would have asked her to celebrate the solution with him. The two of them would have spent the day together, and she didn't want that. Then again, deep down, it was exactly what she wanted, leaving her feeling more confused than she'd been in years.

So she'd come here to preserve her sanity, and she'd return to Boone Creek when things were back to normal. It wouldn't take long. In a couple of days, people would stop talking about the ghosts and the historic homes and the stranger in town. Lexie tugged the blanket tighter around her shoulders. She'd get over him, just as she'd got over the others. But the roiling sea reminded her again of her feelings for Jeremy and it took everything she had to keep her tears in check.

IT HAD SEEMED simple when Jeremy set out. He'd rushed through his room at Greenleaf, making the necessary plans as he did so. Grab the map and his wallet. Put Doris's book in his satchel and bring it along. Write a note for Alvin and leave it at the front desk.

He was in and out in less than ten minutes, on his way to Swan Quarter, where the ferry would take him to Ocracoke, a village in the Outer Banks. From there, he'd head north on Highway 12 to Buxton. He figured it was the route she would have taken, and all he had to do was follow the same path and he'd reach the place in just a couple of hours.

The drive was an easy one, on straight and empty roads, and he'd found himself thinking about Lexie. For one of the few times in his life, he was doing exactly the opposite of what logic demanded, moving on autopilot, thinking only about how she'd react when she saw him.

Just when he thought he was beginning to understand the reason for his odd behaviour, Jeremy found himself at the ferry station staring at a thin, uniformed man who barely looked up from the magazine he was reading. The ferry to Ocracoke, he learned, didn't run with regularity and he'd missed the last departure of the day. 'There's no other way that I can get to Hatteras Lighthouse?' he asked, feeling his heart pick up speed. 'This is important.'

'You could drive it, I suppose.'

'How long would that take?'

The man shrugged. 'Depends how fast you drive. Five or six hours maybe.'

Jeremy checked his watch. It was already coming up to one o'clock; by the time he got there, Alvin would probably be pulling into Boone Creek. No good.

'What if I told you this was an emergency?' he asked.

The man looked up.

'Then I'd call the Coast Guard. Or maybe the sheriff.'

'Ah,' Jeremy said, trying to remain patient. 'But what you're telling me is that there's no way for me to get out there right now?'

The man brought a finger to his chin. 'I suppose you could take a boat, if you're in such a hurry.'

Now we're getting somewhere, Jeremy thought. 'And how would I arrange that?'

'I don't know. No one's ever asked.'

JEREMY HOPPED BACK into his car, admitting that he was beginning to panic.

Maybe it was because he'd already come this far, or maybe because he realised his final words to Lexie the night before had signalled a deeper truth, but something had taken hold of him and he wasn't going back, not after getting this close. Nate would be expecting his call, but suddenly that didn't seem as important to him as it once was. Nor did the fact that Alvin would be arriving; if all went well, they could still film both this evening and tomorrow evening. He had ten hours until the lights would appear; in a fast boat, he figured that he could reach Hatteras in two. It gave him plenty of time to get there, talk to Lexie and come back. He had cash in his wallet and he'd find a way to get there.

Nothing about this entire scenario made sense. But who cared? Sure, he was leaving in a couple of days, but that didn't mean this had to be over. He could visit down here, she could come up to New York and, if it was meant to be, they'd work it out. People did that all the time, right? But even if she was resolute in her determination to end things, he wanted to hear her say it. Only then could he return to New York knowing he'd had no other choice.

And yet, as he came to a sliding stop at the first marina he saw, he realised he wasn't going to Buxton to say goodbye. He was going there to find out if Alvin had been right all along.

LATE AFTERNOON was Lexie's favourite time of day. The soft winter sunlight, combined with the austere natural beauty of the landscape, made the world appear dreamlike. Even the lighthouse, with its black-and-white candy-cane pattern, seemed like a mirage from here, and as she walked the length of the beach, she tried to imagine how difficult it had been for the sailors and fishermen to navigate the point before it had been built.

Her grandfather had been a history buff, and every time they had walked the beach holding hands, he had told her stories about the ships that had been lost over the centuries. Recalling those walks made her miss her grandfather with sudden intensity. The strolls had been part of their daily routine and sometimes they'd see the wild horses.

Usually, the horses kept themselves at a distance, but at dusk they liked to graze, lowering their defences, if only for a few minutes. It was possible to see their distinctive markings and, if you were lucky, to hear them snorting and whinnying.

These days, watching them always made her feel as if she were young again, with all of life's pleasures and expectations ahead of her. She wanted to feel that way now, if only to escape the pressures of adult life. Doris had called to tell her that Jeremy had come in looking for her. It hadn't surprised her. Jeremy was one of those people who were confident in everything they did, forever moving forward without a backward glance.

Avery had been that way, and even now she still remembered how hurt she'd been by his sense of entitlement, his indifference to her pain. Looking back, she knew she should have seen his character flaws, and even more than being disappointed in him, she was disappointed in herself. She'd told herself she would get over it, that she would meet someone better . . . someone like Mr Renaissance, who proved once and for all that she wasn't a good judge of men. Nor, it seemed, could she keep one.

It wasn't easy to admit that, and there were moments when she wondered whether she might have done something to drive both men off. Had she been too pushy? Was she boring? These were the questions she'd never been able to answer.

In the distance, with the sun sinking into the waters of the Pamlico Sound, the town of Buxton looked like a postcard. Staring towards the lighthouse, she saw a small herd of horses grazing in the sea grass. Lexie stopped to watch them, tucking her hands in her jacket pockets. Despite herself, she wondered what Jeremy was doing. Was he preparing to film again? Or deciding where to eat? Was he packing? And why did her thoughts constantly turn to him?

She sighed, already knowing the answer. She was lonely. As much as she thought of herself as independent, she couldn't help but feel a yearning for companionship, for intimacy. It didn't even have to be marriage; sometimes all she wanted was to look forward to Friday or Saturday night.

Lexie shook her head. In coming here, she had hoped to find relief from her thoughts, but as she stood near the lighthouse and watched the horses grazing, she felt the world bearing down hard. She was thirty-one, alone and living in a place without any prospects. Her grandfather and parents were nothing but memories, the state of Doris's health was a source of constant worry to her, and the one man she'd found even remotely interesting in recent years would be gone by the time she returned home.

That was when she started to cry, and for a time, she found it difficult to stop. But just as she was beginning to collect herself, she saw someone approaching, and all she could do was stare when she realised who it was.

SEVEN

Lexie blinked, trying to make sure that what she was seeing was real. It couldn't be *him*, because he couldn't be *here*.

Jeremy smiled as he set his satchel down. 'You know, you really shouldn't stare like that,' he said. 'Men like women who know how to be subtle.'

Lexie squinted at him in the waning light, and it occurred to Jeremy that she was even prettier than he remembered.

'You,' she replied. 'What are you . . .? How did you . . .?'

'It's kind of a long story,' he admitted. When she made no move towards him, he nodded at the lighthouse. 'And this is the lighthouse where your parents were married?'

'You remembered that?'

'I remember everything,' he said, tapping his temple. 'Little grey cells and all that. Where exactly were they married?'

He spoke casually, as if this were the most ordinary of conversations, which only made everything feel even more surreal to her.

'Over there,' she said pointing. 'On the ocean side, near the waterline.'

'It must have been beautiful,' he said. 'I can see why you love it here.'

Instead of responding, Lexie took a long breath, trying to settle her turbulent emotions. 'What are you doing here, Jeremy?'

It was a moment before he answered. 'I wasn't sure you were coming back,' he said. 'And I realised that if I wanted to see you again, the best option was to come to you.' He paused. 'It felt like I didn't have a choice.'

As they stood near the lighthouse, the sun began to sink below the horizon. The breeze, damp and cold, skimmed the surface of the sand. Lexie could feel the shock of Jeremy's appearance beginning to wear off. Part of her wanted to be angry; yet another part, the greater part, was flattered that he'd come to find her. Avery had never bothered to come after her, nor had Mr Renaissance. Rodney would never have thought of coming here. It was beginning to dawn on her that Jeremy was different from anyone she'd met before and that she shouldn't be surprised by anything he did.

The horses in the distance had begun to wander off. The coastal mist was rolling in, merging sea and sky. Jeremy cupped his hands and blew into them. 'Are you angry that I came?' he asked finally.

'No,' she admitted. 'Surprised, but not angry.'

He smiled, and she returned it with a flicker of her own.

'How did you get here?' she asked.

He motioned towards Buxton. 'I got a ride from a couple of fishermen,' he said. 'They dropped me at the marina.'

'They gave you a ride just like that?'

'Well, people are people,' he said. 'Even strangers can sense the urgency of a request and will usually do the right thing.' He stood straighter. 'But when that didn't work, I offered to pay them.'

She giggled at his admission. 'They took you to the cleaners, didn't they?'

He nodded. 'But they did make sure I understood it was a one-way trip. So I guess I'm stuck here.'

She raised an eyebrow. 'Really? How did you plan to get back?'

He gave an impish grin. 'Well, I happen to know someone who's staying out here, and I was planning on using my dazzling charm to convince her to give me a ride back to Boone Creek.'

'And where did you intend to stay while you were out here?'

'I haven't figured that part out yet.'

'At least you're honest about it,' she said, smiling. 'But tell me, what would you have done if I wasn't here?'

'Where else would you have gone?'

She glanced away, liking that he'd remembered this about her. 'Are you hungry?' she asked. 'Would you like to have dinner?'

'Do you know a nice place?'

'I have a pretty good place in mind.'

'Do they take credit cards? I used all my cash to get here.'

'I'm sure,' she said, 'that we'll be able to work something out.'

TURNING FROM THE LIGHTHOUSE, they made their way back down the beach, walking along the water's edge. In the silence, Jeremy mentally replayed his journey here, feeling a pang of guilt about Nate and Alvin. He'd missed the conference call—there had been no reception at all as he was crossing Pamlico Sound—and figured that he should call from the land line as soon as he was able. Nate would go ballistic, but Jeremy planned to suggest a meeting with the producers next week, complete with footage and the outlines of the story, an idea that he suspected had been the whole point of the call, anyway. If missing a single call could end his career before it started, then he wasn't sure he wanted to work in television.

And Alvin . . . well, there was no way Jeremy could get back to Boone Creek to meet Alvin tonight, but Alvin had a cellphone, and he'd explain what was going on. Alvin was one of those rare people who never let anything bother them for more than a day.

Yet, being honest with himself, Jeremy admitted that he didn't care about any of that now. All that seemed to matter was that he was walking with Lexie on a quiet beach and that as they trudged into the salty breeze, she quietly looped her arm through his.

Lexie led the way up the warped wooden steps of the old bungalow. 'Do you like pasta?' she asked.

'Are you kidding? My mother happens to be Italian.'

'Good,' she said. 'Because that's what I planned on making.'

'We're eating here?'

'I guess we have to. You're out of cash, remember?'

The kitchen was small, with fading yellow paint, scuffed cabinets and a small painted table.

'Do you need a hand?' he asked.

'No, I've got it, thanks,' she said. 'Do you want something to drink? I have beer in the refrigerator.'

Jeremy moved to the refrigerator and pulled out two bottles. Leaning against the counter, he crossed one leg over the other. 'Just to let you know, I'm pretty good at chopping if you need help.'

'I'll keep that in mind,' she said.

He smiled. 'How long has your family owned this place?'

'My grandparents bought it right after World War Two. Back then, there wasn't even a road on the island. You had to drive across the sand to get here. There are some pictures in the living room of how this place looked back then.'

'Would you mind if I took a look?'

'Go ahead. There's a bathroom down the hall if you want to wash up before dinner. In the guest bedroom on the right.'

Moving to the living room, Jeremy examined the pictures of rustic shore life, then headed down the hall. On the left, he saw an airy room with a large pedestal bed topped by a seashell-patterned comforter. Crossing the hall, he entered the other room. It was nautical in theme, and as he slipped off his shoes and socks at the foot of the bed, he wondered what it would be like to sleep in here while knowing Lexie was alone across the hall.

At the bathroom basin, he looked at himself in the mirror. His skin was coated with a thin layer of salt and, after washing his hands, he splashed water on his face as well. Feeling somewhat better, he went back to the kitchen and heard the melancholy notes of the Beatles' 'Yesterday' coming from a radio on the windowsill.

'Ready for some help yet?' he asked. Beside her, he saw a medium-size salad bowl; in it were chunks of tomatoes and olives.

Lexie nodded towards the onions. 'I'm almost done with the salad, but would you mind taking the skin off those two?'

'Sure. Do you need me to dice them, too?'

'No, that's OK. Just take off the skins. There's a knife in the drawer.'

Jeremy pulled out a steak knife and reached for the onions on the counter. For a while, they worked without speaking. Lexie tried to ignore how close they were standing together. But from the corner of her eye, she couldn't help admiring Jeremy's broad shoulders, his high cheekbones.

He held up a bald onion, oblivious to what she'd been thinking. 'So you're just going to put these big onions in the sauce?'

'No. I'll cut them in half first.'

'Can I at least do that?'

'No, thanks.' She smiled. 'I'm the cook, remember?'

He glanced at her. Since they'd come in from the cold, the rosiness in her cheeks had faded, leaving her with a fresh, natural glow.

Lexie pulled out a pot, then turned on the gas and lit the fumes under the burner. The blue flame whooshed to life. She poured two cans of tomatoes into the pot, then added a stick of butter to the sauce before adding all four onion halves. Stirring with a long wooden spoon, she let it come to a boil, then set the heat on low.

'OK, then,' she said, satisfied, 'we're done for now.'

As she washed her hands, Jeremy peeked into the saucepan. 'That's it? No garlic? No meatballs?'

She shook her head. 'Three ingredients only,' she said. 'We'll pour it over linguine and top it with fresh-grated Parmesan cheese.' She turned the tap off, shook her hands over the sink and dried them on a dishcloth. 'But since we've got some time, I'm going to clean up before dinner. If you'd like, you can take a shower. I'll set some towels out for you.'

Still feeling the salt on his neck and arms, it took only an instant for him to agree. 'Thanks. That would be great.'

She smiled as she squeezed past him, feeling his eyes on her hips. She wondered whether he was feeling as self-conscious as she was.

At the end of the hall, she opened the closet door, grabbed a couple of towels and put them on his bed. Beneath the basin in his bathroom were assorted shampoos and a new bar of soap, and she set those out as well. As she did, she caught a reflection of herself in the mirror and had the sudden image of Jeremy wrapped in a towel after showering. The image made something jump inside.

'Hello?' she heard him call. 'Where are you?'

'I'm in the bathroom,' she answered, amazed by how calm her voice sounded.

He came up behind her. 'I wanted to ask if it's OK to use your phone. I have to make a couple of calls.'

She nodded. 'The phone's in the kitchen.'

Edging past him, she sensed him watching her again, though she didn't turn round to check. Instead, she went to her room, closed the door and leaned against it, embarrassed at the foolish way she'd been feeling. Nothing had happened; nothing would happen, she told herself again. She locked the door, hoping it would be enough to block out her thoughts. And it worked, at least for a moment, until she had to admit that she'd been lying to herself all along.

By THE TIME Jeremy returned to the kitchen after his shower, he could smell the sauce as it simmered on the stove. Locating the phone, he dialled Nate's number and was put through immediately. For the first twenty seconds, he held the receiver away from his ear while Nate went off the deep end, but he finally calmed down. Jeremy ended the call with a promise to talk to him again tomorrow.

Alvin, on the other hand, was impossible to reach. It was almost six and Jeremy figured that Alvin was somewhere on the highway. Hopefully, they'd have a chance to talk before he went out tonight.

He headed back into the darkened living room. Peering down the hall, he noted a light beneath Lexie's closed door. Unsure of what to do next, he turned on a small reading lamp near the fireplace. Then he remembered that he hadn't looked at Doris's notebook yet. After pulling it out of his satchel, he took a seat and felt the tension in his shoulders begin to ease.

Now, this was nice. This felt like the way things should be.

EARLIER, AS SHE HEARD Jeremy close the door to his room, Lexie stood near the window and took a pull of her beer, glad she has something to calm her nerves. Both of them had kept their kitchen conversation superficial, keeping their distance until things were sorted out. She knew she should stay the course, but as she set her beer aside, she realised that she didn't want to keep her distance. Not any more.

Despite the risks, everything about him had drawn her closer—the surprise at seeing him walking towards her on the beach, his easy smile and tousled hair, the nervous, boylike gaze—and in that instant, he'd been both the man she knew and the man she didn't. She wanted to know the part of him he'd kept hidden from her, wherever it might lead.

After showering, she sorted through her suitcase until she found her favourite pair of jeans. Deeply faded, they were ripped at the knees and the turnups were frayed. But she was aware of how they accentuated her figure. She felt a secret thrill at her certainty that Jeremy would notice.

She slipped into a long-sleeved white shirt and rolled the sleeves up to her elbows. Smiling, she tried to remember the last time looking good had really mattered to her.

Jeremy was sitting in the chair when she came into the room. He looked up at her, and it seemed as if he wanted to say something, but no words came out. Instead, he just stared.

Unable to look away, he knew why it had been so important to find her again. He'd had no choice, for he knew then that he was in love with her.

'You look . . . incredible,' he finally whispered.

'Thank you,' she said, hearing the raw emotion in his voice and revelling in the way it made her feel. Their eyes met and held, and in that instant, she understood that the message in his gaze was mirroring her own.

For a moment, neither of them seemed able to move, until Lexie glanced away. She headed for the kitchen on unsteady legs to check on the sauce. Opening the refrigerator, she took out a jar of olives. She tried to open it, but her hands were trembling.

'Need a hand with that?' Jeremy asked.

She looked up, surprised. She hadn't heard him come in, and wondered if her feelings were as obvious as they felt.

Jeremy took the olives from her. She watched the sinewy muscles of his forearms as he twisted the cap off. Then he leaned against the counter. She was close enough to reach out and touch him and for a fleeting moment almost did; but instead, she turned away and went to the cupboard.

She took out some olive oil and balsamic vinegar and put some of each in a small bowl, along with salt and pepper.

'Everything smells delicious,' he said.

Finished with the dressing, she put the olives into a bowl. 'These will have to do for an appetiser.'

He led the way back to the living room, picked up Doris's book, then watched as Lexie took a seat on the couch. When he sat beside her, he could smell the sweet, floral scent of the shampoo she'd used. From the kitchen, he heard the faintest strains of the radio.

'I see you have Doris's notebook,' she said.

He nodded. 'She let me borrow it. I had a chance to look over a few pages. It has a lot more detail than I thought it would.'

'Now do you believe she predicted the sex of all those babies?'

'No,' he said. 'You can't predict the sex of babies by holding someone's hand.'

'Because you say so.'

'No. Because it's impossible.'

'Mr Sceptic. So how's your story going?'

'Good,' he said. 'I'd still like to finish looking through the diaries, though. Maybe find something to spice up the story.'

'Have you figured it out?'

'Yes,' he said. 'Now all I have to do is prove it. Hopefully, the weather will cooperate.'

'It will,' she said. 'It's supposed to be foggy all weekend.'

'The solution isn't nearly as much fun as the legend. But I wouldn't have missed this trip for the world.'

Hearing his tone, she knew exactly what he meant. She turned towards him, propping her chin on her hand. 'So what is it?' she asked. 'Can you tell me the answer?'

The lamplight behind her gave her the faintest halo and her eyes glowed violet beneath dark lashes.

'I'd rather show you,' he said.

She smiled. 'Since I'm driving you back, you mean?'

'Right.'

'And you want to go back . . .?'

'Tomorrow, if we can.' He shook his head, trying to regain control of his feelings. 'I've got to meet Alvin, a cameraman from New York. He's coming to get some professional footage. He's probably arriving in town as we speak.'

'He's coming to Boone Creek? Shouldn't you be there?'

'Probably,' he admitted.

She thought about what he'd said, touched by the effort he had made to come today.

'OK,' she said. 'There's an early ferry. We can be back around ten.'

'Thanks,' he said.

'And you're going to film tomorrow night?'

He nodded. 'I left a note telling Alvin to go to the cemetery tonight, but we have to film elsewhere, too. And tomorrow's going to be a full day.'

'What about the barn dance? I thought we had a deal that if you solved the mystery, I'd dance with you.'

Jeremy lowered his head. 'If I can make it, I will. Believe me. There's nothing I want more.'

Silence filled the room.

'When are you going back to New York?' she finally asked.

'Saturday,' he said. 'I have to be in New York for a meeting next week.'

Her heart sank at his words. 'Back to the exciting life, huh?'

He shook his head. 'My life in New York isn't all that glamorous. Actually, it can get pretty lonely at times.'

She raised a brow. 'Don't try to make me feel sorry for you, because I'm not buying it.'

He glanced at her. 'I don't live in New York for the excitement, whatever you might think. I live there because my family's there, because I'm comfortable there. It's home to me. Just like Boone Creek is home to you.'

'I take it your family is close.'

'Yeah,' he said, 'we are. We get together almost every weekend at my mom and dad's in Queens for these great big dinners. It's always a real zoo: a bunch of kids running around, Mom cooking in the kitchen, my brothers and their wives standing around in the back yard. Of course, they all live nearby, so they're over there even more often than I am.'

She tried to picture the scene. 'Sounds nice.'

'It is. But it's hard sometimes.'

She looked at him. 'I don't understand.' Perhaps it was the way he said it that kept her from saying anything else; in the silence, she watched him closely, waiting for him to continue.

'Did you ever have a dream?' he asked. 'Something you wanted so badly and just when you think you're about to reach out and grab it, something else takes it away?'

'Everyone has dreams that don't come true,' she answered, her voice guarded. 'I'm not sure what you're trying to tell me.'

'There's something you don't know about me,' he said.

'You're married,' she said, leaning back.

He shook his head. 'No. I was married. And divorced.'

Expecting far worse, she almost laughed aloud in relief, but his sombre expression restrained her.

'Her name was Maria. We shared the same values and beliefs about all the big things in life. Including our desire for children.' He hesitated. 'We didn't know there was a problem right away, but after six months, when she still wasn't pregnant, we went in for some routine tests. She turned out to be fine, but I wasn't. Just one of those things. When she found out, she decided she didn't want to stay in the marriage any more.'

Lexie stared at him. 'Your wife left you because you found out that you couldn't have kids?' she asked.

'Not right away. But in the end, yes.'

'And there was nothing the doctors could do?'

'No.' He seemed almost embarrassed. 'I mean, they didn't say it was utterly impossible for me to have a child, but they made it clear that it would most likely never happen.'

'What about adoption? Or finding a donor? Or . . .'

Jeremy shook his head. 'We could have adopted; I suggested all of that. But her heart wasn't in it. Things started going downhill. But it wasn't just her. I changed, too. I was moody . . . I started travelling even more for my work . . . maybe I drove her away.'

Lexie studied him. 'Why are you telling me all this?'

'Maybe it's because I want you to know what you're getting into with someone like me.'

At his words, Lexie felt the blood rush to her cheeks. She shook her head and turned away. 'Don't say things you don't mean.'

'What makes you think I don't mean them?'

Outside, the wind began to pick up, and she heard the faint tones of the wind chime near the door.

'Because you can't. Because it's not who you are,' she said. 'You have a big family that you see frequently; I only have Doris, and she needs me here. You like cities, I like small towns. You have a career you love, and I . . . well, I have the library, and I love that, too. If one of us is forced to change what we have, what we've chosen to make of our lives . . .' She closed her eyes briefly. 'One of us would have to sacrifice. And if I don't want to have to sacrifice, I don't think it's fair to expect you to sacrifice, either.'

She lowered her gaze. Her lovely face was clouded with sadness and he was suddenly gripped by the fear that he might be losing any chance he had with her. Reaching over, he used his finger to turn her cheek towards him. 'What if I tell you that I'd rather be with you than go back to my old life?'

His finger felt electric against her skin. Trying to ignore the sensation, she held her voice steady. 'Then I would tell you that I've had a wonderful time in the last couple of days, too. That meeting you has been . . . well, amazing. And that I'm flattered.'

'But you don't want to try to make this work.'

Lexie shook her head. 'Jeremy . . . I . . .'

'It's OK,' he said, 'I understand.'

'No,' she said, 'you don't. I have things in my past that left me wounded, too.' Calmly, she told him about Mr Renaissance. 'Maybe that's why I'm trying to be practical. Can you honestly say we'll feel the same way about each other if we have to travel to spend time together?'

'Yes,' he said, his voice firm. 'I can.'

She looked almost sad at his answer. 'You can say that now, but what about tomorrow? What about a month from now?'

Outside, the wind made a whistling sound. The curtains swayed as the air forced its way through the old panes.

Jeremy stared at Lexie, realising once again that he loved her.

'Lexie,' he said, his mouth going dry. 'I . . .'

Knowing what he was going to say, she raised her hands to stop him. 'Please,' she said. 'Don't. I'm not ready for that yet, OK? For now, let's just enjoy dinner.'

With a sinking feeling, Jeremy watched as she rose from the couch. Pausing, she turned round to face him.

'And just so you know, I think what your ex-wife did was terrible. And the fact that you can say anything kind about her at all says that she's the one who made the mistake.'

She turned in the direction of the kitchen, vanishing from sight. Billie Holiday was singing 'I'll Be Seeing You' on the radio. With his throat tightening, Jeremy rose to follow her.

He leaned against the doorway of the kitchen. 'Thank you for saying what you said,' he said.

'You're welcome,' she responded, refusing to meet his eyes.

'Will you do me a favour?' he asked, reaching out his hand. 'Would you dance with me?'

'Here?' She looked up, startled, her heart racing. 'Now?'

Without another word, he moved closer. With his eyes locked on hers, he slipped his arm round her back and gently pulled her towards him.

The melody played softly in the background. As his hand tenderly skimmed her back, she closed her eyes and leaned into him, dropping her head onto his shoulder and feeling the last of her resolve slip away. This, she realised, was what she had wanted all along, and in the tiny kitchen, they moved in rhythm to the gentle music, each of them lost in the other.

When at last she lifted her head to meet his eyes, he wrapped his arms around her. He brushed his lips against hers once, and then twice, before pressing them close. After pulling back slightly to make sure she was OK, he kissed her again and she kissed him back, revelling in the strength of his arms. She brought a hand to his face, tracing the stubble on his cheek, and he responded to her touch by kissing her cheek and neck. They kissed in the kitchen for a long time, both of them savouring the other. Then, taking his hand again, she led him to her bedroom.

Hours later, Lexie rose from the bed and slipped into a bathrobe. Jeremy put on his jeans and joined her in the kitchen, where they finished cooking dinner. Lexie lit a candle and they ate together at the table.

Afterwards, they went back to bed, and he pulled her close, content to simply hold her. When Lexie eventually fell asleep in his arms, Jeremy watched her sleep. Every now and then, he brushed the hair from her eyes, reliving the evening, remembering it all, and knowing in his heart that he'd met the woman with whom he wanted to spend the rest of his life.

JUST BEFORE DAWN, Jeremy woke and realised that Lexie was gone. He snapped on his jeans and made his way to the living room, where he found her in the easy chair near the fireplace. In her lap was Doris's notebook.

In the dim light, he sensed that something was wrong. He sat on the armrest and slipped his arm round her. 'Are you OK?' he murmured.

'Yeah,' she said. 'I couldn't sleep. And, besides, we have to be up in a little while to catch the ferry.'

He nodded, though he wasn't completely satisfied by her answer. 'Are you sorry about what happened?'

'No,' she said. She didn't, however, add anything else and Jeremy pulled her closer, trying to believe her.

Lexie smiled. 'It's been a while since I've looked through the notebook.' She pointed down at the open page in her lap. 'Did you get to this entry?'

'No,' he answered.

'Read it,' she said.

Jeremy saw the names of the parents, their ages, and the fact that the woman would have a girl. When he finished, he looked at her.

'The names Jim and Claire don't mean anything to you?'

'No.' He scrutinised her face. 'Should they?'

Lexie lowered her eyes. 'They were my parents.' Her voice was quiet. 'We think we know each other, but you didn't even know the names of my parents. And I don't know the names of your parents.'

Jeremy felt a knot in his stomach. 'And that bothers you? That you don't think we know each other that well?'

'No,' she said. 'What bothers me is that I don't know if we ever will.'

Then, with a tenderness that made his heart ache, she wrapped her arms around him. For a long time, they sat in the chair holding each other.

'SO THIS IS YOUR FRIEND, huh?' Lexie asked. She gestured discreetly to the holding cell. Although Lexie had lived in Boone Creek all her life, she'd never visited the jail—until today.

Jeremy nodded. 'He's not normally like this,' he whispered.

Earlier in the morning, they had packed their belongings and closed up the cottage, each reluctant to leave it behind. When they drove off the ferry in Swan Quarter, Jeremy's cellphone picked up a signal. Nate had left four messages about the upcoming meeting; Alvin had left a frantic one, saying he'd been arrested.

Lexie had dropped Jeremy off at his car, and he'd followed her back to Boone Creek. He worried about Alvin but worried about Lexie as well. Lexie's disconcerting mood, which had started in the predawn darkness, had continued. When she smiled, it was only a flicker, and when he took her hand, she didn't squeeze his.

Meanwhile, Alvin was in jail, looking—to Lexie's eyes, at least—like he belonged there. Dressed in leather trousers and jacket and a studded wristband, Alvin was staring at them with wild eyes. 'What kind of a cracker town is this? Can you *please* get me out of here?'

Behind them, Rodney stood scowling, ignoring Alvin, as he had been for the last eight hours. The guy whined way too much, and besides, Rodney was far more interested in Jeremy and Lexie. According to Jed, Jeremy hadn't come back to his room last night and Lexie hadn't been at home, either. Which wasn't good at all.

'I'm sure we'll figure something out,' Jeremy said, not wanting to rile Rodney any further. 'Tell me what happened.'

Alvin took on a crazed look. 'You want to know what happened? This whole place is nuts, that's what happened! First, I get lost trying to find this stupid town, since there doesn't seem to be a town. And so I finally get to Greenleaf, right? And the gigantic hairy guy gives me the evil eye, hands me your note, and sticks me in this room with all these dead animals—'

'All the rooms are like that.'

'Whatever!' Alvin grunted. 'So I got your note and follow your directions to the cemetery, right? And I get there just in time to see the lights, and it's fantastic, you know. So I head down to this place called Lookilu for a nightcap. I get to talking to this gal named Rachel. We're hitting it off, and then this guy walks in looking like he just swallowed a porcupine . . .' He nodded towards Rodney, who smiled without showing his teeth.

'So, a little later, I go out to my car, and the next thing I know, this guy is tapping on my window, asking me to step out of the car and asking me how much I've had to drink. So I tell him I'm fine and that I'm here working with you, and the next thing I know, I'm locked up for the night! Now, *get me out of here!*'

Lexie looked over her shoulder. 'Is that what happened, Rodney?'

Rodney cleared his throat. 'He forgot the part where he called me a stupid musclehead. He seemed so irrational that I thought he might be on drugs or get violent, so I brought him in.'

'You were harassing me! I didn't do anything!'

'You were drinking and driving.'

'Two beers! I had two beers!'

Rodney shrugged. 'I was just doing my job.'

It was clear that the two of them had been going on like this most of the night.

'Let me talk to Rodney,' Lexie finally whispered.

When she left with the deputy, Alvin fell silent.

'We'll get you out of here,' Jeremy reassured him. 'Let Lexie handle it. She'll take care of it.'

OUT IN THE HALLWAY, Lexie looked up at Rodney. 'What's really going on?'

Rodney wouldn't meet her eyes. 'Where were you last night?' he asked.

She crossed her arms. 'I was at the cottage at the beach.'

'With him?'

Lexie hesitated. 'I didn't go with him, if that's what you're asking.'

Rodney nodded, knowing she hadn't answered completely, but suddenly realising he didn't want to know any more.

'Why did you arrest him? Honestly.'

'I wasn't planning to. He brought it on himself. He was hitting on Rachel, and you know how she can get when she drinks: all flirty and without a speck of common sense. I know it's none of my business, but someone has to watch out for her.' He paused. 'Anyway, he was drinking and planning on driving. And that's illegal.'

'Was he over the legal limit?'

'I don't know. I never bothered to check.'

'Rodney!' she whispered loudly.

'He made me angry, Lexie. He's rude and weird-looking and hitting on Rachel and calling me names; then he says he's working with this guy . . .' He motioned with his head towards Jeremy.

Lexie laid a hand on his shoulder. 'Listen to me, OK? You know you will get in trouble if you keep him in here. Especially with the mayor. And besides, you know that the sooner you let him out, the sooner the both of them can leave.'

'You really think he'll leave?'

Lexie looked Rodney in the eye. 'His flight is tomorrow.'

Rodney held her gaze. 'Are you going with him?'

It took a moment for her to answer the question she'd been asking herself all morning. 'No,' she whispered. 'Boone Creek is my home. And this is where I'm staying.'

TEN MINUTES LATER, Alvin was walking out to the parking lot beside Jeremy and Lexie. They reached the car and Jeremy motioned for Alvin to get in. 'This isn't the end of it,' Alvin grumbled. 'That guy should be fired.'

'The best thing you can do is forget about it,' Lexie said, looking through the open car door at him.

'Forget about it? Are you insane? He was wrong!'

'Yes, he was. But since no charges were filed, you'll let it go.'

'Who are you to tell me what to do?'

'I'm Lexie Darnell,' she said, drawling out her name. 'And not only am I a friend of Jeremy's, but I have to live here with Rodney and I feel a lot safer with him around. Everyone in town feels safer because of him. You, on the other hand, are leaving tomorrow, and he's not going to bother you again.' She smiled.

He stared at her in disbelief before glancing at Jeremy. 'She's the one?' he asked.

Jeremy nodded.

'She's pretty,' Alvin commented. 'Maybe a little on the pushy side, but pretty.' He was silent for a moment. 'I take it you think she's right about dropping this whole thing.'

'I do. She understands this place better than you or me.'

'Can we go now?' Lexie asked.

Alvin seemed to be considering his options. 'I'll forget any of this ever happened. On one condition.'

'What's that?' Jeremy asked.

'I haven't eaten since yesterday. Buy me lunch, and not only will I drop the whole thing, but I'll tell you how the filming came out last night, too.'

HIS ANGER FADING, Alvin paused in the doorway of Herbs when he saw Jed sitting at one of the tables. Jed scowled and crossed his arms as soon as he saw Alvin, Jeremy and Lexie take their seats at a booth near the windows.

'Our friendly concierge doesn't seem too pleased to see us,' Alvin whispered across the table.

Jeremy stole a glance at him. Jed's eyes became slits. 'Gee, that's strange.

He's always seemed so friendly. Maybe he doesn't like the way you look.'

'What's wrong with the way I look?'

Jeremy winked at Lexie; while she smiled in return, her expression was distant, as if her mind was elsewhere.

'The filming went great last night,' Alvin said, reaching for a menu. 'Caught it all from two angles. Amazing stuff. The networks are going to love it. Which reminds me, I've got to call Nate. Since he couldn't reach you, he kept calling me all afternoon.'

When Lexie looked perplexed, Jeremy leaned towards her. 'He's talking about my agent,' he said.

'Is he coming down, too?'

'No. He's too busy dreaming up my future career.'

She flashed a quick smile.

'So what's with you two?' Alvin demanded. 'How did you meet?'

When Lexie showed no inclination to answer, Jeremy shifted in his seat. 'Lexie's a librarian and she's helping me research the story,' he said vaguely.

'And you two have been spending quite a bit of time together, huh?'

From the corner of his eye, Jeremy saw Lexie glance away.

Alvin looked at his friend, sensing that something was off. It seemed as if they'd had a lovers' quarrel and had got over it but were still licking their wounds. He decided to drop it as Rachel came sauntering towards the table.

'Hey, Lex, hey, Jeremy,' she said. 'Hey, Alvin.'

Alvin looked up. 'Rachel!'

'I thought you told me you were coming in for breakfast,' she said. 'I'd just about given up on you.'

'I'm sorry about that,' he said. He glanced at Jeremy and Lexie. 'I guess I slept in.'

Reaching into her apron, Rachel pulled out a pad and retrieved the pencil she kept behind her ear. 'Now, what can I get y'all?'

Jeremy ordered a sandwich and Alvin asked for one as well. Lexie shook her head. 'I'm not hungry,' she said. 'But is Doris around?'

'No, she decided to take the day off. She worked late last night getting things ready for the weekend.'

'I should go check on her,' Lexie said.

'Would you like me to come with you?' Jeremy asked.

'No, that's OK,' she said. 'You've got work to do and I've got things to do, too. Would you like to meet up at the library later? You wanted to finish looking through the diaries. How about if I meet you there at four?'

'That's fine,' he said, stung by the nonchalance in her tone.

She looked at Alvin. 'Nice meeting you, Alvin.'

'You, too.'

A moment later, Lexie was gone and Rachel was on her way back to the kitchen. As soon as they were out of earshot, Alvin leaned across the table. 'OK, my friend, spill it.'

'What do you mean?'

'First you fall for her. Then you spend the night together. Now you both act like you barely know each other. And she makes the first excuse she can to get out of here. Did you two have a fight or something?'

'No,' Jeremy said. He paused, glancing around the restaurant. 'Actually, I don't know what it was. One minute everything was great, and then . . .'

When he didn't continue, Alvin leaned back in the booth. 'Yeah, well, it wasn't going to last, anyway.'

'It might have,' Jeremy insisted.

'Oh, yeah? What? Were you planning to move down here to the Twilight Zone? Or is she coming to New York?'

Jeremy folded and refolded his napkin without answering, not wanting to be reminded of the obvious.

In the silence, Alvin raised his eyebrows. 'I haven't seen someone get under your skin like this since Maria.'

EIGHT

Jeremy stood on the porch at Herbs, waiting for Alvin to finish his conversation with Rachel. Alvin was giving it his best shot, but Rachel seemed less interested in Alvin than in simply being polite.

When at last they parted and Alvin joined Jeremy, he had a big grin on his face, as if he'd already forgotten about the events of last night. 'Did you see that?' he whispered when he was close. 'I think she likes me.'

'What's not to like?'

'Man, she's something. I love the way she talks. It's so sexy.'

'You think everything is sexy,' Jeremy observed. 'Maybe you'll see her tonight at the dance. We might be able to drop in before we head out to film.'

'There's a dance tonight?'

'At the old tobacco barn. I'm sure Rachel'll be there.'

'Good,' Alvin said, stepping off the porch. But then, almost to himself, he added, 'I wonder why she didn't mention it.'

MEANWHILE, RACHEL WATCHED Alvin leave the restaurant with Jeremy. As flattering as Alvin was, she made it a point never to date someone who had more piercings than she did. But that wasn't her only reason for her lack of interest, she had to admit; Rodney also had something to do with it.

Last night, Rodney had come into the Lookilu and spotted Rachel at the bar. Usually, he would smile and come over to talk, but this time, when he saw her with Alvin, she thought he looked almost hurt. It was an unexpected reaction, but almost as quickly as it appeared, it passed, and he looked angry. It seemed almost as though he was jealous. Later, when she was lying in bed, she concluded that she wouldn't have been upset at all if Rodney had been jealous.

Maybe, she thought, there was hope for them yet.

AFTER PICKING UP Alvin's car, which had remained parked in the street near the Lookilu, Jeremy and Alvin drove to Greenleaf and spent the next couple of hours going over what Jeremy had learned. For Jeremy, it was a method of escape; concentrating on work to keep himself from worrying about Lexie. Alvin's tapes had a clarity and crispness that made it easy to pick out details that he had missed, and Jeremy knew there were a few frames that he could isolate and freeze for the television viewers.

Afterwards, he drove Alvin across the bridge to the paper mill so that Alvin could see the place himself. They spent a few minutes looking round the yard and Jeremy pointed out where they'd be filming later. From there, they headed to the cemetery so that Alvin could get some daytime footage.

He set up the camera in various locations while Jeremy paced on his own, the stillness of the cemetery forcing his thoughts back to Lexie. Despite her denials, he knew she was feeling regret about what had happened, but that didn't make sense to him. Last night, he'd been sure that she felt the same way that he did. But now . . .

Jeremy sighed, and then became aware that he'd drifted to the part of the cemetery where Lexie had vanished from sight the first time he saw her.

Suddenly, a hunch took root in his mind and he began searching the grounds; a minute later he spotted the obvious. Making his way over a small ridge, he stopped at the foot of an untamed azalea bush. Twigs and branches surrounded it, but the area in front seemed to have been tended to. Squatting down, he suddenly understood why neither Doris nor Lexie wanted people trampling through the cemetery.

In the grey light, he stared at the graves of Claire and James Darnell, wondering why he hadn't figured it out before.

JEREMY DROPPED Alvin off at Greenleaf for a nap, then returned to the library. People were milling on the pavement in groups, pointing upwards and gazing at the architecture, as if getting an early start on the Historic Homes Tour. Jeremy walked past the children's room and continued up the stairs. Lexie's office door was open and he paused for a moment to collect himself before entering. Lexie was bending down near the desk, which had been nearly cleared. Like everyone else in the library, she was doing her best to get rid of clutter, stacking various piles under the desk.

'Hey,' he said.

Lexie looked up. 'Oh, hey,' she said, standing. She smoothed her blouse. 'You caught me making the place look presentable.'

Instead of moving towards him, she reached for another pile, then ducked her head beneath the desk again.

'How's Doris doing?' he enquired.

'Fine,' she said. 'If you get the chance, you might swing by before you head out. I'm sure she'd appreciate that.'

For a moment, he simply watched her, but when he realised the implication of what she was saying, he took a step towards her. 'What's going on?' he asked.

She shuffled a few more items on her desk. 'I'm busy.'

'I meant what's going on with us,' he said.

'Nothing,' she said. Her voice was neutral.

'You won't even look at me,' he said.

She finally looked up. He could sense her simmering hostility. 'I don't know what you want me to say. Believe it or not, I am in sort of a rush here.'

Jeremy stared, realising that Lexie was looking for any excuse to start an argument.

'Is there anything I can do to help?' he asked.

'No, thanks. I pulled the diaries out for you again. They're on the desk in the rare-book room.'

Jeremy gave a weak smile. 'Thanks,' he said.

'If you can think of anything else before you leave,' she added, 'I'll be here for at least another hour. The tour starts at seven, so you should be out of here no later than six thirty.'

'I thought the rare-book room closed at five.'

'Since you're leaving, I figured I could relax the rules.'

'And because we're friends, right?'

'Sure,' she said. She smiled. 'Because we're friends.'

Jeremy left the office and made his way to the rare-book room, replaying the conversation in his head and trying to make sense of it. As much as her behaviour bothered him, on some level he knew it made sense. Everything came back to the fact that he lived in New York and she lived here. Yesterday, it had been easy to fool himself with the belief that things would magically work out between them. And he *had* believed it. That was the thing. When people cared about each other, they always found a way to make it work.

He glanced at the stack of diaries as he took his seat and began separating the ones he'd already skimmed from the ones that he hadn't, leaving four to go. To this point, none of them had been particularly helpful.

The next two diaries proved to be largely personal accounts written in the 1920s, so he expected the third one to be another waste of time, too. He leaned back in his chair and skimmed passages at random for any mention of Cedar Creek. Calling it quits would mean leaving, and he couldn't imagine doing so without talking to Lexie again. Yesterday he could have strolled in and said the first thing that came into his mind, but now it was impossible to figure out what he should say or how he should act. Should he try to talk to her? Or just take her in his arms?

Yeah, he loved her. And yeah, he, too, was concerned about their future. But where he wanted to try to figure things out, she was acting as if she was willing to throw in the towel already. He thought again about their conversation and her final comment. *Sure,* she'd said, *because we're friends.*

Friends? he should have said. *After last night, all you can say is that we're friends? Is that all I mean to you?*

It wasn't the way you talked to someone you cared about. It wasn't the way you treated someone you hoped to see again. He stared out of the window, his lips pressed together. He wasn't going to play this game any more. If she wanted to talk to him, fine. But if not . . . well, then, that was the way it was going to be.

Rolling his shoulders to ease the tension, he reached for the final diary. It took only a few seconds for him to realise that this one was different from all the others. Instead of short, personal passages, the diary was a collection of dated and titled essays. Jeremy, vaguely recalling that one of the diaries belonged to an amateur historian, began flipping through the pages more quickly . . . scanning the headings . . . stopping suddenly when he realised he had seen something. He leaned back in his chair, blinking as he moved his fingers down the page.

Solving the Mystery of the Lights
in Cedar Creek Cemetery
Some residents of our town have made the claim that ghosts are present in Cedar Creek Cemetery. After conducting my own investigation, I believe I have solved the riddle of why the lights appear at certain times while not at others.

I will say definitively that ghosts are not present. Instead, the lights are actually those of the Henrickson Paper Mill and are influenced by the train as it crosses the trestle, the location of Riker's Hill, and the phases of the moon.

As Jeremy continued reading, he found himself holding his breath. Though the writer hadn't attempted an explanation as to why the cemetery was sinking—without which the lights would probably not be visible at all—his conclusion was otherwise essentially the same as Jeremy's.

The writer, whoever it was, had nailed it almost forty years ago.

He marked the page with a piece of paper and flipped the book to the front cover, looking for the name of the author.

Owen Gherkin.

The journal had been written by the mayor's father. Who, according to Mayor Gherkin, 'knew everything there was to know about this place'. Who understood what was causing the lights. Who had undoubtedly told his son. Who then knew there had never been anything supernatural at all about the lights. Which meant that Mayor Gherkin had been lying all along, in the hope of using Jeremy to help make a buck from unsuspecting visitors.

And Lexie . . . the woman who'd hinted that he might find the answers he was looking for in the diaries. Which meant that she'd read Owen Gherkin's account. Which meant that she, too, had been lying, playing along with the mayor.

He wondered how many others in town had known the answer. Doris? She *had* to have known. And that meant . . . this whole thing had been a joke all along. The letter. The investigation. The party. The joke was on him.

And now Lexie was pulling away, after she'd told him that story about Doris bringing her to the cemetery to see the spirit of her parents.

Coincidence? Or planned all along? Right now she was acting . . . as if she wanted him to leave. As if she had known what would happen . . .

Had *everything* been planned? And if so, why?

Jeremy grabbed the diary and headed to Lexie's office. He barely noticed that he slammed the door on the way out, nor did he notice the faces of the volunteers who turned to watch him. Lexie's door was cracked open, and he pushed it wider as he stepped in.

Lexie looked up. 'Oh, hey.' She forced a smile.

Jeremy stared at her. 'You can quit the act,' he announced.

Even from across the room, she sensed his anger and instinctively tucked a strand of hair behind her ear. 'What are you talking about?'

'This,' he said, holding up the diary. 'You have read this, haven't you?'

'Yes,' she said, recognising it as Owen Gherkin's.

'Did you know there's a passage that talks about the lights at Cedar Creek?'

'Yes,' she said again.

'Why didn't you tell me about it?'

'I did,' she said. 'I told you about the diaries when you first came to the library. And if I remember right, I said you might find the answers you were looking for, remember?'

'Don't play games,' Jeremy said, his eyes narrowing. 'You knew what I was looking for.'

'And you found it,' she countered. 'I don't see the problem.'

'The problem is that I've been wasting my time. This diary had the answer all along. There is no mystery here. There never was. And you've been in on this little charade all along.'

'What charade?'

'You lied to me. You lied right to my face.' He held up the diary. 'You knew!' he shouted.

She put her hands on her hips. 'No,' she said. 'I didn't.'

'But you read it!'

'So what?' she shot back. 'I read the article in the paper, too. And I read the articles by those other people. How was I supposed to know that Owen Gherkin got it right? And that's assuming I even cared about the subject. Do you honestly think I've ever spent more than a minute thinking about it until you got here? You're the one down here investigating. And if you'd read the diary two days ago, you wouldn't have been sure, either. We both know you would have done your own investigation, anyway.'

'That's not the point,' he said. 'The point is that this whole thing has been a scam. The tour, the ghosts, the legend.'

'What are you talking about? The tour is about historic homes, and yeah, they added the cemetery to it. Whoop-de-do. All it is, is a nice weekend in the middle of a dreary season. Come on, do you really think most people actually believe they're ghosts? They just like to say they do because it's fun.'

'See,' he said, raising his finger like a teacher emphasising a point to a student. 'That's what I don't understand. If you didn't want the cemetery as part of the tour, and Doris didn't want it as part of the tour, then why didn't you just go to the newspaper with the truth? Why did you involve me in your little game?'

'It's not a game. It's a harmless weekend that you're blowing completely out of proportion.'

'I didn't blow it out of proportion. You and the mayor did that.'

Her eyes narrowed. 'Then why did I give you the diary? Why didn't I just keep it hidden from you?'

'I don't know. I'm trying to figure out why I was brought down here in the first place.'

She raised her hands. 'I don't want to hear this. You don't belong here, and I don't want to talk to you any more. Go back to where you came from.'

He crossed his arms. 'At least you finally admitted what you've been thinking all day.'

'Oh, now you're a mind-reader?'

'No. But I don't have to read minds to understand why you've been acting the way you are.'

'Well, then, let me read your mind, OK?' She knew her voice was loud enough for the entire library to hear, but she didn't care. 'Let me tell you what I see, OK? I see someone who's really good at saying the right things, but when push comes to shove, doesn't mean a thing he says.'

'And what's that supposed to mean?'

She started across the room, anger stiffening every muscle in her body. 'You don't think I know how you really feel about our town? That you can't understand why anyone would live here?'

'I didn't say that.'

'You didn't have to!' she shouted, hating the smug way he sounded. 'That's the point. When I was talking about sacrifice, I knew full well that you thought I should be the one to uproot. That I should leave my family, my friends, my home, because New York is so much better. That I should be the good little woman who follows her man wherever he thinks we should be. The thought never crossed your mind that you'd be the one to leave.'

Jeremy simply stared at her, unable to deny her accusations.

'Nothing to say?' she demanded. 'Then tell me this. What did you mean exactly when you said that we'd find a way to make it work? Did you think I was interested in waiting around for you to visit every now and then for a quick roll in the sack?'

The anger and pain in her voice were unmistakable. To her dismay, Lexie felt tears begin to well in her eyes. 'You came into my world. I was content until you arrived. Maybe a little lonely, but I like my life here. I like being able to check on Doris. I like reading to the children at story hour. And I even like our little Historic Homes Tour, even if you're intent to turn it into something ugly so you can make a big impression on television.'

They stood facing each other, frozen and wordless. With everything out in the open, both of them felt drained. Lexie reached for her jacket and bag. Slinging them over her arm, she headed for the door. Jeremy moved aside to allow her to pass and she brushed by him without another word. She was a few steps away from the office when Jeremy finally summoned the will to speak again.

'Where are you going?'

With a sigh, she turned round. 'I'm going home,' she said. She wiped away a tear on her cheek. 'Just like you will.'

LATER THAT NIGHT, Alvin and Jeremy set up the cameras near the boardwalk on the Pamlico River. In the distance, the sounds of music drifted from Meyer's tobacco barn as the dance got under way.

'And then what?' Alvin asked.

'That's it,' Jeremy said. 'She left.'

'You didn't follow her?'

'She didn't want me to,' he said.

'How do you know?'

Jeremy rubbed his eyes, replaying the argument for the umpteenth time. The last few hours had passed in a haze, his feelings of anger mingling with those of sadness and regret. All Jeremy knew was that he was exhausted, and despite the fact that he had to film, he was fighting the urge to find Lexie and mend things.

Jeremy sighed, his thoughts going back to their final moment in the library. 'I could see it in the way she looked at me,' he said.

'So it's over?'

'Yeah,' Jeremy said, 'it's over.'

AT THE DANCE, Mayor Gherkin sat alone at a table. He'd hoped that Jeremy would swing by, preferably with Lexie, but as soon as he'd arrived, he heard about the argument in the library. Apparently, it had been a big one and had something to do with one of the diaries and some sort of scam.

Thinking about it now, he decided he shouldn't have donated his father's journal to the library, but at the time, it hadn't seemed all that important. Who could have guessed what would happen in the next fifteen years? Who could have known the textile mill would be closed or the mine abandoned? Who could have known that hundreds of people would be out of work and the town would end up fighting a battle of survival?

Maybe he shouldn't have added the cemetery to the tour. Maybe he shouldn't have publicised ghosts when he knew they were simply the lights from the night shift at the paper mill. But the fact was that the town needed something to build on, something to get people to visit. It was, he thought, the town's only hope. Thanks to the cemetery and its mysterious lights, they'd sold a few hundred extra tickets to the tour, and Jeremy's presence offered them the opportunity to get the word out nationally.

Oh, he'd always figured that Jeremy would puzzle it out on his own. That part didn't bother him. So what if Jeremy exposed the truth? People around the country would still hear about Boone Creek. Any publicity was better than no publicity. Unless, of course, Jeremy used the word 'scam'.

It was such a nasty-sounding word. Sure, he knew what the lights were, but what was the harm? There was a legend, there were lights, and some people did believe they were ghosts. Others played along, thinking it made the town seem special.

Jeremy Marsh with fond memories of the town would understand that. Jeremy Marsh without them might not. And right now Mayor Gherkin wasn't sure which impression Jeremy would be leaving with tomorrow.

'THE MAYOR looks sort of worried, don't you think?' Rodney remarked.

Rachel looked over, feeling rather proud that they'd been standing together most of the night. Even the fact that he sometimes glanced towards the door and seemed to scan the crowd for Lexie did nothing to diminish the feeling. He seemed happy to be with her as well.

'Sort of. But he always looks that way.'

'No,' Rodney said, 'it's not the same. He's got something on his mind.'

Like the mayor—like everyone else, it seemed—Rodney had heard about the argument at the library. And now the mayor, he suddenly knew, was worried about the way Jeremy was going to present their little mystery to the world.

As for the argument, he'd tried to warn Lexie it was coming. It had been inevitable. She could be volatile and Jeremy had finally got a taste of it. Though Rodney wished Lexie wouldn't have put herself through the wringer again, he was relieved to know the affair was just about over.

On his way here, he'd driven past her house and had seen her lights on and the car in the driveway. Earlier, he'd received a report from another deputy, noting that City Boy and his cartoon-character friend were setting up their camera on the boardwalk.

If Lexie's lights were still on after the dance ended, he supposed he could drop by on his way home, like he'd done the night after Mr Renaissance had left. He had a feeling she wouldn't be entirely surprised to see him. She'd open the door, brew some coffee, and, just like the last time, he'd sit on the couch and listen for hours as she berated herself for being so foolish.

Even so, he wasn't ready to do that just yet. He was tired of being the big-brother type, and he wasn't in the mood to listen to her. From the corner of his eye, he watched Rachel swaying to the music, pleased that she'd sought him out for company, just as she had the other night at the party. The strange thing was that lately, every time he saw her, she seemed prettier.

Rachel noticed him watching her and grinned in embarrassment. 'Sorry,' she said, 'I like this song.'

Rodney cleared his throat. 'Would you like to dance?' he asked.

Her eyebrows shot up. 'Really?'

'I'm not much of a dancer, though—'

'I'd love to,' she said, reaching for his hand.

Following her to the floor, he decided then and there that he'd figure out what to do about Lexie later.

DORIS SAT in the rocker in the living room, staring absently out of the window and wondering if Lexie would drop by. She knew her granddaughter was upset and that it had everything to do with Jeremy leaving.

In some ways, she wished she hadn't pushed Lexie towards him. Looking back, she knew she should have suspected it might end this way, so why had she done everything she could to set their affair in motion? Because Lexie was lonely? Because Lexie was stuck in a rut? Because she'd come to believe that Lexie was frightened by the thought of ever falling for someone again?

Why couldn't she have just enjoyed Jeremy's company? Really, that was all she'd wanted Lexie to do. She simply needed to see that there were men like him out there. She needed to realise that not every man was like Avery or the man from Chicago. What did she call him now? Mr Renaissance?

Oh, she'd be all right in the long run, Doris knew. No doubt she would find a way to move on. If she'd learned one thing about Lexie, it was that Lexie was a survivor.

Doris sighed. She knew Jeremy was smitten. If Lexie had fallen for him, he'd fallen even harder. But Lexie had learned the art of putting relationships behind her and living her life pretending they never happened.

Poor Jeremy, she thought. It wasn't fair to him.

WITH THE TRAIN approaching shortly—according to Jeremy's schedule—Alvin made one final check on the camera facing Riker's Hill. That was the tricky shot. The one on the trestle was easy, but because Riker's Hill was both distant and shrouded in mist, he wasn't certain the camera would work.

Meanwhile, Jeremy was standing at the rail with his arms crossed, staring into a cloud bank.

'Did I mention that Nate called earlier?' Alvin asked, trying to engage his friend.

'He did? What did he want?'

'He woke me up from my nap,' Alvin said, 'and began screaming at me because you didn't have your cellphone on.'

Despite his preoccupied mood, Jeremy smiled. 'I've learned to keep it off as much as possible.'

'I wish you would have told me. But get this: he asked if you'd be able to get a sample of the ghosts—if there was ooze or something that you could show to the producers at the meeting next week.'

'Ooze?'

Alvin raised his hands. 'His word, not mine. He also said you should call,' he added.

'I would,' Jeremy said, 'but I left my cellphone back at Greenleaf.' He paused. 'You didn't tell him about the diary, did you?'

'I didn't even know about it then,' Alvin said.

'If he does call you again, just keep it to yourself, OK?'

'You don't want him to know that the mayor's running a scam?'

'No,' Jeremy said. 'Not yet.'

Alvin squinted through the lens. 'The lights are one thing,' he said, 'but you have to realise the solution isn't all that interesting for television. I'm not so sure they're going to be interested in the fact that a passing train causes the lights.'

'It isn't just the passing train,' Jeremy corrected. 'It's the way the lights from the paper mill are reflected by the train onto Riker's Hill and how the greater density of the fog in the sinking cemetery makes the lights appear.'

Alvin feigned a yawn. 'Sorry,' he said. 'You were saying?'

'It's not boring,' Jeremy insisted. 'Don't you realise how many things had to come together to create this phenomenon? How the quarries changed the water tables and made the cemetery sink? The phases of the moon, since it's only dark enough to see the lights at certain times? The legend? The location of the paper mill and the train schedule?'

Alvin shrugged. 'Trust me. It's boring. It would have been more interesting if you hadn't found the solution. If you're serious about this gig, you're going to need to spice it up, and the diary just might be enough to do that. You can spring it at the end.'

'You think I should throw the town to the wolves?'

Alvin shook his head. 'I'm just telling you that if you can't come up with some ooze, you'd better give the diary some thought.'

Jeremy looked away. The train, he knew, would be coming in just a few minutes. 'Lexie would never talk to me again if I did that,' he said. 'What do you think I should do?'

Alvin drew a long breath. 'I think,' Alvin said, 'that it all comes down to what's most important to you, doesn't it?'

JEREMY SLEPT POORLY on his last night at Greenleaf. He and Alvin had finished up filming and decided the resulting film was good enough to prove Jeremy's theory.

He began once again to replay the last few days in his head. He remembered the first time he'd seen Lexie in the cemetery, and their spirited exchange in the library. Was it really possible for so much to have happened in only a couple of days? And when had everything started going wrong? He wasn't sure, but it seemed to him that she'd been trying to run away from her feelings, not simply from him. So when had she realised that she had feelings for him? He had no answers. All he knew was that he loved her and that he couldn't imagine never seeing her again.

The hours passed slowly; with his flight leaving from Raleigh at noon, he would be leaving Greenleaf shortly. He rose before six, finished packing his things and loaded them in his car. After making sure that he saw Alvin's light shining from his own room, he made his way through the chilly morning air to the office.

Jed, as he expected, scowled. Jeremy set the key on the desk.

'Quite a place you have here,' Jeremy said. 'I'll make sure to recommend it to my friends.'

If possible, Jed's expression grew even meaner, but Jeremy merely smiled ingratiatingly in return. On his way back to the room, he saw headlights bouncing in the fog as the car slowly made its way up the gravel drive. For an instant, he thought it was Lexie, and he felt a surge in his chest; when the car came into view, his hopes sank just as quickly.

Mayor Gherkin, bundled in a jacket and scarf, emerged from the car. Showing none of the energy he had at their previous meetings, he groped his way towards Jeremy in the darkness. 'Packing up, I suppose,' he called. 'Jed didn't slap you with the bill, did he?'

'No,' Jeremy said. 'Thanks for that.'

'It was the least we could do. I hope you enjoyed your stay.'

Jeremy nodded, noting the worry on the mayor's face. 'I did,' he said.

Gherkin seemed at a loss for words. As the silence grew uncomfortable, he retucked the scarf into his jacket. 'Well, I just wanted to drop by to tell you that the folks around here sure enjoyed meeting you. You've made quite an impression.'

Jeremy put his hands in his pockets. 'Why the ruse?' he asked.

Gherkin sighed. 'About adding the cemetery to the tour?'

'No. I mean about the fact that your father recorded the answer in his diary and that you hid the answer from me.'

A sad expression crossed Gherkin's features. 'You're absolutely right. My daddy did solve that mystery. But as I see it, I didn't have much of a choice. Every town needs something to call its own, something to remind folks that their home is special. In New York, you don't have to worry about that. But down here, after all the business closings, I looked around and realised all we had was a legend. And a town needs more than that to survive. That's all I was trying to do, searching for a way to keep this town alive, and then you came along.'

Jeremy glanced away, thinking about the boarded storefronts he'd seen when he first arrived. 'So you came by this morning to give me your side of the story?'

'No,' Gherkin said. 'I came by to let you know all this was my idea. It wasn't the town council's, it wasn't the folks' who live here. I did what I thought was right for this place, and all I ask is that when you do your story, you keep in mind that no one else was involved. If you want to sacrifice me, I can live with that.'

Without waiting for a response, Gherkin went back to his car, and it soon vanished into the fog.

WITH DAWN turning the sky an overcast grey, Jeremy was loading the last of the equipment when Lexie arrived.

She emerged from the car looking much the same as she did the first time he'd seen her, her violet eyes unreadable even as she met his gaze. In her hand was Gherkin's diary. For a moment, they faced each other as if neither one knew what to say.

Jeremy took a deep breath. 'I'm glad you came.' The grey light reminded him of their walk on the beach near the lighthouse, and he felt with a twisting arc of pain how much he'd come to love her.

She nodded towards his car. 'You're ready to go, I see.'

'Yeah,' he said. 'All packed up.'

'I came to apologise for the way I treated you yesterday at the library. I shouldn't have acted the way I did. It wasn't fair.'

'It's OK,' he said. 'I'll get over it. And I'm sorry, too.'

She held up the diary. 'I brought this for you.'

'I didn't think you'd want me to use it.'

'I don't,' she answered. 'But I should have told you about it, and I don't want you to think that anyone here is engaged in some cover-up. I can see how you might have thought the town was up to something. But I assure you that it wasn't some big scheme—'

'I know,' Jeremy interrupted. 'The mayor came by this morning.'

She nodded, and her eyes dropped before rising to meet his again. 'Well, I guess that's it. I've never been a fan of long goodbyes.'

'So this is a goodbye?' he asked.

She looked sad as she tilted her head. 'It has to be, doesn't it?'

'So that's it, then? You just came by to tell me it's over?'

Her voice was quiet when she answered. 'We've been through all of this, Jeremy. I didn't come here to argue. I came because I was sorry about the way I treated you yesterday. And because I didn't want you to think that the week meant nothing to me. It did.'

'What if I told you that I love you?'

She turned away. 'Don't say that.'

'But I do,' he said. 'I can't help the way I feel.'

'Jeremy . . . please . . .'

He sensed that he was finally breaching her defences. 'I want to make this work.'

'We can't,' she said.

'Why not?'

'Because I'm going to marry Rodney, OK?'

Her words stopped him cold. 'What are you talking about?'

'After the dance, he came by. We talked for a long time. He's honest, he's hard-working, he loves me, and he's here. You're not.'

He stared at her, stunned. 'I don't believe you.'

She stared back, her face impassive. 'Believe it,' she said.

When Jeremy failed to say anything, she handed him the diary and began to walk backwards with him in her sights, much the way she had that day at the cemetery.

'Goodbye, Jeremy,' she said before turning to get in her car.

Jeremy heard the ignition turn over. He strode forward to put his hand on the bonnet, trying to stop her. But as the car started to move, he let his fingers glide along the damp surface and finally took a small step back as the car slid into drive.

For an instant, Jeremy thought he caught the flash of tears in her eyes. But then he saw her look away, and he knew once and for all he wasn't going to see her again.

NINE

The rest of the day passed as if he were watching it through someone else's eyes. Hurt and angry, he barely remembered following Alvin back to Raleigh. More than once, he glanced in his rearview mirror, staring back over the black asphalt, watching the cars that followed in the distance, hoping that one of them was Lexie.

On the plane, he stared out of the window as Alvin slept. In the cab from LaGuardia Airport, Jeremy was bombarded with noise and the hectic pace of the city. As he looked out of the car window, he thought of Greenleaf and the utter silence he'd experienced there.

Back at his apartment building, his mailbox was stuffed with advertisements and bills; he grabbed it all and trudged up the stairs. After stowing his suitcase in his room, he opened a bottle of beer and carried his computer and satchel to his desk.

He had all the information he'd accumulated in the past few days: his notes and copies of the articles, the digital photographs of the cemetery, the maps and the diary. As he began unpacking, a packet of postcards fell onto the desk, and it took him a moment to remember that he'd picked them up on his first day in town. The top postcard was a view of the town from the river. Removing the wrapper, he began to thumb through the rest of them. Halfway through, he found himself pausing at a picture of the library.

He sat motionless, thinking of Lexie and realising again that he loved her.

But that was over now, he reminded himself, and he continued shuffling through the postcards. He saw a photograph of Herbs and another of the town as viewed from Riker's Hill. The final postcard was an old black-and-white photo of downtown Boone Creek, *circa* 1950. In the foreground was the theatre with well-dressed patrons waiting near the ticket window; on the pavements, couples could be seen peeking in windows. As Jeremy studied the picture, he found himself thinking about Mayor Gherkin. The postcard depicted not only Boone Creek's way of life half a century before but also the way that Gherkin hoped the town could be again. He held the postcard for a long time, thinking about Lexie and wondering again what he was going to do about the story.

THE MEETING with the television producers was scheduled for Tuesday afternoon. Nate met Jeremy at his favourite steakhouse, Smith and Wollensky's, beforehand. Nate was his buoyant self, excited to see Jeremy; as soon as he sat down, he began talking about the footage that Alvin had shot, describing the images as fantastic, like 'that haunted house in Amityville, but real'. The television executives would love them. Jeremy sat in silence, listening to Nate jabber on.

'So it's not ghosts, right?' Nate said.

'No,' Jeremy said. 'It's not ghosts.'

'What are they, then?'

Jeremy spent the next few minutes telling Nate what he'd learned. When he had finished, Jeremy could see wrinkles of concern forming on Nate's forehead. 'The paper mill?' he said. 'I was hoping it was some sort of government tests. Secret weapons programmes, things like that. Or maybe you heard something out there that you couldn't explain.'

'Sorry,' Jeremy said, his voice flat, 'it's just light that ricochets off the train. There weren't any noises.'

'Look,' Nate said, 'I don't mean to be picky here, but you've got to pump this up if you want it to work. If you're not enthusiastic, they're not going to be excited, either. Am I right or am I right? Of course, I'm right. But be honest with me. You found something else, didn't you?'

'What are you talking about?'

'Alvin,' Nate said. 'He mentioned that you found something else that was interesting.'

Jeremy's expression didn't falter. 'He did?'

'His words, not mine,' Nate said. 'He didn't tell me what it was, though. He said that was up to you.'

Staring at Nate, he could practically feel the diary burning a hole through his satchel. 'Well,' Jeremy began, knowing his time to make his decision had finally run out.

When he didn't continue, Nate leaned forward. 'Yes?'

THAT EVENING, after the meeting was concluded, Jeremy sat in his apartment, absently watching the world outside. It had begun to snow and the flakes were a swirling, hypnotic mass under the glow of the streetlamp.

The meeting had started out well; Nate had revved up the producers. Afterwards, Jeremy told them about the legend, noting their growing interest as he spoke of Hettie Doubilet and the painstaking way he'd approached the investigation.

But as he sat alone later that night, the diary in his lap, he knew he wouldn't be working with them. His story—the mystery of Boone Creek's cemetery—was akin to an exciting novel that petered out at the end. The solution was too simple, and he'd sensed their disappointment by the time he said good-bye. Nate had promised to keep in touch, as they did, but Jeremy knew there would be no further calls.

As for the diary, he'd kept that to himself, as he had with Nate earlier.

Later, he made a phone call to Mayor Gherkin. Jeremy's proposal was simple: Boone Creek would no longer promise visitors on the Historic Homes Tour a chance to see ghosts in the cemetery. The word 'haunted' would be removed from the brochure, as would any claims that the lights had anything to do with the supernatural. While some tourists might see the lights and wonder if they were the ghosts, the volunteers who conducted the tours were told never to suggest as much. Finally, Jeremy asked the mayor to remove the T-shirts from his department store downtown.

In exchange, Jeremy promised he would never mention anything about Cedar Creek Cemetery on television, in his column, or in an independent article, nor would he tell anyone in the town that the mayor had known the truth all along.

Mayor Gherkin accepted the offer. After hanging up, Jeremy called Alvin, whom he swore to secrecy.

IN THE DAYS following Jeremy's unsuccessful meeting with the producers, he tried to return to his previous routines. He spoke to his editor at *Scientific American*. He agreed to do a column about the possible dangers of a low-carbohydrate diet. He spent hours on the Internet, scanning the news, looking for other stories that might be of interest. Though he still often thought of Lexie, wondering whether she was busy preparing for her marriage to Rodney, he did his best to force those thoughts out of his mind.

By Monday noon, as another winter storm was settling in, he'd convinced himself that it was really over. She hadn't called and neither had he. At times, those few days with Lexie seemed like nothing more than the mirage he'd been investigating.

He ordered lunch from the Chinese restaurant down the block. When the intercom buzzed, he grabbed his wallet and headed to the door. Through the static of the intercom, he heard a female voice.

'It's open. Come on up.'

He reached for the door just as he heard the knock. 'That was fast,' he said. 'Usually it takes . . .'

His voice trailed off as the door opened and he saw who was standing before him.

In the silence, he and his visitor stared at each other before Doris finally smiled.

'Surprise,' she said. She stamped the snow off her shoes. 'Are you going to invite me in?'

'Yeah . . . of course.'

Doris moved past him and set her bag on the end table near the door. She glanced round his apartment and removed her jacket. 'This is nice,' she said, walking into the living room. 'It's bigger than I thought it would be.'

'What are you doing here?'

'I came to talk to you, of course.'

'About Lexie?'

She sighed, then said evenly, 'Among other things. You wouldn't happen to have any tea, would you? I'm a little chilly.'

Jeremy went into the kitchen and heated a cup of water in the microwave. After adding a tea bag, he carried the cup back to the living room, where he found Doris sitting on the couch. He handed her the cup.

'I'm sorry that I didn't call,' she said. 'I know I should have. You must be pretty shocked. But I wanted to talk to you in person.'

'How did you know where I live?'

'I talked to your friend Alvin. He had given his phone number to Rachel, so I called him.'

The buzzer sounded again. 'That's my lunch,' Jeremy said. 'Give me a minute, OK?'

He met the deliveryman, came back in, and was just about to set the bag of food on the kitchen counter when he heard Doris behind him. 'It smells good.'

The way she said it made him smile. 'Would you like me to make up a couple of plates?'

'I wouildn't want to take your food.'

'There's plenty,' he said, reaching for some plates. 'And, besides, didn't you tell me that you like to talk over a good meal?'

He spooned out the food, then brought it to the table. Doris sat next to him, and they ate in silence for a few minutes.

'I know you probably think Lexie is tough and strong,' she said finally, 'but that's just what she wants others to believe. Underneath, she's like everyone else. She was crushed by what happened with Avery. She was quite a wreck back then.' Doris hesitated. 'She told you about him, right?'

'Yes.'

'She kept up the brave front, but I knew how upset she was. She hid it by keeping busy, running from here to there. You can't imagine how helpless that made me feel.'

'Why are you telling me this?'

'Because she's acting the same way now.'

Jeremy moved his food around with his fork. 'I wasn't the one who ended it, Doris.'

'I know that, too.'

'Then why talk to me?'

'Lexie won't listen. I'm hoping you're not as stubborn as she is.'

'Even if I'm willing to try again, it's still up to her.'

Doris watched him carefully. 'Do you really believe that?'

'I tried to talk to her. I told her I wanted to find a way to make the relationship work.'

Instead of responding to his comment, Doris said, 'I have the sense that you understand what women want. But for some reason you're unwilling to give yourself completely.'

'What's this got to do with anything?'

'Women want the fairy tale. Not all women, of course, but most women grow up dreaming about the kind of man who would risk everything for them.' She paused. 'Kind of like the way you went to find Lexie at the beach. That's why she fell in love with you.'

'She's not in love with me.'

'Yes, she is.'

Jeremy opened his mouth to deny it but couldn't. Instead, he shook his head. 'It doesn't matter now. She's marrying Rodney.'

Doris stared at him. 'No, she isn't. She only said it so that if you did leave, she wouldn't lie awake at night wondering why you never came back for her.' She paused, letting that sink in. 'And besides, you didn't really believe her, anyway, did you?'

It was the way Doris said this that made him remember his initial response when Lexie first told him about Rodney. No, he suddenly realised, he hadn't believed it then.

Doris reached across the table and took his hand. 'You're a good man, Jeremy. You deserved the truth, which was why I came here.' She stood up from the table. 'I've got a flight to catch. If I don't get back tonight, Lexie's going to know something's up.'

'That's quite a trip.'

'I know. But I had to see your face. I wanted to know if you were in love with her, too.'

'Did you find the answer you were hoping for?'

She smiled. 'The real question is, did you?'

JEREMY PACED the length of the living room. There wasn't time for indecision. Not now, knowing what he knew. He had to go back. Talk to her, convince her that when he'd told her he loved her, he'd never been more serious about anything in his life. Tell her that he would do whatever it took so they could be together.

Before Doris had even hailed a cab outside his building, he was reaching for the phone and calling the airline. The last flight to Raleigh was leaving in ninety minutes.

Grabbing a duffle bag from the closet, he tossed in jeans, shirts, socks and underwear. Then he rushed to the bathroom, threw his razor and toothbrush into his washbag and ran back to the living room, where he pulled on his jacket and stuffed his cellphone in his pocket. He picked up his keys, took one last look around, then locked the door before charging downstairs.

He hailed a cab, told the driver he was in a hurry and sat back with a sigh, hoping for the best. The snow flurries, which had temporarily stopped, started up again. Forty-five minutes until his flight.

They finally reached the exit for the airport and headed towards the terminal. The moment the cab came to a stop, Jeremy opened the door and tossed two twenties to the driver. Inside the terminal, he got his electronic ticket, then headed towards security. He started to jog, then run. Weaving through the crowds, he reached for his driver's licence, counting the gates.

'Did I make it?' he panted.

'Only because of a brief delay,' the woman at the counter said. The attendant near the door glared at him.

When he reached the plane, he moved down the aisle, amazed that he'd made it, and spotted his seat halfway down. He was storing his duffle bag in the overhead locker when he caught sight of Doris, three rows behind him.

Returning his gaze, she simply smiled.

THE PLANE TOUCHED down in Raleigh at half past three, and Jeremy walked with Doris through the terminal. 'I've got to get a rental car,' he said.

'I'll be happy to take you,' she said. 'I'm going that way.' When she saw him hesitate, she smiled. 'And I'll let you drive,' she added.

He never let the speed drop below eighty and shaved forty-five minutes from the three-hour drive. With random images of Lexie floating through his mind, he tried to rehearse what he wanted to say or anticipate how she would respond, but he realised he had no idea what was going to happen.

The streets of Boone Creek were quiet as he approached town. Doris turned to him. 'Would you mind dropping me off at home?'

He glanced at her, realising they'd barely spoken since leaving the airport. 'But don't you need your car?'

'Not until tomorrow. Besides, it's too cold to be walking around tonight.'

Following Doris's directions, Jeremy pulled to a stop in front of her house. Knowing that he was only minutes from seeing Lexie, he ran his hand through his hair.

Doris patted him on the leg. 'It's going to be OK,' she said. 'Trust me.' She leaned across to kiss him on the cheek. 'Welcome home,' she whispered.

TYRES SCREECHED as Jeremy sped towards the library. He saw the lights blazing on both floors. He parked the car and, taking a deep breath, strode quickly to the front door.

With no one at the front desk, he hurried down the corridor and up the stairs. He noted that her office door was closed, no light spilling out beneath it. It was locked.

He ran down the stairs, where one of the volunteers emerged with an armful of books. Her eyes lit up when she saw him. 'Mr Marsh?' she called out. 'What on earth are you doing here?'

'I was looking for Lexie.'

'She left about an hour ago.'

He ran past her and out to the car, then pulled onto the main road, followed the curve to the edge of town. He found her house and felt something give way when he saw no lights and no car in the drive. If not at the library, if not at home, where was she? Had she passed him on the way to Doris's? He was sure he would have recognised her car.

Suddenly he realised where she was.

Jeremy gripped the steering wheel. His chest was tight and he was breathing too quickly. It was hard to believe he'd started his day in New York thinking he would never see Lexie again, and now here he was in Boone Creek, planning to do what he thought was impossible. He drove the darkened roads, unnerved by the thought of what Lexie's reaction might be.

Moonlight lent the cemetery an almost bluish colour, and the tombstones seemed to glow as if lit dimly from within. As Jeremy approached the entrance, he saw Lexie's car parked near the gate. He pulled up behind it and climbed out. He passed through the gate and saw the magnolia, its leaves black and shiny. He moved round a crumbling crypt, walking slowly, climbing the incline. Above him, the moon hung in the sky. He crested the small hill, knowing that Lexie's parents were buried on the other side. It was almost time. He would settle it once and for all, here where it all began.

Lexie was standing just where he imagined she would be, bathed in silvery light. She was dressed for the weather—a scarf round her neck, black gloves that made her hands mere shadows.

She looked up. For the longest moment, their eyes held each other.

Lexie seemed frozen in place. Finally, she looked away. Her eyes focused on the graves again. He suddenly felt that it had been a mistake to come here. She didn't want him here. His throat tightened, and he was about to turn away when he noticed that Lexie wore the slightest smirk on her face.

'You know, you really shouldn't stare like that,' she said. 'Women like a man who knows how to be subtle.'

Relief flooded his body, and he smiled as he took a step forward. When he came close enough to touch her, he reached out and placed his hand on her lower back. She didn't pull away; instead, she leaned into him. Doris had been right. He was home.

'No,' he whispered into her hair, 'women like a man who will follow them to the ends of the earth, or even to Boone Creek, if that's what it takes.'

Pulling her close, he lifted her face and kissed her, knowing that he would never leave her again.

EPILOGUE

Jeremy and Lexie were sitting together, cuddled beneath a blanket, staring down at the town below. It was Thursday evening, three days after Jeremy's return to Boone Creek. The white and yellow lights of the town seemed to be flickering, and Jeremy could see plumes of smoke rising from chimneys. The river flowed black like liquid coal, mirroring the sky above. Beyond it, the lights from the paper mill spread in all directions.

Over the past couple of days, he and Lexie had spent a lot of time talking. She confessed that driving away as Jeremy stood on the road at Greenleaf had been the hardest thing she'd ever done. She described the misery of the week they'd been apart. He told her that while Nate wasn't thrilled with his move, his editor at *Scientific American* was willing to let him work from Boone Creek, provided he made it back to New York regularly.

Sometimes he found it hard to believe that he was really here with her; yet it was hard to believe he'd ever left in the first place. Being with Lexie felt natural, as if she were the home he'd been seeking. Although Lexie seemed to feel the same way, she wouldn't let him stay at her house, insisting, 'I wouldn't want to give the folks around here something to gossip about.' Nevertheless, he felt comfortable at Greenleaf, even if Jed still hadn't cracked a smile.

'So it's serious between Rodney and Rachel?' Jeremy asked.

'It seems that way,' Lexie said. 'She beams when he shows up at Herbs, and he blushes. I think they'll be good for each other.'

He pulled her closer, watching a shooting star skim the sky. 'I'd like to take you to New York some time. My mom's insisting that she meet you.'

'I'd like to meet her, too. Besides, I've always loved that city. Some of the nicest people I've ever met live there.' Jeremy rolled his eyes.

In time, she turned towards him. 'Thank you for coming back. For moving here . . . for everything.'

'I had no choice. Love does funny things to people.'

She smiled. 'I love you, too, you know.'

'Yeah, I know.'

'What? You're not going to say it?'

'Do I have to?'

'You bet you do. Use the right tone, too. Say it like you mean it.'

He grinned. 'I love you, Lexie.'

A train whistle sounded, and Jeremy saw a pinprick of light in the darkened landscape. Had it been foggy, the lights would soon be appearing in the cemetery. Lexie seemed to follow his thoughts.

'So tell me, Mr Science Journalist, do you still doubt the existence of miracles?'

'You're my miracle.'

She rested her head on his shoulder. 'I'm talking about real miracles. When something happens that you never believed possible.'

'No,' he said. 'There is always an explanation if one digs deep enough.'

'Even if a miracle were to happen to us?'

Her voice was soft, almost a whisper, and he looked at her. 'What are you talking about?'

She took a breath. 'Doris shared some news with me today.'

Jeremy watched her face, unable to grasp what she was saying. She gazed at him, waiting for him to say something, and still his mind refused to register her words.

There was science and then there was the unexplainable, and Jeremy had spent his life trying to reconcile the two. He dwelt in reality, scoffed at magic, and felt pity for the true believers. But as he gazed at Lexie, trying to make sense of what she was telling him, he found his old sense of surety slipping.

No, he couldn't explain it. It defied the laws of biology; it shattered his assumptions about the man he knew himself to be. Quite simply, it was impossible, but when she gently placed his hand on her stomach, he believed with sudden, euphoric certainty the words he never thought he would hear.

'Here's our miracle,' she whispered. 'It's a girl.'

NICHOLAS SPARKS

Born: Nebraska, December 31, 1965
Hobbies: Tae Kwon Do, running
Website: www.nicholassparks.com

'The genesis of a novel is always a tricky process. It takes me longer to think of a plot than to write it,' says Nicholas Sparks, whose record of eleven phenomenally successful novels, several of which have been made into films, suggests that, despite his modesty, he has the right formula soundly in his grasp.

When he set out to write *True Believer*, his tenth book, Sparks was determined to create a fresh and unusual story with a new twist. The romantic ingredients at the heart of all his books would still be there, but he dislikes the term 'romance novels' and always strives to transcend the genre. 'I write love stories but I don't want to write the same story over and over. Writing is always a challenge, especially when trying to conceive of an interesting and original story that everyone can relate to, and universal characters that readers feel they know. You may think: It's a love story, you just write, how hard can it be? But for me it's a very difficult genre. My books are love stories where the relationship between two people is the primary focus. But the characters are universal—they are meant to be anybody. When you read my books, you say, "Hey, that could have been my dad or my grandfather, or a neighbour I knew. He was just like that with his wife." These are people you knew growing up. It could have been you!'

True Believer, Sparks decided, should have a strong ghostly element—something he had never tried before. His first step was to research the ghosts of his home state of North Carolina and, in doing so, he came across the local legend of the Brown Mountain Lights, a mysterious phenomenon that is reported to have occurred with regularity over the centuries. Intrigued, he began to develop the idea in his novel, having similar lights appear in a cemetery in a fictitious town, Boone Creek, which stands in the shadow of a fictitious mountain, Riker's Hill.

Nicholas Sparks describes himself as a sceptic when it comes to ghosts and things that go bump in the night, although he remembers one unnerving occasion that gave him pause for thought. 'I once visited a house of a friend that may—or may not—have been haunted. All I know is that I regularly saw movement from the corner of my eyes; when I would glance that way, I would see nothing at all.' His wife Cathy remains convinced that there was a ghostly presence.

All Nicholas Sparks's novels contain autobiographical elements that give them an emotional power and an honesty that has won him the devotion of fans the world over. Lexie, in *True Believer*, is named after his daughter and modelled on the character of Cathy, the love of his life, whom he married in 1989. His first novel, *The Notebook*, was inspired by the marriage of his wife's devoted grandparents; *The Rescue* draws on his experience of dealing with the learning difficulties that beset one of his sons; and *A Walk to Remember* was influenced by his sister's battle with illness.

Sparks is an avid reader and is convinced that it's impossible to become a successful writer without reading a wide range of different authors. 'I read over a hundred books a year and have done since I was fifteen years old,' he says. 'Every book I've read has taught me something. I like to read a book that moves me—in any way except in anger. When I close a book, I almost feel sad, because I've come to know these characters so well. I've just spent a week of my life with them, and now they're gone.'

MYSTERIOUS LIGHTS

The mysterious lights described in *True Believer* are far from being an unusual phenomenon. As well as the Brown Mountain lights that Nicholas Sparks came across, there are also many other examples of lights produced by specific atmospheric conditions around the world. These include two of the most famous: the Northern Lights (also known as the aurora borealis, pictured right), which can sometimes be seen on clear, dark nights in the Northern Hemisphere; and the Green Flash, which is a striking spot of bright green light that appears, on rare occasions, as the sun slips below the ocean horizon at sunset, or rises above it at dawn.

Douglas Preston

Tyrannosaur
Canyon

It's believed that in prehistoric times an asteroid
fell to earth and wiped out the dinosaurs.

Millions of years later, when
striking new evidence of that
cataclysmic event comes to light,
the news travels fast.

And the race is on to lay claim
to what promises to be the
discovery of a lifetime.

Prologue

On December 11, 1972, the last manned Apollo mission to the moon touched down at the Taurus-Littrow landing site, a spectacular mountain-ringed valley at the edge of the Sea of Serenity. The area promised to be a geological wonderland of hills, mountains, craters, debris fields and landslides. Of particular interest were several curious impact craters that had punched deep holes in the valley floor. The Apollo 17 mission had high hopes of returning with a treasure trove of lunar samples.

Eugene Cernan was the commander of the lunar module and Harrison 'Jack' Schmitt its pilot. Cernan was a veteran of two prior missions, Gemini IX and Apollo 10, while Schmitt, a geologist with a PhD from Harvard, had been involved in planning earlier missions. For three days the two men explored Taurus-Littrow with the help of the Lunar Rover. On their first venture across the lunar landscape, it became obvious to all that they had hit the jackpot, geologically speaking. One of the most exciting discoveries of the mission occurred on the second day at a small, deep crater known as Shorty. As Schmitt got out of the Rover to explore the crater rim, he was astonished to see that his boots were kicking through the grey lunar dust to expose a layer of bright orange soil underneath. He dug a quick trench and discovered that the orange soil graded down to a brilliant red.

The 'Backroom' at Houston excitedly debated the meaning of this strangely coloured soil, and they asked the two men to take a double-core sample. After Schmitt took the core, the two men hiked to the rim of Shorty crater, where they saw that the impactor had blasted through to the same orange layer, which lay exposed along the sides of the crater.

Houston wanted samples of orange soil from a second location, so they placed on the exploring itinerary for Day 3 a small unnamed crater close to Shorty, which Schmitt christened Van Serg Crater, after the pen name of a geology professor he had known at Harvard.

Day 3 turned out to be long and gruelling. Dust fouled their equipment and hampered their work. Cernan and Schmitt had driven the Lunar Rover to the base of the mountains ringing Taurus-Littrow to explore an area called the Sculptured Hills. By the time they reached Van Serg Crater, both men were exhausted. To approach the meteorite crater, they had to drive through a field of football-sized rocks. Their observations were captured on the transcripts of the mission:

'I'm not sure what's happened here, yet,' Schmitt said. Everything was coated in thick dust. There was no sign of the orange layer they were after. They parked the Rover and picked their way through the debris field to stand on the rim, Schmitt arriving first. He described the crater top as covered in dust with a mound of blocks measuring around thirty metres in diameter in its centre.

Cernan arrived. 'Holy Smoley!' he said, gazing into the crater.

Schmitt described it for Houston. 'The rocks are intensely shattered in that area, as are the ones that are on the walls.' But as he looked around for orange soil, he saw none, just a lot of grey lunar rock. Mission control was disappointed. Nevertheless, Schmitt and Cernan began collecting samples.

'These are very intensely fractured rocks,' Schmitt said, handling a specimen. 'And it comes off in small flakes. This one will be the best oriented one for documentation. Plus, why don't you get that one you've got there?'

As Cernan took a sample, Schmitt picked up another rock in his scoop. 'Got a bag?' he asked.

'Bag 568.'

'That's a corner, I think.' Schmitt held out another empty bag. 'We'll get another sample that'll be from inside the block.'

'I can get it with the tongs real easy,' Cernan replied.

Schmitt cast about and saw another sample that he wanted—a curious-looking rock about ten inches long. 'We ought to take that just as is,' he told Cernan, even though it was almost too big for a single sample bag.

'Let me hold this end and you put the bag on,' said Cernan as they tried to manoeuvre the specimen into the bag. Then he paused, looking closely at the rock. 'Well, see that? See the white fragments in there?'

'Yeah,' said Schmitt, examining the white spots embedded in the rock. 'You know, these might be pieces of the projectile . . . OK. Pin it down.'

When the rock was safely bagged, Schmitt asked, 'What's the number?'

'It's 480,' responded Cernan, reading out the number printed on the side.

Meanwhile, Houston had became impatient, now that they had determined there wasn't any orange soil there. They asked Cernan to quit the crater and take some photographs of North Massif, while Schmitt did a 'radial survey' of the ejecta blanket surrounding Van Serg. By this time, Schmitt and Cernan had been out exploring for nearly five hours. Back at the Rover, they took one last soil sample and returned to the lunar module. The next day, Cernan and Schmitt lifted out of the Taurus-Littrow Valley, returning to Earth with a splashdown on December 19, 1972.

Lunar Sample 480 joined 842 pounds of other lunar rocks from the Apollo missions at the Lunar Receiving Laboratory at the Johnson Space Center in Houston, Texas. Eight months later, with the end of the Apollo programme, the laboratory was closed and its contents transferred to a newly built, super-high-tech facility at the Johnson Space Center.

Sometime during that eight-month period, the rock known as Lunar Sample 480 vanished. Around the same time, all entries related to its discovery disappeared from the computer catalogue and hard-copy card files.

Chapter 1

Stem Weathers scrambled to the top of the Mesa de los Viejos, tied his burro to a dead juniper, and settled himself down on a dusty boulder. Catching his breath, he mopped the sweat off his neck with a bandanna. A steady wind blowing across the mesa top plucked at his beard, cooling him after the hot, dead air of the canyons.

Studying the familiar landmarks, he silently recited the names—Daggett Canyon, Sundown Rocks, Navajo Rim, Orphan Mesa, Mesa del Yeso, Dead Eye Canyon, the Echo Badlands and Tyrannosaur Canyon. The closet artist in him saw a fantastical realm painted in gold, rose and purple, but the geologist in him saw a set of Upper Cretaceous fault-block plateaus, tilted, split, stripped and scoured by time, as if infinity had laid waste to the earth.

Weathers slipped a packet of tobacco out of a greasy vest pocket and rolled a smoke with gnarled, dirt-blackened hands. Striking a match on his pant leg, he fired up the quirly and took a long drag. For the past two weeks he had restricted his tobacco ration, but now he could splurge.

All his life had been a prologue to this thrilling week.

His life would change in a heartbeat. He'd patch things up with his daughter, Robbie, bring her here and show her his find. She would forgive him his unsettled life, his endless absences. He'd be able to free her from waiting tables and finance the art studio she dreamed of.

Weathers squinted up at the sun. Two hours off the horizon. If he didn't get moving he wouldn't reach the Chama River before dark. Salt, his donkey, hadn't had a drink since morning. Weathers stubbed out the cigarette and untied the burro, leading him eastwards across the barren sandstone mesa. A quarter of a mile distant, the vertiginous opening of Joaquin Canyon cut a spectacular ravine in the Mesa de los Viejos, the Mesa of the Ancients. Falling away into a complex web of canyons known as the Maze, it wound all the way to the Chama River.

Weathers scouted the rim until he found the faint, sloping trail leading to the canyon floor. A treacherous descent, it had landslided out in various places, forcing the traveller to navigate thousand-foot drop-offs. The only route from the Chama River into the high mesa country eastwards, it discouraged all but the bravest souls.

For that, Weathers was grateful.

He picked his way down towards the dry wash along the bottom. It would take him past the entrance to the Maze and from there to the Chama River. By tomorrow afternoon he'd be in Abiquiú. First thing he'd phone Harry Dearborn (the battery on his satphone had died some days back) to let him know . . . Weathers tingled at the thought of breaking the news.

The trail finally reached the bottom. Weathers glanced up. The canyon face was dark, but the late-afternoon sun blazed on the rimrock. He froze. A thousand feet above, a man, silhouetted on the rim, stared down at him.

Weathers swore under his breath. It was the same man who had followed him up from Santa Fe into the Chama wilderness two weeks ago. He recalled the man: a scraggy type on a Harley, some biker wannabe. The man had trailed him through Española, past Abiquiú and Ghost Ranch, hanging 200 yards back, making no effort at deception. He'd followed him on foot up Joaquin Wash from the Chama River. Weathers had lost his pursuer in the Maze and reached the top of the Mesa of the Ancients before the biker found his way out. Two weeks later, here he was again—a persistent little bastard, hoping to jump his claim, no doubt.

Stem Weathers studied the rock spires marking the mouth of the Maze. He would lose him in the Maze again. And maybe this time the son of a bitch would remain lost.

He continued scrambling down the canyon, periodically checking his back trail. Instead of following, however, the man disappeared. Weathers felt his anxiety subside. It wasn't the first time a fool had followed him out into the desert only to find himself lost. They all wanted to be like Stem, but he'd been doing this all his life, and he had a sixth sense. He succeeded where others failed, using nothing more than a donkey and a homemade radar unit built on the back of an old IBM 286.

Weathers's ebullient mood returned. That bastard wasn't going to spoil the greatest week of his life. He rounded the great rock pillar marking the entrance to the Maze. The canyon had a cool, hushed feeling, like the interior of a Gothic cathedral. The air was perfumed by salt cedar. He breathed deeply, and continued into the warren of canyons. In the Maze, not even a map would help you, and the great depth of the canyons made GPS and satellite phones useless.

The first round struck Weathers in the shoulder from behind, and it felt more like a hard punch than a bullet. He landed on his hands and knees, his mind blank with astonishment. It was only when the report cracked and echoed through the canyons that he realised he'd been shot. There was no pain yet, just a buzzing numbness, but he saw that shattered bone protruded from a torn shirt, and pumping blood was splattering on the sand.

He staggered back to his feet as the second shot kicked up the sand next to him. The shots were coming from the rim above him and to his right. He had to return to the canyon 200 yards away—to the lee of the rock pillar. It was the only cover. As he ran for all he was worth, a third shot kicked up sand in front of him. If he could reach that stone pillar, he might escape. He might actually live. Fifty yards, forty, thirty—

He heard the shot only after he felt the bullet slam into his lower back, pitching him face down. He tried to rise, sobbing, furious that someone would steal his find. He writhed, clutching his pocket notebook, hoping to throw it, destroy it, to keep it from his killer—but there was no place to conceal it, and then, as if in a dream, he could not think, could not move . . .

TOM BROADBENT reined in his horse. Four shots had rolled down Joaquin Wash from the great canyons east of the river. It wasn't hunting season and nobody in his right mind would be out in those canyons target shooting.

He checked his watch. Eight o'clock. The sun had just sunk below the horizon. The echoes seemed to have come from the cluster of hoodoo rocks at the mouth of the Maze. It would be a fifteen-minute detour, no more, and Sally wasn't expecting him home before midnight anyway.

He turned his horse Knock up the wash and towards the canyon mouth, following the fresh tracks of a man and burro. Rounding a turn, he saw a dark shape sprawled in front of him: a man lying face down.

He rode over, swung off and knelt, his heart hammering. The man, shot in the back and shoulder, still oozed blood into the sand. Tom felt the carotid artery: nothing. He turned him over, wiped the sand out of the man's mouth and gave him mouth-to-mouth resuscitation. Then, leaning over the man, he administered heart massage, pressing on his rib cage, once, twice, then another breath. Air bubbled out of the wound.

Incredibly, the heart had restarted.

Suddenly the man's eyes opened, revealing a pair of bright blue eyes that stared at Tom from a dusty, sunburnt face. He drew in a shallow breath. The blood-flecked lips parted. 'No . . . You bastard . . .'

'Wait,' said Tom. 'I'm not the man who shot you.'

The eyes peered at him closely, the terror subsiding—replaced by something else. Hope. The man's eyes glanced down at his hand.

Tom followed the man's gaze to a small, leather-bound notebook.

'Take it . . .' the man rasped.

Tom took the notebook. The cover was sticky with blood.

'It's for Robbie . . .' he gasped, his lips twisting with the effort to speak. 'My daughter . . . give it to her . . . She'll know how to find it . . .'

'It?'

'The treasure . . .'

'Don't think about that now. We're going to get you out of here. Just—'

The man clutched at Tom's shirt with a trembling hand. 'It's for . . . Robbie . . . No one else . . . Not the police . . . You must . . . *promise*.' His hand twisted the shirt with shocking force.

'I promise.'

'Tell Robbie . . . I . . . love . . .'

His eyes defocused. The hand relaxed and slid down.

He'd stopped breathing. Tom recommended CPR. Nothing. After ten futile minutes, he untied the man's bandanna and laid it over his face.

That's when it dawned on him: *The man's killer must still be around.* His eyes searched the rimrock and the surrounding scree. The silence was so profound it seemed that the rocks themselves held vigil.

Get out now. Tom rose, caught his horse's reins, swung up and dug in his heels. The horse set off down the canyon at a gallop, and rounded the opening to the Maze. Only when he was halfway down Joaquin Wash did Tom slow him to a trot. A great buttery moon was rising in the east. If he really pushed his horse, he could make Abiquiú in two hours.

JIMSON 'WEED' MADDOX hiked along the canyon floor, whistling 'Saturday Night Fever', feeling on top of the world. Although he had spent the better part of a week tramping around lost in the Maze, it hadn't been a waste of time: now he knew the Maze and much of the mesa country beyond. He'd had time to plan his ambush of Weathers—and he'd pulled it off perfectly.

He rounded the sandstone pillar at the entrance to the Maze. The man he had shot lay on the ground, a dark shape in the twilight.

He halted. Fresh hoofprints in the sand headed to and from the body.

He broke into a run.

The body lay on its back, bandanna carefully spread over its face. Someone had been here. The person might even have been a *witness.*

Maddox forced himself to calm down. It would take the man a couple of hours to ride back to Abiquiú and several more to get the police and return. He had enough time to get the notebook, hide the body and get the hell out.

Maddox searched the body, turning out the pockets and rifling the man's day pack. His fist closed over a rock in the man's pocket and he pulled it out and examined it by flashlight. It was definitely a sample, something Corvus had pointedly asked for. But where was the notebook? He looked around. The man's burro stood a hundred yards off, still packed, dozing.

Maddox undid the diamond hitch, pulled off the packsaddle and emptied the panniers onto the sand. Everything fell out: a piece of electronic equipment, hammers, chisels, maps, a handheld GPS unit, frying pan, empty food sacks, dirty underwear, and a folded-up piece of parchment.

Maddox seized the parchment. It was a crude map covered with clumsily drawn peaks, rivers, rocks, dotted lines, old-time Spanish lettering—and there, in the middle, had been inked a heavy, Spanish-style X.

An honest-to-God treasure map.

He refolded the greasy parchment and stuffed it into his shirt pocket, then resumed his search. Combing through the spilt equipment, he found everything a prospector might need—except the notebook.

He sat back, his head throbbing. Was it coincidence the man on horse-back had shown up—or something else? A terrible idea came to him: the man was a rival. He had also been trailing Weathers and hoping to cash in on his discovery. Maybe he'd taken the notebook.

Well, Maddox had found the map. And that, it seemed to him, would be as important as the notebook, if not more so. He studied the electronic device, a dented metal box with switches, dials and a small LED screen. Corvus hadn't mentioned it but it looked important. He'd take that, too. He removed the rock sample from his pocket, and turned it over in the moonlight. That, the map and the machine should more than satisfy Corvus.

In the meantime, he had a body to bury.

DETECTIVE LIEUTENANT Jimmie Willer sat in the back of the police chopper, tired as hell, feeling the thudding of the rotors in every bone. He glanced down at the ghostly nightscape slipping by underneath them. The chopper pilot was following the Chama River, every bend shimmering like the blade of a scimitar. They passed small villages along the banks, little more than clusters of lights. Here and there a lonely car crawled along Highway 84, throwing a tiny yellow beam into the great darkness. North of Abiquiú reservoir all lights ceased; beyond lay the Chama wilderness and the vast high mesa country, uninhabited to the Colorado border.

Willer shook his head. It was a hell of a place to get murdered.

He fingered the pack of Marlboros in his shirt pocket. He was annoyed at being roused out of his bed at midnight, annoyed that they couldn't find the medical examiner, annoyed that his own deputy was out at the casino, blowing his miserable paycheque on the tables, cellphone turned off. On top of that it cost $600 an hour to run Santa Fe's lone police chopper, an expense that came straight out of his budget. And this was only the first trip. There would have to be a second with the ME and the scene-of-crime team before they could move the body and collect evidence. Then there would be the publicity . . . Perhaps, thought Willer hopefully, it was just another drug murder and wouldn't garner more than a day's story in the *New Mexican*.

Yeah, please make it a drug murder.

'There. Joaquin Wash. Head east,' said Broadbent to the pilot.

Willer shot a glance at the man who'd spoilt his evening. He was tall, rangy, wearing a pair of worn-out cowboy boots.

The chopper banked away from the river, and Willer could see the canyon rims awash in the moonlight.

'The Maze is right down there,' Broadbent said a few minutes later. 'The body was just inside the mouth where the Maze joins Joaquin Canyon.'

The chopper slowed and descended. The moon illuminated most of the canyon bottom. Willer saw nothing but silvery sand.

'Put it down in that open area.'

The pilot began the descent, the chopper whipping up a whirlwind of dust before touching down. The moment it came to rest, Broadbent piled out and Willer followed, keeping low, his eyes covered against the flying dust, until he was beyond the backwash. Then he straightened up, slid the pack out of his pocket and fired one up. Broadbent walked ahead.

Willer switched on his Maglite and shone it around. 'Don't step on any tracks,' he called to Broadbent. 'I don't want the forensic guys on my case.' He shone the Mag up the mouth of the canyon. There was nothing but a flat bed of sand between two walls of sandstone.

'What's up there?'

'The Maze. A whole lot of canyons running up into Mesa de los Viejos. Easy to get lost in there, Detective.'

'Right.' He swept the light back and forth. 'I don't see any tracks.'

'Neither do I. But they have to be around here somewhere.'

'Lead the way.'

He followed Broadbent, walking slowly. He switched off the flashlight. Ahead, the canyon was bathed in moonlight, and it looked empty.

Broadbent hesitated, looking around. 'The body was right in this area. And the tracks of my horse should be plainly visible over there . . .'

Willer said nothing. He was starting to get a bad feeling. He bent down, snubbed his cigarette out in the sand, put the butt in his pocket.

'The body was right in this area. I'm sure of it. The burro was over there,' Broadbent continued, 'a hundred yards off.'

There were no tracks, no body, no burro, nothing but an empty canyon in the moonlight. 'You sure this is the right place?' Willer asked.

'Positive.'

Willer hooked his thumbs into his belt and watched Broadbent walk around and examine the ground. He was a tall, easy-moving type. In town they said he was Croesus—but up close he sure didn't look rich, with those crappy old boots and Salvation Army shirt.

Willer hawked up a piece of phlegm. There must be a thousand canyons out here—Broadbent had taken them to the wrong canyon. Willer could see with his own damn eyes that the canyon was wall-to-wall empty. The moonlight was so bright it was like noon.

'Well there's nothing here now. No tracks, no body, no blood. It's time to call it a night, Mr Broadbent.'

'You're just going to give up?'

Willer took a long, slow breath. 'All I'm saying is, I see no evidence of a crime here. We'll return tomorrow morning with maps, a GPS unit—and find the right canyon.'

'I am not going anywhere until I've solved this problem, Detective.'

'Suit yourself. You know the way out.' Willer walked back towards the chopper, climbed in. 'We're out of here,' he announced to the pilot.

The pilot took off his earphones. 'And him?'

'He knows the way out.'

'He's signalling you. Looks like he found something.'

Willer swore under his breath, looked out at the dark figure a few hundred yards off. Waving, gesturing. 'Christ Almighty.' Willer heaved himself out of the chopper, hiked over. Broadbent had scuffed away a dry patch of sand, exposing a black, wet, sticky layer underneath.

Willer swallowed, unhooked his flashlight, clicked it on.

'Oh, Jesus,' he said, taking a step back. 'Oh, Jesus.'

WEED MADDOX bought a blue silk jacket, silk boxer shorts and a pair of grey slacks from Seligman's on 34th Street, along with a white T-shirt, silk socks and Italian shoes, and put them all on in the changing room. He paid for it with his own American Express card—his first legitimate one—and stepped out into the street. The new clothes drove off some of the nervousness he'd been feeling about his upcoming meeting with Corvus.

He caught a cab, gave the address, and was whisked uptown.

Ten minutes later he was being ushered into a panelled office overlooking Central Park. Dr Iain Corvus was standing at the side of his desk, restlessly sorting through some papers.

Maddox halted in the door, hands clasped in front, waiting to be acknowledged. Corvus was as wound up as ever, his nonexistent lips tight as a vice, his chin jutting out like the bow of a boat, his black hair combed straight back. He wore a well-cut charcoal suit and a crisp Turnbull and Asser shirt set off by a blood-red silk tie.

Corvus paused in his sorting and peered over the tops of his glasses. 'Well, well, if it isn't Jimson Maddox, back from the front.' His British accent seemed plummier than ever. Corvus was about his own age, mid-thirties, but the two men couldn't be more different. Corvus held out his hand and Maddox took it, suppressing a welling of emotion.

This was the man who got him out of Pelican Bay.

Corvus took Maddox's elbow and guided him into a chair in the little sitting area at the far end of the office. Corvus went to his office door, said something to his secretary, shut and locked it, then sat down opposite him, restlessly crossing and uncrossing his legs until he seemed to get it right. He leaned forward, his eyes shining. 'Good to see you, Jim.'

Maddox liked the way Corvus always gave him his full attention, spoke to him like an equal. Corvus had moved heaven and earth to free him from prison, and with one phone call he could put him back in.

'Well,' said Corvus, sitting back.

Maddox withdrew the map from his pocket and held it out. 'I found this in the guy's pack,' he said.

Corvus took it with a frown, unfolded it. His face reddened. 'Where's the notebook?' he asked brusquely, flipping the map onto the table.

Maddox didn't answer directly. 'It was like this . . . I followed Weathers into the high mesas, but he shook me. I waited two weeks for him to come back out. When he did, I ambushed him, killed him.'

There was an electric silence. 'You *killed* him?'

'Yeah. You want the guy running around, telling everyone you jumped his claim? Look, trust me, the guy had to die.'

A long silence. 'And the notebook?'

'That's the thing. I didn't find a notebook. Just the map. And this.' He took the metal box with the switches and the LED screen out of the bag he was carrying and laid it on the table.

Corvus didn't even look at it. 'You didn't find the notebook?'

Maddox swallowed. 'Nope. I shot him from the top of a canyon, and by the time I'd hiked five miles to get to the body someone had gotten there first, another prospector, hoping to cash in. I searched the dead man, turned everything inside out. There was no notebook. I took everything of value, swept the site clean, and buried him.'

Corvus looked away.

'I tried to follow this other guy's tracks, but lost him. Luckily the guy's name was in the papers the next day: a horse vet, name of Broadbent.'

'Broadbent took the notebook,' Corvus said in a monotone.

'That's what I think, and that's why I looked into his background. He's married, lives on a ranch north of Abiquiú. Everybody says he's rich— although you'd never know it from looking at him.

Corvus locked his eyes on Maddox.

'I'll get the notebook for you. But what about the map? I mean—?'

'The map's a fake.'

Another agonising silence.

'And the metal box?' Maddox said, pointing to the object. 'It looks to me like there's a computer in there. Maybe on the hard disk—'

'That's the central unit of Weathers's homemade ground-penetrating radar device. It has no hard disk—the data's in the *notebook*.

Maddox turned his eyes away from Corvus's stare, slipped his hand into his pocket and retrieved the chunk of rock, putting it down on the glass table. 'Weathers also had this in his pocket.'

Corvus stared at it, his whole expression changing. He reached out with a spidery hand and plucked it gently from the table. He retrieved a loupe from his desk and examined it more closely. Finally he looked up. Gone was the tightness, the glittering eyes. His face had become almost human.

'This is . . . *very* good.' Corvus rose, went to his desk, slipped a Ziploc bag out of a drawer and placed the rock inside with the utmost care.

'It's a sample, right?' Maddox asked.

Corvus unlocked a drawer and removed an inch-thick stack of hundred-dollar bills bound with rubber bands. 'For any unexpected expenses,' he said, pressing the block of notes into Maddox's hand. 'You know what to do.'

Maddox nodded, stood up and parked the money in his jacket. Corvus walked to the door and held it open. Maddox stepped through it.

'Goodbye, Mr Maddox.' Corvus placed a firm hand on his shoulder, gave a squeeze too sharp to be affectionate. '*The notebook*,' he whispered.

His shoulder released, Maddox heard the door close softly. He walked through the secretary's office into the vast, echoing corridor.

Broadbent. He'd take care of that son of a bitch.

TOM SAT at the kitchen table, leaning back in his chair, waiting for the coffee grounds to settle in the tin pot on ⬤ stove. A June breeze rustled the cottonwood leaves outside, stripping the trees of their cotton, which drifted past in snowy wisps. Across the yard Tom could see the horses in their pens, nosing the timothy hay Sally had pitched them that morning.

Sally came in, still wearing her nightgown. She passed before the sliding glass doors, backlit by the rising sun. They had been married less than a year and everything was still new. She looked into the tin coffeepot on the stove and made a face. 'I can't believe you make coffee that way,' she said, and began foaming the milk for her own coffee.

Tom watched her, smiling. 'You look bewitching this morning.'

She glanced up, swept her golden hair out of her face. ·

'I've decided to let Shane handle the clinic today,' Tom said. 'I was up most of the night with that . . . business up in the Maze.'

'The police have no theories?'

'None. No body, no motive—just a few buckets of blood-soaked sand.'

Sally winced. 'So what *are* you going to do today?' she asked.

He reached into his pocket and removed the battered notebook. 'I'm going to find Robbie, wherever she is, and give her this.'

Sally frowned. 'Tom, I still think you should have given that to the police. It's irresponsible to keep evidence from them. He was probably up to something illegal.'

'Maybe, but I made a promise to a dying man. If you'd seen the look of desperation on his face, you'd understand.'

Sally sighed. 'So how are you going to find this mysterious daughter?'

'I thought I'd start by going to see Ben Peek,' Tom said. 'He spent years prospecting in those canyons. He might have an idea who the guy was or what this treasure was he was looking for.'

'And there's nothing in that notebook?'

'Nothing except numbers. No name or address, just sixty pages of numbers—and a pair of gigantic exclamation marks at the end.'

'You think he really found a treasure?'

'I could see it in his eyes.'

The man's desperate plea still rang in his ears. It had affected him deeply, perhaps because his father's death was still fresh in his mind. His father, Maxwell Broadbent, had also been a prospector of sorts—a tomb robber, collector, and dealer in artefacts. While he had been a difficult father, his death had left a huge hole in Tom's psyche. The dying prospector, with his beard and piercing blue eyes, had even reminded him of his father. He felt the promise he had made to the unknown man was inviolate.

'Tom? You've got that lost look again.'

Tom blinked. 'Sorry.'

Sally topped off her coffee with a dash of powdered dark chocolate, and sat down. 'Do you realise that we found this place one year ago today?'

'I'd forgotten.'

'You still like it?'

'It's everything I always wanted.'

Together, in the wild country of Abiquiú, they had found the life they'd dreamed of: a small ranch with horses, a garden, a riding stable for children, and Tom's vet practice with his partner Shane—a rural life without the hassles of the city, pollution or long commutes in traffic. The work was mostly outdoors, the people were great and he loved horses.

It was a little quiet, he had to admit.

He turned his attention back to the notebook. It was evidently written in some kind of code, laid out on each page in rows and columns in a fanatically neat hand. There were no erasures or rewrites, no mistakes, no scribbles—as if it had been copied from something else, number by number.

Sally stood up and put an arm round him. Her hair swung down over his face and he inhaled the fragrance of it, fresh shampoo and her own warm biscuit smell. 'Promise me one thing,' she said.

'What?'

'Be careful. Whatever treasure that man found, it was worth killing for.'

Chapter 2

Melodie Crookshank, Technical Specialist First Grade, kicked back and cracked a Coke. She took a sip, gazing pensively around her basement lab. When she went to graduate school at Columbia in geophysical chemistry, she had imagined a very different career path for herself—trekking through the rain forest of Quintana Roo to map the crater of Chicxulub, or excavating dinosaur nests at the legendary Flaming Cliffs

in the Gobi Desert. Instead, she had found herself in this windowless basement lab, doing dull laboratory research for uninspired scientists, many of
whom had an IQ half of her own. She'd sent out hundreds of CVs, and
received no offers in return. It was a brutal market, where every year sixty
freshly minted graduate students chased half a dozen openings, a game of
musical chairs in which, when the music stopped, most were left standing.

Yet Melodie was an incorrigible optimist, and she felt, deep down, that
she was destined for something greater, so she continued to apply for any
and all positions that came up. In the meantime, the present was tolerable.
The lab was quiet, and all she had to do to escape was close her eyes and
step into the future, that vast and wonderful country where she could have
adventures, make wonderful discoveries, and have tenure.

Melodie's reverie was interrupted by a low buzz, which indicated that
someone had entered her empty laboratory. She waited, Coke in hand, for
the intruder to come around the corner.

Soon she heard the confident click of wing tips on the linoleum floor,
and a slender, elegant man appeared—Dr Iain Corvus.

She swiftly removed her feet from the table, and brushed her hair out of
her reddening face. Curators almost never came to the lab, preferring not to
associate with the technical staff. But here, against all probability, was
Corvus himself, who cut quite a figure in his Savile Row suits and hand-
made shoes—handsome too, in a creepy kind of Jeremy Irons way.

'Melodie Crookshank?'

She was amazed he even knew her name. She looked into his lean, smiling face, beautiful teeth, hair black as night.

'Right,' she finally said, trying to keep her voice easy. 'That's me.'

'I'm so glad I found you, Melodie. Am I disturbing you?'

'No, no, not at all.' She collected herself, blushing like an idiot.

'I wonder if I could interrupt your busy day with a sample that needs
analysing.' He held a Ziploc bag up and let it swing back and forth. 'I have
a little, ah, *challenge* for you. Something just between us.'

Melodie paused, then said carefully, 'What do you mean?'

He handed her the sample bag. The label read *New Mexico, specimen #1.*
'I'd like you to analyse the sample in here without any preconceived notions
about what it might be. A complete mineralogical, crystallographical,
chemical and structural analysis. Don't cut any corners.'

'No problem.'

'Here's the rub. I'd like to keep this secret. Don't write anything down or store anything on a hard drive. When you run tests on it, download the data onto CDs and hard-delete the data from the system. Keep the CDs locked up at all times. Don't discuss your findings with anyone. Report to me directly.' He gave her another brilliant smile. 'Are you game?'

Crookshank felt a tingle of excitement at the fact that Corvus had chosen to take her into his confidence. 'Why so hush-hush?'

Corvus leaned forward. She caught the faint scent of cigars and tweed. 'That, my dear Melodie, you shall know—*after* you've done your analysis. As I said, I don't want to give you any preconceived notions.'

The idea intrigued her. Corvus was one of those men who radiated power. At the same time, he was disliked in the museum by many of the other curators, and all this false friendliness only confirmed in her own mind that he was a bit of a rogue—albeit a handsome, charming one.

'What do you say, Melodie? Shall we *conspire* together?'

'All right.' Why the hell not? She knew what she was getting into, at least.

'Good.' He grinned as she eyed the specimen. 'Go on, take a closer look.'

She turned her attention to the chunk of rock. Right away she could see what it was, at least in general terms. There was some really unusual structure in there. She felt her pulse quicken. This was going to be fun.

She lowered the bag and her eyes met his. He was looking at her intently, his pale grey eyes almost colourless in the fluorescent glow of the lab.

'This is amazing,' she said. 'If I'm not mistaken this is—'

'Ah!' He placed a finger gently against her lips, and winked. 'Our little secret.' He removed his hand, rose as if to go, then turned back. He reached into his jacket pocket and pulled out a long velvet box. 'A little thankyou.' He held it out to her. *TIFFANY* was written on the front of the box.

Yeah right, Crookshank thought, taking it. She snapped it open and was dazzled by the sight of gemstones, blue stars. She blinked. A bracelet of star sapphires set in platinum. Real, not synthetics. She felt a lump in her throat, a hot tickling in her eyes. No one had given her anything like this, ever.

She said in an offhand way, not looking up, 'Nice collection of aluminium oxide you got here.'

'I was hoping you would like star sapphires, Melodie.'

Crookshank swallowed. She loved them. Sri Lankan star sapphires were her favourite, each one unique—mineralogy incarnate. She knew she was being shamelessly manipulated, but at the same time she thought: Why not?

She felt Corvus's hand come to rest on her shoulder, giving it the gentlest of squeezes. It was like an electric shock. An erotic charge ran through her like a bolt of lightning, and she flushed and tingled all over.

'Melodie, I'm awfully grateful for your help. I know how good you are at what you do. That's why I entrusted this sample to you. That's why I gave you the bracelet. It's not just a bribe—although it *is* a bit of that.' He chuckled. 'It's an expression of my faith in you, Melodie Crookshank.'

She nodded. 'OK,' she whispered.

WHEN TOM'S FATHER died, and Tom inherited an ocean of money, his sole indulgence had been his truck, a 1957 Chevy 3100 pick-up with a turquoise body, white top and chrome grill. It had once belonged to a classic car collector in Albuquerque who had lovingly rebuilt the engine, machined the parts he couldn't find, and rechromed everything down to the knobs on the radio. The poor man had died of a heart attack before he could enjoy the fruits of his labour. Tom had paid the widow every penny it was worth—fifty-five grand—and still he felt he'd got a bargain.

It was already noon. Tom had driven everywhere, asked around at the Sunset mart, but all he had learned was that he was merely retracing the footsteps of the Santa Fe Police, who were also trying to find out if anyone had encountered the murdered man before his death.

Tom had decided to visit Ben Peek, who lived in the funky hamlet of Cerrillos, a former gold-mining town that had seen better days. The mines had played out decades ago but Cerrillos had avoided ghost-town status by being revived by hippies in the sixties, who bought up abandoned miners' cabins and installed pottery studios, leather shops and macramé factories in them. It was now inhabited by a curious mixture of old Spanish families who once worked the mines, ageing hippies and curious eccentrics.

Ben Peek was one of the eccentrics. He'd been a professional prospector for forty years until a jack mule broke his hip. A sign nailed to his old battenboard house said: THE WHAZZIT SHOP: EVERYTHING FOR SALE. But Peek had an MS in geology from the Colorado School of Mines. He knew his stuff.

Tom mounted the crooked portal and rapped on the door. A moment later a face appeared, distorted by the old rippled glass, then the door opened.

'Tom Broadbent!' Peek's rough hand grasped Tom's and gave it a bone-crushing squeeze. Peek had a five-day growth of beard, and crow's feet around a pair of lively black eyes.

'How are you, Ben?'

'Terrible, just terrible. Come on in.'

He led Tom through his shop, the walls covered with shelves groaning under heaps of old rocks, iron tools and glass bottles. Everything was for sale, but nothing, it seemed, ever sold. The price tags were yellowing antiques themselves. They passed into a back room, which functioned as a kitchen. The old man snagged a battered coffeepot off the stove, poured out two mugs, and limped over to a wooden table, inviting Tom to sit with him.

'How's Sally?'

'Fantastic, as always.'

Peek nodded. 'Wonderful woman you got there, Tom.' He rapped a pipe out on the edge of the fireplace and began filling it with Borkum Riff. 'Yesterday morning I read in the *New Mexican* that you found a murdered man up in the high mesas.'

'There's more to the story than what was in the paper.' Tom told Peek the story—omitting the part about the notebook. 'Any idea who the prospector was?' he asked Peek at the end.

Peek snorted. 'Treasure hunters are a pack of credulous half-wits. But no, I haven't heard anything about a treasure hunter up there.'

'Any idea what the treasure might be? Assuming it exists.'

'I was a prospector, not a treasure hunter. There's a big difference.'

'But you spent time up there. You must have heard stories.'

Peek lit a wooden kitchen match and held it to his pipe. 'Sure did.'

'Humour me.'

'When this was still Spanish territory, they say there was a gold mine up there north of Abiquiú called El Capitán. They say they took out almost ten thousand ounces, cast it into ingots stamped with the Lion and Castle. The Apaches were tearing up the country, so they walled it up in a cave, waiting for things to settle down. It so happened that one day the Apaches raided the mine. They killed everyone except a fellow named Juan Cabrillo, who'd gone to Abiquiú for supplies. When Cabrillo came back and found his companions dead, he took off for Santa Fe and returned with an armed group to collect the gold. But a couple of weeks had passed and there'd been heavy rains and a flash flood. The landmarks had changed. They found the mine all right, but they never could find that cave. Juan spent years looking for it—until he disappeared in those mesas, never to be seen again.'

'Interesting.'

'There's more. Back in the 1930s, a fellow named Ernie Kilpatrick was looking for a maverick bull in one of those canyons. As the sun was setting he claimed he saw where a fresh landslide—just up Tyrannosaur Canyon—had unseated what looked like a cave. He climbed up and crawled along a narrow tunnel until it opened up into a chamber. He just about died when his candle lit up a whole wall of crude gold bars stamped with the Lion and Castle. He pocketed one and rode back to Abiquiú. That night he got drunk in the saloon and started showing the gold bar around. Someone followed him out, shot and robbed him. Of course, the secret died with him and the gold bar was never seen again.' He spat a piece of tobacco off his tongue. 'These treasure stories are all the same. I don't believe a damned word.'

'Ben, I talked to the man. He found something big. Is there anything else he might have found of value up there?'

Peek shrugged. 'Sure. There's all kinds of minerals and precious metals up there. Uranium is sometimes found in the upper member of the Chinle formation, which crops out in Tyrannosaur Canyon and all around lower Joachin. I looked for uranium back in the late fifties, didn't find squat.'

'Is uranium worth anything these days?'

'Not unless you have a private buyer on the black market. The feds sure aren't buying—they've got too much as it is.'

'Could it be of use to terrorists?'

Peek shook his head. 'You'd need a billion-dollar enrichment programme.'

'Why do they call it Tyrannosaur Canyon?'

'There's a big basaltic intrusion right at the mouth, weathered in such a way that the top of it looks like a *T. rex* skull. The Apaches wouldn't go up it, claim it's haunted. It's where my mule spooked and threw me. Broke my hip. Three days before they medevacked me out. I never went back.'

'What about gold? I heard you found some back there.'

Ben chuckled. 'Sure I did. Gold is a curse to all who find it. Back in '86 I found a quartz boulder all spun through with wire gold in the bottom of Maze Wash. Sold it to a mineral dealer for nine thousand dollars, then spent ten times that amount looking for where it came from. Never did find the mother lode.' He drew another cloud of smoke from his pipe.

'Anything else you can think of?'

'This "treasure" of his might have been an Indian ruin. There are a lot of Anasazi ruins up in there. And then there's the Lost City of the Padres.'

'What's that?'

Peek sucked on his pipe. 'Back around the turn of the century, a French padre named Eusebio Bernard got lost up on Mesa de los Viejos. While wandering around, he spied a huge Anasazi cliff dwelling hidden in the rock below him. It had four towers, hundreds of room blocks, a real lost city. No one ever found it again.'

'A true story?'

Peek smiled. 'Probably not.' He stirred the ashes of his pipe with a tool, tamped it down, relit it. 'If this unknown prospector of yours was looking for ghosts, well, they say they're quite a few up there. The Apaches claim they've heard the *T. rex* roar.'

'We're getting off the subject, Ben.'

'You said you wanted stories.'

Tom held up a hand, smiling. 'I draw the line at ghost dinosaurs.'

TOM DROVE back home, disappointed that he hadn't made more progress. He went to his study and pulled the notebook out of his pocket.

Shoving the other papers aside, he opened the notebook and laid it on the table. The numbers beckoned—in there, he felt sure, was the secret to the man's identity. And to the treasure he found.

Sally poked her head in. 'How did it go today?' she asked.

'I'm not having much luck. If I could only figure out what that guy had written in this journal of his, it would probably tell me who he was.'

'It probably would.' She hesitated.

'What is it?'

'You remember last year, you went to that monastery up the Chama River to treat a sick ewe?'

Tom nodded.

'Didn't you tell me that, while you were up there, you heard about a monk who used to be a code breaker for the CIA?'

'Yeah. I remember something like that.'

'Why don't you ask him to take a crack at the notebook?'

Tom stared at her. 'Now that's the best idea you've had all week.'

MELODIE CROOKSHANK adjusted the angle on the diamond wafering blade and upped the rpm. It was a beautiful piece of precision machinery—you could hear it in the clear singing noise it made. She tightened the sample in the cutting bed, then turned on the laminar water flow. The water bathed the specimen, bringing out flecks of colour in it, yellow, red, deep purple. She made some final adjustments, set the automatic guide speed and let it rip. In a moment the specimen had been cut in half, the treasure of its interior exposed to view. Deftly she washed and dried it, flipped it, embedding the other side in epoxy resin on a steel manipulator.

Once the epoxy had hardened, she placed the sample back in the cutting bed and sliced again on the other side. Now she had a slender wafer of stone, perfectly cut, about half a millimetre thick. She quickly dissolved the resin, and cut the wafer into a dozen smaller pieces. Taking one of the chips, she mounted it on a slide and placed it on the stage of the Meiji polarising scope, switched it on and put her eyes to the oculars.

With a rapid adjustment of the focusing knobs, a rainbow of colour leapt into her vision. This was truly an incredible specimen. The structure was perfect—astonishing. She could now understand the secrecy. If there were more of this in situ it would be of the utmost importance to keep it secret. This would be a stunning coup, even for a man as distinguished as Corvus.

She leaned back from the eyepieces, a new thought entering her head. This might be just the thing *she* needed to leverage a tenure-track position for herself, if she played her cards right.

CHRIST IN THE DESERT Monastery lay fifteen miles up the Chama River, deep in the Chama wilderness and hard alongside the enormous cliff-walled bulk of Mesa de los Viejos, the Mesa of the Ancients. Tom drove up to the monastery with excruciating slowness, on a potholed road that threatened to shake loose every bolt in his precious Chevy.

After what seemed like a journey to the very ends of the earth, Tom spied the adobe church tower rising above the junipers. Gradually the rest of the Benedictine monastery came into view—a cluster of brown adobe buildings scattered on a bench of land above the flood plain of the river.

Tom parked his truck in the dirt lot and walked up the trail to the monastery's shop. As he opened the door, a bell tinkled, and a young monk came in from the back and took a seat on a high stool behind the counter.

'Hello,' said Tom.

'Welcome.'

Tom stood there indecisively, looking at the humble products of the monastery: honey, dried flowers, hand-printed cards, wood carvings. 'I'm Tom Broadbent,' he said, offering his hand.

The monk took it. 'Pleased to meet you.'

Tom cleared his throat. This was damned awkward. 'I'm a veterinarian, and last year I doctored a sick ewe up here.'

The monk nodded.

'While I was here, I heard mention of a monk who'd been in the CIA.'

The monk nodded again. 'That would be Brother Ford.'

'Right. I was wondering if I could talk to him.'

The monk glanced at his watch. 'Sext is just over. I'll go get him.'

He vanished up the trail. Five minutes later Tom was startled to see a gigantic figure marching down, his enormous feet in dusty sandals, his brown robes flapping behind him. A moment later the door was flung open, and without a beat he strode up to Tom and enveloped his hand in a large but surprisingly gentle grasp.

'Brother Wyman Ford,' he gravelled out in a distinctly unmonkish voice.

'Tom Broadbent.'

Brother Ford certainly didn't look like a typical monk, with his powerful six-foot five-inch frame, craggy face, black beard and unruly hair.

A silence ensued and Tom once again felt the awkwardness of his visit. 'Do you have a moment to talk?'

'Technically, we're under a vow of silence within these grounds,' said the monk. 'Shall we take a walk?'

The monk set out at high speed along a trail that wound down to the river, Tom struggling to keep up with him. After they'd hiked for ten minutes, the trail ascended, terminating at the top of a bluff. Brother Wyman tossed back the skirt of his robe and sat on a dead juniper trunk.

Tom sat beside him. 'I hope I haven't taken you from anything important,' he said, still unsure where to begin.

'I'm missing a terribly important meeting in the Disputation Chamber. One of the brothers swore at Compline.' He chuckled.

'Brother Ford—'

'Please call me Wyman.'

'I wonder if you'd heard about the murder in the Maze two days ago.'

'I gave up reading the paper a long time ago.'

'Well, two nights ago, a treasure hunter was murdered up there.' Tom recited the story of the man, finding the body, the notebook.

Ford was silent for a while, looking out over the river. Then he turned his head and asked, 'So . . . where do I come in?'

Tom removed the notebook from his pocket.

'You didn't give it to the police?'

'I'd made a promise.'

He found the monk's steady grey eyes on him. 'What can I do for you?'

'I've tried everything I know to identify the man so I can give this to his daughter. Without success. The police haven't a clue and it may be weeks before they find the body. The answer to the man's identity lies in here—I'm sure of it. Only problem is, it's written in code.'

A pause. The monk continued to gaze steadily at Tom.

'I heard you were a code breaker for the CIA.'

'A cryptanalyst, yes.'

'Well? How about taking a crack at it?'

Ford hesitated, then said, 'I'm sorry, Tom, but I came up here to get away from just that sort of thing. In less than a month I'm going to take my vows. Being a monk is more than wearing a habit. It's taking on a new life. That'—he pointed to the book—'would be a throwback to my old life.'

'You must've had a pretty rough time of it, to run away to a monastery.'

Ford's brow contracted. 'Monastic spirituality is not about running away, but about running *towards* the living God. But yes, it was rough.'

'What happened? If you don't mind me asking.'

'I do mind. I guess I'm no longer used to the kind of prying inquisitiveness that in the outside world passes for conversation.'

Tom was stung by the rebuke. 'I'm sorry. I'm out of line.'

'Don't be sorry. You're doing what you feel is right. And I think it *is* right. It's just that I'm not the man to help you.'

Tom nodded and they both rose.

'I don't think you'll have much trouble with that code. Most homemade codes are just numbers substituted for letters. All you need is a frequency table of the English language.'

'What's that?'

'A list of the most to least common letters in the English language. You match that list up with the most to least common numbers in the code. You'll crack it in a jiffy, I bet.' Ford hesitated. 'Let me take a quick look. I might be able to do it on the spot.'

'You sure you don't mind?' Tom handed it to him.

Ford leafed through it, taking his time. 'Funny, but this is looking a lot more sophisticated to me than a substitution code.'

The sun was descending into the canyons, suffusing the arroyos in a bright golden light. The river tumbled by below, a whisper of water.

He shut the book with a slap. 'I'll keep the book for a few days. These numbers are intriguing—all kinds of weird patterns in there.'

'You're going to help me out after all?'

Ford shrugged. 'It'll help this girl learn what happened to her father.'

'After what you told me I feel a little uncomfortable about this.'

'Sometimes I get a little too absolutist about things. There's no harm in giving it a quick try.' He grasped Tom's hand. 'I admire your stubbornness. The monastery doesn't have a telephone, but we do have an Internet connection via satellite dish. I'll email you when I crack it.'

WEED MADDOX REMEMBERED the first time he had blown through Abiquiú on a stolen Harley Dyna Wide Glide. Now he was just another asshole in khakis and a Ralph Lauren Polo shirt driving a Range Rover. Beyond the town of Abiquiú the road followed the river, past green alfalfa fields and groves of cottonwoods, before climbing out of the valley. He took a left on 96, drove over the dam and up along the southern side of the valley, until the left-hand turn to the Broadbent place appeared.

Maddox slowed at the gate, passed it, continued on for another quarter of a mile, and parked the car in a thicket of gambel oaks. He got out and eased the door shut. Three o'clock. Broadbent would probably be gone, at work or out. They said he had a wife, Sally, who ran a riding stable.

Maddox slung the rucksack over his shoulder. First thing, he thought, was to reconnoitre the land. If no one was home he'd search the place, get the notebook if it was there, and get out. If the little woman was home that would make things easier. He had yet to find the person who wouldn't cooperate with the business end of a gun grinding the back of their mouth.

He hiked along the bank of a dry creek that ran parallel to the road. Cutting to the left, he passed through a grove of cottonwoods before coming up behind Broadbent's barn. Moving slowly, he climbed through a barbed-wire fence and edged along the back wall of the barn. Crouching at the corner, he had a view of the back of the house.

He took it in: a low adobe, some corrals, a couple of horses, a feeding area. He heard a high-pitched shout. Beyond the corrals there was an outdoor riding arena. The wife—Sally—held a lunge line with a kid riding on a horse, going round and round in circles.

He raised his binoculars and she leapt into focus. A breeze caught her long hair and she brushed it from her face. Jesus, she was pretty.

He turned his attention back to the house. They said in town that Broadbent was loaded—big time. His old man had died a year ago and he'd supposedly inherited $100 million. Looking at the house, you'd never know it. There was no sign of money anywhere, not in the house, the barn, the garage, the dusty yard and gardens. If Maddox had inherited $100 million, he sure as shit wouldn't live in a dump like this.

Maddox set down his pack. Taking out his sketchbook and a freshly sharpened pencil, he made a quick sketch of the layout of the house and yard, then he crawled round behind the barn and through some brush to get a fresh angle to sketch the front and side yards. Through a pair of patio doors he studied a modest living room. Beyond was a flagstone patio with a Smokey Joe barbecue and some chairs, bordered by a herb garden. No swimming pool, nothing. The house looked empty. Broadbent, as he had hoped, was out—at least his '57 Chevy was gone from the garage and Maddox figured he'd never let anyone drive that classic except himself.

He finished his sketch and examined it. There were three sets of doors to the house: a back door to the kitchen, a front door, and the patio doors leading to the side yard. Assuming they were all locked, the patio doors would be the easiest to get into. They were old, and with the pair of shims he carried in the rucksack it would take less than a minute.

Hearing a car, he crouched. A moment later a Mercedes station wagon came round the back of the house and parked. A woman got out and walked over to the arena, waving at the kid on the horse. The kid waved back. The horse slowed and Broadbent's wife helped the kid off the horse. The kid ran over to the woman, hugged her. The lesson was over. They chatted for a while, then the kid and his mother got in the car and drove off.

The wife, Sally, was left alone.

He watched her every movement through the binoculars as she led the horse to a hitching post, unsaddled it and groomed it. When she was done, she led the horse to a corral and turned it loose, then headed towards the house. Was there going to be another lesson? Unlikely—at four o'clock.

She went in the back door to the kitchen, letting the screen door bang.

He rose, scurried across the lawn to the patio door, flattened himself against the side of the house. Waited, listening for a minute or two. Then he took a long, flexible shim out of his pocket, began working it in between the door and the frame. He would be inside in less than sixty seconds.

Suddenly he paused. A door had slammed. He heard footsteps crunching on the gravel of the drive. He ducked down, crouching behind a bush next to the patio door, and through the screen of leaves he saw her striding to the garage, keys jangling from her hand. She disappeared inside. A moment later came the roar of a car engine and an International Scout nosed out, went down the driveway and out of the gate in a swirl of dust.

Maddox felt an impotent fury take hold. The bitch didn't know how lucky she was. And now he'd have to find the notebook without her help.

Chapter 3

D r Iain Corvus strolled to the window of his office facing Central Park. He could see the park pond, a bright sheet of metal reflecting the afternoon sunlight. As he watched, a rowing boat drifted across the water—a father and his son on an outing together, each manning an oar.

Father and son. Corvus felt a faint sickness in his gut. The charming little scene reminded him of his own father, late of the British Museum, one of the most famous biologists in England. By the time his father was thirty-five, Corvus's present age, he was already a fellow of the Royal Society, winner of the Crippen Medal and on the Queen's birthday honours list to receive a KBE. Corvus felt a shiver of old anger as he recalled his father's mustachioed face, veiny cheeks and military bearing, his spotted hand perpetually closed round a whiskey-and-soda, his voice offering sarcastic correction. The old bastard had died ten years ago of a stroke. Sure, Corvus had inherited a bundle, but neither that nor his name had helped him get a job at the British Museum, the only place he'd ever wanted to work.

Now he was thirty-five and still Assistant Curator in the Department of Paleontology, awaiting tenure. Without tenure, he was only half a scientist—half a human being, really. *Assistant Curator.* He could almost smell the odour of failure clinging to it. He had come up for tenure three years before but the decision had been deferred. Since then he'd been running around like a blue-arsed fly with precious little to show for it. Until now.

He glanced at his watch. Time for the bloody meeting. He walked briskly along the corridor to the office of Dr W. Cushman Peale, president of the museum. The suite occupied the southwestern tower of the museum, and it commanded a sweeping view of Museum Park and the neoclassical façade of the New-York Historical Society. Peale's secretary ushered Corvus in.

Peale came from behind his desk to greet Corvus, gave him a firm, manly handshake, then seated him in an antique Shaker chair before a marble fireplace. Only when he was assured that Corvus was comfortable did he take his own seat, in a display of old-world courtesy.

'Iain, how are you?' Peale settled back into his armchair.

'Very well, thank you, Cushman,' said Corvus, crossing his legs.

'Good, good. Can I offer you anything? Water? Coffee? Sherry?'

'No, thank you.'

'I myself enjoy a small glass of sherry at five o'clock. It's my one vice.'

Right. Peale had a wife thirty years his junior who was making an ass of him with a young curator, and if playing the doddering old cuckold wasn't a vice, marrying a woman younger than your daughter was.

The secretary brought in a small crystal glass filled with amber liquid.

Peale took it, sipped fastidiously, then set down the glass. 'I won't beat about the bush, Iain. As you know, you're up for tenure again. The department begins deliberations the first of next month. We all know the drill.'

'Naturally.'

'As you know, the department makes a recommendation to me. Technically, I have the final say, although in my ten-year stint as president of the museum I haven't once gone against a departmental tenure decision. I don't know which way the department's going to fall on your case. I haven't spoken to them about it. But I am going to give you some advice.'

'Advice from you, Cushman, is always welcome.'

'We're a museum, not a university burdened with having to teach undergraduates. We can devote ourselves one hundred per cent to research and publishing. So there's no excuse for a weak publication record.'

He paused, one eyebrow rising slightly as if to signal the subtlety of his point, which as usual was about as subtle as a blunderbuss.

Peale picked up a piece of paper. 'Your list of publications. You've been here nine years, and I count eleven papers. Roughly one per year.'

'What counts is quality, not quantity.'

'No one has ever questioned the quality of your work, Iain. But eleven? We have curators here who publish eleven papers a *year.*'

'Anyone can knock out a paper. Publication for the sake of publication. I prefer to wait until I have something to say.'

'Come now, Iain, you know most of what we do here at the American Museum of Natural History is world-class. But I'm getting off the point. A year has gone by without you publishing anything. The reason I called you in here is because I assume you're working on something important.'

Corvus could feel the muscles round his mouth straining from the effort of smiling. 'As it happens I *am* working on an important project. Right now it's at a somewhat delicate juncture, but within a week or two I'll be able to bring it to you and the tenure committee.'

Peale gazed at him a moment, then smiled. 'That's splendid, Iain. The point is, I think you're a fine addition to the museum. I'm asking these questions only in the spirit of giving counsel. We take it to heart when a curator fails to make tenure; we look on it more as a failure on our part.' Peale rose with a broad smile, extended his hand. 'Good luck.'

Corvus left the office and walked back down the long corridor. He was so full of silent rage he could hardly breathe. But he kept his smile, murmuring greetings to colleagues who were on their way out of the museum at the close of day, the herd heading back to their split-level ranches in faceless suburbs in Connecticut and New Jersey.

THE WHITEWASHED ROOM behind the sacristy of Christ in the Desert Monastery contained only four things: a hard wooden stool, a rough table, a crucifix and a laptop computer running on DC solar power. Wyman Ford sat before the computer, tingling with anticipation. He had just finished downloading two cryptanalysis programs and was about to unleash them on the code he had typed in from the dead man's notebook. This was no simple code; it had not yielded to any of his usual tricks. It was something special.

He lifted his finger and brought it down smartly: the first program was off and running.

It wasn't exactly a decryption program, but rather pattern analysis software that looked at the code and made a determination as to what class of code it belonged to. It was only a matter of five minutes for the program to return a beep, indicating the first analysis was complete. Ford was startled when the conclusion popped up: UNABLE TO DETERMINE CODE TYPE.

Far from being discouraged, Ford felt a shivery thrill. The more sophisticated the code, the more interesting the message. He ran the next program in the module, a frequency analysis on single digits, number pairs and triplets, matching it against frequency tables of common languages. But that, too, was a failure. Ford glanced at his watch. He'd missed Terce. He'd been at it now for five hours straight. Damn.

He went back to the computer screen. The fact that each number had eight digits—a byte—implied a computer-based code. Yet he had already tried translating the eight-digit numbers to binary, hexadecimal and ASCII, still with no success. This was getting fun.

Ford paused, picked up the notebook, flipped it open, ruffled through the pages. The numbers were written with a sharp pencil, in neat rows and columns. He turned the notebook over. There was a stain on the back of the worn leather cover, a smear that was still slightly tacky, and he realised with a start that it was blood.

Wyman Ford wondered just what he was getting himself into.

He suddenly felt a presence behind him, and turned. It was the abbot, a faint smile on his face. 'We missed you, Brother Wyman.'

Wyman rose. 'I'm sorry, Father.'

The abbot's gaze shifted to the numbers on the screen. 'What you're doing must be important.'

Wyman said nothing. He wasn't sure it was important in the way the abbot meant. He felt ashamed. This was just the kind of obsessive work habit that had got him into trouble in real life.

'*Ora et Labora*, Prayer and Work,' said the abbot gently. 'The two are opposites. Prayer is a way of listening to God, and work is a way of speaking to God. The monastic life seeks a strict balance between the two.'

'I understand, Father.' Wyman felt himself colouring. The abbot always surprised him with his simple wisdom.

After the abbot had left, Wyman saved his work and shut down the computer. He wondered: had he really got the spook trade out of his system?

He returned to his cell, where he bowed his head and prayed.

TOM BROADBENT watched Detective Lieutenant Willer pacing back and forth in his living room, the policeman's slow, heavy steps somehow conveying insolence. The detective wore a plaid sports jacket, grey slacks, and a blue shirt with no tie, and his arms were short with bony, veined hands swinging at the end. He was about forty-five, with a narrow face, bladelike nose, and sagging black eyes rimmed in red: the face of a true insomniac.

Standing behind him, notebook flopped open in his hand, was his side-kick, Hernandez, soft, plump and agreeable. They had arrived in the company of a no-nonsense woman with iron-grey hair who introduced herself as Dr Feininger, the medical examiner.

Sally sat on the sofa next to Tom.

'A human hair was recovered at the crime scene,' Willer was saying as he slowly turned on his heel. 'Dr Feininger wants to find out if it came from the killer, but we need to eliminate all others who were at the site.'

'I understand,' said Tom.

'If you don't have any objection, then, sign here.'

Tom went over to the table to sign the permission form.

Feininger picked up her little black bag. 'Would you take a seat?'

Tom attempted a smile. 'I didn't know it was going to be dangerous.'

'I'll be pulling them out by the roots,' came the crisp answer.

Tom sat down, exchanged a glance with Sally.

'In the meantime,' said Willer, 'there are a couple of points I'd like to clear up. Mind?'

Here we go, thought Tom. 'Do I need a lawyer?'

'It's your right.'

'Am I a suspect?'

'No.'

Tom waved his hand. 'Lawyers are expensive. Go ahead.'

'You said you were riding along the Chama river the night of the killing.'

'That's right.' Tom felt the doctor's fingers in his hair, poking around.

'You said you took a short cut up Joaquin Canyon?'

'It's not really a short cut.'

'That's just what I was thinking. Why'd you go up there?'

'As I said before, I like the route.'

Silence. He could hear Hernandez's pen scritching on the paper.

The ME plucked one hair, two, three. 'Done,' she said.

'How many more miles did you have to ride that night?' Willer asked.

'Ten, twelve.'

'How long would that have taken you?'

'Three to four hours.'

'So you decided to take a short cut that was actually a long cut, at sunset.'

'It was the night of the full moon and I'd planned it that way. I *wanted* to ride home by moonlight—that was the whole point.'

'Your wife doesn't mind you coming home late?'

'No, *his wife* doesn't mind him coming home late,' said Sally.

Willer continued, not varying from his stolid tone. 'And when you heard the shots, you went to investigate and found the man, dying. You administered CPR, which is how you got his blood all over your clothes.'

'Yes.'

'And he spoke to you, told you to find his daughter to tell her what he'd found. But he died before he could say what that was. Correct?'

'We've been over all this.' Tom had not told, and had no intention of telling, that the prospector had a notebook or had mentioned a treasure. He had no confidence in the police's ability to keep it confidential.

'Did he give you anything?'

'No.' Tom swallowed. He was surprised at how much he hated lying.

After a moment Willer grunted. 'I'm told that yesterday afternoon you went to the monastery up in the wilderness, Christ in the Desert.'

Tom rose. 'Who told you that? Are you having me followed?'

'Take it easy, Mr Broadbent. You drive a distinctive truck and I might remind you that most of that road is visible from the top of Mesa de los Viejos, where my men are searching. Now, did you go up to the monastery?'

Tom swallowed again. 'Yes, I went up there, to see a friend of mine.'

'Name?'

'Brother Wyman Ford.'

Scritch, scritch went the pen. Willer made a sucking noise through his teeth. 'What did you go up there to see this Brother Ford about?'

'I wondered if he'd heard anything related to the killing up in the Maze.' He felt terrible lying again. He began to realise that Sally may have been right, that he never should have kept back the notebook.

'And had he heard anything?'

'No. He didn't even know about it. He doesn't read the newspapers.' If the cops went to see Ford, Tom wondered if he would lie about the notebook. It seemed most unlikely—he was, after all, a monk.

Willer rose. 'You going to stick around here for a while? Case we need to talk to you again?'

'I don't have any travelling plans at the present time.'

Willer nodded again, turned to the ME. 'Got what you needed?'

'Yes.'

Tom saw them to the door. As he was leaving, Willer paused, his black eyes fixed on Tom. 'Lying to a police officer is obstruction of justice.'

'I'm aware of that.'

Willer turned and left. Tom watched them drive out, then came back in and shut the door. Sally was standing in the living room, arms crossed.

'Tom, you're sinking in quicksand. You've *got* to give them the notebook. You can explain. They'll understand.'

'The hell they will. How many times do I have to say it? *I made a promise.*'

She sighed, uncrossed her arms. 'You're impossible.'

He put his arm round her. 'Would you have me any other way?'

'I suppose not.' She sighed. 'On top of all this, when I came home this afternoon, I got the feeling that someone had been in the house.'

'How so?' Tom said, alarmed.

'Nothing was stolen or moved. It was just a creepy feeling—like I could smell some stranger's BO.'

'We should report it.' Tom said, alarmed.

'Tom, you report a break-in and Willer will be all over you. Anyway, I'm not sure at all—it was just a feeling.'

Tom thought for a moment. 'Sally, this is serious. We already know that someone thinks the treasure is worth killing for. I'd feel better if you kept that Smith & Wesson of yours handy.'

'I wouldn't go that far, Tom. It's not necessary.'

'Humour me.'

Sally rose, slid open a drawer under the phone, took out a key and went to unlock a cabinet in the den. A moment later she came back with the gun and a box of .38 cartridges. She opened the cylinder, pushed five rounds into the chambers, snapped it shut. 'Satisfied?'

THURSDAY MORNING, Tom received an email from Wyman Ford.

> Tom: I 'deciphered' the journal. You are not going to believe this. Come up to the monastery a.s.a.p. and prepare to have your mind blown. Wyman

Tom had left the house immediately. By the time his Chevy pulled into the monastery parking lot, his impatience had reached fever pitch.

In a moment Brother Wyman came flying down from the church, his robes flapping behind him, like a giant bat on the wing.

'How long did you take to crack it?' Tom asked as they climbed the hill.

'I never did crack the code.'

'I don't get it.'

'Every test I ran on the numbers indicated that they were not random, that they were highly patterned. I was stumped—until it occurred to me that it wasn't a code at all. It was "data".'

'Data?'

'I was a complete idiot. I should've seen it right off.' Wyman broke off as they neared the refectory, putting a finger to his lips.

They walked inside, down a hall, and into a small, cool, whitewashed room. A laptop sat on a crude wooden table underneath a crucifix.

Ford shut the door. 'We're not really supposed to be talking in here,' he whispered. 'I feel like the bad boy at school, smoking in the john.'

'So what kind of data was it?'

'You'll see.' They pulled chairs up on either side of the computer. Brother Wyman began typing rapidly. 'I'm connecting to the Internet via a broadband satellite connection. Your man was using a remote-sensing instrument and copying the data into his notebook.'

'What kind of instrument?'

'It took me a while to figure it out. It's a ground-penetrating radar or GPR device. It basically fires pulses of radar at the ground and records the echo. Depending on the type of ground and how dry it is, the radar can penetrate as deeply as five metres before being reflected back up. You can get a rough 3D image of something hidden in the ground or in certain types of rock. It lets you see voids, caves, old mines, buried treasure chests, metal-bearing veins, ancient walls or graves—that sort of thing.'

He paused to catch his breath, and went on in a rapid undertone. 'It turns out the numbers in your notebook were the data stream from a custom-built ground-penetrating radar device. Luckily the imagery could be processed by off-the-shelf software.'

'So did he find a treasure?'

'He certainly did.' Wyman smiled. 'And you're about to see a radar image of it, mapped using the GPR data.' He typed some more, then rapped his finger down on the ENTER key, executing the program.

Tom stared intently at the white screen as an image began to take shape.

'Takes a while to process,' murmured Wyman.

The first pass was complete, but the image remained a shadow, a blob. A second pass began, the image sharpening, line by line. Tom caught his breath as the blob became an object. An unmistakable object. He felt it must be an optical illusion, that it was actually something other than what it seemed. On the third pass he realised it was no optical illusion.

'My God,' Tom said. 'It's no treasure. It's a dinosaur.'

Wyman laughed, his eyes sparkling. 'I told you it would blow your mind. Look at the scale bars. It's a *T. rex*, and according to some research I did, it's by far the biggest ever found.'

'But it's the whole thing, not just the bones.'

'Correct.'

Tom fell silent, staring. It certainly was a *Tyrannosaurus rex*—the outline was unmistakable—lying twisted and on its side. But it wasn't just a fossil skeleton—much of the skin and flesh appeared to have been fossilised along with the bones. 'It's a mummy,' said Tom, 'a fossilised mummy.'

'That's right. It's virtually complete, except for a few teeth, a claw, and the last foot of tail, anyway.'

'So the murdered man was a *dinosaur* prospector.'

'Exactly. This "treasure" he was talking about may simply been a manner of speaking. That *is* a treasure, only one of the palaeontological variety.'

Tom gazed at the image, knowing that he was staring at what had to be one of the most stupendous dinosaur fossils of all time.

'There's your murder motive,' said Ford. 'That dinosaur's worth a fortune. I did some poking around the Web. A tyrannosaur auctioned at Sotheby's ten years ago pulled down $8.36 million.'

Tom gave a low whistle. 'This one must be worth a lot more. Where is it?'

Ford smiled and pointed to the screen. 'You see that fuzzy outline encasing the dinosaur? That's a cross-section of the rock outcrop the fossil's embedded in. It's such an unusual shape that it should be easily recognisable. All the location information you need is right there. It's merely a question of hiking around until you find it.'

'That could take for ever.'

'I don't think so. I've spent a lot of time hiking around the high mesas and I believe I could find it in less than a week. Not only do you have the shape of the formation, but you can see that part of the dinosaur's head and upper body are exposed along the side. That must be quite a sight, the dinosaur's jaws emerging from the rock like that.'

'Like that rock that gave Tyrannosaur Canyon its name?'

'I know that monolith—it's got nothing to do with the fossil. With this plot, now we know just what to look for—eh, Tom?'

'Wait a minute. Who says we're going to look for it?'

'I do.'

Tom shook his head. 'I thought you were studying to be a monk. I thought you'd left this sort of thing behind.'

Ford looked at him for a while, then dropped his eyes. 'Tom—the other day you asked me a question. I'd like to answer it.'

'I was out of line. I really don't want to know.'

'You weren't out of line. I've bottled it all up, I've used silence as a way to avoid the issue.' He paused. 'I was an undercover operative. I studied cryptology but I ended up working undercover as a systems analyst for a large computer firm. I was, in reality, a CIA hacker.'

Tom listened.

'Let's say—theoretically speaking, of course—that the government of, say, Cambodia buys servers and software from, say, a large American firm with a three-letter acronym which I shall not mention. Unbeknownst to the Cambodians, a small logic bomb has been hidden in the software code. The bomb goes off two years later, and the system starts acting funny. The government of Cambodia calls the American company for help. I get sent in as systems analyst, bringing my wife, who's also a Company employee. I fix the problem, while at the same time burning onto CD-ROMs the entire contents of the Cambodian government's classified personnel files. The CD-ROMs are tarted up to look like bootlegged copies of Verdi's *Requiem*, music and all. You can even play them. Again I'm speaking theoretically. None of this may have actually happened.' He paused, exhaled.

'Sounds like fun,' said Tom.

'Yeah, it was fun—until they car-bombed my wife, who happened to be pregnant with our first child.'

'Oh, my God.'

'It's all right, Tom,' he said quickly. 'I've got to tell you. When that happened, I just walked out of that life and into this one. All I had were the clothes on my back, my car keys and wallet.'

'No one knows you're here?'

'Everyone knows I'm here. The CIA understood. Good people for the most part. Julie—my wife—and I knew the risks. We were recruited together out of MIT. Those personnel files I scooped up exposed a lot of former Khmer Rouge torturers and murderers. That was good work. But for me . . .' His voice trailed off. 'The sacrifice was too great.'

'I hardly know what to say, Wyman. I'm sorry—I'm really sorry.'

'No need to say anything. It's a good life here. When you deny your own needs by fasting, poverty and celibacy, you get closer to something eternal. Call it God, call it whatever you like. I'm a fortunate man.'

There was a long silence. Tom finally asked, 'And how does this connect to your idea that we should find the dinosaur? I promised to give the notebook to the man's daughter—and that's it. The dinosaur's hers.'

Ford tapped the table. 'I hate to tell you this, Tom, but all that land out there, the high mesas and the mountains beyond, belong to the Bureau of Land Management. It's all federal land. The American people own that land and everything on it and in it, including the dinosaur. You see, Tom, your man wasn't just a dinosaur prospector. He was a dinosaur *thief.*'

DR IAIN CORVUS softly turned the handle of the metal door labelled MINER-ALOGY LAB and stepped into the room. Melodie Crookshank was sitting at a work station, her back turned, typing.

He crept up to her, laid his hand softly on her shoulder. She gave a muffled gasp and jumped.

'You didn't forget our little appointment, did you?' asked Corvus.

'No, it's just that you snuck up on me like a cat.'

Corvus laughed softly, gave her shoulder a little squeeze. 'I'm grateful you were willing to stay late.' He was glad to see she was wearing the bracelet. She was pretty, but in an athletic and unglamorous way, as if one of the prerequisites of being a serious woman in science was to wear no make-up and avoid the hairdresser. But she had two important qualities: she was discreet and she was alone. He had quietly enquired into her background; her parents were both dead, she had no siblings, few friends, no boyfriend. On top of that, she was competent and *so* eager to please.

He dazzled her with his finest smile and took her hand, which was hot in his. 'Melodie, I'm delighted you've made such splendid progress.'

'Yes, Dr Corvus. It's . . . it's incredible. I've burned it all onto CDs.'

He lowered himself into a chair before the big flat-panel computer screen. 'Let the show begin.'

Melodie seated herself next to him, picked up the top CD in a stack, slid it into the drive bay and typed in a command.

'First, what we've got here,' she began, switching into professional speech, 'is a piece of the vertebra and fossilised soft tissue and skin of a large tyrannosaurid, probably a *T. rex*. It's fantastically well preserved.'

An image appeared on the screen.

'Look at that. It's an imprint of skin.' She paused. 'Here it is closer up. You see those fine parallel lines?'

Corvus felt a momentary shiver. This was even better than he had imagined, much better. 'It's the impression of a feather,' he managed to say.

'Exactly. There it is: proof that *T. rex* was feathered.'

The theory had been advanced a few years ago by a group of young palaeontologists. Corvus had derided it in the *Journal of Paleontology*. And now, here was proof that *they* were right and *he* was wrong. His feelings were complex. He would have to admit that he was mistaken, but here was a rare opportunity. With this in hand, they would *have* to give him tenure. But then he wouldn't really need it, would he? He could get a job anywhere— even at the British Museum. Especially at the British Museum.

'Yes, indeed,' he murmured. 'The old gentleman was feathered after all.'

'It gets better.' She rapped a key and another image appeared. 'Here's a polarised image at times a hundred of the fossilised muscle tissue. It's petrified, of course, but it has to be the most perfect fossilisation on record. What we're looking at is an actual image of the muscle cell of a dinosaur.'

Corvus found he could not speak.

She rapped again. 'Here it is at times five hundred . . . look, you can see the nucleus.' *Click.* 'Mitochondria.' *Click.* 'Ribosomes.'

Corvus stood up, steadied himself with a hand on the back of the chair and took a deep breath. The future flashed through his mind—the awards, the best-selling book, the lectures, the money, the prestige. Tenure was only the beginning. He looked at Crookshank. Did she, too, see it?

'Melodie . . .'

'Yeah. It's awesome. And I'm not done. Not by a long shot.'

He managed to sit down. Could there really be more?

'Let's go to the electron micrographs.' A black and white image leapt into focus. 'Here's endoplasmic reticulum at times a thousand. True, you can't see much—but to see *anything* at times a thousand is incredible. You're looking at the microbiology of a dinosaur, right there.'

It was extraordinary. And to think that there was probably a whole dinosaur like that, if his information was correct. The perfectly fossilised carcass of a *T. rex*, complete—the stomach, no doubt with its last meal, the brain in all its glory, the skin, the feathers, the liver, kidneys, spleen—the diseases it had, its wounds, its life history, all perfectly duplicated in stone. It was the closest they were going to get to *Jurassic Park* in the real world.

She clicked to the next image. 'Here's the bone marrow.'

'Wait.' Corvus stayed her. 'What are those dark things in that last image?'

'Oh, those.' She backed up to the previous picture.

Corvus pointed to a small black particle. 'What is it?'

'It's probably an artefact of the fossilisation process.'

'Not a virus?'

'It's way too big. And it's too sharply defined to be part of the original biology anyway. It's probably a microcrystalline growth, like hornblende.'

'Quite right. Sorry. Keep on.' He watched as she clicked through another series of micrographs. 'This is stupendous, Melodie.'

She turned to him, her face flushed, radiant. 'Can I ask a question?'

He hesitated, collecting himself. He was going to need her help, that much was clear, and doling out a few grains of glory to a female lab assistant would be a lot better than cutting another curator in on the deal.

He put his arm around her, leaned close. 'Of course.'

'Is there any more of this out there?'

Corvus couldn't help smiling. 'I suspect, Melodie, that there's a whole dinosaur like this out there.'

SALLY FELT a lot more disturbed than elated at the computer-plotted image that Tom had spread out on the kitchen table.

'This just gets worse and worse,' she said.

'Better and better, you mean. This is exactly the kind of information I needed to identify the man and find his daughter.'

'Look, Tom—this man was illegally prospecting for fossils on public land. He was a thief and he got murdered. And even if you *found* his daughter, the fossil wouldn't belong to her. It belongs to the feds.'

'I made a promise to a dying man and that's the end of it.'

Sally sighed in exasperation.

Tom circled the table like a panther prowling around a kill. 'You haven't said what you think of it yet.'

Despite herself, Sally was drawn to the strange image. It was blurry, indistinct, but it was clearly a dinosaur, entombed in the rock. It lay on its side, its head thrown back, jaws open, its two front limbs raised up.

'Amazing how fresh it looks, almost as if it should stink.'

Tom chuckled. 'It's not the first discovery of a mummified dinosaur. At the turn of the last century a mummified duck-billed dinosaur was found in Montana. I remember seeing it as a kid at the natural history museum in New York, but it isn't nearly as complete as this one.'

She picked up the plot. 'Looks like he died in agony, with his neck twisted back and his jaws open like that.'

'It's a she. Female tyrannosaurs were bigger than the males. And since this is the biggest *T. rex* ever found, it's a good guess it was female. And that twisting of the neck was caused by the tendons drying and contracting. Most dinosaur skeletons are found with contorted necks.'

Sally whistled. 'What now? You have a plan?'

'I sure do. There's a thriving black market in dinosaur fossils out there. A lot of collectors, especially in the Far East, will pay almost anything for a spectacular dinosaur fossil. The thing is, the biggest and best-preserved dinosaurs still come from the American West—and most of them are found on federal land. If you want one, you have to go steal it.'

'Which is just what this man was doing.'

'Right. He was a professional dinosaur hunter. There can't be too many of them in the world. He'll be easy to identify if I ask the right people. All I have to do is find the right people.'

Sally looked at him suspiciously. 'And how do you propose to do that?'

Tom grinned. 'Meet Tom Broadbent, agent for Mr Kim, the reclusive South Korean industrialist and billionaire, who is looking to buy a spectacular dinosaur, money no object.'

'Oh, no.'

He stuffed the paper into his pocket. 'I've worked it out. Shane can handle the clinic on Saturday while we fly to Tucson, fossil capital of the world.'

'We?'

'I'm not leaving you here alone with a murderer roaming around.'

'I've got a gymkhana planned on Saturday with the kids. I can't leave.'

'I don't care. I'm not leaving you here alone.'

'I won't be alone. I'll be surrounded by people all day long. You go to Tucson and do your Mr Kim song and dance. I'll be fine.'

'No way.'

She gave it one final push. 'If you're so worried, go to Tucson for the day. Fly out early Saturday morning and get back before dark. Tom, I'm not some helpless female who needs watching over. I can take care of myself.'

Chapter 4

The morning sun burned over the high mesas, cauterising the land. Jimmie Willer halted in the shade of a juniper, easing himself down on a rock. Hernandez took a seat beside him, his plump face beaded with sweat. Willer slipped a flask of coffee out of his rucksack, poured a cup for Hernandez and one for himself, shook out a Marlboro.

'What a scorcher.'

'Yeah,' said Hernandez.

Willer took a deep drag, looked out over the endless landscape of red and orange canyons, domed rocks, ridges, buttes and mesas. The body could be buried at the bottom in any one of a hundred canyons or in God knows how many caves and alcoves, deep-sixed down some crevasse.

'Too bad Wheatley didn't get his dogs on the trail when it was fresh,' said Hernandez. After the murder a hard rain in the high mesas had got all the washes running and swept the Maze free of tracks and scent trails.

The K-9 chief, a nervous, carrot-haired man, appeared beyond the rise in front of them, struggling up a long incline, four heavy canteens slung over his shoulders. His two unleashed bloodhounds tumbled along ahead of him.

'Bet Wheatley's sorry now,' said Willer. 'He has to carry water for himself and his dogs.'

Hernandez chuckled. 'So what do you think? Got any theories?'

'At first I figured it was drugs. But now I think it's something bigger. The scene-of-crime guys haven't come up with anything—apart from the two rounds and ten and a half quarts of blood-soaked sand. But there's something going on out here, and both Broadbent and the monk are in on it.'

'Like what?'

'I dunno. They're looking for something. Think about it. Broadbent claims he spends a lot of time riding around here, for "pleasure". Well look out there at that son of a bitch. Would you ride around here for pleasure?'

'No way.'

'Then he just happens to come across this prospector, right after he's shot, eight miles from the road . . . Coincidence? Give me a break.'

'You think he shot him himself?'

'No. But he's involved. Anyway, a couple of days after the shooting, he goes up to visit this monk. I've checked up on this guy and it seems he too goes hiking all over the desert, for days at a time.'

'Yeah, and what are they looking for?'

'Exactly. And here's something else. I asked Sylvia to see if there was anything in the system about Brother Wyman Ford. Guess what? He was CIA.'

'You're shitting me.'

'I don't know the whole story, but it seems he quit suddenly, showed up at the monastery, they took him in. Three and a half years ago.'

Willer took one more drag, threw the butt down. Suddenly he sat up. He had spied a black dot moving on a low ridge in the distance, framed against some high bluffs. He brought his binoculars to his eyes, stared.

'Well, well. Speak of the devil.'

'Broadbent?'

'No. The monk. And he's got a pair of binoculars dangling from his neck. Hell, I'd give my left testicle to know what he's looking for.'

WEED MADDOX came out onto the porch of his rented cabin, inhaled the scent of pine needles warmed by the morning sun, and marvelled once again at his luck in finding a set-up like this. He smiled as he remembered the woman at Cowboy Country Realty. She had really been taken in by his story about being a novelist who needed a quiet place to finish his first novel. And the lodge at Perdiz Creek was certainly perfect for his purposes.

He raised the mug of coffee to his lips and took a noisy sip. He'd slept late; it was almost ten o'clock. Beyond the tops of the ponderosa pines he could see the distant peaks of the Canjilon Mountains gilded with silver light. He strolled across the porch, his cowboy boots thunking hollowly on the wood, and stopped beneath a fancy sign that read *Saloon*. He gave it a little push sending it squeaking back and forth on rusty hinges.

Perdiz Creek had once been a gold-mining town. The Civilian Conservation Corps had put a camp there in the thirties for the men building trails in the national forest, a dozen or so wooden cabins surrounding an old lodge. There wasn't much left of the old CCC camp now; most of the buildings had collapsed into pancaked slabs of rotting wood, overgrown with bushes and small trees. A guy from Texas had bought the camp and renovated the lodge. He lived there for a while, found it lonely and began renting it out.

Maddox drained his coffee, set the mug on the rail and strolled down the wooden steps. He began walking down the dusty old main street, whistling tunelessly. At the far end of town the road petered out into a weedy trail going up the ravine. He walked on, swishing his boots through the tall grass. He picked up a stick, beheading tall weeds as he went. After two minutes, he reached a sign planted in the trail that read:

DANGER: UNMARKED MINE SHAFTS
NO TRESPASSING. OWNER NOT RESPONSIBLE FOR ACCIDENTS

Maddox slipped past the sign, and followed the trail to an old clearing, then up an open hillside to the right. The trail ran parallel to but below the summit for a quarter of a mile before coming to a decrepit shaft house enclosing the entrance to an old mining tunnel. The shaft-house door sported a fresh padlock and chain, along with another NO TRESPASSING sign, both of which Maddox had affixed the day before.

He slipped a key out of his pocket, unlocked the padlock and stepped into the cool, fragrant interior. A pair of old railroad tracks led into a dark hole in the rock, covered by a heavy iron grate, also padlocked. He unlocked the grate and swung it open on freshly oiled hinges, inhaling the scent of damp stone and mould. Then he flashed his light around and proceeded carefully along the tunnel. A hundred feet further on his light illuminated a fork in the tunnel. He took the left branch. It soon came to a dead end, across which Maddox had built a wall of timbers bolted into the mine cribbing to create a small prison cell. He walked up to the timber wall and gave it a proud smack. Solid as a rock. He had begun at noon the day before and had worked until midnight, twelve hours of backbreaking labour.

He slipped through the unfinished opening into a small room built into the dead end of the tunnel. He plucked a kerosene lantern off a hook, raised the glass chimney, lit it and hung it on a nail. The friendly, yellow glow illuminated the room, perhaps eight by ten feet. He'd laid a mattress in one corner, covered with a fresh sheet. Next to it stood an old wooden cable spool serving as a table, a couple of old chairs, a horse bucket for drinking water, another bucket for a toilet. Opposite him, in the stone of the far wall, he had sunk four half-inch steel eye bolts, each with a chain and manacles—two for the hands, two for the feet.

A few more beams and he'd be done. Instead of a door, he would bolt three beams over the opening—a simpler, stronger and more secure solution. He would only need to go in and out at most a few times.

The cave was humid and warm. Maddox stripped off his shirt and picked up the heavy-duty cordless drill and slapped in a fresh battery. He went to the old pile of beams he'd found stacked up at the end of the mine, probed a few with a screwdriver until he had found a good one, measured it off, marked a spot with a pencil and began drilling.

In an hour Maddox had finished all, leaving only the door opening. He strolled the length of the finished wall, caressing the beams, grinning.

Nobody was going to bust out of his jail. Nobody.

WYMAN FORD shook the dust out of the hem of his robes and sat down on the fallen trunk of an ancient juniper. He had hiked almost twenty miles from the monastery and had reached the heights of Navajo Rim, a great long mesa running along the southern boundary of the Echo Badlands. Far behind him lay the vermilion canyons of Ghost Ranch, and the view to the northwest was framed by the snowcapped peaks of the Canjilon Mountains.

Ford removed four 1:24,000 topographical maps from his backpack, unfolded them and laid them side by side on the ground. He took a moment to orientate himself, visually matching various landmarks to their corresponding outlines on the maps. With his binoculars he began searching the Echo Badlands, looking for a rock formation resembling the one on the computer plot. Whenever he saw something promising, he marked its location on the map in red pencil. He was convinced that the formation containing the *T. rex* would be found here, since the domelike shape of the rock in the plot seemed to be typical of the badland formations.

He continued searching until he had covered all that he could see from that vantage point. It was time to move on to a point he had marked on the map as Vantage Point 2, a small butte at the far end of Navajo Rim. It would be a long hike, but well worth the trouble. From there, he'd be able to see almost everything in the badlands.

He picked up his canteen, shook it, estimating that it was still more than half full. He had another, completely full, tucked away in his pack. As long as he was careful, he would have no problems with water.

He took a small sip and set off, following the edge of Navajo Rim.

Ford had told the abbot that he needed some spiritual time by himself in the desert, and he'd promised to be back by Terce the following day. That was now out of the question, and if he went into the badlands it might be two more days before he got back. The abbot wouldn't mind—he was used to Ford going off into the desert on spiritual retreats. Only this time Ford felt that he was doing something wrong. He had misled the abbot as to the purpose of this trip; he had allowed himself to be swept up in the intrigue, the mystery of it. Why *was* he doing this? It wasn't to recover the dinosaur for the American people, as much as he'd like to think he was acting from altruistic motives. It wasn't for money, and certainly not for fame.

He was doing this because of something deeper, a flaw in his character, a craving for adventure. Three years ago he had made a decision, impulsive at the time but by now confirmed by prayer, to retreat from the world and devote his life to serving God. Was this little expedition serving God?

Somehow, he didn't think so.

Despite these thoughts, as if in thrall to a power not his own, Brother Wyman Ford continued to hike along the windswept cliffs of Navajo Rim, his eye fixed on the distant butte.

SIX O'CLOCK. The sun had fallen below the canyon rim and the heat of the day was going down, but it was still stuffy and dead between the sandstone walls. Willer, trudging up yet another endless canyon, suddenly heard an eruption of baying from the dogs from just round the bend.

He glanced at Hernandez. 'Looks like K-9 found something.'

'Lieutenant!' he heard Wheatley's panicked shout. 'Lieutenant!'

The hysterical baying of the dogs and Wheatley's yelling echoed down to him distorted by the narrow canyon walls.

'About time,' said Hernandez, his short legs churning him forward.

'I hope to hell Wheatley's got those dogs under control,' Willer said.

When he rounded the bend, he saw that Wheatley had lost the leash of one dog and was unsuccessfully trying to haul back the other, as both dogs were frantically trying to dig into a patch of sand at the base of a tight curve in the canyon wall. Hernandez and Willer rushed forward and snatched up the leashes, hauling the dogs back and tying them up to a boulder.

Huffing and red-faced, Willer examined the scene. The bed of sand had been disturbed by the dogs, but it was no great loss, considering that rain would have already swept it clean of traces. He could see nothing to indicate that anything lay under the sand—beyond a faint, unpleasant odour that the breeze wafted past his nostrils. Behind him, the dogs whined.

'Let's dig.'

'Shouldn't we wait for the SOC team and the ME?' asked Hernandez.

'We don't know we've got a body yet. Could be a dead deer. We can't chopper a whole SOC team out here until we know.'

Willer heaved off his backpack and slipped out the two trowels he had brought, tossing one to Hernandez. He began scraping the trowel across the loose sand, removing one layer at a time. Hernandez did the same at the opposite end of the area, making two careful piles that the forensic team would later sift through. As he swept the sand aside he kept an eye out for clues—clothing or personal articles—but nothing came to light. There was something down there, for sure, Willer thought, as the smell intensified.

At three feet his trowel scraped against something hairy and yielding. A sudden wave of stench, thick as soup, hit his nostrils.

'It's not human,' said Hernandez. 'Maybe it *is* a deer.'

Willer scraped some more. The fur was too coarse and matted to be a deer, and as he tried to clear more sand off it, the fur and skin began coming away in patches, exposing slimy, brownish-pink flesh underneath. This was no deer: it was a burro. The prospector's burro.

He stood up. 'If there's a stiff, it'll be next to it. You take that side, I'll take the other.'

Once again they began scraping away the sand. Willer lit a cigarette and held it between his lips, hoping to chase off some of the stench.

'Got something.'

Willer went over to where Hernandez was crouching. He trowelled some more sand away, exposing something long and swollen like a boiled kielbasa. It took Willer a moment to realise that it was a forearm. A second foul wave of odour struck him, a different and far worse smell.

'OK. That's good enough. It's a stiff—that's all we need to know.'

FRIDAY MORNING had dawned a flawless blue, with flocks of jays squawking in the piñons, the cottonwoods casting long shadows across the meadow. Tom had fed the horses, given them an hour to eat, and now he led his favourite horse, Knock, over to the rail. Sally joined him with her buckskin gelding, Sierra, and together they saddled and tacked up for a ride.

'Where to, cowboy?' Sally asked.

'Barrancones Spring.'

'Perfect.'

They rode in silence to the bluffs, then began climbing the narrow trail up the side of the mesa. A hawk circled above them, whistling.

'Damn, I love this country,' Sally said.

The trail wound into the cool ponderosa pines. In half an hour they reached the top and Tom turned his horse to look at the view. He never tired of it. To his left was the steep flank of Pederna Peak, to his right the sheer orange cliffs of Pueblo Mesa. Ahead, on the far side of the Piedra Lumbre Valley, rose the Mesa of the Ancients, notched by canyons—the beginning of the high mesa country. Somewhere out there was the fossil of a fabulous tyrannosaur—and a half-crazy monk looking for it. Tom glanced at Sally.

'Not a bad view,' she said with a laugh.

As they rode on, the only sound was the rhythmic creaking of their saddles. Then the country opened up to high grasslands of Mesa Escoba.

'Let's go a little faster,' Sally said, giving Sierra a nudge with her heel.

He broke into an easy lope. Tom kept pace, and they abandoned the trail, riding across windblown grass dotted with Indian paintbrush and lupins. At the far end of the meadow Tom could see the cluster of cottonwoods marking Barrancones Spring, at the base of a red cliff.

'All right,' cried Sally. 'Last one to the spring is a rotten egg! Giddyap!' She gave Sierra one final touch of heel. The horse shot forward, stretching out into a dead run while Sally gave a whoop.

Knock needed little urging to follow suit, and soon they were tearing across the meadow, neck and neck. Sally began to pull ahead, her hair streaming behind like a golden flame. The horses whipped over the grass and into the cool of the trees. At the last minute, Sally reined in and Tom followed; the horses leaned back and dug in, sliding to a stop.

Sally hopped off the horse, her face in high colour. 'That was fun.'

They were in a grove of cottonwoods, with an old fire ring in the centre and a couple of logs for seats. *Genízaro* cowboys from days gone by had built a line camp here, with tables shaped from rough-hewn logs of ponderosa, a broken piece of mirror wedged into the fork of a tree, and a chipped enamel washbowl hung from a nail. The spring itself lay at the bottom of the cliffs, a deep pool hidden behind a screen of desert willows.

Tom unsaddled the two horses and staked them out to graze. When he returned, Sally had spread out the picnic on a blanket and was pouring orange juice into plastic tumblers. Tom took a bite from his sandwich and watched Sally eat. A green light filtered through the foliage, and every time a breeze blew the trees rustled. When he had finished eating he lounged back on the blanket. Through the cottonwoods, he could see the horses grazing out on the distant flats, dappled in sunlight. Suddenly he felt a cool hand on his temple. He turned and found Sally was bending over him.

'What are you doing?'

She smiled. 'What does it look like?'

She laid her hands on either side of his face.

Tom tried to sit up, but the hands gently pushed him back down.

'Hey . . .' he said.

'Hey yourself.'

One of her hands slid inside his shirt, caressing his chest. She bent down and put her lips to his. He reached up to stroke her hair and ran his hand down to the hollow of her back. As he drew her down, he felt her slender body and soft breasts glide up against him.

Afterwards, they lay next to each other on the blanket. Tom's arm was thrown over her shoulder and he was looking into her turquoise eyes.

'Doesn't get much better than this, does it?' he said.

'No,' she murmured. 'It's so good it almost makes me afraid.'

THE HELICOPTER transporting Willer, Hernandez and the forensic team had to land half a mile down the canyon, and the team was forced to hike their equipment up the wash. They arrived in a ferocious mood, but Calhoun, head of forensics and always the wit, had turned it around with jokes, slaps on the back and the promise of cold beer all round when it was over.

Calhoun had run it just like an archaeological dig, the site mapped out on a grid, his men trowelling down layer by layer, the photographer documenting every step. They ran all the sand through one-millimetre wire mesh and then through a flotation tank to recover every hair, thread and foreign object. It was brutal work and they'd been at it since eight that morning. Now it was three o'clock and the temperature had to be close to 100°. The flies had arrived in force, and their droning filled the confined space.

Finally it was time for the 'scoop'—the moment when a corpse is rolled into a body bag. Three of the men stood on one side of the body.

'Ready?' said Calhoun. 'One . . . two . . . three . . . roll.'

With a smooth motion they rolled the body onto the open body bag, which had been prepositioned on a stretcher, and one of them zipped it up. All they had to do was carry the stretcher down to the chopper.

'Put the animal head in that one,' Calhoun directed.

They duly placed the burro's head in a wet-evidence bag and zipped it shut. At least, thought Willer, they had agreed to leave most of the burro behind, just taking the head, with the gaping hole made by a 10mm round fired at point-blank range. The round had been found embedded in the soft sandstone of the canyon wall, an excellent piece of evidence. They had also uncovered the prospector's equipment; the only thing they hadn't found, it seemed, was any indication of his identity. But that would come in time.

Willer checked his watch. Three thirty. He wiped his brow, pulled an iced Coke out of the cooler, rolled it against his forehead and his cheek.

Hernandez came up beside him, nursing his own Coke. 'You think the killer expected us to find the stiff?'

'He sure went to a lot of trouble to hide it. He had to strap the body on the burro, lug it up here, dig a hole big enough for the burro, the man and all his shit . . . No, I don't think he figured we'd find it.'

'Any theories, Lieutenant?'

'The killer was looking for something on the prospector. Look at his kit.' Willer gestured to the plastic tarp on which all the prospector's gear had been laid out for labelling. 'You see how the sheepskin padding on the packsaddles is torn off, the other stuff slit open? And you see how the guy's pockets were turned inside out? Not only was our man looking for something, but he was pissed that he wasn't finding it.'

Hernandez grunted. 'So what was he looking for? A treasure map?'

A slow smile spread across Willer's face. 'Something like that. And I'll bet you the prospector gave it to his partner before the shooter could hike down from the rim into the canyon.'

'What partner?'

'Broadbent.'

Chapter 5

It was midafternoon on Saturday by the time Tom drove into the parking lot of the Silver Strike Mall on the outskirts of Tucson, Arizona. The Fossil Connection was at the far end of the mall, where Tom found a modest storefront, with a few fossils on display in a window that was mostly whitewashed out. A sign on the door announced: WHOLESALE ONLY.

The door was locked. He buzzed, the door clicked and he stepped in.

It looked more like a law office than one of the largest fossil wholesalers in the West. Two secretaries were working at desks flanking a beige-carpeted waiting area, with taupe chairs and a glass and chrome table.

One of them looked up, took in Tom's $2,000 Valentino suit and hand-made shoes, and raised her eyebrows. 'May I help you, sir?'

'I have an appointment with Robert Beezon.'

'Name?'

'Broadbent.'

'Please have a seat, Mr Broadbent. Can I get you anything to drink?'

'No, thank you.'

Tom sat, flipped through a magazine. He felt a twinge of anticipation thinking about the deception he planned. The suit had been sitting in his closet, along with others he never wore, bought for him by his father.

A moment later the phone on the secretary's desk chimed. 'Mr Beezon will see you now.' She nodded towards a door that said, simply, BEEZON.

Tom rose as the door opened, framing a heavyset man in shirtsleeves with a combover. He looked indistinguishable from a small-town lawyer.

'Mr Broadbent?' He held out his hand.

The office itself finally betrayed the man's business: there were posters on the walls of fossil specimens, and an array of fossils in a glass case—a curious fossil plaque in the centre containing a fossil fish, with a fish in its belly, which in turn had a minnow in its belly.

Tom sat in a chair and Beezon took a seat behind his desk.

'You like my little gem? It reminds me that it's a fish-eat-fish world.'

Tom gave the obligatory chuckle to what was obviously Beezon's standard opening line. 'Nice.'

'Now, Mr Broadbent,' Beezon went on, 'I haven't had the pleasure of working with you before. Are you new to the business? Do you have a shop?'

'I'm a wholesaler.'

'We sell to a lot of wholesalers,' he said, his eyes flickering up and down Tom's suit, 'but it's odd I haven't run into you before.'

'I'm just getting into the business.'

'Well then, what can I do for you, Mr Broadbent?' He cocked his head.

'I was hoping to see some samples.'

'I'll give you the cook's tour round the back.' Beezon heaved up from his desk, and Tom followed him through the office suite to an unassuming door in the back. Beezon unlocked it, and they stepped into a cavernous room heaped with fossils, thousands of them. Men and women drove about with forklifts or hand-pushed flatbed carts loaded with rocks. A smell of stone dust drifted in the air.

'It's a warehouse, showroom and pick-and-pack operation all rolled up into one,' said Beezon. He took Tom's elbow and led him forward. 'We're the largest dealer of ammonites in the world, polished or rough, in matrix or no, sell by weight or by number, prepared or unprepared.' He kept walking, passing shelf after shelf covered with boxes of ammonite shells.

'If you're interested in insects, I just got some beaut spiders from the Nkomi Shales of Namibia. Agatised wood—sell that by the pound. Great for tumbling. Crinoids, concretions with ferns. Coprolites—kids love 'em.'

Tom followed. At one point Beezon stopped, pulled out a concretion. 'Lot of these haven't even been split. You can sell them that way, let the customer split them. Usually there's a fern or leaf inside. Once in a while a bone or jaw. It's like gambling. Here—' He handed Tom a concretion, then swiped a rock hammer off an anvil. 'Go ahead, split it.'

Tom took the hammer and fumbled with it a bit before placing the fossil on the anvil.

'Use the chisel end,' said Beezon quietly.

'Right, of course.' Tom turned the hammer round and gave the concretion a whack. It split open, revealing the single leaf of a fossilised fern.

He found Beezon eyeing him thoughtfully.

'What do you have as far as, er, higher-end material goes?' Tom asked.

Beezon went silently to a locked metal door and led him into a smaller, windowless room. 'This is where we keep the good stuff—vertebrate fossils in here, mammoth ivory, dinosaur eggs.' He moved to a long, coffin-shaped metal box, unlocked it to reveal an irregular plaster lump about four feet by three. 'Here's something really sweet, a *Struthiomimus*. Just came in from South Dakota. Legal, strictly legal, came from a private ranch.'

He gave Tom a rather pointed look. 'Everything we deal in here is legal, with signed and notarised documents from the private land owner.' He paused. 'Just what *are* you after, Mr Broadbent?' He was not smiling now.

'Just what I said.' The encounter was going exactly as he had hoped: he had aroused Beezon's suspicions.

Beezon leaned forward and said in a low voice. 'You're no fossil dealer.' His eyes flicked over the suit again. 'What are you, a fed?'

Tom shook his head, putting on a sheepish smile. 'You smoked me out, Mr Beezon. You're right, I'm no fossil dealer. But I'm no fed. I'm an investment banker and I work with a small, exclusive clientele in the Far East— Singapore and South Korea. We invest our clients' money. Sometimes our clients seek eccentric investments—old master paintings, gold mines, racehorses, vintage wines . . .' Tom paused, then added, 'Dinosaurs.'

There was a long silence. Then Beezon echoed, 'Dinosaurs?'

Tom nodded. 'I guess I didn't cut a convincing figure as a fossil dealer.'

Some of Beezon's friendliness returned, combined with a look of a man taking satisfaction in not having been fooled. 'No, you didn't. First of all, there was that fancy suit. And then as soon as you held that rock hammer I knew you were no fossil dealer.' He chuckled. 'So, Mr Broadbent, who is this client of yours and what kind of dinosaur is he in the market for?'

'May we speak freely?'

'Naturally.'

'His name is Mr Kim, and he runs a multibillion-dollar industrial enterprise in South Korea. He wants a display for the corporate headquarters that will make a statement about who he is and how he does business.'

There was a long silence. Then Beezon asked, 'And just what kind of dinosaur might that be?'

Tom stretched his lips in a smile. 'What else—but a *T. rex*?'

Beezon gave a nervous laugh. 'Surely you're aware that there are only thirteen tyrannosaur skeletons in the world and every one is in a museum.'

'I am also aware that there may be one or two others for sale—quietly.'

Beezon coughed. 'It's possible.'

Tom lowered his voice. 'You will understand, Mr Beezon, when I tell you he is none too particular about how or where the specimen might have been found. What is important is that it be *the right specimen,* and he is expecting to pay up to fifty million for such an investment.'

Beezon licked his lips. 'Fifty million? That's a bit out of my league.'

'Then I am sorry to have wasted your time.' Tom turned to leave.

'Now hold on a minute, Mr Broadbent. I didn't say I couldn't help you. I might be able to introduce you to someone. If . . . well, if my time and effort is compensated, of course.'

'In the investment banking business, Mr Beezon, everyone involved in a deal is remunerated to the extent of his contribution.'

'That's exactly what I was hoping to hear.' A faint smile spread on his

round face. 'I think we can do business, Mr Broadbent. I know a gentleman—you might call him a dinosaur seller. He lives not far from here.'

There was a silence.

'Well?' said Tom, pitching his voice to just the right level of impatience.
'What are we waiting for?

WEED MADDOX crouched behind the barn, watching. Children were riding
round the arena in circles, shouts mingling with laughter. He had been there
an hour and only now did the gymkhana seem to be winding down. As the
kids unsaddled the horses, Maddox waited, his muscles aching. Finally the
soccer-mom SUVs were driving out of the parking area behind the house
amid a lot of waving and shouting goodbyes.

He checked his watch. Four o'clock. Nobody seemed to have stayed on
to clean up—Sally was alone. She wouldn't go out like she did last time. It
had been a long day and she was tired. She'd go inside and rest, take a bath.

He watched her cross the yard carrying an armload of bridles. She was a
knockout, dressed in western riding boots, jeans and a white shirt, her long
blonde hair streaming behind her. She entered the barn and he could hear
her moving around, just a few feet from him on the other side of the flimsy
wooden wall. Ten minutes later she emerged and went into the house by the
back door. He could see her through the kitchen window, filling a kettle and
putting it on the stove, bringing out a mug. The making and drinking of the
tea would take at least five minutes, giving him the opportunity he needed.

Working quickly, he pulled out his equipment. He slipped the green surgical booties on over his shoes, the hair net over his hair, then the shower
cap, and over that a stocking. Then he put on the four-dollar plastic raincoat. He slid on a pair of latex gloves and took out his Glock 29 10mm
Auto, popped out the magazine and slapped it back in place. As a last step
he unfolded his sketch map of the house and gave it a final scrutiny.

Maddox moved round to the other side of the barn, where she couldn't
see him from the kitchen window. Then he straightened up, walked easily
across the yard to the patio, and quickly flattened himself against the side of
the house, with the patio doors on his right. Swiftly he inserted a shim into
where the door latched, worked it through to the other side, then pulled it
down. The door latch released with a loud click; he slid the door open,
ducked inside, shut it and flattened himself behind an angled wall where the
hall led from the living room to the kitchen.

He heard the chair scrape in the kitchen. 'Who's there?'

A few soft, tentative footsteps into the hall. 'Is someone there?'

Maddox waited for her to come in and see what made the noise. She might go back to the kitchen. She might go for the phone. But she wasn't sure . . . it could have been anything—a falling twig hitting the window. Maddox knew exactly what she was thinking.

A low whistle started from the kitchen. The kettle was boiling.

Damn. He heard her footsteps receding down the hall to the kitchen.

Maddox coughed, not loudly, but distinctly, as a way to bring her back.

The footsteps halted. 'Who's that?'

The whistle in the kitchen got louder.

She suddenly came charging back into the living room. He leapt out at the same time that he saw, to his complete shock, that she had a .38 in her hand. She whirled and he dived at her legs just as the gun went off; he hit her hard and dropped her to the carpet. She screamed, rolled, her blonde hair all in a tangle, her gun bouncing across the carpeted floor, her fist lashing out and dealing him a stunning blow to the side of the head.

He struck back wildly, connecting with his left in a soft place, and it was just disabling enough for him to get himself on top of her. She gasped, struggled, but he pinned her to the floor and pressed the Glock to her ear.

'You bitch!' His finger almost—*almost*—pulled the trigger.

She struggled, screamed. He pressed down harder, pinning her flailing legs in a scissor grip between his. 'I'll kill you if I have to. I will.'

More struggling, incoherent sounds. She was strong, a wildcat.

'Don't make me do it, but so help me I *will* if you don't stop.'

He meant it, and she heard that he meant it and stopped. As soon as she was quiet he slid around with his leg until he got his foot on the .38. He pulled it to him, picked it up and shoved it in his pocket.

He pushed the barrel of the Glock into her mouth and said, 'We're going to try this again. Now you know I'll kill you. Nod if you understand.'

She suddenly twisted hard and gave a vicious backward kick to his shins, but she had no leverage and he checked her struggling with sharp, wrenching constriction of his arm round her neck.

'Don't fight me.'

More struggling.

He twisted the barrel so hard she gagged. 'It's a gun, bitch, get it? Do what I say and nobody'll get hurt. Nod if you understand.'

She nodded and he loosened his grip, slightly.

'You're coming with me. Nice and easy. But first, I want the notebook. The one your husband got from the prospector. Is it in the house?'

Shake of the head.

Her husband had it. That much he was sure of already. 'Now listen to me carefully. One false step and I'll kill you. It's that simple.'

He meant it, and once again she got the message.

'I'm going to get off you and step back. You will go to the telephone answering machine over there on the table. You will record the following message: "*Hi, this is Tom and Sally. Tom's away on business and I'm out of town unexpectedly. Sorry about the missed lessons; I'll get back to everyone later. Leave a message, thanks.*" Can you do that in a normal voice?'

A nod.

He removed the gun barrel. 'Do what I said. I'm going to check the message on my cell as soon as you're done, and if it isn't right, you're dead.'

The woman got up slowly and walked over to the phone machine. She pressed a button and spoke the message.

'Your voice is too stressed. Do it again. Naturally.'

She did it again, and a third time, finally getting it right.

'Good. Now we're going to walk outside like two normal people, you first, me five feet behind. My car is parked in a grove of scrub oaks about a quarter mile up the road. That's where we're going.'

As he pushed her across the living room, he became aware of a sensation of wetness on his thigh. He looked down. The plastic raincoat was torn and there was a small, dark patch of blood on his pant leg. Maddox was astonished because he had felt nothing, still felt nothing. He scanned the floor but saw no evidence that any blood had dripped onto it. He felt the wound.

Son of a bitch. The blonde had winged him.

He marched her out of the house and alongside the creek, soon arriving at the hidden car. Once in the cover of the scrub oaks he took a pair of leg cuffs out of his rucksack and told her to put them on.

She bent over, fumbled with them for a while, snapped them on.

'Put your hands behind your back.'

She obeyed and he spun her round and snapped on a pair of handcuffs. Then he opened the front passenger door. 'Get in.'

She managed to sit and swing her feet in. He took off his knapsack, took out the bottle of chloroform and the diaper, poured a good dose.

'No!' he heard her scream. She swung her feet up to kick him but she had little room to manoeuvre, and he had already lunged in on top of her, pinning her manacled arms and mashing the diaper into her face. She struggled, writhing and kicking, but in a few moments she went limp.

He made sure she had breathed in a good dose, then got in the driver's side and slid behind the wheel. He reached over, hefted her and propped her up against the doors so she looked like she was peacefully asleep.

He powered down the windows to get the stench of chloroform out of the car, then pulled off stocking, shower cap, booties, hair net, gloves and raincoat, balling them up and stuffing them inside a garbage bag. He started the car, eased out of the grove and drove down the dirt road to the highway. Ten miles north he turned onto the unmarked Forest Service road that ran up into the national forest, and to the CCC Camp at Perdiz Creek.

The woman lay against the door, eyes closed, blonde hair all in a mess. He paused, looking at her. Damn, he thought, she was a real beauty.

'THEY SAY it used to be a bordello,' Beezon said to Tom as they stood in front of a shabby Victorian mansion, which rose incongruously from a desert sprinkled with palo verde, teddy bear cholla and ocotillo.

'Looks more like a haunted house than a whorehouse,' said Tom.

Beezon chuckled. 'I warn you—Harry Dearborn's kind of eccentric. His brusqueness is legendary.' He clomped up onto the porch and lifted the ring on the big bronze lion doorknocker. It fell once, with a hollow boom.

A rotund voice inside said, 'Come in, the door is unlocked.'

They entered. The house was dark with most of the drapes drawn, and it smelt of mustiness and cats. The walls were lined with oak display cases, mineral specimens crowding their shadowy depths. Standard lamps with tasselled shades stood here and there, throwing pools of feeble yellow light.

'In here,' came the deep rumble of the voice. 'Don't touch anything.'

Beezon led the way into a sitting room. In the middle, a grossly fat man was embedded in an oversized armchair of flowered chintz.

'Hello, Harry,' said Beezon, his voice a little nervous. 'Long time, eh? This is a friend of mine, Mr Thomas Broadbent.'

A large hand emerged from the darkness of the chair, made a vague flicking motion towards a pair of wing chairs. They both sat down.

The man was dressed in a white suit with a dark shirt and yellow tie, his thinning hair combed back, neat and tidy despite his corpulence. His broad forehead was as smooth as a baby's and gold rings winked on his fingers.

Beezon cleared his throat. 'Mr Broadbent here—'

Dearborn stopped Beezon and turned to Tom. 'Broadbent? You aren't by chance related to Maxwell Broadbent, the collector?'

Tom was taken aback. 'He was my father.'

He grunted. 'Interesting man. Ran into him a few times. Is he still alive?'

'He passed away last year.'

Another grunt. A hand came out holding a huge handkerchief, dabbed away at the fleshy, slabbed face. 'I'm sorry to hear that. He couldn't have been more than sixty.' A pause. 'So, what can I do for you, Tom?'

'Mr Broadbent is interested in purchasing a dinosaur,' Beezon began.

'A dinosaur? What in the world makes you think I sell dinosaurs?'

'Well . . .' Beezon fell silent, a look of consternation on his face.

Dearborn extended a large hand to him. 'Robert, thank you for introducing Mr Broadbent to me. Excuse me if I don't rise. It seems Mr Broadbent and I have some business to discuss, in private.'

Beezon stood and hesitatingly turned to Broadbent, wanting to say something. Tom guessed what it was.

'About that agreement we made? You can count on it.'

'Thank you,' said Beezon.

Tom felt a pang of guilt. There wouldn't, of course, be any commission.

Beezon said his goodbyes, and a moment later they heard the thump of the door, the whine of the car engine starting.

Dearborn turned to Tom, his face creasing into the semblance of a smile. 'Now what I said is true, Tom. I don't sell dinosaurs.'

'What exactly *is* it that you do?'

'I'm a dinosaur *broker*.' Dearborn leaned back in his chair with a smile.

Tom gathered his wits. 'I'm an investment banker with clients in the Far East, and one of them—'

The fat hand rose up yet again, halting Tom's prepared speech. 'That may work with Beezon but it won't wash with me. Tell me what it's really about.'

Tom thought for a moment. The shrewd, cynical glitter in Dearborn's eye convinced him that he would be better off telling the truth.

'Perhaps you read about the murder in New Mexico, in the high mesas, north of Abiquiú?'

'I did.'

'I was the man who found the body. I happened to come across him as he was dying. He pressed a journal into my hand and made me promise to give it to his daughter, Robbie. I'm trying to keep that promise. The problem is, the police haven't identified him or, as far as I know, even found his body.'

'Did the man tell you anything else before he died?'

'He was lucid for only a moment,' Tom said evasively.

'And this journal? What does it say?'

'It's just numbers. Data to a GPR survey, I believe.'

'Yes, yes, of course, that's how he did it. May I ask what *your* interest is in this, Mr Broadbent?'

'I made a promise to a dying man. That's my interest—no more, no less.'

Harry Dearborn seemed amused. 'I do believe, Mr Broadbent, that you are that rarest of things, an honest man. Or a consummate liar.'

'My wife thinks I'm merely stubborn.'

He gave a flabby sigh. 'I did indeed follow that murder up in Abiquiú. I wondered if it wasn't a certain dinosaur hunter of my acquaintance.'

'You know his name?'

The fat man shifted in his chair. 'Marston Weathers. The top dinosaur hunter in the country. His friends called him Stem, because he was tall and stringy. Tell me, did old Stem find what he was looking for?'

Tom hesitated. Somehow, he felt he could trust this man. 'Yes.'

Another long, sad sigh. 'Poor Stem.'

'What can you tell me about him?'

'A great deal. And in return, you will tell me what he found. Agreed?'

'Agreed.'

Chapter 6

Wyman Ford could see the tapering point of Navajo Rim a few hundred yards ahead, where the mesa ended in a small, thumb-shaped butte. The sun hung low in the sky, a disc of red-hot gold. Ford felt exhilarated. He had been on half rations for two days, eating only a slice of bread drizzled with olive oil for breakfast, and then for dinner half a cup of lentils and rice. Hunger had given him a feeling of euphoria and boundless energy that was curiously spiritual.

He skirted the butte, looking for a way up. The view was incredible, but from the top he would be able to see even more. He edged along a sandstone ledge no more than three feet wide, where the mesa plunged a thousand feet down into the blue depths of a canyon.

He rounded the curve of the butte, then stopped in delighted astonishment. There, wedged into the side of the bluff, was a tiny but almost perfect Anasazi cliff dwelling—four small rooms constructed from stacked pieces of sandstone and mortared with mud. He edged round further, then knelt down and peered in through the doorway. The tiny room inside was empty, save for a scattering of burnt corn cobs, and there were recent footprints in the dust of the floor made by someone wearing hiking boots with chevron-shaped lugs. Ford wondered if these belonged to the prospector.

He continued along the ledge past the ruin, where he encountered an ancient trail pecked into the sandstone, going to the top of the butte.

The summit afforded a dazzling vista across the Echo Badlands. To his left, the enormous profile of Mesa de los Viejos loomed up, level after level like a great stone staircase, rising to the foothills of the Canjilon Mountains.

Ford sorted through his maps and removed one. He traced the quadrants of the map with his eye and mentally drew those same lines on the badlands in front of him. Then he took out his binoculars and began searching the quadrant furthest to the east. When that was done he moved on to the next one, methodically working his way across the landscape.

While many rock formations looked similar to the one he was after, none was a perfect match. As his eyes roved about, one of the canyons captured his attention. Tyrannosaur Canyon. It was the longest canyon in the high mesas, deep and tortuous, cutting more than twenty miles across the Echo Badlands. He identified the great basalt monolith that marked its opening, and he followed its sinuous length with his binoculars. The canyon petered out in a distant valley jammed with strange, domelike rocks. Some of the domes looked uncannily like the image in the computer plot, jumbled together like a crowd of bald men knocking their heads together.

If he hurried, he could reach the domes before dark and continue his exploration at the crack of dawn tomorrow. Sunday. The day of the Lord.

He pushed that thought out of his mind.

Ford took one last look through his binoculars at the deep, mysterious canyon. Something twisted in his gut. He knew the *T. rex* was down there—in Tyrannosaur Canyon. The irony of it made Ford smile.

HARRY DEARBORN drew in a long breath of air, his face hidden in shadow. 'My goodness, it's four thirty already. Would you care for tea?'

'If it isn't too much trouble,' Tom said.

Dearborn moved his foot slightly and pressed a small bump in the floor; a moment later a servant materialised out of the back of the house.

'Tea.'

The man withdrew.

'Now where were we? Ah, yes, Stem Weathers's daughter, Roberta. Her father called her Robbie. Unfortunately, she and her father were estranged. Last I heard she was trying to make it as an artist in Marfa, Texas. A small town—she should be easy to find.'

'How did you know Weathers. Did he collect dinosaurs for you?'

A fat finger tapped on the arm of his chair. 'Nobody collects *for* me, Thomas. Most fossil hunters are looking for small stuff. Once in a while they stumble over something important, and that's when they come to me. I have clients who are looking for something quite particular: businessmen, foreign museums, collectors. I match buyer and seller and take twenty per cent commission. I never see or touch the specimens. I am not a field man.'

Tom stifled a smile.

The servant appeared with an enormous silver tray carrying a pot of tea, plates heaped with scones, cream puffs, small eclairs and miniature brioches, jars of preserves, butter, clotted cream and honey. He placed the tray on a table to the side of Dearborn and vanished as silently as he had come.

'Excellent!' Dearborn pulled the cosy off the pot, filled two china cups, added milk and sugar. He handed the cup and saucer to Tom.

Tom took his cup, sipped.

Dearborn reached out with a plump hand and plucked a brioche from the tray, opened it steaming, slathered it in clotted cream and popped it in his mouth. 'Please, help yourself,' he said in a muffled voice.

Tom took an eclair and ate it, licking up the thick whipped cream that squirted out onto his hand.

Dearborn dabbed his lips with a napkin and went on. 'Stem Weathers spent his whole life looking for that one big strike, something of enormous rarity and value.' He raised his cup to his lips, drained it halfway in a single loud sip. 'I handled Stem's finds but otherwise left him alone. He rarely told me what he was doing, but word got out that he was on to something big in that high mesa country. Everyone knew how he operated—his homemade

GPR and that notebook were both legendary—so it doesn't surprise me someone went in there after him. On top of that, the high mesa country is all federal land—overseen by the Bureau of Land Management. Anything taken off BLM land without a permit is grand theft—pure and simple. And they only issue permits to a select few museums and universities anyway.'

'Why would he take the risk?'

'It's not much of a risk. Most BLM land is so remote the chances of getting caught are almost nonexistent. Anyway, his problem wasn't finding the dinosaurs; it was what to do after he found them. The financial side always tripped him up. Sure, he might find a dinosaur he could sell for half a million dollars, but just to get that fossil out of the ground and ship it to a lab might cost him a hundred grand. It takes about thirty thousand man-hours to clean and prepare a large dinosaur—and that doesn't include mounting it. Weathers cared too much about his dinosaurs and as a result he was always broke. But he sure could find them.'

'Do you have any idea who murdered him?'

'No. But my guess is he was murdered by a claim jumper.'

Tom leaned forward. 'Anyone in particular?'

Dearborn shook his head. 'I know everyone in the business. Black-market dinosaur hunters are a rough lot. They rob each other's quarries, they lie, cheat, steal. But murder? I can't see it. I would guess the killer is a newcomer, or perhaps a hired hand who takes his work a little too seriously.'

He drained his cup, picked up an eclair and swallowed it.

'These rumours you spoke about?'

'For a couple of years, Weathers had been trying to trace a layer of sandstone known as the Hell Creek Formation down into New Mexico. Almost all the *T. rex* in existence have come out of this immense sedimentary formation, which crops out in various places across the Rocky Mountains but has never been found in New Mexico. Weathers was in search of more than just Hell Creek rocks, however. He had an obsession with the KT boundary itself.'

'The Cretaceous–Tertiary boundary?'

'That's right. You see, the Hell Creek Formation is topped by the KT boundary layer. That layer of clay, which is only half an inch thick, records the event that killed off the dinosaurs—the asteroid strike. There aren't many places in the world where there's an interrupted sequence of rocks at the KT boundary. I think that's what brought him to the high mesa country of Abiquiú—looking for the KT boundary layer.'

'Why was he looking for the KT boundary specifically?'

'The KT boundary is about the most interesting layer of rock ever found. It contains the debris from the asteroid impact along with ash from the subsequent burning of the earth's forests. The asteroid struck where the Yucatán Peninsula of Mexico is now, coming in at an angle that sprayed molten debris across much of North America. They've named the asteroid Chicxulub, a Mayan word meaning 'The Tail of the Devil'—cute, eh?'

He chuckled and used the opportunity to eat a crumpet.

'Chicxulub struck the earth at a speed of Mach forty. It vaporised a major chunk of the earth's crust on contact, blasting up a plume of material a hundred kilometres wide that punched through the earth's atmosphere and went into orbit, some of it rising halfway to the moon before plunging back at speeds of over twenty-five thousand miles an hour. The falling material superheated the atmosphere, igniting gigantic wildfires that swept the continents, releasing hundreds of billions of tons of carbon dioxide, methane and soot. The thick smoke and dust made the earth so dark that all photosynthesis stopped and food chains collapsed. At first a kind of nuclear winter set in, and the earth froze, then the carbon dioxide and methane caused a galloping greenhouse effect. It took a hundred and thirty thousand years for the earth's atmosphere to cool down and return to normal.'

'I'm still puzzled why Weathers would be interested in the KT boundary if he was just after dinosaur fossils.'

'Maybe he was using that layer as a way to locate *T. rex* fossils. The late Cretaceous, just before the extinction, was when tyrannosaurs ruled the earth.'

'What's a good *T. rex* worth these days?'

Dearborn poured himself another cup of tea. 'I've got two dozen customers waiting to bid on the next *T. rex* that comes on the private market, and I'd guess that some of them would be willing to pay a hundred million.'

Tom whistled.

Dearborn drained his cup, ate one final scone, dabbed his face and wiped the tips of his fingers with his napkin. 'Now it's your turn to talk, Tom. Tell me what Stem Weathers found. Naturally, you can count on my discretion.' His eyes glowed.

Tom slipped the computer-plotted drawing from his pocket and unfolded it on the the tea table.

Slowly, inexorably, but with huge momentum, Harry Dearborn raised his great bulk from the chair in silent astonishment.

MADDOX STOOD above the woman, who lay on the bed, her blonde hair spread out on the pillow like a halo. She had just begun to stir, and finally her eyes opened. He watched the look in her eyes go from confusion to fear.

He raised the gun so she could see it. 'No monkey business. You can sit up, but that's it.'

She sat up, wincing, and the manacles round her wrists and ankles clinked.

He gestured around. 'So . . . what do you think?'

No answer.

'I worked hard making it nice for you.'

He had spread a tablecloth on the cable spool table, even put some fresh flowers in a jam jar. The kerosene lantern threw a yellow glow across the room, which was pleasantly cool compared to the heat outside.

'When's Tom coming back?' Maddox asked.

No answer. The blonde looked away. This was starting to piss him off.

He raised his gun. 'Look at me.'

She turned her head slowly. Her green eyes blazed with hatred.

'Like what you see?'

She said nothing. The look on her face was so intense that Maddox found it disconcerting. She didn't look afraid. But she *was* afraid, he knew that.

He stood up and gave her his winning, lopsided smile, holding out his arms. 'Yeah, take a good look. I'm not so bad, right?'

No reaction.

'Now I'm going to show you the tattoo on my back. You know why?'

He paused but she said nothing.

'Because that tattoo is the reason I'm here with you today. Now listen carefully. I want that notebook. Your husband has it. When he gives it to me, I let you go—simple. But I need to get in touch with him. He got a cell-phone? Give me the number and you could be out of here in a few hours.'

Finally she spoke. 'Look him up in the phone book.'

'Aw, now why do you have to be a bitch about it?' It was obvious he would have to break her like a young filly. 'Stand up.'

She remained seated.

He carefully pointed the gun at her ankle, aimed just to the left, fired. The noise was deafening in the enclosed space, and she jumped like a deer.

'Darn. Missed.' He aimed again. 'You'll limp for the rest of your life. Now stand up.'

She stood up, her cuffs jingling.

'Shuffle over there where those manacles are set in the wall. You're going to take off your cuffs and put those on.'

Now he could see fear leaking through on that arrogant face of hers, despite her efforts to control it.

'Are you going to do what I say or do I have to shoot you in the foot? Last warning and I'm not kidding.'

'I'll do it,' she said in a smothered voice.

'Smart girl. Here's how. The same key goes to both sets. Switch off your ankles first, one at a time. Then your right wrist. I'll do your left myself.'

He tossed her the key. She bent down and picked it up, awkwardly unlocked the cuffs round her ankles, and followed his instructions.

'Now drop the key.'

She did, and he retrieved it. Then he stepped over to the table, placed the gun down on it, went over and shackled her left wrist.

'Now. Your husband's got the notebook. I want it.' He aimed the Glock at her foot again. 'Give me his number and we can get the ball rolling.'

She gave him a cell number.

'Now you're going to get a real treat.'

He grinned, stepped back, and began unbuttoning his shirt.

THE USUAL HUSH prevailed in the reading room of the Amsterdam Club. The oak-panelled walls, dark paintings, old books and heavy furniture gave the place a feeling of elegance and timelessness.

In one corner, ensconced in a deep chair, Iain Corvus was flipping through the pages of the latest *Scientific American*, not really reading. He tossed the magazine onto the side table with impatience. At seven o'clock on a Saturday evening the reading room was beginning to empty, with the members going in to dinner. Corvus had no appetite for either food or conversation. It had now been seventy-two hours since Maddox last contacted him. Corvus had no idea where he was or what he was doing. So much depended on Maddox; *everything* depended on Maddox. Corvus's career was at a crisis point, and he was at the mercy of an ex-con.

Yet he had prepared well. He'd heard the rumours more than six months ago that Marston Weathers was on the track of something big, that he was in northern New Mexico hoping to score an illegal dinosaur on BLM land—*public* land. Corvus had seen that here was a perfect opportunity: to expropriate a dinosaur from a thief and recover it for science. He would be performing a valuable public service—as well as doing himself a good turn.

Corvus had been more than a little disturbed when he learned that Maddox had killed Weathers, but once he'd got over the initial shock he realised that it had vastly simplified matters. It removed from circulation a man who had been responsible for more thefts from public land of more irreplaceable scientific specimens than anyone else, living or dead.

In fact, Maddox had proved to be a remarkably intelligent individual, a smooth talker, good-looking, presentable. Corvus congratulated himself on recognising the fellow's usefulness. Had he been born under different circumstances, Maddox might have made a rather decent scientist. Corvus knew that he really should relax, and trust Maddox to carry through on the assignment and get the notebook. The notebook was the key to everything.

He glanced at his watch, then picked up the *Scientific American* again. His mind was now calm.

IN THE DIM LIGHT of the kerosene lantern, Sally Broadbent watched the man take off his shirt. She could feel the cold steel round her wrists and ankles, her head ached and there was a coppery taste in her mouth.

He was shirtless now, a lopsided grin covering his face. 'Ready?' He swung round and turned his back to her.

She gasped. There, completely covering his back, was the tattooed image of a charging *Tyrannosaurus rex*, claws raised, jaws agape, so real it almost seemed to be leaping from his back.

'Cool, huh?'

Sally stared. He flexed his muscles, and the dinosaur seemed to move.

'When I was in prison, I decided I needed a tattoo. It's a tradition, know what I mean? It says who you are and defines your alliances. That's why I chose a *T. rex*. Nothing meaner's ever lived on this planet. But then I had to find the design for it. So I wrote to the world's expert on *T. rex*. Of course, he didn't answer my letters. Why would a guy like that correspond with a convicted murderer in Pelican Bay?'

He chuckled softly, flexed again. 'Take a good look there, Sally. There's never been a more accurate depiction of a *T. rex*—not in any book, not in any museum. All the latest scientific research is in there.'

Sally swallowed, listened.

'Anyway, after a year of no answer, all of a sudden this dinosaur expert wrote me back. We had quite a correspondence. He sent me drawings in his own hand. He was really into it, making sure this *T. rex* was the real thing. We got to be friends. And then—you know what he did?'

Sally worked her mouth, managed to say, 'What?'

'He sprung me from the slam. I was doing ten to fifteen years, aggravated manslaughter, but he vouched for me at my hearing, gave me money and a job. So when he asked me for a favour, I wasn't in a position to refuse. You know what that favour was?'

'No.'

'To get that notebook.'

She swallowed again, fought against a fresh wave of fear. He would never be telling her this unless he planned to kill her.

He turned back round, pulled on his shirt. 'You see now why I'm going to so much trouble? But I've got to go make a phone call. I'll be back.'

Then he turned and walked out of her little prison-room.

AS THE CAR neared Tucson, Tom checked his watch again. Half past five. He was going to have to hustle to make his six thirty flight back.

He dialled his home number to check in on Sally. The phone rang a few times and the answering machine kicked on. '*Hi, this is Tom and Sally. Tom's away on business and I'm out of town unexpectedly. Sorry about the missed lessons; I'll get back to everyone later. Leave a message, thanks.*'

The beep followed and Tom hung up the phone, suddenly concerned. What was this about being out of town unexpectedly? Why hadn't she called him? He dialled again, listened to the message more carefully. She didn't sound normal at all. Tom felt his heart pounding in his chest. He dialled the Santa Fe Police and asked for Detective Willer.

'It's Tom Broadbent,' he said, when the familiar stolid voice answered.

'Yeah?'

'I'm out of town and I just called home. My wife should be there but she's not, and she left a message on the answering machine that makes no sense. I think she was forced to leave that message. Something's happened.'

A silence, and then Willer said, 'I'll go out there right now and take a look. Do we have permission to break in, if the door's locked?'

'Yes, of course.'

'When are you getting back to town?'

'My flight from Tucson's landing at seven thirty.'

'Give me your number, I'll call you from the house.'

Tom gave his cellphone number and hung up. A feeling of self-reproach washed over him. What a fool he'd been, leaving Sally by herself.

He floored the accelerator. No way could he miss this flight.

Fifteen minutes later his cellphone rang.

'Am I speaking to Tom Broadbent?'

'Look, I'm running late for a flight—'

'Shut up, Tommy boy, and listen.'

'Who the hell is—?'

'I said shut up.' A pause. 'I got your little lady. Sally. She's safe—for now. All I want is the notebook. You follow? Just answer yes or no.'

Tom gripped the phone as if to crush it. 'Yes,' he managed to say.

'I want you to listen to me very carefully. After your flight lands, get in your car and drive to Abiquiú. Go through town and get on Highway 84 north of the dam. Don't stop for anything. You got the notebook on you?'

'Yes.'

'Good. I want you to take the notebook, put it in a Ziploc bag and pack it full of trash to make it look like garbage. The trash has to be yellow. You get it? Drive back and forth on Highway 84 between the dam turnoff and the Ghost Ranch turnoff. Drive at *exactly* sixty miles an hour with your cellphone on. I'll call you then with more instructions. Understand?'

'Yes.'

'What's your flight number, and when's it due to land?'

'Southwest Airlines 662. Seven thirty.'

'Good. I'm going to check and find out when you actually land, and I'll expect you up by Ghost Ranch one hour and twenty-five minutes later. Don't stop at home, just drive straight up to Abiquiú. You understand?'

'Yes. But if you hurt her—'

'Sally's going to be taken care of real good, provided you do everything I say in the way I say it. And Tom? No cops. You call the cops and you'll lose control, I'll lose control and Sally will die. Understand? You'll be kissing your wife goodbye on a stainless-steel gurney. Have I made myself clear?'

'Yes.'

The man clicked off.

Tom could hardly drive, hardly see the road. Almost immediately, the phone rang again. It was Willer.

'Mr Broadbent? We're at your place, in the living room, and I'm afraid we've got a problem.'

Tom swallowed, unable to find his voice.

'We got a round in the wall here. The SOC boys are on their way.'

Tom realised he was veering all over the highway. He made an enormous effort to concentrate. 'Detective Willer, I want to thank you for your trouble, but everything's fine. I just heard from Sally. She's fine. Her mom's sick, she had to go to Albuquerque.'

'But the Jeep's still in the garage.'

'She took a cab; that car doesn't work.'

'I see. About this round.'

Tom managed an easy laugh. 'My gun went off accidentally. Couple of days ago.'

'Is that so?' The voice was cold. 'Mind telling me the make and calibre?'

'Thirty-eight Smith & Wesson revolver.' There was a long silence. 'As I said, Detective, I'm sorry to have bothered you, I really am. False alarm.'

'Got a spot of blood here on the rug, too. That also yours?'

Tom didn't quite find an answer to that. He felt a wave a nausea. If those bastards had hurt her . . . 'A lot of blood?'

'Just a spot. It's still wet.'

'I don't know what to tell you about that, Detective. Maybe someone . . . cut himself.' He swallowed. He had to make that flight and he had to cooperate with the man. He never should have left Sally alone.

'Mr Broadbent? Are you familiar with the term "probable cause"?'

'Yes.'

'That's what we've got here. We entered the house with your permission, we found probable cause that a crime had been committed—and now we're going to search it. We don't need a warrant under those circumstances. You say your plane lands at seven thirty?'

'Yes.'

'I'd like to see you and your wife—sick mother or not—tonight. At the station. Nine o'clock sharp.'

'I can't. Not at nine. It's impossible. And my wife is in Albuquerque'

'This is not an optional appointment, Broadbent. You be there at nine or I'll get a warrant for your arrest. Is that clear?'

Tom swallowed. 'My wife has nothing to do with this.'

'You don't produce her and your problem will get worse. And let me tell you, pal, it's bad already.'

The phone went dead.

Chapter 7

Wyman Ford paused, looking down the great cleft in the earth named Tyrannosaur Canyon. Ten miles back he had passed the black basaltic intrusion that gave the canyon its name, and now he was deep within it. Nothing, it seemed, lived in the canyon beyond a few saltbushes and a plethora of rattlesnakes. The canyon walls rose higher the deeper he went, with many side canyons peeling off into nowhere. Ford hiked on, his long legs eating up the ground. Towards sunset, as the canyon made yet another turn, he could see the great crowd of rocks up ahead, the ones he had seen from Navajo Rim, which he had whimsically named the Bald Ones. The lower part of the canyon was already in shadow, bathed in a warm orange glow of reflected light from high up on the eastern rim.

Ford felt grateful that the day was over. He had been rationing water since morning and the cooling brought a lessening of his thirst.

When night arrived in the desert, it came fast. He would not have much time to pick out a good campsite. With a jaunty step he continued down the canyon, looking left and right, and soon located what he was after: a sheltered spot between a pair of fallen boulders with a soft, level bed of sand. He unshouldered his rucksack and took a swig of water, rolling it about in his mouth before swallowing. He still had fifteen, maybe twenty minutes of light left. Leaving his gear, he hiked up the canyon to the beginning of the Bald Ones. From the closer vantage point they looked more like gigantic toadstools than skulls.

He walked into the forest of sandstone pillars holding up the domes of rock. None of the rocks looked like the one he was after, but the family resemblance was strong. He felt a shiver of excitement, sure that he was getting closer to the dinosaur. He squeezed his way among the rocks, sometimes forced to crawl, until he reached the far side. To his surprise he discovered that the Bald Ones hid the entrance to another canyon—or what was actually a continuation of Tyrannosaur Canyon.

He hiked on for a quarter of a mile, then the canyon took a twist and opened into a stupendous valley where three tributary canyons came together like a train wreck of rock, creating a spectacle of erosional ferocity. Ford halted, awe-struck by the frozen violence of it. As he stood, the last of the sun winked out on the canyon rim and the evening crept across the strange valley, cloaking it in purple shadow. It was truly a land lost in time.

Ford turned back. It was too late to explore further; he had to get back to camp before dark. The stones had waited millions of years, the monk thought. They could wait one more day.

WILLER GLANCED UP at the clock from a stack of paperwork: 9.15 p.m. He looked over at Hernandez, whose face appeared almost green in the sickly fluorescent glare of the office.

'He blew us off,' said Hernandez. 'Just like that.'

'Just like that . . .' Willer rapped his pen on the stack of papers. It didn't make sense, a guy with so much to lose. 'He's playing some kind of game.'

'What's he up to?'

'Hell if I know.'

The room became heavy with silence. Willer finally coughed and lit up.

'Here's what we know for a fact: there's fresh blood on his living-room rug and a fresh round in his wall. He missed an interview with the police. That classic Chevy he drives was parked at the airport and now it's gone. Maybe he's in trouble or running scared. Maybe he argued with his wife, things got out of hand . . . and now she's buried in the back forty. Maybe he's just an arrogant bastard who thinks we don't rate. It doesn't matter: we got to track his ass down.'

'Right.'

'I want an all points for northern New Mexico, checkpoints on 84 at Chama, 96 at Coyote, 285 south of Española, I40 at Wagon Mound and the Arizona border.' He paused, shuffling through some papers on his desk, pulled one out. 'Here it is: he's driving a '57 Chevrolet 3100 pick-up, turquoise and white, NM licence plate 346 EWE. We got one thing going for us: driving a truck like that, he'll stick out like a sore thumb.'

MADDOX PARKED the Range Rover in front of the Sunrise Liquor Mart and checked his watch. Nine twenty-one. He knew, from earlier research, that from here he would see the headlights of a southbound car two minutes and forty seconds before it passed.

He got out, shoved his hands in his pockets, leaned on the car, drew in a deep breath of cool desert air. Nine twenty-two. He had passed Broadbent in his '57 Chevy eleven minutes ago, and if the man followed directions, turned round quickly and maintained his speed, his headlights should appear in the north in just over six minutes. Maddox got back in the car and waited.

Nine twenty-seven. Nine twenty-eight.

Bingo: a pair of headlights emerged from the sea of blackness in the north. The headlights slowly grew in size and brightness as the truck approached—then it passed in a flash of turquoise, the red taillights receding into the blackness to the south. Nine thirty and forty seconds.

He waited, his eyes on the watch, counting out one minute exactly, then he pressed the speed-dial button on his cell. Tom answered immediately.

'Listen carefully. Maintain your speed. Roll down the passenger window.'

'What about my wife?'

'You'll get her in a moment. Do as I say.'

'I've got the window down.'

Maddox watched the second hand on his watch. 'When I tell you, take your cellphone, hang up but *leave it on*. Put it in the Ziploc bag with the notebook and throw them all out the window. Then keep driving.'

'Listen, you son of a bitch, I'm not doing anything until you tell me where my wife is.'

'Do what I say or she's dead.'

'Then you'll never see this notebook.'

Maddox checked his watch. Already three and a half minutes had passed. He started the engine, pressed the accelerator and turned out on the highway, leaving a line of smoking rubber in the parking lot. 'She's in the old campground at Madera Creek, forty miles south of here. She's with my partner. If you don't do what I say I'm going to call him and he'll kill her and split. Now put the cell in the bag and toss it, *now*.'

'If she dies, I'll follow you to the ends of the earth and kill you.'

'Stop the grandstanding and *do what I say*!'

'I'm doing it.'

Maddox heard a rustling sound and the line went dead. He checked his watch, noted the time to the second, looked at his speedometer. He knew within a quarter-mile stretch where the notebook must be.

Maddox passed the mile marker and slowed down, unrolled his windows and called Broadbent's number. A second later he could hear the faint answering ring: and there it was, lying by the side of the road, a plastic Ziploc bag full of bright yellow trash. He cruised past, at the same time switching on a mounted lamp on his Range Rover and shining it around, to make sure Broadbent wasn't waiting in ambush. But the prairie stretched out empty on all sides.

He pulled a U-turn, drove back to the bag, hopped out, and scooped it up. As he accelerated back onto the highway he ripped the bag open with his right hand and groped through trash for the notebook.

There it was. He pulled it out, looked at it. It was bound in old leather and there was even a smudge of blood on the back cover. He opened it. Rows of eight-digit numbers, just as Corvus said. This was it. He'd done it.

Now it was time to get rid of the woman.

ABOUT HALF A MILE south of where he had tossed the Ziploc bag containing the notebook, Tom shut his lights off and veered off the highway, bounced over a ditch and drove into the dark prairie until he felt he was far enough away from the road. He shut off the engine and waited, his heart pounding.

When the man said that Sally was in the Madera Campground, Tom knew he was lying. The campground was overrun with small children at that time of year; it was too public, too exposed. The story was designed to draw him south.

A few minutes later he saw the headlights of a car far behind him. He had passed a Range Rover earlier, and seen the same car in the liquor mart, and he had no doubt this was the kidnapper's car now, as he saw it slowing down along the stretch of highway where he had thrown the bag. A side lamp went on, scouring the prairie. The car pulled a U-turn, came back; a man jumped out and picked up the bag, then headed north with a screech of rubber.

Tom waited until the car was well ahead on the highway, then, keeping his headlights off, he started his car and drove back onto the road, following the receding glow of the taillights. But the car ahead was moving fast, and he realised he had no hope of keeping up without turning on his lights.

At that moment he was approaching the liquor mart, and he saw that a shabby Dodge pick-up had pulled in for gas. He braked hard, swerved into the station, pulled up on the opposite side of the pumps. The truck was sitting next to the pumps with the keys dangling from the ignition while the driver paid inside. He could just see, in the door pocket, the handle of a gun.

Tom jumped out of his truck, climbed into the Dodge, started the engine and peeled out with a squeal of rubber. He floored it, heading north into the darkness where the pair of taillights had vanished.

THE CALL CAME in at 11.00 p.m. Even though Melodie had been waiting for it, she jumped when the phone trilled in the silent, empty lab.

'Melodie? How's the research going?'

'Great, Dr Corvus, just great.' She swallowed, realising that she was breathing hard into the mouthpiece. 'Those results, they're . . . incredible.'

'Tell me everything.'

'The specimen is riddled with iridium.'

'What type of iridium?'

'It's bound up in various isometric hexoctahedral forms in a concentration of four hundred and thirty parts per billion. That, as you know, is the exact type identified with the Chicxulub asteroid strike.'

Melodie waited for a response but it didn't come.

'This fossil,' she ventured, 'it wouldn't happen to be located at the Cretaceous–Tertiary boundary . . . would it?'

'It could be.' Another long silence.

'In the outer matrix surrounding the specimen,' Melodie continued. 'I found an abundance of microparticles of soot. As you know, the KT boundary layer contains soot laid down by worldwide forest fires following the Chicxulub asteroid strike. So it seems to me . . .' She paused, almost afraid to say it. 'Or rather, my conclusion is that this dinosaur was actually *killed* by the asteroid strike—or it died in the ecological collapse that followed.'

This dynamite conclusion fell into the void. Corvus remained silent.

'This would account for the fossil's extraordinary state of preservation.'

'How so?' came the guarded response.

'After the asteroid impact, there'd have been no scavengers to tear apart the body and scatter the bones. The strike heated up the whole earth, and in many areas the air temperature reached two, even three hundred degrees— perfect for flash-drying a carcass. On top of that, all the dust would trigger gigantic weather systems. Immense flash floods would have buried the remains.' Melodie took a deep breath, waited for a reaction.

'Anything more?' asked Corvus.

'Well, then there are the Venus particles.'

'Venus particles?'

'That's what I call those black particles you noticed. Under a microscope they look sort of like the symbol for Venus—a circle with a cross coming out of it. I did some tests on them. They're not a microcrystalline formation. The particle is a sphere of inorganic carbon with a projecting arm; inside are a bunch of trace elements I haven't yet analysed. I need to do a lot more work, but I wonder if they aren't some kind of infectious particle.'

There was that strange silence on the other end of the telephone. What was wrong with Corvus? Didn't he believe her?

When he finally spoke, the Curator's voice was so calm it was almost spooky. 'Melodie, this is fine work you've done. I commend you. Now listen carefully. I want you to gather up all your CDs, the pieces of specimen, *everything* in the lab connected with this work, and lock it all up securely in your specimen cabinet. If there is by chance anything left in the computer, delete it using the utility program that completely wipes files off the hard disk. Then I want you to go home and get some sleep.'

She felt incredulous. Was that all he could say, that she needed sleep?

'Can you do that, Melodie?' came the low voice. 'Lock it all up, clean the computer, go home, get some sleep. We'll talk again in the morning.'

'All right.'

'Good.' A pause. 'See you tomorrow.'

AFTER HANGING UP the telephone, Melodie sat in the laboratory, feeling stunned. After all her work, her extraordinary discoveries, Corvus acted as if he hardly cared—or didn't even believe her. *I commend you.* Here she'd made one of the most important palaeontological discoveries in history, and all he could do was *commend* her? And tell her to get some sleep?

She felt a growing burn of resentment, and began to wonder, for the first time, just how Corvus planned to handle their discovery. And it was *their* discovery—he couldn't have done it on his own. He didn't know how to work the equipment, he was practically computer-illiterate and he was a lousy mineralogist. She had done the analysis, asked the right questions of the specimen, teased out the answers, developed the theories.

It began to dawn on her why Corvus wanted to keep it all so secret. A spectacular discovery like this would set off a furore of competition, and a rush to get the rest of the fossil. Corvus might lose control of the discovery, and with it lose credit. Credit was the cold cash of the scientific world.

Her eye fell on the sapphire bracelet. She took it off and let it dangle in front of her eyes, the gems winking seductively. She shoved it in her pocket in disgust. Corvus had thought that the bracelet would buy her silence. Now he was worried that she had found out too much.

Melodie Crookshank suddenly knew what she had to do.

THE M-LOGOS 455 Massively Parallel Processing Object Unit System was the most powerful computer constructed by the human race. It sat in a perpetually air-conditioned, dust-free, static-free basement deep beneath the National Security Agency headquarters at Fort Mead, Maryland. It had not been built to predict weather, simulate a fifteen-megaton thermonuclear explosion or find the quadrillionth digit of pi. It has been created for a more mundane purpose: to listen.

Countless nodes distributed across the globe collected a gargantuan stream of digital information. It intercepted more than forty per cent of all traffic on the World Wide Web, more than ninety per cent of all cellular telephone conversations, virtually all radio and television broadcasts and a large portion of the data flows from governmental and private networks.

The digital torrent was fed into the M455MPP at the rate of sixteen terabits per second. The computer merely listened.

It listened with almost every known language on earth, every dialect, every protocol, almost every computer algorithm ever written to analyse language. But that was not all: the M455MPP was the first computer to employ a new, highly classified form of data analysis known as Stutterlogic. The role of Stutterlogic was to identify a 'communication of interest', or a CI in the jargon of its operators, and forward it to a human for review.

Most of the CIs that emerged from the M455MPP were emails and cellular telephone conversations. The latter were parcelled out among 125 human listeners. Their job required an enormous knowledge base, fluency in the language in question and an almost magical sense of intuition. Being a good 'listener' was an art, not a science.

At 11:04.34.98 EDT, four minutes into an eleven-minute cellular telephone call, module 3656070 of the M455MPP identified the conversation under way as a potential CI. The computer began analysing it, even while it was still in progress. When the CI concluded at 11:16.04.58, the conversation had already passed through a series of algorithmic filters that had parsed it linguistically and conceptually, scrutinising the voice inflections for dozens of psychological markers, including stress, excitement, anger, confidence and fear. Object programs identified the caller and the receiver and then went out to examine thousands of data bases to retrieve every particle of personal information about the two interlocutors that existed in networked electronic form anywhere in the world.

At 11:22.06.31 the CI was forwarded to a human listener.

AT A TERMINAL in his locked cubicle, Rick Muzinsky, one of the Homeland Security 'listeners', punched the READY button to indicate he was free to receive the next CI. His role was to forward those CIs he identified as threatening to an appropriate agency for further analysis. The computer sent him no preliminary data or background information about the call, nothing that might influence his mind about what he was about to hear.

A hiss and it began. There was the sound of a phone ringing, an answer, the sound of breathlessness on the other end, and the conversation:

'*Melodie? How's the research going?*'

'*Great, Dr Corvus, just great.*'

SALLY'S LEGS ACHED from standing in the same position, unable to move, her ankles and wrists chafing under the cold steel. A chill flow of air from the back of the mine penetrated her to the bone. The dim glow from the kerosene lantern wavered and spluttered, filling her with an irrational fear that it would go out. But what got to her most as she stood in the same position, unable to move, was the silence, broken only by the monotonous drip of water. She found it impossible to tell how much time had passed, whether it was night or day.

Suddenly she stiffened, hearing the rattle of someone unlocking the metal grate at the mouth of the mine. He was coming in. She heard the grate clang shut behind him and the chain rattle as he relocked it. And now she could hear his footsteps approaching. The beam of a flashlight flickered through the bars and a moment later he arrived. He unbolted the bars over the door frame with a socket wrench and tossed them aside. Then he shoved the flashlight in his back pocket and stepped inside the small stone prison.

Sally sagged in the chains, her eyes half closed. She moaned softly.

'Hi Sally.'

She moaned again. Through half-lidded eyes she could see that he was unbuttoning his shirt, a grin splitting his face.

'Hang in there,' he said. 'We're going to have ourselves a good time.'

She heard the shirt land on the floor, heard the jingle of his belt buckle.

'No,' she moaned weakly.

'Yes. Oh, *yes*. No more waiting, baby. It's now or never.'

She heard the jeans slide off, drop to the floor, then his underwear. She looked up weakly, her eyes slits. There he was, standing before her, naked, priapic, small key in one hand, gun in the other.

'Please, don't.' Her body sagged—lifeless, weak, utterly helpless.

'Please *do,* you mean.' He advanced towards her, grasped her left wrist, and inserted the key into the manacle. As he did so he leaned close over her bowed head, nuzzled down her neck with his lips, scraping her cheek with his unshaved chin. She knew he was about to unlock her left hand. Then he would make her unlock the others. That was his system.

She waited, maintaining her slackness. She heard the little *click* as the key turned the tumbler and she felt the steel bracelet fall away. In that moment, with all the force she could muster, she lashed out with her left hand, striking at his gun. It was a motion she had rehearsed in her mind a hundred times, and it caught him off guard. The gun went flying. She whipped her hand round and clawed her fingernails into his face—fingernails she had spent an hour sharpening into points against the rock. She just missed his eyes but managed to score deeply into his flesh.

He stumbled back with an inarticulate cry, throwing up his hands to protect his face, his flashlight landing on the mine floor.

Immediately her hand was on the unlocked manacle. *Yes!* The key was still in there, half turned. She pulled it out, unlocked her foot in time to kick him hard in the stomach as he was rising. She unlocked the other foot, unlocked her right hand. *Free!*

He was on his knees, coughing, his hand reaching out for the gun.

In yet another motion she had rehearsed in her mind countless times, she leapt for the table, one hand closing on a book of matches, the other sweeping the kerosene lantern to the floor. It shattered, plunging the cavern into darkness. She dropped to the ground just as he fired in her direction, the shot deafening in the enclosed space.

'I'll kill you, *bitch*!' came the gargled scream, followed by another shot.

The muzzle flash showed her the way to the door, and Sally scuttled blindly through it. She knew she couldn't escape through the outer tunnel—she had heard him lock the grate. Her only hope was to go deeper into the mine. She crawled down the tunnel, hoping, praying, that it would take her to a second exit or a safe place to hide.

IAIN CORVUS, waiting in an idling cab across from the museum, finally saw Melodie leave the building and turn left on Central Park West, heading uptown—no doubt to some dismal Upper West Side studio.

Corvus cursed his stupidity yet again. Almost from the beginning of their conversation that evening, he'd realised the colossal mistake he'd made. He'd tossed into Melodie's lap one of the most important scientific discoveries of all time. Sure, as senior scientist his name would be first on the paper, but the lion's share of the credit would go to her.

Fortunately, there was a simple solution to his problem, and Corvus congratulated himself on thinking of it before it was too late.

He tossed a fifty to the cabbie and stepped out. He strode across the street to the security entrance, went through security with a swipe of his card and in ten minutes was in the Mineralogy lab. Using his master key he opened her specimen cabinet, and was relieved to see a stack of CD-ROMs, and sections of the specimen arranged neatly in their places. It amazed him how much information she had extracted from the specimen in just five days.

He picked up the CDs, each labelled and categorised. Without these she couldn't even begin to claim credit. It was only right he should have the credit. After all, he was the one who was risking everything—even his own freedom—to claim the tyrannosaur fossil for the museum. He was the one who had snatched it from the jaws of a black marketeer. Without him taking those risks, Melodie would have nothing.

Corvus carefully packed all the material in his briefcase. Then he went to the computer, logged on as system administrator and checked all her files. Nothing. She'd done as he'd said and wiped them clean. He turned and was about to leave when he had a sudden thought. He needed to check the equipment logs. Anyone who used the lab's expensive equipment had to keep a log of time in, time out and purpose, and he wondered how Melodie had handled that requirement. He flipped open one of the logs, perused it. He was relieved to see that she had recorded her name and time but put false entries under 'purpose', listing miscellaneous work for other curators.

In his bold, slanting hand, he added log entries under his own name. Under 'Specimen' he put: *High Mesas/Chama River Wilderness, NM, T. rex.* He paused, then added under 'Comments': *Third examination of remarkable T. rex vertebral fragment. Extraordinary! This will make history.*

He signed his name, adding the date and time. He flipped back, and, finding some blank lines at the bottom of previous pages, he added two similar entries at appropriate dates and times. He did the same in the other equipment logbooks. Then he locked the CDs and specimens in his briefcase and left the laboratory, turning off the lights and locking the door on his way out.

The dim basement corridor stretched ahead of him, lit with a string of forty-watt bulbs and lined with sweating water pipes. Horrible place to work—he wondered how Melodie could stand it.

At the first dogleg in the hall, Corvus paused. He felt a tickling sensation on the back of his neck, as if someone were watching him. He turned, but the corridor behind him was empty. Bloody hell, he thought, he was getting as jumpy as Melodie.

He strode down the hallway, turned the corner, then hesitated. He could have sworn he'd heard behind him the soft scrape of a shoe on concrete. He waited for someone to round the corner, but nothing happened. He swore to himself; it was probably a graduate student, or a guard making the rounds.

Clutching his briefcase, he strode on, approaching the double set of doors leading to the vast dinosaur bone storage room. He paused at the doors, then quietly swiped his key card in the magnetic reader. The security light blinked from red to green and the door softly unlatched. He pushed it open, stepped inside, and closed it behind him. There was a small window in the door, with wire-mesh glass, through which he could see into the corridor beyond. Now he would be able to identify who was following him.

A minute passed, then a sudden shadow fell across the pane. A face appeared in profile, then turned with a snap and looked in the window.

Jolted, Corvus hastily stepped back into the darkness of the storage room, but the man, he knew, had seen him. He waited, wrapped in a cloak of absolute darkness, looking at the man's face. It was lit from behind and partially in shadow; but he could still see the outline of the man's features, the skin stretched tightly over prominent cheekbones, a thatch of jet-black hair, and a pair of lips that looked like two thin coils of clay. It was not a face he recognised. This was no museum employee, no graduate student.

Corvus hardly breathed. There was something about the utter calmness in the man's expression that frightened him—and those grey, dead lips. The man lingered at the window, unmoving. Then there was a soft brushing noise, a scraping, a faint click. The door handle turned a quarter turn, then back again. Corvus couldn't believe it: the bastard was trying to get in. Fat bloody chance. Only half a dozen people had access to Dinosaur Storage—and this man certainly wasn't one of them.

Another soft brushing noise, a click, another click. The security light on the inside of the door continued to glow red—as Corvus knew it would. He almost felt like laughing out loud, taunting the blighter, except that the sheer persistence of the man alarmed him. What the devil did he want?

Corvus slipped his cellphone out of his jacket so he could call security—but of course there was no coverage this far underground. The man was still working the knob, making various clicking and scraping noises as he tried to get in. It was unbelievable.

More soft sounds, a sharper click—then Corvus stared in disbelief.

The security light on the door had just gone green.

AFTER PASSING the kidnapper's car, which had pulled off the highway and shut off its lights, Tom had driven on until he was out of sight, then made a U-turn. The road behind him remained dark. The man had evidently turned off on one of the many forest roads going up into the Canjilon Mountains.

Tom made a U-turn and headed back. In a few minutes he found the place where the man had pulled off, leaving a clear set of tracks in the sand. He followed in the Dodge, driving slowly, resisting the impulse to turn on his headlights and charge ahead; surprise was his only advantage.

The road switchbacked up a steep ridge covered with a dense stand of ponderosa, and at the top it skirted a cliff. Soon a chain-link fence loomed up out of the darkness, gleaming new, with a pair of gates across the road.

A weather-beaten sign read: CCC CAMP, PERDIZ CREEK. A new sign on the fence read: PRIVATE PROPERTY: TRESPASSERS WILL BE PROSECUTED.

It was some kind of inholding in the national forest. Tom pulled off the road, shut off the engine. Now that he had a moment, he pulled the gun out of the door pocket. It was a well-used J. C. Higgins '88' revolver, .22 calibre. He checked the cylinder—nine chambers, all empty.

He yanked open the glove compartment and searched it, scattering old maps and empty bottles, and in the bottom found a single beaten-up round, which he inserted into the cylinder. He shoved the gun in his belt, pocketed a Maglite from the glove compartment and got out of the truck. The gate was padlocked. He peered through. The road curved off into the trees, and there, in the far distance, he could see the faintest glimmer of light.

A cabin.

Tom climbed the chain-link fence, dropped down the far side, then headed down the road at a fast, silent run.

AS SALLY CRAWLED down the tunnel, she could hear the man scrabbling about and swearing, evidently looking for his flashlight. She peered ahead into the darkness. Where did it go? She felt her matches but didn't dare light one, realising that it would turn her into a silhouetted target. She crawled ahead blind, cutting her knees on the rocky floor of the mine. In a few minutes her hand made contact with something cold—a length of slimy, rotten wood that swayed under her grasp. She could smell a cold exhalation of damp mine air coming from below. She felt past the railing, her hand encountering a sharp edge of rock. She inched forward, feeling downwards—it was slick and wet, evidently the vertical side of a shaft.

Hoping there might be a way round, she crawled sideways, feeling the railing as she went, but she reached the tunnel wall. The pit, it seemed, stretched all the way across. She paused, her heart pounding in her chest.

A voice rang out. 'Look, I'm sorry about all that. I got carried away. Let's be reasonable. Let's talk.'

She could still hear him rummaging around for his flashlight. She had to find a way down the shaft, and fast. She felt her way back along the railing until she came to a gap. Was this where a ladder descended? She lay flat on her stomach and leaned over the lip of the pit, feeling down the wet wall of stone—a ladder! The top rung felt spongy from rot.

'Hey, I know you're there. So be reasonable. I *promise* I'll let you go.'

She felt for the box of matches, slid it open, took out a match. Then she leaned out over the edge and struck it, keeping the flame below the edge of the shaft. The rising air caused it to flicker and blue, but she could see a rotting wooden ladder descending into a black, seemingly bottomless pit.

Wham! A shot rang out, snipping the rock just to her right and spraying the side of her shoulder with chips of stone. She dropped the match with an involuntary gasp, and it spiralled into the darkness.

'Bitch! I'll kill you!'

She swung herself over the black void and felt downward with her foot, encountering a rotten rung, tested it with her weight, then lowered herself slowly, trying the next rung.

She heard a muffled exclamation of triumph, then a click—he'd found the flashlight. Suddenly a beam of light swung past her head.

She ducked and scrambled down the ladder. Almost immediately one of the rungs snapped and her leg swung out over the pit before she could reestablish her footing. The entire ladder creaked and swayed.

Down she went, rung after rung, slipping and gasping with effort, the ladder shaking, drops of water cascading about her.

The beam of the light suddenly appeared at the lip of the shaft, fixating her in its glare. She threw herself sideways as the gun went off, the round tearing a hole in the rung, the entire ladder swaying.

A laugh echoed down. 'That was just for practice.'

She looked up again, gasping. He was leaning over the lip, twenty feet above her, flashlight in one hand, aiming the gun with the other. It was a no-miss shot. He knew he had her and was taking his time.

'No,' she gasped. 'Please don't.'

He extended his arm, the steel muzzle of the gun gleaming in the light.

Sally did the only thing she could do: she launched herself from the ladder, letting herself fall into the dark pit.

CORVUS STARED at the green LED, paralysed with fear. How could the man have penetrated the museum's security? What the hell did he want?

The door eased open, casting a widening stripe of yellow light across the floor. As his pursuer took another step forward, Corvus saw that he had a long-barrelled weapon of some kind in his hand.

The sight of it spurred Corvus into action. He turned and fled back towards the dark recesses of the storage room, flying down a narrow corridor lined on both sides with massive steel shelves, past stacks of bones and skulls. He came to a jog and turned right, then ran down another aisle and stopped, panting and crouching behind a large *Centrosaurus* skull, looking back to see if the man was pursuing. His heart was pounding so hard he could hear the rhythmic whoosh of blood in his ears. This was insane: he was being hunted in his own museum.

A voice came from the darkness, quiet and neutral in tone. 'I should like to speak with you, Professor.'

Corvus did not respond. He had to get to a more secure hiding place. He felt his way forward, crawling on his hands and knees, moving carefully so as not to make any noise. There was, he recalled, the massive torso of a *Triceratops* back there under a sheet of plastic; he could hide in the beast's rib cage. The great horned casque of the dinosaur would act like a hood.

'Dr Corvus, we are wasting precious time. Please make yourself known.'

Corvus was shaken: the voice was coming from a different place—closer and to his right. The man had been moving silently through the darkness.

Corvus continued to crawl forward with infinite caution, feeling the mounted foot bones of each dinosaur, trying to identify it and then place it within his mental map of the jumbled storeroom.

He bumped something and a bone fell with a rattle.

'This is getting tiresome.'

The voice was closer—a lot closer. Corvus scurried to the right, feeling his way, until he encountered a tail vertebra, and another, along with the bent iron rod supporting them. It was the *Triceratops*. He reached up, encountered a thick sheet of plastic, then carefully raised it and wriggled underneath. Once inside, he felt a rib and another, and inched painstakingly into the hollow where the beast's heart and lungs once sat. He waited, crouching, unmoving, his heart pounding in his own rib cage.

'It is useless trying to hide. I am coming to you.'

The voice was even closer. Corvus felt a hum of terror, like a swarm of bees unloosed in his head. He could not get the image of that long gun barrel out of his mind. This was no joke: the man was going to kill him.

'Dr Corvus?' the voice asked. 'All I want is some information about the *Tyrannosaurus rex*. When I get that, our business will be concluded.'

Corvus crouched there, in foetal position, trembling uncontrollably. The voice was not more than ten feet away.

Chapter 8

Tom sprinted through the forest towards the yellow light shining through the trees. He slowed when he came to the cabin, and moved forward cautiously. It was a large, two-storey structure with a porch, and in the glow of the porch light he could see the Range Rover parked in front.

Tom pressed himself against the rough logs of the cabin, creeping along until he came to a window. He peered in. The view was of a timbered living room with a stone fireplace, Navajo rugs on the floor. Only a single light was on. The place was silent and the second-floor windows were dark.

Keeping low, pausing every now and then to listen, he crept up next to the car and put his hand on the hood—the engine was still warm. Crouching by the passenger door, he pulled out the Maglite he'd found in the Dodge's glove compartment and turned it on. In the loose sand he could see a confused muddle of cowboy boot prints. Just beyond the car, he saw what looked like two parallel drag marks made by boot heels. He followed the marks with the beam of the flashlight and saw that they headed up the dirt street towards a ravine at the far end of town.

His heart flopped wildly in his chest. Was it Sally who had been dragged? Was she unconscious? His hand went instinctively to the butt of the pistol tucked into his belt. *One round.*

He followed the drag marks down the dirt track to the far end of the old camp, where they vanished into the woods at the mouth of the ravine. He continued along the trail, and after a quarter of a mile came out into an open area. The trail ran up the hillside and he sprinted up it through a stand of ponderosas. It ended at the old wooden shaft house of a disused mine.

Sally was imprisoned in the mines.

Tom scrambled up to the door of the shaft house. It was chained and padlocked. Resisting the impulse to bash it down, he paused and listened. Silence. He examined the padlock and found it unlocked. He switched off his light, eased the door open and slipped inside.

Cupping his hands round the flashlight, he turned it on just long enough to examine his surroundings. The mine opening lay ahead, securely barred with a heavy iron grate, locked with a fat, case-hardened steel padlock.

Tom tried to sort out his options. He had to get in—or attract the man to the door and shoot him as he approached.

A faint sound came from the mine, breaking the silence. Tom froze. A shout? He hardly dared breathe. After a moment he heard another sound, distorted by its long travel down the throat of stone. It was a man's voice.

He grasped the padlock and shook it, but it wouldn't budge. The grate was cemented into the stone. He had no hope of breaking it.

As he was casting about, he heard another angry shout, this one much louder and clearer, in which he could just make out the word *bitch.*

She was alive in there. Then he heard the muffled boom of a gunshot.

FOR A MOMENT, Sally lay in a shallow pool of water, stunned by the fall. It hadn't been a long drop after all, and she was more frightened than hurt. But she was far from out of danger. Even as she was recovering her thoughts, the flashlight beam was probing down from above. A moment later it fixed her and she jumped sideways as the shots came, the bullets striking the water around her with a zipping sound. She thrashed through the water towards where the flashlight beam had revealed a tunnel running off into darkness. In a moment she had turned the corner, beyond his range.

She leaned against the wall, taking great gulps of breath. Her whole body ached but nothing seemed to be broken. She felt in her breast pocket for the box of matches. Miraculously, while the outside of the box had got damp, the inside was still dry. She struck a match against the rock wall, one scratch, two. It flared on the third try and it cast a faint illumination down a long corridor cribbed with rotting oak beams. A shallow stream flowed along its bottom. The tunnel's condition looked disastrous; beams had fallen down, while small cave-ins from the walls partially obstructed the passage. What hadn't already fallen looked like it was about to go.

She jogged down the tunnel, shielding the match until it burned down to her fingers and she was forced to drop it. She kept going as long as she dared in the darkness, then stopped and listened. Was he following? It seemed unlikely he would risk going down the ladder—she had broken too many rungs in her descent. He would have to find a rope, but that would give her no more than a moment's reprieve; she remembered seeing a rope in her cell, coiled up at the foot of the bed.

Sally struggled to think rationally. She had read somewhere that all caves breathed and that the best way to find your way out was to follow the 'breath' of the cave—that is, the flow of air. She lit another match. The flame bent back, towards where she had come from. She went in the opposite direction, deeper into the mine. The tunnel opened into a large gallery, with pillars of raw rock holding up the ceiling. A third match showed two tunnels. She paused, there being just enough flame to see where the air was flowing from, and decided to take the right tunnel, which sloped upwards.

The match burned down, and she tried moving forward by feel. She soon realised her progress was too slow. She had to put as much distance between herself and him as possible. Now was the time to use the matches, not later. She lit another, continued up the tunnel, turned a corner—and found the tunnel blocked by a cave-in. She stared up at the dark hole in the roof from which an enormous mass of rock had fallen into a disorderly pile below.

Sally retraced her steps and took the left-hand tunnel, the one that sloped downward with the stream. Her panic was rising; at any moment the kidnapper would be down there after her. She followed the running water, hoping it might lead her to an exit, wading through a series of pools. The tunnel sloped downward and levelled out. The water got deeper and she realised it was pooling; soon it was almost up to her waist. Round the next turn she saw the cause: a cave-in that had completely blocked the tunnel and backed up the water. She swore to herself. In five minutes she had explored all of the mine that was still accessible. In short, she was trapped.

She retraced her steps yet again, recklessly lighting match after match, until she came back to the first cave-in. It was a compact mass, offering no obvious holes. She looked up at the hole in the roof. The light from her match was too feeble to penetrate its recesses, but still, it looked like there might be a crawl space up there where she might at least hide—if she were willing to risk the precarious, sloping pile of loose boulders.

It was a crazy risk. As she stood there, trembling and indecisive, she heard a distant voice, echoing raucously through the tunnels of stone. 'Ready or not, bitch, here I come!

CORVUS CROUCHED inside the rib cage of the *Triceratops*, blood pounding in his ears. He heard the faint scuff of a shoe on the concrete floor, then the ever-so-small crunch of fossil grit under the man's sole as he approached. *How the hell was the man moving around so well in the dark?*

'I can see you,' came the soft voice, as if reading his mind, 'but you can't see me. You look silly crouching there.'

Corvus's heart felt like a bass drum. The voice was right next to him.

'All I want is the locality data. GPS coordinates, name of a canyon, that sort of thing. I want to know where the dinosaur is.'

Corvus swallowed, shifted. It didn't make sense hiding any longer; the man knew where he was. He was probably wearing a night-vision device.

'I don't have that information,' Corvus croaked. 'I don't know where the bloody dinosaur is.' He sat up, clutching his briefcase.

'If that's the game you want to play, then I'm afraid I'll have to kill you.' The man's voice was so quiet, so gentle, that it left Corvus without the slightest doubt that the man meant what he said.

'I don't have it. I really don't.' Corvus heard himself pleading.

'Then how did you acquire the specimen?'

'Through a third party.'

'Ah. And the name and place of residence of this third party?'

There was a silence. Corvus felt his terror mingling with something else: anger. His whole career, his life, hung on getting that dinosaur. He wasn't going to give up his discovery to some bastard holding him at gunpoint—he'd rather die. If he could just get to one of the light banks it would eliminate the man's advantage. He could use his attaché case as a club—

'The name and place of residence of this third party, please?' the man repeated, his voice as soft as ever.

'I'm coming out.'

'A wise decision.'

'Corvus crawled towards the tail of the skeleton and out though the back. He slipped under the plastic and stood up. It was still pitch-dark.

'The name of this third party?'

Corvus lunged at the voice in the darkness, swinging his case by the handle in an arc, striking him somewhere; the man grunted and was thrown back in surprise. Corvus turned, groping blindly through the forest of skeletons towards where he remembered the back light switches were. He stumbled against a skeleton and fell, just as he heard a sharp pneumatic hiss followed by the sound of surgical steel striking fossil bone.

The bastard was shooting at him.

He lunged sideways, collided with a skeleton, which creaked in protest, sending a few bones clattering to the ground. He scrabbled desperately among bone forest, then suddenly he was free of the crowd of skeletons and sprinting towards the bank of electrical switches. With another shout he clawed at the panel, the lights clicking on by the dozen.

He spun round, at the same time grasping a petrified bone off one of the shelves, wielding it like a club, ready to fight.

The man stood there placidly, not ten feet away, legs apart, not even looking as though he'd moved. He was dressed in a blue track suit, night-vision goggles on his forehead. His hands were in firing position and the shiny tube of a strange-looking weapon was aimed straight at Corvus. He heard the *snap-hiss!* of compressed air, saw the flash of silver, felt the sting in his solar plexus. He looked down and saw a stainless-steel syringe sticking out of his abdomen. Already a darkness unlike any other was rushing upon him like a tidal wave, burying him in its roaring undertow.

FORD SAT with his back against a rock, soaking in the warmth from a meagre fire he had built, and savouring the bitter, smoky flavour of the coffee he had boiled up in the burning ashes. He smiled ruefully to himself, thinking of the crowded little café he and Julie used to go to round the corner from the Pantheon in Rome, where they drank perfect cups of espresso at a tiny table. What was the name of that place? The Tazza d'Oro.

He was a long way from there.

He drained the last bit of moisture from the cup and leaned back on the rock with a sigh, pulled his robe more tightly about himself and raised his eyes to the stars. The glowing skein of the Milky Way stretched across the sky; he located the constellation Cygnus, the Swan, frozen for ever in its flight across the galactic centre. He had read there was a gigantic black hole in the centre of the galaxy, called Cygnus X1, 100 million suns compressed into a mathematical point—and he wondered at the audacity of human beings to think they could understand anything about the true nature of God.

Ford sighed and stretched out in the sand, wondering if such musings were proper for a soon-to-be Benedictine monk. He sensed that the events of the past few days were propelling him towards some kind of spiritual crisis. The search for the *T. rex* had awakened that same old hunger, that longing for the chase that he thought he had purged from his system. God knows, he had had enough adventure for one lifetime already. He had suffered unbearably for it, and still suffered.

Unwillingly, Ford's mind travelled back to that fateful day in Siem Reap, Cambodia. His wife Julie and he had left Phnom Penh and stopped for a few days to see the temples of Angkor Wat on their way to Thailand. Only a week before they had learned that Julie was pregnant, and to celebrate they booked a suite at the Royal Khampang Hotel. He would never forget his last evening with her, watching the sun set over the temple's five great towers while Buddhist monks chanted in the monastery in the forest nearby.

After sunset they had a long dinner in one of the cheap open-air restaurants along the Siem Reap River, the frogs hopping about the floor and moths bumbling against the light bulbs strung on wires. They'd gone back to their hotel room and passed a good part of the evening cavorting on their bed. They slept until eleven, ate breakfast on their terrace. And then Julie had gone to get the car while he brought down their luggage.

He heard the muffled explosion just as the elevator doors opened into the lobby. He assumed that an old land mine had gone off—Cambodia was still plagued with them. He remembered walking through the palm court and seeing, through the lobby doors, a column of smoke rising in front of the hotel. He ran outside. The car lay upside-down, almost split in half, billowing acrid smoke, a crater in the pavement.

As he stood there, a piece of torn fabric, caught in a gust of wind, fluttered up to the steps of the hotel, and settled almost at his feet—and he recognised it as the collar of the blouse Julie had put on that morning.

With a wrenching mental effort, Ford brought himself back to the present, to the campfire, the dark canyons, the sky sparkling with stars. All those terrible memories seemed far away, as if they had happened in another life, to another person.

But that was just it: was this really another life—and he another person?

SALLY BEGAN CLIMBING up the unstable pile of rocks, match clenched between her teeth, seeking out footholds and handholds. With every step she could feel the rocks shifting, some dislodging and tumbling to the bottom.

Her breathing came so hard that it put the match out.

She felt in the box—only one match left. She decided to save it.

'I'm coming!' the hoarse voice echoed down through the tunnels, maniacally distorted. Sally kept climbing, moving upward by feel, more stones rattling down. Then she heard, above her, a deep groan of shifting wood and rock, followed by a cascade of pebbles. It was about to go.

She reached up, fumbled for a handhold and drew herself up, grasping a length of beam above her. Leaning her weight on it, she tested it. It shifted slightly, but seemed to hold. She paused, trying not to think of what it would be like to be buried alive, then lifted herself up. Another flurry of falling pebbles, then her hands encountered a tangle of splintered wood.

She would have to light the last match.

It scraped against the side of the box and flared to life. Above, she could see the dark hole she had to go into. She held the matchbox over the flame until it caught fire, casting a much brighter light into the dark space, but it was still not enough to see where it went.

With one hand holding the burning box, she hoisted herself over the next shifting beam. In a moment she was standing on a precarious ledge just inside the dark opening. By the dying light of the burning matchbox she saw that the hole ended in a broad, half-moon crack going off at a shallow angle of about thirty degrees. The crack looked just wide enough to fit in.

There was a sudden crash below her as a large rock from the ceiling fell to the ground. The flame went out.

'There you are!'

The beam of a flashlight lanced through the darkness, scouring the rock pile below her. She reached up, grabbed a handhold and scrabbled up towards the two damp faces of stone and into the broad fissure. The crack was wide enough for her to wedge herself in and move up by wriggling and inching.

She had no more matches, no way to see if the crack went anywhere.

'I know you're up there, bitch!'

She heard the rattle of falling rocks as he began to climb the rockfall. She drew up her feet, twisted her torso, and was able to get her arm loose and slide it in front of her, to feel her way forward. If she could push herself past this narrow section, the crack might lead to another tunnel.

She braced herself, and with a mighty push shoved herself deeper into the crack. The terror of being squeezed in the darkness was almost overwhelming. Water dripped down and ran over her face. Now she knew she could never back out. She braced, pushed—and she felt forward with her hand. The crack narrowed sharply to something less than an inch wide. She felt wildly, looking for a wider place—but there was none.

Sally felt an unspeakable terror bubbling up, beyond her ability to control. She tried to wriggle back out, but she had no leverage and her arms were not strong enough to force herself back. She was wedged in. There was no going forward. And there was no going back.

TOM TRIED EVERYTHING to break the lock on the grate. He bashed it with boulders, rammed it with a log, but it was useless. The faint sounds from inside the mine had ceased, and he felt the silence would drive him mad. Anything could be happening to her—a minute might mean the difference between life and death.

Perhaps the mine had another entrance. He hiked up to the top of the ridge and gazed down the other side. About 200 yards below stood another shaft house, at approximately the same level as the other.

Surely they would connect.

He ran down the hill, sliding and leaping boulders, and in a moment had reached it. Pulling out his gun, he kicked down the door and went inside, shining the light around. There was another mine opening, and this one had no metal grate sealing it. He ventured inside and probed the beam down a long, level tunnel. A feeling of urgency almost choked him now. He jogged down the tunnel, and at the first fork stopped to listen.

Suddenly he heard it: the faint echo of a yell. The two mines connected.

He dashed down the tunnel that the sound had come from, his light disclosing a series of air shafts on the left-hand side. He turned a corner and his flashlight revealed two other tunnels, one going up, the other down. He stopped to listen, waiting—and then came another distorted shout.

The voice of the man again. Angry.

Tom ran down the left-hand shaft, sometimes having to duck because of a low ceiling. More sounds came echoing down the tunnel from ahead, still faint but getting clearer. The tunnel made a few sharp turns, then dead-ended in a vertical shaft surrounded by a railing.

The pit was too deep for his light to reach the bottom. There were no ladders or ropes. He examined the rough edges of the shaft, then tore off his shoes and socks and tossed them over the edge, counting the time it took for them to hit the bottom. One and a half seconds: thirty-two feet.

Sticking the gun back in his belt and holding the Maglite between his teeth, he let himself over the edge, gripping the bare rock with his feet. With maddening slowness, he climbed down the shaft until finally, with a sense of relief, he felt solid ground. He shone the light around, collected his shoes and socks and put them back on. He was in yet another mining tunnel going straight back into the mountain. He listened. All was silent.

He jogged down the tunnel, stopped after a hundred yards to listen again. Coming from behind him he heard what sounded like a muffled shout. He shut off his light, holding his breath. It was a voice, still coming from distance, but much clearer than before. He could just make out the words.

I know you're up there. Come down or I shoot.

Tom listened intently, trying to locate the direction of the voice.

You're dead, bitch.

The words filled him with a rage so sudden that he lost his breath for a moment. The sound seemed to be coming from below, as if through the very rock. Some ten feet to his left he could see a web of cracks in the stone floor of the tunnel, where it had sagged and broken. He knelt, held his hand over one of the cracks. Cool air flowed out. He put his ear to the crack.

There was the sudden *crack!* of a large-calibre gun, followed by a scream—a scream so close to his ear he jumped.

WILLER AND HERNANDEZ sped north on Highway 84, the empty blackness of the desert wilderness mounting in front of them. It was almost midnight and Willer was beside himself that they had wasted so many precious hours. The owner of the Dodge that Broadbent stole hadn't reported the theft but, finding that the thief had left a classic Chevy, worth at least ten times more than his old truck, parked at the gas station with its keys dangling in the ignition, had simply taken it in recompense and driven it to Española.

Willer slid a butt out of his shirt pocket and inserted it between his lips. He wasn't supposed to smoke in the squad car but he was beyond caring.

'Broadbent could be over Cumbres Pass by now,' said Hernandez.

Willer sucked in a lungful. 'Not possible. They've logged all the vehicles coming over the pass and that half-wit's Dodge wasn't one of them. It hasn't gone through the roadblock south of Española either.'

'He could've ditched the Dodge in some back lot in Española and gone to ground in a motel.'

'He could've, but he didn't.' Willer gave the car a little more pedal. The speedometer inched up from 110 to 120.

'So what do you think he did?'

'I think he went to that so-called monastery, Christ in the Desert, to see that monk. Which is where we're going.'

'What makes you think that?'

'I don't know why I think it but I think it,' Willer snapped. 'Broadbent and his wife are mixed up in it, the monk's in on it, and there's a third party out there—the killer—who's also up to his ass in it. They've found something in those canyons and, whatever it is, it's big—so big that Broadbent blew off the police and stole a truck over it. I mean, Jesus, Hernandez, you got to ask yourself what's so important that a guy who's already got everything would risk ten years in Santa Fe Correctional over it.'

'Yeah.'

'Even if Broadbent's not at the monastery, I want to have a little chat with that so-called monk.'

TOM RECOGNISED, with a freezing sense of disbelief, that the scream came from Sally. He pressed his mouth to the crack. 'Sally!'

A gasp. 'Tom?'

'Sally! What's happening? Are you all right?'

'My God . . . Tom! It's you.' She could hardly speak. 'I'm stuck. He's shooting at me.' Another sobbing gasp.

'Sally, I'm here, it's OK.' Tom shone the light down and was shocked to see Sally's face wedged in the crack not two feet below him.

Another *boom!* from the gun, and Tom heard the zing and rattle of a bullet in the rocks beneath.

'Tom, I'm trapped, and he's shooting into the crack!'

'I'm going to get you out of here.' He shone the light around. The rock was fractured already and it would just be a matter of breaking up and prising out the pieces. He cast around with the light, looking for a tool. In one corner was a pile of rotting crates and ropes.

'I'll be right back.'

Another shot.

Tom ran to the pile, threw off a rotten coil of rope, searched through a heap of rotting sacks of burlap. Underneath was a broken piece of miner's hand-steel. He grabbed it, and as he ran back, there was another shot.

Sally screamed. 'I'm hit! He hit me! In the leg. Oh, my God, get me out.'

'Close your eyes.'

Tom jammed the steel wedge into the crack, picked up a loose rock and slammed it down on the wedge, slammed it again and again. The fractured rock began to loosen. He dropped to his knees and began scrabbling and pulling out the pieces with his hands. All the while he talked to Sally, telling her over and over that she was OK, that she'd be out of there soon.

Another shot.

'*You bitch! You're dead as soon as I reload.*'

Tom prised a piece of rock out, threw it aside, prised out another and another, working furiously. The tip broke off the wedge and he swore, turning it around and prising with the other side.

'It's big enough!' Sally cried.

Tom reached down, took her hand and pulled as she pushed from below, scraping up through the broken rock. It wasn't enough; her hips stuck.

'*You're dead meat!*'

Tom drove the hand-steel into the rock, splitting off a chunk of brittle quartz. He tossed it away, prised out another.

'Now!' He grabbed her under the arms and pulled her free.

Sally lay on the ground, filthy, wet, her clothes torn.

'Where are you hit?' He searched her frantically.

'My leg.'

Tom ripped off his own shirt and wiped away the blood, finding a series of shallow cuts on her calf. He picked out some fragments of stone from a ricochet. 'Sally, it's OK. You'll be fine.'

'*Bitch!*' The scream sounded hysterical, unbalanced. Then another shot.

'We've got to block this hole,' Sally said.

But Tom was already rolling rocks over. They jammed them into the crack, hammering them down. In five minutes it was blocked.

Suddenly his arms were round her, squeezing tightly.

'God, I thought I'd never see you again,' said Sally with a sob. 'I can't believe it, I can't believe you found me.'

He held her again, hardly believing it himself. He could feel her heart beating wildly. 'Let's go.'

They ran back down through the tunnels until they came to the shaft. He helped her climb the shaft and in another five minutes they had exited it.

'He'll be coming out the other shaft,' said Sally.

Tom nodded. 'We'll go around the long way.'

Instead of going back over the ridge, they ran into the darkness of the trees at the bottom of the ravine. There they stopped to catch their breath.

'How's your leg? OK with walking?'

'Not bad. Is that a gun in your belt?'

'Yeah. A .22 with one round.' Tom looked back over the silvered hillside, his arm supporting Sally. 'It was in the truck I had to steal to get out here.'

They set off down the ravine, pausing from time to time to listen and see if the kidnapper was following, but all was silent. After ten minutes the gulch levelled out into a broad dry wash. Ahead and slightly below shone the lights of the cabin. But the kidnapper's Range Rover was gone.

'You think he panicked and took off?' Sally asked.

'I doubt it.'

They bypassed the cabin and moved swiftly through the trees, paralleling the dirt road till they came to the chain-link fence. Tom gave Sally a leg up, and in a moment she was over. He followed. They ran along the fence line until Tom saw a gleam of moonlight off the stolen Dodge, still parked where he'd left it near the locked gate. Except now the gate was wide open.

'Where the hell is he?' Sally whispered.

Tom squeezed Sally's shoulder and whispered, 'Keep to the shadows, head down at all times, and get in the truck as quietly as possible.'

Sally nodded. She crept round to the passenger side, crouching below the level of the cab; Tom eased open the door and climbed in the driver's side. Keeping his head down, Tom fished out the key, inserted it in the ignition.

'Hold on tight.' He threw the switch.

The Dodge roared to life. He jammed it into reverse and gunned the engine, the truck backing up while he spun the wheel. In that same moment, bright headlights went on from a turning space at the edge of the woods. There was a sudden *thwang! thwang!* of heavy-calibre rounds hitting steel, and the interior of the truck exploded in a storm of shattered glass and plastic.

'*Down!*'

Throwing himself sideways on the seat, Tom rammed the truck into first and floored it, fishtailing onto the road, spraying a shower of gravel. Jamming it into second, he accelerated as he heard more rounds hitting the Dodge. The wheels were spinning, and the back of the truck slewed back and forth. He raised his head up but could see nothing: the windshield was a spiderweb of shattered glass. He punched his fist through it, ripped out a hole big enough to see out of, and continued accelerating down the dirt road.

'Stay on the floor!'

He made the first turn and the shooting temporarily stopped, but he could now hear the roar of a car engine behind them—and a moment later the Range Rover skidded round the corner, its headlights stabbing past them.

Thwang! Thwang! More shots hit the truck. Tom jerked the wheel sideways and back, making them a weaving target. He felt the rear suddenly vibrating and he knew that at least one of the rear tyres had been shot out.

'Gas!' Sally screamed from the floor. 'I smell gas!'

The tank had been hit. Another *thwang!* followed by a dull shuddering *whoosh*. Tom instantly felt the heat, saw the glow from behind.

'We're on fire!' Sally screamed. She grabbed the door handle. 'Jump!'

'No! Not yet!'

He steered the truck round another curve in the road, and the firing ceased for a moment. Up ahead, Tom saw where the road skirted the edge of the cliff. He gunned the engine, accelerating straight for it.

'Sally, I'm taking it off that cliff. When I say *Now*, jump. Roll away from the wheels. Then get up and run, towards the high mesas. Can you do it?'

'Got it!'

He gunned the engine, the cliff approaching. He grabbed the door handle and half opened the door, keeping the accelerator floored.

'Get ready!'

A beat.

'*Now!*'

He threw himself out, hit the ground and rolled, regained his feet running. He could see Sally's dark figure on the far side, scrambling to her feet just as the flaming truck disappeared over the cliff, engine screaming. There was a muffled roar and a sudden orange glow from the bottom of the cliff.

The Range Rover braked just in time, and Tom glimpsed a shirtless man leaping out, a handgun in one hand and a flashlight in the other, with a rifle slung over his shoulder. Tom ran towards the steep slope just beyond the cliff, but the man had spotted Sally and was running after her.

'Hey, you son of a bitch!' Tom screamed, hoping to draw him off.

But the man kept after Sally, rapidly gaining ground. Fifty feet, forty . . . He'd soon be close enough to put a bullet through her.

Tom pulled his .22. 'Hey, you bastard!'

The man coolly dropped to one knee, unshipped the rifle, snugged the gun against his cheek and took aim. Tom stopped and braced himself, aiming with the .22. He'd never hit the man, but the shot might distract him.

Tom fired. Instinctively, the man hit the ground.

Tom ran at him, waving the revolver like a madman. 'I'll kill you!'

The man rose back up and took aim, this time at Tom. He squeezed the trigger—as Tom threw himself to the ground and rolled sideways.

The man looked back to where Sally had been—but she was gone. He threw the rifle over his shoulder, drew his handgun and ran towards Tom.

Tom scrambled to his feet and ran downhill, leaping over boulders and fallen trees, glad that the man was now chasing him. He heard a double *crack! crack!* of a handgun, the sound of a round smacking a tree to his right. He dived forward, rolled, was back on his feet and leaping diagonally down the hillside. The man was about a hundred feet behind.

Tom leapt, weaved, zigzagged among the trees. The hill was getting steeper. More bullets ripped past him, tearing a piece of bark off a tree to his right.

Tom kept running.

WEED MADDOX saw that he was steadily gaining on Broadbent. He'd stopped three times to fire, but each time he was too far away, and the pause let Broadbent regain lost ground. He had to be careful; Broadbent had some kind of small-calibre weapon, no match for his Glock, but still dangerous. He had to take care of him first, then the woman.

He saw Broadbent veer to the left. Maddox cut the corner, gaining more ground. Broadbent kept dodging, trying to put trees between him and his pursuer. The hill was plunging ever steeper, and Maddox was now only seventy, eighty feet behind. The game was almost over; Broadbent was being funnelled between two ridges.

Broadbent disappeared behind some thick trees. A moment later Maddox rounded the trees and saw an outcrop ahead—a cliff, about 200 yards wide, forming a 'V' where the dry wash went over. He had Broadbent trapped.

He halted. The man had vanished.

Maddox swept his light from one end to the other. No Broadbent. The crazy bastard had jumped off the cliff. Or he was climbing down. He stopped at the edge, shining his light down, but Broadbent was nowhere to be seen. Maddox felt a surge of fury. Had he turned and run back uphill? He swept the light up the hill, but the slopes were empty. He went back to the cliff face, playing his light across it, searched the rocks below for a body.

About fifteen feet from the cliff stood a tall spruce. He heard the crack of a branch and saw the lower branches on the opposite side moving.

The son of a bitch had jumped into the tree.

Maddox whipped his rifle round and knelt, aiming for the disturbance. He squeezed off one shot, a second, a third, to no effect. Broadbent was climbing down on the far side of the trunk, using it as cover.

Maddox sprinted along the edge of the cliff looking for a better shooting angle for when Broadbent reached the base of the tree. He knelt, aimed, held his breath and waited for him to appear.

Broadbent dropped out of the lowest branch just as Maddox fired. For a moment Maddox thought he'd nailed him—but the bastard had anticipated the shot and had rolled as he hit the ground, then was up and running again.

Shit.

Maddox looked around for the woman, but she was long gone. He stood at the edge of the cliff, beside himself with fury. They had escaped.

But not completely. Maddox knew how to track. He'd find them.

To allow them to escape would mean going back to prison for the Big Bitch—life without parole. He had to kill them or die trying.

WILLER PUT ONE FOOT out of the cruiser onto the dirt parking lot of the monastery, then goosed the siren, just to let them know he was there. He was pretty sure that at 1.30 a.m. the monks would be in bed. The place was as dark as a tomb. A moon had risen above the canyon rim, casting a spooky light.

'You really think Broadbent's here? The parking lot's empty.'

Willer felt a fresh wave of irritation at the doubt he heard in Hernandez's voice. He plucked a cigarette from his pocket, stuck it between his lips, lit it. 'We know Broadbent was on Highway 84, driving that stolen Dodge. He hasn't gone through any roadblocks. Where else would he be?'

'There are plenty of forest roads going off both sides of the highway.'

'Yeah. But there's only one road into the high mesa country and this is it.'

He sucked in, exhaled. A flashlight was now bobbing down the trail. A hooded figure approached, face hidden in shadow.

The monk arrived with his hand outstretched. 'Brother Henry, abbot of Christ in the Desert.' The man was small with brisk movements, bright eyes and close-cropped goatee.

Willer shook the monk's hand, feeling nonplussed at the friendly, confident welcome. 'Lieutenant Willer, Santa Fe homicide,' he said, removing his shield, 'and this is Sergeant Hernandez.'

'Fine, fine.' The monk examined the badge by the light of his flashlight. 'Would you turn off your warning lights, Lieutenant? The brothers are asleep.'

'Right. Sure.'

Hernandez ducked into the police car, switched them off. Willer felt awkward and defensive. Maybe he shouldn't have goosed the siren like that.

'We're looking for a man by the name of Thomas Broadbent,' he said. 'Seems he's friendly with one of your monks, Wyman Ford. We have reason to believe he might be here.'

'I don't know this Mr Broadbent,' said the abbot. 'And Brother Wyman's not here. He left three days ago for a solitary prayer retreat in the desert.'

Prayer retreat, my ass, thought Willer. 'And when's he getting back?'

'He was supposed to be back yesterday.'

'That so?' Willer looked closely at the man's face. It was about as sincere a face as you could find. He was telling the truth, at least. 'So you don't know this Broadbent? My information is that he was up here a couple of times. Sandy hair, tall, drives a '57 Chevy pick-up.'

'Oh yes, the man with the fabulous truck. I know who you mean now. He's been here twice, as far as I'm aware.'

'He was up here four days ago, according to my information. The day before this monk of yours, Ford, went into the desert on his "prayer retreat".'

'That sounds correct,' said the abbot, mildly.

Willer took out his notebook, made a note.

'May I ask, Lieutenant, what this is all about?' asked the abbot. 'We're not accustomed to getting visited by the police in the middle of the night.'

Willer snapped his notebook shut. 'I've got a warrant for Broadbent's arrest. We think he may be involved in something of an illegal nature—something connected to the murder up in the Maze last week. And I have reason to believe that Wyman Ford may also be involved.'

The abbot gazed disconcertingly at Willer for a moment. 'I find it impossible to believe that Brother Wyman would be involved in anything illegal, let alone murder,' he said. 'He is a man of sterling character.'

'Has Ford been out in the mesas a lot lately?'

'No more than usual.'

'You aware he was CIA?'

'Lieutenant, we do not enquire into the past lives of our brothers, beyond what needs to be addressed in the confessional.'

'You noticed any differences in Ford's behaviour lately?'

The abbot hesitated. 'He was working on the computer quite a lot recently. But as I said, I am sure he would never be involved—'

Willer interrupted. 'Any idea where Ford went on this "spiritual retreat"?'

'No.'

'And he's late coming back?'

'I expect he'll be back at any moment. He promised to be here yesterday. He usually keeps his promises. Is there anything else?'

'Not at the moment.'

'Then I'd like to retire. We rise at four.'

'Fine.'

Willer and Hernandez watched the monk walk back to the monastery.

'What do you think?' Hernandez asked.

'The whole thing stinks. I'm going to sweat that monk Ford if it's the last thing I do. "Spiritual retreat"—give me a break.' Willer lit up, and gestured with his head to the car radio. 'Call Santa Fe for a chopper, and while you're at it, ask for a warrant to seize the monastery's computer. I want the chopper here at first light. We're going in to find those mothers.'

'Sure thing, Lieutenant.'

Willer watched Hernandez climb into the police cruiser, and he heard the crackle and hiss of the radio. An unintelligible exchange went on for a long time, then Hernandez rejoined him.

'They just closed the airspace from Española to the Colorado border.'

'Who's "they"?'

'The FAA. Nobody knows why; the order came from on high.'

'For how long?'

'Open-ended.'

'Beautiful. What about the warrant?'

'No dice. They woke up the judge; he's pissed, he's Catholic and he wants a lot more probable cause before seizing a monastery's computer.'

'I'm Catholic too. What the hell's that got to do with it?' Willer sucked the last ounce of smoke from the cigarette, dropped it on the ground and stomped on it with his heel. Then he nodded towards the dark mass of canyons and bluffs rising behind the monastery. 'Something big's going down in the high mesas. And we don't have the slightest frigging idea what it is.'

Chapter 9

A black speck appeared against the rising brightness of the eastern sky above White Sands Missile Range, New Mexico. It slowly resolved itself into the twin-tailed, swept-wing shape of an F14 Tomcat, coming in straight for a landing, the rumble of its engines shattering the predawn stillness. The fighter touched down, reversed its thrusters, turned and taxied to a stop in front of the terminal building.

The cockpit opened and the thin figure of a man climbed out of the copilot's seat and leapt lightly to the ground. He was dressed in a blue track suit and carried a battered leather briefcase. He strode across the tarmac to the terminal, crisply saluting a pair of soldiers guarding the door.

Everything about the man was cold, clean and symmetrical, like a piece of turned steel. His hair was black and straight and lay across his forehead. His cheekbones were prominent, the two sharp knobs pushing out the smooth skin of his face. His lips were thin and grey, the lips of a dead man. He might have been Asian if it weren't for his piercing blue eyes, which seemed to leap from his face, so strongly did they contrast with his black hair and white skin.

J. G. Masago entered the cinder-block terminal and paused, displeased that no one was there to meet him. Masago had absolutely no time to waste.

The pause allowed him to reflect that, so far, the operation had gone perfectly. He had solved the problem at the museum and sequestered the data. An emergency review and examination of the specimens at the National Security Agency had produced results exceeding all expectations. This was it: the momentous event that Detachment LS480, the classified agency he headed, had been waiting for ever since the return of the Apollo 17 mission more than thirty years ago. The endgame had begun.

Masago was sorry about what he had done to the Brit in the museum. It was always regrettable when a human life had to be taken. But sacrifices had to be made. Others would take care of the laboratory assistant, who was a lower priority now that the data and samples had been fully secured.

Masago was the child of a Japanese mother and an American father, conceived in Hiroshima in the weeks after the bombing. His mother had died several years later, screaming in agony from cancer caused by the Black Rain. His father had, of course, disappeared before he was born. Masago had made his way to America when he was fifteen. Eleven years later, the Apollo 17 landing module touched down at Taurus-Littrow on the edge of the moon's Sea of Serenity. Little did he know then that this Apollo mission had made what was arguably the greatest scientific discovery of all time—and that this secret would eventually be entrusted to him.

By that time, Masago was already a junior officer in the CIA. From there he followed a convoluted career path through the Defense Intelligence Agency, succeeding by virtue of ultracautious behaviour, self-effacing brilliance and achievement cloaked in diffidence. Eventually he was given the leadership of a small classified detachment known as LS480, and the secret was revealed to him. For ten years he had kept the lowest profile. They had been in a holding pattern, a waiting game, an interregnum. But he had been ready. And when the time came he had acted swiftly and with decision.

Masago knew a simple truth that none of his colleagues had the courage to face. He knew that humanity was finished. Mankind had gained the capability of destroying itself, and therefore it would destroy itself. QED. It was as obvious to Masago as two plus two. But he knew also that it was in his power to delay the event. If he performed his duty, he personally might be able to give the human race five years more, maybe ten—perhaps even a generation. This was the noblest of callings, but it required moral discipline. If some had to die prematurely, that was a small price.

Masago's sapphire eyes gave the terminal a second sweep. He had been waiting two minutes; it was close to becoming intolerable. Finally, out of an office stepped a man in rumpled desert camouflage, with two stars on his shoulder and a thatch of iron hair.

Masago extended his hand. 'General Miller?'

The general took the hand in a firm, military squeeze. 'And you must be

Mr Masago.' He grinned and nodded out towards the Tomcat refuelling on the runway. 'Navy man once? We don't see many of those around here.'

Masago neither smiled nor responded to the question. Coldly he asked, 'Everything is ready as specified, General?'

'Of course.'

The general turned and Masago followed him into a spare office at the far end. On the metal desk lay some folders, a badge and a small device that might have been a classified version of a military satellite phone. The general picked up the badge and phone and handed them to Masago, along with the first folder, which had a number of red stamps on it.

Masago took a few minutes to scan the folder. It was exactly what he'd requested, the UAV equipped with synthetic aperture radar, multi- and hyperspectral imagery. He noted with approval the diversion of one SIGINT KH-11 infrared photographic satellite for his mission.

'And the men?'

'A team of ten assigned from the Combined Assault Group and DEVGRU to a branch of the CIA Operations Directorate. You won't get any better men than these ten. They're the best damn soldiers I've got.'

'I will rely on that. Tell me about the chalk leader.'

'Sergeant First Class Anton Hitt, bio in the folder.'

Masago flashed an enquiring glance at Miller. '*Sergeant?*'

'You asked for the best, not the highest ranking,' responded the general, dryly. He paused. 'The mission isn't here in New Mexico, is it? We'd appreciate a heads-up if this op's in our back yard.'

'That information falls into the need-to-know category, General.'

'My USAF crew needs a briefing—'

'Your air crew will be given mission cards and coordinates once in the air. I want a cargo helo standing by, ready to fly at a moment's notice to pick up a cargo of up to fifteen tons.'

'May I ask the range?' the general asked. 'We might have a potential fuel problem.'

'The bird will fly seventy-two per cent fuelled.' Masago slapped the folder shut, slipped it into his briefcase. 'Escort me to the helipad.'

He followed the general out through a side door and across a broad, circular expanse of asphalt, on which sat the sleek black Sikorsky Pave Hawk, rotors whapping. The eastern sky had grown brighter, turning from blue to pale yellow in the approaching sunrise.

Masago strode over, not bothering to shield himself against the back-wash of the rotors, his thick black hair whipped about. He leapt aboard and the sliding door closed. The rotors powered up, the dust rose in sheets, and a moment later the big bird took off, nosed towards the north and accelerated into the dawn sky.

Tom Broadbent paused to catch his breath. Sally came up behind him and rested her hand on his shoulder. After managing to find each other in the upper canyons, they had hiked all night long, guided by the light of a gibbous moon. The badlands stood in silent repose, thousands of small grey hills like heaps of ash. In front of them lay a depression in the sand, with a cracked bed of silt whitened by alkali crystals. The sun was about to rise.

Sally gave the silt a kick, sending up a whitish plume that drifted off. 'That's the fifth dry waterhole we've passed.'

'Seems the rain last week didn't extend out this far.'

She eased herself down on a rock and gave Tom a sideways look. 'I do believe you've ruined that suit, mister.'

'Valentino would weep,' said Tom, mustering a smile. 'Let's have a look at your cut.'

She let him peel off her jeans, and he carefully removed the improvised bandage. 'No sign of infection. Does it hurt?'

'I'm so tired I can't even feel it.'

He discarded the bandage and took a clean strip of silk from his pocket, earlier ripped from the lining of his suit. He tied it gently in place, feeling an overwhelming rage against the man who had kidnapped her.

'I'm going up on that ridge to see if he's still following us. You take a rest.'

'Gladly.'

Tom scrambled up the slope of a nearby hogback, crawled the last few feet and peered over the edge. In the past five hours they had hiked at least twenty miles, trying to put as much distance as they could between themselves and their pursuer. He didn't believe the man could have tracked them through the night, but he wanted to make sure they'd really shaken him.

He settled in for a wait. The landscape behind him looked devoid of human life, but many low areas and canyon bottoms were hidden; it might be a while before the pursuer emerged into the open. Tom lay on his belly, scanning the desert. Five minutes passed, then ten. Tom felt a growing sense of relief. The sun rose, a cauldron of fire, throwing an orange light that nicked the highest peaks and ridges, creeping down their flanks like slow-motion gold. Eventually the light invaded the badlands themselves.

Still he saw no trace of their pursuer. The man was gone. He was probably still up in Daggett Canyon, staggering around, dying of thirst.

With that pleasant thought in mind, Tom descended the ridge. He found Sally with her back against a rock, resting.

'Any sign?' she asked.

Tom shook his head, yet for some reason doubt lingered in his mind.

'We've got to keep moving,' she said, and groaned as Tom helped her to her feet. 'I'm so stiff. I never should have sat down.'

They set off hiking down the wash, Tom letting Sally set the pace. He tried to ignore his growing thirst. They weren't likely to find water until they hit the river, another fifteen miles distant. The night had been cool, but now that the sun was coming up he could already feel the heat.

It was going to be a scorcher.

WEED MADDOX lay on his belly behind a boulder, looking through the 4x scope of his AR-15, watching Broadbent helping his wife to her feet. His body still ached from the kick she'd given him, his cheek was inflamed by her vicious scratch and he was getting thirstier by the minute. The sons of bitches had been hiking at an almost superhuman pace. If it hadn't been for the moon he would surely have lost them. But this was good tracking country, and he knew where they were headed—to the river. Where else would they go? Every source of water they'd passed had been dry as a bone.

He watched them set off down the canyon. From where he was he could probably drop Broadbent, but the shot was dicey. No, the key here was not to betray his presence. If they believed he was still following, they would be a lot harder to surprise.

With the scope of his rifle he scanned the landscape ahead, being careful to keep the lens out of direct sunlight; nothing would give him away faster than a flash of light off ground glass. To the southwest he recognised the great ridge known as Navajo Rim, rising 800 feet above the surrounding desert. Between here and there, he recalled, lay a broken country called the Echo Badlands, riddled with deep canyons and strange rock formations. Perhaps fifteen miles ahead, Weed could just see the termination of the Mesa of the Ancients. Cut into its flanks were a number of canyons, of which Joaquin Canyon was the biggest. That led to the Maze, where he had killed the dinosaur prospector, and from there it was a straight shot to the river.

They'd be heading for the one trail across Navajo Rim, so if he made a southward loop, skirting the base of Navajo Rim, he could come back up north and ambush them at the head of the valley. He would have to move fast, but in less than an hour it would be all over.

He crept down from his vantage point and set off at a fast pace southwards. This time tomorrow he'd be boarding that early flight to New York.

MELODIE CROOKSHANK slotted her museum pass through the card-reader outside the mineralogy lab and pushed open the door. She'd had a long, sleepless night, but her mind was unusually clear. She felt inside for the light switch. The fluorescent lights stuttered on.

Through the shelves of specimens she could see that Corvus was already in—asleep over the stereozoom, his attaché case at his side. She took a tentative step inside, cleared her throat. He did not stir.

'Dr Corvus?' She stepped forward more confidently.

The curator had fallen asleep on the desk, head laid on his crooked arm. He had been looking at a specimen under the stereozoom.

She walked over to the table. 'Dr Corvus?' she repeated. Still no response. She moved round to the other side of the table and leaned over to look into his face. She jerked back with an involuntary gasp.

The curator's eyes were wide open, staring and filmed over.

A heart attack? Surely he was way too young. She took another step back, reached out for the museum phone—then noticed the specimen that Corvus had been looking at under the microscope: a trilobite. An ordinary trilobite from the Cenozoic. The museum had thousands of them. Corvus, who was sitting on the most spectacular palaeontological discovery of the century, had chosen that moment to examine a common trilobite? No way.

Then she remembered that the lights had been off when she entered the lab. If Corvus had had a heart attack, who had turned off the lights?

A feeling of dread invaded her gut. She walked over to her specimen locker, spun out her combination on the lock, jerked it open. The CDs and specimens that she had locked up there at midnight were gone.

She picked up Corvus's attaché case, laid it on the table, unlatched it, rifled the contents. Nothing.

It felt like a piece of dry ice had just formed in her stomach. She had to handle this carefully. Whoever had killed Corvus might come after her too.

LIEUTENANT WILLER stood at the entrance to the monastery and watched the sun rise over the buttes above the river. The sound of chanting drifted down from the church behind him, rising and falling in the desert air.

Ford hadn't returned and there'd been no sign of Broadbent. Hernandez was down at the cruiser, making one last call. Santa Fe already had a chopper standing by at the police heliport, flown up from Albuquerque—and still the airspace was closed with no word on when it would reopen.

He saw Hernandez duck out of the cruiser. A few minutes later the deputy came toiling up the trail, shaking his head. 'No go.'

'Any word on Broadbent or the vehicle?'

'None. Seem to have vanished into thin air.'

Willer swore. 'We're doing nothing here. Let's start searching the Forest Service roads off Highway 84.' He took a last glance up at the church, then headed down the trail, Hernandez following. They'd grab some breakfast burritos and a couple of gallons of coffee at Bode's.

Willer seized the door handle of the cruiser and was about to jerk it open when he became aware of a distant throbbing in the air. He looked up and saw a black dot materialise in the dawn sky.

'Hey,' said Hernandez, squinting, 'isn't that a chopper?'

'It sure as hell is.'

'They told me it was still on the tarmac.'

'Idiots.'

Willer watched the helicopter approach, his feeling of frustration evaporating. 'Now we can get this show on the road.'

He felt pretty sure that the action was up in the Maze, and that's where he'd direct the chopper first. He'd get a kick out of seeing how that millionaire vet liked sharing a basement cell with a crackhead.

The black speck was beginning to resolve into something larger, and Willer stared with growing puzzlement. This was no police chopper, at least none that he'd ever seen. It was black and a lot bigger, with two pods hanging off either side like pontoons. He turned to Hernandez.

'You thinking what I'm thinking?'

'FBI.'

'Exactly.' Willer swore softly. It was just like the feds to let local law enforcement stumble along like idiots and then arrive in time for the bust.

The chopper banked slightly as it approached, slowed, and hovered for a landing in the parking lot. With the rotors still whapping, the side slid open, and a man in desert fatigues and holding an M4 carbine, hopped out.

'What the hell is this?' Willer said.

Nine more soldiers hopped down, several loaded with packs of electronic gear. Last to jump was a tall man, thin, with black hair, wearing a blue track suit. Eight of the men jogged single file up the trail towards the church, while the other two stayed with the man in the track suit.

Willer sucked on the last of his butt, chucked it on the ground, and waited. These weren't even feds—or at least any feds he knew.

The man in the track suit strode over, stopped in front of him. 'May I ask you to identify yourself, Officer?' he said in the neutral voice of authority.

'Lieutenant Willer, Santa Fe Police. And this is Sergeant Hernandez.'

'May I ask you to please step away from the cruiser?'

Willer said, 'If you've got a shield, mister, now's the time to show it.'

The man in the track suit spoke calmly. 'I am Mr Masago with the National Security Agency of the US government. This area has been declared a special operations zone, closed under a state of military emergency. These men are part of a combined Delta Force commando team here on a mission involving national security. Now, final warning: step away from the vehicle.'

'Until I see—'

The next thing Willer knew, he was on the ground, doubled up, desperately trying to suck some air into his lungs, while one of the soldiers deftly relieved him of his service weapon. Hernandez stood there, dumbfounded.

Willer watched in disbelief as the other soldier went into his cruiser—*his cruiser*—with a screwdriver. He emerged a moment later with the radio in one hand, wires dangling. In the other he had the cruiser's keys.

'Surrender your portable radio, Officer,' said Masago.

Willer sucked in another lungful of air, handed over the radio.

'Surrender your nightstick, cuffs, pepper spray, and all other weapons and communication devices. As well as any other keys to the vehicle.'

Willer obeyed. He could see Hernandez being put through the same drill.

'Now we will walk up to the church, and you will tell me all about why you're here and who this fugitive is.'

THE SUN HAD RISEN hours ago and the hidden valley had turned into an inferno of boulders reradiating the pounding heat of the sun. Ford sat down on a rock, unshouldered his canteen and took a sip. He screwed the top back on and hefted the canteen, estimating that less than a litre remained.

His feelings of being close to discovering the fossil had faded in the harsh reality of the landscape. Three big canyons and many smaller ones came together in an absolute chaos of stone—a dead land gutted by erosion, ripped by flash floods, scarred by avalanches. On top of that, Ford had seen no sign of any fossils at all—not even bits and pieces of petrified wood, so common elsewhere in the high mesas. It was truly a lifeless landscape.

He checked his watch: 10.30. He had searched about half the valley, and still had at least another day's work. But he would have to set off for the river no later than dawn the next day if he didn't want to die of thirst.

He slung the canteen over his shoulder and trudged on across the sandy flat. His legs ached, his feet were blistered, his eyes were red from the dust, and his stomach had that hollow feeling of a hunger beyond mere hungriness. A broken leg, even a sprained ankle, would be a death sentence with so little water. But Ford had taken far worse risks in his life.

He hiked on. The dry wash turned in a tight curve against a wall of sandstone, forming an undercut some fifteen feet high, creating a half-moon of shade. Ford rested for a moment, fighting the impulse to drink again. Up the canyon he could see where part of the cliff face had collapsed into a gigantic rockslide, a 500-foot pile of car-sized boulders.

In that pile of boulders he saw something. The smooth face of one of the boulders was turned at just the right angle to receive the raking light of the sun. And there, outlined with perfect clarity, was an exquisite set of dinosaur footprints—a large, three-toed dinosaur with massive claws, which had evidently crossed what had once been an ancient mud flat. Ford slung his canteen back over his shoulder and walked to the base of the slide, feeling an electric surge of energy, all his weariness evaporating.

He climbed up the heap of fallen rocks to examine the footprints more closely. The rock had cleaved along the bedding plane, exposing a ripple-marked surface of mudstone, almost black in colour, compared to the brick-red of the layers above and below. If these were *T. rex* footprints—and they certainly looked like them—that dark layer was like a marker indicating the layer around which the *T. rex* would probably be found.

As he climbed down to the canyon floor, he heard a buzzing noise. He looked up, squinting against the glare and saw a flash of sunlight off a small aircraft passing almost directly overhead. He pulled out his binoculars and searched the sky, finally locating it in the harsh glare.

Ford stared in surprise. It was a small, windowless white aircraft, about twenty five feet long, with a bulbous nose and a rear-mounted engine. He recognised it as an MQ-1A Predator Unmanned Aerial Vehicle, a drone that could operate independently when out of contact with its remote human pilot. This one was carrying a pair of Hellfire C laser-guided missiles.

He tracked it with his binoculars, wondering what the heck the CIA would be doing flying a highly classified piece of aviation over public land. He watched it pass by, flying west. Then, perhaps five kilometres from his position, it banked in a lazy turn and came back round towards him. It was losing altitude and gaining speed—fast. What in the world was it doing? He continued watching it through the binoculars, spellbound. It appeared to be engaged in a simulated attack.

There was a faint puff and the Predator seemed to take a small leap upwards—it had just launched a missile. This was unbelievable; what could possibly be the target?

A split second later, he realised that the target was himself.

MADDOX CLIMBED over the last ridge and surveyed the canyon below. Here, two canyons joined to become one larger canyon, creating a rock amphitheatre with a smooth floor of yellow sand. He was breathing hard and felt light-headed—from the heat and from thirst. But he knew that Broadbent and the bitch had to be suffering at least as much as he was.

His eyes traced the deep cleft of the central canyon, the one the Broadbents would be coming down. Then he cast around for a good position from which to kill them. The many boulders that had rolled down from the canyon rims gave him plenty of options, and he picked out a spot where a couple of giant stones had jammed up—directly opposite the central canyon. It was an ideal place for an ambush, but he needed an easy shot: he had two kills to make, and Broadbent was armed.

He picked his way down the ridge, slipping and sliding as he went, knowing that he had only ten minutes, at most, before they appeared.

He paused at the cluster of boulders and looked around. It was in the direct sun and hotter than hell, but it provided an ideal view of the opposite side. He unslung his .223 AR-15, gave it a quick check and moved into shooting position. He found a perfect firing notch between two boulders leaning together. As he rested the barrel in it, a deep rumble, not unlike thunder, rolled across the badlands, echoing strangely through the canyons.

Maddox looked up. Funny, he thought. There's not a cloud in the sky.

FORD LAY HUDDLED in the lee of the cliff, face down, arms wrapped round his head, as the deafening roar of the missile strike rolled away, reverberating down the canyons. A rain of sand and gravel continued as the echoes died away. He waited until all was silent, then raised his head.

He was inside a dull orange cloud. He coughed, covered his mouth with the hem of his robe and tried to breathe, still half stunned from the blast wave. The roar had been so powerful that it almost seemed as if the sound itself could have killed him. And yet here he was, alive and unhurt.

He stood up, steadying himself against the canyon wall, his head pounding and his ears ringing. He had taken refuge in the scooped-out undercut in the canyon wall, a lucky decision. Great shattered chunks of stone littered the ground all around him, but the overhang had protected him well. Slowly the dust began settling and he retreated back under the overhang, away from the penetrating eyes of the video cameras onboard the Predator drone.

When the sound of the drone had completely faded away, Ford staggered to his feet, slapping the dust from his robes, shaking it out of his hair and wiping his face. He was only now beginning to grasp what had just happened: a Predator drone had deliberately fired a missile at him. Why?

It had to be a mistake, a test gone awry. But even as the thought came into his mind, he discounted it. He knew that a classified drone would never be tested over public land, not in New Mexico, which had White Sands Missile Range, the nation's largest proving ground. Nor could the Predator have somehow escaped from WSMR and ended up there—it didn't have the range. The turn, dive and fire manoeuvre the drone had executed was beyond ICCG capability; a remote human pilot had been controlling it.

Was it a case of mistaken identity? Could they be hunting someone else? Ford supposed it was possible, but that would be a gross violation of the first rule of engagement: secure visual identification of the target. How could he, in his monk's robes and sandals, be taken for someone else? Was the CIA after him specifically for something he knew or had done? But it was inconceivable the CIA would murder one of its own, and even if they did want to kill him, they wouldn't send a 40-million-dollar classified drone after him when it would be much simpler to assassinate him in his cell in the monastery, and dress it up to look like the usual heart attack.

Something else was going on here, something truly strange.

Ford began walking down the canyon, his ears still ringing. What had just happened was still inconceivable, but he began to feel that the attack had something to do with the dinosaur fossil. He couldn't say why, but nothing else made sense. For some unfathomable reason, he mused, a government agency was so desperate to get their hands on that dinosaur fossil and leave no witnesses that they were willing to kill a US citizen. But how did they know he was out hunting the dinosaur? Only Tom Broadbent knew that.

During his CIA years, Ford had sometimes dealt with various classified subagencies, special task forces and 'black detachments'. The last of these were small, highly classified teams of specialists formed for specific investigative or research purposes, disbanded as soon as the particular problem had been solved. The Black Dets—as they were called in CIA lingo—were supposed to be under the control of the NSA, the DIA or the Pentagon, but in fact they were rogue agencies, accountable to no one, run by cowboy types who felt the end justified the means—whatever means and whatever end.

This situation fairly reeked of Black Det.

Chapter 10

Melodie watched the last group of guards leave the mineralogy lab. She closed the door after them, locked it and leaned against it, exhaling. It was almost one o'clock. The coroner had come, signed a bunch of papers; the body had been carried off; a bored cop had made a perfunctory walk-through. Everyone assumed it was a heart attack, and Melodie felt sure the postmortem would confirm it.

Only she suspected that it was murder. The killer was after the dinosaur, of that Melodie felt certain—why else would he have stolen all of their research, *her* research? She had to work fast.

She grabbed a heavy metal chair and carried it to the door, jamming it underneath the knob. If anyone asked why she had blocked the door, she could always say the death had spooked her. She would have plenty of time to work undisturbed.

Melodie hastened into the storage area contiguous with the lab. Here, tens of thousands of mineral and fossil specimens were arranged in drawers and on metal shelves rising from floor to ceiling, numbered and categorised. A railed library ladder on wheels allowed access to the highest shelves.

Her heart beating with anxiety, Melodie pushed the library ladder around until it was in the row she wanted. She climbed up. On the top shelf sat an old wooden crate with a faded label that read: '*Protoceratops andrewsii* egg clutch, Flaming Cliffs, Access No. 1923-5693A'.

The wooden lid looked nailed shut, but it wasn't. Melodie lifted it, laid it aside and pulled up a layer of straw matting.

Nestled among the eggs of a fossil dinosaur nest were the copies of the CD-ROMs that Melodie had burned, containing all her data and images. Next to it was a tiny plastic case containing three wafer-thin sections of the original specimen, too small to have been missed.

Leaving the CDs in place, Melodie removed the plastic specimen case, replaced the straw matting, refitted the lid, climbed down the ladder and rolled it back to where it had been before.

She carried the case over to the polisher, removed one sliver and fixed it to a polishing plug. When the epoxy had dried she began to polish it, aiming for a perfect, microthin section, enough to get some really good images out of the transmission electron microscope. When the specimen was ready she carried it into the TEM room to turn on the machine and let it warm up. As she did so, she noticed the logbook open next to it. The last entry, written in a bold, slanting hand, leapt out at her:

Researcher: *I. Corvus*
Specimen: *High Mesas/Chama River Wilderness, N.M. / T. rex.*
Comments: *Third examination of remarkable T. rex vertebral*
    fragment. Extraordinary! This will make history. I.C.

Third examination? She flipped back in the book and found two other entries, both written at the bottom of the page where Corvus had obviously found some blank lines. She went into the SEM room and flipped through the logbook there, finding a similar number of phoney entries. So that's what he'd been doing in the lab late last night: doctoring the logbooks. She had suspected something like this, but nothing quite so blatant.

She found herself breathing hard. There was only one way to ensure credit and protect herself from the killer at the same time: finish up her research and beat the murderer into print. If she submitted her results online to the *Journal of Vertebrate Paleontology,* they would be peer-reviewed and published electronically within three days.

Naturally she would give due credit to Corvus for supplying her with the specimen. Sure, there would be controversy. The specimen might have been obtained illegally. But that was not germane to her work; she'd been given a sample to analyse and that was what she had done. Once her research was in print, there'd no longer be any point in killing her.

The only loose end was the Venus particle. She was determined to tie that one up before submitting her paper for publication. Otherwise some other scientist would tie it up for her—and she was so close.

She selected the last of the prepared wafers, slipped it into a micro-mortar and carefully broke it up, gently grinding it with water to a fine slurry, which she poured into a plastic beaker.

She went to the locked cabinet and removed a bottle of twelve per cent hydrofluoric acid. It was unwise of her to handle such a dangerous chemical—one that would actually dissolve glass—after so much stress, but it was the only acid capable of dissolving the replacement mineral of the fossil without attacking the carbon coating of the Venus particles. She brought the bottle over to the fume hood, then put on splash goggles, nitrile gloves, a rubber apron and sleeve protectors. She lowered the fume hood to six inches to protect her face, turned it on and began work, pouring a small amount of HF into the plastic test tube containing the ground fossil.

She watched as it foamed and clouded, then diluted it fifty to one to stop the acidic reaction, poured off the excess, diluted it again to get rid of the acid, and was left with a thin layer of sediment at the bottom of the test tube.

With a micropipette she sucked up most of the sediments, dried them, then, using a sodium metatungstate solution, floated off the lighter sediments from the heavier grit. A further rinse, then she sucked up a small quantity of particles and let them drift over a gridded slide. A quick count at 100x revealed about thirty Venus particles, largely intact.

Time to take a look at this sucker in the round, she thought.

IN POSITION behind the boulders, Maddox shifted his weight and stretched out his foot, trying to get the stiffness out. His tongue felt coated with rust, his lips cracked. Christ he was thirsty. Twenty minutes had passed and the Broadbents hadn't showed. He took a look through the scope, sweeping it up and down the empty canyon. Had they found water? If so, they might have turned and headed north towards Llaves. If he had lost them—

And suddenly there they were.

Fitting his eye to the scope and resting his finger on the hot curve of the trigger, he forced himself to relax, waiting until they reached the range of 200 yards. He could see the butt of the gun in Broadbent's waistband. He wouldn't even have time to pull it out, let alone fire it.

In another minute, they were in position.

He squeezed the trigger, firing a protracted burst, full-auto. He looked up, and saw them both sprinting back up the canyon. Both of them.

What the hell—?

He'd missed. He returned to the scope, tracked the woman, fired another burst, another—but the bullets were kicking up sand ahead of them, each round high as his quarry ran zigzagging towards the canyon wall. They were going to escape round the lee of the canyon bend.

He rose with a roar of frustration. How could he have missed? He was exhausted, thirsty, injured—but still, how could he have missed? Then it hit him. Unaccustomed to shooting at such acutely high angles, he had over-compensated for the bullet's drop-off.

Still, he had a chance. The canyon had sheer walls—they were trapped. He could still kill them—if he could run them down.

Slinging his rifle over his shoulder, he charged down the slope and sprinted after them. In a minute he rounded the bend. He could see them 400 yards ahead, running, Broadbent helping his limping wife along.

He ran after them, not fast, but keeping to a sustainable pace. They began to falter and lag. One, two, three more bends he pursued them. By the time he rounded the third, Maddox had narrowed the gap to less than 200 yards.

He dropped to one knee, fired a burst. They threw themselves down, and when they scrambled back to their feet he'd closed to less than a 100 yards.

She fell and Broadbent helped her up. Forty yards now. He tried to encourage her, but she staggered again—and then they just gave up. Turned and faced him defiantly.

He aimed, thought better of it, walked closer. Twenty-five yards. Flicked off the auto, knelt, aimed, and fired.

Click!

Nothing. The full-auto bursts had emptied the magazine. With a roar, both of them were sprinting at him full bore. He fumbled for his pistol, but the woman was on him like a wildcat, grabbing at his pistol. They fell together, struggling, and then he got the gun and rolled on top of her, pressing it to her head, fumbling to get his finger through the trigger guard.

He felt a gun on the back of his own head.

'Count of three,' said Broadbent.

'I'll pop her! I will!'

'One.'

'I swear, I'll blow out her brains! I'll do it!'

'Two.'

Knowing he couldn't get off two shots, he whipped round, going for Broadbent first, and fired wildly but practically into his face, and the man went down. He aimed to follow up with another shot, but the bitch dealt him stunning kick to the groin, so hard that his hand spasmed and the pistol went off, and it felt as if something had jerked his leg hard, followed by a numbness—and a gush of crimson on the sand.

'My leg!' he shrieked, dropping the gun. The blood was jetting out of the wound, and so much of it. 'I'm bleeding to death!'

The woman stepped back, covering him with his own Glock.

'No! Wait! Please!'

She didn't fire. There was no need. The blood—geysering out of his severed femoral artery—inundated the leg of his jeans.

She shoved the gun in her belt and hastened to kneel over Broadbent. Maddox watched her, overwhelmed with relief that she hadn't killed him, but then he began to feel dizzy and the canyon walls started to move around. He tried to rise, but he was so weak that he sank back to the sand. A remoteness crept into his head, as if he had become smoke and was rising, expanding, dissipating into nothing.

And then he was nothing.

WYMAN FORD halted next to a rock pillar and listened. He had heard the shots distinctly, three bursts from an automatic weapon, possibly an M16, followed by two deeper-sounding shots from what was probably a large-calibre handgun. The sounds seemed to have come from the northeast.

He waited, listening for more reports, but after those few quick bursts of shooting all was quiet.

Something extraordinary was going on. If his CIA training had taught him anything, it was that the guy with the better information survived. Engagements were won with information. And that was what he lacked.

Ford hefted his canteen and took a small sip. He was down to about half a litre and he had no business doing anything but going straight for water. Still, the shots had been close, and it would be a matter of twenty minutes to hike to the head of the valley where they had come from. He turned back, determined to find out what was going on.

He headed northeast across an area of low sand dunes towards the mouth of a canyon. As he approached, he could see that the canyon walls on either side were stepped back as sandstone alternated with shale and volcanic tuff. Dead-end side canyons branched out, many containing clusters of bald domes of rock. It was a complicated and confusing country. Somewhere in this very area was the dinosaur fossil.

He shook his head. What a fool he was, still thinking about finding the dinosaur. He'd be lucky to get out of there alive.

TOM OPENED HIS EYES to find Sally bent over him, her blonde hair spilling over his face. She was dabbing his head with a torn piece of cloth.

'Sally? Are you all right?'

'I'm fine. You, on the other hand, got creased by a bullet.' She tried to smile but her voice was shaky. 'Knocked you out for a moment.'

'What about *him*?'

'Dead—I think.'

Tom relaxed for a second, then tried to raise himself up.

Sally eased him back down. 'I'm not finished. It's a crease, maybe a concussion, but it didn't crack the bone.' She finished tying a strip of blue silk round his head. 'A quarter of an inch to the right and . . . never mind.'

He reached out and took her hand.

'Help me up. My head seems to be clearing.'

She raised him into a sitting position, then helped him to his feet. He staggered but the dizziness cleared.

'You sure you're OK?' she asked.

'I'm a lot more worried about you than me.'

'I have an idea: you do my worrying, I'll do yours.'

Tom steadied himself, trying to ignore his thirst. His eye fell on the man in a puddle of blood—the scumbag who had kidnapped, then tried to rape and murder his wife. He lay on his back shirtless, arms by his side, almost as if he'd gone to sleep. Both legs stuck straight out, but the jeans covering his right leg sported a large hole and were soaked black with blood.

He knelt and felt the man's neck for a pulse and was shocked to find it.

'Is he dead?' Sally asked.

'No.'

'What do we do?'

Tom removed a knife from the man's belt, and slit up the leg of the jeans. The leg and groin were a mess and blood was still feebly pulsing out.

'Help me pull him into the shade against this rock.'

They propped him up. Tom cut a shirttail off and fashioned it into a tourniquet. He rummaged around in the man's pockets and extracted his wallet. He opened it, pulled out an Ohio driver's licence.

'Jimson A. Maddox,' he read aloud. He searched the wallet, pulling out a wad of cash, credit cards and receipts. A soiled business card stopped him:

IAIN CORVUS, D. PHIL. OXON. F.R.P.S.
Assistant Curator, Department of Vertebrate Paleontology
American Museum of Natural History

He passed it to Sally. 'That's the guy he was working for,' she said. 'The guy who got him out of prison.'

'I find it hard to believe that a scientist from a great museum like that would be involved in kidnapping, theft and murder.'

'When the stakes are high enough, some people will do anything.'

She handed the card back and Tom quickly searched the other pockets. He found the notebook, pulled it out, held it up.

'Well, well, what do you know,' said Sally.

Tom stuck it in his own pocket, along with the driver's licence and the business card. In a small bag buckled round the man's waist, he found an extra magazine for the handgun. He glanced around, saw the gun lying on the ground where Sally had dropped it. He picked it up, shoved it in his belt and buckled the bag round his own waist. 'Let's go,' he said.

'And him?'

'The only thing we can do for him now is get out of here and find help. If the truth be told, he's a goner.' Tom put his arm round her. 'You ready?'

Arm in arm, leaning on each other, they set off limping down the wash. For ten minutes they walked in silence, and then Tom halted in surprise.

A robed figure was striding up the wash towards them, hand raised. It was the monk—Wyman Ford.

'Tom!' the figure called, breaking into a jog. 'Tom!' He was gesturing frantically, now running towards them. At the same time Tom heard a faint droning noise and saw a small, windowless plane with a bulbous nose come flying over the rim of the canyon, making a slow turn towards them.

J. G. MASAGO STOOD in the whitewashed computer room of the monastery, now serving as the ground control station for the Predator. His eyes were fixed on a flat-panel video screen displaying the feed from the Predator's main camera. The wooden monastery table was covered with an array of advanced electronics, manned by three operators. The central operator was wearing a UAV FlightSim helmet. The console he worked displayed the basic controls a normal aircraft would have: yoke, throttle, air-speed indicator, heading and altimeter, along with an F16-style joystick.

Masago's eyes flickered away from the screen for a moment to the two CAG/DEVGRU support operators: one worked the payload console, which controlled the reconnaissance capabilities of the Predator; the second operator worked the UAV's three targeting systems. The Predator had already expended one of its two Hellfire C missiles killing the monk.

Masago's attention drifted back to the video display. He stiffened.

'Got something,' one of the operators murmured in Masago's headset.

Masago could see two people being approached by a third, approximately a hundred yards away. A quarter of a mile up the canyon, a figure lay supine.

'Zoom in to 900mm on the southernmost target,' said Masago.

The new image jumped on the screen. A man, lying against the canyon wall. A large stain—blood. A dead man. He'd known of the monk and these two from his debriefing of the cop, Willer. But the dead man was an unknown.

'Back out to 240mm,' he instructed.

Now he could see the three figures again. The one to the north had broken into a run. Masago stared in surprise. It was the CIA meddler.

'Looks like we missed the monk,' murmured the targeting controller.

Masago stared at the picture. 'Give me a closer look at the middle target.'

The camera jumped and the figure of a man filled the screen—Broadbent. He was the man who had found the dying dinosaur prospector, so he was the one most likely to know the location of the fossil. How the others were involved wasn't clear. Nor did it need to be. Masago's goal was simple: obtain the locality of the fossil, get the fossil and get out.

'Activating moving target indicator,' said the controller.

'No,' murmured Masago. 'I need these targets alive.' He scanned the canyon. It was 800 feet deep with stepped-back walls, narrowing at a bottleneck before opening up to the big valley of stone. 'See that point where the canyon narrows? About two o'clock on your screen.'

'Yes, sir.'

'I want you to hit that canyon wall in such a way to bring down enough material to block their route forward. We've got a chance to trap them.'

'Yes, sir.'

'Heading one-eighty, descend to two thousand,' said the pilot.

'Tracking stationary target. Ready to fire.'

'Hold until my signal,' Masago murmured into his head set. 'Wait.'

He watched the figures as they cleared a bend in the canyon and reached a straight stretch. They were running, faltering, clearly exhausted. The woman fell, and was helped up by the two men. They were now 400 yards from the target . . . 350 yards . . . 325. . .

'*Fire.*'

TOM RAN just behind Sally, the roar of the explosion still ringing in his ears, dust from the explosion boiling down the canyon towards them. They rested for a moment, waiting for Ford to join them.

'What the *hell* is going on?' Tom gasped. 'What was that firing at us?'

'A forty million dollar drone. It's still up there, watching us.' The monk shook his head. 'I think it fired only to block the canyon. They want to trap us.'

'Who's *they*?'

'Later, Tom. We've got to get out of here.'

Tom squinted up and down the canyon, examining the walls. His eye was arrested by a broad, sloping crevasse offering plenty of handholds. 'There,' he said. 'We can climb that crack. There's a good climbing line up the right-hand side to that ledge.' He turned to Sally. 'Can you do it?'

'Yeah.'

'You, Wyman?'

'No problem. You lead the way.'

Tom looked down at his $400 handmade Italian shoes, battered beyond recognition but still holding up. At least these ones had rubber soles. As he looked back up, the tail end of dust from the explosion came rolling lazily over them, casting a sulphurous-coloured pall across the sky.

'Let's go.' He grabbed the first handhold and hoisted himself up. 'Watch where I put my hands and feet and use the same holds. Maintain a ten-foot gap. Sally, you come next.'

Tom braced his knee against the stone and worked his way up. Heat radiated off the canyon wall. He tried to ignore the fact that his mouth felt like it was full of grit. Thirst had become physical pain.

It was hard climbing, but there were plenty of handholds. Tom checked every minute to see how Sally was doing. She was athletic and got the hang of it quickly. Ford climbed fearlessly, like a monkey—a true natural. As they ascended, space yawned below, vast and terrifying. It was what climbers euphemistically called a 'no-fall pitch'—you fall, you die.

Tom focused his eyes on the rock face in front of him. When they were 200 feet up the pitches began to get easier. In another five minutes they had scaled the sheer part of the cliff. The rest of the climb consisted of an exhausting scramble up steep scree. At the top, Sally stretched herself out on the flat stone, gasping, Tom next to her. He looked up at the empty sky, which was silent, the plane apparently gone.

Ford slipped a tattered map from his pocket and opened it.

'Where are we?' Tom asked.

'Just off the map.' Ford folded it back up.

Tom looked up, examining the landscape ahead. The mesa top was slick-rock, a plateau of naked sandstone hollowed and carved by the action of wind and water. Here and there a wind-blasted juniper clung to a crack. The mesa ended a quarter of a mile away in blue sky.

Tom squinted, peering ahead. 'I'd like to see what's beyond that rim. We're sitting ducks up here.'

'We're sitting ducks everywhere, with that eye in the sky,' said Ford.

'They're still watching us?' Sally asked.

'You can be sure of it. And I have little doubt they're sending a helicopter after us. I'd say we've got ten to twenty minutes.'

'This is truly insane. You've really no idea what's going on?'

Ford shook his head. 'The only thing I can think of is that it's something to do with the dinosaur.'

'What interest could they possibly have in a dinosaur? It seems to me a lot more likely that a classified satellite crashed—something like that.'

Ford shook his head. 'Somehow, I don't think so.'

'But even if it was the dinosaur, why come after us?' Tom asked.

'To get information. You've got the notebook and I've got the GPR plot. With either of those, they could find it in a few days.'

'And when they get what they want from us?'

'They'll kill us.'

'You don't really believe that.'

'I don't believe it, Tom. I know it. They already tried to kill me.'

Ford climbed to his feet, Tom painfully following suit and helping Sally up. The monk set off across the stone plateau at his usual breakneck pace, his brown robes sweeping the ground with each step, heading towards the rim on the far side.

THE ROTORS were already spinning up as Masago hopped into the chopper, threaded past the seven members of the CAG/DEVGRU chalk that made up the operation and took a rear-facing seat near the front. The sun was over-head as the bird lifted off and skimmed above the red-hot buttes and mesas.

On the floor of the chopper, Masago unrolled a 1:24,000 topographical map of the target area. When he had finished marking up the map with a red pencil, he passed it to the chalk leader, Sergeant First Class Anton Hitt.

Hitt examined the map in silence and began punching the way points marked on the map into his GPS unit. The men had received their final patrol order just before liftoff without comment, even when Masago briefed them on the possible need to kill American civilians. Of course, he'd laid it on about how they were bioterrorists in possession of a doomsday microbe.

He watched Hitt work. The chalk leader was an African-American man of few words, in superb physical condition, with a high mahogany brow, clear pale brown eyes and a demeanour of great calmness. He was dressed in desert multi-cam fatigues and combat boots, carrying an M4 with Aimpoint electronic sights. As a sidearm he had a .22 Magnum revolver, an eccentric choice for a special forces soldier, but one that Masago approved of. Masago had allowed Hitt to make the decisions regarding equipment: and the sergeant had decided his men should go in light and fast, carrying no extra ammo, one-litre canteens only, no grenades, and without the usual Kevlar body armour. No squad automatic weapons, either.

When Hitt was finished, he passed the paper map back to Masago.

'The four men we're dropping in won't need to maintain radio silence. We're setting up a perimeter round our objectives and drawing it tight.'

Masago nodded, pausing for a second. 'Sergeant Hitt,' he asked slowly, 'the time is coming when I will ask you to kill several unarmed American citizens. These individuals are too dangerous to entrust to the courts. Will you have a problem with that?'

Hitt turned his clear eyes on Masago. 'I'm a soldier, sir. I follow orders.'

Masago nodded and settled back, arms crossed. General Miller had been right after all: Hitt was good.

Chapter 11

Ford reached the rim first, and looked down into a valley. With a shock, he recognised that they had circled back round. It amazed him that this landscape was so complex it had confused a man of his wilderness experience and knowledge of the desert. He took out his map, checked it and saw that they had just entered the area from the northwest.

He glanced around, expecting at any minute to see a black dot on the horizon and hear the familiar sound of a rotary aircraft approaching.

He had been in plenty of tough situations in his life, but nothing quite like this. What he always had before was *information*; now he was operating blind. He knew only that his own government had tried to kill him.

Ford paused, waiting for Tom and Sally to catch up. They were amazingly resilient considering that both of them were injured and severely dehydrated. He squinted into the brilliant light. The mountains were fifteen miles away on one side, the river twenty miles on the other. They had less than a third of a litre of water left and it was over a hundred degrees.

Ford looked at the cliff with a growing feeling of dismay.

'Here's a possible way down,' said Tom, from the edge.

Ford paused, looking down on a horrendous vertical crack. A faint throbbing sound impinged on the threshold of his hearing. He stopped, scanned the horizon and saw the speck, two, maybe three miles away. He didn't even need to check with his binocs: he knew what it was.

'Let's go.'

MELODIE CROOKSHANK stared at the three-dimensional SEM image of the Venus particle on the video screen with a sense of awe. It was 65 million years old, yet it looked as if it had been created yesterday—a perfect sphere with a tube sticking out of it, with two crosspieces at the end of the tube like spars on a ship. The crosspieces had bunches of tubules at their end that resembled a dandelion seed-head.

An X-ray diffraction analysis confirmed what she'd suspected, that the sphere of carbon was what chemists call a fullerene or a 'buckyball'—a hollow shell of double-bonded carbon atoms arranged like a Buckminster

Fuller geodesic dome. The primary feature of a buckyball was that it was almost indestructible: only the most powerful enzymes carefully manipulated in a laboratory setting could split open a buckyball.

Which is exactly what Melodie had done.

She cracked a warm Dr Pepper and leaned back, sipping meditatively. After the removal of Corvus's body it had been quiet as a tomb, even for a Sunday. People were staying away. It reminded her once again of how few friends she had in the museum. Nobody had called to check and see how she was or to cheer her up. It was partly her fault, holing herself up in the basement lab like a sequestered nun. But a lot of it had to do with her lowly status and the whiff of failure that clung to her.

All that was about to change.

She called up some of the earlier images of the particle she had captured on CD-ROM, looking for more evidence to support a theory that had been developing in her mind. As she examined some of the images she had taken earlier for Corvus, she noticed something significant: many of the cells in which the particles appeared were elongated. Not only that, but many of the particles seemed to inhabit pairs of cells side by side. The two observations were directly related, and Melodie quickly put them together. She felt a prickling sensation at the base of her neck. The Venus particles had infected the dinosaur's cells and were actually *triggering* cell division. Many modern viruses did the same thing; that was how they eventually killed their host—with viral-induced cancer.

Various palaeontologists had proposed that the mass extinction of the dinosaurs had been caused by a Black Plague-like epidemic. As species intermixed as the result of the joining of Asia with North America, they spread new germs. But as the asteroid-impact theory of the mass extinction had gained acceptance, the plague hypothesis was gradually forgotten.

Now, it seemed it was right after all. In a way.

The dinosaurs *had* been killed off by a plague. But it wasn't caused by the joining of continents; it was triggered by the impact itself. The asteroid strike had caused worldwide forest fires, darkness, starvation, catastrophic loss of habitats—the landscape would have been littered with dead and dying animals, the rest starving, burned, injured, their immune systems in collapse. Under those conditions, a devastating epidemic wouldn't just be possible . . . it would be *inevitable*. The asteroid killed off most of the dinosaurs; and the plagues that followed killed the rest.

There was another twist to Melodie's theory. She was still undecided if this twist was too crazy to put in her paper. It was this: the Venus particle did not look like a terrestrial form of life. It looked, well, *alien*.

Maybe, just maybe, the Venus particle had arrived *with* the asteroid.

MASAGO HOPPED OUT of the chopper, and looked around the badlands as he cleared the landing area. The Predator drone indicated that the targets had descended from the rim of the plateau above them into this unnamed valley. Four of the men had already been dropped, at the only four exit points of the canyon. The chopper had landed in the middle of the valley, in the centre point towards which these four men would draw.

Hitt came up beside Masago, followed by Privates Gowicki and Hirsch. The terrain was difficult, but their targets were trapped in the valley, cut off by cliffs. The four men on the perimeter were tightening the noose. Now all that remained was for Hitt and his two men to go in and flush them out. There was no chance—none—that they could escape.

The chalk leader led his men up the wash until it broadened out and divided. Here they paused while Hitt climbed a butte and reconnoitred. A few minutes later he came down with a shake of his head. They continued, spreading out as the wash levelled, then entering the shady confines of a curious forest of mushroomlike standing stones.

They came to where several enormous rocks leaned together, necessitating a crawl through a gap underneath. Hitt waited while Masago caught up. He pointed to some fresh prints in the hard sand. They had come through here, and not long ago at all. Masago nodded.

Hitt went first, dropping to his hands and knees. Masago went last. As he rose, he saw flaming cliffs mounting like staircases on all sides. Their quarry seemed to have walked into a box canyon, a dead end.

Masago murmured into his headset: 'I want them alive until I get the information I need.'

'WAIT HERE,' Ford said. 'I'm going up there to take a look.'

Tom and Sally rested while Ford scrabbled up a boulder and reconnoitred. They were in the middle of badlands, with hoodoo rocks all around. They had seen the helicopter land less than a mile away in the middle of the valley, and Ford felt sure that their trail had been picked up. He also knew, from his CIA training, that they must have dropped men at potential exit points, who would be moving in to cut them off. Their only chance was to find an unexpected route out of the canyon—or a hiding place. He glanced down at Sally and Tom. He didn't think they would be able to continue much longer. They had to find a place to go to ground.

He climbed down.

'See anything?' Tom asked.

Ford shook his head, not wanting to get into it. 'Let's keep going.'

They continued up the wash and into the forest of standing rocks. An oppressive heat had collected in the enclosed space. They drove as deeply as they could into the mass of rocks, sometimes crawling on hands and knees.

Suddenly they came out against the face of a cliff, which curved back on both sides, forming a kind of coliseum. At the far end, about fifty feet above the canyon bottom, a long-gone watercourse had hollowed out a cave. Ford could see a faint series of dimples in the rock, where ancient Anasazi Indians had pecked out a hand-and-toe trail up into the cave.

'Let's check that out,' Ford said.

They walked to the base of the cliff, and Tom examined the ancient trail.

'They'll find us in there, Wyman,' he said.

'There's no other option. The cave may go somewhere. And it's *possible* they may miss us, if we erase our footprints down here.'

Tom turned to Sally. 'What do you think?'

'I'm beyond thinking.'

'Let's do it.'

It was not a difficult climb, and in a few minutes they were in the cave. Ford paused, breathing hard. He was getting towards the end of his own endurance, and he wondered how Sally and Tom could even walk. For better or worse, this cave was the end of the road.

The cave was shaped like a soaring cathedral dome, with a floor of smooth sand. An enormous boulder sat at the far end of the cave, apparently having fallen from the ceiling aeons ago, worn and rounded off by the action of water coming through a web of crevasses in the roof.

As they walked deeper into the cave, they disturbed a colony of canyon swallows, which flitted about in the shadows, making shrill cries.

'The cave may continue behind that large rock,' said Ford.

They walked towards the back of the cave.

'Look,' said Tom. 'Footprints.'

The sand had been carefully brushed, but in the gap between the huge rock and the side of the cave they could see marks from a chevron-lugged hiking boot. They squeezed through the gap into the back part of the cave.

Ford turned and there it was, the great *T. rex*, its jaws and forelimb emerging from the rock.

No one spoke. It was an extraordinary sight. The beast looked as if it were engaged in a fierce struggle to tear itself free from the tomb of stone. It lay on its side, but the tilt of the fallen rock had set it almost upright, giving it a grotesque illusion of life.

In silence, they approached the base of the rock. Scattered on the sand lay a few pieces that had weathered from the fossil—including one long, black, scimitar-shaped tooth. Tom picked it up, ran his thumb along the viciously serrated inner edge. He gave a low whistle and handed it to Ford.

'Incredible,' murmured the monk.

'Look at this,' said Tom, pointing to some ancient figurines partly buried in the sand. He knelt down and brushed away the sand, uncovering more figurines below and a small pot filled with arrowheads.

'Offerings,' said Ford. 'That explains the Indian trail up here. They were *worshipping* the monster. And no wonder.'

'What's that?' Tom pointed to a rim of metal that poked from the sand.

He swept the sand aside to reveal a burnt tin can. Inside was a Ziploc bag enclosing a bundle of sealed envelopes addressed to 'Robbie Weathers'. The first one had written on it: *For my daughter Robbie. The T. rex is all yours. Love, Daddy.* Without a word, Tom put the letters back in the can.

Sally, standing nearer the front of the cave, suddenly hissed. 'Voices!'

Ford started, as if coming out of a dream. The reality of their situation came back in a rush. 'Let's see how far back the cave goes.'

Tom shone his feeble flashlight into the back of the cave. They all stared in silence. The cave ended in a narrow, water-worn crack, far too narrow to admit a person. He directed the beam up, around, back and forth.

'We've walked into a dead end,' Ford said quietly.

'So that's it?' said Sally. 'What do we do now? Give up?'

Ford did not answer. He moved swiftly to the mouth of the cave, flattened himself against the wall and peered down. 'They're in the canyon below, three soldiers and a civilian.'

Tom joined him and looked down into the small amphitheatre. Two men with assault rifles were examining the ground where they had brushed out their tracks. A third appeared, then a fourth. One pointed up to the cave.

'That's it,' said Ford quietly.

'Bullshit.' Tom pulled the handgun out of the bag at his waist.

'You take a pot shot at those D-boys and you're looking at instant suicide.'

'I'm not going down without a fight.'

'Neither am I.' Ford paused, his craggy face deep in thought. As if absentmindedly he removed the dinosaur tooth from his pocket, hefted it. Then he slipped it back in. 'Tom, do you have the notebook?'

Tom pulled it out.

'Give it to me. And the gun.'

'What are you—?'

'No time to explain.'

MASAGO WATCHED from below as Hitt and the two other D-boys edged up the steep sandstone slope and flattened themselves just below the lip of the cave, spreading out to cover the occupants within from three angles.

'*You in the cave,*' Hitt called out. '*You're outgunned and outnumbered. We're coming in. Don't move, and keep your hands in sight.*'

Hitt rose, exposing himself to the unseen targets inside. The other two remained covering him. '*Hands above your heads. Nobody's going to get hurt.*' He gestured to the other two D-boys, who rose from their cover.

It was over. The three targets were standing in the open central area of the cave, hands raised.

Hitt walked over and patted them down, ensuring they weren't armed. He spoke into his comm. 'Sir, we've secured the cave. You may come up now.'

Masago seized the first handhold, hefted himself up and in a few minutes stood in the mouth of the cave, looking at the three sorriest bastards he'd seen in a long time: the monk, Broadbent and his wife.

'Search them again,' he said. 'I want to see everything they have on their persons. Everything. Lay it out on the sand here in front of me.'

Hitt nodded to one of his boys, who began searching the bedraggled group. Out appeared a flashlight, wallets, keys, a driver's licence, an empty canteen, matches, a few empty tin cans and other camping gear.

The last thing to come out had been hidden in the monk's robes.

'What the hell's this?' the D-boy asked, holding it up.

Without changing expression, Masago said, 'Bring it to me.'

The boy handed it to him. Masago gazed down at the serrated tooth, flipped it over, hefted it.

'You.' He pointed to the monk. 'You must be Ford.'

The monk gave an almost imperceptible nod.

He held up the great tooth. 'So you found it. You know where it is.'

'That's correct,' said the monk.

'You will tell me where it is.'

'I'm the only one who has the information you want. And I'm not talking until you answer my questions first.'

Masago unholstered his Beretta, pointed the gun at Ford.

Ford said. 'Kill me and you'll never find the dinosaur. Never.'

Masago smiled thinly. 'All right then—you get one question.'

'Why do you want the dinosaur?'

'It contains highly dangerous infectious particles, which could be transformed into a bioterror weapon.' He would say nothing more—nothing that would contradict the patrol order that had been distributed to the men.

'The name of your detachment?'

'That's two.'

'You can go to hell, then,' said the monk.

Masago made a quick step forward and sank his fist in the monk's solar plexus; the man went down in the sand like a sack of cement.

'The dinosaur, Mr Ford: where is it?'

Ford was coughing, sinking into the sand. 'Water . . . please . . .'

Masago unhooked his canteen and shook it. 'When I hear the location of the dinosaur.' He unscrewed the cap and bent down towards the monk.

The monk exploded like a striking snake. His hand came out of the sand—unexpectedly holding a gun. Before Masago could react, Ford's left arm had locked round his throat. Masago felt the gun barrel jammed in his ear, his arms pinned back, unable to reach his Beretta.

'Now,' said Ford, using Masago as a shield as he spoke to the soldiers, 'this man's going to tell all of us what's really going on—or he's dead.'

MELODIE CROOKSHANK finished editing the short article she had written in a burst of furious activity. She was running on empty—sixty hours with no sleep—but she still felt buoyed up. This was going to be one of the most significant papers in the history of vertebrate palaeontology. There would be naysayers and there might even be accusations of fraud—but the data was good. What's more, she still had one raw slice of the specimen that she intended to offer to the Smithsonian for independent examination.

She was done—or almost done. Her finger was poised over the ENTER button, ready to email the article to the *Journal of Vertebrate Paleontology*.

A knock came at the door and she jumped, turned. The chair was still up against the knob. 'Who is it?'

'Maintenance.'

She sighed, walked over to the door, and unhooked the chair. She was about to open the door when she paused. 'Frankie?'

'Who else?'

She unlocked the door, noting with relief the ninety-eight-pound Frankie she knew so well, a sack of unshaven bones stinking of bad cigars and worse whiskey. He shuffled in and she locked the door behind him. He began going around the lab, emptying wastebaskets into a huge plastic bag, whistling tunelessly. He ducked under her desk, grabbed the overflowing wastebasket, bumped his head as he pulled it out, dropping an empty Dr Pepper can on the desktop, splattering the stereozoom scope.

'Sorry about that.'

'No problem.' She waited impatiently for him to finish, wondering briefly how it was that some human beings could invent the calculus while others couldn't even empty trash. 'Thank you, Frankie.'

'See you.' Frankie left, slapping the bag on the door as he went out.

With a sigh, Melodie examined the stereozoom. Droplets of Dr Pepper had sprayed the side of the scope, and some had landed on the wet slide. She glanced through the oculars to make sure no damage had taken place.

The slide was fine. The Dr Pepper would make no difference—a few sugar molecules could hardly damage a particle that had survived a 65-million-year burial and a twelve per cent hydrofluoric acid bath.

Suddenly she paused. If her eyes weren't playing tricks on her, one of the crosspieces on the arm of a particle had suddenly moved.

She waited, staring at the magnified particles, a crawling sensation at the nape of her neck. As she watched, another arm of a particle moved, and the particle propelled itself forward like a little machine. She watched, fascinated and alarmed, as the others began to move in the same fashion, towards where the Dr Pepper was most highly concentrated on the slide.

The particles were still alive.

It must have been the addition of sugar to the solution.

Melodie felt the prickle of apprehension grow. She hadn't even considered that they might still be alive and infectious.

In the herpetology lab down the hall, one of the curators had been breeding parthenogenetic lizards as part of an experiment. The lab contained an incubator of *in vitro* cell cultures, which would make an excellent testing bed for whether the particle would infect a modern-day lizard.

She exited the lab. The hall was empty—after five o'clock on a Sunday she would be most unlikely to meet anyone. The herp lab was locked but her card key worked, and it was a matter of five minutes to obtain a petri dish full of growing lizard cells, and transfer them onto the slide.

Then she put her eyes to the oculars.

The Venus particles stopped moving towards the higher concentration of sugar. They turned in unison and headed for the lizard cells. In a moment they clustered round the group of cells, attaching themselves to the cell membranes by their long appendages; then, with a swift cutting motion, each one entered a cell, triggering an orgy of cell division.

It wasn't long before Melodie realised that these cells were not dividing like normal cells in a culture, nor even like a cancerous growth of undifferentiated malignant cells. No—these cells were *differentiating*.

Three hours later, the group of cells had begun to take on the characteristics of a blastocyst, the ball of cells that form from a fertilised embryo.

Melodie, at the limit of exhaustion, raised her head. What the hell was she doing? These particles need to be studied under biosafety conditions, not in an open lab like hers. She had no idea what they were, how they worked. They were an alien life form that had hitched a ride to Earth on the Chicxulub asteroid. This was over her head—way over her head.

Melodie began to consider what she had to do. She cast around and her eyes lit on a bottle of eighty per cent hydrochloric acid. She unlocked the cabinet, took down the bottle and poured a few ounces of it into a shallow glass tray under the fume hood. With infinite care she slipped the slide into the hydrochloric acid. There was a hissing noise as the acid instantly destroyed the hideous growing blob of cells until nothing was left.

She breathed a sigh of relief. That was the first step, to destroy the organism growing on the slide. Now to destroy the Venus particles themselves.

She added a strong base to the acid, neutralising it and causing the precipitation of a layer of salt at the bottom of the dish. Setting up a Bunsen burner under the hood, she put the glass dish on the burner and began boiling away the solution. In a few minutes all the liquid had evaporated, leaving behind a crust of salt. She now turned up the burner as high as it would go. Five minutes passed, then ten minutes, and the salt began to crust up, glowing red-hot as the temperature approached the melting point of glass. No form of carbon, not even a buckyball, could survive that kind of heat.

She still had one more thing to do, and that was to finish the article, adding what she had just discovered. She spent ten minutes writing up two final paragraphs, describing what she had just observed.

Melodie silently criticised her own lack of caution. Whatever the particles were, she now believed they might be very dangerous. She felt a chill, wondering if she was infected. But that was impossible—the particles were too big to become airborne and besides, apart from those she had painstakingly freed from the rock, the rest were securely encased in stone.

She attached the article to an email and readied it for sending.

She hit ENTER then leaned back in her chair with a great sigh, feeling suddenly drained. With that keystroke her life was changed. For ever.

Chapter 12

Ford manhandled the man in the track suit back into an angle of the rock, where he was covered from the back and sides. The sergeant made a motion with his hand and the other two soldiers began moving to either side of him, weapons trained on Ford.

'Stop moving, all of you, and lower your weapons.'

The leader motioned them to halt.

'Like I said, this man's going to tell all of us what's going on or I'm going to kill him. Understand? You wouldn't want to report back to base with your handler in a body bag, would you?'

'You'll be in a body bag next to his,' said Hitt.

'I'm doing this for you, Sergeant. You need to know what's going on.'

Silence.

Ford pressed the gun to Masago's head. 'Talk.'

'Release him or I'll open fire,' Hitt said quietly.

'Wait,' said Tom. 'We're American citizens. We've done nothing wrong. Is this why you went into the military—to kill American civilians? Don't blindly follow orders. At least wait until you know what's going on.'

The sergeant hesitated. The two other soldiers were looking to him. Hitt lowered his weapon.

'You lied to these men, didn't you?' Ford said quietly to Masago.

'No.' He was already sweating.

'You did. And now you're going to tell them the truth, or I'll kill you. A bullet to the brain and then I'll take what's coming to me.'

Ford meant it and that was key. The man knew it.

'OK. First question. Who do you work for?'

'I'm director of Detachment LS480, established in 1973 after the Apollo 17 mission. Its purpose was to study a lunar sample known as LS480.'

'Go on.'

Masago swallowed. 'It was a piece of ejecta from a crater known as Van Serg. The rock contained fragments of the meteorite that formed the crater. In those contaminants were particles, microbes that appeared to be an alien form of life. Biologically active. They could be weaponised.'

'And the connection to the dinosaur?'

'The same particles were found in the dinosaur fossil. The dinosaur died of an infection caused by the LS480 particle following the asteroid impact that caused the mass extinction of the dinosaurs.'

'Go on.'

'Van Serg crater was made by a fragment from that same asteroid. It appears that the asteroid itself was riddled with the LS480 particles.'

'What's the purpose of this op?'

'To clear the area, eliminate all knowledge of the dinosaur and recover the dinosaur for classified research.'

'When you say "clear the area and eliminate all knowledge of the dinosaur", you're talking about killing us—am I right?'

'This is an issue of the gravest national security. You were CIA. You understand.' He paused, fixing Ford with pinpoint eyes. 'Those LS480 particles caused the mass extinction of the dinosaurs. In the wrong hands, those same particles could cause a second mass extinction—of the human race.'

Ford released him.

Masago jumped away and backed up, breathing heavily, then unholstered his Beretta. He positioned himself slightly behind Hitt.

'Sergeant Hitt, eliminate these three people. I don't need their information. We'll get it another way.'

There was another long silence.

'You're not going to do this,' said Sally. 'Now you know it's murder.'

'I'm waiting for you to carry out my orders, soldier,' said Masago.

No one spoke. No one moved.

'You're relieved of command, Hitt. Private Gowicki, carry out my order. Eliminate these people.'

'No,' said Hitt.

Masago pointed his Beretta at Hitt's head. 'Gowicki? Carry out my order.'

Tom hit Masago's knees with a flying tackle, the gun going off harmlessly into the air. Masago spun, recovered, but with an adroit movement Hitt landed a blow to his solar plexus. Masago fell heavily, and lay doubled up, unable to make a sound.

Hitt kicked the gun away. 'Cuff him.'

Gowicki and the third soldier came forward and in a moment had secured Masago's arms behind his back in plastic cuffs.

'All right,' said Hitt to his soldiers. 'I'm taking charge of the op. And it seems to me these three people need some water.'

Gowicki unslung his canteen and passed it round. They all drank deeply.

'We've still got an op to finish.' said Hitt. 'Seems to me we're supposed to locate a dinosaur fossil. And you know where it is.' He faced Ford.

'What do you plan to do with us?'

'I'm taking you three back to White Sands. General Miller'll decide what to do with you—he's the real commanding officer around here, not this'—his voice trailed off and he cast a glance at Masago—'civilian.'

Ford nodded towards the great boulder that dominated the back of the cave. 'It's right behind there.'

'No shit?' He turned to Gowicki. 'Keep an eye on them while I confirm.'

Hitt vanished behind the boulder and came back a few moments later.

'Now that,' he said, 'is one *mean* mother.' He turned to his men. 'Far as I'm concerned, the first part of the op is accomplished. We've located the fossil. I'm calling in the rest of the chalk. We'll return to base, report to General Miller with these three individuals and await further orders.' He turned to Masago. 'You'll come quietly, sir, and make no disturbance.'

THE CHOPPER SQUATTED on the alkali flats like a giant black insect about to take flight. They approached in silence, Tom limping on his own, Sally being helped along by a soldier. Hitt came last with Masago in front of him. The man hadn't said a word. His face looked strangely blank.

The four other members of the chalk waited in the shade of a nearby rock, smoking cigarettes. Hitt motioned them towards the chopper and they rose, tossing away their butts. Tom followed them into the chopper and the sergeant gestured for them to sit on benches along the wall.

A soldier slid the cargo door shut and the chopper rose out of the steep-walled valley and skimmed southwestwards over the mesa tops. The sun was a large drop of blood on the horizon, and, as the chopper gained altitude, Tom could see Navajo Rim and the Mesa of the Ancients beyond.

The chopper made a lazy turn to the southeast, and Tom saw a sudden movement out of the corner of his eye. Masago had jumped up and was running for the cockpit. Tom hurled himself at him, but the man twisted free. Masago pulled a knife from his trouser-leg sheath with his cuffed hands and bounded through the open cockpit door. The other men jumped from their seats to pursue him, but the chopper suddenly yawed, throwing them into the netting, while a gargling scream came from the cockpit.

'He's crashing the chopper!' Hitt cried.

The bird took a sickening downward lurch, and a deep shudder came from the rotors. Tom staggered to his feet, fighting against the deceleration as the chopper screamed and spiralled downwards. He caught a glimpse through the cockpit door of the copilot struggling with Masago—and the pilot lying dead on the floor awash with blood.

As the chopper pitched back, Tom used the motion to launch himself into the cockpit. He slammed into the flight console, righted himself on a seat, threw a punch at Masago, clipping his ear. As he staggered back, the copilot seized the man's cuffed wrists and slammed them down on the console, knocking the knife from his hands. The yawing chopper threw them both down and Tom managed to slam Masago's head against the floor.

'Take the controls!' Tom screamed at the copilot.

The man needed no encouragement. He scrambled to his feet and seized the controls. With a roar from the back rotors and a gut-wrenching deceleration, he righted the chopper. Masago was still thrashing wildly, but Tom and Hitt now had him pinned. Above the screaming engines, Tom could hear the copilot calling in an emergency while he fought with the controls.

Suddenly, through the windscreen, the face of a cliff came rushing past, followed by a bone-breaking jolt and a rapid series of *whangs* as pieces of rotor tore through the fuselage. The copilot was hammered to one side by the flying debris, his blood splattering against the shattered Plexiglas windscreen.

There was a weightless moment of free fall, and then a massive crash.

Silence.

Tom felt as though he were swimming out of darkness. and it took him a moment to remember where he was. He was jammed up in a corner of the chopper, debris piled over him. He could hear screaming as if coming in from a distance, smelt the stench of aviation fuel and burnt electronics. All motion had ceased. A huge gash had ripped open one side of the chopper, and through it he could see that they had come to rest on a steep slope. The helicopter groaned and shifted. Smoke filled the air.

Tom climbed over the debris and found Sally all tangled up with a heap of netting and plastic tarps. He pulled the netting aside.

She stirred, opened her eyes.

'I'm getting you out.' He grasped her round the shoulders and hauled her free, relieved to see she seemed to be only dazed.

'Tom!' came the voice of Wyman Ford.

He turned. Ford was crawling up the pile of debris, his face running with blood. 'Fire,' he gasped. 'We're on fire.' At the same time there was a whooshing sound and the tail section burst into flame.

Tom wrapped his arm round Sally and carried her towards the tear in the fuselage. He grasped the netting and struggled up, hooked an arm over the sill and hauled her up through the hole, and onto the top of the fuselage to the ground. He could see that the fire was spreading rapidly along the tail, crawling along fuel and electrical lines.

'Can you jump down?'

Sally nodded. He eased her down the side, and she dropped.

'Run!'

'What the hell are you doing staying there?' she screamed from below. 'It's going to blow—!'

But Tom had turned his attention back into the chopper, where Ford was trying to climb up the netting. One of his arms dangled uselessly.

Tom lay on his stomach, reached through the hole, grasped the man's good arm and hauled him up. Black smoke billowed out in a great wave just as he pulled Ford up on top of the fuselage, then slid him to the ground.

'Tom! Get off there!' Sally screamed, helping Ford away from the wreck.

'There's still Hitt!' Smoke was now pouring through the opening. Tom dropped down into the layer of air beneath it and crawled towards where he had last seen Hitt, keeping low. The unconscious sergeant lay on his side in the cockpit amid a shower of debris. He slid his arms around Hitt's torso and pulled, but the man was huge and Tom couldn't manage it.

There was a muffled thump as something burst into flame inside the fuselage. A wave of heat and smoke rolled over Tom, scorching his skin.

'Hitt!' He slapped the man across the face. The man's eyes rolled. He slapped him again, and the eyes came into focus. 'Get moving!'

Tom wrapped his arm round the man's neck and heaved him up. Hitt struggled to his knees. The smoke was now so thick that Tom could barely see.

'Climb, damn you!' he shouted.

Hitt started climbing, almost like a zombie. Tom followed alongside, dizziness filling his head. He was going to pass out; it was too late . . .

And then arms reached down, pulling him up and throwing him off the side of the chopper. He fell heavily in the sand, and a moment later Hitt landed heavily next to him, with a groan. Sally jumped down beside them—she had climbed back up on the chopper to haul them out.

They stumbled and crawled, trying to get as far away from the burning chopper as possible. Tom finally collapsed, gasping and coughing, able to go no further. Lying in the sand, he heard a dull thud and felt the sudden heat as the last of the chopper's tanks blew, engulfing the wreck in flame.

As Tom began to lose consciousness, he saw a man emerge from the fire, sheeted in flame, his arm raised with a gun in his burning fist. With strange deliberation he stopped, aimed, fired a single wild shot—and then the figure slowly toppled like a statue back into the burning inferno and was gone.

Tom opened his eyes. The sun lay in stripes across his bed, a monitor beeping softly somewhere in the background, a clock on the wall. Through a haze of pain, he managed to locate Sally sitting in a chair opposite.

'You're awake!' She jumped up, taking his hand. 'You're in the hospital.'

It all came rushing back: the pursuit in the canyons, the helicopter crash, the fire. 'Sally, how are you?'

'A lot better than you.'

Tom looked at his bandaged body. 'So what's wrong with me?'

'Nothing more than a nasty burn, a broken wrist, cracked ribs, concussion, bruised kidney and a seared lung. That's all.'

'And Ford? How's he?'

'He should be coming to see you at any moment. He had a broken arm and a few cuts, that's all. He's a tough bird. You were hurt worst.'

Tom grunted, his head pounding. As clarity returned, he noticed a heavy presence sitting in the corner. Detective Lieutenant Willer.

'What's he doing here?'

Willer touched his forehead in a greeting. 'Glad to see you awake, Broadbent. Don't worry, you're not in any trouble—although you should be. I just dropped in to see how you were getting along.'

'That's kind of you.'

'I figured you'd probably want to know what we found out about the killer of Marston Weathers, the same man who abducted your wife. In return, when you're ready, I'd like a complete debriefing from you.' He raised his eyebrows in query.

'Fair enough.'

'Good. The man's name was Jimson Maddox, a convicted murderer who appears to have been working for a fellow named Iain Corvus, a curator at the American Museum of Natural History in New York. Corvus himself died the same night Sally here was kidnapped, apparently of a heart attack. Given the timing, the FBI is looking into it.'

Tom nodded. 'So how did this Corvus know about the dinosaur?'

'He heard rumours that Weathers was on to something big, sent Maddox down to follow him. Maddox killed the guy and took a sample off him, which Corvus had analysed at the museum. Something just went up on the Web about it and there's been a hullabaloo like you've never seen before.'

'What's happening to the fossil?'

'The government's sealed off the high mesas and are taking it out. They're talking about building some kind of special lab to study it.'

'And Maddox? He's really dead?'

Willer nodded. 'We found his body where you left it.'

'What about the Predator drone, all that business?'

Willer eased back in his chair. 'We're still untangling that one. Looks like some kind of rogue government agency.'

'Ford will tell you about that when he comes,' said Sally.

As if on cue, a nurse came in and Tom could see Ford's craggy face behind her, one side of his jaw bandaged, his arm in a cast and sling.

'Tom! Glad to see you awake. You've been out for two whole days.' He came and leaned on the foot of the bed. 'How are you?'

'Been better.'

Ford cautiously settled his huge frame down in a cheap plastic hospital chair. 'I've been in touch with some of my old pals in the Company. Apparently, the agency that ran the op has been disbanded. A government panel's looking into the whole business, but you know how it is . . .'

'Right.'

'There's something else. A scientist at the American Museum of Natural History in New York got hold of the piece of the dinosaur, studied it and has released a paper about it. It's explosive stuff. Seems the *T. rex* died of an alien infection—brought in on the asteroid that caused the mass extinction.'

Ford told him how Apollo 17 brought back some of the particles on a moon rock. 'When they saw that the rock was impregnated with an alien microbe, they diverted it to the Defense Intelligence Agency, and they've been studying these particles for the last thirty years, all the while keeping their antennae out in case any more showed up.'

'But it still doesn't explain how they found out about the dinosaur.'

'The NSA has a ferocious eavesdropping capability. Seems they intercepted a phone call and jumped on it immediately.'

Tom nodded. 'How's Hitt?'

'Still in bed upstairs. He's doing fine. Pilot and copilot are both dead, though. Along with Masago and several soldiers. A real tragedy.'

'And the notebook?'

Willer stood up, took it out of his pocket, laid it on the bed. 'This is for you. Sally tells me you always keep your promises.'

MELODIE HAD NEVER been inside the office of Cushman Peale, the museum's president, and she felt oppressed by its atmosphere of old New York privilege. The man behind the antique rosewood desk added to the effect, dressed in Brooks Brothers grey, with a gleaming mane of white hair and an unshakable assumption of superiority.

Peale guided her to a wooden chair placed to one side of a marble fireplace and seated himself opposite. He laid a copy of her article on the table.

'Well, well, Melodie. This is a fine piece of work.'

'Thank you, Dr Peale.'

'Please call me Cushman.'

'All right. Cushman.' Melodie leaned back in the chair. She had a bad case of impostor syndrome—but figured she'd get over it, eventually.

'Now let's see . . .' Peale consulted some notes he had jotted on the first page of the article. 'You joined the museum five years ago, and you've been

in the mineralogy lab ever since as a . . . Technical Specialist First Grade?'
He seemed almost surprised by the lowliness of her position.

Melodie remained silent.

'Well, it certainly seems time for a promotion.' Peale leaned back and
crossed his legs. 'This paper shows great promise, Melodie. Of course, it's
controversial, but it seems likely the results will withstand scrutiny.'

'They will.'

'That's the right attitude, Melodie.' Peale cleared his throat, delicately.
'The committee did feel that the hypothesis that this, ah, Venus particle
might be an alien microbe is perhaps a bit premature.'

'That doesn't surprise me, Cushman.' Melodie paused, finding it difficult
to say his first name. 'Any major scientific advance involves going out on a
limb. I'm confident the hypothesis will stand up.'

'Delighted to hear it. Of course, I'm only a museum president'—and
here he gave a self-deprecating chuckle—'so I'm hardly in a position to
judge your work. They tell me it's quite good.'

Melodie smiled pleasantly.

He leaned back, placed his hands on his knees. 'I had a talk with the
Committee on Science and we'd like to offer you a position as Assistant
Curator in the Department of Vertebrate Paleontology. This is a fine, tenure-
track position that will lead, in time, to an appointment to the Humboldt
Chair. Naturally there will be a commensurate increase in salary.'

Melodie allowed an uncomfortable amount of time to pass before
responding. 'That's a generous offer,' she said. 'I appreciate it.'

'We take care of our own,' said the president pompously.

'I wish I could accept it.'

'You're turning us down, Melodie?' Peale looked incredulous.

Melodie kept her voice even. 'Cushman, I spent five years in the basement doing first-class work. Never once did I receive one iota of recognition. My salary was less than the guys who emptied my trash.'

'Of course we noticed you . . .' Peale was nonplussed. 'And let me say
our offer to you isn't engraved in stone, either. An associate curatorship
with tenure might be possible.'

'I already turned down a tenured position at Harvard.'

Peale's brows shot up in astonishment, quickly concealed. 'My, they're
quick on the draw.' He managed a strained chuckle. 'And you turned it down?'

'Yes. I'm going with the dinosaur . . . to the Smithsonian.'

'The Smithsonian?' At the mention of their big rival, his face reddened.

'That's right. The government plans to build a laboratory in the White Sands Missile Range in New Mexico to study the dinosaur and the Venus particles. They've asked me to be the assistant director in charge of research, which comes with a tenured curatorial appointment at the natural history museum. Being able to continue my work on the specimen means a lot to me.'

'That's your final decision?'

'Yes.'

Peale rose, extended his hand and mustered a weak smile. 'In that case, Dr Crookshank, allow me to be the first to congratulate you.'

Breeding had produced one fine quality in Peale, thought Melodie: he was a good loser.

Epilogue

The van bounced along the dirt road, running like an arrow across the desert. The landscape was flat and empty as the ocean. They were deep in the White Sands Missile Range, a 3,000-square-mile proving ground for the nation's most advanced weaponry.

'We're almost there,' said Melodie Crookshank, sitting in the front next to the military driver.

They passed a cluster of burnt and boarded-up buildings, enclosed by a double perimeter fence. Beyond that stood a gleaming, new structure, faced with brushed titanium panels, surrounded by its own high-security fence.

'This area used to host some kind of genetic engineering lab,' said Crookshank, 'but they closed it down after a fire. The Smithsonian is leasing a part of it. Since it had once been a biosafety level four facility, it'll be a perfect place to study the dinosaur—in terms of isolation and security.'

'It looks like a lonely place to live,' said the attractive, curly-haired woman who was sitting in the back with the Broadbents and Wyman Ford.

Robbie Weathers had accepted the Smithsonian's invitation to attend the unveiling of the dinosaur. The museum had wanted to name its new facility after her father, but Tom Broadbent had persuaded them to christen their newest acquisition, 'Robbie', just as Marston had intended. In an emotional meeting with Robbie, Tom and Sally had given her the notebook and the letters addressed to her that they had found with the dinosaur.

'Not at all!' said Crookshank. 'The desert has a Zen-like purity about it. And this is a fascinating area, with ancient Indian ruins, lava flows, caves with millions of bats. They've got stables. I've been learning how to ride horses. It sure beats a windowless basement lab in New York City.'

The van bounced over a cattle grid. A guard waved it along. They parked in a gravelled lot in front of the building, which was already packed with cars, television vans, Humvees, Jeeps and other military vehicles.

They stepped out into the intense July heat and walked across the parking lot towards the titanium building. A guard held open the door and they entered a large atrium. A man in uniform, with two stars on his shoulder, came over, his hand extended.

'General Miller,' he said, shaking hands all round. 'Commander of White Sands Missile Range. Welcome.'

The General led them through a set of doors into the laboratory complex itself. They headed down a long, white corridor towards a larger set of double doors at the far end. The room beyond was a kind of conference room, with rows of seats facing a long white curtain across one wall. The place was packed with scientists in lab coats, grey-suited government types, curators and military officers; the media were roped off to one side.

'It's behind that?' asked Robbie, nodding to the curtain.

'That's right. The whole lab was designed so we could work under high security and level four biosafety—but openly, not secretly. That's the key. The results will be posted online for all to see. A discovery like this is . . . well . . . momentous, to say the least.'

'I wish like hell my father were here,' Robbie said softly.

Melodie greeted various people. More dignitaries arrived, and then, in response to an announcement, people took their seats.

'I'm on,' said Melodie.

A hush fell as she took to the podium.

'Welcome,' she said, nervously spreading out half a dozen index cards, 'to the Smithsonian's new Desert Paleontology Research Station.'

A burst of applause.

'I'm Dr Melodie Crookshank, the assistant director, and I guess you all know why we're here.' She shuffled her cards awkwardly. 'We're gathered to unveil—and christen—the greatest palaeontological discovery ever made. Some would call it the greatest scientific discovery of all time. But first I'd like to mention the man who found this incredible specimen: the late Marston Weathers. You all know the story of Weathers's discovery of the fossil and his murder. Few know that Weathers was probably the greatest dinosaur hunter since the days of Barnum Brown and Robert Sternberg. He's represented here by his daughter, Roberta. Robbie? Please stand up.'

There was a thunderous round of applause as Robbie stood, blushing.

'I want to thank a few other people. Tom and Sally Broadbent, first of all, along with Wyman Ford, without whom this dinosaur would not have seen the light of day.'

More thunderous applause. Tom glanced at Ford. The man was no longer dressed in brown monk's robes. Now he was wearing a sleek suit, his unruly hair combed neatly back. He looked sophisticated and at ease.

Melodie reeled off a list of people to be thanked, then paused, consulted her cards again, smiled nervously. A hush fell.

'The MIT physicist Philip Morrison once pointed out that either there is life elsewhere in the universe or there isn't—and that either possibility boggles the mind. Today we stand here knowing that there is indeed life elsewhere in the universe. The discovery of alien life has long been the subject of speculation. And now this discovery has come to pass, but in a way that was totally unexpected—as an alien microbe entombed in a fossil.

'Here, at the Smithsonian Desert Paleontology Research Station, we'll be able to study this new life form in safety and security—but openly, sharing our discoveries with the world for the benefit of humankind. The fossil will tell us volumes about theropod dinosaurs, particularly *Tyrannosaurus rex*—their anatomy, how they lived and reproduced. And we will learn a great deal more about that momentous event sixty-five million years ago, when the Chicxulub asteroid struck, causing the greatest natural disaster ever to befall our planet. We already know that these mysterious alien microbes, these Venus particles, were carried to Earth on the asteroid and were spread by the impact, because a fragment of that same asteroid was found on the moon by the Apollo 17 mission.

'These alien microbes were the last nail in the dinosaurs' coffin. Whatever dinosaurs survived the impact were killed by a deadly pandemic, a plague to end all plagues. Without the total extinction of the dinosaurs, mammals would never have evolved into anything larger than a rat, and human beings would never have existed. So you might say that these particles cleared the earth for us. The asteroid and the epidemic started the great chain of evolution that led to the appearance of human beings.'

Crookshank paused, breathed deeply. 'Thank you.'

Applause filled the room. The director of the Smithsonian, Howard Murchison, strode to the podium, a bottle of champagne in one hand, and shook Crookshank's hand. He turned to the audience, smiling broadly.

'May I ask Robbie Weathers to come up?'

Robbie flashed a smile at Melodie and walked to the podium. There the director grasped her hand and placed the champagne in it.

'May I introduce Robbie Weathers, daughter of Marston Weathers. We've asked her to officiate at the christening.'

There was a burst of applause.

'We can't actually break a bottle of champagne *over* the dinosaur, but we can at least raise our glasses to it. And who better to do the honours?' He turned to Robbie. 'Would you like to say a few words?'

Robbie held up the bottle. 'This one's for you, Dad.'

'Drumroll, please,' said the director.

A canned drumroll sounded over the PA system, and at the same time the draperies at the end of the hall drew back, exposing a brightly illuminated laboratory behind a thick sheet of glass. On a set of massive steel tables in the laboratory, the astonishing fossil had been laid out in pieces, still partly jacketed in matrix. Much of the dinosaur's skull, gaping jaws and twisted neck had already been exposed, along with its clawed hands and feet.

The director held up his hand and the drumroll stopped. 'Time to pop the cork, Robbie.'

Robbie struggled with the cork, twisting it back and forth. With a pop the cork flew over the heads of the crowd, champagne gushing from the mouth of the bottle. There were cheers and clapping.

Murchison caught part of the stream with his glass, raised it to the great fossil, and said, 'I christen you Robbie, the *Tyrannosaurus rex*.'

A huge cheer went up, and as waiters walked through the crowd, bearing silver trays loaded with flutes of champagne, Melodie joined Tom, Sally and Wyman Ford. They clinked glasses all round.

'It'll be such a kick, unlocking the mysteries of that fossil,' said Melodie.

'It must be the dream of a lifetime,' said Ford.

She laughed. 'I was always a dreamer, but in my wildest dreams I never thought of anything quite like this.'

'Life is full of surprising turns, isn't it?' said Ford, winking. 'When I entered the monastery, I never would have guessed it would lead me here.'

'You don't look much like a monk,' said Melodie.

Ford laughed. 'I'm not, never was—and now never will be. The hunt for this dinosaur made me realise I'm not cut out for a life of contemplation.'

'What are you going to do?' Tom asked. 'Rejoin the CIA?'

He shook his head. 'I'm going to hang up my brass plate as a private investigator.'

'What? A detective? What would the abbot say?'

'Brother Henry approves. He says he always knew I'd never become a monk, but it was something I'd have to discover for myself. And so I did.'

'What kind of detective?' Sally asked. 'Chasing cheating husbands?'

Ford laughed. 'Not at all. Corporate and international espionage, cryptography, science and technology. Similar to what I did for the CIA.'

There were some more cheers as the director opened another bottle and began circulating among the press corps.

Ford sipped his champagne and turned to Crookshank. 'While you were giving your speech, Melodie, a rather offbeat idea occurred to me.'

'What's that?'

He glanced at the dinosaur, then back at the palaeontologist. 'Let me ask you this: what makes you think the Venus particle is alive?'

Crookshank smiled, shaking her head. 'Well, technically it doesn't meet our current definition of life, because it isn't DNA-based. But it meets all the other definitions of life in terms of its ability to reproduce, to grow, to adapt, to feed, to process energy, to excrete waste products.'

'There's a possibility you don't seem to have considered.'

'And what's that?'

'That the Venus particle is a machine, built to ensure the extinction of the dinosaurs and manipulate evolution, which was seeded on an asteroid headed towards Earth—perhaps even on an asteroid *pushed* towards Earth.'

'But why?'

'You said it yourself. To make way for the evolution of human beings.'

There was a brief silence, then Melodie laughed uncomfortably. 'That *is* an offbeat idea. Only an ex-monk could have dreamed up something as crazy as that.'

DOUGLAS PRESTON

Born: 1956, Cambridge, Massachusetts
Home: Maine
Website: www.tor.com/preston

RD: How did you get the inspiration for *Tyrannosaur Canyon*?

DP: Many years ago I worked at the American Museum of Natural History in New York. I had a chance to see the great dinosaur bone storage vaults there, where thousands of fossil bones are stacked up like cordwood on huge metal shelves, with giant skulls parked in the corners. There were crates, covered with Chinese and Mongolian script, which contained dinosaur remains shipped to the museum in the 1920s and never opened! I began to wonder: Who collected all this stuff? I learned that the dinosaur hunters were a rare breed: daring, adventurous men who explored the far ends of the earth, fighting bandits, harsh deserts, and sometimes each other, to find these behemoths. That was when I had the idea to write about a dinosaur hunter and the greatest find of them all.

RD: What started your fascination for dinosaurs and all things ancient?

DP: I've wanted to be a palaeontologist ever since I was five. I never outgrew that early fascination with dinosaurs. My mother was an avid fossil hunter and a lover of geology, and I picked up my interests from her.

RD: How did you feel when you heard about the very recent discovery in Montana of a *T. rex* with soft tissue attached to the bones?

DP: I could hardly believe it. Before that, scientists believed that no soft tissue could survive more than a hundred thousand years or so. This tissue had survived, intact, for sixty-five million years. And not just tissue—the micrographs I've seen show actual dinosaur blood cells. That is spectacular, and it means that DNA may be recoverable.

RD: What do you believe to be the most exciting scientific frontier?

DP: One of the most exciting frontiers is all the fascinating (and frightening) research being done on exactly what happened when the asteroid struck the earth, triggering the extinction of the dinosaurs. It came within a hair's breadth of wiping out all life on earth. If you think of the earth as a living organism, it was like a shot to the heart. The earth almost died. The big question now is, how did the mammals survive?

RD: And what's next for the world of palaeontology, do you think?

DP: Here's a reasonable prediction: within the next thirty years, scientists will clone a woolly mammoth from DNA recovered from a frozen carcass. Since the mammoth has a close living relative, the elephant, a female elephant could serve as a surrogate mother. This will happen. Later, much later, it might be possible to clone a dinosaur from DNA recovered from soft tissue. That is a far more difficult proposition.

RD: Would you travel into space if you could, and why?

DP: Naturally. What an adventure that would be!

RD: What other great adventures would you like to undertake?

DP: I am a member of the Long Riders' Guild, an organisation of horse riders who have gone more than a thousand miles in a single journey. I would love to undertake another long horseback journey riding across South America, or along the US Continental Divide, or around Iceland. I would also like to sail solo around Cape Horn.

RD: If you had to give one piece of advice for living, what would it be?

DP: Don't be totally sane.

RD: Using three adjectives, how would you sum yourself up?

DP: Restless, curious, a dreamer.

IT'S ALL IN THE BONES

A giant dinosaur, later to be named *Tyrannosaurus rex*, was first found in 1902 in Montana. Since then, only seven skeletons, more than 50% intact, have been unearthed and, of these, the largest and by far the best preserved is 'Sue' (pictured right), now on permanent display in Chicago's Field Museum.

(www.fieldmuseum.org/sue). Millions of years after her death, she is 90% complete, with bones in such excellent condition that it is possible to see where muscles, tendons and other soft tissue were attached. Found in South Dakota in August 1990, Sue was named in honour of Sue Hendrickson, the fossil hunter who made the discovery.

Quite Honestly

Robin   **Timbo**   **Lucy**

Giving something back to society
by helping those less fortunate than herself
is Lucy Purefoy's innocent aim.
And volunteering to help newly released
ex-con Terry Keegan to go straight appears
to be the perfect first project.
Until she goes just a bit too far in her
enthusiastic attempts to get a feel
for Terry's lifestyle . . .

One

I don't know why, but I've always wanted to do some sort of good in the world. I used to have a boyfriend, Jason, who laughed at me and called me a 'do-gooder'. 'Meet my girlfriend, Lucy,' he would say. 'She's a do-gooder, of course.' And then he'd laugh. I don't know what he wanted—a 'do-badder'? A person who sets out to do one bad turn to somebody every day? No one wants that, surely? Anyway, I got tired of being called a 'do-gooder' and Jason and I split up, which I did regret, because I found him rather attractive and quite funny at times. But I didn't know why he was so irritated by my ambition to do a bit of good in the world.

I ought to introduce myself—I'm always called Lucy, but I was born Lucinda Purefoy. 'Purejoy', Jason used to call me when he was in a good mood. When I was young my father was a vicar in a big North London parish and Mum always said that he'd been spotted as having 'bishop potential'. This made Mum laugh, because she's more than a little irresponsible and tends to OD on gin and tonic before dinner. Anyway, Mum was right and Dad got made the bishop of a large chunk of Surrey and Hampshire. He gets into the papers quite a lot because he can't see what's wrong with gay marriages, if that's what people want. He's extremely tolerant and told me I must make up my own mind about God. I have to admit that I haven't got round to doing it yet. Probably that's because I'm always kept pretty busy. I don't want to boast, but I did manage to get four decent A levels which took me to uni (Manchester), where I tended towards politics and sociology.

It was there I got interested in crime and the causes of crime, which I put down to poverty, a failing system of education and the values of the monetarist society which regards success as owning a four-wheel drive to take the children to school in and a second home in the Dordogne. At the time I hadn't even met a criminal.

After my degree, and work experience at the *Guardian,* I really longed to do some good in the world. I'd had a lot of privileges. Although my father being a bishop was more than a little embarrassing, I had, like I say, a secure and loving family. So I felt I had to repay my debt to society. But I really had no idea how to do it until I heard about 'praeceptors' and met Terry Keegan. Quite honestly, it wasn't until then that I found a real purpose in life.

I first heard about praeceptors from my friend Deirdre Bunnage. Deirdre was one of those irritating girls at school who were always telling you about their marvellous new boyfriends or the fact that they'd been asked to spend a long weekend in Acapulco with someone who'd been on television. Anyway, I hadn't long left uni when I bumped into her in the bar of the Close-Up Club in Soho. My then boyfriend, Tom, was very keen on getting into television so he joined the Close-Up and we went to hang out there in the hope of meeting someone in a television company who wanted to give Tom a job. Most of the people we met were also hanging out in the faint hope of meeting someone from a television company with a job to offer, so Tom wasn't getting very far. I was sitting with him at the bar, when Deirdre came over.

'I suppose your life seems pretty empty since you finished at Manchester,' she said. She was wearing that sort of surprised smile which I always found annoying. The fact that she was accompanied by someone she introduced as a 'well-known rap artist' added considerably to my irritation.

'It's not at all empty,' I told her, not altogether truthfully.

I told her I'd had the offer of a PA job with an advertising agency, and I really wanted to do some sort of good in the world.

To my surprise, Deirdre's smile was no longer one of lofty disdain. 'That's wonderful, Lucy! You're a perfect candidate for SCRAP.'

'For what?' Her suggestion didn't sound entirely complimentary.

'SCRAP. I've joined and it's fascinating work. You befriend young criminals fresh out of prison. Help them to lead an honest life. Make decent citizens out of them. You'd be perfect at it.'

'Why is it called SCRAP?'

'Social Carers, Reformers and Praeceptors. You know what a praeceptor is, don't you? Don't you remember any Latin from school? Anyway, we've got to go. Come on, Ishmael.' And with that, Deirdre went off with her rap artist.

And I rang the office of SCRAP near to King's Cross Station on the off chance that I might be able to do some sort of good in the world.

'WHY DO THEY go on doing it? They've been to detention centres, youth custody, prison when they're seventeen or over and they just come out and do it again! So they have to go back to prison, to their boredom and our considerable expense. Why can't they ever stop? Have you any ideas on the subject?'

'Poverty? Lack of education? The monetarist society?' I remembered some of my essays from Manchester.

'No, none of that.' The large grey-haired man, with brown appealing eyes and a crumpled suit, swung gently in his office chair. He was Orlando Wathen, criminologist and chairman of SCRAP. 'Some of these lads come from quite decent homes. They could hold down a reasonable job. What's so great about pinching laptops from the cars of sales reps who've stopped for a pee in a service station? There's a piece in here.' He searched his desk. 'Here it is! It's by a doctor. He suggests it's all because they take too much salt in their food. Seventy-five per cent of those convicted of theft in the Grimsby area admitted they liked their food well salted. Bloody nonsense! I take salt with my food and I don't steal laptops.' Mr Wathen looked up at me. 'Perhaps you'll discover what makes your customers pinch things.'

'I'll certainly try.'

'All our praeceptors say that, but they haven't enlightened me yet. I got your father's letter.' He found it under a pile of pamphlets. 'He signs himself Robert Aldershot. That's not your name, is it?'

'He signs like that because he's the Bishop of Aldershot.'

'Your father's a bishop?'

I had to admit it.

'We all have to rise above the unfortunate circumstances of our birth.' Mr Wathen was shaking with suppressed mirth. 'What's in a name anyway? My parents called me Orlando. No doubt they thought they'd produced a handsome wrestler who'd win the heart of the beautiful Rosalind. Instead they got a fat criminologist who's completely mystified by the causes of crime. You do realise, don't you, that your customers are likely to resent you and refuse to cooperate?'

'Oh yes,' I told him, 'I'm expecting something like that.'

THE ONE PERSON who had no doubts at all about the cause of crime and the rising number of young criminals being locked up was SCRAP's chief executive, Gwendolen Gerdon. Gwenny, as everyone called her, was an oversized, blonde-haired, pink-cheeked woman, in her forties I suppose, who spoke in a high-pitched, rather breathless little-girl's voice. She never blamed the criminals we were meant to reform for any part of it. Instead she blamed the judges mostly and then the police for their unfair and unjust persecution of so many really quite harmless young men.

Gwenny was clearly the power behind the SCRAP office. She did the work while Orlando Wathen swung in his chair, speculating fruitlessly on the deeper causes of housebreaking, fraud and grievous bodily harm. It was Gwenny who organised our training sessions, every weekday evening for a month. We got talked to by prison officers and someone who worked in prison education. But the one who depressed me most was a probation officer. Mr Markby had sandy hair, a small sandy moustache and a dry, breathy sort of voice like the sound of wind over the desert.

'Just remember that you and the client' (he meant ex-prisoner) 'aren't "friends",' Alexander Markby told us. 'You're his, or perhaps her, guide, philosopher and teacher. So don't offer him a cigarette, or he'll start to expect cigarettes all the time. Don't tell him what a good time you had at the pub the night before. That would put you on the same level. You must never step down from your position as a teacher. Keep your distance.'

Gwenny seemed to approve of the probation officer's advice. And she added, laughing. 'For heaven's sake, don't sleep with a client of either sex. We have had that happen in the past and it has always led to disastrous results. Keep in touch. That's the main thing. See that he's got somewhere to live and get someone to give him a job—part-time if it has to be.'

On the final day of the course, Gwenny told us who our prisoners were going to be. 'Alex Markby has suggested you for one of his very own clients,' she told me. 'He was impressed when I told him your father was a bishop and he said you might be able to give this chap a bit of moral backbone.' Not for the first time I cursed my father's choice of a job. What was moral backbone anyway, I wondered, and did I really have any of it to spare?

'The client's name is Terry Keegan.' Gwenny chuckled. 'He operated round the Ladbroke Grove area. Uncle almost in the big time, played a minor role in a Notting Hill Gate bank robbery. His grandmother lived round Bethnal Green and she can remember the Krays and the Richardsons.

Terry began offending when he was about twelve. He was in a detention centre by the time he was fourteen. Last time he got four years for housebreaking from that bastard Judge Bullingham down at the Old Bailey. I have little doubt that he was stitched up by the police.'

'You mean he hadn't done the housebreaking?'

'Well, yes. I suppose he had. But that doesn't alter the fact that Judge Bullingham's a bastard. You'll soon find out. The entire judicial system is completely hopeless. Anyway, Terry's coming out of the Scrubs on Thursday morning. He's been told to expect you. It would be rather nice if you met him at the prison gates. He's got black hair, rather curly. Oh, and an unusually cheerful grin.'

So that's why I was waiting, at 8.30 a.m. on a wet March morning, outside the gates of Wormwood Scrubs.

Which is where this story begins.

A GOOD MANY PEOPLE down our end of Ladbroke Grove came from one-parent families. I'm still not too sure who my dad is, and certainly Mum never told me. I always went by her name, which was Keegan, and it was only her family I ever met, so I reckon my dad was no more than a passing moment in her life.

What I remember most about Mum was that when I was first at school she would come and fetch me with this music stuck in her ears. You couldn't hold much of a conversation at home either because she liked her music loud. When I remember talking to Mum, it was all shouting over Duran Duran, at full volume.

I remember the kitchen where we lived on the estate, with plates stacked up by the sink, and I remember wondering why there was so much washing-up because we weren't a big family. No dad, no brothers and sisters—just me. I suppose more got eaten because Mum often had guys she called my uncles around. Most of the time, of course, these uncles weren't uncles at all and then Mum would hustle me off to bed extra early and I'd lie awake listening to her *Music for Romantic Evenings* tapes until they moved to the bedroom and I could get a bit of sleep. Anyway, I put up with Duran Duran and her Romantic Evenings until one of the uncles, someone called Jack Levenhall, made it horribly plain that he fancied me more than he fancied my mum, so I moved out as quick as I could and I never lived at Mum's place after that.

Well, my mum knew where I was if she wanted to come after me, which she didn't. First I went to my gran's place, in the Bethnal Green area, but she was always on about the big heavy villains she had known and how they could draw, with their razors, a perfect semicircle on the faces of those who disagreed with them. Gran seemed to admire this about the heavy men of her younger years, but hearing about it pissed me off, quite honestly, which is why I went to live with Aunt Dot up near Kensal Rise cemetery.

Aunt Dot was the best. She was Mum's aunt, but a lot younger than Gran. She always talked to me without the incidental music, and it seemed like she always took an interest in me, and when I got into trouble and had to go away, Aunt Dot always seemed pleased to see me back.

Of course, my Aunt Dot was used to people going away, seeing as she was married to my Uncle Arthur. He was good to me also. He was in a business way out of anything I've ever attempted, robbing banks and building societies, threatening cashiers and customers with a shooter which he kept carefully cleaned and never ever let me hold. This paid Uncle Arthur very well when he was working, and we used to go out to posh restaurants and even for holidays in Spain. The trouble was he went away for a long time, so we stayed on in Kensal Rise, where the rent was reasonable, and Aunt Dot went off to the West End to do bits of cleaning.

It all started when I was about thirteen. This may surprise you, but I was quite a bright boy at school. For one thing I got the hang of the isosceles triangle long before anyone else in the class understood it. It was at school I met Tiny McGrath. He wasn't called Tiny because he was especially small but to distinguish him from his very much older stepbrother, known as Chippy, because of his huge appetite at that time for chips.

Chippy was always tall and in spite of what he ate he was quite skinny. He had a strange smile. He only smiled with one side of his mouth. One side went up quite cheerfully while the other side stayed down as though it couldn't see the joke.

He had the gift of getting other people to work for him. He used to ask Tiny and me and some of our friends round to his place and give us sweets or cigarettes, or a bit of money, to do little jobs for him. Such jobs usually consisted of stealing things, like bottles of whisky and that from the off-licence, while he kept the woman in charge amused with requests for crisps and sweets. All this led to us, but not Chippy, having to appear before the desk sergeant at the Paddington nick, where he told us that a life of crime would lead to misery. Looking back on it now, I'm still not sure that he was telling us the truth.

We graduated from there to car radios and the opening of car doors with a wire coat hanger. It was when I got caught at this that the friendly warnings stopped and I got seriously beaten up by members of the Metropolitan Police with time on their hands. After that I went inside for the first time as a Youth Offender.

It was after I left the Youth Offenders that Chippy and I got together seriously. We took to watching the smart houses in the Holland Park area, and noting when the milk and the papers were stopped because of the owners being away on holiday.

We got skilled in the way of breaking and entering, and Chippy's cousin Ozzy Desmond had made a study of disconnecting burglar alarms. We did well enough, and I was about to give my Aunt Dot some of life's little luxuries when I got caught. I got four years from a judge who'd decided from the word go that I was a menace to society. Chippy, by the way, was in the getaway car near the house we got caught in, and he just drove off.

When I was in real prison I decided I wouldn't get into no more trouble at all. I kept myself to myself. I'd get my meals and take them back to the cell and eat them on the table, which was the lid of the toilet. There was a lot of violence and you could quite often get into a fight in association, so I kept out of it. I stayed in my cell about twenty-three hours a day and I got used to it. I got so I didn't really want to be with other people. Near the end of my sentence, when I was allowed days out with close relatives, I went out with my Aunt Dot, who told me Uncle Arthur had gone away again for ten years. She was always nice to me, my Aunt Dot, but all I could think of was how nice it would be to get to my cell for a bit of peace and quiet.

Of course, being alone so much, I had time to read a lot of books. Most of them were a load of rubbish, crime stories, so called, by people who didn't know the first thing about crime. Then a prison visitor gave me a crime book by some Russian. It was about murder. Of course, I never did a murder. In fact, there's no violence in my record whatsoever. But I got stuck into this book and I found it interesting. Then I kept on getting called away for education classes, which taught me that three and three make six, a fact I already knew, and I lost the thread of the Russian book from time to time. But I persisted with the book.

By then I was able to work the system. We had ETS classes, which stood for Enhanced Thinking Studies. They asked you what you were thinking and you had to say, 'I was thinking how great it'd be to go out and get pissed and hit someone's head with a hammer.' If you said something like that, you started from a low point and your thinking could only improve you. So the ETS person gave you a good report, which helped towards parole.

Then I began to get visits from a woman who asked me to call her Gwenny and said she was from an outfit called SCRAP. She asked if I'd like SCRAP to fix up for some sort of person to look after me when I got out and help me to lead an honest life. I realised that SCRAP was another of those things, like ETS. It was better to go along with it if you wanted to leave the Scrubs as quick as possible.

This got a bit delayed, however, by my probation officer, Mr Markby, when the question of parole came up. He said that I was extremely intelligent (ha, ha) and that I knew exactly the right answers to give (which I did) but that I didn't seriously mean them (which perhaps I didn't) so I should stay inside because I couldn't be trusted. Which was why I didn't get parole. It just shows that I wasn't as good at working the system as I thought I was.

Anyway, this incident made me very suspicious of probation officers and all suchlike who say they're only trying to help you. All the same I felt relieved, because quite honestly, I wasn't ready to face the outside at that particular moment and I had to finish the Russian book, which I was able to do before my eventual release.

One week before I got out, I got a visit from the chaplain who said that SCRAP had found a praeceptor, whatever that might mean, Lucinda Purefoy. I smiled at him, of course, but I'd already decided not to have much more to do with probation officers and SCRAP women. Being out of prison means that you're free, doesn't it? At least that's the way I looked at it at the time.

THEY WERE A BIT SLOW at the office that morning. They gave me the clothes back that I was wearing when I got arrested. I got £46.75 and a travel warrant and then they opened the gate and I was out in the rain.

I hadn't taken more than a couple of gulps of fresh air when this girl came towards me, all smiling. She was wearing black trousers, a long overcoat and a white shirt. It looked as if she'd dressed up for the occasion. Now I'm not sure why that annoyed me so much.

Which is where the story begins.

Two

He had dark curly hair and what I think they call 'prison pallor'. What he didn't have was a cheerful grin. Quite honestly, he looked distinctly uncheerful. All the same I managed a big smile. Probably I was breaking Mr Markby's number one rule and looking too friendly. But I had to form some sort of relationship, even if he was going to be my pupil.

'Hi there!' I said. 'You must be Terry Keegan.'

He stood looking at me in silence. He seemed astonished, as though he'd been approached by some sort of lunatic. Eventually, he spoke.

'What if my name's Terry Keegan? What do you want to make out of it, man?' He spoke in a low gruff voice, which came as an unpleasant surprise.

'I don't want to make anything of it. And I'm not a man, actually.' I thought this was quite a funny thing to say, all things considered. Anyway I laughed, but Terry didn't. 'I'm sure SCRAP have warned you about me. I'm your praeceptor. It means I'm your guide and philosopher. I'm here to help you find a job, a place to live and that sort of thing. Support you in any way I can. And to see you don't ever go back inside that place again.'

The going-to-work traffic had grown and heavier rain was splattering the pavement. I had to raise my voice to be heard as I said the last sentence, so a small party of girls on their way to school turned their heads to stare. This caused Terry to look even more crossly at me.

'I don't need no help,' he growled, 'so fuck off, will you?'

'My name's Lucinda Purefoy,' I told him, 'but it's perfectly all right if you call me Lucy.'

'I don't need to call you anything. In fact I don't need you, full stop.'

'Don't lose your temper with your client. Never give him that particular satisfaction.' I was finding Mr Markby's instructions hard to follow. All I could think of doing was to look my client between the eyes and say, 'Well then, fuck you!'

The effect of this was surprising. Terry seemed deeply shocked. Had I said that in front of my father, the tolerant bishop, he wouldn't have batted a single eyelid. Terry Keegan, with a string of convictions, was far more easily shocked. He said, 'What do you mean?'

'I mean I've been training for a month. I've postponed a job in an advertising agency. I'm prepared to spend time away from my boyfriend, Tom, who's good-looking, never swears at me, and is going to end up with an important job in television. And I've done all that to help you.'

'I don't need no help!' He was still angry.

'Oh yes, you do. Eighty-five per cent of criminals reoffend within two years of their release from prison. If I take my eye off you you'll be back pinching laptops on garage forecourts or whatever you used to do.'

'Breaking and entering premises by night.' It seemed I had insulted him by talking about the laptops.

'All right then. Breaking and entering, whatever. Now tell me what you want to do that's free and legal and has nothing to do with sex and we'll do it.'

He stood there, looking at me, and then he said, 'Burger King.'

'What?'

'I've had Scrubs food for nearly three years. I want to go to Burger King.'

'All right,' I said, and I waved at a passing taxi. Talk about extravagance. I'd already broken practically every rule that Mr Markby had ever given us.

In the Burger King, Terry's behaviour improved slightly. I bought him a Whopper burger with fries and onion rings and a big milky coffee with five spoonfuls of sugar. After he'd finished that, he ordered another Whopper and I'm sorry, Mr Markby, but I paid for all this because I couldn't stand any further argument.

As he finished the second burger I went on to more important business.

'I have to make sure you've got a mobile phone.'

'You want to give me a few minutes to pinch one?' He gave me his first grin, but I decided to stand no more nonsense.

'Of course not. I've bought you one to save you getting into trouble.' I gave him the phone I had paid for, although my instructions from Mr Markby were simply 'to make sure the client had a mobile.' I couldn't think of any way I could be sure of that without buying the thing.

'Does it take photographs?' Terry was looking at it critically.

'No, it doesn't take photographs. And you've got to ring me on that every morning and at six o'clock every evening so I know how you're getting on. Is that understood?'

'Yes, man,' he gave me a sort of mock salute.

'Now, your probation officer tells me he's got you a place in a hostel.'

'I'm not going to no hostel.'

'Why not?'

'Because I'm free now, aren't I? I don't have to spend another night in no sort of prison place. Forget it, man.'

The worst of it was that I could see his point. That's my greatest weakness, being able to see other people's points.

'All right,' I said, 'where do you want to go?'

'My Aunt Dot's.'

'Where's your Aunt Dot live?'

'Up the end of Ladbroke Grove. Kensal Rise area.'

I looked at him. He seemed to mean what he said. Once again I disobeyed instructions. 'OK then. But call me as soon as you settle in. 'I'll try and smooth it out with Mr Markby.'

Terry stood up. 'I'll be getting along then.'

'I don't suppose you'll say "thank you"?'

'Thank you for what?'

'Taxi here, two Whoppers with fries and onions, and letting you choose your accommodation.'

'I never asked you to do any of that,' he said, and he sounded serious. 'It was you did all the asking.'

'YOU MUST BE Terry Keegan.' That's what she said to me. The first thing. All smiles she was as she crossed Du Cane Road to get to me.

You know what I felt? Like I was being arrested all over again. I'd done nearly three years. All I wanted was to breathe a bit of fresh, free air that didn't smell of toilets and disinfectant and stale food and men's bodies. I wanted to decide what I was going to do for a change and not leave it to other people. I wanted to be shot of all those concerned-looking individuals who thought they knew more about Terry Keegan than Terry Keegan knew about himself.

And there was one of them waiting for me, the very moment I got out.

I'd worked out a way of dealing with her, of course. I remember how Chippy McGrath used to put off girls he wanted to get rid of. He used the expression 'Fuck you, man', and the result was that they didn't hang about near him for very long. So when this one came on to me with all that bright 'let's be friends' kind of chatter, I gave her the full McGrath, delivered with his special sort of grunt.

It didn't seem to have any effect on her whatever. Talk about persistent! What worried me was that she swore back at me. I don't like to hear a woman swear. It reminds me of my mum and seems to go against the laws of nature, like women getting drunk. My Aunt Dot wouldn't do either of those things and I didn't see why this girl, who took it on herself to improve me, had to swear like Chippy McGrath.

Well, I knew we'd never get on with each other after that. But there was one thing she could do for me. I still felt the old prison hunger for a decent bit of food, and I didn't want to break into my £46.75. So I expressed my need for a Whopper with fries and onions.

Can you believe this? She put up her finger for a taxi. We could have gone to the bus stop or down the tube. Anyway, I bet we were about the only customers to arrive at Burger King in Notting Hill Gate by taxi. And when I'd polished off a Whopper with all of what comes with it I felt a lot calmer.

At the Burger King I got given a mobile phone. Of course I'd had phones, and plenty of them, but not ones that were given up voluntarily. I remember thinking, this is rather dull, being given a mobile without the interest attached to stealing it. She told me her number was in the phone and I should call her every morning and evening, which I hadn't the slightest intention of doing.

One thing she did do was to agree to me going to Aunt Dot's. She said she'd deal with Mr Markby and I suppose, looking back on it, I should have said thank you for that, because I had no wish to deal with Markby.

At the end of the meal, she said I ought to thank her. What I said was I hadn't asked her to do anything for me, and it was her who was doing all the asking. Well, that was true, wasn't it?

'OLD LADY no longer live here.'

'Why, where's she gone?'

'Old lady dead.'

When we parted, my teacher, lecturer, whatever she was, reminded me to phone or text her when I was settled in. I'd walked up to the far end of Ladbroke Grove so as not to disturb my £46.75. The high tower block looked only a little more inviting because some graffiti artist had decorated its lower walls with a pattern of hearts. I got out at the tenth floor and walked along the concrete balcony. I opened Aunt Dot's flat with the keys they'd given me back in the Scrubs that morning and let loose a great burst of Chinese voices. Probably they thought that I'd come to rob them. There were so many of them, at least three or four men, one of them picked up a baseball bat, three or four women, some small children and a baby who screamed at me.

It wasn't until I'd quietened them down and explained who I was that they told me. My Aunt Dot had passed over.

And Uncle Arthur? I didn't need to be told where my Uncle Arthur was. Gone away. No doubt after some bungled robbery or other. That was the trouble with prison. They never told you anything. Aunt Dot had died and there was I, alone in my cell, and not knowing anything about it.

When I was leaving the buildings, I have to say I felt really lonely. It suddenly struck me, I'd stepped out of prison into nothing at all. The whole day stretched in front of me like a long sentence. The worst was that I had no idea where I was going to serve it.

I'd walked as far as Bayswater when I had the idea of phoning Chippy McGrath.

'You're out! In the land of the free. I'll buy you a drink!' That was what Chippy said when I got to him through the small army of protectors, minders and hangers-on that seemed to be around him.

'I need a bit more than a drink, Chippy.' I had to tell him. 'Would you mind if I kipped down at your place? Just till I can get something fixed up.'

'No problem. Meet you for that drink and we'll fix it all up. Beau Brummell Club.'

'Where the hell's that?'

'Harrowby Street. Bright lights, bouncers in the doorway, you can't miss it.' And my old school friend rang off to attend to more important business.

Well, at least I've got friends, I thought. But it was a long time till six o'clock. I invested in cigarettes and a toothbrush and toothpaste plus an evening paper and a packet of sandwiches from Marks, which I took to a bench in Regent's Park. The rain had stopped. There was a sky like a grey prison blanket all over the lake but I sat there reading the paper. By this time, my wealth was down to £36.

'SO YOU'RE OUT! We can work together again.'

'No, I don't think so. I'm not too keen on going back inside.'

'So what're you going to do?' Chippy had changed over the time I'd been away. He looked older, but he was much smoother. He had the self-satisfied smile of a successful person.

'I suppose get some sort of job,' I told him, a bit uncertainly.

'What sort of a job? Not much use with your convictions.' Chippy spoke as though he had the cleanest character ever, which was far from the truth. 'You work along with me, Terry, and you could live like me.' He waved his hand round the club as though he owned the place. There were tables with girls with dickie bows round their bare necks and naked shoulders who were dealing out cards and raking in money. In and out of the shadows round the bar there were easy-to-come-by women and men straining the buttons on their dark suits. I heard four posh voices piping excitedly away and I thought, this is where the tip-top people come to mix with the crims.

Chippy himself was perched on a high bar stool, staring at what seemed to be his personal bottle of champagne. Give him the credit, he poured me a glass without hesitation.

'Bubbles, Terry. I bet you didn't get many of them in the Scrubs.'

'Too right,' I agreed.

'You ought never to have got caught on that last job, Terry.'

We'd made sure the couple who owned the house were away on holiday. It was just our luck they'd left a key with their daughter. She arrived with a pack of beefy young men just as I was packing up the last of the silver! Chippy, of course, heard their arrival and escaped in the getaway car.

'It was a bit careless of you, Terry, to choose that particular gaff. I was lucky to get away.'

'Of course. You're always lucky. When you get nicked you'll have had no previous convictions.'

'What do you mean when I get nicked? I'm a law-abiding citizen, Terry. Let me give you one of these.' At which he produced a wallet and extracted a business card that read 'Leonard McGrath, Financial Adviser. Environmentally Friendly Investments. Mortgages and Home Loans Negotiated' and gave the address of his maisonette in Connaught Square.

'Are you really a Leonard?'

'Of course I am. Anyway, as I say, it was careless of you, Terry, to get us into that particular house. I can't take you out for a job if you're going to be careless.'

I explained again that I'd finished with that side of life and all I wanted was somewhere to kip down for the night. Could Chippy help?

'I don't see why we shouldn't fit you into a corner of the maisonette.' Then there was a burst of music from his top pocket and he got deep into a conversation. As soon as he'd put his phone away he stood up. 'Sorry, my lad, got to go. Urgent business. Oh, and the maisonette's going to be chock-full, so you'll have to make other arrangements. But do finish the bottle.'

I wasn't too upset, because I knew I had enough for a room for a couple of nights at least. So when my phone rang and I knew it was Lucy, I didn't feel the need to reply.

And then my first day of freedom began to fall apart. Just after I'd knocked back the last glass, the barman asked for money, saying my friend had said he'd leave me to settle up. When I parted with £36, apparently the price of a bottle of bubbles at the Beau Brummell Club, my remaining capital was nil.

With the prospect of a decent bed for the night fading away, and still determined not to surrender to Mr Markby and his prison hostel, I thought I'd try and do what had worked for me a time or two when I was teenager, which was to head off to the super-loo on Euston Station.

It wasn't bad in there, with a few creature comforts such as shower, and I still felt able to ignore Lucy ringing my phone. However, there was a bloke in that super-loo who was giving me the sort of looks my mum's boyfriend was so free and easy with. I didn't want to get into trouble fighting on my first night out, so I moved to a bench on platform four, which I had entirely to myself from around ten o'clock. I woke up with a mouth like the floor of a parrot's cage and stiff legs. Some unseen visitor must have visited my bench when I was asleep and made use of the opportunity for a good vomit. When my phone rang at 6.48 I gave up the fight and answered it.

'Terry Keegan speaking.' I tried to sound self-confident.

'Where on earth are you?'

'Honeymoon suite. The Ritz Hotel.'

'You're not!'

'Of course I'm bloody not.'

'Are you at your Aunt Dot's?'

'I couldn't stay at Aunt Dot's. It wasn't convenient for her.' I didn't want to tell her the truth and have her feeling sorry for me.

'So where did you sleep?'

'Not a bad bench. Handy for platform four at Euston.'

'Why didn't you get a room somewhere? You've got money.'

'Not now I haven't.'

'What did you do with it?'

'Spent it all on a bottle of champagne.'

'You're joking!'

'I wish I was.'

She was quiet then and I wondered if she was going to cut off on me. Oddly enough, I hoped she wouldn't.

She didn't. 'Get yourself over to Waterloo Station. Meet you by W.H. Smith's at, let's say, 8.30. I'm telling you, it's your last chance.'

'IT WAS YOU did all the asking.' That was what he said to me, remember? After I'd bought him a mobile and second helpings at the Burger King and rung his probation officer to get him out of staying in the hostel. I'd done all that and all he could find to say was, 'It was you did all the asking.' It was as if he expected me to go down on my knees and thank him for allowing me to spend out on him. You can tell how disappointed I felt with this doing-good business. After he'd failed to answer my calls all evening, I decided to ring the advertising agency and tell them I'd be able to start next week.

It was when I'd been kept awake all night with anger and frustration I decided to give him the chance of one last call. Miracle of miracles, he answered me. And he told me he'd spent all his prison money on a bottle of champagne. You know what that was, don't you? That was a cry for help.

It's a bit of a thankless task doing any sort of good in the world, but if you ever set out to do such a thing, you can't ignore them, not cries for help. I told him to be at W.H. Smith's on Waterloo Station. If he wasn't there that would be a definite end to my trying to do good in the world. But before I met him I had to speak to my father.

'YOU'RE HERE THEN.' I looked at Terry in amazement. I'd got to W.H. Smith's at 8.40 and there he was, looking a bit tired, certainly, but alive and apparently unrepentant.

'I've been buying you a ticket,' I told him. 'And it's about the last thing I'm buying you if you don't remember to phone me every night and every morning. I'm very disappointed in you, Terry.' I was beginning to realise you can't do good to people without being quite nasty to them occasionally.

'All right then. Where are we going?'

'To visit my parents.'

'Oh yes.' He seemed determined not to show any sign of surprise. 'Where do they live then?'

'Not very far. Aldershot.'

'No, I mean what they got? A house or just a maisonette?'

'As a matter of fact it's a palace,' I said truthfully. At which I clearly succeeded in surprising Terry.

'Pull the other one,' he said, 'it's got bells on it!'

MY DAD is very handsome for a bishop, or indeed for anyone. He has chis-
elled features, clean-cut, regular. His hair is going grey, in rather an attractive manner. He keeps thin by riding for miles uphill on a stationary bike in
the bathroom. He wears the thinnest of dog collars and a pectoral cross said
to have formed part of the pulpit where Archbishop Cranmer preached a
sermon—though I'm not sure that the ecclesiastical outfitter wasn't having
Robert on a bit there. (My father always encouraged me to call him
'Robert' and not 'Dad', just as I had to call my mum 'Sylvia'.)

When I collared him in the bathroom, and found him panting a bit to get
up the hill, he was wearing black socks, a quite flattering pair of Gucci
underpants and a T-shirt he'd bought as a joke at an Episcopalian congress.
This garment had written across the chest the words 'Skanky Danky'. I'm
not sure that my dad had any idea of what those words meant.

As a Christian, my dad was, I thought, an expert at doing good in the
world, and he'd already shown considerable interest in the Terry Keegan
story. As a professional forgiver of trespasses, he seemed to take Terry's
appalling behaviour less seriously than I did.

'Sounds a bit of a character,' he said. 'Still with the possibility of
redemption.'

'He spent all his money on a bottle of champagne. I thought it might be a
cry for help.'

'Or just a cry for champagne.' My dad smiled and got off his bike.

Then I told him we had to have a last-chance plan for Terry. And once I
told him that, Dad became extremely helpful.

THE BISHOP'S PALACE at Aldershot isn't really all that palatial. It's old and
draughty. To me, it always seems to have the smell of Sunday lunch, to which
my dad invited whoever had preached that morning in the cathedral, and at
which my mum was inclined to drift off into a snatch of sleep, having been in
charge of the pre-lunch cocktails. That morning my dad greeted Terry as
though he were some strange and wonderful being from outer space.

'Do sit down, Mr Keegan. Darling, wouldn't Mr Keegan like a biscuit with his coffee?'

'Or something a little stronger than coffee?' Mum was looking longingly at the trolley with the gin bottle on it.

'Too early,' Robert was unusually decisive. 'Far too early for anything of that nature, wouldn't you agree, Mr Keegan?'

'He answers to the name of Terry,' I told them.

'Terry. Yes, of course, Terry. Coffee all right for you, is it Terry?' Here Robert stood up to offer Terry a biscuit, which he took in silence.

Dad resumed his seat and went on in the friendliest way possible. 'Well then, Terry. Lucy's told us you're just out of bird?'

'Out of what?' Terry seemed genuinely puzzled.

'Porridge. The nick. The cooler. Whatever you call it.'

'I call it prison.' Terry wasn't giving my father any marks for trying.

'Ah yes, prison—of course. Well, Lucy tells us you're just out of prison.'

'Yesterday.'

'Well, that must have come as a great relief to you. I'm only sorry you didn't have better weather for it.' My heart went out to Dad, who was clearly growing desperate.

'I don't care about the weather,' Terry told him.

'No, I don't suppose you saw much of it in prison, did you?'

'Not a lot, no.' Terry allowed himself to smile.

Dad smiled back. 'And what exactly were you in prison for, if it's not a rude question? Lost your temper, did you? Had a moment of blind rage and stabbed someone?'

'I've got no violence on my record.'

'Well done, Terry. Terribly well done! So what was it that got you into trouble—what was your *specialité de la maison*?'

'My what?'

'What particular brand of expertise landed you in chokey?'

I saw no particular future in this conversation, so I supplied the answer. 'Terry's *specialité*, if you have to call it that, was breaking into houses at night and stealing stuff. Terry was a thief.'

'Ah,' Dad nodded, still smiling. 'A blagger. That's good.'

'You don't mean that, do you?' Terry seemed profoundly shocked.

'What?' Dad looked puzzled.

'You don't mean that it's good at all. You think it's very bad, don't you?

It's what they teach you in church. If you do it, you'll go down to hell.'

'Hell?' Dad looked puzzled, as though Terry were speaking a foreign language. 'What do you mean by that exactly?'

'You know.' Terry looked surprised at my father's ignorance. 'Hell, the place you go to after you're dead. Lots of big fires and devils there with red-hot forks to torment you.'

'Oh dear me.' My father was trying hard to stop himself laughing. 'I'm afraid that's seriously out of date. We don't believe in devils with red-hot toasting forks any more.'

'So you think it's all right then? Thieving. And that.'

'No, no.' My father was now laughing openly. 'Of course it's not all right. But we must always try to understand.'

I was pleased, in a way, that Terry and Dad seemed to have struck up a conversation that at least caused Terry to say more to him than he ever had to me. I was only a little worried because Terry was looking with particular interest at the silver loving cup on the mantelpiece which had been presented to Dad when he left his London parish.

'I suppose,' my father said, 'it all comes down to poverty. Poverty makes you steal.'

'We didn't have poverty.' Terry seemed rather offended by the suggestion. 'My Uncle Arthur brought home a pretty good wage, when he was in business. Not when he was away, of course. And Aunt Dot went up the West End, charring, until she passed over.'

'How extremely interesting. And what was your Uncle Arthur's job?'

'Jobs? He did banks, building societies. All sorts of offices.'

'You mean he worked in them?'

For the first time since I'd known him, Terry laughed. 'No. I mean breaking into them. Not always successful, Uncle Arthur. That's why he was away a good deal.'

'Yes, of course.' Dad seemed to be getting out of his depth. 'Of course he would have been.'

Dad retreated into clerical solemnity. 'Well, we must have a long talk about all that sort of thing. Remember, my door is always open. Now, down to business. Lucy tells us you've been sleeping on Euston Station.'

'That was only temporary.' Terry said, as though we might have expected him to stay there for the rest of his life.

'I've got a chaplain. Tim Rideout. Everyone calls him Timbo. Timbo has a sizeable flat in the High Street. Church property, of course. He's unmarried and happens to have quite a good-sized spare bedroom.'

'It's a really nice room,' I assured Terry. 'And the Burger King is just down the High Street.'

'And Lucy's going to look round for a job for you,' Dad said.

We all of us, including Mum, sat smiling at Terry hopefully. I'm sure if he'd turned us down I'd have given up being a praeceptor for good.

Terry looked thoughtful and then astounded me by saying. 'Well, thank you very much. I'm extremely grateful.'

You know what about the praeceptor business? I clearly had a talent for it. Something I'd said or done had got through to Terry. It was then that Mum, who came from a nautical family, said, 'The sun's over the yardarm. Who's for a little G and T?'

Terry looked confused so I explained that Mum meant a gin and tonic. He then asked if he could have it without the gin. Mum said, 'I *suppose* you could. But I don't think there'd be very much point in it.'

Later, Dad rang Mr Markby, Terry's probation officer, who approved of our scheme. 'At times being a bishop comes in useful,' my Dad said.

On our way to inspect his new quarters, Terry said, 'Don't you think it's a bit dangerous of your dad?'

'What, finding you somewhere to live?'

'No. Keeping his door always open. Don't you remember, that's what he said?'

What I did remember was Terry's long look at Dad's silver loving cup. 'Don't think about it, Terry,' I said in what I hoped was an impressively warning tone of voice. 'Don't even give it a thought.'

Three

'At least we learnt the difference between right and wrong in the Youth Offenders wing.'

Believe it or not, I was sitting with Lucy in the bar of the Intimate Bistro somewhere in Aldershot. I had a Becks beer, my praeceptor had ordered a Pernod with ice and water. The drinks were on her.

'Who taught you that? The chaplain?'

'No! It was the other inmates. They had a code.'

'They taught you morality?'

'They had their morals, yes. Anything you did wrong to children you got pushed in the scalding shower. You couldn't rob from poor people, like hurt them. There was one big offender there called Jim. He'd set fire to an old tramp asleep on a park bench. He got enough cocoa poured on his head to float a ship.'

'So what *could* you do then?'

'Rob from building societies. Places where they had more money than they knew what to do with. Sort of jobs my Uncle Arthur did.'

'What about breaking into houses by night?'

'Like I said, that was all right. If you stuck to rich people.'

'Lot of Robin Hoods then in the Young Offenders. Stole from the rich. Did they give to the poor?'

'Not often,' I had to admit. 'But your dad, he said it was all right. All of it. I mean, he's a vicar and he's never heard of hell.'

'I think Robert goes more for understanding than passing judgment.'

'Who's Robert?'

'My dad. Whenever I remember to call him that.'

I looked at her. She had her fair hair parted at the side so it fell across her forehead. Her trousers stopped way before her T-shirt started, leaving her bellybutton open to the world. Her beaten-up old leather jacket was on the seat beside her. She hadn't dressed up at all to visit her mum and dad.

Anyway, I've got myself too far ahead, telling you about us sitting at the bar of the Intimate Bistro waiting for the arrival of its owner, Robin Thirkell.

I suppose I've had low times, like when I stood up in the dock at the Old Bailey and the red-faced judge, with his black cloak and dirty grey wig, said 'Keegan, you've clearly grown up to be a habitual criminal. The least sentence I can pass upon you, in the interest of the public, is four years' imprisonment.' But oddly enough, the lowest of all my moments was when I woke up beside a pile of sick in Euston Station. I had no Aunt Dot, no cash and no bed for the night unless I gave into Mr Bloody Markby's hostel. It was then I decided I needed the help of Lucinda (call me Lucy) Purefoy.

I did find her mum and dad a bit strange. He wore this red shirt with a great big wooden cross hanging over it. But he didn't seem to believe in religion, anyway not as we learnt about it from a teacher at my primary school, who made it pretty obvious that in her view heaven was up there and very pleasant and hell was down below and extremely hot. And her mother seemed very anxious to get on the sauce, which in her case was gin mixed in with tonic. But who am I to criticise after my experience of mothers? In a way I'm sorry for 'call me Lucy' if she hasn't got someone like my Aunt Dot, who was always good to me and kept off the gin. What did become clear when I was in the palace (so called!) was that they had fixed up somewhere for me to sleep nights and even discussed the situation with the probation officer who delayed my parole.

So I was going to play along with them. That way at least I'd get a bed for the night and hopefully a bit of loose change in my pocket and, when that was accomplished, I could walk free of them. I told the dad that I was extremely grateful. When I said that, 'call me Lucy' looked as though Christmas had come and she'd struck lucky with her first offender, who was now well on the way to reform.

All the same, when I happened to remark that it was a bit unusual of Lucy's dad never to lock the door, she gave me a suspicious look. 'Don't think about it, Terry,' she said. The truth was no decent fence would offer anything much for even the one small silver cup on the mantelpiece, so I wasn't that interested.

TIMBO'S FLAT, however, was absolutely stuffed with silver cups. Sorry. His name was the Reverend Timothy Rideout. 'Call me Lucy' said I was always to say Mr Rideout. Whatever you called him, he was not very tall, with broad shoulders, bright little eyes and hair cropped so short it was almost a number two. He had a sort of soft voice and a funny way of speaking so that the r's came out like w's. He'd won all these cups for cricket and football and the walls were covered with pictures of Revd Timbo holding a bat or a ball in the middle of a team of men who looked much taller than him.

He showed me my room. There was an iron bed and a cross, this time with Jesus on it, hanging beside another photograph of the Revd Timbo, this time wearing shorts and boxing gloves.

'Suit you well, will it?' Timbo looked around at what seemed a bit like a cell without the toilet. 'Better than Wormwood Scrubs anyway.'

'Oh yes,' I told him, my idea being to keep everyone happy till I could plan my escape. 'A whole lot better.'

'Good! Jolly good! Now I expect you'd like a cup of char?'

Lucy seemed to know that he meant tea. She refused in favour of a cigarette, but said I'd have it with milk and sugar. As we sat round in his lounge, Timbo looked me straight in the eye and said, 'What's your usual position?'

'I'm afraid my usual position for the last three years has been in one of Her Majesty's prisons.'

'What I meant,' Timbo was smiling, 'was your position on the field. Is it in the slips? Silly mid on? Or perhaps you retreat to third man?'

'I'm sorry, Mr Rideout. I'm not quite sure what you mean.'

'My dear fellow, have you never played cricket?"

'Never.'

'Not wugby? I'm sure you must have played wugby.'

I had to admit that, whatever it was, I hadn't played it.

'Footie then.' Footie seemed to come as the last resort. 'I'm sure you enjoy your footie.'

'Oh yes.' I tried to sound enthusiastic. All I could remember was kicking a ball round the estate with Tiny McGrath.

'Sport!' Timbo told us while he poured out mugs of tea. 'That's what'll keep you out of crime. Haven't you found that, Lucy, in your life dealing with those who have strayed from the straight and narrow?'

'I really don't know.' Lucy blew out smoke and looked doubtful.

'Take it from me, young lad. Get your head down in a good wugby scrum and you won't want to go thieving any more. It's been an exciting time the past year, hasn't it? I tell you, I had to do a good deal of heavy knee work.'

By now he'd lost me. It was like listening to someone talking a foreign language. What did he mean? I could only repeat 'knee work' with a big question mark at the end of it.

'On my knees. In the cathedral. Silent prayer, of course. Night and morning. I prayed for our success in the European Championships. But Almighty God moves in a mysterious way. In his infinite wisdom he decided not to help us when it came to the penalty kicks. Well, there it is.'

'Yes,' said Lucy, stubbing out her fag on one of the Reverend's saucers. It didn't seem to me that she was enjoying all this talk about God and knee work. 'But we've got no time for playing games. Terry needs a job as well as a bed to sleep on. Thanks, Timbo, we'll be on our way.'

'Yes, of course, Lucinda.' Timbo was on his feet. 'Do send my salutations to the dear bishop. The photograph on the way out,' he told us as though he was passing on an important secret, 'is Cathedral Clergy and

Staff versus the Aldershot Biscuit Factory. What a game that was. Three goals, all in extra time. I'm sure you remember it, Lucinda?'

'No,' 'call me Lucy' told him, 'I don't remember that at all,' which I thought was really rude of her, quite honestly.

SO, WHEN I'D PLANTED my toothbrush in Revd Timbo's bathroom, Lucy took me to the Intimate Bistro. We sat in the small, stuffy bar waiting, Lucy said, for someone she called Robin ('you'll adore Robin'), who, it seemed, ran the joint but only popped in occasionally.

'My God, what an ass that Timbo is!' Lucy shook her hair out of her eyes and took a big gulp of her white drink.

I told her that I didn't get much help thinking about crime from either the bishop or Timbo. In fact more sense seemed to have been talked about the subject in the Youth Offenders wing. So the chat started that kept us going until Robin Thirkell blew in and gave Lucy one of the longest French kisses I'd witnessed since before I got four years from Judge Bullingham.

ALTHOUGH I SAY IT MYSELF, I think this praeceptor business is going rather well. I mean, just look at the difference it made to Terry Keegan in only a few days! When I met him he couldn't have been worse. Rude, sulky, non-cooperative. And yet here we were having a drink and a really good conversation. He even managed to be polite to Timbo, who as usual made a bit of an ass of himself talking about the 'wugby'. I remember him taking me to watch that when I was still at school. Quite honestly, I thought it was rather a disgusting game, with grown men pushing their heads up against each other's bottoms. I couldn't see the point.

I'm not quite sure if prison works, but, as I say, the praeceptor business seems to be working excellently, as witness our conversation in the bistro.

I haven't told you about Robin, have I? I went out with Robin after I'd finished with Jason and before I met Tom. I suppose I'd have to admit that Robin Thirkell was the most exciting of the three of them. He not only owned the Intimate Bistro but also Nifty's, the dress shop in the High Street. He was always looking out for the latest trends and was so cool that one of the local newspapers called him 'the Giorgio Armani of Aldershot'. He had a suntan almost all the year round, which I think owed a good deal to Tone Up, the local health and fitness club, but it suited him rather, as did the shades he wore even on cloudy days.

Robin makes quite a lot of money, I mean serious money, out of property. Lots of pubs are closing and Robin bought some of them up and turned them into desirable residences for weekenders. He's obviously charmed someone on the local county council, so he doesn't have any problems about getting planning permission.

Anyway, having fixed a bed for Terry, I had to get him a job and I thought immediately of Robin.

Gwenny in the SCRAP office had explained to us that our 'clients' found it hard to get work because people who might employ them checked up on their criminal records. If they'd been caught thieving, as Terry had far too often, the job offer was off. So, by and large, I thought Robin was the best hope for Terry.

Robin arrived, as usual nicely browned and smelling strongly of Gucci aftershave. He gave me an enormous kiss, which reminded me of the old times, and when I emerged from it I introduced him to Terry.

'Is this your little criminal, Lucy? How tremendously exciting!'

I could see that this particular remark had not gone down at all well with Terry, so I did my best to save the situation. 'He's not a criminal any longer. So, Robin, it's up to you to give him a job in the Intimate Bistro.'

'Can you wash up? Clear tables? Bring dishes in?'

'Course I can.'

It was obvious that Terry had not yet fallen victim to Robin's undoubted charm. I thought he thawed a bit, however, when Robin said, 'How about £120 a week?'

AFTER THAT FIRST TALK in the Intimate Bistro it wouldn't be an exaggeration to say that I became good friends with Terry. We had more chats in the bistro and two or three times we drove out into the country in the clapped-out old Polo I mainly keep at home. He talked to me about his ghastly mum (neither Terry nor I seem to have had much luck in the mum department) and it was clear how much he had loved his Aunt Dot, although his Uncle Arthur obviously suffered from praeceptor deprivation and couldn't help reoffending.

Anyway, we were getting on so well and the days were full of spring sunshine and I thought Terry probably hadn't had many picnics in his life, so why shouldn't we have one? I got things together and Terry brought some bits of salami and pâté, together with a bottle of red Rioja which he might or might not have stolen from the bistro. But anyway, I thought, Robin could well afford it and he probably wouldn't have minded. And why would I want to spoil a picnic lecturing Terry again on how to be honest? Instead we drank Rioja out of plastic cups and laughed at something. I can't quite remember what because now, after all that's happened, it seems a long time ago.

When we'd almost finished the Rioja, I asked him how he liked his new job.

'Not bad. It doesn't pay so well as my old one.'

'You mean thieving?' I felt I had to say it, although I still didn't want to lecture him.

'Well, yes. I didn't do no crime for nothing, you know. Not like that mad Russian.'

'Which mad Russian was that?'

'The one who hit the old pawnbroker woman with an axe. Sort of just for the hell of it.'

'You mean you've read *Crime and Punishment*?' I knew what I sounded. I sounded patronising.

'Course I have. Do you think I haven't read books? I've read Dickens.'

'Really? Which one?'

'The one where the boy finds the old con in the marshes and gives him a slice of the ham. Something like my Uncle Arthur that old con was.'

'I suppose so,' I said, although I couldn't see the connection. '*Wuthering Heights*. That was a good one. *Wuthering Heights*.'

I have to say I was surprised at the width of Terry's reading. I realised that there was undoubtedly a good deal more to him than met the eye.

'You surprised I've read books?' He was smiling at me. 'I tell you, you get lots of time for reading in the Scrubs. Probably I've read more books than you have.'

'Probably.' I looked at him. He was still smiling and he looked younger than he had done at any time since I met him. I thought he might be going to make a pass at me, but he didn't.

Instead he stuffed what remained of the food into my basket. But things were definitely better between us.

'IT'S ALL GONE extraordinarily well,' I told my boyfriend, Tom, when he came down to stay with me at my parents' place and we were having dinner, just the two of us, in the Intimate Bistro. Tom had given up looking for a job in a television company and was spending his time writing a documentary script about the tube called *Underground*, which he was sure any television company would want to do when it was finished. So we were both in a good mood, holding hands and smiling at each other.

'It wasn't too easy at first,' I told Tom. 'I felt he resented me. But then I got him this job and we've kind of, well, hit it off.'

Tom said, 'I hope you haven't hit it off too far. I mean, you don't fancy him, do you?'

'Of course not, darling. It's purely a platonic relationship.'

Looking back on it, what I said may not have been entirely true, but I didn't want Tom to get into one of his sulky moods, so I squeezed his hand.

It was then that Terry emerged from the kitchen to collect our plates, piling them up on his forearm with the dish that had contained the veg balanced a little insecurely on the top. I was pleased to see that he was learning some of the tricks of a professional waiter.

'Terry,' I said. 'This is my friend, Tom Weatherby.'

'Lucy tells me you're getting on so well, Terry,' Tom was concerned enough to say, 'and you're enjoying the Intimate.'

'Am I?' Terry's answer was, I thought, quite rude. 'Well, I can see you are,' with which he buzzed off with our dirty plates. As he went down the steps into the kitchen, we heard an almighty crash. Terry had clearly dropped the lot. Our dessert, coffee and the bill were served to us by Hermione, who is Robin's current girlfriend, and I saw no more of Terry that night, nor for a good many nights to come.

It was quite late when we got back to the palace. Robert was still up and gave that sort of deeply understanding look he usually saves for people who've lost a husband or wife, or at least a close relation.

'Lucy,' he said, 'I'm afraid I have bad news for you.'

'Is it Mum?' I steeled myself to listen to an account of one of Sylvia's regular falls in the bathroom.

'No, darling, it's not Sylvia. It's young Terry Keegan.'

'He's not hurt?' I found myself unexpectedly anxious.

'No. Not him. So far as I know he's not hurt at all. The one who was hurt was poor Timbo. He rang me about an hour ago. He was in quite a state.'

'About what?'

'Now, Lucy, you mustn't let this shake your faith. We must follow the sinner down to the end of his chosen path.'

'What happened?' I'm really fond of Dad, but I was in no mood to hear one of his Radio 4 'Thoughts for the Day'.

'Well, it seems that your Terry came home at about ten o'clock and assaulted Timbo and went off with one of my chaplain's favourite silver cups. The one he got for the inter-denominational boxing tournament.'

'Terry attacked Timbo?' I was still trying not to believe it. 'But he had no violence in his record.'

'Well, he has now,' my dad told me. 'Poor Lucy! It just makes your job that bit more difficult, doesn't it?'

Of course, Robert and Sylvia have no objections to Tom and me sharing a bedroom in the palace. 'Sex is rightly regarded by today's Church as one of God's most generous gifts,' was what my dad always said.

So we said goodnight and made our way upstairs, where I found I wasn't at all in the mood for sex. It was a terribly low moment and I was extremely depressed. All the same, I told Tom, 'I'm not going to give up. It was all working so well. It's just a temporary setback. I won't let him go.'

'Quite honestly,' Tom said, 'I thought he was bloody rude to us in the restaurant.' Which didn't make me feel any better.

I HAVE TO SAY that I found her behaviour disgusting. When I got my job with the Intimate Bistro she welcomed Robin Thirkell by allowing him to put his tongue halfway down her neck. Three weeks later, there she is holding hands with this Tom and staring into his eyes as though he was the only man in the world for her. It reminded me of my mother. There she was pretending she was always in the right, knowing how to behave and teaching it to what her boyfriend Robin called her 'little criminal'—and yet there she is putting herself about to all-comers. I just couldn't be doing with it any longer.

All this happened a good three weeks after I'd started work. Things hadn't been so bad during that time. I did my work, got my £120 a week and, seeing as I lived rent-free with Revd Timbo, it wasn't too bad.

Anyway, I made my view of what was going on pretty clear by the way I picked up their plates. I left them to whatever they had in mind as quick as I could, with the result that I had a bit of a crash going down the steps to the kitchen. So I wasn't in a very good mood when I went home to Timbo's. I'd hardly got into the lounge when an extraordinary thing happened. I felt a bloody great bash to my chin, a vicious sort of upper cut that made my head spin and bloody near unhinged my jaw.

When I opened my eyes, what should I see but the Reverend, who must have been waiting for me behind the door. All he was wearing was shorts, a

T-shirt with a picture of Aldershot Cathedral on it, socks and trainers and boxing gloves that looked about the size of footballs. I could also see another fat pair of boxing gloves on the coffee table.

'Come on, Terry,' Timbo was shouting. 'Why don't we go a couple of rounds before bedtime? Blow away the cobwebs. A decent punch-up to get rid of your criminal tendencies. I've helped a lot of lads this way.'

And there he was, aiming another upper cut at my chin.

A lot of them I got to know in the Scrubs were there for violence of various kinds and I could never see the point of it myself. There was no profit in violence of any kind. But this was an exceptional moment. The next time I'm up for a sentence of any kind, I'll have to ask for the following to be taken into consideration: a couple of knocks to the side of the Reverend's head, a temporary grip to his throat, a knee in his groin and a bit of a push that saw him falling backwards across the coffee table.

I collected my money, toothbrush etc. On my way out I also collected just one of Revd Timbo's silver cups, just as a memento really.

'Terry, that's my boxing cup. Where're you going with it?' he called out from the chair.

'Away,' I told him. And I left.

Four

Was I going to let him get away with it? No, I wasn't! Was I going to go on trying to do a bit of good in the world by turning Terry Keegan away from a life of crime no matter how bleak things looked? Yes, I was!

So I called a council of war at twelve noon in the sitting room of the palace. The interested parties present were my dad, Robert, Robin Thirkell, Tom Weatherby and Sylvia, my mother, who, I must say, didn't have much to contribute. Oh, and me of course, as the person primarily responsible for the irresponsible Terry Keegan.

'Tim's not coming,' Robert told us. 'He said he wanted to give young Terry a boxing lesson for his own good, but that your friend reacted in an unsportsmanlike way. Below the belt, Timbo called it.'

'You mean Tim started the fight?' I asked hopefully.

'Oh yes, but purely as a matter of sport.'

'It was all going so well with Terry,' I felt I still had to defend my client, 'until Timbo hit him.'

'I'm not so sure,' Tom said. I know he didn't approve of my doing good in the world so far as Terry was concerned. It was as though he was ridiculously jealous of Terry or something. 'He was bloody rude to us in the restaurant and he broke a lot of plates.'

'Oh, everyone breaks plates to start with,' Robin said. 'I thought you were doing a marvellous job with that young man, Lucy. In fact I'm going to see if I can't get a load of wrong 'uns and find them jobs at my farm. Loads of fresh country air might make them go straight!'

'Or not,' said Tom, who doesn't like Robin for reasons, I would say, of jealousy.

'The first problem we have to face,' I did my best to call the meeting to order, 'is Terry's probation officer. I propose we ring up Mr Markby and say . . . well, let's say he's living with Robin on the farm.'

'But wouldn't that be a lie?' Tom pretended to ask an innocent question.

'I was visiting the cottage hospital out at Frimley,' began Robert, about to embark on one of his 'Thoughts for the Day'. 'There was an old chap there, obviously dying. And he said to me, "Bishop," he said, "it's bad weather now but I'll be in beautiful weather up there, won't I? Sitting on a cloud I'll be, with all the angels and me singing and playing on harps." Of course, we no longer believe in harps and angels sitting on clouds. But what did I say to the old fellow—"Of course you'll be sitting on a cloud, Ted, and I look forward to joining you there in due course." All I'm trying to say is that on many occasions what many folk call a lie is in fact an act of mercy.'

'All right,' I told them, 'that's decided then. I'll do an act of mercy tomorrow and tell the probation officer that Terry's gone off to live on Robin's farm. Then we'll start looking for him.'

'LUCINDA PUREFOY HERE. I'm ringing about Terry Keegan. I'm his praeceptor. On behalf of SCRAP.'

'Oh yes.' Mr Markby's voice revealed a complete lack of interest.

'I'm just ringing to report that Terry's changed his address.'

'I know.' He gave a heavy sigh. 'He has to report regularly to me as he's still on licence, you know. He told me about his change of address.'

I thought this was bit off as I hadn't been able to find Terry or tell him where we'd pretend he was living. I thought I'd better say my piece quickly.

'He's staying with a family friend, Robin Thirkell, at God's Acre Manor, near Farnham. Terry's going to work on the farm for Robin.'

'He isn't.'

'What?'

'He has a room in a maisonette in Connaught Square belonging to a Mr Leonard McGrath, a financial adviser with no convictions or criminal connections of any sort.'

'Well, neither has Robin Thirkell got any criminal connections.'

'That's as may be. If you'd take my advice, Miss Purefoy, you'd be far better off leaving this sort of job to professionals. I understand Keegan's helping Mr McGrath in his financial business, so he's doing rather well. Now, if you'll excuse me, I have a great deal of work to do. He's not my only client, you know.'

MY EFFORTS to do good in the world had clearly been the most pathetic failure. It was the second time Terry had walked out on me and by now I had to wonder if there was any point in trying any more. He'd walked out on me without a word of thanks. He hadn't even sent a thank-you letter to Robert for all the trouble my dad had taken over him. Added to which, all the time I'd wasted on Terry had left me a bit short of money, so I decided to take up the job at the Pitcher and Pitcher Advertising Agency, where my immediate boss was a workaholic woman who'd been put in charge of several important accounts ranging from sanitary towels to garden furniture. Tom had got really stuck into his documentary script about the London Underground, so he mostly didn't want to go out in the evenings, or if he did it was to observe tube stations like Dollis Hill and Neasden, where he could record the unusual experiences of typical travellers. He thought this script was going to land him a writer-director's job in television. I couldn't see it myself. What I'm trying to get across is a picture of my life at that moment, which I can only describe, quite honestly, as dull and boring, with an emphasis on dull.

Pitcher and Pitcher's offices are in Oxford Street and in my lunch hours I began to walk round Connaught Square. It's a big square with tall houses, some of which are divided into flats. You go up the front steps and you are met with a row of bells with various names attached to them. I began to walk round the front doors without any luck until, on my second or third visit, I found it, a card that read 'Leonard McGrath, Financial Adviser. Environmentally Friendly Investments. Mortgages and Home Loans Negotiated.' I felt a sort of excitement, I don't know why, as I rang the bell.

'Who's that?' The voice that emerged from the intercom sounded cautious. It wasn't Terry's voice.

'My name's Julie Connaught.' I didn't want to warn Terry if he was up there that I was coming back into his life so, rather unimaginatively, I adopted the name of the square. 'I've come for some advice about taking on a mortgage.'

Then the voice said, not quite so suspiciously, 'You prepared to meet the usual fees for a consultation?'

'I suppose so.'

'Come up then. Top-floor maisonette.' There was a loud buzz and the door clicked open and I started to climb endless stairs. Somewhere near the top a tall, thin man with sharp, enquiring eyes was standing outside an open door. He was wearing a sort of Middle Eastern robe with slippers.

'Miss Connaught?'

'Yes. Are you Mr McGrath?'

'Oh yes indeed. We're quite informal in the office here. As you can see, I'm working from home. Come right in.' He gave me a curious sort of twisted smile and led me into a room that contained a good deal of white furniture, a large sofa and a complete absence of office desks or computers.

'This is Diane, my secretary.'

Diane was lounging on the sofa, her feet up on a leather stool. I can only describe her appearance as tacky. When I tell you that she was wearing a ridiculously short denim skirt with chains on it, torn fishnet tights, biker's boots, a tight T-shirt with 'Foxy Woman' written on it in sequins and blue varnish on her fingernails, you get what I mean. Business in Environmentally Friendly mortgages couldn't have been brisk because she was reading, or at least turning over the pages of *Heat* magazine.

Mr McGrath invited me to sink into a white armchair, and went on about how he would take all the worries about my mortgage off my shoulders. Looking round the room, I was surprised to see some quite unexpectedly good pictures and then I noticed on the mantelpiece a familiar-looking silver cup. I stood up while Mr McGrath was still wittering on, took the cup off the mantelpiece and read, 'To the Revd Timothy Rideout, Inter-denominational

Boxing Trophy: St Crispin's Theological College, 1984'.

'What are you looking at that for?' Mr McGrath was not best pleased at my interest in the cup, and Diane (did I forget to tell you that she had dyed red hair?) looked up with obvious suspicion.

'It's just something I seem to recognise.' Before I could explain myself any further, the door opened and in came Terry.

'Oh, Terry,' Mr McGrath introduced me, 'this is Miss Connaught, come after some advice about her mortgage.'

'No, it isn't, Chippy.' This seemed to be Terry's name for Mr McGrath. 'It's Lucy Purefoy, come after me.'

'What the hell do you mean?' Mr McGrath, or Chippy as I'm going to call him from now on, looked confused. Then he turned on me. 'Are you going under a false name then?'

'Well, yes.' I had to admit it. 'Entirely false!'

I thought for a moment that Chippy was going to attack me, and hurl me down the stairs. But Terry calmed him down when he said, 'Back off, Chippy. She's a friend of mine.'

IT'S ALL VERY WELL to say you're going away, but where the away is, that's what matters. When I got on the train to London my future was uncertain. I had a bit of money, but not enough to pay for some decent accommodation. I got out of the train at Waterloo and stood for a while looking at people, all going to places with some sort of definite plan in mind.

I arrived in London just before midnight and I spent out on a room in a small hotel near Waterloo, where the bleary-eyed woman in charge looked as though she wasn't used to singles. The bed was home to various insects who stung me during the night and so in the morning, not wishing to spend any longer in such a place, I decided to give Chippy a tinkle in the faint hope he might have improved since our last meeting.

'Leonard McGrath, Environmentally Friendly Investments, Diane speaking. How can I help you?'

'By cutting all the crap,' I told her, 'and giving me Chippy McGrath.'

'May I ask who's calling?'

'Tell him it's Terry Keegan. His old friend.'

My old friend came on the line. 'Terry, you old devil! I thought you were coming to stay at the maisonette.'

'So I was. Until you told me not to.'

'Did I? Did I really do that to you, old friend?'

'You did. And you left me to pay for a bottle of champagne. That cleaned me out. I had to sleep in Euston Station.'

'Did you really?' Chippy was laughing his head off. 'You still sleeping there, are you?'

'No, I went to Aldershot.' Chippy found this quite funny too. But then he said, 'Come round. There's still a spare bed for you in the maisonette.'

He gave me the address in Connaught Square and it was there I unpacked my toothbrush, shirts and razor in Chippy's spare room. It was when we were sitting in the white armchairs in his lounge and Diane brought us two large whiskies that I asked Chippy what all the stuff about Environmentally Friendly Investments was about. Was it a cover?

'Call it that if you like, Terry. Mention the environment and everyone's on your side.'

I asked Chippy if he was doing environmentally friendly crime.

'I suppose you could call it that,' he said, laughing. 'We can go back to being partners now, can't we, Terry? It'll be quite like old times.'

'Possibly,' was all I said about that. However, I gave Chippy Timbo's silver cup and explained that I couldn't pay much rent until I found work.

'We'll find you work,' Chippy said. 'Don't worry about that. Where did you get this?' He examined the writing on the cup closely. 'You wouldn't get much for it even melted down.'

'I know. I thought you might like to have it. Just as an ornament.'

Chippy stood up and put it on his mantelpiece. 'We'll be partners,' he repeated. 'Just like old times.'

IT WAS LIKE, when I got that upper cut, something snapped inside of me. I couldn't take it any longer, all these people trying to reform me as though I had some sort of nasty disease. I felt sick of having to be so grateful for everything, from a job in that Robin's bistro, to being socked on the jaw for my own good. It was also that they seemed sort of excited by the idea of me being a real live criminal. 'Is this your little criminal?' Robin had asked Lucy. I began to think I was just there as an entertainment.

SO BY THE TIME I rang Chippy I'd decided to break with the past, at least as far as Aldershot was concerned. I got Chippy to ring Mr Markby to tell him that I'd got accommodation with Leonard McGrath of Environmentally Friendly

Investments, with a good prospect of getting a job with him eventually.

While I had been away, Chippy had formed an extremely efficient organisation. Bent burglar-alarm salesmen gave him news of particularly well-stocked houses. Bent insurers told him where the best pictures and the finest silver could be found. His personal fence had a house in Brighton where art treasures could be turned into ready money, and he even found a bent art expert to tell him which pictures were valuable, but not so famous that you could never get rid of them. From time to time, Chippy'd enlarge the team to include a peterman to blow safes. They'd do warehouse breaking and one time they got away with a whole safe full of expensive watches. Chippy was in a pretty prosperous line of business and, as luck would have it, I was able to share a bit in his prosperity.

Working with Mr Leonard McGrath of Environmentally Friendly Investments in a number of posh houses to the north of Oxford Street, I earned quite a bit of cash, which enabled me to order drinks in the Beau Brummell Club, which I no longer considered lousy but an excellent place to meet up with blaggers, reliable sources of information, as well as some quite well-known footballers and personalities on television.

I suppose it all started again when we got news about a house in Dorset Square which was shared by a couple of blokes. We got the information from the firm they used for a bit of cleaning. So I was in there one night, sorting out the silver and a few small pictures, when I suddenly saw it, a photograph pinned to a notice board in the study. I'd shone a torch on it during my search of the place and there it was. A group of girls around a grey-haired man in a crumpled suit in front of a door marked 'SCRAP Central Office'. And I saw her smiling out shyly at the camera: Lucinda 'call me Lucy' Purefoy, who had tried to stop me from doing exactly what I was doing when I saw her photograph.

I'd decided to go back to the life I knew and that was it. All the same I felt, well, I won't say it was guilt exactly, but I had to admit Lucy had done her best to help me and we'd also had some good conversations. And I'd gone off without a single goodbye, which, looking back on it, seemed a bit mean. On the other hand, there was nothing much I could do about it now, so I dismissed her from my mind.

But she kept coming back. I could see her in the bistro, fair hair falling across her forehead, her bellybutton out on view, and that look she gave as though she was genuinely worried about me. In some weird sort of way I was beginning to miss her. Perhaps it was because she was so different from Chippy's Diane or the brass you got to meet round the Brummell. But if we ever met again I was certain she would give me up as a hopeless case, so I told myself to stop thinking about her.

About three months after I left Aldershot, which would make it June, I walked into Chippy's lounge and there she was, holding Revd Timbo's silver cup in her hands and admitting that she had gained access by the use of an assumed name. I could see that this had irritated Chippy and I told him to calm down, at which I thought Lucy looked surprised and grateful.

'You come to get Reverend Tim's cup back, have you?' I asked her.

'Not necessarily.' And much to my surprise, she put the silver pot in question back on the mantelpiece. 'I came here to find you. I thought we might have a drink together some time. And a bit of a chat. You know, like we did at the Intimate Bistro.'

She certainly knew the right thing to say because, as I say, that was the chat I remembered. But she wasn't pushy about it, not at all pushy.

'Ring me if you feel like it. I'm working for Pitcher and Pitcher in Oxford Street. Ring me any time.'

She gave me a card, and then she left us. When she had gone, Chippy said, 'What the hell is she? Working for the Serious Crime Squad, is she?'

'She's not working for any nick, you can be sure of that.'

'All right then. But I'll hold you responsible for her and anything she might do that's uncalled for. I want you to be aware of that.'

I told him I was well aware.

OF COURSE I never expected to hear from him again.

So I worked away at Pitcher's and they gave me an account (Tell-All Beachwear) of my very own and Tom stayed with me in my one-bedroom flat in Notting Hill and nothing enormously exciting was happening at all.

Mr Orlando Wathen from SCRAP rang me and asked me if I was still seeing my client Keegan. For some reason I told him that I'd rather lost touch with him.

'Typical,' Orlando said. 'You can't do anything for some of these little bastards. Hopeless cases, entirely hopeless!'

'Do you really think so?'

'I know so. We were away at our place in the Dordogne and they got into Dorset Square. All the silver has gone and some pretty valuable pictures. I'm sorry, Lucy, the only place for some of these little menaces is back in the prisons where we found them. Longer sentences. That's the only answer.'

'Is that SCRAP policy from now on?' I was more than a little surprised.

'SCRAP? Oh, I'm leaving SCRAP. I'm doing voluntary work at the Home Office. Advising on the parole system.'

Then, one morning at work, the switchboard girl told me that someone called Terry Keegan was on the phone.

'Where've you been hiding, Lucy?' he said, as though it was my fault. 'What about meeting up for a drink or something?'

'Of course, I'd like that. Where exactly?'

'How about my club?'

'What's your club then?' I asked. I had a momentary absurd vision of Terry in the bar of the Athenaeum, holding forth to senior civil servants, judges and professors on life in the Scrubs.

'It's the Beau Brummell in Harrowby Street. Would you be free Thursday, shall we say round six o'clock?'

Terry's club turned out to be a far cry from the Athenaeum. There were two burly men wearing top hats at the entrance who I took to be bouncers. The girl at the desk said that Mr Keegan was waiting for me in the club room and I went up in the lift to find him.

Pools of light lit up the tables, where girls wearing bow ties and very little else were dealing out cards or spinning roulette wheels. There were hardly lit areas where large men and shadowy women were sitting talking. By the bar, I saw Terry sitting beside an ice bucket and a bottle of champagne.

He was wearing a dark suit and, extraordinarily enough, a tie, his hair was neatly brushed and he gave off an expensive smell of aftershave.

'Hello there,' he said. 'Can I offer you a glass of bubbles?'

I said I didn't see why not and then there was a silence, as though neither of us was quite prepared to explain the strange situation in which we now found ourselves. Then he said, 'I brought you this.' He fished up a plastic bag from the floor beside his bar stool. 'He can have it back,' he said.

It, of course, was Timbo's boxing cup.

'Are you sure?' I had made a point of leaving it with him as a recompense for Tim's ridiculous attack.

'Of course I'm sure. Anyway, you couldn't get much for it.'

'Thank you. Have you got a new job now, Terry?'

'Oh yes. I've got a job.'

'What is it exactly?'

'Helping Chippy out with his business.'

'You mean the Environmentally Friendly Investments business?'

'That's the one.'

Before I could ask any more, Terry, looking towards the roulette table, gave a great show of 'Sandy!' At which a pink-cheeked plump little man got up and crossed towards us.

'This is Sandy, a friend of my Uncle Arthur's.' Terry introduced us in a way I found even more encouraging. 'This is Lucy, a friend of mine.'

'Good to meet you, Lucy.' Sandy took my hand and pumped it energetically. 'Your Uncle Arthur, Terry,' he said when he'd finished, 'dreadful bad luck that was, the job he got put away for.'

'I was away myself,' Terry explained. 'I don't really know what happened.'

Sandy looked at me doubtfully and then said, 'Can we talk freely?'

'Quite freely,' Terry assured him. 'Lucy's used to it. Her father's a bishop.' I suppose this was meant to be a joke. He was obviously in a good mood.

What Sandy wanted to say was that Uncle Arthur was doing ten years for his part in an armed robbery. 'The Bright Penny Friendly Society office in Peckham. They kept a lot of cash there. Of course, he never ought to have got caught. It was all Jim Nichols's fault. A tragedy really, but we had to laugh.

'They're in the getaway car, with Big Jim Nichols driving, and the rozzers that got called after the party was over chasing them, when the freestanding phone in the car rings and this male voice asks, "Hello, is Jim Nichols there?" So Jim answers, "Yes," and the voice goes on, "This is Chris Tarrant from *Who Wants to Be a Millionaire?* We've got your friend Harry Stoker here. He's up to £32,000, but he's stuck on one question so he's chosen you as his friend."

'"OK," Big Jim Nichols says, "put him on."'

For any of you who don't know, *Who Wants to Be a Millionaire?* is a programme on television in which Chris Tarrant is the quizmaster and competitors, who may win large sums of money, are allowed to phone a friend to help them with one of the general knowledge questions.

'"The next voice you hear will be Harry's." "You ready, Jim?" "Yes, mate," Jim says, already slowing down slightly.

'Harry said, "The question is, which king died of a surfeit of lampreys? Was it a) King John, b) King Charles, c) King Harold or d) King Henry I?"

'"King Charles?" Big Jim wondered out loud, and your Uncle Arthur chipped in with, "No. It couldn't be him. He died of having his head chopped off." And then they were all arguing about who died of lampreys and what lampreys were anyway, and Jim slowed down so much that the rozzers got them. Funny, isn't it? I heard the story from a bloke who was with your Uncle Arthur in Parkhurst.'

I had to laugh too, but Terry looked serious. 'I never heard that,' he said. 'I never heard about my Aunt Dot either.'

'No. She was a good woman was your Aunt Dot. There's Rosanne waving at me. I've got to go back to her.' A woman in a green top was signalling to him from the roulette table. So he went off.

'I never knew all that about Uncle Arthur.' Terry repeated, without smiling, when we were left alone together. His mood seemed to have deteriorated a bit.

'You know,' I said to him, 'all that Environmentally Friendly Investments stuff is a load of nonsense, isn't it?'

'What do you mean?' He began to look angry and defensive.

'I mean that whatever's bought you a new suit and a tie and a bottle of bubbles in this extraordinary club wasn't investments that were at all friendly to the environment.'

There was a bit of silence after that. He was frowning as he said, 'You still trying to reform me, are you?'

If I said yes I knew we'd lose contact altogether, so what I said was, 'Certainly not! I gave you up months ago as a completely hopeless case.'

'A hopeless case, am I? So you gave up on me?'

'What else could I do?'

'Yeah,' he said thoughtfully. 'What else could you do? You lot will never begin to understand.'

'You mean we don't understand why you need smart suits, fast cars and all that sort of thing?'

'None of you understands the real reason.'

'And what is the real reason, Terry?'

'It's the excitement. That's what you lot don't understand.'

'What do you mean, the excitement?'

'People do all sorts of dangerous things, don't they? They climb up bloody great precipices. They drop out of aeroplanes or something equally daft. What do they do it for? The excitement. I tell you honestly, Lucy, all that's nothing compared to the excitement of a decent bit of crime.'

508 | JOHN MORTIMER

'You mean pinching things?'

'All right then. Pinching things. Even taking Timbo's bloody boxing cup gave me a little bit of a thrill when I nicked it.'

'Now you're giving it back.'

'Of course. It was taking it that was worthwhile. I remember what my old Uncle Arthur told me about his friend Springy Malone, so called because he could hop across roofs and so forth. Springy did serious crime until he got reformed and took up religion. But he told Arthur how disappointing it was when he went to the bank to draw out money. He stood watching the cashier count it out and he thought, in the good old days I'd have pulled out a shooter and taken the lot off you. How dull life has become! Can you understand that?'

'I might try to.'

'Forget all the mountain climbing and falling out of aeroplanes and all that. Being in someone else's house at night. Getting the silver out of the drawers and the pictures off the walls and wondering all the time if they're going to wake up and you'll be caught. I tell you, Lucy, there's nothing so exciting. People can't get cured of it.'

'You mean you can't.'

'You still don't understand it,' he said, not angrily, but smiling. Then he picked up his cuff to display a classy sort of watch that I hadn't seen before. 'I've got to go,' he said, 'I've got an appointment.'

It was not really that he seemed, at that moment, better-looking, more in control, than he ever had before. It was like, quite honestly, he was going off into a world in which there was no place for me at all.

'But like I said,' he went on, 'you lot will never understand it.' And then he smiled unexpectedly. 'We might do this again. Some time soon.'

'Yes,' I said, 'some time soon.'

The truly worrying thing, I realised, was that I had done what no decent praeceptor should ever do—fallen in love with the client.

'I JUST RANG to see how you were getting on with your client.'

'I think we've reached a pretty good understanding.'

'He's kept out of trouble?'

'So far, yes. I don't think he's in any trouble at all.'

Gwenny had called me at Pitcher's. Then she said, 'We're having a bit of trouble here at SCRAP.'

'Oh, I'm sorry to hear that.'

'Orlando Wathen resigned. He suddenly announced that the main cause of crime was the soft and soppy liberal view we took of it in the sixties. He wrote to the *Daily Telegraph* calling for life sentences for a second conviction for housebreaking.'

'Did that have something to do with his house being broken into?'

'It may have done. Anyway, we couldn't have the head of SCRAP saying things like that, so he resigned and we're looking for a replacement. That's why I rang you actually. Alex Markby said there's a wonderful chap called Leonard McGrath. Apparently he found a job for your client, Terry Keegan, and helped him go straight since he came out of the Scrubs. Do you know anything about him?'

'Oh yes. I know quite a lot about Leonard McGrath.'

'Do you think he'd be interested in helping young criminals?'

'Yes, I think he might be very interested.' I had to put the phone down before I started to giggle.

Anyway, I had more important things to do than talk to Gwenny. I had to go down to my parents' in Aldershot.

'TIMBO WILL BE DELIGHTED,' Robert said when I got down to Aldershot.

'Delighted to get his cup back?'

'Delighted that young Terry repented. There is more joy in heaven over one sinner that repents than over ninety and nine just persons who need no repentance.'

'I'm not so sure about his repenting. Apparently you couldn't get much for the cup.' I was trying to bring Robert down to the harsh reality of the situation, but he was off on another 'Thought for the Day'.

'Rather odd that, you may think. I mean, it seems, on the face of it, a bit unfair on the ninety and nine just persons who don't get God's attention at all. What he really likes are the sinners. How many of us are troubled, deeply troubled, by that thought?'

'Not many of us,' would have been my answer. But I didn't want to spoil what Robert told me would be the theme of his Sunday sermon. Then he changed the subject. 'Tonight we're invited for drinks with the dear Smith-Aldeneys,' my dad told me. 'You remember them, don't you, Lucy?'

'Of course. I used to go to pony club with Persephone.'

'They're good people. She does a lot for charity and he's chair of the

Save the Cathedral Committee. I'm afraid they're part of the ninety and nine just persons who bore God. They bore me too, if I have to be entirely honest about it.'

'But we're going to drinks with them?'

'In this life, Lucy, we must take the rough with the smooth,' my dad told me.

There was nothing really wrong with the Smith-Aldeneys. In fact they did everything right. They lived in just the right size of converted farmhouse to the south, that is to say the better, side of Aldershot. They had just the right amount of money since Christopher Smith-Aldeney worked for a City bank, and the right number of children. Persephone, who was my age and just returned from back-packing in Cambodia, and a younger son, Billy, who was reading economics at Cardiff. Their mother, Olive Smith-Aldeney, controlled the whole family with determined charm. You could be quite sure at a party of the Smith-Aldeneys that nothing embarrassing or outrageous would occur and probably nothing very interesting either.

Persephone wanted to discuss the time when we were all at pony camp together, and then Christopher Smith-Aldeney came up and asked if I'd like to see his new acquisition. Long ago, when I was about fourteen, I'd shown a sort of polite interest when Christopher showed me his collection of ancient coins and he had been sure that I was a budding numismatist. So I never visited Fallowfield, the Smith-Aldeneys' home, without Christopher opening his glass cases and taking me on a brisk tour through the ducats and louis d'ors, the crowns and the florins and the first pounds of the British Raj in India. But now there was something entirely new—a Roman coin with the head of the Emperor Claudius.

'Don't you think it's beautiful, Lucy?' Christopher said, and although it seemed an ordinary bit of bronze to me, I agreed that it brought the whole history of the Roman Empire back to the drinks party in Fallowfield. With that he gave me a squeeze and the sort of distinctly damp kiss I used to get when I came back to the farmhouse after pony club events with Persephone.

However, just as Christopher was uttering the corniest of lines, Mrs Smith-Aldeney came up considerably worried, not about her husband's squeezing but about the conduct of my mother. 'Sylvia says she didn't come out to drink sherry in glasses the size of eggcups and could she have a G and T. I told her I'd ask you to find something or other.' At which her husband put his Claudius coin down on the table and went buzzing off.

'I'm terribly sorry,' I told Olive after Christopher had gone.

'What have you got to be sorry about, Lucinda?' Olive wasn't in the best of tempers.

'My mum,' I told her.

'Oh, don't worry.' She became more sympathetic. 'We've got used to her.'

I left the party and drove myself straight back to London as I had to be up early for a breakfast meeting with the Tell-All Beachwear account. I'd hardly started when my mobile rang its little tune ('Toreador').

Christopher was sounding desperate. 'I've lost the Claudius coin.'

'You can't have done.'

'I thought I put it back in the case. But when the party was over I looked and it wasn't there. You didn't see what I did with it?'

'I'm afraid not. But I'm sure it will turn up somewhere.'

'I've searched every corner of the room.'

'And you couldn't find it?'

'Nothing so far. It's a complete mystery.'

'Yes,' I said. 'I suppose it is.'

Five

'Let me see now. You're still working with Environmentally Friendly Investments?'

'Oh yes, I am.' I told Mr Markby, my probation officer, nothing but the truth.

'Good! I'm glad to hear it. There's nothing more vitally important in our world today than global warming.' Mr Markby ticked another box on his form. 'I sometimes wonder how you managed to land a job with Mr McGrath. Have you had any training in business studies?'

'Not much,' I had to admit. 'I think he took me on as a favour.'

'Leonard McGrath wanted to help you go straight!' Mr Markby seemed deeply impressed. 'How long have you known him?'

'I was at school with his young brother.'

'Good. Excellent.' Mr Markby seemed easy to please that day. 'They're looking for a new man to head up SCRAP. I put Leonard McGrath's name forward. I hope he won't mind.'

'I'm sure he'll be pleased.' Of course I could see the funny side of it. Then my probation officer leaned back in his chair and said, 'By the way, are you seeing any more of your so-called praeceptor, that Miss Purefoy?'

'Not much.' I lied. I didn't think he needed to know about my friends.

'Good. I'm glad of that. Those girls rush in where we probation officers are careful where we tread. My advice to you is to give that Miss Purefoy a wide berth.'

'All right then.'

'So long as you hold down your job with Mr Leonard McGrath and report to me regularly, I'm quite happy.'

I'd never really forgiven Mr Markby for delaying my parole, although he seemed a good deal more friendly since I moved in with Chippy. However, I was determined not to take his advice about giving Lucy 'a wide berth'. The hell with that, Mr Markby. It was a bit surprising, but it seemed that I wanted to see Lucy more than ever I had before. I suppose life's like that, isn't it? When she was busy trying to reform me I wanted to get as far away from her as possible. But when she said she'd given me up as a bad job I felt I couldn't get enough of her. It wasn't just the way she looked, I swear to you it wasn't. I'd found out you could have a good conversation with her, and good conversations weren't easy to come by around the maisonette.

So I was seriously thinking of giving Lucy a bell again, but before I got round to doing that she rang me and sounded, I thought, a bit less sure of herself than usual.

'I wonder if you'd like to go out with me some time. Have dinner together or something?' See what I mean? That wasn't the usual Lucy, who knew exactly what she wanted. It also reminded me of the different sort of worlds we came from. When I was a kid, 'dinner' was something you got on Sundays if you were lucky. What you had in the evening was your 'tea'.

'No,' I said. 'I'll take you out.' Let her pay a bill, I thought, and she'll be back feeling she's in control and trying to reform me. 'Thursday?'

'I'd love to see you on Thursday.' She seemed to be genuinely pleased.

'All right, I'll ring you. Time and place. I'll pick a good one.'

The truth was that I had no idea where to pick. I had to consult a well-known member of the smart set—Mr Leonard McGrath.

'The in place now is definitely La Maison Jean Pierre,' Chippy told me. Jean Pierre is a personal friend. Only trouble is you won't get a table in less than six months' time.'

'We can't go there then.'

'Unless we ask for it in my name. Lift the phone, would you, Diane? When do you want to go?'

'Say . . . Thursday?'

'Oh, it's Leonard McGrath's office here,' Diane told the 'in place'. 'Mr McGrath would like a table for two on Thursday. Yes, dinner. Shall we say eight o' clock? Cool.' She put down the phone. 'They're looking forward to seeing us.'

'But they'll be seeing me.'

'Just say I came down with a heavy cold,' Chippy told me, 'so I sent you to take my place as you run my accounts department and it's your birthday.'

THE RESTAURANT was in a room with white walls and steel furniture, like a hospital wing. There were a few pictures on the walls, but they didn't seem to be pictures of anything, just plain colours. They were the sort of thing I'd have left on the walls of any house I'd broken into. The place was very busy and it was quite a while before some sort of top waiter arrived. 'Tonight, Jean Pierre recommends,' he said, and made it clear that it was what we'd choose unless we were a couple of idiots who'd never seen the inside of a five-star restaurant before.

The food was big let-down. The idea of a good feed never seemed to have entered the mind of Jean Pierre. The starter was something to do with marinated seaweed, which wasn't anything I'd eat again. The fish didn't look much like any fish I'd ever met before and had a taste of meat about it, and a salad of plums and raspberries, with not a chip in sight. On the whole I think we did better, food-wise, in the Burger King. But what I'll never ever forget is what happened when all this rubbish had been cleared away.

Lucy had been sort of excited during the meal with lots of 'Mmmmm, this is delicious!' which I think she did more out of politeness to me than because she genuinely enjoyed what we were eating. And then, when we got to the coffee part, she opened her handbag and put something down on the tablecloth.

What she'd got was a dirty old coin that might have been shiny years ago but was now a sort of dirty green colour. I could just make out a bald head and some letters I could hardly read.

'That's very kind,' I said. I didn't want to seem ungrateful. 'Did you buy this for me?'

'No,' she said, and by now she was almost laughing. 'I stole it for you.'

'You did *what*?' I was so surprised that I asked her while the waiter was hovering. 'But *why*?' I asked her as the waiter moved away. It seemed like, well, like the whole world had turned upside down.

'I suppose because I wanted to understand you properly. It was what you said about the excitement. You said it was the extraordinary excitement that made you do it.'

'That's part of it, of course. And earning a living, of course.'

'I suppose there is that,' she seemed a bit disappointed, 'but you said it was the excitement you'd miss.'

'I may have said that.'

'But you're not missing it now, are you?'

'No, not exactly. I'm working.'

'Well, I want to work with you. To be together. That was what was wrong before. We came from separate worlds.'

I thought of my world. According to the likes of my Uncle Arthur and Aunt Dot, a woman's place was in the kitchen or looking after the kids if there were any, not out robbing banks and building societies, blowing safes or holding up security guards.

'You see, when I was being trained by SCRAP,' she said, 'we learned all about what it was like trying to reform people, getting them cheap places to sleep and not very well-paid jobs. They never taught us what it was like to live by stealing things. Nobody told us anything about the excitement.'

'I wish I never had.' I can't say I really approved of what was going on.

'No, Terry, I'm so glad you did. I feel we've come together. We can really bond.' She put her hand on mine on the table.

I looked down at the coin. 'What did you say this was exactly?'

'A Roman coin from the time of the Emperor Claudius. It was found in a field near St Albans.'

'What do you expect me to do with it?'

'Fence it,' she told me, 'through your usual chap.' She was getting to know some of the ropes already.

I had to pull off a number of tenners to pay the bill. Lucy watched me doing this and said, 'Ill-gotten gains!'

'What do you mean?'

'I expect everyone's paying with gains that are more or less ill-gotten. Faked expense accounts, pretending to be entertaining for business reasons, tax fiddles. It's just that yours are more openly ill-gotten, aren't they darling?'

It was the first time anyone had called me that for years.

I took Lucy back to Notting Hill in a taxi. She seemed happy enough until we got to her flat, but she looked up and saw that the lights were on. Then she said, 'Oh damn!' and gave me a sort of fluttering kiss that just missed my mouth and landed on my nose. Then she jumped out of the taxi and ran away from me.

Lucy might have gone a long way to understand me, but she was still a bit of a puzzle so far as I was concerned.

IT HAPPENED. It finally happened. And I must say it was a relief, although it's hard to explain and you probably won't understand unless you've done it yourself, which I don't for a second advise you to do, for reasons you'll discover before this story ends.

When I began to have feelings for Terry that no praeceptor is meant to have for a client, I realised that I was from another world entirely. In the world I came from, bishops and chaplains and praeceptors and probation officers, they all talked about sin and crime but they couldn't really understand it. Take Robert. He preached hours of sermons about sin, but I don't believe he'd ever committed the smallest sin in his life. Orlando Wathen, Gwenny and Mr Markby all set themselves up as experts on crime, but Mr Wathen confessed he couldn't understand the first thing about it. He hadn't had Terry explain the excitement. It was what turned a dull party at the Smith-Aldeneys into the most exciting turning point of my life.

When Christopher was showing me his collection, the thought of doing it hadn't crossed my mind. It was when he was called away to get Sylvia a gin and left the Emperor Claudius out lying on the table that the sudden irresistible urge came over me. It was the sudden feeling of understanding Terry and being near him, closer to him than I could ever get in any other way. I felt everything change when I picked up the Claudius coin and put it in the back pocket of my jeans.

I know what you're going to say. You're going to say, 'What happened to that Lucinda Purefoy who wanted to do a bit of good in the world?' And I suppose I'd find that a hard one to answer. I suppose I might say that what I was doing was trying to do some good to Terry by understanding him, and I think that's what I told myself. It sort of made sense to me at the time.

I tried to explain some of this to Terry. Poor sweet, he insisted on taking me out to the most expensive restaurant in London run by the ghastly Jean Pierre O'Higgins, who does those wretched television programmes about how rude he has to be to the customers who criticise his awful cooking. I had to pretend to be thrilled and oooh and aaah over the crystallised seaweed and the bacon and egg ice cream! It was at the end of this gastronomic nightmare that I did what I'd been longing to do. I produced the Emperor Claudius coin and told Terry I'd stolen it for him.

Honestly, I thought he might have congratulated me on what I'd done. I thought he might have welcomed me into his exciting world of thieves, where we could sink or swim together. I have to admit I felt really let down when he didn't welcome me into it at all.

Of course they'd warned us at SCRAP about this male chauvinist thing that criminals have, like they don't want women committing crimes, or especially, trying to reform them. It's the same thing again, isn't it? I mean, Tom Weatherby thinks that him writing scripts for documentaries no one in television seems to want is a serious business whereas my job in advertising is just a sort of hobby, like Pilates classes. Even my dad, for all his liberal views, seems a good deal more enthusiastic about gay marriages than he is about women bishops.

All I can say is that if being a woman is a hurdle in me getting closer to Terry, it's one I've got to get over as soon as possible.

In all this, Tom was no help at all.

I was particularly glad when Terry suggested Thursday because that was when Tom planned to do some late-night research and spend the night with his sister in Sidcup. So I thought the flat would be empty and I could invite Terry up after dinner, and we could do whatever we wanted to do. I was sure he'd be in a pretty good mood after I'd shown my solidarity with him by handing over the coin. I was really angry with Tom when I found his plans had changed and all the lights were on in the flat when Terry took me home. All we could manage was a quick frustrated kiss. I suppose we could have gone on to the maisonette, but Terry never invited me.

Of course, Tom had some feeble excuse, it wasn't convenient for his sister to have him to stay. Then he said, 'I suppose you wanted to bring the little thief up here?'

'Terry's not particularly little,' I reminded him.

'But he is a thief. I know you find that tremendously exciting. I'm terribly sorry. I do apologise! I've got no criminal convictions!'

I suppose if I'd listened to Tom at the time, I might have saved myself a great deal of trouble but of course, I didn't want to listen. All I knew was that our relationship, such as it was, had definitely fizzled out.

A FEW WEEKS went by after that dinner when I didn't see Lucy. I suppose I was a bit shocked when she told me she'd stolen something. Of course, you'll say I stole things, which is true, but it just didn't seem to me to be in Lucy's character. I never fenced that old green coin she gave me, but I kept it on the table by the side of my bed, to make sure she hadn't really become part of our business.

Which was growing all the time. Chippy had taken on more part-time workers, who did the smaller odd jobs for us, and a character known as 'Screwtop Parkinson', who, Chippy said, drove a getaway car so fast no one would ever catch it. It may be that this talent came from the fact that he was slightly mad, as his name indicated, but Chippy said he could rely on Screwtop to get us out of any nasty situation.

Chippy also told me what he thought was a good joke. 'They want me to be chairman of SCRAP. You know what that is, don't you, Terry?'

'Of course I know what it is.'

'They help young cons go straight. Do you think I'd be good at that?'

'I don't think you'd be good at it at all.'

Chippy gave me his one-sided smile. 'Do you not?' he said. 'I think I know a good deal about young cons. Anyway, the lady from SCRAP wants me to help in her drive for funding.' And then Chippy further amazed me by saying, 'Reckon if you do a job like that you get made a "sir" in the end. Play your cards right and you get knighted by the Queen.'

I couldn't get my mind round it.

Then, once again, everything changed. It was a Sunday and I'd got up late. I was in my bedroom in the maisonette when I heard a furious hooting in the square below my window. I looked out and there she was, standing beside this clapped-out Polo.

'I ought to go down and see my dad,' she told me when I joined her in the square. 'And I thought we might have another picnic on the way down.'

I had nothing much to look forward to except a long and boring Sunday with Sir Leonard in the maisonette. So I hopped in. We went round an Arab shop in Queensway and bought kebabs and pitta bread, taramasalata and hummous and all that stuff including olives, all things Lucy knew about.

Then we found an off-licence and got a bottle of Rioja like we'd had at our first picnic. Lucy said we were off to Folly Hill.

So we got round the M25 and turned off down the M3 towards woods with spiky trees and sandy soil. Although I'd been driven by Lucy before, I hadn't remembered that the experience was, well, frightening. Lucy's idea of driving was to put her foot down on dangerous corners. She passed fast cars and lorries without any clear idea of what was going on ahead. I had to bite my tongue to stop myself saying, 'Hang about! You're not Screwtop Parkinson in the getaway car, let's go a bit slower and admire the scenery.' Of course, I didn't say this. I didn't want to spoil her day.

So it was a bit of a relief when we turned off on to the country roads and we got to this spot looking out over woods and fields. She parked the Polo not far from a farm gate and she set off, with a rug, plates and glasses. She called out at me to bring the lunch and follow her.

Lucy had laid out the rug not far from the road. I joined her and we sat down. I opened the Rioja and we took big swigs out of plastic cups. The sun was shining and there was a bit of a breeze stirring the pointed trees and lifting Lucy's hair occasionally. She was smiling and laughing, looking happier, I thought, than at any time since we met.

When we'd finished eating Lucy produced another plastic bag from somewhere. It was heavy and clinked a bit as she handed it over to me with a big smile and said, 'It's for you, Terry.'

I looked into it. Then I put the things out on the rug. There was a silver cigarette case, a couple of snuff boxes which I knew were quite valuable, an expensive Rolex watch, a gold pen and a pair of binoculars.

Lucy had stood up and was looking down at me and her collection, smiling proudly. 'Stuff I blagged. For you.'

'I told you I didn't want you to do that.'

'But I want to.' She was kneeling beside me now. 'You said it was exciting and it is. I could feel it. I could really understand.'

'I didn't need you to understand me,' I told her.

'But I want to, Terry. Don't you know how much I want to? You don't know how close I felt to you when I was doing it.'

Well, all I can say is that it didn't make me feel close to her. But she looked that proud of what she'd done, she seemed so bubbling over with it, that I just couldn't bring myself to say it. And then I suddenly found her mouth was on my mouth and her fingers were after the zip in my trousers. I won't say that I didn't hope that something like this might happen when I got into the clapped-out Polo but I wanted to make the suggestion and now there was obviously no need to do so.

So there we were together on the rug and occasionally I caught sight of the things she'd stolen, but I tried not to think about them. I heard a car stop and then go on again, but after that, apart from the birds twittering, everything was quiet.

That's really all that has to be said about it, except that when it was over I felt different. As though my prison days were well over.

WHEN DEIRDRE (you remember Deirdre? I was at school with her and she told me to join SCRAP) asked me and Tom Weatherby to dinner at her Uncle Charles's spread near Ascot, I told her it had all fizzled out with me and Tom, so I went alone. On my way to and from the loo, I managed to pick up quite a few items, including the snuff boxes I knew Terry would think had a bit of value to them. In all this I was following the morality of the Youth Detention Centre and strictly confined myself to robbing from the rich without necessarily having to give to the poor. And I knew I needed these bits and pieces to bond with him. Well, thank goodness, it worked at last.

Mind you, even before I showed him the new stuff, he was nicer than he'd ever been. He seemed really pleased to drive out into the wilds of Hampshire. Of course he gripped his seat when I drove round corners, but all men do that because they think women can't drive. At least he didn't whimper, 'Please don't kill me,' like Tom sometimes did.

Well, then I showed him the things I blagged and I think he was pleased. What I hadn't quite thought through was what we should do once we'd bonded. And then all that was put on hold, in a manner of speaking, because I took one look at him and you know what I said to myself, and this may surprise you, I said, 'Heathcliff'. Well, I knew he'd read *Wuthering Heights* and I'd read it at school (another sort of a link between us) and there he was, my favourite character, who was irresistible but dangerous to know, sitting on the rug with the wind in his black curly hair.

Of course you can guess what happened next. I really don't want to go into it, because although I think sex is great to do it's quite boring to read about. I heard a car stop once and start again on the road above us; apart from that it all seemed wonderfully still and quiet round Folly Hill.

I'd promised Robert we'd have dinner at the palace before we drove back to London, and during the shepherd's pie (Dad and Mum have always been strong supporters of nursery food) my father came out with what I imagined was going to be his next 'Thought for the Day'.

'God gave the joy of sex,' he said, shaking the tomato ketchup bottle sharply over his shepherd's pie, 'to our forefather and mother in his garden of Eden. We must assume that our common ancestors enjoyed the heavenly gift of coitus in the open air.'

'Why?' Terry asked in surprise, a forkful of potato about to enter his mouth.

'Well, that's a very good question. Because we don't read of Adam and Eve having built any sort of shelter in the garden. We must assume that the climate was always favourable in those far-off days.' Robert's thoughts seemed to me to be getting a little too close for comfort. 'I said that to Charlie Fawcett today. We'd met at an inter-diocesan conference in Basingstoke and I was giving him a lift back. We'd just got to Folly Hill when he suddenly said, "Stop the car!" I thought he'd heard the exhaust drop off or something so I stopped, but all Charlie said was, "Look at that! Isn't it disgusting?" Well, all I could see was a couple on a rug apparently enjoying God's great gift of sexual intercourse al fresco under the arch of heaven.'

'Did you see who they were?' I had to ask him.

'Certainly not! I just took a quick look and drove on, but Charlie Fawcett went on and on about people using the English countryside as though it were their own private bedroom.'

I looked at Terry. He was chomping away without any expression at all.

'So, no one need be ashamed.' Robert was completing his 'Thought' of enjoying the gift God has given us, in all weathers.

Sylvia, who'd brought her gin and tonic into dinner, made no comment.

Six

'Quite honestly, I'm worried about her. Seriously worried.'

'And what is it that worried you about her exactly? Has she got what I suppose you'd call "a bun in the oven"?' Mr Markby gave me a rare Scottish sort of a smile that flickered only for a moment.

'No, it's not that. It's her thieving.'

I'd called to make my routine visit to my probation officer. I sat opposite him and we talked across the desk in a cold office with a big filing cabinet and a pot plant that looked as if it hadn't got long to live. As you know, I never liked Mr Markby, not since he robbed me of my parole, but I was stuck for someone to come to for advice. The fact I'd come to him seemed to be an unexpected point in my favour.

'You're worried and you've come to tell me about it?'

'I didn't know who else I could tell.'

'Quite right, come to the professional. I don't suppose that girl from SCRAP's any help at all in this situation.'

'I'm afraid she's not.'

'Just as I thought. Now, let's see.' He turned over his notes. 'You're still living in Mr McGrath's accommodation and working for Environmentally Friendly Investments.'

'I'm still working with him, yes.'

'He's a good man, Terry. He's been a good man to you.' Mr Markby was looking extremely serious. 'A force for good in the world.' Then he said, 'You're really concerned about this friend of yours, aren't you?'

'Most concerned.' I really was.

'That shows how much the Probation Service has done for you. What does she steal, by the way?'

'Bits and pieces. Old coins. A gold pen. Snuff boxes she got. They might be worth a bit actually. A good watch.'

'The menopause.'

'What?'

'It happens to women of a certain age. Is she of a certain age?'

'Twenty-five.'

'Then the menopause has got nothing to do with it. Just plain simple crime. And greed. That's what it was, wasn't it, Terry, when you used to do it yourself?'

'When I used to do it, yes.'

'Well, you can point this out to her. Where did it get you, all that thieving you did? Into prison for a long time, that's where it got you.'

'I'll try that.'

'Yes, you try that. Really scare her. Tell her she wouldn't enjoy Holloway. Be gentle with her of course. Gentle and understanding. But be perfectly clear. She's committing crimes and she'll end up in prison. Oh, and keep an eye on her. If she's going to go straight and resist the temptation to steal things, she'll need continued support.'

'I'll remember that,' I told him.

Then he looked at me, sort of sizing me up. 'I don't suppose you've ever thought of joining the Probation Service, have you?'

I could quite honestly tell him that I hadn't.

'Pity,' he said. 'We could do with lads like you.'

BECAUSE MR MARKBY had told me to keep an eye on Lucy, I agreed to move in to her flat in Notting Hill Gate. In the flat I could still go out on any of the big jobs when Chippy needed my help. Apart from that, I saw that Lucy got up in time for work and left thieving to the professionals. During the day I did the shopping, cleaned up and read some of the books Lucy had on the shelves in the lounge. In the evenings, Lucy either got me cooking with her or we went out locally for a Chinese or an Indian. Looking back, it was about the best time of my life, but nothing much happened. Except perhaps I ought to just mention the evening Lucy said she'd take me to the Close-Up in Soho. She said it was her club but it seemed that her ex, Tom Weatherby, was the member and she told the girl on the desk we were waiting for him, which of course we weren't.

'Well, well, I see you've got a new friend.' A tall woman with a sort of commanding voice, bright red hair and permanently raised eyebrows came up to us. She was with a smallish, grinning man who I put down as Caribbean. Lucy said, 'This is Deirdre,' and told her that I was Terry Keegan. Then Deirdre asked if Lucy had picked me up at SCRAP. When Lucy admitted it, Deirdre said that was where she picked up Ishmael. She seemed very proud of him. 'He's a terrific rap singer, you know.'

Then Deirdre went on to tell us that after the dinner at her Uncle Charles's spread it was discovered that a few little things were missing. Deirdre's uncle suspected Ishmael, although he was busy entertaining them all with his rap and never went off around the house on his own—pure bloody racism.

'How ridiculous!' Lucy was saying, cool as cold beer.

'IT'S IN THE *Guardian*,' I told Terry at breakfast. 'Leonard McGrath made chairman of SCRAP. That couldn't be anything to do with your friend in the maisonette, could it?'

'It is my friend in the maisonette—Chippy reckons he's in with the chance of a knighthood.' Terry was buttering toast.

'But that's ridiculous!' I said.

'Yes, it is. Very ridiculous.' But he wasn't laughing.

'Do you think SCRAP ought to be told?'

'I don't think Chippy would like that.'

'I suppose we needn't take SCRAP seriously any more,' I suggested.

'No, we needn't take it seriously.'

This was a kind of relief, but then Terry said he'd been to see Mr Markby, his probation officer.

'Routine visit?' Quite honestly, I didn't have a lot of time for Mr Markby.

'Not quite routine.' Terry looked unusually serious. 'I told him how worried I was about you. Of course, I didn't say you by name. I called you a friend. He advised me to tell you that it would land you in prison like it did me.'

'But isn't that why it's so exciting? The risk, I mean.'

'I don't want you to take any risks, Lucy.'

'Why not? I'm not objecting to you taking risks.'

'I'm different,' Terry said. 'Completely different.'

'Because you're a man?' I'd got Terry cooking but I still couldn't get rid of the male chauvinist side of him.

'Not that I'm a man, Lucy. Because I do the big, serious jobs. The bits and pieces you bring home aren't either here or there.'

'Not even the snuff boxes?'

'Well, the snuff boxes might bring in a bob or two,' he had to admit.

'Stop doing that male superiority thing then. Anyway, you know I'm only doing it to understand you. To be at one with you. You know that, don't you, Terry?' I don't think I could have put it more nicely. But I was not altogether pleased by his reply.

'You'll never be like me because you don't do serious jobs. It's just a sort of game to you, isn't it, Lucy? But it's not to me. It's how I earn a living. That's why I want you to stop doing it.'

'You mean you want to reform me.' I'm afraid I rather snapped at him.

'Something like that, I suppose,' he had to admit.

When I came back that evening I dialled 1571 for my messages and immediately got the high-pitched sound of Robin Thirkell.

'Lucy, darling!' Robin was carolling. 'I'm inviting you to no end of champagne and caviar and I hope it's going to be an amusing evening.

Come alone, if you don't mind. I really want to enjoy your company far away from that little criminal.'

I told Terry that Robin had invited me to a rather grand dinner party in the country. 'But you'll probably be too busy to come.' I didn't tell him that the invitation was only for me, because I knew he wouldn't fancy it anyway.

'Yes,' Terry said, 'I probably will be busy.'

WHEN I DROVE into the yard of God's Acre that Saturday at 7.30, I saw no other cars. I didn't know who had been invited or where they might have got to. As I climbed out of the Polo I got the usual long hysterical barks from the four bull terriers, who seemed about to attack me until I called them by their names, Judy, Greta, Marlene and Virginia, then they calmed down and started licking my hands.

The door was opened by Max, Robin's sort of butler, who wore a short white jacket that was never entirely clean. Max had ginger hair and had never shaved adequately at the top of his cheekbones. 'His nibs is in the living room, Lucy,' he told me, then returned to the kitchen to finish the large whisky he'd no doubt been drinking.

Robin had done up God's Acre Manor like a homage to Cecil Beaton. There were a lot of heavy curtains held back by ties with massive gold tassels, statues of marble cherubs on marble columns and a selection of gold-framed photographs on top of the grand piano, many of them of Robin as a winsome child. I remembered a time when I found Robin's decor rather grand and exciting, but now I thought it just poncey.

'Where's the party?' I asked him.

'There isn't a party. Just me.' Robin was wearing a blue velvet smoking-jacket thing and offering me strips of toast with caviar on them.

'But you said . . .'

'What's it matter what I said?' He gave me that roguish little-boy look that I now found mildly irritating. 'I thought you wouldn't come if it was just me. Isn't that true? Not now you've taken to rough trade from Her Majesty's prisons.'

'I can't stay tonight,' I told him quite firmly.

We were soon alone in the dining room, being served by Max, who winked at me over the roast pheasant as though he knew exactly what I'd come for. I was almost moved to shout at him, 'I'm going home tonight!' But by then Robin was being quite bitchily funny about all the neighbours so I decided to ignore Max completely and merely disappoint his expectations later.

Towards the end of dinner, when I'd had the champagne and a good deal of red wine, Robin suddenly said, 'I've got a Bonnard.'

Now, you'll have to excuse me. I'm not really up in the world of art. At that time I didn't know what a Bonnard was. It might have been a brand of dog, or a vintage car, or a type of Italian suit. Then Robin said, 'My Uncle Everard left it to me in his will. This wonderful picture. You should see it.'

'I'd like to.'

Well, of course, after dinner it became clear that the great Bonnard picture was upstairs, in his bedroom. However, I felt so completely attached to Terry and so confident of my powers of refusal that I let Robin take me into the familiar room with the big four-poster bed with carved wooden leaves at the top of each column and a shield on the crossbar with some sort of coat of arms that was certainly not Robin's.

There on the wall a slim, pinkish youngish woman was drying her thighs near a big white bathtub. She looked utterly uninterested in what was going on anywhere else in the world, totally absorbed in what she was doing.

'I like it,' I told Robin. I really did.

'I like it too. Of course she's not *in* the bath. It would go for millions if Mrs Bonnard was *in* the bath. But that little thing's worth £300,000.'

'Really?' My interest in the picture increased.

I examined Robin's 'little Bonnard' more closely, and I asked him if he wasn't afraid of burglars.

'Not a bit. The dogs would just fly at anyone they didn't know. They'd wake up Max and he's a match for any burglar. Shall we go to bed now?'

'Go to bed? Whatever for?' I asked him, looking innocent.

'Sex, of course. With all the trimmings.'

'I don't think so.'

'Are you turning me down?'

'Flat!'

Robin looked thoughtful and then said casually, 'What did you do with the Emperor Claudius coin?'

'I don't know what you mean.'

'Oh yes, you do. Either we go to bed now or I tell the neighbourhood.'

'That's blackmail.' I was profoundly shocked. 'It's a crime.'

'I know it is. Almost as bad a crime as thieving.' Robin turned on the charm. His shirt was now wide open, his face lit up with a smile. 'Hop into bed, why don't you? You know you want to.'

As he tried to embrace me all I could do was to bring my knee up smartly, a gesture met with a cry of pain. And, in less time than it takes to tell, I was out of the house, across the yard and in the Polo. Luckily the key was still in the ignition and I left God's Acre at around sixty miles an hour.

I DIDN'T THINK I was getting anywhere. Nothing I said to Lucy about the danger of ending up inside stopped her from lifting small bits and pieces of other people's property and giving them to me, with the sort of proud look I used to see on my Aunty Dot's cat when it brought in a dead bird and laid it on the carpet.

Whenever I told Lucy what I thought about it she said she was doing it for my sake 'so we could share a common experience'. It seemed to me there was only one person who might have a bit of clout with Lucy so I took the Polo and headed off in the direction of Aldershot.

I found Lucy's mum in the palace, wandering vaguely from room to room, but when she asked me to join her in a snifter I had to refuse politely and ask where my girlfriend's dad might be found. It turned out he was in the cathedral, preparing for a special service on 'Family Values' to be broadcast over the radio next Sunday.

I'd never been in a cathedral before, never much in church if it comes to that. The one in Aldershot seemed to be very cold and grey and there were rows and rows of empty chairs. Around the walls were statues of dead people lying on marble boxes with their legs crossed.

Up at the far end there were lights and a bit of activity. Some man was fixing up a mike. An organ somewhere stopped and started and a row of young kids was going through a song, over and over in a way that would drive you bananas if you had to listen to it too long.

I stood blinking in the shadows for a minute and then I spotted Lucy's dad in the back row of the chairs. He was wearing a sort of long black skirt arrangement and scribbling away in a notebook.

'Terry!' I have to say he gave me a great welcome as I made my way towards him. 'You've come to church! There's more joy in heaven over one sinner that repenteth—well, I've told you that before, haven't I?'

'I just wanted to find you.'

'And here I am.' He spread out his arms as though he'd performed some sort of miracle just by being there. 'What's your trouble?'

'It's not my trouble exactly. It's your daughter's.'

'You mean Lucy?'

'Yes, I do mean Lucy. She's been stealing.'

'Whatever do you mean?' He was still smiling, as though I'd made a joke.

'Money and other things. Snuff boxes. Bits of silver. That's what I came to tell you, Mr Purefoy.

'Bishop Purefoy.'

'Sorry.'

'It doesn't matter. Now what is it you're trying to tell me?' He leaned forward as though he didn't want to miss a word of what I was saying.

'That your daughter's a thief, Bishop Purefoy.'

'Classic!' he said. 'It's a classic situation!'

'You mean a lot of bishops have thieving daughters?'

'No. Not that. Not that at all. God sent Jesus down to redeem our sins and then sent Freud down to explain them. Oh, I'm sorry,' Lucy's dad seemed suddenly embarrassed, 'I don't suppose you know much about Freud!'

As a matter of fact he was wrong. He made the usual mistake of thinking I didn't know much about anything. Having spent years in a cell reading books, I knew enough about Freud to be sure he had nothing to do with our present discussion.

'You see, you're the thief, Terry.'

'I've got to admit that.' I didn't want to go into further detail.

'You're the thief and not Lucy.'

'Me *and* Lucy. I just told you.'

'You told me because that's what you want to believe. You probably need to. You'd rather not have it, this guilt. This is where our old friend Freud comes in.' The bishop was now rubbing his knees in excitement. 'It's a classic case! The transference of guilt!'

'Transference of *what*?'

'You don't like your guilt. So you hand it on to my daughter.'

'But I came down here to see you. So you could help.'

There was a burst of music and the kids up by the altar started singing again. The bishop stood: 'Robin Thirkell came to see me with some ridiculous story about Lucy stealing old coins from Christopher Smith-Aldeney. No doubt you'd been spreading rumours. My advice to you, Terry, is to keep your guilt to yourself. Now I must go and see to our service. Next

Sunday on Radio 4, if you happen to be listening. It's all God's work.'

After he'd gone I sat for a while looking at the grey walls and marble boxes full of old bones. I thought that Lucy's dad knew about Freud and God, but he didn't seem to have much understanding of his daughter.

Seven

He told me he'd been down to see my dad about reforming me and of course I was furious. I remembered how far apart we'd been when I was trying to be the reformer, and how much he'd hated me for it. Something had to be done about it and it was at this time that I had what I called 'the Great Idea'.

The more I thought about the idea the greater it became. At least it would wipe off that patronising, worried little smile that arrived far too often on Terry's face. At best it would bind us together for always, equals with a full understanding of each other. We'd be real partners, and not that come and go sort of partner people like Deirdre called whoever they happened to be sleeping with at the time.

Speaking of Deirdre, she still phoned me from time to time. When Terry was out one evening on business he wasn't going to tell me about (well, when I got the Great Idea going, all that would have to change), I promised to meet her again for a drink in the Close-Up Club.

She was as usual with Ishmael, her rap artist. We sat at the bar fingering our glasses of white wine.

'Hello, praeceptor!' Deirdre had greeted me. 'How's the little crook you're busy turning into a little angel?'

'I'm not a praeceptor any more actually. And Terry's moved in with me.'

'Terry Keegan has moved in with you?' It was almost the first time that the rap singer had spoken directly to me. His sudden interest surprised me.

'Why? Do you know Terry Keegan?' I asked him. Ishmael muttered, 'I may have heard of him.' I suppose that in the underworld Ishmael inhabited quite a lot of people would have heard of Terry.

Deirdre said, 'You remember that Gwenny told us never to sleep with anyone we met through SCRAP?'

'She said it would have disastrous results,' I agreed. 'But it hasn't, has it?'

'Not so far!' the suddenly loquacious rap artist cheerfully agreed. And then he ordered another bottle of New Zealand Chardonnay. It was an evening full of surprises.

When we got down to the end of the bottle, I heard myself say to Deirdre, 'It's a problem, isn't it? We come from such different worlds, Terry and me and you and Ishmael. Don't you find it difficult to, well, bridge the gap?'

'Not really.' Deirdre would never admit that there was anything the slightest bit difficult about her perfect existence. 'Do you find it difficult to get close to Terry?'

'Of course we're close,' I couldn't help saying. 'But I've got a great idea about how to get even closer. I mean, I want to understand exactly how he feels. I want to be part of his life. Not some superior sort of reformer.'

'Really?' The rap singer looked at me, apparently fascinated. 'And we'd be so very interested to hear what that great idea is.'

'I might tell you when it's all over,' was all I could say. 'On the other hand, I might not.' I raised my glass and drank a discreet toast to the future.

IT'S NO GOOD THINKING now of what my Great Idea led to or all its results which I didn't even consider at the time. I have to think myself back to when the Great Idea filled up my mind and I got more and more excited about it. I also found it exciting to keep it a secret from Terry, as though it was something special I was buying him for Christmas and I was saving it up as a huge surprise.

My first thought was to get myself really fit for the experience. So I spent a lot of time in the Lysander Club. I was a regular at the aerobics class, where the loud-voiced girl with the cropped top and the microphone fixed to her head shouted, 'Tits, bums, stomachs, squeeze now, squeeze!', her voice rising high above the dance music. There was I, working away in Lycra leggings, perfecting my core stability and doing cardiovascular exercises to make sure my heart was strong enough to put the Great Idea into practice. My core stability became amazing and my legs, which I might have to depend on, were in first-rate condition. Terry wasn't best pleased that I was spending so many evenings at the Lysander, but then, as I say, he had no idea that I was doing it entirely for him.

When I felt ready, I rang the SCRAP office and asked Gwenny if I could speak to Leonard McGrath. I didn't want to meet him at the Connaught

Square maisonette, where my Great Idea would get known to everyone, including, no doubt, eventually Terry.

'Leonard gives us an hour and a half at lunchtime on Thursdays.'

'I'll call in on Thursday then.'

'Can I help? Is young Terry in trouble again?'

'Not at all. So far as I know.'

'You've managed to find him accommodation.'

'Oh yes. I got him settled in a flat in Notting Hill Gate.'

'Well done! And is he working?'

'Regularly. Mainly at nights.'

'Well, I suppose that pays better than day work.'

'Yes, it seems to.'

You see how confident I'd become since I had the idea? When I got to the SCRAP office in my Thursday lunch hour I marched straight into Orlando Wathen's old room in spite of Gwenny's protests. The new chair was munching a sandwich and reading some no doubt boring SCRAP report.

As he looked up at me I closed the door behind me and said, 'Chippy, they say you're doing a marvellous job at SCRAP.'

He looked at me, clearly furious. 'Don't you ever call me that in here.'

'Why not? I can't wait to tell Gwenny that you planned the jobs Terry went to prison for. Of course, I might keep calling you "Leonard" if you'll cooperate with me.'

'What's that mean? Money?'

'Not at all. Just your help.' By this time I was sitting comfortably down beside the new chair.

'What for? Something to do with Terry?'

'Eventually perhaps. This has more to do with Bonnard.'

'Bonnard?' Chippy was momentarily puzzled.

'French painter,' I explained.

Chippy supplied the rest. 'Influenced by Gauguin and Van Gogh.'

'You studied History of Art?'

'My art expert and I,' he explained, with his curious little twisted smile, 'have been on the lookout for a Bonnard.'

'He painted a picture of a naked woman standing beside a bath and drying her thighs.'

'That would be his wife, Marthe. He painted her lots of times, in and out of the bath. She was his favourite subject.'

'So how much do you think a painting of Marthe might be worth?'

His fingers drummed on his desk. He pursed his lips and looked thoughtful.

'The dealer said £300,000,' I told him.

Chippy looked impressed. 'Is it in good condition?'

'Perfect!' Of course I didn't really know whether it was or not.

'I suppose it's locked up in some museum or other?' Chippy said after more thought.

'No,' I told him. 'It's hanging on someone's bedroom wall.'

And it was then, of course, I told him my Great Idea and he promised his full cooperation.

On my way out, Gwenny looked up at me expectantly from her desk and asked if I'd had a good meeting with Chair.

'Yes,' I said. 'He was a considerable help.'

After work I knew Terry was out for the evening, so I went for a swim and cranial massage. I was on my way across the gym to get an organic cheese and beetroot sandwich when I passed a familiar figure on the stationary bicycle.

'Ishmael,' I said. 'I didn't know you'd joined the Lysander Club.'

'Oh yes.' He gave me one of his sweetest smiles. 'You have to keep fit in my job.'

'Your job as a rap artist.'

'Of course, my job as a rap artist. By the way, how's that great idea of yours going?'

I did nothing but smile and went on my way. I wasn't going to tell anyone except for Chippy McGrath about my idea. Not yet anyway.

LUCY HAD BEEN ANGRY when she found out I'd visited her father. She said I'd hated her when she was trying to reform me. 'We only got close to each other when I stopped trying to change you,' she said. When I told her I'd wanted to stop her stealing little things she told me she wasn't going to steal little things any more, but she had a surprise for me that would make us really close for ever. When I said that'd be nice she said, 'It won't just be nice. It'll be amazing!'

It wasn't that Lucy changed towards me. In fact she seemed more loving than ever before. But she went around with a secret sort of smile on her face. So naturally, from time to time, I felt that something was going on, although I had no idea of quite what. I suppose everyone feels, don't they, when their girlfriend looks unusually happy, that it's a dangerous signal.

Chippy too treated me to a lot of his twisted little smiles, as though he was busy with something that was far too important for me to know about. Of course I still did jobs for him and when I called round to the maisonette there were Screwtop Parkinson, the getaway driver, and Ozzy Desmond, the burglar alarm man, all the old lot. But they all seemed to stop talking when I went into the room and I had the feeling they had plans I wasn't meant to know about.

Funny thing was that with all this feeling of things going on that I didn't know about and people not telling me, I began to feel more at home with Mr Markby. Of course I had a few secrets from him, like the way I earned my living. I told him that I was helping round a couple of restaurants in Notting Hill, where I'd found a flat. He seemed to be happy with that. Then he asked me how that friend of mine was doing, the one who'd fallen into the habit of stealing small articles of no great value.

'I think I've stopped her doing that,' I told him.

'Well, congratulations!' There was a delighted grin on his face, as though he'd just won on the horses. 'You reformed her!'

'I did my best.' I tried to sound modest.

'Reforming people is a real talent!' The grin seemed to fall from Mr Markby's face and he looked troubled. 'I'm not sure I have the gift myself.'

I felt I had to cheer him up. 'Oh, I'm sure you have,' I told him.

'So many people come through this office. They've just come out of prison and we're here to help them reform. And what do they do? Something calculated to send them back for even longer in prison. When I was young I used to believe prison was like the National Health. You were meant to go in bad and come out better. But what would doctors feel like if everyone who came out of hospital felt they had to go back there immediately?'

'I suppose a bit depressed.' I felt really sorry for him.

'Depressed is the right word for it.' Mr Markby was clearly in a mood to tell me all his troubles. 'I have a Jack Russell dog called Rosemary. An intelligent dog. But if a strange man appears in the house she has an irresistible urge to bite the ends of his trousers. I've tried everything I could think of to reform her. I've put her into her bed when she does it. I've given her extra biscuits on the rare occasions when she doesn't. But I really have to admit, I can't change her behaviour patterns.'

'I'm sorry,' was all I could think of to say.

'Sir Jonathan Peebles, Her Majesty's Inspector of Prisons, did us the honour of coming to a small dinner party my wife and I gave a week or so ago. I'd hardly given him a glass of sherry before Rosemary fixed her teeth in the ends of his trousers.'

'That was embarrassing?' It seemed to be the wrong way round, having Mr Markby expecting help and reassurance.

'Terribly embarrassing! They were fine trousers, Savile Row, Scottish tweed, all that sort of thing. Sir Jonathan has perfect manners of course, but he was certainly irritated. He said something like, "Can't you call your bloody dog off?" I did my best of course, but I've simply failed to reform Rosemary. And yet you've managed to reform this friend of yours.'

At first I didn't see the connection. But then I said, 'I seem to have per-suaded her.'

'Persuaded her?' He seemed to think hard about it. 'Perhaps that's because you've been a criminal yourself. It takes one to reform one.'

'Perhaps.'

Quite suddenly he said, 'I suppose you're over twenty-five?'

I admitted it.

'And I suppose you left school before A levels?'

I told him I'd been self-educated in Wormwood Scrubs.

'So, A level passes wouldn't be necessary. Maybe a Diploma in Probation Studies instead. You know what I'm talking about?'

I had to tell him I had absolutely no idea.

'It's just something to keep in mind for the future. We can discuss it when we meet again.'

But before we met again, something happened that changed everything.

MY PHONE RANG at the office and, after a small click that seemed to infect the telephones I used at work and at home, a voice said, 'Is that Miss Purefoy? My name is Screwtop. I've been instructed to meet you concern-ing the lady coming out of the bath.'

'Oh yes,' I said. 'I've been expecting a call.'

'We better have a meet. Shall we say 6.30 tomorrow in the Brummell?'

'Is that safe? Terry goes there. I wouldn't want him to know.'

'He won't be there tomorrow evening. I can promise you that. He'll be out at another job. I'll be at the bar. Red hair, stocky build, sweet smile. You'll recognise me.' And he rang off.

In the days that followed, the fear and the excitement seemed to die away, and I remembered my date at the Brummell Club as though it was just another meeting with a client to discuss a campaign for an organic shampoo.

So I walked down Harrowby Street and into the club with the feeling that I was going to just a routine meeting. At one end of the bar I saw a small hunched-up figure with red hair and a cheerful smile. As I got nearer he straightened his back and said, 'You must be Lucy.'

I sat down on a stool beside him. 'And you must be Screwtop,' I told him.

As he gave no signs of buying me a drink, I got myself a glass of white wine and a Bacardi Breezer, which Screwtop told me was his 'usual poison'.

'The governor says you're to come along with us on the job.' He looked doubtful. 'We don't usually take amateurs with us.'

'I'm not exactly an amateur.'

'Why, you done jobs before?'

'One or two so far, yes.' I didn't tell him what Terry thought of my efforts at stealing.

'So where are we going then?'

'It's called God's Acre Manor. It's near Aldershot. About an hour out of London if there's no traffic.'

'There won't be much traffic at two in the morning.'

'Is that when we're going?'

'Take your average house. Everyone's asleep around three. Big family, is it?'

'Only one.'

'Single gent?'

'You got it! Oh, and a man-servant, a sort of butler. He drinks a lot of whisky. With any luck, he'll be out for the count.

'Ground-floor kitchen, is there?'

'Yes, at the back of the house.'

'Sash windows?'

'I think so. It's an old manor house.'

'And you know where the gent keeps—whatever we're after?'

'Oh yes. I know exactly where he keeps it.'

'We'll take Ozzy Desmond along with us. He knows his burglar alarms and he'll be useful. He knows his silver so we might pick up all we can. All right then.' Screwtop pulled out a Filofax and looked for a date in his diary. 'Next Friday, 21 July, if that suits you?'

'I'm sure it will.' I hadn't thought it would be so soon.

'Be in your car. What is it by the way?'

'A Polo. A bit beaten up, I'm afraid.'

'Don't worry. Always best to have an anonymous-looking motor. Be parked in the underground car park at Charing Cross. We'll pick you up there at two. Wear dark clothes. Jeans and a sweater. Trainers on your feet not to make a noise. You got all that?'

'Oh yes, I've got it. I just wonder what I'm going to tell Terry. It's all come a bit soon.'

'You'll think of something, won't you?'

Screwtop suddenly felt the call of duty. 'Better report to the governor. I think we've covered everything.'

Then he was gone and I was alone in the Beau Brummell Club finishing a glass of white wine. I was aware of a figure further down the bar and moving to sit next to me.

'Ishmael?' I said. 'Is Deirdre with you?'

'No. This place is not her sort of thing at all.'

'No, I suppose it isn't.'

'You came here with a friend. I saw you.'

'Not a friend. It was business. My advertising business.'

'Yes, of course,' he said. 'For a moment I thought I recognised him. Must be mistaken.'

'Sorry, Ishmael,' I told him, 'I've got to get back to Terry.'

'Yes, of course. Of course, I understand.'

I'll say one thing for Deirdre's Ishmael. Although he seemed to bob up everywhere, he was perfectly polite.

I TOLD TERRY I was going to a hen party in Aldershot. I know it was a lie but I'd planned that he'd know the truth soon enough. 'It might go on till quite late, so don't wait up for me.'

'Who are these girls anyway?'

'Oh, just people I used to know. Some of them I went to school with.'

'And where's this party taking place?'

Oh, if only he knew, I thought, he wouldn't be cross-examining me as though he was some sort of police officer or something. But if he even got a hint, I knew he'd be trying to stop me. He went on looking at me suspiciously and he said, 'You're not going to see that Robin Thirkell, are you?'

'Why do you ask that?' His question made me a bit nervous.

'You were all over him one time. And you had that lucky escape last time—or at least that's what you told me!'

'Well, I'm not going to see him, I hope. He'll hardly be invited to a hen night.' What I really meant was I hoped he didn't see me. 'You don't mind me going out with the girls, do you?'

'Of course not. You can come and go as you please.' But he didn't sound exactly sure about it.

'Well,' I said, 'thank you very much.' I pretended to be quite upset that he was questioning me about my movements. 'So what are you doing this evening?' I asked.

'Staying in. Mr Markby gave me a book. About the Probation Service.'

'You don't want to read that, do you?'

'I might have a look at it.'

'I won't be gone long,' I promised him.

And then he smiled and said, 'I'll miss you,' which was all I needed to speed me on my way.

THE DIFFICULTY was knowing how to fill in the evening. You see, I had to leave Terry at what might be a reasonable time to set off for a hen party in Aldershot and my actual date wasn't until two o'clock in the morning.

I went and sat in a cinema, watching car chases and shootings in a film with a story that I had too much else to think about to understand.

When I came out, the long light July evening seemed to stretch out like a lifetime before me. I parked near the Close-Up Club and took my suitcase from the boot of the Polo. In the lavatory, I changed into my jeans, sweater and trainers. There was no one in there I knew. I had ordered a plate of pasta and thought that crime was rather like the National Health Service. There was a great deal of hanging about attached to it. I almost gave it all up then, but I remembered that by the morning I would truly have understood Terry, and we would be together completely, absolutely and for always. I finished the spaghetti and drove to the underground car park.

There was nothing to do but go to sleep in the car. I switched off the radio and, suddenly tired, wondered what I was doing, alone in an underground car park, until I fell asleep.

I was woken up by someone knocking on the window. I turned my head and opened my eyes to see Screwtop's grinning face. I opened the window and felt the first tingle of excitement.

I COULDN'T QUITE CREDIT the story about the hen party. I got a feeling that I didn't like at all that Lucy was lying to me. Why didn't I believe her? I suppose I'd seen so many people telling lies in court. Made-up stories about what they were doing on the night in question, told with a sort of wide-eyed look of sincerity—the look Lucy gave me when she talked about the hen party. I mean, she'd never mentioned this lot of girlfriends before. Yes, she'd mentioned her friend Deirdre, from time to time, but that was all.

Then I noticed that nearer the date she got, well, sort of excited. A lot of the time she seemed to be thinking of something else entirely and then she'd keep coming back to the subject, saying, 'You don't mind really, do you?' or 'I'm sure it's better for our relationship that I do things on my own from time to time.' What sort of things was she thinking of doing on her own? That was what I couldn't help wondering. I suppose you'd say I was unreasonably jealous but just look at her previous. When we first met she had this boyfriend, Tom, who fizzled out but was no doubt somewhere still alive on the face of the earth. Then there was that Robin, who had his tongue halfway down her throat in the Intimate Bistro. I know he had tried his luck when she went for a dinner party in his house.

I know what you're going to say. That I was well in love with Lucy by this time and that was perfectly true. It all seemed to be going well. I was sure I'd put her off the habit of stealing little things which didn't suit her at all. Lucy kept saying there was something needed to make us feel really close, but to be honest I felt close enough already. Which is why I got more than a little upset when she spun me what I suspected was a false alibi.

Then there was the business of the suitcase. The evening before the alleged hen night, I was cooking in the kitchen and I looked out of the window and saw her put her small suitcase in the boot of the Polo. There was something about the way she did it, looking to see there was no one watching. When I asked her about it she got quite angry. 'I told you I might have to stay the night with one of the girls,' she said. 'What's the matter? Do you want to search my luggage?'

We sort of made things up, though I was still not entirely convinced. Then the time came when she set off in the Polo and I was left alone in the flat, still not quite sure she'd told me everything.

I went to bed quite early but I couldn't sleep. Eventually it got to past two in the morning. I'd had a very restless few hours, imagining all kinds of stuff. I was still not sure of her, so I decided to ring her on her mobile.

Perhaps, I thought, she'd still be partying with the girls.

Well, she must have pressed the green button to answer my call and I heard her voice and man's voice I thought I recognised but couldn't place. Then she cut me off and the line went dead. After that there was no point in trying to go to sleep.

THE CAR THAT WOULD become the getaway and was now the get-to-it was an anonymous Rover. Ozzy Desmond, a tall, thin person with long, bony fingers, wound himself up in the seat next to the driver. He'd obviously decided neither to speak nor to look at me, as though I were a quite unnecessary complication in the job ahead, which, from his point of view, I suppose I was. So I sat alone in the back of the car.

As we were crossing Clapham Common my mobile rang. I pulled it out must have pressed the green button as I answered Screwtop's question: 'Know God's Acre well?' 'Every inch of it,' I told him. Then I put the phone to my ear and heard Terry's voice as Screwtop almost shouted, 'Put that bloody thing away. Don't answer it.' So I had to switch Terry off. Screwtop was right, of course, I couldn't speak to Terry then.

We'd sped, and I mean sped, round the M25 and turned off along the M3 and then I could see in the headlights the tall familiar trees round Folly Hill, where Terry and I had made love for the first time. I leaned forward to give Screwtop directions.

Like all the smart houses in our neighbourhood, God's Acre had big gates between pillars. You had to press a number on one of the pillars for the gates to swing politely open and invite you in. When we stopped in front of the main gate I dug my Filofax out of my bag and found the magic number. I got out, pressed the numbers and the gate swung open. From that moment, it all seemed like a dream.

As the car crunched the gravel, there came what seemed to me an ear-splitting chorus loud enough to wake the dead. The dogs were barking in the stables. 'We should give them a whiff of something,' Screwtop said.

I promised to deal with it. The stable door wasn't locked and I saw the bright eyes of four dogs glowing in the shadows. I suppose they could smell someone they knew and so the loud barks turned to low grumbling whimpers. I called them softly by their names. They licked my hands and them composed themselves for another long sleep. I felt I'd been a huge success with the dogs and after that nothing else was going to be a problem.

Robin had told me Max'd be a match for any burglar. I rather doubted it. Max's intake of whisky was such that I felt sure the short chorus of barks wouldn't have disturbed his sleep in his rooms over the garage.

When I got to the back of the house where the car was parked my mates (that's what I called them to myself) had cut a pane of glass out of the kitchen window, and, as I came round the corner to join them, Ozzy Desmond was oozing, like some long and dark-suited snake, over the window sill. Screwtop helped me in through the window and he squirmed across the sink after me. And then we were in the house with our torches switched on, and I felt the extraordinary excitement Terry had described. We were taking the great risk for the great prize and I felt almost like laughing at the danger. Now I knew exactly what Terry felt. From now on Terry would have no secrets from me.

As we moved quietly from room to room our torches picked out familiar objects, a cherub on a marble column, photographs on the piano of Robin as a boy, an empty champagne bottle on an inlaid table. In the dining room as Ozzy Desmond finished removing the silver from the sideboard I whispered to Screwtop, 'Shall I go and get it now?'

'You want a bit of help?' the whisper came back.

'No, thanks. I can manage it perfectly well on my own.' I felt invisible. I could manage anything.

I remember going up the staircase in the old days, probably a bit drunk, laughing at one of Robin's ridiculous bits of gossip. But all that was long ago. In the days before I met Terry and my life seemed to change. I felt elated but not guilty. We really weren't taking anything Robin couldn't afford to lose.

As I reached the bedroom door I switched off my torch and put it in my pocket. I stood in the pitch dark, gripping the cold china door handle.

Of course I knew how Robin slept. It was a deep sleep and it was hard to wake him. It was so dark that I had to feel along the wall until I got to the picture frame and, as I touched it, some dark cloud must have moved in a gusting wind and faint moonlight crept across the room. I could see the tall posts of Robin's bed and even made out the naked woman engrossed in drying herself after her bath. She came off the wall with no trouble at all. As Robin muttered something incomprehensible I was out of his room with £300,000 worth of Pierre Bonnard swinging at my side.

As I carried the picture down the dark passage, I heard a car driving away fast. Then I started down the stairs and suddenly found myself walking into the brilliant light of Robin's great candelabra. There were people in the hall. And, much to my amazement, I saw Ishmael step forward.

'Ishmael,' I greeted him, but he wasn't smiling.

'Detective Sergeant Ishmael Macdonald, C Division.'

I felt sure he must be joking until he said, 'Are you Lucinda Agnes Purefoy?'

'You know I am,' I told him.

'I'm arresting you for suspected burglary.'

As he said this one of the policemen took the Bonnard and I looked up the stairs to see Robin in a silk dressing gown staring down at me. Ishmael was reciting some rigmarole about anything I said being used as evidence against me at my trial, but I wasn't listening. It all seemed part of the dream. Then I felt something on my wrist and I looked down and saw that Ishmael and I were joined by a single handcuff. 'But you're a rap singer,' I told him.

'Only as a hobby.' He was actually smiling. 'At work I'm DS Ishmael Macdonald, one of the Met's few Caribbean detective sergeants. Shall we go out to the car?'

'Deirdre never told me.' I don't know why I said that.

'No, I think she finds it rather embarrassing.'

As I went out of the front door I passed Max wearing pyjama trousers and a none too clean vest top. When we got out into the driveway, the dogs started howling. I think it was then I woke up. The dream was over.

Eight

After Lucy cut me off, I lay awake, thinking the worst things about her and really surprised at how much I minded. I thought about leaving her, but then decided that life wouldn't be much good without her. Only I wanted to know the truth, and at about 3.30 in the morning the telephone rang and I found it out.

'Hello.' It was Lucy's voice. 'Sorry to wake you up.'

'I wasn't asleep. Where the hell are you?'

'I'm in Aldershot Police Station.'

'What are you doing there?'

'Just about to be taken down to my cell. This is the one telephone call I'm allowed.'

'What is it? Were you drunk driving?' She had had quite a bit to drink when she drove back from Robin Thirkell's place that time previously.

'Not exactly.'

'Then what?'

'Burglary.' She stopped talking then and I heard some male voices in the background. Then she said, 'I shouldn't say any more about it now. They're going to interview me later.'

'I can't believe it!'

'Why not? You know what it's like, don't you?'

'But what do they say you took?'

'I can't explain it all now. I did it all for you, Terry. I've got to go now. I'm going to miss you, Terry.'

And then the line went dead. I got up, made tea and smoked until it was morning and I could do something about getting a brief for Lucy. I didn't want to ask Chippy, as all the briefs he'd recommended to me had seemed to get me guilty verdicts. In the end, I rang my probation officer, Mr Markby. I told him that my friend who I'd tried to stop thieving had been arrested for burglary.

'Then you'd better tell me who she is.'

'Lucy Purefoy.' I couldn't hide her any longer. Anyway, she'd soon be in all the papers.

'Lucy Purefoy! That's the trouble with these girls from SCRAP. They start off falling in love with the criminal and end up falling in love with crime.'

He recommended a guy called Peter Bethell, and managed to persuade him to get himself down to Aldershot by the time Lucy got interviewed.

Interview conducted with Lucinda Agnes Purefoy at 10.30 a.m. on 22 July 2005 by DS Ishmael Macdonald in the presence of DC Gutteridge. Also present Mr Peter Bethell of Bethell, Sherman and Pensotti.

DS MACDONALD: I am Detective Sergeant Ishmael Macdonald and this is Detective Constable Gutteridge, who is taking a full note of this interview. You are Lucinda Agnes Purefoy?

PUREFOY: You know perfectly well who I am.

DS MACDONALD: This is for the record. Would you like a cup of tea?

PUREFOY: No thanks. Your tea's disgusting.

DS MACDONALD: Right. Now, you were found leaving God's Acre Manor at 3 a.m. in possession of a valuable painting.

PUREFOY: What I want to know is how you got there.

DS MACDONALD: Because of what you told me.

PUREFOY: What I told you when?

DS MACDONALD: It's not for you to ask the questions.

MR BETHELL SOLICITOR: I think my client is entitled to know what you suggest she said and on what occasion.

DS MACDONALD: Oh, very well then. It was in the Close-Up Club and you said you had a great idea that would bring you closer to Terry Keegan, a man with a lengthy criminal record. It seemed possible that you were planning to participate in some crime to please your lover. So you were kept under observation.

PUREFOY: Is that why you kept bobbing up wherever I went? And were my telephone calls getting interfered with?

DS MACDONALD: Once again, I must warn you not to ask me questions. How did you get to God's Acre Manor last night?

PUREFOY: I'll leave you to find that out.

DS MACDONALD: As we approached the house, a car drove rapidly away from the back entrance. Did you come in that car?

PUREFOY: Why didn't you drive after it and find out?

DS MACDONALD: At that stage we couldn't drive through the main gates.

PUREFOY: You mean because you hadn't got the secret number?

DS MACDONALD: As I have clearly said, it would be better if you confined yourself to answering my questions. Did you enter the house through the kitchen window?

PUREFOY: That's for you to find out.

DS MACDONALD: We found no fingerprints. Did you and your companions wear gloves?

PUREFOY: I didn't say I had any companions.

DS MACDONALD: We found foot marks. There must have been at least three of you.

PUREFOY: Must there?

DS MACDONALD: You were seen lately in the company of a man called

Parkinson, sometimes known as Screwtop. How did you know him?

PUREFOY: I think he once knew Terry.

DS MACDONALD: What were you talking about when you were with him in the Brummell Club?

PUREFOY: I think we discussed the weather. Oh, and American foreign policy.

DS MACDONALD: Was he with you when you stole the picture?

PUREFOY: I've told you, I was alone. There was no one else with me.

DS MACDONALD: Then who was driving away in the car? Was it perhaps your lover, Terry Keegan?

PUREFOY: No, it certainly wasn't.

DS MACDONALD: Who was it then?

PUREFOY: I don't know. I have no idea and I don't want to answer any more questions. I want to go to sleep.

DS MACDONALD: We'll see how you feel about it later.

PUREFOY: I still won't want to answer any questions. Oh, by the way, tell Deirdre she might have warned me you were a sneaky member of the Metropolitan Police.

This interview ended at 10.55 a.m.

AFTER THE INTERVIEW I stretched out on the bed in my police cell and went back to sleep. Sleep seemed to be the only way of getting through the next days, weeks, maybe years of my life. I realised that I was a bit rude to the rap artist cop, but I couldn't help that. I was more sorry that I had to disappoint Mr Bethell.

Peter Bethell looked like a middle-aged schoolboy. He had a lock of brown hair that fell untidily over his forehead. He had a ready grin that varied between the ingratiating and the cheeky. He spoke rather fast, sometimes as though the general excitement of entering prison was almost too much for him. He was, as I was to discover, a sort of criminal's groupie. He spoke of the well-known felons he had defended as though they were great stars of the stage and screen and he was their agent. He was obviously delighted to meet me.

'Of course it was a joke,' he told me when we first met. 'You took away your friend's picture as a prank, meaning to give it back to him, didn't you?'

'No, it wasn't a prank. It was a serious attempt to commit a serious crime. Unfortunately it turned out that I wasn't very good at it.'

'You're not telling me you did it to get a share of £300,000?'

'No, I'm not telling you that.'

'Then for what?'

'Because I wanted to really understand Terry. Because I wanted to feel what he felt. Because I wanted us to be really together. Because I love him.'

'Please don't say any of that in the interview.'

'Why not? It's the truth.'

'Oh, good heavens! If everyone I defended felt they had to tell the truth in interviews we wouldn't get many of them off.'

'I can't help it. I just feel I've got to tell the truth.'

'What's Terry do? I mean what's his job exactly?'

'Thief.'

Mr Bethell looked as though he had walked through an open door that had then banged shut and struck him smartly on the head. 'Then for God's sake let's keep his name out of this.'

'All right. I won't mention Terry.'

'The detective sergeant says you came with two other people, who drove away. Were they thieves as well? Men of bad character, perhaps, who forced you to help them steal the picture?' Mr Bethell looked suddenly hopeful.

'It's just me that's responsible for all this. I'm not blaming anyone else.'

'The police would be grateful if you gave them some names.'

'I'm not naming names. I'm not going to get anyone else into trouble.'

He looked like a schoolboy who'd been told that he'll be off sweets at least for a week.

It was then they called us for the interview and I was determined to irritate the rap artist at least as much as I'd managed to irritate poor Mr Bethell, who, after all, was only trying to help me out of a hopeless situation.

HER FATHER TOLD ME that she was coming up the next day in the Aldershot Magistrates' Court. He said the question of bail would be considered.

'I can't believe it,' he said. 'Is this something you planned together?'

'Absolutely not! I told you. I wanted to make her stop stealing.'

'Oh yes.' He seemed surprised. 'I didn't take you seriously. I should have done, I suppose.'

'You certainly should.'

'It's so difficult.' The bishop seemed lost in a world he couldn't understand any longer. 'God has sided with President Bush, my dear daughter has been arrested for stealing, and you're at liberty.'

'For the moment, yes.'

'I just don't know how Lucy will cope with life in the cells. Luckily we sent her to boarding school, which may have given her some sort of training for it.'

'Let's hope she gets bail.'

'Oh yes. Let's hope profoundly and of course I shall do some solid knee work for it. Although,' now the bishop sounded doubtful, 'I'm not sure God really appreciates being prayed to any more. The world seems to be full of unanswered prayers. Her solicitor wants me to give evidence on the bail application. He says they won't be able to refuse a bishop. Would you agree, with your experience of courts?'

'My experience is you never can tell what they're going to do.'

THE ALDERSHOT MAGISTRATES' COURT was crowded. I guessed there were a lot of journalists wanting to write 'Bishop's Daughter on Theft Charges'. I could feel their excitement at Lucy's troubles and I hated them for it. But what I wanted most of all was to see Lucy. There was a fat bloke wandering round with a list and I asked him if I could see Lucy Purefoy.

'Purefoy, Purefoy . . . bail application. We should get to it around twelve o'clock.'

'I just wanted to see her before then. Where should I go?'

'You want to see Purefoy?' A smiling character came up to me. 'I'm Detective Sergeant Macdonald, officer in charge of the case. And you are . . . ?'

'Terry Keegan,' I told him.

'Of course.' The DS's smile broadened. 'I'm afraid you can't just "pop" down into the cells. Prisoners here are not able to receive visitors.'

'I must see her though.'

'Of course you will see her. You will be able to see her from the public gallery. I advise you to go up there now to be sure of a place in the front row.'

So I sat in the public gallery and in time the magistrates came in. In the middle was Madam Chair who was a large grey-haired woman. On one side of her was a burly-looking character with the physique of a nightclub bouncer. I told myself he was the sort that might take a fancy to Lucy and want to do the best for her. I wasn't too hopeful about the bloke on the other side of Madam Chair. He was a hawk-faced person with rimless glasses who might have been an off-duty headmaster and looked at everyone as though they had been caught having sex in the playground. The most active person in the court was the little clerk who sat under Madam Chair and kept bobbing up to give her advice, which sometimes she seemed to take.

I saw the bishop, Lucy's dad, sitting behind a brief who took his place in the solicitor's row. I guessed that man was Mr Bethell. On the other side there was a small bald-headed man who I was sure was there from the Director of Public Prosecutions as he plumped himself down in front of DS Macdonald, the Old Bill representative.

'R. v. Purefoy,' The clerk read. 'Application for bail. Put up Purefoy.'

And there she was, Lucy in the dock. She had half a smile and a look that meant that she hoped they would like her, but deep down she didn't care whether they did or not.

There was a bit of droning on. The DPP man, who turned out to be called Mr Hastie, took a while to explain that the accused was charged with stealing a picture of enormous value. During this, Lucy glanced up at the public gallery. She saw me and smiled, and I did my best to smile back. For a moment it seemed we were alone in the court and then Madam Chair told Lucy she could sit down. Lucy sat down obediently and didn't look back to me again.

Then her brief, Mr Bethell, got up on his hind legs and said he was applying for bail. He said it in a silky sort of a purring voice which I'm sure he thought would get the magistrates on his side, but Madam Chair and her two supporters didn't seem to be all that impressed. He obviously expected a better reaction when he announced that he was going to call the Bishop of Aldershot to give evidence. There was certainly no round of applause from the bench. Then the chat went on, beginning with Mr Bethell asking Lucy's dad if he was the Right Reverend Robert Purefoy, Bishop of Aldershot.

'Yes, I am.'

I could see the newspaper people in court licking their pencils and turning to a new page in their notebooks to write their 'Bishop Gives Evidence for Arrested Daughter' stories.

Mr Bethell asked, 'And you are the father of Lucinda Purefoy, who is here in the dock?'

'Yes, I am. In fact we always call her Lucy. Everybody does.' He gave what he hoped was a winning smile at Madam Chair, but it was not returned.

'As we know, your daughter is of good character with no convictions.'

'Only one or two for going too fast in that Polo car of hers. Women drivers! Well, you know what they are.'

I suppose the bishop thought this might get a laugh from the bench. In which case he was wrong.

'But Lucy has no convictions for dishonesty. She has never been arrested before?'

'Certainly not! Indeed she has worked hard helping convicted criminals to reform and lead an honest life. She joined SCRAP as praeceptor.'

'Which means—for the benefit of those of us in court who may not have had a classical education . . . ?'

'Being a guide, philosopher and friend to some young offender freshly out of prison. Lucy has always wanted to do a bit of good in the world.'

I looked at Madam Chair. Her expression was unchanged.

'If the bench grants her bail,' Mr Bethell was asking, 'would Lucy come and live with her parents at the Palace?'

'I imagine not.' The answer seemed to have disappointed Mr Bethell. 'I imagine she will continue to live in her flat in Notting Hill Gate. With her boyfriend. They are in a stable relationship.'

Madam Chair looked as though she knew what a stable relationship meant and she didn't think much of it.

'But she can visit you and you'll be able to keep an eye on her?' Mr Bethell asked.

'Yes, of course! Lucy and Terry will always be welcome.'

'Thank you, Bishop Purefoy.' Mr Bethell sat down, looking like a man who has done as much as possible with some pretty ropy material.

But now the man from the Director of Public Prosecutions was on his feet and Madam Chair's 'You have some questions, Mr Hastie?' was warmer than anything she had handed out to Mr Bethell.

Hastie began. 'When you say that your daughter is in a "stable relationship", Bishop, does she live with this young man as his wife?'

'They're not married.' The bishop looked puzzled.

'No, but they are living together and having sexual intercourse?'

'Let us hope so. God gave us our bodies as a source of pleasure.'

'So you approve of sex before marriage? Some sections of the church wouldn't agree with you.'

'Some sections of the Church have failed to move with the times.'

'Is it true that you're in favour of gay marriages in church?'

'I really can't see why not.'

'Doesn't the Bible forbid homosexuality?'

In his answer Lucy's dad asked a surprising question. 'Do you enjoy prawn cocktail, Mr Hastie?'

The clerk jumped up to speak urgently to Madam Chair, who told the bishop that he wasn't there to ask questions and that the bench failed to see what a prawn cocktail had to do with a bail application.

'I'm quite prepared to answer the question.' Mr Hastie was showing how fair he could be even though he was there for the DPP. 'Yes, Bishop. I do enjoy a prawn cocktail.'

'Then let me remind you. It's true that the book of Leviticus says, "Though shalt not lie with mankind, as with womankind: it is abomination." But it also says, "Whatsoever hath no fins nor scales in the waters, that shall be an abomination." Therefore no shellfish and, in particular, no prawn cocktails!'

'What's that meant to prove?' Hastie obviously felt he'd been outsmarted.

'It proved that we needn't take too much notice of those ancient bits of desert law.'

'Is the man she's living with called Terry Keegan?'

'He is. And he's here in the public gallery.'

Almost everyone except Lucy turned to look at me. The DPP's man handed a bit of paper in to the clerk of the court.

'That's a list of Keegan's convictions. All for theft.'

Madam Chair and her two sidekicks received the list gratefully.

'So, Bishop, if your daughter is granted bail on this serious theft charge she will be living, as man and wife, with a convicted criminal. I suppose you'll tell this court that you thoroughly approve of that?'

'Of course,' the bishop plunged in happily. 'Jesus Christ was a convicted criminal,' he told Mr Hastie.

'But this man Keegan is a thief.'

'And Jesus was crucified between two thieves. May I remind you of the gospel according to Saint Luke? One of the thieves said to Jesus, "Lord, remember me when thou comest into thy kingdom," and Jesus said, "Today thou shalt be with me in Paradise."'

'Are you suggesting that Terry Keegan is going to heaven?' Mr Hastie asked, to which the bishop replied, 'I think he's got a better chance than most of us.'

'So this court is being asked to grant bail so your daughter can live with a thief?'

'A thief who may enter the Kingdom of Heaven.'

'Thank you, Bishop.' And Mr Hastie sat down. I suppose he thought he'd done a great job.

Mr Bethell made a short speech after that, stressing the fact that Lucy had never been in trouble before. Then Madam Chair announced that they'd retire. I told myself that there was still a small hope, but I didn't really believe it.

I don't know why they retired. Probably to have a coffee, or go to the loo. Anyway, they were back ten minutes later and for the first time there were smiles on the faces of Madam Chair and both the sidekicks.

'We have decided that we cannot grant bail in this case,' Madam Chair was delighted to say. 'The defendant will be remanded in custody. Take her down.'

Lucy stood up and was removed to the cells. She didn't turn to look at me but I was ready, however badly I felt, with smiles of encouragement.

As we left court I asked DS Ishmael Macdonald when I could get to see Lucy. 'You'll be able to visit her in Holloway,' he said.

Nine

What I really couldn't bear about that so-called bail application was the way they treated my dad.

All right, I know Robert lives in a world of his own. All sorts of things seem important to him that have never seemed particularly important to me, although I'm sure we felt close to each other in the days when I wanted to do some sort of good in the world. He had some really interesting ideas about thieves getting into heaven which that awful woman up on the bench might have been well advised to listen to, instead of allowing Robert to be teased and baited by that poncey little man from the Prosecution Service. It must have been a horrible experience for Dad and I'm really sorry.

Those charming policemen in Aldershot had told me terrible things about Holloway, but to tell you the truth I didn't find it so bad as all that, compared with the horrible boarding school I went to. Robert and Sylvia sent me there because they thought I was an only child who'd be lonely at home, so they packed me off to St Swithen's where I was a good deal more lonely, at any rate to start with. I think I was made more welcome in prison.

I was in a dorm with four others (at Holloway, that is). We had to share one loo, which at times was difficult, but we could wear our own clothes and not those dreadful gym tunics they forced us into at St Swithen's. The food was equally stodgy, but at least in Holloway you got bacon and eggs for breakfast. It's true that there were cockroaches in Holloway—you could watch them marching along the window sills—but it didn't have St Swithen's smell of overboiled cabbage mixed with the drains. And as for the girls—well, I'll tell you more about them later.

I was what they called a 'remand prisoner'. That's to say, I hadn't been tried and convicted. So I could have as many visits as I wanted. I had hardly looked around the place, when Terry came to see me.

We sat at a table in the crowded visiting hall. I hadn't seen Terry since he was looking at me in that dreadful magistrates court, and I looked away because I couldn't stand the idea that we were going to be separated.

When they told me I was going to have a visit I couldn't wait to see Terry. But now, as we sat at the table and he looked at me, strangely silent, I felt a space between us that was much wider than the table.

'Well, here's a funny situation!' I said, as brightly as I could manage. 'I'm in prison and you aren't. But we're more together than we ever were before.'

'I don't know what's funny about that. I'm in Notting Hill Gate and you're in bloody Holloway. How can we be more together than we were before?'

'Because now we've done all the same things.'

'That's what you always say.' He gave a big sigh, heavier than I thought was necessary.

'But now it's true! I did a more important burglary. I planned it on my own. All right, I wasn't particularly good at it.'

'You can say that again.'

'And I landed up in prison. Like you did, Terry.'

'Are you saying that's a good thing?'

'I'm saying now I can understand you completely. And of course I felt the excitement, just like you said. You said it was the greatest excitement in the world, being in a house when no one knew you were there.'

'I might have said a lot of things. But you didn't have to try it.'

'I didn't have to. I wanted to.'

'And now look where it's got you.'

'It's not so bad. You can get bacon and eggs for breakfast.'

'I could cook you that at home.'

'I know you could, darling.' I put my hand on his across the table. Things were going better. 'I'm going to miss you.'

'I'll miss you too.' Then he kissed me. I wasn't behind a screen or anything. It was a moment to enjoy, because it wasn't much use thinking about the future.

As I SAY, I was in a dorm with four other girls. I say girls because that's what we called ourselves, as though we were quite young and not really responsible for our actions—although, of course, the crimes we were in for were, I suppose, quite serious.

There was Devira, a serious Indian girl who wore glasses and talked in a precise voice quite slowly as though everyone she talked to had only a moderate understanding of English. There was Martine, a sensible and cheerful girl who had done a burglary to pay for crack cocaine that her mother had started her off on around her fourteenth birthday. There was Daisy, who was pretty, blonde and so quiet that you couldn't believe she'd ever been part of a gang of street muggers. Then there was Rachel, a dark-haired girl whose conversation usually started off with phrases like, 'I met this guy in Zanzibar', because she had gone round the world on stolen credit cards.

There had also been a girl called Louise, who was a professional 'carer'. No one, it seemed, had been quite clear what she was in for, but then someone discovered what had happened. Louise had found the old man she was caring for so irritating that she had smothered him with the cushion off his wheelchair, pressing it tight across his mouth and nose until he died. This was a crime that the other girls thought unforgivable and Louise was in constant danger of being smothered or worse by the harsh judges of the Holloway establishment. She had been removed to a security wing to protect her from the other girls and I suppose I took her place.

'I WORK IN THE LAUNDRY,' I told Terry on one of his visits. 'And then I work out in the gym. Rachel's wonderful on the trampoline. She does sort of somersaults.'

'And Martine? You told me about Martine.'

'Martine doesn't do it because she's pregnant!'

'I hope you're not.' Terry looked worried.

'No, I'm not.' I didn't tell him that I wouldn't have minded. I wouldn't have minded at all. Then he began questioning me. 'When you got into Robin's house, you got in through the kitchen window, didn't you?'

'Yes, that's how I got in.'

'You weren't alone, were you? You had other people with you. Screwtop, for instance.'

'Who told you that?'

'Never mind who told me. Tell them that Screwtop and Ozzy Desmond led you into it.'

'That wouldn't be true. They didn't.'

'Who did then?'

'You!'

Well, it was true, so I had to say it. Terry went rather quiet, but he still kissed me before he left.

THE LAST GIRL to be hanged in England was Ruth Ellis, executed in Holloway. Of course, we all knew about her. Rachel had read a book on her and told us all about it.

Ruth was only twenty-eight when it happened—not all that much older than me. She'd been a waitress and a nightclub hostess and married a dentist called George Ellis, but they soon parted.

She fell in love with a glamorous young racing driver. His name was David Blakely. They lived together but she saw other lovers. They quarrelled and he drank a lot. David tried to leave her from time to time and he refused to tell her when he was going out and who he was going with. She'd had an abortion and got insanely jealous. In the end, when she found him outside the Magdala Tavern, a pub near Hampstead Heath, she shot him dead.

At her trial Ruth was asked what she'd intended to do when she found her lover. It was her chance to say, 'I only wanted to scare him' or 'I'd just recovered from losing my baby and I think I went mad for a moment'—that sort of thing.

But all she did was to tell the truth. 'I intended to kill him,' was what she said. I respected her for that.

'I THOUGHT I saw a ghost.' I told Terry on his next visit.

'Of course you didn't.'

'Yes, I know I didn't. I just thought I did. The ghost of Ruth Ellis.'

'She was a murderer.' Terry sounded deeply disapproving. 'There's no excuses, not for murder.'

'I suppose not,' I said. 'All the same, they were wrong to hang her.'

Terry didn't answer that one. He changed the subject.

'I've been reading some of your books,' he said. The books you used to pass your A levels with.'

'My school books? Yes, I kept some of them.'

'*Paradise Lost*, that's a good one.'

'I never really cared for it,' I had to admit.

'What's wrong with it then?' Terry seemed unexpectedly protective of Milton.

'No jokes. I liked Shakespeare better. There are jokes in Shakespeare. Were you honestly reading *Paradise Lost*?'

'Quite honestly.'

'But why?'

'Maybe I want to better myself.'

'I don't want you better, Terry. I want you exactly as you are,' I told him, but then they rang the bell and the visit was over.

'LIFE! THEY GAVE ME LIFE!'

I was working in the laundry with Devira, who ironed sheets with grim thoroughness. She folded them so she was only doing a quarter of a sheet at a time, then slammed down the iron and flattened the pile mercilessly. She finished a sheet long before I had got mine under control so she attacked that as well. When the sheets were ironed we stood apart, held one end each with part of it tucked under our chins and then we approached each other, refolding it neatly.

'I read in the paper "Life should mean life." Well, it does. That's what it means exactly. My life is in here. What have I got when I get out—an old woman no one wants around the shop?'

In general, we didn't discuss the reasons for us being in Holloway, but Devira talked about what she'd done quite freely.

'He was my husband, you know. Igbal. A horrible man.' One sheet was now thoroughly folded and we parted to either end of another.

'Your husband?'

'The husband they decided I had to marry. They sent for him all the way from Chandigarh. Travel expenses paid for by my father out of the profits of our corner shop in the Edgware Road area. I tell you, Igbal was a truly horrible man.'

'Why did you marry him then?'

'It was long ago decided by our families. I had no choice whatever in the matter. Igbal was a very sexual person. He couldn't keep his hands still because of it.'

I smiled, trying to lighten her mood a little. 'Is that such a terrible thing?'

'It is when you're as bad as Igbal. He looked bad. He smelt bad. His temper was bad and he was bad at sexual relations. But he wanted them. Even in the shop. He wanted me to come behind the bead curtain and do it for him. Even when I was busy serving a customer.'

'I'm sorry.' That was all I could say.

'Don't be sorry. I was just explaining why I had to kill him.'

We'd folded all the sheets we'd ironed and Devira sat down while I pulled another lot out of a big pile on the floor.

'How did you manage it?' I genuinely wanted to know.

'I set fire to him when he was asleep,' Devira said.

'Wasn't that very difficult?' I asked.

To this, the quiet, calm Indian girl answered simply, 'Petrol.'

'Now, you two. This is work time, not a mother's meeting.'

'Yes, Miss,' Devira stood up obediently and we went back to work.

ALL THE TIME I had been talking to Mr Markby, and having discussions about my future, I was still working for Chippy, no longer doing the important jobs but some of the routine housebreakings. Why? Because crime had been a way of life to me since I was a kid and there didn't seem to be another way to make a reasonable income. I don't say I didn't feel bad about going on with crime when Mr Markby was doing so much to help me, because I did. But once I was away from his office I could put him to the back of my mind.

I was no longer part of the 'A' team and I was kept well away from Screwtop and Ozzy Desmond, I suppose because of my connection with Lucy. They were always afraid she was going to tell the police about them. They needn't have worried, because Lucy may have slipped into dishonest ways but grassing was not one of them. In fact she kept to the code of ordinary decent criminals as though it was something she'd been brought up to since her school days.

So I was sent out with what was definitely a 'B' outfit, with Romeo Robinson and Alfie Barnet, who could be relied on provided the instructions were brilliantly clear. Romeo looked less like a heart-throb than a lightweight boxer grown old before his time. He'd been put into a number of fights to entertain the paying customers when he was younger and his nose had been well broken and his ears well cauliflowered. Alfie had probably, like me, never followed any entirely honest occupation. He was small, cheerful, able to squeeze through small windows and climb drainpipes. He could deal with simple burglar alarms and locks.

It seemed like a routine job. It was a house on the edge of Hampstead Heath. Romeo had been keeping observation and he was quite sure the family were away on holiday. The back door could probably have been forced by an intelligent child with a penknife, but Alfie seemed to expect a round of applause when he managed it. The burglar alarm was also no problem. So we made a routine entrance in search of such routine articles as silver, television sets and money.

I told the others I'd take the bedrooms and walked up the main staircase. Oddly, there was a light on in the corridor and I remember wondering vaguely why. But the feeling I'd described to Lucy, the excitement of being in someone's house wondering if you were going to get caught, had gone completely. Quite honestly, if I felt anything at all it was boredom. I was sick and tired of the whole business. And then I heard the soft sound of music coming from an open doorway.

It seemed that I was past caring what happened, because I went to the doorway and looked. There was enough moonlight for me to see an old man with wispy grey hair fast asleep. The radio at his bedside was still playing. Of course I could have gone in and nicked the radio, but you know what I did? You won't believe this, and I hardly believed it of myself. I went and switched the radio off for him.

Then I went down the stairs and out of the front door while the others were still at work. I was away across Hampstead Heath, away from the crime I didn't want to commit, and then back in Notting Hill Gate, still amazed at the change that had come over me.

Most of all I was looking forward to telling Lucy about it.

THAT NEXT VISITING DAY Terry seemed very excited and said he had something important to tell me. When I asked him what, he said, 'I've been thinking.'

'Thinking about what?' I always feel a certain amount of dread when people say they've been thinking.

'Since you told me that I'd introduced you to crime. And of course I feel bad about it.'

'You needn't. It was quite exciting while it lasted.'

He looked a bit nervous, as though he had a confession to make.

'I told Mr Markby I felt bad. And now I'm going to tell him the big thing. But I'm telling you first.'

Then he began to tell me a long story about being in a Hampstead house at night and leaving suddenly. Just clearing off home.

'Why did you do that?'

'Because I was bored with it.'

'Bored with what?'

'Crime. And then I made the big decision. To get out of it. Once and for all.'

He looked at me with what I thought was a superior sort of smirk, as though he'd moved into a higher, better world.

'That's just great!' I said. 'I get into all this to understand you. To bond with you. To feel like you. So we could be together. So now you're giving it all up, are you, to become Mr Markby's favourite good boy, and leaving me in this dump!' Well, it was what I felt and I had to say it.

'I don't want to leave you,' Terry said. 'I want to be with you. Always.'

'We'll have to see about that.' I got up. 'I'd better get back to the girls. They'll be needing help with the laundry.'

So I left him looking completely surprised and ten minutes before the visiting time was over.

IT WAS CLEAR that Lucy and me had drifted apart and, quite honestly, I couldn't work out the reason why.

If anyone was to blame for our troubles I should have said she was, for taking part in a burglary which, of course, was a complete cock-up. From what she told me, it was pretty obvious that Detective Sergeant Ishmael Macdonald was on the case from the start. So what Lucy did was to walk straight into the arms of the law.

But what was it all for, for God's sake? During an earlier visit Lucy had told me what she took was a picture of a naked woman drying herself after a bath. Was the amount of trouble she'd got into worth it? When I said that, she told me that I really didn't understand anything about her. She was probably right.

All she seemed to be was angry with me and disappointed. She seemed to be happier with the women in Holloway—them that set fire to sleeping husbands and all that sort of thing. When we discussed that Lucy's case might not be heard for around six months, Mr Bethell said he'd apply to a judge this time for bail, but Lucy didn't want it. She said her friend Martine was due to have her baby at any moment and she didn't want to leave her.

Whatever she thought about it or me, I was going to do my best to help Lucy. I couldn't believe she planned a job like that by herself. She must have been forced into it by the old firm I used to work for.

I thought I should be a bit more sure of my ground before I accused Chippy. Then I remembered that a picture was the cause of all the trouble. So I rang Chippy's art expert, a bit of an old fart called Hughie Whitcombe. I got an invitation to a drink with Hughie at his club in Pall Mall. To get in there I had to look respectable and remember to wear a tie.

The Gainsborough was nothing like the old Brummell Club. The Gainsborough seemed to be a place mainly used for sleeping. The porter was asleep behind his desk in the marble-tiled entrance hall. He thought Hughie was in there somewhere, but having been asleep he couldn't be quite sure where he'd got to. He led me across the hall and we had a peep through the half-open door of the 'smoking room', but there was no sign of Hughie there. Finally we discovered him alone at the bar, where the bloke in charge was leaning back against the shelf of bottles, his arms crossed, one hand clutching a dishcloth and his eyes closed. The few members at the tables talked quietly, afraid of waking this person up. Only Hughie sat with his eyes wide open, a grey-haired man whose glasses were continually slipping down his nose, wearing a tweed suit and a spotted bow tie.

'You'd like a drink,' he welcomed me. He then called 'Clive!' loudly so that the barman opened his eyes, looked startled and delivered a couple of whiskies quite quickly.

'Thank you.' Hughie gulped his and then asked me, 'How is Leonardo de Medici?'

'I don't know him.'

'I'm sorry. I always think of our friend Leonard as like the great Medicis of Florence. A brigand, of course, but deeply interested in art.'

The words came tumbling out of Hughie, high-pitched and quite excited. I knew he'd written for one of the posh papers and then been sacked. He'd got involved in the stolen picture business, first of all as a go-between, agreeing ransoms for stolen stuff, and then as Chippy's adviser on what was worth stealing or how to turn stolen art into money.

'Did Chippy ever say anything to you—'

'You mean Leonardo?' he corrected me. 'Let's show the greatest respect for an important patron of the arts.'

'All right, Leonardo. Did he say anything about a picture of a woman drying herself after a bath?'

'Oh! You mean little Bonnard. Leonardo was going to "find" one for us. Picture of the painter's wife, Marthe, having got out of the bath. It would have been worth more if she'd been in the bath, but all the same it would have been a nice little earner.'

'Chippy—sorry, Leonard said he was going to get this picture?'

'It was going to come to us through the system.'

'But it never came?'

'I suppose there must have been some hitch.'

I didn't tell him that the hitch was that the thief in question had landed up in Holloway Prison.

'YOU'VE DONE IT all my bloody life. We did all the stealing for you and then we did the prison for you. All for you, you jammy bastard, while you sat in that maisonette and got richer and more respectable. You just used me. All my life. But this time you went too far. You used Lucy to do your stealing and now she's in prison because of you, Chippy.'

I had caught him at work in SCRAP and I didn't, as you can see, mince my words.

'Don't ever use that word in here.'

'What word is that?'

'Chippy!' He scarcely whispered it.

'Chippy!' I said quite loudly. 'I'm going to use it. And I'll make sure Lucy uses it in court. She'll have to explain why she went out stealing to get a picture for you. You organised the entire job.'

'She volunteered. She made sure I'd help her do it. She threatened to make trouble if I didn't lay on a team for her. I meant her to have her share.'

'Well, you'll get your share, Chippy. She's going to tell them the whole story in court.'

Chippy was sitting at his desk. He looked hunched-up, smaller than usual. He stared up at me, pleading. 'What can I do about it?'

'I don't know. Give her some sort of a defence. She was with other people. Can you find someone to say they forced her to do it? Threatened her? You think of something. You'll find someone else to take the blame. That's your special subject, isn't it, Chippy?'

He said quietly, 'I ought to get you killed, Terry.'

'That wouldn't do you any good. She'll tell the story in court anyway. So you just think of a way of helping her out.'

I left him then. He did think about it, and he found a way out that was no help to Lucy. No help at all.

Extract from the minutes of the Council, Social Carers, Reformers and Praeceptors

Present:

GWENDOLEN GERDON, EXECUTIVE DIRECTOR (ED)
LADY DOUGHBERRY, Bunyan Society for Prison Reform
PROFESSOR MAXWELL HEATHERINGTON, Reader in Criminology at the University of East Surrey
CAMPBELL DYSON, Chair of Dyson Soft Furnishing
PETER BETHELL, Bethell, Sherman and Pensotti, Solicitors
THE REVD HARVEY TYLER, Rector, St Barnabas, King's Cross
ALEX MARKBY, Probation Service

Gwendolen Gerdon (the ED) read out the letter received from the chair, Leonard McGrath.

My doctors have informed me that the British climate is seriously damaging my health and it is essential that I move to a place abroad where I can enjoy the benefits of sunshine and warmth. It has been a pleasure and an honour to have been chair of SCRAP. Carry on with the good work!

Yours sincerely,
Leonard McGrath

The ED told the meeting that she had no information as to the whereabouts of our former chair. She had made enquiries and discovered that his maisonette in Connaught Square was 'up for sale'.

A motion was proposed by the Revd Harvey Tyler and seconded by Lady Doughberry thanking Leonard McGrath for his inspirational leadership of SCRAP, to be sent to him as soon as the ED discovered his address.

Professor Maxwell Heatherington suggested that the meeting should proceed to elect a new chair. Peter Bethell said that we need look no further than this room to find an excellent chair and he proposed Mr Alex Markby and he was seconded by Mr Campbell Dyson. Mr Markby said he was taken aback at such a great honour but after further thought he was persuaded that his long experience of the reform of ex-prisoners would be of value in a chair. 'Leonard McGrath,' he said, 'would be a hard act to follow, but I can only do my best.'

The proposal to elect Mr Alex Markby chair was carried nem. con. There being no further business, the ED declared the special meeting closed at 3.30 p.m.

TIME PASSED IN HOLLOWAY, where the days were all the same: get up, breakfast, laundry, dinner, more work, association and locked up for the night. Martine was getting nearer to having her baby and I began to tell the passing of time by the progress of her pregnancy. Otherwise, we were killing time, waiting in my case until the date of my trial, when I expected to find out how much more time I would have to kill.

When Terry came to visit, he looked at me sadly as though I hadn't done what I did to be close to him, and I felt he was getting further and further away from me. Finally we didn't seem to have much to say to each other. All he wanted to talk about was how well he got on with Mr Markby, his probation officer, now chairman of SCRAP since that Chippy McGrath had done a runner. He told me that he'd threatened to expose Chippy unless he admitted he'd forced me to steal the picture. That was why Chippy left the country. I told him no one forced me to steal the picture, which had been entirely my Great Idea. After that we found even less to say to each other.

Persephone Smith-Aldeney visited me from Aldershot and showed me one of the tabloids with a huge article by Robin Thirkell under the screaming headline 'Bishop's Daughter Invaded My Home because I'd Ended Our Torrid Love Affair'. I thought at least someone had profited from this mess.

So the days passed, working in the laundry, waiting for Martine's baby. Then they told me I had another visitor and, surprise, surprise, who should I find sitting in the visitors' centre but my usually not very talkative mother.

Sylvia had scrubbed up for the occasion. Her hair looked as though it had been done specially and she'd brought me a box of chocolates.

'What an extraordinary place!' She looked round at the tables where girls were meeting their husbands or boyfriends and bored children were longing for the visits to end. 'I've never been in a prison before. And it's not too bad in here?'

'No, it's not too bad. A bit better than St Swithen's. At least we have a heated swimming pool.'

I wondered how long it was since we last sat down to have a talk to each other. The prison atmosphere was clearly bringing the best out in my mother.

'I'm afraid there's bad news,' she said. 'Will London's about to retire. He's got something wrong with his brain. Robert's been strongly recommended as his successor.'

'Bishop of London?'

'Of course the idea's ridiculous but Robert's enormously excited about it. It'll be very controversial and there are already letters against him in the *Daily Telegraph*. Robert likes that.'

'Well, who's for him then?'

'The Prime Minister apparently thinks he's a "moderniser" who's prepared to draw a line under the old conservative Church of England. Oh, I do so hope it never happens.'

'Why, exactly?'

'I've got used to the palace at Aldershot. I know the stairs. I love the peculiar little scullery. I don't want to go to London, Lucy. I prayed to God it doesn't happen. But I'm not sure he was listening. All I can say to you is, don't ever marry a man with bishop potential.'

'Don't worry. My boyfriend's a burglar.'

'I know, dear. Your father told me.'

'Even though he may be my ex-boyfriend now.'

'Don't worry, Lucy. You've done something with your life.'

'Have I?'

'You've had an extraordinary experience. I never had an extraordinary experience and I don't suppose I ever shall.'

Then it was time for her to go. I put my arms round her and told her that I loved her. She left me then, smiling sweetly to herself.

THE VISIT from my mother went well, but the same couldn't be said of my visits from Terry. He kept telling me he was going straight and divided his time between chatting up his probation officer and helping out in various restaurants. He also said that I shouldn't get too close to the girls as they were probably all reoffenders and I might end up by being as bad as them.

This attitude of Terry's to my girlfriends got under my skin more than a bit, particularly as the great excitement for all of us was the arrival of Martine's baby. I told him I thought it would be better if he didn't visit me any more. He seemed quite startled when I told him that, but he just muttered, 'OK then,' and left. I didn't see him after that, not for a long time.

Martine had been moved into the mother and baby unit with three other mothers-to-be. Then we heard that she'd been moved to the labour ward of the Whittington Hospital, where she could stay for no more than seventy-two hours. But that was long enough to produce what she came back with. We got passes to see him and of course everyone agreed that he was just the most marvellous baby that had ever been born. His name was Nicholas, but she called him Nick—which I thought was an appropriate name if he grew up pinching things like his mother.

Martine was now in a single room with Nick. She wasn't locked up at night, but she couldn't leave the room without permission. So we marked the passage of time by Nick's various achievements, the first day he smiled, when he started on solid food and when he sat up.

Behind all these achievements, though, there was a horrible worry for Martine. Each step forward brought Nick nearer to being nine months old, when he and his mother would have to be parted. And if Martine had no home to send him to, he would be put into care and it would be good-bye to Nicholas.

Well, she hadn't got a home. Martine's mother was a crackhead who'd only left Holloway a month or so before we arrived. Of course she had friends, but they were airheads and regular offenders. There seemed to be no one to look after Nick. This worried me more than thoughts of my coming appearance at the Old Bailey.

I got another visit from Peter Bethell, who brought with him a youngish, tallish and enthusiastic man who seemed to find everything he said himself irresistibly funny, although he never laughed when Mr Bethell made anything at all like a joke.

'We've briefed Mr Frobisher for your case, Lucy,' Mr Bethell told me. 'I used him the other day in the Court of Appeal.'

'I managed to tie them up in knots on the quality of criminal intent.' Mr Frobisher laughed heartily.

'So you did, Mr Frobisher. You had the Lords Justice "appealing" for mercy.' Mr Bethell laughed loudly, but Mr Frobisher didn't crack a smile.

'We thought a brilliant young junior was better than a QC in your particular case,' Mr Bethell said. 'And Mr Frobisher says it's not too late for you to say it was all a joke on your old friend Robin Thirkell.'

'Just a bit of a prank.' Mr Frobisher seemed overcome by laughter. 'We'll get a judge with a sense of humour. They do exist, you know.'

'Mr Frobisher knows his judges,' Peter Bethell assured me.

Honestly, I needed to put an end to this nonsense. 'It wasn't a joke,' I said, 'It was deadly serious.'

'I told you.' Peter Bethell turned to the barrister sadly. 'It was deadly serious. She was deeply in love at the time.'

'I can't see why being deeply in love should make you go around stealing.' Saying this made Mr Frobisher laugh again.

'Then you can't understand my case at all,' I told them. 'I'm just going to say I'm guilty. Oh, perhaps now you're both here you could think of a legal way of stopping Martine having her child taken away from her when he's nine months old.'

But they couldn't. They weren't any use at all.

TIME PASSED. I'd stopped visiting Holloway, quite honestly because Lucy didn't want to see me again. Talk about attitude! Hers seemed to have changed from love, real proper love, to what you might call irritation. Just because I wanted to be what she once wanted me to be.

Of course I'd had girlfriends before, plenty of them, and the truth is that I'd never been given the push before. It always either fizzled out or I was the one who decided we weren't best suited. It was different with Lucy. Come to think of it, everything was different with Lucy. If I was to be honest about it I'd have to admit that it was because I cared for her more than I'd ever cared for any of the others. So I suppose that's why I felt so badly about it.

As she'd ended our relationship I thought it wasn't fair to stay on in her flat, so I moved away. I found myself a room above a Japanese restaurant down the Goldhawk Road. Never mind I had to share a bathroom with the head sushi cook. He was spotlessly clean and would send me up a few bits of sushi when he thought I looked hungry. It was a long way from cooking up a rack of lamb for Lucy in her flat, but it was a lot better than being locked up inside like she was.

I went over to the Brummell Club in the days when I still had a bit of money and one night there, drinking at the bar, was Screwtop. I sat down beside him, allowed him to order me a large vodka on the rocks and then I accused him of leading the scam that had landed my ex-girlfriend inside.

'She hasn't told you that, has she?' Screwtop looked seriously worried.

'No, she hasn't told anyone.'

'She's a good girl.' Screwtop looked horribly self-satisfied.

'She's not a good girl,' I told him. 'And that's why she's in Holloway.'

'And what about you? You done any good jobs lately?'

'Helped out in the kitchens of Il Deliciosa in Westbourne Terrace.'

'You mean you're going legitimate?'

'That's what I mean.'

'That can't be very profitable.'

'No, it isn't. But it gives me time to study. I hope to get a few more qual-ifications. What about you?'

'Been abroad.' Screwtop looked very pleased with himself. 'Came back to clear up a few things and then I'll be away again.'

'Like Chippy?' it occurred to me to ask him.

'Yes. Very like Chippy.' Screwtop gulped down his glass and said, 'We may be working together again. Somewhere you can make money by the bucketful.'

'Oh yes? Where's that exactly?'

Screwtop leaned forward and whispered one word in my ear: 'Iraq.'

Screwtop left the Brummell then and I never saw or spoke to him or Chippy again.

LIKE I SAY, time passed. Thanks to Mr Markby I got lessons through the post. It wasn't the Milton book I had to read but one about animals talking about politics and one from America about a half-witted man. I wrote down my thoughts about these books and posted them off, and got quite encouraging letters back. When it came to Christmas, Mr Markby invited me to lunch at his home in Enfield.

So I sat round a table with Mr and Mrs Markby and her sister and her sister's husband and we all put on paper crowns out of the crackers and Mr Markby's little dog, who seemed dead set on eating the ends of my trousers. Mr Markby told them all that we'd first met when I was in prison and they looked at me with a sort of respect as though he'd told them that I'd swum the Channel or crossed the Arctic with dogs.

After a few glasses of port and a few more crackers, Mr Markby told them all how he'd delayed my parole. 'I thought he gave me all the right answers but he didn't seem to mean them. Now I know he's changed. He's particularly anxious to stop a friend getting into trouble. Terry's a fine example of the way that prison works.'

Mr Markby, whose paper crown was now a bit askew, raised his glass to that and I didn't argue. The fact that I'd come a long way from my sort of home with my Aunt Dot and Uncle Arthur, who was continually away, to the Markbys' Christmas dinner was, I thought, a bit of an achievement. So I told them that I was grateful for what Mr Markby had done for me, and I suppose I meant it. All the same, I went and got a bit drunk in a pub down the Goldhawk Road the next night. All I'd done to keep my friend out of trouble had got me no further than Christmas dinner with the Markby family.

MORE TIME PASSED and I found myself in another public gallery, this time in Number 2 Court down at the Old Bailey. Mr Bethell had told me my ex-girlfriend had made up her mind to plead guilty. Lucky for Lucy it wasn't Judge Bullingham, who had seen me off for four years the last time I visited the Old Bailey. It was a small, neat, pocket-sized judge called Springer. From the way he handed out prison sentences in the guilty cases before Lucy he seemed a polite sort of person who always said, 'The least sentence I could possibly pass in this case is . . .'

When the turn came to 'Bring up Purefoy' I craned forward to see Lucy looking round the court as though she was already bored with the whole proceedings. Whether she was just putting on an act I didn't honestly know, because I'd got so far out of touch with Lucy's feelings.

She didn't even give a glance up to the public gallery although I was staring at her so hard that I thought she must have felt it.

The prosecution told the story of the stolen picture and then the brief got up to make his speech. He was a tall, lanky sort of person who didn't seem able to control his giggles.

'Your Lordship,' he started off merrily enough, 'may well feel there is a good deal of comedy about this particular case.'

'I find it difficult, Mr Frobisher,' the judge told Lucy's brief, 'to see a comic side to burglary.' This ought to have given the lanky brief a fair warning, but he went on doing his stand-up stuff.

'The whole business was such a disaster that I must say I find the facts as they have been outlined by my learned friend most amusing.'

'Do you indeed?' Mr Justice Springer looked determined to be serious. 'May I remind you that the purpose of the Central Criminal Court in England is not to amuse you, Mr Frobisher.'

Even this didn't wipe the grin off Mr Frobisher's face. 'She undertook this picture-stealing operation having first alerted Detective Sergeant Macdonald who was able to guess that she had some such ridiculous enterprise in mind.'

'Are you suggesting, Mr Frobisher,' the judge asked, 'that the inefficiency of a burglar should lead to a shorter sentence?'

'Let me put it this way, My Lord,' Mr Frobisher invited the judge to enjoy what he clearly thought was an excellent joke, 'Lucy Purefoy was helping the police with their enquiries.'

The judge didn't even crack a smile. 'It seems clear that she arrived at the scene with some professional accomplices and she has refused to name them. That was hardly helping the police with their enquiries, was it, Mr Frobisher?'

Lucy was told to stand. I can still hear what the judge said to her now.

'Lucinda Purefoy, you were caught in the act of stealing a very valuable picture from a friend to whom you stood in a position of trust. I utterly reject Mr Frobisher's speech in mitigation. You will go to prison for three years. Take her down.'

I thought that Lucy would at least glance up at the public gallery to see if I was there, but she did nothing of the sort. She went down from the dock to the cells as though she couldn't wait to get away from the whole courtroom including me if I happened to be there. I didn't see her again for some considerable time.

Ten

After my so-called trial, Mr Bethell and that ass of a barrister came down to the cells, I suppose to say goodbye. They were both angry with the judge, not because of my sentence, but because he'd ticked Mr Frobisher off for his so-called comic speech. 'Speaking to learned counsel like that in public. It's not what we expect of Her Majesty's judges,' was what Mr Bethell said.

Although I hadn't been treated so badly by the judge as his barrister had, Mr Bethell seemed to feel I might need a little consoling. 'Three years doesn't really mean three years,' he told me.

It turned out that I'd get a third off for good behaviour and that the time I'd been in prison waiting for a trial would be taken into consideration, so I should be out early next year.

'So that's not so bad then, is it?'

I had a strange feeling, a sort of dread at being let out to join the world again, but I said nothing and Mr Bethell changed the subject.

'Your friend Terry Keegan was in the public gallery. Did you notice him?'

'No,' I told him. 'I didn't notice him at all.'

I was never going to notice him again. Not so long as I lived.

I SHOULD HAVE MADE IT CLEAR that my dad was visiting me all the time I was in Holloway. He was lovely of course and kind, but so anxious not to appear what he called 'judgmental' that he did not have anything really valuable to say.

'I'm still not altogether sure *why* you wanted to take Robin's picture,' he said when we finally got round to a discussion of the subject.

'You could say I did it for love.'

'Indeed? People do strange things for love. Very strange things indeed.' And then he returned to the subject that really excited him, his possible promotion to be Bishop of London. 'It's caused a great deal of controversy. In the newspapers, on the radio and television. It's regarded as one of the most controversial issues that's faced the Church for generations.' He was glowing with pride.

'Mum's against it,' I reminded him. 'She loves the scullery in the palace at Aldershot.'

'Who knows? We may find a better scullery in London. The progress of the spiritual life can't be entirely decided on the convenience of sculleries.'

'She thinks it'd be too much of an upheaval.'

'The history of our Church is one of continual upheavals.'

'She's praying to God you don't get the job.'

'Is she really? She's not the only one, I can tell you.' My dad seemed flattered by this attention. 'There is a whole new movement within the General Synod opposing my promotion! They call themselves the Play It by the Rules Movement. They say—' now Robert was chuckling with delight at the idea of a new controversy, 'that the Church of England has certain age-old, always respected rules, like sport. So you must play it by the rules in Church. No same-sex marriages etc., no gay clerics, because that would be hitting below the belt. I tell you Lucy, the movement's attracting a lot of supporters and they'll make quite a lot of fuss at the synod. You'll never guess who their leader is.'

I told him I never would.

'Who else but my former chaplain, Timbo. He knows all about sport.'

Timbo, I remembered, who tried to start a fight with Terry and, instead, started another chapter in our lives. 'How are you going to deal with him?'

'By trying to point out that there are considerable differences between religion and cricket.' And having thought of this line, my dad hurried off to give it to the press.

I REMEMBERED Robert coming over after I'd been sentenced and looking at me sadly and asking if there was anything he could do to help. Rather to his surprise, I said there was. I told him about Martine's baby, Nick, who was going to be taken away from her when he reached nine months old.

'What can I do about it?' Dad asked.

'I don't know. Do some knee work. Get God on the case. Put it in your friendly newspapers. Get the Archbishop of Canterbury to say it's a major sin to part mothers from their children.'

Dad considered this and then his eyes lit up. 'It might make quite an effective "Thought for the Day".'

'Do it,' I told him. 'Do it as soon as you can.'

Nick had just reached his nine-month birthday when they came to take him away. Martine couldn't satisfy them she had a respectable home for him. They didn't hang about, the so-called Welfare Services. They came and took Nick away to put him in so-called 'care'.

Martine came back to our dorm from the mother and baby unit when she lost her child. It was as though Nick had died on her. She didn't say much about it, but at night she cried. She kept us awake with her crying but no one complained. We'd loved Nick too, but of course not in the way Martine had. I was glad I was still in Holloway to help her.

So we fed Martine with hopes that she'd manage to find Nick when she got out and get him back because she'd get a job and make a good home for him that even the welfare people would approve of. She presumably didn't believe this, deep down, any more than we did. But it kept her from crying so much at night, except on important days, like when Nick would have been one year old and she had no idea where he was or what had happened to him.

Robert did a 'Thought for the Day' about it that someone heard on the radio and said it was very good and effective. It made absolutely no difference at all.

THEY CERTAINLY don't make giving up crime easy. Mr Markby had some idea of me ending up in a university, but no university was going to take me with a criminal record. There were better jobs going than helping out in the Notting Hill restaurants, but I had to fill in a CV and Mr Markby told me I had to mention all my form because they'd check with the police records anyway and the result was that I never got any of the jobs concerned.

When Lucy stepped down from the dock and never even looked at me, I knew it was well and truly over. So I decided to forget her, but it was hard. Just as hard, it seemed, as getting into university or a decent job.

One of the restaurants I worked in was called Il Deliciosa in Westbourne Terrace. Alysia was the manageress, a tall dark-haired woman with greenish eyes that were always wide open in surprise at finding a dirty ashtray or unswept crumbs on any of the Deliciosa's tables. She definitely ruled the place, and most of them in the kitchen and all the girls who did temporary waitressing to pay their university debts were scared stiff of her. I wasn't scared because I got the feeling she fancied me, and I thought she wasn't so bad with all the flashing eyes and dark hair she pushed away from her face when she was really angry. One day she said, 'We ought to have a date. I'll take you dancing.' It seemed a sort of order, like, 'We'll do Italian meatballs for the special tonight.' So I agreed to go.

'I'm going to take you real dancing,' she told me, 'not this present-day rubbish where you just wiggle your bottom and wave your fists in the air. None of that at all. Strictly ballroom.'

We met at a bar in Shepherd's Bush. Alysia had high-heeled shoes and a skirt full of pleats. I was wearing the only suit I'd been able to save up for. Alysia took me to a place called the Palais Glide off Hammersmith Broadway. I looked round in astonishment. There was a three-piece band playing tunes I didn't recognise and couples with their arms round each other's waists and holding up each other's hands.

Before I could draw breath, Alysia had grabbed me and had me joining in. She was going backwards but she led me definitely. She occasionally leaned right back and made me lean over her. Then she pushed me back and leaned over me. She called out for me to do something called 'chassé at the bends', and I gave a little hop because I had no idea what she was talking about. We went on dancing for what seemed like hours.

There was no licence in the Palais Glide so from time to time we stopped for a Diet Coke. In one of these rest periods Alysia asked me where I lived. It was then she asked me if I had a big bed.

Well, by now you'll have guessed what happened, and at midnight Alysia got out of my bed, which isn't as big as all that, and started to put on her clothes. When I asked her what the matter was she told me. 'You're not good at ballroom and you were thinking of someone else. Go on, admit it.'

I should never have done it, I suppose, but I'd got in a way of trying to be honest. 'All right,' I said, 'I did sometimes think of her.'

'Sometimes! Who was she anyway?'

'Someone I knew. She said she wanted to do some good in the world when I met her.'

'Do some good!' The green eyes were very angry. 'What is she, a missionary or something?'

'No, she's in Holloway Prison. She's doing three years for burglary.'

'How disgusting!' Alysia was buttoning up as though she couldn't wait to get out of my place.

'Not too disgusting. I think she wanted to be like me.'

'Well, you haven't done three years for burglary, have you?'

'Not really. The last time I was inside I got four.'

She was still then, very still. Then she said. 'Does Geoffrey know that?' Geoffrey Parsons being the owner of Il Deliciosa. It was one of the few jobs where I didn't have to produce my CV. That's why I took it.

She was out of my place like a flash. It was the end of our conversation and the end of my job too, because Mr Geoffrey Parsons gave me the sack. I had no one to blame but myself.

'I WAS TRYING to be honest,' I told Mr Markby when I next saw him. 'That was a mistake, wasn't it?'

'Not necessarily. Honesty's quite important in our sort of work.'

'You think I should be a probation officer?'

'You might be quite a good probation officer, with all your experience of prisons. Unfortunately it seems that your convictions make it impossible. Though I have thought of one job,' he was actually smiling at me, 'where you might be rather successful.'

'What's that?' I wasn't expecting very much.

'I just have to consult a few people,' he said. 'I'll tell you later.'

IT WAS HARD WORK saying goodbye. I really didn't want to leave them, particularly as it now seemed I was going out into a world where I found it hard to remember what to do exactly.

Devira gave me a handkerchief she had embroidered for me and held her hands together in what I supposed was a sort of blessing. I promised Martine that I'd set about finding out where they'd put Nick, though I'd no idea how to do that or even where to begin.

They were a bit slow in the office that morning and it took a long time to give me back the clothes I wore when I was arrested—the jeans and sweater and trainers that I'd put on to climb into Robin Thirkell's house for the sake of excitement. And then the screw unlocked the door and let me out into an uncertain future with a travel warrant and £46.75.

It was a grey, damp morning early in the year and the traffic outside Holloway, after the calm silences of prison, sounded almost unbearably loud. I only had time for one quick look round before I saw him. I don't know why but I found it irritating that he hadn't changed at all. He still had dark curly hair and a determinedly cheerful smile as he bore down on me.

And then he said, as though it was a joke, 'You must be Lucy Purefoy.'

'You know damn well who I am.'

'But you don't know who I am.' He gave me the news as though he thought he was giving me good news. 'I'm your praeceptor.'

'My *what*?'

'Of course you know what a praeceptor is. It means I'm your guide, philosopher and friend, although Mr Markby warned me not to get too friendly, at least at first. I'm here to see you get a job, settle you back in the flat, see you never go inside that place again.'

'Well, don't bother!' I felt I had to tell him. 'Anyway, what's Mr Markby got to do with it?'

'He's the new chair of SCRAP. I was having a hard time getting a job so he found me one at SCRAP. Paid praeceptor in charge of special cases. You're one of them. I'm here to help you.'

'I don't need your help now, Terry.'

'That's what they always say. You know perfectly well that 85 per cent of prisoners reoffend within two years of their release. I'm going to help you stop that habit of stealing things.'

'You mean you're here to reform me?'

'You could say that, yes.'

'Well, you can fuck off then.'

Just as he had once long ago, Terry looked surprised and pained as I said that. Women weren't meant to swear. Terry's male chauvinism was coming out again. This time, though, he was making a bit of an effort to control it.

'All right then,' he said, 'if that's the way you feel, that's all right. All I'd suggest is we do one thing together. If you don't want to see me after that, I'll piss off and leave you alone.'

'One thing?' I was extremely doubtful. Did he mean sex?

'I got up early to get here on time and I missed breakfast. Are you feeling hungry? What would you say to a burger?'

The rain was falling steadily and the traffic was even noisier. I was facing a day with nothing much to do. Also I suddenly felt, having been too busy saying goodbye to eat breakfast, unexpectedly hungry. I looked at Terry and for another inexplicable moment I didn't want to disappoint him.

'All right,' I said. 'If you mean just one hamburger.'

'Just one,' he promised. 'But a Whopper!'

There was a taxi passing and SCRAP must have been paying expenses because he stopped it.

And that's where this story begins again.

SO THERE I WAS, waiting outside the gates of Holloway Prison one grey morning with the rain coming down. And then I saw her coming towards me, not much changed, but a bit paler. People coming out of prison always seem paler than those of us on the outside. She didn't look at all pleased to see me.

'You must be Lucy Purefoy,' I said. I thought she might see the joke. I thought she might remember how she greeted me when she was waiting for me outside the Scrubs what seemed like all those years ago. She wasn't in the mood for laughter. 'You know damn well who I am,' was what she said.

Then I explained to her about Mr Markby. How he'd given me the job at SCRAP and got me to be paid wages so I would not be tempted to reoffend. I told her I was the praeceptor now, her guide, philosopher and friend.

She didn't take it well. I didn't take it well when she said she was going to get me to go straight when we first met. But so much had happened since then that I sort of hoped she'd have been thinking about that and changed her attitude.

No way, in fact no way at all. She said she didn't need my help. Then she actually told me to fuck off. I didn't like hearing her say that, just as I don't like the idea of women doing serious crimes. I still expect women to be feminine, if you know what I mean. I think it suits them better.

But. 'Never lose your temper with a client,' Mr Markby had told me. 'Never give him, or her, that particular satisfaction.' I suddenly had an idea. I told her that if she really felt like that I'd leave her alone. But I felt we ought to do just one thing together before that was decided on.

Of course she thought I meant sex but I didn't mean that at all. At SCRAP they made it clear that the praeceptor mustn't have sex with the client. Well, not during the reforming process anyway. So remembering how we first met, I told her I hadn't had breakfast, which was nothing but the truth, and if she was at all hungry, what about a hamburger.

She thought about it and I was anxious about how she'd take to this suggestion. In the end she said, 'If you mean just one hamburger.'

'Just one,' I said. 'But a Whopper!'

So there it was. It was a start. I had money for expenses and a taxi was crawling by in the rain so I flicked my fingers and we set off towards the Burger King. At least we were together.

And that's where this story begins—again.

JOHN MORTIMER

Born: Hampstead, London, April 21, 1923
Home: Oxfordshire
Publications: over 50 books, plays & scripts

Described as 'our greatest living Englishman' by London's *Evening Standard* and 'an institution' by the *Independent*, Sir John Mortimer has earned a special place in British hearts. Knighted in 1998 for services to the arts and the recent recipient of a Lifetime Achievement Award for his literary skills, he is of course, most admired as the creator of the irascible, maverick barrister, Horace Rumpole (below), who was brought to life on television in the seventies by actor Leo McKern. His numerous stories about Rumpole earned Mortimer many fans on both sides of the Atlantic. The fictional character was even alluded to in the O.J Simpson trial, when an attorney for the defence remarked that 'as Mrs Rumpole would have put it, I think we have a case of premature adjudication'.

Rumpole made his first screen appearance in 1975 in *Rumpole of the Bailey*, a one-off play for the BBC. It attracted so many viewers that Thames Television later commissioned a series under the same name, which proved enormously popular and ran for many years. A new Rumpole series is planned for 2006, with Jim Broadbent in the starring role.

Mortimer, like his alter-ego Horace Rumpole, knows the legal system inside out. He read law at Oxford and was admitted to the Bar in 1948, becoming a Queen's Counsel in 1966. At first he specialised in matrimonial and divorce law, like his successful father before him, but he later switched to criminal law, claiming, with typically dry wit, that murderers were nicer to work with than divorcing couples.

Mortimer's legal career received a boost in the 1970s for his part in defending two of the editors of the underground magazine Oz against obscenity charges.

The defence was unsuccessful at first but later won on appeal. Always a firm and vocal advocate of free speech, Mortimer continues to stand up for civil liberties, and remains a strong opponent of the 'nanny state'. He often touches on issues that concern him in his books and once remarked, 'The best way for me to comment about the world is by doing a Rumpole story.'

Over the years Mortimer has continued to write many short stories, film scripts and plays for radio and television, including *A Voyage Round My Father*, which depicts his relationship with his blind barrister father. He also worked on the highly popular television adaptation of Evelyn Waugh's *Brideshead Revisited*. His books include novels such as *Summer's Lease*, *Paradise Postponed* and *Titmuss Regained*, as well as two volumes of autobiography. Eventually, as his fame as the creator of Rumpole began to impinge on his court appearances, he stopped practising as a barrister.

Now in his early eighties, Mortimer lives with his second wife in the house his father built and in which he grew up. He shows no signs of slowing down and explains his still prodigious output by saying that since he gave up the law he hasn't 'had anything else to do. So I have written quite a lot. I just have to do something to keep myself from dying of boredom'. His attitude to ageing is equally robust: 'You do the same silly things, you get glasses of wine flung in your face. You're like you always were, except you can't see very well and you fall over.'

QUOTABLE QUOTES

- 'I refuse to spend my life worrying about what I eat. There is no pleasure worth foregoing for an extra three years in a geriatric ward.'
- 'No brilliance is required in law, just common sense and relatively clean fingernails.'
- 'To escape jury duty in England, wear a bowler hat and carry a copy of the *Daily Telegraph*.'
- 'The only rule I have found to have any validity in writing is not to bore yourself.'
- 'The freedom to make a fortune on the stock exchange has been made to sound more alluring than freedom of speech.'
- 'The shelf life of the modern hardback writer is somewhere between the milk and the yogurt.'
- 'People who write Hollywood scripts always think that characters have to learn things and change and develop. I think nobody learns anything. I think they make the same mistakes throughout their lives till they drop.'
- 'The worst fault of the working classes is telling their children they're not going to succeed, saying: "There is life, but it's not for you."'